A Crooked College

1974... 1975... 1976... 1977

A Murder Mystery set in the mid-1970's when there was no DNA for criminal investigations, sexual harassment was not recognized as an offense, gender equality was a euphemism and the drive-thru beverage barn returned 2 cents for every empty bottle.

E. Timothy Lightfield, Ph.D.

authorHOUSE®

AuthorHouse™
1663 Liberty Drive
Bloomington, IN 47403
www.authorhouse.com
Phone: 1 (800) 839-8640

Published by AuthorHouse 10/31/2018

ISBN: 978-1-5462-5344-0 (sc)
ISBN: 978-1-5462-5343-3 (e)

Library of Congress Control Number: 2018909582

Print information available on the last page.

CONTENTS

There was a crooked man, and he walked a crooked mile.
He found a crooked sixpence upon a crooked stile.
He bought a crooked cat, which caught a crooked mouse,
And they all lived together in a little crooked house.

James Halliwell-Phillipps

There also was also a crooked college . . .

PREFACE

"The following story is fictional and does not
depict any actual person or event."

This cryptic, enigmatic statement appears in the opening of many murder mystery television episodes. However, the disclaimer fails to clarify that the episode unabashedly addresses a current and actual happening, adjusted to assure no direct connection to persons, places or events and appease attorneys.

A Crooked College is a nonfiction novel, based on actual persons, real events and undeniable behaviors. The murder mystery did not happen in any one state, or at the same time, and the college is a fictional institution set in central New Jersey. Each character is a composite of persons and behaviors captured over the years. There is some hyperbole in the characterization, but only some, and readers may care to search out same as part of the puzzle. Most likely, you would be wrong.

The behaviors and incidents are taken from the author's thirty years of working at or with different colleges in numerous states as well as assorted federal and state government agencies. The suspect behaviors are altered by person and timeframe, but they are real. The characters are a collectively accurate mosaic of personalities and a portrayal of cultural norms dominating the campus and reflecting society at that time.

The book is set from 1974 – 1977, a time of unparalleled expansion of colleges, as states competed to launch new community/junior colleges. This was a period when higher education dealt with the turbulent societal matters of integration, sexual equality, Watergate, genetic vs. environmental influences on personality and the Bicentennial.

The College President, J. Paul Kelleher, despised by some and distinguished by few, is found dead the same year as Jimmy Carter is inaugurated as President and Elvis dies. This is a year after the premiere of *Rocky*, two years after the Vietnam War ends, Microsoft is founded and NBC's *Saturday Night Live* debuts.

The President's surprise death is three years after his appointment and when a 55 MPH speed limit is mandated nationally to preserve gas and at the height of shag carpet popularity and the Pet Rock craze.

Each chapter reveals clues to the President's death and crooked behaviors within the college. The mystery begins before J. Paul Kelleher is appointed College President and continues during his administration and after he dies, as the County Sheriff conducts his investigation and completes the medical examination.

The intriguing investigation comes together when the Coroner holds an official day-long Inquest. During the showcase judicial proceeding, Arthur Clough faces off against an array of suspects. He systematically interrogates witnesses and disarms the entanglements, restoring order, uncovering facts of the President's death and exposing the deceptive nature of the testimonies. The courtroom becomes the arena where layers of conspiracy are exposed, alibis are discarded and wicked alliances are betrayed.

A Crooked College divulges the reality of crooked behaviors and leadership deceit – even in higher education. The mystery deals with college life *outside* of classrooms, fraternities, libraries and locker rooms, demonstrating that college characters too can be flawed humans even with their advanced degrees, tenure tracks and privileged parking permits.

As with the disclaimer statement, if a former colleague or consort is upset by a characterization, know that no direct depiction of any person was intended. However, you know who you are and what you did.

Irish Leprechaun

PROLOGUE

*May your trails be crooked, winding, lonesome, dangerous,
leading to the most amazing view. May your mountains rise
into and above the clouds.*
Edward Abbey

President Kelleher's Office

Nothing seemed to be different about the President's Office this morning. At least at first. Something was very different.

The President's daily calendar was resting conspicuously on the extreme right corner of the desk, stuck on the day before – Wednesday, October 19, 1977. The date showed an evening meeting with the Board of Trustees.

There was the short stack of four pancaked manila folders on the right side of the leather-edged desk blotter.

A clear Waterford crystal paperweight in the shape of a Shamrock was properly placed on top of the folders. It had been given to the President by his wife as a gesture of love and recognition for his appointment almost three years ago. The paperweight was about four inches from top to bottom and side to side, with intricate vertical cuts. Shaped as the national flower of Ireland, the crystal piece was a fitting and functional addition to the office.

The executive three-pen set was perched to the right of the engraved, wood-grained nameplate of *J. Paul Kelleher, President*. His preferred coffee cup and saucer, holding fourteen ounces rather than a standard eight-ounce version, rested to the left of the blotter.

The President favored a cup and saucer to a coffee mug, a faux effort at elegance. Everyone else in the office, if offered hot coffee, would drink from an assortment of thick porcelain diner mugs.

A hefty, amber glass ashtray, overflowing with cigarette remnants and guilty as the source of lingering stale air, stood at the top of the blotter. Remnant ash that didn't quite make the unloading dock was sprinkled on a trail from the saucer to the ashtray. A brass cigarette lighter, engraved with

JPK, stood proudly next to the ashtray as if auditioning for guard duty at Vatican City.

All those office standards on the President's desk were in place, yet something was different this morning.

There was an abiding odor of cigarette smoke, masked only by the early morning sun streaming into the room and highlighting the fog of dust in the air. The President smoked fervently, as many others did in these mid-1970's years when anti-smoking campaigns tickled warnings by the Surgeon General that *Cigarette smoking may be dangerous to your health.* Phillip Morris and other manufacturers cried foul at the medical claims that cigarette smoking could be linked to cancer or other health conditions.

This President innocently walked alone in his office late last night, after most everyone else had left the building. Well, most everyone. Big mistake when you're Irish. Now he's probably going on a wild ride.
Irish Pooka Spirit

It would not have mattered to the President had anti-smoking appeals been an intimidating forewarning of throat or lung cancer or had a skull and crossbones image been plastered on the package. J. Paul was going to smoke his manly *Marlboro* cigarettes.

The four folders incorporated the quadruple divisions Mr. Kelleher inherited when he became President of Central Jersey Community College. The divisions encompassed his latest reorganization which had upset the Vice Presidents. Inside each folder, there would be red, blue and green ink marks on the papers signifying the range of priority for his attention.

Kelleher's first reorganization was declared shortly after a bitter, divisive and highly political presidential selection campaign. The search was advertised nationally, but the Board of Trustees eventually arrived at two local finalists, J. Paul being one. Crusty Donald L. Winters, long-time Vice President of Academic Affairs, had been the other.

The four Vice Presidents made up the President's Cabinet as head of Kelleher's divisions: Academic Affairs, Administrative Affairs, Student Affairs and Institutional Support. Apparently, the staff in Institutional Support, the recently re-engineered and re-modeled division, had sufficient assignments and consternation not to merit any affairs.

The Executive Assistant to the President, Samantha Bartell, was included on President Kelleher's Cabinet. Her position did not warrant a manila folder. She did not reign over a division or supervise employees. The Executive Assistant could contribute to the Cabinet discussions but held off when votes were taken. J. Paul never explicitly told her not to vote or that she did not have a vote. She figured casting a vote might be presumptuous and unnecessary.

Samantha had enough on her work plate just to keep meeting notes and affect decisions made outside of the meetings, and in more compelling ways. She always had enough on her mind not to lose composure at the occasional verbal outbursts emanating from the all-male peer group language, power displays and gorilla roars.

The votes were typically advisory anyway. While each Vice President had one vote, Mr. Kelleher had five votes and enjoyed overruling one or more consensus ballots during the meeting. More frequently, he would have the vote recorded but then decide outside of the meeting to ignore the majority. The President's recurring hand of five aces always beat the four-of-a-kind cards shown by the Vice Presidents in a stacked deck.

The President's high-backed power chair was positioned behind the desk. The leather throne was disguised as a chair balanced on caster wheels. The chair enabled a 360-degree swivel as well as lateral maneuvering across the work-space. The European Renaissance design adapted well to the magisterial function as did the rich, wood finish with the burgundy button-tufted cushioning.

Predecessor President, Dr. Robert T. Greenleaf, who had been lured to St. Louis to fill the vacant presidency in that system, had selected the office desk and credenza, not J. Paul. The desk had an array of features; some not readily apparent.

Mr. Kelleher merely re-appropriated and re-claimed the office aura for himself, with a few carefully selected furniture placements and possession replacements to mark the territory, much as a dog might pee on a tree. He did stalk, snare and eventually acquire his signature desk chair throne, while the former chair was summarily appropriated to another office as were the complementary vinyl reception armchairs.

Everything about his desk was in order. Yet something was different this morning.

The office walls were comparatively bare, given the array of proprietary and egoistic artifacts on the desk and credenza. The art was mostly still-life pieces intentionally left behind by Dr. Greenleaf. The paintings were about as stately and sentimental as one would find in a modestly priced motel room.

The uninspired and unassuming art work was balanced by an octagon vintage schoolhouse clock in mahogany wood, with the pendulum weight in neutral. Kelleher was not fond of the incessant ticking noise, especially when he was alone. He liked that the beautiful time-piece no longer functioned as a clock. The two hands were set at high noon or midnight, with one number twelve hand disguising the other number twelve hand, making a crooked time-keeper.

A framed photograph of Governor Brendan Byrne, a Democrat, hung unceremoniously on the wall near the door to the outer office area where his

Executive Secretary, Mrs. Edith Reynolds, guarded the doorway. Byrne had been elected New Jersey's Governor in 1974 and was pushing a State Income Tax. He argued the new tax would be offset by reduced property taxes. The Governor's office was in Trenton, but his residence was in Princeton, comparable to driving Ford's *Pinto* to work and having Cadillac's *Eldorado* in the garage at home.

Nothing seemed different. Something was.

Kelleher made it a point to cozy up to both Democrats and Republicans. He voted Democratic most of the time but kept his vote and party affiliation ambiguous and undisclosed. Gerald Ford had been President as a Republican last year. A southern Democrat, Jimmy Carter, was President now. The County Commissioner was a Democrat and his Board Chairman a Republican. None of that mattered to J. Paul. He knew how to work the angles and was a master at political maneuvering and posturing.

If you had taken a vote of his seven Trustees or the seven-member County Board of Chosen Freeholders on whether Kelleher was Democrat or Republican, they would have had a three-to-three vote, with one person abstaining. Had the vote been taken again, a month or two later, the results would be the same, although each person might vote differently. Kelleher was cagey and clever. He had to be.

Next to the Governor's obligatory, drab photo was a laminated framed version of Kelleher's MBA sheepskin from New York University and his M.A. in English Literature from Rutgers. The two college degree plaques of dark oak wood were same-sized, equally aligned and balanced, not displaying any preference or favoritism for degree or institution.

The eight-drawer and four-panel aircraft-carrier credenza would transport one to the romantic villas and artisan ambiance of Tuscany, the birthplace of Italian Renaissance. The Old-World flair balanced the President's grandiose historical allure, owing to his preference for English Lit.

The shelf behind the credenza's bottom left door housed an assortment of crystal glassware supported by a mini-collection of alcoholic beverages including Irish Whiskey. The mini-Executive Refrigerator positioned to the side held bottles of *Coke, 7-Up* and *Michelob*.

A 12-inch tall version of Ireland's national flag, resplendent with the vertical green, white, and orange tricolors, sat on top of the polished but smudged credenza. An Irish Shamrock adorned a pair of Belleek bone-china coffee mugs which were perfectly aligned with the Irish flag. No hot or cold beverage had ever graced those mugs – likely ever would.

The desk-top displayed a modest, framed photograph of wife Isabella, known to everyone as Izzy. Her photo may have been placed more out of duty and obligation than emotional support and partiality. The credenza displayed an immodestly framed photograph of the President's two teenage sons – Connor and Ian – with their arms around the family German Shepherd, Cerberus.

The dog was pretentiously named in honor of the canine warrior assigned, as per Greek mythology, to guard the gates of the Underworld to prevent the dead from departing. From his position in the photograph, the Cerberus Kelleher hound mythically served as a sentinel for the President's Office, even though he never materialized in the President's Office, the Administration Building or on campus.

"There's a photo of my two teen sons here on the credenza," Kelleher would tell most everyone who came before him. "There's a photo of Izzy around here someplace too," he would add quickly, waiting for a commiserating chuckle, as if from a deadpan Rodney Dangerfield monologue. The trouble lately was that J. Paul seemed more enamored of the unimposing photo than the woman.

The elongated credenza would not be complete without a throw pillow portraying a hand-stitched version of the *Irish Wedding Blessing*. The worn pillow made from Irish linen was a sentimental gift from long-departed Mamo Kelleher or, more likely, unclaimed when she died. He liked the pillow more for the line about *May He Crown Your Work with Success and Fulfillment* than *May the Good Lord Watch Over You as You Grow in Love*.

Inconspicuously hiding behind the Irish Blessing was a hardwood gavel, an unenhanced symbol of authority. The gavel bore the brass labeling to record J. Paul as having served in Student Government at his New Jersey high school twenty-five years ago. Like the Irish coffee cup, the gavel merely sat on the credenza, never in use for meetings or to pound the desk or hammer picture hooks into the wall.

Another coffee mug rested innocently to the far right on the credenza with the lettering *Greatest Boss*, the product of a past mistaken Boss's Day tribute. The tribute piece was purposefully rotated to face the wall as if the superlative was yet in judgment. More likely, one or more colleagues repositioned it to face the corner, much as a child might be disciplined in the classroom and told to wear a dunce cap. Kelleher didn't care much about the mug or how it faced. *Greatest Boss* was not a coveted or sought-after title.

Two chrome armchairs upholstered in burnt-orange fabric were placed strategically in front of the royalty desk. The depressed chair cushions showed evidence of guests having squashed the seats, due more to extended seat time than poor chair construction. The distressed armchairs were much older and decidedly more worn than any other furniture in the President's Office, but they were never intended to be comfortable or stylish.

J. Paul had unceremoniously appropriated the two office chairs from the Admissions Office waiting area. He contended that they matched the orange threads that were apparent, if not dominant, in the Persian rug he transported to his office to accent the drab commercial carpet. The costly rug had been spread under the desk and chairs, much like a magic carpet.

The over-used chairs were meant to exemplify the inferiority and vulnerability of all who sat in them. President Kelleher delighted in their rightful presentation in front of his desk and underlying side-by-side representation. He could rationalize that he did spend public dollars on his new desk throne but little on the reception chairs and none on the Persian rug.

Something, nevertheless, was different this morning. Very different.

The President's Office was accessed via the outer office, where Mrs. Reynolds reigned, and via the hallway adjacent to the back of the office. That hall led to the Executive Bathroom with the Executive Shower, Executive Closet, Executive Sink and Executive Toilet and then to the Board Room. Most often, the President used the Board Room door to enter and exit his office, given he could enjoy his realm for hours without anyone, including the Executive Secretary, assured of his presence.

We Irish Spirits are real even if not on the same physical plane as humans. We'll determine soon whether J. Paul spends eternity prowling the streets or roaming the graveyard. Be forewarned. Don't insult Irish honor.

Irish Banshee

The office drapes were drawn on the south side and open on the east side. This meant that humbled employees and others confined were to the uncomfortable burnt-orange armchairs, getting to see the pulled boring, beige drapes. That's how they were this morning.

The President, however, could gaze at the impressive eighteen-year old campus of Central Jersey Community College off to the east. He could marvel at his spacious realm and career success.

Not that President Kelleher had anything to do with the campus property acquisition, building architecture or site construction that began in 1958. That was all accomplished by predecessor Dr. Robert T. Greenleaf. The founding President had insisted before the General Assembly and the County Freeholders that the original campus be built in an all-at-one-time, fully comprehensive manner, rather than building-by-building construction as a capital-project-by-capital-project over an extended period.

Thus, the College had a 200-seat Little Theatre, a Public Auditorium, Olympic indoor swimming pool and 2,200-seat Fieldhouse, as well as a Library, Media Center and parking lots surrounding the campus and designed for twice as many students as initially enrolled.

The founding President had insisted the County post directional road signs to the campus throughout the service district. That meant a Monroe County resident could drive down any road and eventually come across a CJCC logo sign with an arrow pointing the way. It was also grand strategic thinking that the beautiful campus was placed in the exact geographical center of the County on former agricultural flat land.

There was a set of architectural program plans ruminating on the President's desk that morning. Another set had been filed in Trenton for the $5.2 million State-approved Library expansion. There were assorted locally funded projects for HVAC upgrades, office conversions and still more parking spaces. But the Library was a major addition, and the College had been through a disciplined, albeit conflicted, process to select the architectural firm.

J. Paul was peculiarly obsessed with the campus grounds and property maintenance. He would regularly point out trees and shrubs that needed attention. He would report if the hedges or grass needed to be trimmed or cut, much as a doting mother might suddenly conclude her son's hair warranted an urgent barbershop visit.

As he drove through or walked about the campus, he would make notes for work orders he would later have prepared. No project was too small or too dopey to warrant his attention. The campus was picturesque and the buildings well-maintained – the grounds needed to be too. CJCC was a source of pride for the community.

J. Paul Kelleher would customarily rise early at his home and arrive at the College by 7 AM wearing some combination of running shorts and t-shirt. He donned additional layers when the seasons changed. He would park his car in the President's designated space and commence his run around the perimeter campus road. However, his pace was more like an elderly senior citizen attempting to race-walk than a middle-aged man athletically running.

The President's shuffling motion as he jogged reinforced his athletic motto: *Start Slowly and Then Taper Off*. Since he smoked up to three packs of the filtered *Marlboro* cigarettes daily and coughed sporadically, his lungs would probably not be too responsive to a faster pace. He had never mounted a horse, worn a rugged cowboy hat or worn a yellow wagon-train raincoat, but he was a *Marlboro Man*.

After his constitutional, unhurried campus jaunt, J. Paul would end up at the office where he would shower and dress for the day. The closet in the Executive Bathroom held multiple business suits, business ties, long-sleeve pinpoint oxford white shirts and wing-tipped and cap-tipped *Johnston & Murphy* shoes, far more than closeted at his home. Probably more underwear and socks as well.

However, he would suit-up for duty in an array of sequences or stages.

Mr. Kelleher's habit was to appear before his office callers in unraveled progressions of dressing, more modestly having pants sans belt when ladies were before him. The wardrobe progression would start with underwear and the signature white, medium-starched, collar-button shirt.

He would typically be absent suit pants before male staff, with white boxer shorts the underwear of choice. Gradually, sometimes hours later, the pants, socks and tie would be added, and the white shirt fully buttoned, as if there was a prize for the slowest dresser in town. Had there been, J. Paul would have won.

One could marvel at his laid-back, even lackadaisical approach to readying himself for work. The method was to demonstrate and thereby affirm the power of his position. He could dress in whatever Emperor's Clothes he preferred, and however long it took him to do so. Everyone else needed to come to work fully clothed, with buttons fastened and zippers closed. The message was unavoidable: *Perhaps when you become President of the College one day, you too can get dressed in your office in front of your employees.*

Another habit of President Kelleher was to polish his shoes during a meeting in the office or even in the Board Room, while dangling a cigarette clenched securely between his teeth, leaving his lips free to maneuver. A ventriloquist can speak for the figurine mannequin without moving his or her lips. J. Paul could carry on a conversation, without the dummy, and with the lips rapidly moving, as the filtered cigarette remained cradled between his upper and lower incisors.

Sometimes he would halt the morning footwear buffing to listen to a point or two from the person seated in one of the two saggy-bottom, burnt orange chairs. More often, he would continue with the shoe-shining ritual. As commonplace, he would re-polish and re-buff the footwear in the afternoons, as if the shoes had a five-o'clock shadow.

Irish Spirits inhabited the President's Office as haunting intermediaries between this life and an afterlife. These entities lingered not as spirits of dead people but as conversational testimonials. The ghosts told stories of crooked designs, structures and patterns within the College and crooked actions and attitudes by its people.

Even with the Irish Spirits, something else on this autumn morning did seem different about the President's Office. Maybe it was that the tufted executive desk chair throne was docked to the far right of the desk as if more space was needed for something located to the left. When Kelleher wasn't perched in the chair, it was meticulously positioned in the true center of the desk. It was placed not too far right or too far left, reflecting his political preference and compulsion for order.

President Kelleher was not in the Executive Bathroom this Thursday morning. He was not sitting at his desk, shining his shoes, sipping coffee from his oversized coffee cup or clenching a cigarette between is teeth.

Something surely was different.

There was an air of suspicion as if Alfred Hitchcock or Rod Serling were about to divulge the ominous incertitude of that moment. One could hear the eerie sounds of the theme songs from these sagas and sense the Twilight Zone.

Indeed, suspicion became a reality. Substance overtook imagination. What was different this morning became obvious, more and more evident.

There was a long-sleeve, white-shirted arm reaching-out on the rug from behind the desk and in front

I was summoned here this morning to meet J. Paul. Claim his soul. He's been haunted by me for a few months. Maybe this guy will carry his head too and ride a black horse in the darkness.

The Dullahan

of the elongated credenza. The arm was visible from an angle to the right, with the remainder of the body camouflaged by the desk's undersides and shadows. The waist-down portion of the body was stuffed under the desk, as if shoved in a convenient hiding place or just crammed to assure focus on the upper body and uplifted arm.

The customarily polished and buffed shoes were not on his feet but resting adjacent to the figure under the desk, perfectly aligned and perpendicular to the body. The shoes appeared to have been placed and positioned to signify something – to punctuate the vanity of the person or demonstrate respect for order and polished appearances.

J. Paul Kelleher, President of Central Jersey Community College was dead at age 47. He was lying behind the desk, his death the result of natural medical trauma, self-inflicted destruction or a not-so-self-inflicted slaying.

Cerberus, the German Shepherd pet sentinel, had failed to guard the gates of the President's Office. The President had many adversaries, and he had made many an enemy. Had one of them gotten past the gates and invaded the office?

Soon Arthur Clough, the overweight and disheveled County Sheriff, would investigate the death, uncover clues and cause campus chaos and confusion. Soon, the President's wife, the Vice Presidents, Deans and other characters would scramble to understand what had happened and protect their crooked secrets.

Later, Monroe County's Coroner would expose the lies and mysteries in an official Inquest where the Irish Spirits would again reveal themselves. Those people would find themselves trapped and defending *A Crooked College*.

Cerberus – Guarding the Gates of Hell

PAST

The College Before Kelleher Became President

Between a fellow who is stupid and honest and one who is
smart and crooked,
I will take the first.
I won't get much out of him but with that other guy I can't
keep what I get.
Lewis B. Hershey

1

PAST

"Did you get to first base?"

J. Paul Kelleher was born in Paterson, New Jersey, at St. Joseph's Hospital in May 1930, the youngest of three sons. Paterson is within the footprint of New York's metropolitan region, yet more aligned with Jersey. Paterson's residents were crammed into the city, seemingly from the first Italian and Irish settlers. Ethnic groups kept the neighborhood boundaries clear and uncompromising.

Kelleher could not remember ever being called anything but Pauly in his youth, never by his first name, Jacob. Jacob was a particularly common Irish male name, as his parents wanted something traditional. Until high school, most people just thought his first name was Paul or Pauly. A local parish priest went by the name of Father J. Peter, and mother decided that *J. Paul* lent a certain noblesse and flair even if the family lineage was unremarkable.

Dad and his father's father were both butchers, although mother preferred the occupational category of meat cutter. Each had owned his meat market and prospered when families shopped for groceries daily, and dinner had to include meat and potatoes. They took pride in the Prime-rated cattle and fresh-made link and patty pork and Italian sausages for the weekend. After Grandpa Daideo retired and sold his meat market, he worked on Friday nights and Saturdays for his son, breaking down hind-quarters, carving loins into steaks and cooking his spicy spaghetti sauce sold in Mason jars.

J. Paul worked at his father's Superior Market during his high school days after dismissal and on Saturdays. He filled customer orders at the counter, cut up chickens, sliced cold cuts and cleaned up at end of day. Dad paid him $28 for the week, no matter how many actual hours he worked, unceremoniously leaving the money on Pauly's dresser – two $10 bills and eight $1 bills. J. Paul placed most of the earnings in a savings account at Talman Federal.

J. Paul grew up at a time and place where boys tried to please their fathers. Dad was his hero. As a teen he felt no amount of success would make him a man in his father's eyes. It was not that J. Paul lacked confidence – he lacked alternative male role models.

Young Kelleher's preferred job at the meat market was to deliver meat to the housewife regulars who called in orders. He used a bicycle with the store name and slogan of *Prime-Aged Beef Our Specialty* painted on it. The front bicycle wheel was considerably smaller than the rear wheel to accommodate a colossal wire basket suspended from the handlebars. Each meat order would be stowed in the basket along with the bill and address taped to the package.

The ladies who greeted him were generous with compliments about the meats and relatively charitable with tips. When cold or rainy weather made bicycle deliveries dangerous, he would hop out of the car as his father drove around the neighborhoods on the way home from work. Pauly would run the orders up to the front doors. The meat orders got delivered, but the tips were forgotten or dwindled considerably.

When teenage J. Paul had a date or a party to go to on Saturday evening, he could leave the market early but would hear the other butchers mock him. On the following day, the guys would want a post-date debriefing, and the inquiry would be unending. *Hey, Pauly, how was the date? Did you get to first base? What time did you get her home? Did you park in the woods? Did you try for second base? How pissed was her father?*

If a teenage girl came into Superior Market, with or without her mother, the butchers would go out of their way to be sure Pauly waited on her. He would try to be professional in preparing the meat order but was more embarrassed for the boorish butcher behaviors than having a cute girl ask him for frankfurters, ground chuck and split chicken breasts.

After high school, Pauly went to Rutgers University with the intent of becoming anything but a butcher, at least if he wanted to keep peace with mom. Dad was grateful and proud of himself for being able to provide for his family and run a business. Mom adversely compared a butcher occupation with the corporate careers of husbands of her lady friends, thereby whittling dad's self-esteem.

Kelleher ended up an English major in college, after shuffling through preliminary courses in Psychology, Business and Mathematics, hunting for a discipline that grabbed him. Dad was not thrilled that Pauly chose a non-vocational, non-job-prospective major. Mom just kept reminding her son how many pork chops his father had to cut that week to pay the tuition.

His two older brothers had gone into sales occupations after high school. They artfully avoided conversations about taking over the family meat business and about going off to college. They unknowingly served as anti-role models for the young sibling and not just on education and careers.

After college graduation, J. Paul was ready to find a job when it dawned on him that he could get a deferment and continue his sanctuary studies in graduate school. He ended up with a master's degree in English Literature from Rutgers. Now, mom and dad were thoroughly confused: *Why would our son major in Shakespeare, Chaucer and Milton? Why spend his time reading Canter-something Tails and Withering Highs? Why isn't he reading machine manuals, bank ledgers or Wall Street handbooks?*

The master's degree led to two years of teaching high school where J. Paul developed an interest in data analysis, owing to serving on the renewal of accreditation team. He was the only teacher who could apply and decipher the statistics or who admitted to those abilities. He was on the team because of his writing skills, but he became celebrated due to his latent but flourishing computational and analytical skills.

The school principal heaped praise on J. Paul during the post-affirmation of accreditation celebration. He unconvincingly told the other teachers and staff that this young man would be a principal too one day, even with English Literature as his major. J. Paul's faculty colleagues preferred to enjoy the wine and cheese trays rather than follow the accolades, much less vouch for J. Paul's talents.

That is, except for one fellow English teacher who knew how many hours her boyfriend had put into the research analyses and reports. Seeing that loving support, as well as seeing her every day in attractive poses in front of her classes, J. Paul proposed to Isabella Brooke Rhodes, better known as Izzy. The pair of English majors married later that year.

Two years teaching English grammar, punctuation and spelling to high school students were more than enough for J. Paul. There were way too many kids who were high on hormones and low on scholarship. With anti-nepotism championed in the school policy, one or the other of the English-teaching Kelleher's had to change careers or schools.

Instead, J. Paul decided to pursue an MBA degree. He was accepted at New York University, after being rejected at Wharton School, University of Pennsylvania. Finally, mom and dad were fulfilled with the practical major and the explicit career path, to say nothing of the anticipation of one day having grandchildren.

Kelleher spent most of the week on campus in New York, rather than commute from New Jersey daily. But Izzy and J. Paul made-up for the lost time on weekends. Their evenings were spent on the frayed, leather couch with Izzy's head on her husband's lap while he read his business books and made marginal notes. That is until his concentration drifted from the textbooks to Izzy's long red hair draped over his leg and her bare, curled-up legs.

The two newlyweds did not have a great deal in common, other than the

Garden State, garden beefsteak tomatoes, Madison Square Gardens, Three Dog Night and Jim Croce. The love of English Lit and reading meant they accumulated a mini-library of paperback books, carelessly cataloged in corners of the apartment on bookshelves made of cinder blocks and wooden planks.

Occasionally, Izzy lured J. Paul to New York sporting events with the promise of expertly folded-over, thin-crust pizza slices from Little Italy as a reward. J. Paul would drag Izzy to the theater with matinee tickets and promise of a three-inch-tall corned-beef-on-rye sandwich afterward.

Izzy overheard her in-laws tell a story about young J. Paul and how he was called *Pauly* in those years. She adopted that endearing nickname much to the regret of her husband who thought the name was juvenile. When anyone else would accidentally or willfully copy that moniker when addressing J. Paul, he would quickly and emphatically call such misstep to their attention. "My name is J. Paul, not Pauly," he would correct. But he truly loved it that his wife called him Pauly.

The couple shared an earthy sense of humor. They also shared a propensity to swear and an uncompromising ease in applying expletive-not-deleted language, no matter the setting or audience.

J. Paul could trace his vulgarity affinity to having had two older brothers who mastered the vocabulary within their male peer group. Izzy could trace hers to two brothers who never hid the language-use skills or off-color jokes from their sister. The young couple interjected cusswords into their conversations much like chefs season their favorite dishes with assorted zesty spices. Sometimes, however, the recipes did not call for red-hot words or spicy verbal seasonings.

J. Paul and Izzy tempered their cursing when their two sons – Connor and Ian – were young. They prided themselves on their ability to refrain from foul words in the presence of the boys. However, that abeyance was set aside when the sons entered the teens. Then the double-standard was paramount. "Your father may say those words," Izzy would declare. "He and I may cuss in this house, but don't you dare use such language," Izzy-mom would profess, conspicuously comfortable in her hypocrisy.

J. Paul was enamored with telling locker-room jokes on campus, especially after he became an administrator, and using the vulgar language in meetings. But he was not alone. Off-color jokes and pranks were ingrained in locker rooms, Board rooms, ballrooms, living rooms, dining rooms and occasionally classrooms.

This was still the 1970's when male chauvinism was rampant, women were incredulously tolerant, sexual equality was fumbling and the courts were silent. Very silent. J. Paul and other men thought of themselves as robustly masculine for such foul behaviors. A professional or even an amateur Psychologist would attest that the expressions were more a result of insecurities and self-doubts than of confidence and aggression.

Most women on campus thought so. Many men did too.

After completing the MBA and thus earning his unofficial union card for school administration, J. Paul was employed for one year back at the same high school where he had met Izzy and where she had continued to teach. The principal hired him as a temporary understudy to the finance officer, knowing it would only be a few months before the young MBA would bolt to a preferred opportunity. The few months became two years before he left.

Izzy had earned her master's degree in the interim and settled into a teaching career. She mocked her husband. "So, you've finally abandoning the fine arts," she declared. "Must make your parents happy that now you're taking courses in the vocational arts. Another one crosses over."

J. Paul learned of a finance staff position at a community college in Pennsylvania. The job was in accounting with broader responsibilities than counting numbers and balancing school budgets. When he accepted the position, he had no idea what a community college was. But Izzy would get a teaching position at the nearby high school. They could save some money for a house and start a family.

Three years later, with the two toddler sons, J. Paul saw an ad in the *Chronicle of Higher Education* for a community college in Abington, south of Paterson and in the central eastern portion of New Jersey. The position was that of a Dean – supervising several administrative offices and serving on the President's Cabinet.

Central Jersey Community College had completed its building construction, and descriptions of the facilities on campus were impressive. After having classes for two years as an evening-only program at a high school, the College had opened the new, modern and comprehensive campus, providing day and evening classes for residents of Monroe County.

Founding President Greenleaf, wanted to create a new division and find someone to further administrative operations and planning. In 1965, at age 35, J. Paul Kelleher began a brand new career as a community college administrator.

Kelleher was hired to focus on the fiscal chunks and other administrative fragments, but he was not bashful about interjecting himself into the curricular components. Any territorial intrusion was less than appreciated by the Dean employed for that purpose, Donald L. Winters. The two of them would have many a wrestling match over the ensuring years. Each would deliberately and obstreperously cross over the differentiation of authority and responsibilities. President Greenleaf would serve as Field Judge, and the other Deans and Vice Presidents would be entertained with the humor of it all.

As a Dean, Kelleher supervised Personnel, Computer Center, Research and Planning, Registrar and Admissions. Winters ruled over the faculty and instruction. Kelleher's title was Dean for the first couple of years. Then Greenleaf added a layer of Deans in Academic Affairs under Winters. That organizational complexity led to the substituted title of Vice President for the four Cabinet positions.

Suddenly, J. Paul Kelleher was vice president of a college, with an attractive office, Administrative Secretary and expense account. It took him a month in that role and title before he released his ambitions to become a College President. He knew it was just a matter of time before Greenleaf headed off to another college, with Winters his competition on campus for the appointment.

Over the years of their marriage, J. Paul and Izzy's appetites for spur-of-the-moment, unplanned romance gradually diminished. Aging was not necessarily a factor. Neither was physical health, except possibly for the smoking. Gone from those early years was J. Paul's MBA study on the couch while cuddling Izzy, enchanted by her flaming red hair and soft skin.

Those times were replaced by evenings of his wife grading English papers from her new teaching position at Atlantic State College and dealing with two toddlers, then the pre-teen and then teenage boys, including pimples, peers and parties.

Kelleher spent his evenings in the same room watching television out of one eye and reading through countless memos and reports with the other. That was before he would fall asleep in his favorite chair.

Izzy would kiss his forehead and touch his hand. "Pauly, why don't you go to bed?" she asked most evenings. "You've been reading that same page for an hour."

After three years of apartment life, the Kelleher's purchased a four-bedroom house in Ewing Township. The location was ideal – equally distant from Central Jersey Community College, where J. Paul did his administration, and Atlantic State College, where Izzy was an Associate Professor of English. More importantly, it was only a few blocks from the Italian Peoples Bakery and their incredible custard cream puffs with the chocolate icing.

Obligatory romantic liaisons, more directed at self-release than partner gratification, replaced amorous spontaneity for Izzy and J. Paul. They reasoned that such was related to, and justified by, their ongoing years of marriage, graying hair, early morning traffic avoidance and weekend chauffeur duties.

Trips to New York City for sporting and Broadway events, pizza and deli sandwiches were replaced with school activities, college commitments and indulgent parental issues.

The marriage had settled into a predictable pattern, a middle-aged spousal template, especially since J. Paul had become a senior college administrator. His career had evolved into anything but settled.

PAST

"Senator, you need to get with it!"

The first junior college was started in Joliet, Illinois, about 65 years before the New Jersey General Assembly approved funding for Central Jersey Community College in 1957. The State appropriated funds to hire the President, teach assorted classes in the evening in a temporary facility and commence campus construction. It would take two years to complete the capital project.

New Jersey had adopted a funding formula – the State was responsible for one-third of the budget, and the County obligated for a third. The final portion would come from student tuition and fees. Capital funding would be on a priority basis, subject to the political realities of favoritism and pork barrels.

Junior colleges became a national network in the 1960's, with new ones sprouting-up weekly, much like dandelions in an open field. The cumulative total reached over 500 across America within a few years. New Jersey would establish a County System of 19 public community colleges. With only two exceptions, each Jersey county got its own college – for bragging rights.

The robust economy of the 1960's prompted the initiation of these higher education institutions, as did social activism and a competitive "me-too" attitude within the states. The number of these junior/community colleges would triple over the years, and the number of students enrolled and graduating with a two-year Associate Degree would grow exponentially.

Years later there would be over 1,500 such colleges with comprehensive missions and a broad array of General Education, University Parallel, Occupational and Continuing Education programs and courses. Decades later, these two-year institutions would enroll more undergraduate students than all universities combined.

Besides University Parallel coursework designed for transfer to a four-year institution, junior/community colleges added Technical Programs and courses designed to lead directly to employment. Some states adopted the name *Technical College* to demonstrate that emphasis. That name tended to cast a disparaging cloud over the General Education and University Parallel programs and courses and confuse the postsecondary curriculum with that of a vocational high school.

Most of the colleges transitioned to the designation of *community*, rather than *junior*, colleges. The differentiation enabled the institutions to highlight a focus on the local community and the comprehensive nature of the curriculum.

Even into the 1970's, community colleges were having to lobby to retain a comprehensive curriculum. The General Assembly in New Jersey, and in most states, was made up of university graduates who were skeptical of these ambitious institutions and leery that their funding would come at the expense of their alumni universities and private colleges.

As New Jersey State Senator Herman Ravel remarked one day in 1972 when having lunch with President Greenleaf, "I don't understand why you and your junior college presidents need to offer English, math and science courses. It makes no sense. The emphasis should be on job skills. We need more welders, plumbers and mechanics, not more teachers and nurses. Hell, why do you even teach English?"

"The reason is real, sir," Dr. Greenleaf offered while watching the Senator devour his meatball sandwich. "Professional organizations and accrediting associations require high levels of reading and other skills. These groups sanction the credentials, not us."

Ravel never looked up from his eating, so Dr. Greenleaf continued. "Take Health Education, Nursing and Dental Hygiene. They have university sophomore and junior level science and math course requisites in the major."

The President paused to see if the State Senator was absorbing anything he had said. "Gone are the days of the shade tree mechanic who apprenticed his way into a car repair job. The coursework for most Automotive Technology programs is grounded in high-level technical skills and college-level reading. That means considerably high achievement levels in English, reading and math."

President Greenleaf did not expect the State House Senator to change his paradigm. Greenleaf was not about to let the guy shuffle around the State Capital with such a level of misconception and archaic, delusional thinking.

President Greenleaf could speak with conviction, given he had a three-year renewable contract. "With all due respect, Senator Ravel, you need to get with it!"

Greenleaf also knew that he, not Ravel, would pay for lunch.

Focused on local, community educational needs, community colleges became havens for political influence. Central Jersey Community College was no exception. New Jersey was especially susceptible to political influence, given the Board of Chosen Freeholders for each county approved the annual budget and added or deleted items on line-by-line scrutiny.

That meant considerable massaging of the relationships and occasional intrusive demands especially when it came to non-academic jobs and contracts that could be addressed by local firms.

The meddlesome nature of Jersey politics also came into play for the appointment of members to a community college Board of Trustees. While university Trustee appointments were based on statewide influence, power and position, community college Board member appointments were grounded in backroom and alley politics.

The original CJCC Board consisted of seven members, only two of whom had been to college. There were six white males and one lone white female. The woman got the appointment because her husband was too busy and rejected the invitation after being selected. He ran a prosperous interstate trucking business that specialized in overnight hauls and trucks with hidden cargo compartments. She died that first year and was replaced by her widow husband.

Another Trustee ran a wholesale produce company which meant he kept early morning work hours which was a problem when Board meetings lasted past 10 PM. Then he would periodically dose off only to be poked in the arm to wake up. Usually the poking person was the former Precinct Chair who held the record for both longevity and padded expense accounts.

Locals sought out and leveraged the positions because they calculated they could micromanage the College. Some wanted to be a Trustee to use the engagement as a stepping stone to another, more visible County position. Others thought the exposure would be terrific for their businesses.

Dr. Greenleaf was, nevertheless, a master at working the Board. He spent as much time wining and dining each Trustee, out of his pocket, as he did on the campus dealing with organizational and educational matters. He strategized as much on how best to present the budget before the Chosen Freeholders as how best to handle union negotiations.

Before each Board meeting, Dr. Greenleaf would meet individually with each Trustee to go over the agenda and secure support. He would anticipate each one's incredulous questions and boundless biases and

Only crookedness and death can change all things. We track things that are innocently or deliberately crooked.
Irish Leprechaun.

11

address each during these secluded one-on-one private meetings, rather than the public sessions.

Community colleges were teaching institutions. The mission did not encompass faculty research, book contracts and scholarly publications. Their campuses did not include fraternities, sororities or football teams. Faculty members at community colleges taught five or six courses a term with three-hour contacts for each section each week. The rest of the week was consumed by student advising, committee meetings, course preparations, paper gradings and required office hours.

The President of Rutgers University had bragged to the General Assembly: "None of our English faculty teach the Freshman English courses. They teach only junior and senior level or graduate courses. Instead, graduate assistants, studying for their masters teach the English sections in large, 250-person lecture halls. We pursue efficiency."

CJCC's President had heard that admission and decided to boast a different paradigm: "Only faculty with a master's degree teach the Freshman English courses at CCJC, not graduate students. Instead, our class size for those courses is limited to a maximum of 25 students per section. We require effectiveness."

Each CEO thought they had made the convincing argument for their financial support.

PAST

"You're my Dirty Half Dozen."

The Title III Program – *Strengthening Developing Institutions* – was funded through the U.S. Department of Education and the 1965 Higher Education Act. Central Jersey Community College was in its first wave of five-year funding, hoping to be re-funded.

The Dean of Instructional Resources, David Lieber, was the campus hustler. If Edith Reynolds, the President's Secretary, was *Radar* from MASH, then Lieber was *Scrounger* in the 1963 movie, The Great Escape. Lieber loved the comparison, perhaps because he thought of himself as an educated, if more stout, James Garner. Garner's character was cunning and opportunistic. David's version was tricky and a bit sleazy.

Lieber had demonstrated his worth and proficiency by landing the highly competitive federal grant for the initial cycle. CJCC was one of only two New Jersey community colleges to have been awarded the funding.

The grant monies were directed at laboratory equipment, faculty development, tutoring, student counseling and, most significantly, strategic planning and improved fiscal stability. The grant provided compelling, innovative incentives and paid some bills, as well freeing institutional monies for other priorities. Most everyone celebrated the unanticipated achievement.

The grant proposal had been a massive undertaking for the College. President Greenleaf had assembled a six-person task force in 1971 and directed them to give full priority to the grant-writing effort. He had called the half-dozen employees together and toasted them with plastic glasses of Chablis in his office. The President christened them the *Dirty Half-Dozen*, comparing them to the 1967 movie starring Lee Marvin.

"Dean Lieber is your Lee Marvin," Dr. Greenleaf had proclaimed. "For better or worse, David recommended you serve in this Commando Unit.

Blame him if you want to, but receiving this grant is paramount to the next several years of our College. I can't promise you anything, not even a crucial role in spending the grant money. Even if we don't receive the federal funding this year, be assured our grant submission will be fine-tuned and submitted again next year."

Now changing references to television's Mission Impossible with actors Peter Graves and Martin Landau, President Greenleaf redirected his historical and inspirational charge. "Unlike Mission Impossible, one of my all-time favorite shows," he said, "You do not have the right to refuse this mission. Understand, I will disavow I ever said that." The audience of six snickered. Some less than others. But, they had appreciated the President's sincerity if not his lame attempt at humor.

"David is your *Jim Phelps*, and Vice President Kelleher is your *Rollin Hand*," President Greenleaf continued, seeing that his character references were making an impression, and chuckling with his latest humor attempt. "Use whatever means you need, as long as you stay out of jail and don't get captured. Complete this mission, guys, and put together a magical proposal. Your participation has the full support of your Vice President and the Deans. They will adjust your priorities as needed to enable you to fulfill this obligation."

Unfortunately, President Greenleaf had forgotten that actress Barbara Bain was a main character in MI's Elite Unit, as *Cinnamon Carter*. He also forgot there was one female on the Lieber Task Force. But he had remembered to have cleared their selection and participation with his Cabinet and to assure them their workloads would be reasonably adjusted.

The other four members of CJCC's *Mission Impossible*, aka *Dirty Half-Dozen*, were Ralph Hughes, Mathematics faculty; Richard Spurling, Lead Accountant for the Business Office; Frank Richards, Counselor; and Resource Librarian, Donna Phelan, the lone female.

The CJCC proposal had been written in late 1971 to the maximum of 75 pages, plus the required Appendices. The typists were told to set the margins at the maximum and the font size at the smallest amount allowable to squeeze more words, more sentences on each page. Brevity was not a goal of the proposal or a feature of the writing.

The College had exceptionally current and impressive statistics on enrollments, faculty, demographics and finances to incorporate. The *CJCC Fact Book* prepared annually by the Planning Department, under Vice President Kelleher, was a determining element of the proposal. The *Fact Book* made the College stand out among its peers.

Lieber was exceptionally adept at formulating Milestones and Performance Evaluation Measures (PEM), as required by the agency. A

Milestone was an action with a due date. A PEM was a measure of quality. Sometimes, the two measures got confused. But mostly the Milestones and PEMs were ignored once the proposal got accepted.

Dean Lieber was amazing at piling on the exaggerations when describing the rationale for how desperate the College was for the grant. Despite the impressive array of buildings, routinely balanced budgets and ever-increasing salaries, as well as growing enrollments, one would have thought CJCC was bankrupt.

David was a virtuoso artist at "cutting and pasting" – taking excerpts from one grant proposal or report and inserting the text into another one. It wasn't plagiarism as much as patch-work quilting with a typewriter. Embellishment was his specialty; exaggeration was his vice.

Dean Lieber and Vice President Kelleher did not care much for each other, personally or professionally. David was an education major, with a pervasive self-taught appreciation of Art History, especially modern artists. J. Paul was a business major, steeped in the English classics and an imposing management style. President Greenleaf could enact a precarious balance of the two antagonistic personalities. That had been his intention in putting Lieber and Kelleher to cook in the same kitchen, with contrasting culinary talents and menu preferences.

The two men had achieved a remarkable balance when it came time to put the grant proposal together. David was a master at educational jargon. He could make the description of drying paint appear exciting. J. Paul was a master at clarity of expression and interweaving management principles into the proposal. Had either of them attempted writing the CJCC Title III proposal alone, he would have failed. Together they produced a magical piece of narrative, seductive design and compelling direction.

Lieber had been with the College for about three years, being hired by Vice President Donald L. Winters to supervise the Library, Academic Skills Labs, Media Center, Language Labs and the Performing Arts. David knew Washington D.C. and all its bureaucratic agencies and departments. He could work his way around Congressional Halls and into offices, having generated federal and state grant support at a Virginia community college before coming to New Jersey.

David was recently remarried. His divorce had been the reason he was ready to move from his prior position. But, his passion was art, not education. He was a noteworthy amateur art collector whose plan was to use his art collection as his retirement investment. Paintings represented success to him, and he was partial to vibrant colors and visual textures. He was well on the way with thousands of dollars of quality pieces, most of which were growing in value and notoriety.

Lieber's house could have doubled as an art gallery, with two original and early Chagall paintings, one of peasant life and the other a village scene. David had identified with Marc Chagall because of their Jewish origins and that the artist had fled Europe and settled in New York, as he had fled his first marriage.

David was skilled in these retirement investments. He had recently purchased a painting by Adolph Gottlieb, another Jewish artist. He knew the artist was not in good health, and the value of his collection would skyrocket when he died. Lieber also owned a painting by the more obscure Max Weber, the Jewish artist, not the German sociologist of the same name.

David had a Master of Education degree from George Mason University near Washington D.C. His specialization had been Instructional Technology which meant he could design learning resources and media presentations. Vice President Winters was looking for an innovative dean, one who would challenge the faculty and their blackboard and chalk approach to teaching. He got that and much more from Lieber. He also got an ally against Kelleher.

The College did have to revise and resubmit its initial Title III proposal. CJCC's Mission Impossible Task Force completed the second submission in six months. The revised proposal sailed through the Department of Education selection process and was heralded by the Washington D.C. bureaucrats as a model.

After the grant award, Lieber and Kelleher were brought to D.C. on two subsequent occasions to speak to drooling college representatives on how to prepare a grant proposal. David lapped up the accolades. Kelleher would shake his head out of disbelief that the *Cut and Paste* approach was effective, and the hyperbole sanctioned. He, along with the others on the Mission Impossible team were partners in Lieber's crooked crime of exaggeration. Crooked or not, the College received $2.5 million in April 1972, to be awarded over five years.

A significant portion of the revised Title III grant funding was to create a Media Production Studio on campus. David was a pioneer in harnessing television, video and other delivery systems as an educational medium to support teaching. Title III was looking for innovative ways to extend educational opportunity to minorities and others of diminished choices. CJCC was looking to attract the dollars and soak up the prestige.

The federal grant paid for equipment and the hiring of production staff, but the College had to fund all material costs. CJCC also had to pay the costs to set aside and modify a classroom to become the Media Production Studio. The College was expected to absorb the grant-funded staff in the operating budget by the end of the grant period.

Founding President Robert Greenleaf was a physical plant and facilities

CEO, meaning he judged success as overseeing an impressive physical campus, not necessarily measuring student learning or achieving a budget reserve. Thus, creation with grant monies of one of New Jersey's first Media Production Studios was an easy sell to Greenleaf, no matter what the matching costs.

Greenleaf convinced the Board of Trustees, or most of them, on the merits of this technology. He praised Lieber and Kelleher for their innovation and their vanguard approach to media production. He figured he would be gone before the grant dried up. He would be hired away by a bigger college for a higher salary. He was wrong. Dr. Greenleaf would be leaving CJCC in only two years.

Kelleher, however, thought the Media Production Studio was a black hole through which institutional and the federal grant money would flow unceasingly. Kelleher was innovative in organizational development and modern leadership principles, although mostly he preached them. He applied his own set of unpublished, bastardized management principles – *Kelleher's Kreative Kriteria for Execs.*

Kelleher was not creative or innovative regarding the curricula or instructional techniques. "Give me a well-prepared instructor, a decent classroom and eager students, and I will show you a roomful of learning," he had often said.

Vice President Donald Winters would counter in meetings of the President's Cabinet. "Students learn in different ways, and instructors have various teaching styles: In the ideal learning situation, those two variables match – the student's preferred learning way and the teacher's dominant classroom style."

At the next meeting of the President's Cabinet, Kelleher would argue. Winters would counter. President Greenleaf would sigh, shake his head and call for a bathroom break.

PAST

"It's strictly business."

Central Jersey Community College had four negotiated union contracts. That meant four bargaining merry-go-rounds with the unions, including facing real or threatened work slowdowns, showdowns or shutdowns.

The Faculty Association was loosely connected to the American Federation of Teachers (AFT). The Staff Union was known as the Career Employees Association and as affiliated with AFSCME – American Federation of State, County and Municipal Employees. Security and maintenance personnel were joined at the hip with Abington City's comparable employee group, also affiliated with AFSCME but with a separate contract.

The administrative employees did not have a bargaining unit until 1973. The General Assembly reluctantly succumbed to the courts and obstinately acquiesced to the national AAUP (American Association of University Professors) to grant that right.

Accordingly, the Board of Trustees was obligated to separate rank and file administrative employees who were in the Union from Exempt Administrators – those relatively few positions excluded from the bargaining table. The select group amounted to the President, Vice Presidents, Deans and supervisors who accessed key data. A smaller number of support staff with access to confidential information were included as Exempt Personnel.

The faculty contract was inclusive of credentialed full-time Counselors, Librarians and all ranks of teacher personnel – Instructor, Assistant/Associate Professor and Professor. New Jersey adjunct faculty and all part-time employees were without bargaining table rights and benefits in 1974 and years to come.

The four union contracts were on different cycles such that the College, its Board and the President faced artful negotiations in one form or another every year. Significant portions of each contract pertained to salary and financial benefits. Yet, there were plentiful proposals on working conditions, tenure, governance, office privileges, workloads, student advising and whatever else surfaced that was not already spelled out in the agreement.

Often the administration, as well as the respective union, would throw out a non-financial article for debate, only to miraculously cave on how truly important that issue was if they could barter the financial package. Each union pitched a more generous salary increase as a marvelous trade-off for any non-financial issue.

Each negotiations process began with CJCC's President who would provide a detailed report to the Board on contracts across the state. He would outline the key salary, benefit and other items to be brought forth, even though most Board members did not understand or were entirely bored. All they cared about was the percentage salary increase and demonstrating defiance to a higher number.

Some would ask a question, mostly so they would be able to affirm to their fellow Board members that they were really on top of the negotiations process. They would usually prop themselves up in the leather Board Room chairs, while the President reviewed the Other Items which were highly significant to the administrative leadership and dozing inducements for the Trustees.

"We caved to the faculty way too easily on the last contract," Vice Chairman Chuck Harrison moaned whenever President Robert Greenleaf made his report to the Board. "I'll be damned if I'm gonna stand for it again," would be Harrison's refrain. "I don't care what percent increases other community colleges, state colleges, universities, grade schools or nursery schools are showing. We need to be tough this time. Faculty have it easy. If we cave on that percent, the other damn unions will want at least the same."

Chuck Harrison was a 50-something portly male with a nasal voice that sounded like he was holding one of his nostrils. He displayed a comb-over hairstyle that approximated a sail when the wind blew.

The Board Vice Chairman thought of himself as a hardliner, the tough out in any line-up. He and his wife, Julie, ran the profitable costume and magic shop in town – *Chuck's House of Magic*. The sales also included unmagical erotic props and videos for sale in a backroom marked "Adults Only."

Harrison considered himself as the only person in New Jersey who worked a strenuous and grueling job. His wife ran the business while *Chuck the Magic Man* did birthday party shows and dashed around the town on behalf of the Chamber of Commerce. She worked far longer hours, without complaint, comment or accolade.

Harrison and likely one or two other Trustees thought the faculty had it easy. They taught five courses a week, adding up to only fifteen class hours.

The gruff Vice Chairman and some of his ignorant colleagues chose not to take into consideration the two-hour per lecture course preparations, exam and paper grading time, syllabus development, mandated office hours, committee work, etc. that faculty crammed into a 50-hour plus work week.

Faculty negotiations always took the same steps no matter the year, the budget or the contract. There would be plenty of posturing during the early weeks, along with prolonged incongruity of facts and greater amounts of false and deliberately misleading data. As the deadline approached, the antipathy morphed into revulsion and mutual ridicule at the zero hour.

The ever-decomposing relationship would reach a climax when faculty would break out their end-of-time buttons, the ones they used the last time. Then the fun would begin. The buttons would proclaim *Hold the Line, Solidarity Forever, Faculty Know How to Teach* or more creatively, *2 Teach is 2 Excel* and *Silence Never Won Rights.*

The intention was to arouse and inflame students and generate media attention. The goal was to start a chain reaction that would eventually agonize the Board into upping the settlement monies. Sometimes it worked; often not.

Certain elements of the negotiations process were a given. If the time frame for negotiations were six months, there would be no closure on anything until that period had exhausted. These unserious meetings would end abruptly, as would any others until the date on which the contract expired. Had the deadline been a month later, there still would have been no settlement.

Each side had to spar as if employing all possible manners of reaching consensus. Mediation would be avoided at all costs, as neither of the opponent Thespians wanted a third party to discern and deflate technical details or identify preposterous positions.

A Board-appointed four-member administrative team, chaired by the Vice President of Administrative Affairs, conducted the negotiations with the Faculty Union. The team included the Personnel Director and two other administrators rotated with each contract. None of the appointed administrators wanted to serve, preferring Jury Duty, road rage and thirty lashes to negotiations. The meetings were tedious, argumentative and turbulent.

Roseanne Hart, as the Personnel Director, was considered bossy and devious. She had only been in the position for two years, having worked in a middle school before the CJCC appointment. Had she been a man, her moniker would have been reasonable and clever, not bossy and devious.

Hart's predecessor was opinionated, overbearing and more arrogant. But Roseanne was a female in a position most persons felt was the sacred right and obligation of a male to hold. Her famous line from The Godfather was *It's* not personal Sonny. It's strictly business. But she would change the line from Sonny to Sister, or to Brother, depending on the audience. She said it with a mischievous smile and a chilly glare.

There had been only five applicants for the Personnel Director position when the College hired her two years ago. Among the candidates, only Roseanne had prior experience in negotiations and public education.

As head of Personnel, Roseanne Hart had to accept the command performance to serve on each negotiation team and participate in every bargaining session with all four unions. Her role was to affirm that each reference to an article, section, sentence or word in the Board-approved contracts was correct and errorless.

She was unerringly precise, and she was tough. Roseanne guarded the terminology and phraseology of any proposal as if wording the U. S. Constitution, perhaps more so.

Miss Hart was in her mid-forties and never married, probably closer to a spinster than a woman in pursuit of male companionship or marital bliss. But this was Jersey in 1973. If she had a male companion, and they wanted to buy a house together but weren't married, the residence would be listed in the man's name. She would have had *"Spinster Hart"* on the deed.

Roseanne was simply a tentative date. Her cynical trepidation to a commitment was grounded in her romantic code: *What a shame to meet the love of your life after marriage.*

Roseanne had had her hair cut to a shapely pageboy, politely framing her face. She featured a pleasant smile on those rare occasions she chose to smile and preferred tailored clothes for work, cowl-neck sweaters, pinstriped pantsuits and chunky, leather boots. She was no knockout, but she was pleasantly attractive.

Roseanne had been in love twice or thought she was. Each time the guy moved on, the last one without even make-up sex or a farewell kiss. She had no interest in having kids and thought that might be a discouraging element in her relationships, especially since the last boyfriend was divorced with two teenage boys.

Roseanne enjoyed her vintage bungalow home, two cats and a range of library books. She kept to herself on campus and mostly avoided social contact with other administrators, staff or faculty and certainly with students. Because of her position in Personnel, and being on each bargaining team, employees stayed beyond arm's reach with her.

Students had no idea who she was. The Board of Trustees still wondered why a woman was in the job.

Miss Hart was active in her church, singing in the choir on most Sunday mornings unless she slept in. She served food on Friday evenings twice a month at the church's homeless shelter and food kitchen. She was not so much a spiritual proselytizer or a zealot – just someone who felt secure with the happenings of the church and trusted her fellow parishioners. And Roseanne could absolve herself, with God's help, of her clandestine misdeeds from the week, or mainly from the day before.

Occasionally, Roseanne would join a few other women or a mixed church group for an event, such as Christmas caroling or bowling, but rarely on Saturday. Saturday was her day. She earned it all week and was adamant she would enjoy her day. Roseanne spent that day at the track, betting on the jockeys and their horses.

Roseanne Hart really enjoyed playing the horses, driving on most Saturdays to Monmouth Park Racetrack in Oceanport. She would study the racing forms, jockeys, trainers, weather, track conditions, wind directions and her horoscope before making her picks.

She was not addicted to horse racing. She was indefensibly hooked on the gambling. Occasionally, she would take home track winnings. More often, she would drive back home with remorse and a reduced bank account. On Sunday at church, she would repent and pledge to avoid the track forever.

Well at least until the next Saturday.

PAST

"Don't ever call me Candy."

Howard Tucker was extraordinarily sound about, and particularly skilled with, computers. Howard was also adept with a bottle of gin and not-so-extraordinarily adroit at hiding his alcohol penchant.

As Director of the Computer Center, Tucker supervised an office of six employees, five male Programmers and a female Administrative Secretary. He reported to the Vice President of Institutional Support, J. Paul Kelleher. He wasn't particularly fond of President Greenleaf; he was entirely un-fond of Vice President Kelleher.

The College had invested in the latest technology, a generic version of the IBM 360 as a mainframe computer. The IBM 360 was designed to provide organizations with the complete range of applications and 512 KB (Kilobytes) of digital memory. There was no model 359 or a 361 version – the 360 merely represented a full circle of applications, IBM's clever promotional appeal.

The College rented the IBM 360 for $5,530 per month. IBM marketed the product to be rented and thus marginally affordable. The computer functioned with a DOS (Disk Operating System) that employed disk storage to organize, read and write files using punched cards and magnetic tapes and drums.

The computer industry was changing quickly in the mid-1970's. The challenge for Tucker, other than hiding his liquor habit, was to survey the field and decide how best to migrate upward, replace peripheral devices and balance exponentially expanding computing priorities.

The Computer Center had an elevated, false flooring to enable the enclosed area to be chilly enough to protect the mainframe investment and prevent over-heating. The machine itself was comparable to a large U-Haul truck, and most users never got to see the mysterious behemoth. The staff wore long sleeve shirts and sweaters even in the summer. Some wore zippered jackets and wool hats.

The nickname for the Center was *Meat Locker,* owing to the temperature. When Vice President Kelleher would visit the facility, he would recall his father's butcher shop where beef hind-quarters would hang, not house complex data-processing machines.

Faculty and staff had to submit the jobs to the Computer Center to be processed on the mainframe, consistent with specifically written programs or repeated software applications. There were no desktop computers, but employees were thrilled to have the data processing capabilities of the IBM 360.

The staff would take the punched cards, create the program, input the job and eventually retrieve the output. The yield would be in the form of computer paper with perforated outer margins. The pierced sheets unfolded like connected sheets of paper towels, only much larger pages and more elongated rolls.

It was a necessary and acquired skill to tear off the outer belts of the perforated print-out papers without ripping the document. For most computer jobs, the multi-page output pages, if separated and plastered to a building wall, would cover the entire space as substitute wallpaper.

Howard kept his gin in a plain glass bottle in a desk drawer, actually two bottles. There was no prohibition by the College against having liquor in one's office or on campus. Society had no rules against such either. The Computer Center Director drank from paper *Dixie Cups* borrowed from the water cooler parked in the staff lounge. The behavior fooled no one. But the illusion that he was drinking cold water from the water cooler, not the gin from his cloaked bottle, was demeaning and comical.

While Howard Tucker was the Director, Gene Wildwood was the Lead Programmer. That meant Wildwood supervised the other Programmers and ran the operation. Howard preferred to stay in his office, pour through sales and marketing manuals, sort billings, check the air conditioning, serve on College committees and take early morning, mid-morning, mid-afternoon and late afternoon coffee breaks in the Student Center.

Howard was very accomplished at looking busy when he was not. Gene and the other Programmers knew Howard was unindustrious, but they accepted his situation without incidence or ridicule, other than occasional wisecracks. He had hired each of them, served several as a mentor and left them to do their jobs. They could work as hard, or as little, as they chose and on a hurried or lackadaisical pace.

Howard was the figurative leader, but Gene held the power in the Computer Center. He was the one who conducted triage and affixed a priority to each job submitted. According to office policy, preference was to be given to the Vice President of Academic Affairs to manage the efficiency of course schedules and faculty assignments. Regardless, Gene knew Vice President Kelleher needed every one of his requests to have highest priority. Every request from everyone else was to have a lower priority, except jobs for Dr. Greenleaf.

Gene was partial to jobs submitted by the faculty and not afraid to stall even the President if he didn't think the request was a priority. Wildwood decided if a submission could leapfrog another one, just because he wanted to do that. He was manipulatively partial to faculty and staff who saw his priority assignment as a favor, one he could collect on later.

Wildwood became comfortable expecting and receiving bottles of wine, movie tickets and dinner coupons in return for priority processing. The faculty and staff knew that was how to get their programming elevated in the computer queue. Those who appreciated how the crooked system worked asked Gene for what he preferred in wine. Without exception, it was always Italian Chianti Classico. The Lead Programmer particularly enjoyed receiving the wine with the traditional straw basket. Those who did not understand the system had to wait longer for their output.

If students needed computer processing, they had to appeal to a faculty member. Students were not allowed in the *Meat Locker*, much less invited to submit jobs. There were no Work-Study student workers or student interns in the Computer Center. The Financial Aid Office did not want students to witness Howard with his *Dixie Cups*. The Programmers did not want brighter Computer Technology students showing them up.

Wildwood took the late shift on Monday and Wednesday, meaning he worked from 11:00 AM to 7:30 PM, not 9:00 AM to 5:30 PM. Tucker preferred the Tuesday and Thursday shift. Saturday was reserved for the Programmers only, those few who desired overtime when the jobs backed up or holidays approached.

The Computer Center's gatekeeper was the sole female employee, Mrs. Candace Rodewald. Gene may have determined the programming priority, but Candace – *don't ever call me Candy* – set the bar for sequencing before the submissions even got to Gene. If users entered the office and greeted her with "Candace" and showed respect for her and her responsibilities, they got through the gate.

If one called her "Candy" or assumed she was a lowly secretary, that job request got shelved. When the output was eventually completed, Candace would accidentally on purpose stall before notifying the person to pick up the work. She would offer a familiar retort. "Oh, I'm sorry. The job must have gotten stuck somewhere. Hope you won't have to wait too much longer." Users learned not to upset Mrs. Rodewald.

The fact that Howard had settled on the gin, rather than a variety of spirits or vodka, which did not have a telltale smell, only meant Howard was a man of principle. He was going to drink what he wanted to drink. He had fully arrived at his booze of choice.

But Tucker's paper *Dixie Cup* gin-drinking manifested itself into a habit of alcohol over indulgence.

Only Computer Center staff went into Howard's office, at the rear of the *Meat Locker* next to the mainframe. Vice President Kelleher, upset that a job was not done or that Gene and Candace were setting priorities, was the exception. He ventured into the offices to remind the folks who was the ultimate boss. He did so with loud, often vulgar, language and Irish threats.

Because the Computer Center was a *Meat Locker*, it was normal for Candace to display a couple of protruding nipples at times during the day, owing to the cold. Some men, including the Programmers, likened them to *Gum Drops*. The enticing exposure was keenly evident when the lady would wear one of her dark-color sweaters, especially the emerald green choice. The clothing preference in the cold was an occupational hazard.

Candace was aware of the swelling nature of her breasts and had tried stuffing *Kleenex* tissues in her bra to mask the nipples. When that did not work, she once applied *Band Aides,* but that got expensive. She changed bra brands and styles frequently.

The *Wonderbra* had boldly hit the commercial market as an unmentionable at a time when bras were slowly transitioning as an undergarment no longer lurking unseen and disguised beneath a lady's blouse. Women were processing society's acceptance of lingerie as a main attraction. Bras were now marketed as chic, fashionable items rather than as functional garments. Beautiful patterns, lace and lining were becoming normative for the lingerie, not rubbery material with uncomfortable cones and fasteners.

Most women still were wearing highly structured undergarments, including girdles with suspender clips to hold-up nylon stockings. The girdle was considered eminently respectable and modest, albeit uncomfortable.

The Feminist Movement questioned the mores that defined women's roles, as well as their underwear. Changes in fashion trends, such as pantyhose and the mini-skirt, both introduced to mass markets in the mid-1960's, gradually rendered the girdle unattractive and elevated intimate apparel sales in the 1970's

For the first time, TV commercials displayed bras with a discrete woman's torso, not mannequins showing the product. Bras were designed to "Lift and Separate" one's bosom and pad for comfort. There also was the favored *Playtex Cross Your Heart* bra that promoted itself as ever- so-slightly-padded. One could purchase the sexy lingerie in department stores in various colors and styles, not as relegated to Adult Novelty Stores or mail-order catalogs.

Candace wore pantyhose, and she favored mini-skirts over slacks, but never in the office. The exception was for those liquor-dominated faculty and staff Christmas parties. Pantyhose was a revelation for women who could ditch their nylons and garter belts. Rodewald chose *L'eggs*, partly because they were sold stuffed inside a plastic, egg-shaped container.

Candace, in her early thirties and highly attractive with long sandy-brown hair and enchanting green eyes, was charming and self-assertive, not just curvaceous. She was not about to alter her appearance or stop wearing sweaters because of a couple of out-thrusting appendages and more than a couple of ogling males.

Employee males made it a habit and a privilege to volunteer to take over the departmental programming and processing jobs to the *Meat Locker*. The common phrase was, "I have to go to the Computer Center and check out the knockout lady who patrols the outer office. I'll be back, eventually."

Candace, setting aside her looks, knew that her colleagues found her intelligent and honest. She was for the most part.

Mrs. Rodewald approached work with high aptitude and drive. She had had to compensate for being highly attractive all her life and confronting a male-dominated career. She was exceptionally thorough and ambitious.

If there was a polling of faculty and staff to vote for the person with whom you would most likely want to be marooned on a desolate island, it would be Candace. People knew she'd be able to handle every survival necessity and confront every challenge. This lady would successfully address every unknown and unanticipated contingency faced in the *Meat Locker* or on the remote island.

And she would look good in a bikini.

PAST

"Guys don't count on a cheerleading squad."

The *Roaring Raiders* of Central Jersey Community College were one of the more successful men's basketball programs in the Northeast during the early and mid-1970's. They had won the State title twice. They had twice placed second in the Northeastern Regional Tournament but never had made it to the National Championship games.

Basketball at a community college in the 1970's was not a major athletic event comparable to the Atlantic Coast Conference or the Big Ten, or even a mid-major conference. People did not buy pricey tickets, purchase assigned seats or enjoy a variety of concessions for campus home games.

Nevertheless, the games were highly competitive, well-coached contests between two institutions. The spectators were sporadically spaced on wooden bleachers, having paid $4 for entry. No advance ticket purchases necessary. No reserved seating, pep band or half-time show either.

The cheering audience was made up predominantly of family members, assorted faculty and staff, loyal friends, basketball junkies and a nomadic busload from the opponent's town. The College President would not likely be in the stands, or even have the event on his calendar. The Athletic Director would be there, unless he had a hot date. There would not be any scouts from the NBA or the USA Olympics or from the Boy Scouts of America.

The basketball athletes at the College did not receive full or partial scholarships. They did not experience pressured recruitment tactics. Most lived within miles of the respective campus, commuted daily and had on-campus Work-Study and off-campus part-time jobs to handle expenses.

Like most junior colleges, the CJCC basketball team was made up of local kids who had played high school ball and weren't skilled enough, tall enough or academically sound enough to warrant a university scholarship.

These young men played basketball because they cherished the sport and relished playing time. They thrived on competition. Some labored with an idealized, hyperbolic assessment of their skills. Some had delusions of being discovered and signed to a university scholarship or a long-term contract with a professional basketball team. Most gave thanks they could at least play organized basketball for a couple more years.

Solly, the *Roaring Raiders'* Head Coach, was named Nathan Howard Solomon and grew up in Squirrel Hill, a predominantly Jewish community in Pittsburgh. He went by the first name Nathan through grade school and then by Natty in high school. Neither name was endearing to the future basketball coach.

He was named after his grandfathers, Nathan on the paternal side and Howard for his mother's dad. He was proud of both namesakes, just not particularly pleased with how his male peer group friends would consider them as old-man names.

When he got to college, the professor in a freshman English class got his names reversed. He called him *Solomon Nathan*. Nathan immediately corrected the mistake, but his class colleagues started calling him Solomon anyway. In one semester, that handle morphed into Sol and that tag into Solly. Solly stuck.

In younger years, Solly had been a gifted athlete, just a little stubby at 5" 8" in stature to be able to play big time sports. Nevertheless, he persisted pugnaciously. After two years as a walk-on guard for Rutgers, he earned a scholarship for his junior and senior years as well as a starting position for basketball's *Scarlet Knights*. He got the position due to his hustle and because he knew the defensive alignments better than the coach. He understood the weaknesses and strengths of his teammates better than they did.

Once he became a high school coach after college, his signature title became Coach Solly. Few people and none of his players were aware of the Nathan Howard Solomon. Henceforth, Coach became his first name and Solly his surname. His fellow Physical Education faculty members at CJCC knew his full name, as did the Personnel Office. But the rest of the faculty and staff fell blissfully into the Coach Solly title and assumed his passport and driver's license had the same name.

Head Coach Solly attracted several exceptional athletes to play for him. These guys elevated every teammate's play and propelled the team into a championship caliber squad.

Coach Solly knew many Division I and II university basketball coaches. They knew he was a marvelous teacher of fundamental basketball, especially defensive strategies and techniques, and that he cared deeply for his players. Solly held clinics at basketball conventions and gave speeches several times before audiences of Division I coaches. His knowledge, humor and entertaining presentation always filled the room, much as a Las Vegas nightclub act. Despite his antics, there was no disputing his coaching prowess, accomplishments on the court and sales mentality.

Periodically, the university coaches he knew would have a highly skilled player or an exceptionally tall athlete on their recruitment screen. The coach might subsequently learn that the recruit did not earn the prerequisite SAT exam score for admission. If so, the university basketball coach would let Coach Solly know. Or, that coach might be aware of an impressive basketball player who was injured and could not play for several months or a year. If so, he would let Coach Solly know.

CJCC's basketball coach would reach out to these players, smooth-talk them and invite the athletes to play on his team. He could not provide a scholarship, free shoes or even a meal plan. He could assure they would not be a BMOC (Big Man on Campus) unless they were exceptionally tall, and height counted. "Sorry, you're on your own as far as the ladies are concerned. And guys, don't count on a cheerleading squad or pep band."

Coach Solly arranged for a communal apartment for the out-of-town players to serve as a group dormitory. He could provide Work-Study jobs and leads for off-campus part-time work. He could assure the student-athletes would raise their achievement by taking advantage of remedial English, reading and math courses and availing themselves of learning resources and tutors.

To be sure, he could hound them, amplifying and sharpening their on-court performance and their off-court maturity.

The academically challenged athletes would learn to learn, and the wounded high school stars would heal. Both would mature as men and blossom on the court. Both would earn transferable college credits and eventually have a two-year Associate Degree in hand. The same guys who were rejected by the university two years ago would now have multiple opportunities to transfer and play their junior and senior years. But they would be wiser, stronger and far more coachable. Most would be sought out by those same university coaches who had previously referred them to Coach Solly.

The university coach would say, "Thanks Solly for healing them, getting their grades up and teaching them fundamentals and hard play. I'll take them back now. Nice job."

Academically on track as college juniors, fully healed and extremely well-prepared for higher level basketball, these Coach Solly disciples would be granted university scholarships to continue their education and further their basketball careers. Such was the channel Coach Solly used to augment his team roster and champion one of the most well-respected junior college programs in the East.

When the basketball games were over, and the *Roaring Raiders* would win the game, the stands would not erupt with fans streaming across the court to embrace players. There would be no media onslaught to interview the players or hold a press conference for Coach Solly or provide an audio, let alone video, replay of the winning basket.

There would be no congratulatory telephone call from the President of the United States, the Governor or the Mayor, or for that matter the College President. There would not be a parade around the town or the campus the following week. There would be no salary bonus, no comped car. But the coach and players knew they were good, and the team camaraderie in winning was contagious.

Title IX, passed by Congress in 1972, required gender equity for males and females in every athletic program at a college or university receiving federal funding, including student financial aid. The law applied to other aspects of higher education but provided assurances that women would have intercollegiate athletic programs comparable to men.

CJCC was compliant with Title IX. There were four intercollegiate sports for males – basketball, soccer, tennis and baseball. There were four sports for females – field hockey, softball, volleyball and tennis.

Not all community colleges had intercollegiate basketball teams or even an intercollegiate athletic program – for men or women – in the early and mid-1970's. For colleges with intercollegiate basketball programs, the teams often practiced and played in borrowed middle or high school gyms. The teams traveled by a car caravan rather than a university-owned or leased bus or van.

Most coaches were part-time in that profession at a junior college, paid according to a temporary contract rather than hourly. They shared a devotion to the sport and the reality of earning a living from other jobs. Less frequently, coaches like Solly were faculty members at the same college with teaching and student advising load assignments and a partial course reduction as compensation for the coaching.

The minimum wage was $2.10 per hour. Given their hours of work, most coaches made considerably less. Few cared.

PAST

"Don't mess up where you live!"

Early in his administration, President Robert Greenleaf established the culture of the Campus Security Office of Central Jersey Community College. There were eight Security Guards along with the Chief of Security. All were expected to secure and protect campus property while interacting with students and faculty and smiling at them. They were to engage students rather than stand in armed patrol with sour or intimidating expressions.

None of the Security Guards wielded a firearm, although there were two shotguns and two handguns locked in the Chief of Security's office. In deference to the College's color scheme, the guards wore a forest green sports coat, with the College logo sewn on the chest pocket, and a purple tie. Each jacket included a coat of arms emblem with the words *Campus Security*. A white shirt, tan slacks and a black embossed *Campus Security* cap completed the uniform. The guards looked professional, sharp and approachable, much like everyone's favorite uncles.

All the CJCC Security Guards were white males when the College was founded. There was little, if any, conversation during those early CJCC years about workforce diversification in ethnicity or gender. You would have even odds as to whether a future guard would ever be a racial minority or female.

Most of the Security Guards had military backgrounds; none had ever worked for a police force, a sheriff or any other branch of criminal justice. That was the way Greenfield wanted it. "It's better to secure the campus by the force of interactions and relationships, rather than by force of an armed police presence," Greenfield had convincingly argued before the Board of Trustees.

There were few campus incidents to prove him wrong. Indeed, the work of the CJCC Security Guards had mostly to do with parking – keeping students from parking in *Faculty Only* spaces or *Visitor Only* spaces and discouraging necking and romantic interludes in parked cars or darkened hallways. Occasionally, a purse would be stolen, or a vending machine vandalized.

There was a car break-in once in the parking lot when a female student had her cassette tape stolen. That disruption proved to be a dispute as to who owned the machine. By and large, students adhered to the 25 MPH speed limit on the campus access roads, although it was common practice to floor the accelerator once they hit the county road. Then they would peel off in their cars as if at the Pocono Raceway.

There was a memorable incident in the spring of 1973 that was more humorous than menacing, more asinine than perilous. An adjunct art faculty, who taught a section of Life Drawing on Tuesday evenings, had decided to switch models. Normally she brought in young women to pose nude for the amateur artists, sometimes wearing a cape or colossal hat. Mostly the young women wore nothing.

The art professor decided to substitute a pony for the human as the model for the final exam. The trouble was that the classroom was on the second floor, and the disagreeable pony had no interest in climbing stairs.

While students snickered aloud over the stubborn pony, the resourceful instructor decided to lure the animal into the elevator. That was fine until the doors closed and the elevator began its upward movement. Then the 400-pound American Shetland began to howl. Normally, hoofed animals will whinny, neigh, snort or grunt. This fellow decided to moan and groan as if some had placed its sexual organs in a vice.

In apparent agony, the pony let loose with a blow of gas followed by a release of what could only be described as a dump on the elevator floor. The art teacher did not know whether to go back to the first floor or continue to the second. And she did not know whether to cry or laugh. She continued to the second floor and exited with one hand holding the leashed pony and her other hand covering her mouth, so she could breathe.

Campus Security was called and helped retrieve the pony from the second floor. But this was after the students had moved to the hallway near the elevator to assume their Life Drawing class. A maintenance crew was summoned for the clean-up, but they had to retrieve a larger shovel. Their supervisor subsequently filed a grievance petition.

"All I could think about is the scene in The Godfather where the horse head is in bed," said the flustered and frustrated faculty member. And I was wondering how the students would interpret the rather large pony penis in their sketches."

The first Chief of Security had retired in Spring 1974 just before Dr. Greenleaf would take the job in St. Louis and leave the College. There was talk that President Greenleaf would bring in an outside person to head Security.

Instead, he invited all current guards to apply and interview for the position. Three guards did, including Mr. Tyrone Jackson.

Much to the surprise of the faculty and staff, Greenleaf chose the sole African-American guard for the lead position as Interim Chief.

Tyrone Jackson had been with the College since 1972 and had seniority over all but two of the Security Guards. At 6 feet 2 inches, Jackson was the tallest of the guards. At 51, he was a father figure to half of the Security Guards and a role model to the rest.

Jackson had interviewed exceedingly well, and Greenleaf had reasoned that he was as qualified and competent as any, and he would get brownie points for the minority hire. Three months later, the Interim title was dropped, and Tyrone Jackson was officially appointed as Chief of Campus Security.

Tyrone Jackson was born in Newark and had entered the Marines shortly after high school, serving mostly in the Korean War near the Sea of Japan. In 1952, he was severely injured when he and fellow Marines jumped from a helicopter. Tyrone landed poorly on his right leg, severely breaking his ankle.

Jackson was in the military hospital for a month recovering from the surgeries and going through intensive therapy, but he was never able to recover sufficiently to re-enter the Marines. The ankle just did not heal properly despite two surgeries and extended recovery time. He could walk, but not run anymore, at least not without a prominent limp.

Tyrone had been awarded an Honorable Discharge due to his model service record and physical disability. After a few months of out-patient therapy, the former Marine had applied for a prison guard position at Fort Dix Federal Penitentiary, twenty miles southeast of Trenton. He was a prison guard at Fort Dix for sixteen years, arduously monitoring the prisoners by day and trying to forget those contacts by night.

With his honorable military service and exemplary Fort Dix work, Tyrone could retire in 1972 from the prison guard duty with a twenty-year pension. It was time for a different career direction.

Central Jersey Community College had had an opening for a Security Guard, and Tyrone Jackson had applied and was hired. He was more than qualified. However, his wife of sixteen years decided this was the time for separation in anticipation of a divorce. She remained in Pemberton Heights. Tyrone got an apartment in Abington less than a mile from the College. They attempted a reconciliation, but there was no need to pretend.

Ironically, Tyrone had met his wife at the hospital where he underwent extensive physical therapy following surgery after the accident in the Marines. She was a Practical Nurse and tended to his needs including an occasional body sponge bath.

She liked to explain to friends, "I had to give Tyrone a sponge bath over his entire body, well most of it anyway. Normally we give a sponge bath once a day, but Tyrone kept asking me for another one just after he'd had the first one."

They married just before Tyrone got the Fort Dix penitentiary job. He kept asking for sponge baths even after they married. The sponge baths became less frequent and less soothing; the marriage became less satisfying and more annoying.

Two years after his relocation to Abington and the Security Guard appointment, Tyrone's elder daughter, Crystal, had moved in with him after being accepted into CJCC's Associate Degree Nursing program.

Crystal aced her prerequisite science courses but struggled with the Human Anatomy course, owing to the cadaver the students had to study and dissect. "Dad, it's a bit creepy to see this decomposed dead human with various body parts exposed and unlayered for us," Crystal shared with her father. "How come if a person is dead, they're a corpse, but if used for a scientific study they're a cadaver? And, why do we have to peel back the body parts like we might peel the layers of an onion?"

"All I know, is that when the person is dead, the guy's a stiff," Tyrone responded to his daughter. "That's what we called them at Fort Dix."

Crystal had completed the AAS program in two years and a summer. She got her own apartment in Morristown and a Registered Nurse job at a local clinic. At the campus Pinning Ceremony, when the students took the Nightingale Pledge, her father cried with joy. Crystal just went over to Professor Jim White and gave him a huge hug – he was her professor for that Human Anatomy class with the peeled-back body parts cadaver.

There was a sharp increase in cocaine use in the early 1970's, most everywhere. The drug was clean, white and pretty. Cocaine became a gang problem when the crack cocaine market exploded. By mixing cocaine in a saucepan with baking soda and water, novice chemists would create a product of miniature white rocks.

The cocaine product was suitable for smoking and emitted a crackling sound when burned. It was sold as a rock, weighing anywhere from 0.1 to 0.5 gram. Buyers could spend $5 or $50 on the street, and likely get ripped off with either amount.

County Commissioner Dominic Panichi Jr. created a task force in 1973 to study the situation in Monroe County. He knew the College had a Security Guard who had worked in a federal penitentiary, so he asked Jackson to serve on the esteemed group. The study expanded into an analysis of local gangs as well as those that were invading the region from New York and Newark.

Through his former contacts at Fort Dix, Security Guard Jackson found the Newark source of the drug manufacturing and distributorship. That endeared him to the County Commissioner and the County Sheriff and brought considerable public presence to the sole African-American on the College's Security detail.

The front-page story in the *Jersey Star* included a quote by the County Commissioner, "We identified the mainline route for the drugs, thanks to Mr. Jackson's connections. We will never be able to slam the door shut on the trafficking, but we certainly can swing it to where it's almost shut. The mules running the drugs have gone into hiding."

Drugs had never been much of a problem on the College campus. There was an unwritten rule that the gangs consciously or unconsciously honored: *No dealing on campus. Ever.*

The Safety Zone saying was akin to: *Don't mess up where you live!* Or, as Jackson was fond of saying, *Don't shit where you sleep!* There might be some pot left over from the hippie days or stashed in a few faculty offices. Outside of that, the campus was unstained by drugs.

Tyrone Jackson was the only member of the Security Office who was African-American even when he was promoted to Chief in 1974. There were several African-American employees in the Maintenance Department, along with one instructor in Physical Education, one in Automotive Technology and one in Welding Technology. There was a lab assistant in Culinary Arts who was African-American and one Nursing Lab assistant.

There were no Hispanic or Latino-American professors or support staff members. There was one solitary male Asian-American faculty member in Pre-Engineering. Diversity was measured by program majors, hair styles and tastes in beer, not by ethnicity, gender or religion.

It had been twenty years since the Supreme Court ruled in 1954 in Brown v. Board of Education of Topeka, Kansas, that racial segregation in schools was unconstitutional. But admittance of black students to state universities, or community colleges, was not assured or prioritized.

President Greenleaf was injudiciously proud of the racial diversity of CJCC. After all, there were a handful of minority employees and he had promoted Jackson. The bar was set very low.

He was unaware of gender diversity of the campus, nor did he consider it much of a priority. Male domination of all employee positions, other than secretarial, was as natural then as male-dominated football teams, male fraternities and boys in the Boy Scouts.

Greenleaf was not alone in thinking that way. After all, there was a ten-year age differentiation between the oldest white male on his Cabinet and the youngest. In his mind that created sufficient diversity in consideration of decision and issues.

PAST

"Be sure to wrap up that Dissertation Defense."

Of all the five Division Deans at Central Jersey Community College – Communications & Arts, Science & Mathematics, Social Science & Business, Applied Technologies and Instructional Resources – Dr. Vernon T. Carter was the most qualified. When the College hired Carter, he had earned a Ph.D. in Educational Management from Penn State, after an M.A. and B.A. in Biology from Drexel University. None of the other four had a doctorate. None of the four was African-American either.

Vice President Donald L. Winters had initiated the national search in May 1974 for the replacement Dean of Science & Mathematics, coincidentally at the time Carter was finishing up his Penn State doctorate, while teaching Biology as a graduate student. Vernon and his wife wanted to relocate closer to New York in a full-time academic administrative position.

He was attracted by the CJCC job announcement in the *Chronicle of Higher Education*. The position was administrative, but the Division Dean would be obligated to teach one course each semester. To Vernon, that meant the College put a high value on teaching, keeping administrators active in the classroom and interacting with students.

Vernon was part of a national focus on producing more eligible minority doctorate students. He had received a handsome fellowship from Penn State in 1971 and had only recently completed the final draft of his Dissertation. He would now have to present his dissertation to his Doctoral Committee.

Vernon had been looking for a career opportunity at a university, college, academy, high school, junior high or nursery school. His curriculum vitae highlighted his soon-to-be Ph.D. and his productive internship and successful college teaching experiences. He had over-the-top letters of recommendation.

He may have been part of Affirmative Action, but he was a stellar example of how opportunity can be maximized.

Vernon had answered the *Chronicle* ad. He had submitted the glowing letters of recommendation especially the ones highlighting his work ethic and integrity. He had included a Statement of Administrative Philosophy. That document was not difficult or a burden because he had already crafted a similar statement as part of his doctoral examinations.

Subsequently, ABD (All But Dissertation) Vernon had been invited, with expenses paid, to the CJCC campus to spend two days interviewing and meeting with faculty, staff, students and various officials. Members of the Search Committee had been startled when Dr. Carter showed up on campus for the interviews. No one had told them he was a minority candidate. Committee members knew Vernon had stellar credentials. They had not known his ethnicity, and they were confused that a candidate of his stature would want to work at the College and inconceivably make the cut.

Vernon was anxious and suspicious about the upcoming Faculty Forum, expecting it to approximate a feeding frenzy. He had learned that the Division faculty members were mixed on their feelings regarding the predecessor, who left under fire for misrepresenting his academic credentials. Some liked the guy. Some were appalled when they learned what he had done. The rest didn't care.

The departed guy had falsified his master's degree. Picky, picky. The deceit was uncovered when the College had to present notarized copies of college transcripts for all its faculty as part of the 1972-73 Middle States Accreditation reaffirmation report and the February 1974 evaluation visit.

The College had hired the guy as a Division Dean when there were far fewer official materials required to document the credentials. The false transcript from the University of Tampa was accepted, even though the institution's correct name was *Tampa University*. Only when they conducted the audit of faculty credentials did someone catch the bogus name and counterfeit transcript.

After a brief self-introduction that afternoon at the Faculty Forum, Vernon had taken faculty questions one by one. Mrs. Nancy Wiegand, the Screening Committee Chairman, served in the dual capacity as Mistress of Ceremony and Sergeant at Arms. Wiegand was an Associate Professor of Psychology and not even a member of the Science & Mathematics Division.

Vernon had been patient with the initial questions and even more indulgent with the tough questions. He was tolerant of the ugly ones and quickly won over the group with his honesty and humor.

If the faculty had expected Vernon T. Carter to be a token minority candidate, they were way off. Vernon was the leading candidate, even for those with a cynical attitude and misplaced Uncle Tom values.

Academic Vice President Donald L. Winters had been very aware of Vernon's background and his racial identification. He had made it clear to the committee chair that he would not tolerate racial bias in the screening process.

Educational institutions were now subject to Title VI and to Equal Opportunity norms after Congress determined that discrimination against minorities and women in education was as pervasive as other employment areas. Winters had not needed the federal or state government looking over his shoulder. He was resolute to interject diversity into his departments and his deans, if only by the one appointment.

Winters had set up a time for his prime candidate to meet and visit briefly with President Greenleaf. However, he was hoping Greenleaf would be too busy with other priorities or that Mrs. Reynolds, the President's Secretary, would forget to remind him when he went to lunch. Winters knew Greenleaf had other things on his mind these days.

Vernon, the candidate, and Winters, the Academic Vice President, had crossed the campus to the Administration Building and caught Dr. Greenleaf as he had been entering his car parked in the College President reserved space. "Oh, sorry, Donald," Greenleaf shouted as he turned the ignition in his car. "I have to run. Edith was supposed to call you. Is this the other candidate, the one from Penn State you told me about? If I have questions, I'll call you. Nice to meet you, sir. Sorry I have to go now."

Winters hadn't bothered to apologize. Vernon had not done any homework on the President, so he just absorbed what had happened and ignored the awkward moment. But Winters had not wanted to leave the candidate thinking less of the campus CEO, so he had interjected, "The President has pressing off-campus concerns disrupting his normal schedule right now. Greenleaf's a fine person to work with, respectful of our work and not into micro-managing. Another way of saying it, I suppose, is that he's not much into the academics of the College. Fine with me."

The soon-to-be Dr. Carter had been surprised when he got the telephone call from Vice President Winters a day after returning home from the visit to CJCC. He had submitted the paperwork, completed an initial telephone interview and visited the campus for those two days. All that was part of a typical screening and selection process. But now, Winters had wanted to come to State College and spend two days interviewing Vernon's supervisors and colleagues and having dinner with him and his wife.

Mrs. Wiegand, representing the Search Committee, would join the Vice President, which seemed even more unusual. Nancy had been with the College since 1972 and had distinguished herself as a marvelous professor, but why was the Committee Chair not from Science and Mathematics? Winters had

39

been swimming upstream by having chosen a relatively new faculty member, let alone a female, as Chairman. But Nancy had few distractors, and there had been a method to Winters' madness.

Vernon had known that it was not Standard Operating Procedure (SOP) for a prospective candidate to expect an on-site visit. That SOP was almost always reserved for the selection of presidents, seldom for chief academic officers and never for a dean position.

The on-campus visit the prior week had gone well, and Vernon had known he was a finalist among one or perhaps two others, and with no in-house candidate. He had interpreted that news as indicative of a reasonably fair and unbiased search, but then he had been part of a couple of other searches that were anything but beacons for Equal Opportunity. This one might just be a carbon copy of the others.

The Winters and Wiegand duo would fly into State College, Pennsylvania. Winters had asked Vernon to pick them up at the airport and drive back the thirty minutes to where he lived and had reserved hotel rooms. Carter was to follow through with a prescribed agenda, dictated by Winters, including a lengthy listing of people and positions to schedule.

However, on the afternoon of the pick-up, there was an accident on I-99 going to the airport. All traffic headed south came to an abrupt halt. There had been nothing Vernon could do about it, except wait it out. There had been no car phone and no telephone booth on the highway. There had been no way he could drive the shoulder to an exit and find a telephone. All he could do was wait and stew, while his job opportunity dematerialized.

When Carter finally got to the airport, Vice President Winters and Mrs. Wiegand had been sitting pleasantly in the Delta Airlines reception area with their baggage. They had not been agitated or upset. The reaction had been Vernon's clue that he was the final candidate.

Instead the odd couple had chosen to apologize to Vernon. "So sorry you got stuck in traffic, Mr. Carter," Winters admitted with a calm voice and quiet demeanor. "A little late now, but Mrs. Wiegand and I should have rented a car and driven to State College on our own to meet you. Sorry about that."

Fortunately, the rest of the on-site visit had gone exceedingly well, especially the part where Donald, Nancy, Vernon and his wife Katherine had dinner. Katherine had charmed and mesmerized the out-of-town pair. She had a way of captivating others, first with her profound good looks and then with her effervescent, embracing personality.

After lunch the second day, Winters and Carter headed back to Vernon's house to meet Mrs. Wiegand, who had visited with Katherine at her workplace. Now Vernon could ask his burning questions: "Sir, it's unusual for a candidate for Division Dean to receive an on-site visit from the recruiting college. I'm impressed by the thoroughness of your search, but I still ask why? Too, I was wondering why you selected a Psychology professor as Chairman of the Search Committee and not someone from Science or Mathematics?"

Vernon had held his breath for a moment and then continued with his reverse interview questions. "Since we are at the end of your visit, is there anything else you would want to know or accomplish while here in town? And, sir, what are the final steps in the process? When do you anticipate a decision?"

The expression on Vice President Winters' face had been akin to that of a pint-sized schoolboy caught with his hand in a cookie jar, except that the scenario would have included falling off the stool. He had been impressed that his final candidate was so perceptive, but he had not anticipated an astute interrogation.

"Let me be perfectly honest, Vernon," Winters had responded with a highly serious expression on his face and earnestness in his voice. "Few people know, but Dr. Greenleaf, whom you saw as he was getting into his car, is the finalist for another presidency, in St. Louis. Likely he will be leaving the College as soon as June."

"It's just a matter of negotiating his new contract," Winters added. "I knew this. That's why I was hesitant to occupy his time with a meeting. But Robert has confided in me that I'd be his choice to serve as Interim President while the Board of Trustees conducts the replacement search. He also shared I'd be his choice to succeed him as the President, although the Board would have the final say."

Vernon had not expected this explanation. His face had been approximating that of a vigilant mother who suddenly enters her kitchen only to find toddler son on the floor with the broken cookie jar and a chocolate chip cookie dangling from his mouth. But Vernon had quickly returned to a more stoic expression, as the mother would have too.

"We won't know for a few months," Winters confided. "Should all of that happen, I would be searching for an interim and then a replacement Vice President of Academic Affairs. While there is no guarantee that would be you, I wanted to make this screening process very, very thorough. I share this with you because we think highly of you, and we want you to know there will be other opportunities at the College, likely sooner rather than later."

Without hesitation and in the same cadence, Winters had continued. "Mrs. Wiegand understands and is comfortable with that explanation, although she's not aware of what I've just shared with you. Much of the campus knows the President is leaving. The local newspaper carried a feature on him recently, wrongly stating he was a finalist for a position in Florida, not Missouri."

"As for Nancy as Search Committee Chairman," Winters had elaborated,

"I wanted to get a broader, more faculty-wide perspective. There's been all this turmoil among the Division faculty over the former guy's departure. I wanted an objective, non-science and non-math person as Chairman. Besides being an excellent teacher, Mrs. Wiegand played a huge role in the Self-Study her first year for the Middle States re-affirmation of accreditation. She is highly respected, but I still got several complaints that I'd chosen a female as Chairman."

This had been a considerable amount of information for Vernon to process. He had just kept his eyes on the road while his mind trailed off in various directions.

Winters continued, "From what I hear, you handled yourself amazingly well at that Faculty Forum. Your colleagues in the Division were hurt and angry by what the former administrator had done. Hope you don't mind, but we double-checked your credentials."

Then Winters added, "Be sure to wrap up that Dissertation Defense."

PAST

"I love you, but I'm going back to the Library to study."

Vernon Carter had entered Penn State University's Ph.D. program with the career goal of becoming a chief academic officer. But that ambition would normally take several years. Yet, Carter was presented with a storyline that unfolded to that end, far more quickly than he contemplated.

Carter had ended the "Cat and Mouse" contest with Vice President Donald L. Winters by conceding that if offered the position, he would accept. "Katherine and I talked at length last night after our dinner with you and Mrs. Wiegand. My wife is most supportive. Katherine works for a travel agency, as you know, and would be looking for a position at a local agency. Vern Jr. would be looking for a pre-kindergarten school."

Vernon had just wanted to put his potential new boss on the spot with the reassurance from his wife about the move. He wanted to see what might be done to help her land a suitable job.

Winters' comments made Vernon Carter's decision a slam dunk. "That's great news," Winters proclaimed, not hiding his delight. "There are several travel firms in the region, two in town. They're good opportunities especially for a woman of Katherine's experience. With your permission, and once we agree on a salary and a starting date, I'll have my secretary make inquiries."

There had been excitement and anticipation in the air as Vernon picked up Nancy Wiegand knowing he had the job. He had driven his soon-to-be colleagues to the airport, this time without traffic delays or incidents. The Carter family would be moving to New Jersey. Vernon could visualize the U-Haul truck backing up to his apartment to load furniture for the move to the Northeast.

Katherine had been elated, once Vernon shared the wonderful news and the back-story about the soon-to-leave President. She was overjoyed with the proposed salary being $5,000 more than the minimum range. However, Katherine had visualized an Allied Moving Company van, not a U-Haul, unloading brand new furniture at their new house in New Jersey.

Everything was coming together just as the Carters had planned. Vernon had gotten this adjunct teaching position at Penn State a year ago, so he could complete his research and write the Dissertation. The pay wasn't much, but it gave him more classroom experience and kept him on the student health plan. He could use the extra time to finish the Dissertation.

Katherine had continued working at a local travel agency knowing an elusive but impressive income for Vernon was about to happen. Only the Dissertation Defense had been between them and this exceptional opportunity at CJCC in an area nearer their native New York.

For months, Vernon had been saddled with that dreaded title of ABD – All But Dissertation. He had completed the coursework, the oral and written exams and even the final tuition payments. The Dissertation had been demanding to write, especially since he was teaching and looking at job openings. But the document was complete and at final typing. It was ready to submit to the Graduate School.

Carter had explained to Winters that the only thing that had stood before him was to defend his research analyses and conclusions before his Dissertation Committee. He had completed an impressive study of curricular innovations of university vs. community college and public vs. independent institutions.

His methodology was top notch and well-documented. His statistical analyses were sound. He and Katherine had edited the 253-page manuscript several times. Even the pages with typos had been redone.

Vernon had suffered from *Graduate Student Paranoia Plague*. The disease affects persons who pursue a Dissertation. The initial symptom is worry and periodic panic that the research topic is being pursued by another graduate student in another graduate school in another universe. The symptom is elevated with fear that someone will attempt the same study.

Graduate Student Paranoia Plague reaches the critical stage when the research is complete, but the manuscript is not yet written. The fear is that a raging fire, tornado, hurricane or other natural storm or man-made calamity will consume the house, apartment or trailer where the student lives and destroy all notes, drafts and computer printouts.

The initial and elevated symptoms can be addressed by selecting the most obscure and boring topic that one could possibly imagine as the basis of the research. However, the topic must be sound enough and ample enough so that the graduate student can discreetly alter the focus, as necessary, should the research be replicated.

The critical stage of the disease is usually addressed by having two complete sets of notes, drafts and printouts – one kept in the Graduate Library and the other at home, preferably in a fire-proof box.

There is no manual provided for a naïve grad student, and there is no oral history passed down for each wave of students to understand the symptoms and remedies for the disease. Protection of the Dissertation becomes obsessive. It did with Vernon.

Vernon had come home one evening after taking the first day of the two-day written portion of the Ph.D. Qualification Exam. He found Katherine and son Vernon sitting on the stoop of the apartment. How nice, he thought. His family was waiting for him, wanting to know how he did on the exam.

"Vernon, sorry dear, but our son has the measles," was Katherine's greeting to her husband.

"Oh, sweetheart," a shocked Vernon said, weary from writing essay questions all day. "I love you two, but I'm going back to the Library to study."

Usually, the Dissertation Defense step was automatic, sometimes even perfunctory. But Vernon had been experiencing a tug-of-war between two of his three committee members – Dr. Louis Pasternak and Dr. Craig Jones. There had been rumblings that the two disagreed on the direction of the findings.

Pasternak had wanted to affirm that Vernon was his protégé respecting community college administration. Jones wanted the same but for higher education research. Oil and water do not mix. Professor egos do not cope well with each other.

Sure enough, when Carter's Dissertation Committee met, the two antagonists tangled. Vernon was squarely in the middle, with the New Jersey position in limbo. All Vernon had wanted was to get official approval and get on with his professional life and the move to Jersey with the U-Haul truck or the Allied moving van.

Mr. Carter had chosen to demonstrate his leadership skills, as well as his self-control, by forcefully interjecting a resolution. "Gentlemen, I can't believe this," he interrupted. "It's a little late to be having such a disagreement. So, here's my proposal. I will edit the written conclusions in my Dissertation and show two directions – one will emphasize innovations from a management perspective and the other, equally conclusive, for continued research."

Vernon let his proposal soak into the thick skulls of the two rival professors. Then he added, "Dr. Pasternak and Dr. Jones, I have a great job opportunity, and it's time for me to get on with my career."

Pasternak and Jones gulped simultaneously. They were embarrassed that their silliness had been exposed but annoyed with Vernon's attitude. After all, they were tenured professors. They could make Carter rewrite the

Dissertation, re-start his research, change his major or do cartwheels across campus.

The third member of the Dissertation Committee, Dr. Harold Stickler, had been looking at his two colleagues with scorn. He rose to the occasion – literally and figuratively. "Guys, this is an outstanding student and one who will go on to a marvelous career in higher education, likely combining his administrative and research skills," Sticker had bellowed, relying on his seniority. "I'll work with Mr. Carter this next week to accomplish what he proposes. Understand, you two will defer to me and accept this revision without seeing the re-edited version."

Vernon had thought about jumping across the conference table to embrace Dr. Stickler. He hesitated, knowing the moment had to be climaxed by Pasternak and Jones reluctantly consenting or agreeing enthusiastically. He didn't care which.

They did agree, although not without scowls.

His Dissertation got revised and officially approved by the Penn State Graduate School. An exclamation point was added when Dr. Vernon T. Carter had a scholarly version of his Dissertation accepted for publication in the *Higher Education Research Journal* and when Penn State's Graduate School recognized his work as Dissertation-of-the-Year.

Professors Pasternak and Jones had each placed Carter's Dissertation in nomination for the Grad School award. Stickler had co-authored Carter's published research article.

More importantly, the moving boxes could be loaded on the truck and headed to Abington, New Jersey. Now Katherine could go through travel agency job openings, pre-kindergarten schools, real estate listings and furniture catalogs.

10

PAST

"Is there any truth to the chest exam rumors?"

Central Jersey Community College hired Dr. Vernon Carter once the Personnel Office received a copy of the official transcript showing the earned Doctorate. Soon the new administrator set a remarkable standard for competence and job performance. Vernon was like a highly anticipated recruit added to a basketball team who quickly became the star player – as expected. He elevated the play and contributions of each teammate – not so expected.

Dr. Carter did not gloat about his Ph.D. to campus faculty. His usual line was, "Hey, the degree and use of the Dr. title help me get a restaurant reservation. Not much else."

To some of his colleagues, Dr. Carter was overly conscientious and overly preoccupied with fulfilling the job. None of the other Division Deans had ever worked with an African-American professional, let alone one with better credentials, more training and a higher aptitude for the role. Consequently, Carter's appointment triggered a not-entirely welcomed transition, not unlike sibling rivalries.

Vice President Winters had let the Deans pretty much alone, lowering his expectations to fit the reality of the incumbents. But here was this enthusiastic new Ph.D. challenging the status quo and pressing Winters to raise the standards. If this Carter guy got too productive, he might just screw up their cushy jobs.

Vernon and his wife, Katherine, had quickly settled into the mid-Jersey community even though they were upstate New Yorkers and transplanted Pennsylvanians. She had specialized in business travel at the State College, Pennsylvania agency. She knew the chunky OAG (Official Airline Guide) facsimile telephone book backward and forwards.

Mrs. Carter advanced this specialized form of travel and appealed to corporations because she provided efficiency and knew what businesses desired. Her boss at the State College agency had unsuccessfully tried to convince Katherine she should divorce Vernon and stay at his agency.

When Katherine had contacted agencies in central New Jersey for job openings, she found to her delight, an investment opportunity to co-own Global Travel Agency. The owner, Deborah Feldman, had contracted to construct a new and expanded, stand-alone agency facility. Feldman would relocate the seven-year old business from the crowded quarters at the end of a strip shopping center anchored by Sears and a Chevrolet dealership.

As an owner, Deborah wanted the most modernized equipment with an inviting exterior, elegant interior furnishings and classy ambiance. She also wanted a partner to share a little in the capital investment and a lot in employee supervision. She was thrilled that her new partner, Katherine, would oversee and expand the corporate travel component.

Deborah Feldman was married to a local medical doctor whose Family Medical Practice was in the basement of their home about two blocks from the newly constructed Global Travel. Deborah was in her late-40's, while her husband was closer to mid-50's.

Dr. Reuben Feldman was a dead ringer for tough-talking, lollipop-sucking *Kojak*, TV's Telly Savalas, owing to his shining bald head, muscular build and bulb-shaped nose. However, Reuben was proudly Jewish, not Greek, and he had graduated from New York's Hofstra Med School, not a Manhattan police academy.

Reuben liked to cook. He considered himself an above-average home chef, if overly inventive and intolerably messy. He was fond of Jewish matzo ball soup, potato latkes and challah, not Greek moussakas and feta cheese. Having the medical practice in the basement enabled him to cook all day. Often his patients would benefit from homemade soup or a variation on beef stew during their medical visits.

Dr. Feldman had not been concerned about the capital investment in the new Global Travel. He wanted his wife to have a partner to share the challenges of the business and have a least one owner on site. Deborah had wanted to move to a 9 AM to 7 PM daily work schedule, including Saturdays. Having a partner could assure one or the other was on hand to supervise. Reuben wanted his wife to have a highly successful and financially rewarding business for the years ahead, including those years when he would walk away from his medical practice.

Reuben and Deborah Feldman were delighted that Katherine had a college degree and travel agency experience. The soon-to-be co-owner was highly professional and happily married. The latter attribute was relevant because the other seven women in the office were all single, as well as good looking. If measured on an original *Agent Pulchritude Scale*, the non-married ladies would range from adorable to glamorous to seductive. There was something about a career in the travel business that enticed young, pretty ladies.

"I expect you had some travel benefits at your Pennsylvania agency," Deborah had asked Katherine during the interview process. "We are situated in this area with a great many opportunities, especially in this Northeast corridor. All that is very appealing to the female travel agents."

The M.D. and the Mrs. M.D. had not been dismayed or uneasy that Katherine was a minority woman or that her husband was an administrator at CJCC. Instead, they were excited. Katherine would be the only person of color in the agency unless one included Rachel, who spent most of her off hours at the Jersey Shore in the summer and a tanning salon in the winter.

Vernon had been thrilled that his wife had found this opportunity so quickly after the CJCC appointment and their relocation. The agency was only a couple miles from their new home, and Katherine could have flexible hours. Young Vern, Jr. would be in full-days at a nursery school that fall 1974, having graduated from half-days when his daily grade reports were F for Firm, S for Soft or that dreaded D.

Katherine had financially supported the three of them while Vernon was in graduate school, and he now wanted her career to be the focus. Plus, he loved her immensely and was sure she would score highly on the travel company's *Agent Pulchritude Scale*. His wife had high cheekbones and soft black hair that barely touched her shoulders. Vernon was enamored with her shapely legs and her buttocks, which he liked to compare adoringly to an oversized eggplant. Vernon loved his eggplant.

Despite being ten years older than most of the gals at the agency, Katherine did hold her own and then some when it came to looks. Katherine loved the attention and did not mind the metaphor or the high standing on the *Agent Pulchritude Scale*, or that the ranking had come from her husband.

Katherine had wanted to expand the corporate travel component even before construction was completed on the new Global Travel. She had made contacts and visited almost every large and not-so-large business in the region. The new co-owner had wanted to spell out the benefits to a company of doing their travel business through Global. She wanted to demonstrate her professionalism and manifest her ethnicity, in person.

Vernon had not anticipated the other benefits of the agency. The company ran periodic bus trips, so he and Katherine, and sometimes Vernon, Jr., got to go on excursions to Oktoberfest and concerts in Philadelphia and to Rockefeller Center and Madison Square Gardens in New York City. They could tour Ocean City, Atlantic City and New Hope in Bucks County by chartered bus.

Plus, there would be recurring invitations to hop aboard an ocean liner and cruise to St. Thomas, Puerto Rico or Puerto Vallarta. They would only have to pay half-fare for Vernon. Katherine would be comped, and they would receive upgrades in the ship cabins and first-class seats on flights to Miami. Plus, Vernon Jr. would receive a set of plastic pilot wings and visits to the cockpit.

As they finalized the agreement, the Feldman-Carter partners had gone to dinner a few times. The first was at the Old Heidelberg which specialized in a German menu, draft German beer and wait staff wearing Lederhosen and colorful suspenders.

All but Reuben had the braised short ribs and Gruyère cheese mashed potatoes. Reuben ignored his Jewish heritage and had the roast pork, Spätzle dumplings and red cabbage.

"Of course, I'm Jewish," the family practice M.D. had said with pride. "I certainly respect the ancient traditions of our people. However, I have it on good authority that the pigs they use in this restaurant are Kosher."

The tankards of frothy beer undoubtedly had contributed to the tone and elongated toast that Reuben offered at the restaurant before they started to eat their dinners. He took a big breath and spoke:

> *To the health and prosperity of us all and to the corporate health of Global Travel. May our newly found partnership be surrounded and embraced by our friendships. May our challenges strengthen us and not confound or deter us. May we flourish professionally and benefit financially and personally from this business and all our endeavors.*
>
> *Our God, we are very grateful that Katherine and Vernon left Pennsylvania and have made New Jersey their new home. Vernon Jr. too. We are delighted they have become part of the corporate family of Global Travel.*
>
> *May Vernon have a long and successful career at Central Jersey community college and for the benefit and the prosperity of our entire community. May all of us prosper and grow together.*
>
> *And may we all find that . . .*

With a well-placed elbow shot to her husband's side, Deborah abruptly stopped Reuben in mid-sentence. "Dear, the food's getting cold," she said to her husband, not to God. "Our friends are probably quite hungry." Deborah kissed him on the cheek and told him, "Save the flowery language for another day. Finish it up please, or we may never benefit, much less prosper."

Reuben rubbed his side and continued his toast with a snicker and a loving nod to his wife as he became Kojak in person: "Who loves ya, baby?"

Reuben then added: *"And thank you, God, that my wife has a partner with*

Global Travel to share in the long hours and watch over this flock of pretty ladies at work. Amen."

The second dining occasion had been a week later at the Feldman House, with Chef Reuben in charge and wearing his red apron with the black lettering, *Today's Menu – Take It or Leave It.* Dr. Feldman had announced his culinary selections. "True, I eat pork at Old Heidelberg, but Deborah won't let me cook it at home. We're having chicken."

The Chicken Cacciatore with Chef Reuben's homemade and highly seasoned tomato sauce was surely on the *Take It* side. He had passed on the celebratory toast that evening, heeding warnings from his wife and smirks from his dining companions.

Deborah had decided to fill the void, *"Thank you, God, for bringing us together and directing this opportunity. Bless Katherine, Vernon and their son and continue to bring them happiness. Amen."*

If Katherine Carter had had any doubts about her new business partner, there were none now. She said a silent prayer of thanks that Vernon had gotten this opportunity at the College, and she would co-own a travel agency – *Amen and Amen.*

Besides the local travel opportunities, the first-class air flights and the ocean cruises, there was another unusual employee fringe benefit at Global Travel. Medical care was complimentary, as provided by the good Dr. Feldman.

The presumed payoff was that every visit to the office by a female employee supposedly had to include a chest examination, no matter the illness, condition or urgency. A chest cold may have properly precipitated a chest exam, but a headache, infected toe, sore knee or bee sting did not.

As Katherine told her agency partner, with a big smile, "Deborah, I've decided to stick with the health care insurance Vernon has with the College and pass on this other Global Travel fringe benefit. The chest exams under the College's medical plan are optional."

But Vernon would not let the folktale go. "Hey Katherine," he said after only a couple of months at the new job. "Is there any truth to the chest exam rumors for all those ladies in the office? You know, dear, we are co-owners of the agency, and I'm a doctor, too!"

PAST

"I don't see anything wrong with that."

Izzy Kelleher, the President's wife and an Associate Professor of English at Atlantic State College, had been dealing with her own omens and demons. The woman was highly attractive in face and form, yet most men preferred to keep her at a distance. They arrived at that conclusion not because she was married, or her husband was a Vice President at CJCC, but because she could be contentious and intimidating.

Concurrently, Izzy was becoming aware of a subtle but creeping fascination with women. Perhaps as a byproduct of early menopause or drifting attention from her husband, Izzy was meekly aroused when changing clothes at the YMCA. As a highly intelligent, educated person, she was not afraid of such innate impulses and did not label herself as something other than normal. This attraction just seemed to augment her heterosexual orientation, as comatose as it was becoming, not threaten or castigate it.

One morning at the Y, after two competitive racquetball games, Izzy was alone with another woman in the locker room. Her playing partner had left, preferring to shower at home after she got the kids off to school.

The other woman seemed to exhibit traits that one might surmise, perhaps incorrectly, could place her as lesbian. But Izzy was not about to stereotype the lady despite the short hair, self-assured look and boyish clothing style. Izzy knew heterosexual and homosexual women, and men, came in all shapes, forms, personality traits and femininity and masculinity levels.

Something inside Izzy had stirred. She could not discern if the restlessness was a product of her brain, her organs, hormones or hyper-emotions. She could not help to note that this locker-room woman avoided make-up other than a touch of lipstick and mascara. The woman preferred running shorts and a t-shirt to a racquetball outfit, as most of the women chose and as featured at the Y's boutique.

Izzy knew she could not, and would not, succumb to stereotypes.

The woman's name sounded like Ellen or Bella. Izzy could not be sure. She only knew the name from other occasions when the gal would be next in line for a court, and the attendant would call out her name. Whatever this woman's name was, Izzy chose to speak up that morning.

"Guess it's just the two of us left," Izzy said stumbling on the words. "Must be a slow day for racquetball play or for the moms who come early before their husbands go off to work."

Izzy stood between the two rows of lockers, as she continued her greeting. "I see you here a few times a week and admire how you play the game. You're very competitive, with a wicked crosscourt backhand. When I play, I tend to take the glorious scenic route to the ball."

The woman was flattered by the attention and sensed a hint of flirtation in Izzy's eyes, if not noticeably, in her words. "Thanks," she said with a smile. "Having brothers and sisters, I'm used to competition and somewhat obsessed with winning, or at least not losing."

"My name's Izzy," said Mrs. Kelleher. "I think your name is Ellen?"

"Pretty close. The name is Ella, short for Isabella. Ella Cosby. Is your first name Isabella too?"

"Yes, it is, but I've only ever gone by Izzy. My grandmother on my mother's side was an Isabella. She went by Ella."

Ella Cosby finished stuffing her sweaty clothes in her workout bag and pointed herself at the exit. That meant she had to bisect the room and walk directly past Izzy.

Her brunette hair was still damp from the shower and made for an attractive glimmer in the morning sunlight streaming through the windows. Her full figure curves did as well. Ella wasn't overweight, not at all. She was charitable in the bust, hips and buttocks and sturdy in her shoulders and legs.

Izzy interrupted the woman's crisscross maneuver. "Hey, give me a minute," she said. "We can walk out together. That's if you're not in a rush to get to work." Ella paused while Izzy closed her locker and pulled the strap on her workout bag over her shoulder.

They walked past the Juice Bar where she had seen Coach Solly CJCC's basketball coach, from time-to-time. Solly was in another league in playing prowess, but she would sometimes stop, and they would exchange pleasantries. He was not there today, and she was glad, maybe even relieved.

Their cars were parked nose-to-nose in the lot, as if tickling each other and reflective of the bonding to occur. "You drive a Honda Accord," said Ella.

"I had a Honda Hatchback until just a few months ago and then got this used '74 Toyota Corolla."

The cars in the lot were partially covered in autumn leaves, mostly Red Oak and the oversized Silver Maple leaves that were now a fluorescent yellow. This was one of those unusually warm fall days that stayed in people's minds the rest of the year.

Izzy brushed aside the colorful leaves blanketing the rear of her car and tossed her gym bag into the trunk. She headed over to Ella who was waiting next to the Corolla as if wanting to be sure Izzy was secure. "Sometimes I like to get a bite of breakfast after a workout," Ella confessed. "Care to join me? There's this Egg & You place a mile or so up the road, if not out of your way. I'm a Dental Lab Technician and don't have to be at work until 10."

"That would be great," Izzy replied without pausing to consider any reason she might not. "I'm hungry for some reason this morning. Most of my classes at State are in the afternoon, so I can be a bit leisurely in the mornings. I'll follow you, but I know where the diner is. They make a great omelet."

Izzy and Ella entered the breakfast specialty restaurant as the bulk of the morning congregation filed out of the door and charged to the parking lot. Ella chose a booth next to the window and away from the still noisy counter facing the hot grill and chatty waitresses.

The place was a legitimate diner with worn linoleum that had bubbled on the floor in unwanted areas. The peach and turquoise laminated counter was cracked in several spots. Freshly brewed coffee competed with the smell of burnt bacon and sausages on the griddle and a stale cigarette fog.

Izzy slid into the worn leather booth, grateful for the company of her new friend. She hardly got settled before confronted with a heavy mug slapped down before her, a hovering pot of hot coffee and a request. "Morning. Coffee I presume," blurted the pudgy but perky waitress in the off-white and blue-trimmed smock spotted with coffee stains. "Black or cream? Sugar or substitute? I can do decaffeinated, but it would be instant." The questions of customer taste and preference were presented more as directives than options. The answers better be quick.

The other diner patrons were either reading the morning *Jersey Star* or talking about the ascension of Gerald Ford to President when Richard Nixon resigned. The year was 1974, and neither the Yankees or the Phillies were having championship years. Izzy and Ella could not have cared less.

Izzy took her coffee black, as did Ella. Another thing they had in common. Each promptly ordered a cheese omelet, much to the delight of the stressed waitress who thus saved herself another trip to the table.

The diner's customers usually took at least ten minutes to page through the oversized, over-complicated and sticky menu. As the uppity waitress left the table, Izzy remarked, "It's amazing how many things can be created for breakfast with eggs."

"Izzy, I told you I was a Dental Lab Tech, but I'm also an artist," Ella explained. "I work in a lab where we fill dentists' orders for dentures, crowns, bridges and mouth-guards. Much of our work is restoration."

"But you're an artist too – painting, sculpture or what?" Izzy quickly asked, cutting her off, while trying to hide how captivated she was to have time with this woman.

"I like to make silver jewelry," Ella said. "My Dental Tech casting skills transfer well to jewelry-making. I work mostly with Cabochons, shaping and polishing semi-precious stones and agates and creating settings for necklaces, earrings, pendants. I select stones with interesting colors, textures and patterns. When the stones are polished and placed in a setting, the transformation is magical."

Izzy jumped on the explanation and offered a litany of questions. "Is this a business? Do you sell your jewelry? Can I see your work? Is that sweet pendant around your neck one of your creations? Where can I buy some?"

"Mostly I do the jewelry as a change of pace from the tooth-fairy work," Ella offered in response. "I admit I'm a techie by day and a design freak by night."

"I'd be glad to show you some of my work. Mostly, I do this as an avocation, for my amusement and for gifts. The casting process is quite similar. I admit I'm also a rock hound who chases the conventions across the state. Yes, this pendant is my work. The earrings too."

Izzy sipped carefully on her coffee after the enthusiastic waitress hustled back and topped off the cup. She again complemented Ella on her racquetball play. Izzy was taken by the dubious use of the word "closet" and decided to revert their conversation to more racquetball inquiry.

"Have you ever been in a tournament at the Y," Izzy asked. She wanted to be polite and initiate a conversation without revealing so soon what was on her mind. Speaking of the racquetball seemed like a safe opening.

Ella told her that she had been in a couple of tournaments a year or so ago but now just played for fun. "Those ladies are incredible," Ella volunteered, as if to explain why she had stepped aside from competition. "You and I need to play sometime, Izzy. I'd like that."

"I see the ring on your finger with the diamond, so you're married," Ella declared, yet uncertain as to what answer she wanted. "I never overlook a diamond ring or any jewelry on a woman, or a man, for that matter. I can spot a beautiful stone and an original setting from across the room. And you teach at Atlantic State College?"

Ella saw that Izzy was uneasy, given she almost dropped the hot coffee mug. "You seem tense," she quickly interjected. "Is there something wrong or something I said. If so, tell me, please. Something you want to ask? If so, ask away. You're a lovely, mature woman and there's an aura about you that I'm sure your husband and others find attractive."

Izzy was startled by the recognition of an aura and by the mention of a husband. She decided to ignore the questions about being married and teaching. The opening was there, and she leaped, much like a bunch of kids at a summer camp running off the end of the pier into the water. Except the campers would already know how deep the water was when they jumped. Izzy did not.

"I do not know if I'm intruding, and certainly I'm no judge. I was an English Lit major in college. Lately, I've had some stirrings within my body, and many questions as a result. As awkward as this is, I sensed you might listen and offer some advice to help sort this out for me." The last comment had been more of a question than a statement from the 40-something woman.

Ella was not taken back by the comment or the invitation. She had heard such revealing honesty before from a couple of other women, although somewhat younger, and considerably less sophisticated.

"If you're asking me if I'm attracted to women, rather than men, then the simple answer is yes," Ella said. "The more complicated answer is that I'm attracted to both, just more comfortable these past few years with female companionship. I have a good friend. We run around and share intimacy, but we don't live together. We're not stupid. We know society is not ready for that. We enjoy our time together, trust each other and share emotional support as well as physical affection. I have my male friends too, but not in a romantic way."

"Lesbian ladies like me are not that different," Ella Cosby continued, her eyes unflinchingly affixed to Izzy's, as if part of an annexed property and trying not to sound annoyed. "I trust you respect all this."

Not waiting for an answer, Ella continued. "We shave our legs and underarms and wear make-up to one degree or another. We like fashionable bras and panties. We enjoy shopping for contemporary, chic clothes. Some of us express our femininity in non-conventional ways, but we are women. We are not radically politicized, and most are comfortable knowing our sexual orientation comes from within – not something we can or care to change."

Ella paused to gulp some cooled-down coffee and then carried on. "Most lesbians are attracted to a woman who is assured and confident in herself and her sexuality, much as you appear to be. We don't prey on others, and we differentiate our sexual thoughts from our sexual expressions. But certain attributes appeal to each lesbian lady in different ways and at different times in our lives."

Izzy quickly added, "Kind of like being heterosexual. What you say could just as easily describe them."

"Yes, in fact, I have occasional heterosexual fantasies," Ella responded. "I don't see anything wrong with that."

Izzy reached across the table for Ella's hand, which slid freely into hers, squeezing affectionately and communicating a sense of understanding. "I'd like to talk more about all of this if you'd be willing. Perhaps we could meet someplace for a drink after work or have breakfast again?"

"To be sure," Ella quickly answered. "To be sure, we have to play racquetball together! I may even spot you a few points!"

PAST

"Until you get your act together."

Samantha Bartell had led a charmed life, spoiled as a girl, coddled as a teen and indulged as a young woman. Her father, Dr. Daniel Bartell, was the head of Psychiatry at St. Anthony Hospital, north of Abington. He enjoyed a distinguished and lucrative practice. His wife of 30 years was an Oral Surgeon with operating privileges at the same hospital.

Samantha was the middle child between two sons. The first son was the namesake of Daniel. The second son was given the namesake of Ramsey, mother's maiden name.

Samantha was named just because her parents liked it. They were not influenced by the television Bewitched show with its main character. That *Samantha* character was a friendly witch with magical powers trying unsuccessfully to live a normal housewife life. In some ways, Samantha was also trying to live a normal life. It was not easy for her either.

Samantha's father, Daniel, had changed the Bartelli surname when he got married, dropping the "i" at the end so the name became Bartell. The re-spelling was an attempt to camouflage the suspect Italian legacy. The ancestors were notorious for their Mafia connections, with Daniele Bartelli a lieutenant in the syndicate that made its living in illicit cigarette trade.

The Jersey organization smuggled cigarettes from low cost and lower taxation southern states. Then they sold the cigarette cartons to high cost and much higher taxation towns and cities within the eager procurement market of the Northeast. The profitable organized crime group was guilty of tax evasion but never prosecuted.

The elder Daniele Bartelli died just after young son Daniele went off to college, and the namesake had decided to drop the connection in his given name. So, with the two changes, *Daniele* had become *Daniel,* and *Bartelli* became *Bartell*. Samantha, born years later, only knew Bartell as her surname, but she was aware of the name change history and the Mafia connection. She knew her dad was a successful medical doctor and did not transport cigarettes across state lines. He didn't even smoke.

After college, and med school at Drexel University in Philadelphia, Daniel had moved to Monroe County and started a residency at St. Anthony Hospital. There he had met and fallen in love with a beautiful young dental graduate student. They started a family, nurtured successful careers, got involved in high society and led the good life – grand home, fancy cars, fashionable clothes and splendid vacations.

Daughter Samantha was exceedingly bright but not academically motivated during high school. Despite her mediocre grades and dormant ambition, her influential father got her admitted into Princeton University as a legacy freshman. Reluctantly, Samantha headed off to college. The unfocused young lady dropped out of the Ivy League school in the first semester of her sophomore year – before she would have flunked-out.

Hence, the prodigal daughter was summoned home to live with mom and dad. "Samantha, your mother and I love you very much and that's why you are going to have to live with us until you get your act together." Samantha accepted that she would have to live with, and under the supervision of, the dual doctor parents.

Samantha Bartell was pint-sized as a child and she was petite as an adult, standing five-foot-no-inch tall and weighing 115 pounds. She possessed a thin radiant face, fathomless azure blue eyes and curvy, wavy sandy hair.

As a teen, Samantha had a severe overbite and crooked teeth owing to overbearing wisdom teeth. But after she completed Orthodontics, her plaster before-and-after teeth molds became the stars of Dr. Carlson's dental office, highlighting a truly amazing transformation. After the Orthodontics, Samantha's white teeth became locked in a smile and her confidence locked in place.

In her mind, Samantha's distinguishing but dispiriting feature was the array of freckles clustered on the bridge of her nose. In grade school, her peers had made fun of her freckles. Samantha became conditioned to want to hide them.

In her first and only year at Princeton University, Samantha had developed a slight astigmatism and needed to wear eyeglasses. The young lady bought glasses with thick frames to mask most of the freckles above her nose. The glasses also lent a degree of sophistication that enhanced her self-image, if not her grade-point-average.

Now with his daughter living at home, dad Daniel used his influence again. He procured a job for Samantha in Administrative Services at St. Anthony's.

She started doing special projects and odd jobs. Samantha was about to adopt *Odd Jobs* as her career title when the Office Manager invited her to work with him on an analysis of office efficiency. That work led to other assignments and praise for her contributions. Young Samantha was maturing and growing more and more self-assured.

Samantha lapped up the assignments like a hungry dog devours dinner with huge gulps of the chow. She knew then that her future, her career, was to be in administration of non-profit organizations. She thrived in policy-making and loved being in control. She had the aptitude, and now she had the inner drive and a growing track record of contributions.

The Bartell daughter enrolled at Atlantic State College while still living with her parents. She studiously hit the library and the books, majoring in Business Administration. She had to retake three General Education English and math courses from Princeton, as the D grades she had earned did not transfer. She got A grades in all of them.

While at Atlantic State, Samantha got involved in the Future Democrats Society and began to contribute to various local election campaigns. The energy and intensity of elections appealed to her far more than the potential to make positive societal changes. She found herself drawn to the politics of politics, the backrooms as well as the front rooms.

Samantha was profoundly fascinated by her Industrial Psychology and Organizational Development courses in her major at Atlantic State. She saw herself using that knowledge to influence worker behavior and motivation through organizational structure and systems.

Samantha didn't choose to date much at college. At Atlantic State she was three years older than her freshman classmates, having spent the troubled year at Princeton and then two more years living at home and working at the hospital.

Samantha had concluded that all freshman boys had pimples, were incredibly immature and had mommy issues. The sophomore and junior guys were just immature, and the senior studs only wanted their dates to listen to their exaggerated sexual exploits. She was not about to become a notch in some frat boy's belt of conquests.

Samantha was not a virgin, but she was very picky and in no hurry to have a boyfriend, let alone a husband. She did have a lusty crush on one professor, a graduate assistant who graded papers, took roll and held tutoring classes for Macro-Economics. But that connection was more mutual flirtation than romantic connection, more communal triumph than a nurturing relationship.

The Economics grad student and Samantha did go out a few times, once the semester ended, and she had progressed to more advanced courses. But the guy was a better teaching assistant than a potential soul mate or lover.

Samantha was not about to have a man redirect her motivations or deflect her ambitions.

After Samantha finished her bachelor's degree, she began work on a master's at Atlantic State. She contacted the folks at St. Anthony Hospital, but there were no job openings, even with her father's influence and prodding.

Miss Bartell saw an ad for an Administrative Coordinator at the Monroe County Administration Building, and she applied. She began work in County Services which meant she handled issues of fair and affordable housing and community development, reporting to the Director.

Samantha became a star employee the first month on the job. She began to draw attention from the other departmental directors as well as from the members of the Board of Chosen Freeholders and the County Commissioner. She continued to take classes in the evening and weekends, and the young lady accumulated 15 credit hours toward a master's degree in Public Administration in her first year of work for the County.

Most of all, the young lady no longer had to live with her dual-doctor parents.

PAST

"I scratched your back and now you gotta scratch mine."

As the Garden State, New Jersey is known for tomatoes and corn, miles of shoreline, Thomas Edison, 24-hour diners and jug handle turns. Over one-hundred battles were fought in Jersey during the Revolutionary War. Most importantly, street names for the *Monopoly* board game are taken from Atlantic City and its elongated boardwalk along the Jersey Shore.

New Jersey is unusual for its distinctive system of Chosen Freeholders elected as the legislative body to serve each county. The name derives from English tradition, in which "Freemen" were property owners entitled to control their lands and were "Chosen" by the populace. In other states, Freeholders are recognized as commissioners, supervisors or simply board members.

Central Jersey Community College serves Monroe County. The County has a seven-member Board of Chosen Freeholders, constitutionally focused on legislative and oversight matters. Each member serves a staggered three-year term. Just because they are supposed to focus on policy, not management, strategic planning not tactical maneuvers, does not inhibit them from monkeying around in day-to-day decisions.

The Freeholders are elected-at-large, but they run under political party affiliations and are supported by them. Once elected, almost all get re-elected and re-elected again. There are no term limits other than retirement, jail terms or leaving the County. An historical analysis would show there were more retirees than arrests, but it would be close.

The Board has a Chairman and Vice Chairman, with the positions rotated among Board members periodically or seldom. The County departments include Social Services, Sheriff, Coroner, Park Commission, Court House, Improvement Authority, Library and the College.

The party connections mean voting blocs, as well as unwanted pressure on County department directors, including CJCC's President, to abide by their wishes. Their wishes are one thing. Showing partiality and favoritism in employment, contracts and purchases are another.

Partisan and political intrusions were normative. If a party had financially backed a candidate to a local election and had garnered votes, the *I scratched your back and now you scratch mine* mentality resulted. Thus, if a ranking politician had a first or second cousin looking for a job, the Freeholders could assure employment.

CJCC's President Robert Greenleaf had fended off the crooked advances for much of his tenure but not all of it. He had wavered considerably when the College was built heeding the politics of favoritism. With his pending departure, the Freeholders as a group and as individual mavericks were salivating to intrude. The time would be right to encroach. They could pressure the replacement President right from the start.

The County Commissioner, as appointed by the Board of Chosen Freeholders, serves as the executive officer to provide leadership to all Monroe County departments. As a professional position, the incumbent needs Public Administration credentials, but it is highly political in that the person better be connected and able to negotiate the political interference.

Since 1972, the Commissioner was Dominic Panichi Junior, whose father had been in the same position for twenty-one years before the son succeeded him. This was a legacy of control rather than of nobility. When you fall into the family, it is almost a right that you perpetuate that power. The elder Dominic and the replacement younger one both did that.

Junior Dominic had earned a baccalaureate in Economics from Rutgers and a master's degree in Public Administration, also from Rutgers. Daddy Dominic stepped aside just in time for his son to replace him in the election, and the results were never in doubt. It was not that the Panichi father-and-son-tag-team had done exceptional work, but that the citizens had no interest in an alternative, much less a change.

While most people were aware of the good ol' boy nature of Monroe County operations, the engine by and large had propelled good things to happen. Better to see a pimple on your face than not see the hidden mole on your behind. The system functioned well enough. There were no illusions that a different system, borrowed from New York, Pennsylvania, Arkansas or Illinois would produce better results.

The election slogan had said it all: *Keep things rolling as they are.* The 32-year old son took over. On a scale of one-to-ten, with a ten being highly ethical and unblemished, and one being anything but, Dominic would rate about a seven. Some loyal soldiers found jobs with Monroe County for which they were marginally qualified. Some contracts went to companies with prominent Italian or Irish heritage. But only a few. Daddy was encouraging his son to go for a lower score than the seven.

Dominic was not getting rich as the Commissioner. He knew how to avoid aspersions of impropriety and indictments for any of the three "C's" – *Conspiracy, Complicity and Connivance*. Daddy had nurtured him well.

It did not take long for the young County Commissioner, Dominic Panichi, to notice and appreciate the work of one Samantha Bartell. She was skilled and sophisticated beyond her age and had created quite a buzz by her work ethic. When any community development project was initiated, inevitably Miss Bartell would be on both the design and implementation teams.

When Samantha strolled the halls, she exuded a bubbly, bouncy and bright-eyed personality. When she participated in departmental meetings, she displayed a dazzling command of everything on the table, and most of what was not yet there. Some guys were threatened at first, but Samantha knew when to press the agenda engine and when to shift to idle.

When Samantha went to a bar, liquor store or restaurant, she would still get carded and asked to show her Driver's License. She was a youthful 29 years old. Perhaps it was the petite and lithesome figure, the sandy hair, the modest choices in attire or that she wore little makeup.

Maybe it was those freckles, those cute freckles, partially hidden behind the thick-rimmed glasses.

PAST

"We should attract the finest candidates with the best credentials."

The Vice President of Academic Affairs, Donald L. Winters, had sat in his office staring at the two framed degrees from Towson State College. The degrees were awarded 25 years ago when Winters received a master's degree in Education after earning a baccalaureate in History.

This new junior college, being started in Abington, had an opening for an instructor. In 1958, he applied and was hired to teach History at Central Jersey Community College.

But now, sixteen years later, J. Paul Kelleher was to be the President. Not him.

Winters chaired the History Department those early years, although there were only three faculty members who taught History and the Social Sciences. He became Dean of Arts & Sciences in 1962 and Vice President of Academic Affairs in 1968.

Alma mater Towson State College was located near Baltimore and was founded a hundred years ago as a school for teachers. Enrollment had grown exponentially, and the institution was now known and recognized as Towson State University. That had been a year too late for Winters. He couldn't help but daydream about what might have been.

When President Robert Greenleaf left the Central Jersey Community College in June 1974, he had recommended to the Board of Trustees that they appoint Vice President Winters as Interim President. Winters was approved to serve in that capacity until the Board completed the national search. Greenleaf calculated that would give Winters about five months, perhaps six, to demonstrate he could handle the position and blow away all competitors. More likely, that would give Winters time to show his limited value. Greenleaf really didn't care which.

Unfortunately for Winters, his colleague, J. Paul Kelleher, had ideas of his own. He was a schemer who could work and manipulate the process. He intended to do so. All's fair in love, war and presidential searches.

The members of the Board of Trustees were mixed on what they wanted to see in the replacement President. A couple were comfortable with Winters or someone else from within the College taking the reins and skipping the search entirely. They had businesses to run and vacation time to take. They did not want to spend time in any search process. Besides how difficult was it to be a College President?

Board Chairman Dr. Gerald Pitman and Vice Chairman Chuck Harrison were adamant that this would be a straightforward and principled search with Board member involvement. It would not be, however, a democratic process where faculty, staff, students, alumni, citizens or anyone other than a Trustee had more than token involvement.

The Board of Trustees had the authority to design the Presidential Search process as they wanted. The State Board had no requirements other than to submit the name of the final candidate to them for rubber stamp approval.

The Board could make the selection decision with or without input from others. The Trustees were united not to have a paid consultant or head-hunter advise the Board on the search process or on candidates. They were unanimous that the democratic vote would only encompass the Board itself.

The Board also agreed that token representation of faculty and staff was admirable, and that students or anyone from the community had no place in the process.

Vice Chairman Chuck Harrison summed up the Board sentiment well, when interviewed by the reporter from *The Jersey Star*: "It is our job to select the President. We intend do that without interference by faculty and staff, and certainly not students. This is not a union matter or a popularity contest. We'll share the names and credentials of the final candidates, and we'll have interviews of the final men on campus."

The Board of Trustees could have formed a campus-based committee to conduct the search and recommend two or three final candidates. They could have. Instead, the Board named a subcommittee of four Board members plus the Board Chairman as an Ex-Officio member.

The Board's subcommittee, henceforth known as the official Presidential Search Committee, was augmented with two faculty members and two staff members, chosen by the respective union organizations. Their role was advisory – they could participate in committee discussions but would need to leave the room when the Board held a vote or showed them the door.

As Vice Chairman, Harrison would chair the Presidential Search Committee. The group would make a recommendation of two or three candidates to go before the full Board for a vote. The two Board members who wanted the search process to be over, opted-out of serving on the subcommittee or it would have been the entire Board.

Dr. Pitman would vote if there were a tie or if his vote would make the action a tie, as per *Roberts Rules of Order*. Otherwise, the subcommittee was to operate according to *Pitman's Rules of Order*. Those rules were far less complex.

The Board had been unanimous in favor of Donald Winters being the Interim President for up to six months – not a day longer. If desired, he could enter his name into the Presidential Search process.

They were also united in a vow not to make any part of the search and selection subject to partisan politics. However, a couple of Board members had their fingers crossed when they voted. They could not resist sharing progress reports with assorted members of the Board of Chosen Freeholders, local politicians and bocce ball pals.

A major question for the search was whether a Ph.D. or an Ed.D. would be a Minimum Qualification or a Preferred Qualification. "This College is well enough known, thanks to Dr. Greenleaf," Harrison said. "We should attract the finest candidates with the best credentials. Still there may be someone with graduate study who has more experience. I vote to have the degree be a Preferred Qualification that we can waive."

No one challenged him. Some weren't sure of the difference anyway.

The Board announced the vacancy in the *Chronicle of Higher Education* and the *New York Times*, plus the weekend edition of *The Jersey Star*.

The ad was straightforward. Under the *cloak* of an open and fair search process, involving all constituents, the Board of Trustees would proudly hold the *dagger* of making the decision all by itself.

HELP WANTED – ADMINISTRATIVE　　　　The **Jersey Star**

October 4, 1974

President, Central Jersey Community College
Abington, New Jersey
　　The Board of Trustees announces a national search for the next President. The President manages and directs the affairs of the College, working with four bargaining units.
　　He administers adopted policies and procedures under the guidance of the Board of Trustees. He cultivates effective relationships with County and State offices, including the General Assembly.
　　CJCC was founded in 1958 and is fully accredited by the Middle States Association and was recipient of a $2.5 million Federal Grant in 1972 as per the Title III Strengthening Developing Institutions.
　　The Board seeks candidates with demonstrated leadership skills and organizational, finance, budgetary and long-range planning knowledge; the ability to inspire and work with the Board of Chosen Freeholders and County Commissioner; and a working understanding of technology and applications.
　　Skill in streamlining operations and procedures.
　　Knowledge and expertise with accreditation and federal grant processes.
　　Excellent oral and written communication skills.
Qualifications:
　　　Master's Degree
　　　Doctorate preferred
　　　Minimum five years senior-level community college experience.
Inquiries:
Inquiries and requests for Job Description should be directed to:
　　　Mrs. Edith Reynolds, Administrative Secretary, President's Office.
　　　101 Crosstown Drive, Abington, NJ 07700
Application Materials (Required):
　　　Letter of interest not to exceed two pages
　　　Current resume
　　　Three letters of recommendation
　　　Addresses and phone numbers of three professional references
　　　Transcripts from graduate institutions
Application Deadline: October 18, 1974.
　　　Salary Range – $44,000 – $64,000 Negotiable. Dependent on History
　　　Excellent Fringe Benefits Package
　　　Must reside within Monroe County upon employment.

PAST

"We have no idea what went on behind those closed doors."

On October 21, the Monday after the closing date, Personnel Director Roseanne Hart refilled her coffee cup and poured in more sugar. She closed the door to her office and began the process of sifting through the applicant packages. There were 32 of them in front of her. She put them into three triaged piles of applicants: New Jersey, Out-of-State and In-House. All 32 were males.

Three of the 32 folders were incomplete. By her judgment, four others did not meet the qualifications or more likely were on a fishing expedition for a job. She set those seven packages aside and spent the rest of the morning applying a checklist of qualifications to the 25 remaining candidates.

About an hour into the review, and two cups of coffee later, there was a knock on her door. "Hey Roseanne, do you have the folders of the Presidential Candidates," was the voice coming through the door. "How does it look?" The voice belonged to Vice Chairman Harrison. He opened the door without knocking and saw Roseanne at the table.

"Good morning, sir," the Personnel Director said while looking up at the visitor and at the same time re-arranging the folders to hide the names. "Yes, these are the applicant folders. So far so good. I should finish in another hour. I can call you then and advise you on how many candidates there are who meet all the qualifications."

"How many we got now, and are Winters and Kelleher the only two internal candidates?" Harrison asked, dismissing what Miss Hart had just told him.

"I can tell you we have 25 candidates as of today, with Vice President Kelleher and Vice President Winters in the mix."

That seemed to satisfy the Board Vice Chairman who bowed out of the office with the comment, "Keep up the good work. Let's get this done."

About twenty minutes later, Roseanne received a phone call from her boss – J. Paul Kelleher. "Morning Roseanne, just wondering how many candidates did the Board get for the job? Anyone other than Winters and me from New Jersey? Any sitting Presidents?"

Roseanne looked in her desk to see if she had any bourbon she could add to her coffee.

When the Board's Presidential Search Committee got together two days later, Roseanne presented a grid showing how each of the 25 candidates met the qualifications. She also provided notations on degrees, universities and present position for each applicant. The Vice Chairman had already been through the 25 folders and offered an observation, as Roseanne passed out copies of the grid. "Folks, I've taken the liberty of going through all the files. We can eliminate 11 of the 25 based on lesser credentials.

Roseanne, you agree with me, right," he added as more of a statement than a question.

Roseanne started to feel contracted and began to condition herself to accept the box that Harrison had just placed around her. Roseanne had thought the earlier meeting with Harrison, when they whittled the 25 to 14 was preliminary and not consequential. But she decided to go along with the desire to reduce the candidates to the 14. She knew when to go along.

After a pause to collect her thoughts on the awkward moment, the Personnel Director offered an escape. "Mr. Harrison, I would agree. Let me suggest we put the 11 in a separate pile and let the Committee members see if they want anyone of those added. If so, we can include him. If not, we can concentrate on the remaining 14."

The four Board members, along with the Board Chairman and four token employees, spent the next two hours going through the 14 folders. Only the two faculty members bothered to look at any of the 11 Harrison discards. They decided to leave well enough alone.

Harrison went around the table one-by-one, asking each of the four Board members and the four employees to put forth one name. Harrison suggested that, for the time being, they exclude consideration for candidates Winters and Kelleher, and focus on the 12 external candidates.

With that Round-Robin iteration, the Committee had arrived at a reduced list of five outside candidates that all members could agree on. With Winters and Kelleher, that made seven candidates to be contacted and interviewed via telephone. There was no discussion on the pros and cons of the two in-house candidates – their inclusion was automatic and presupposed. The meeting adjourned. Everyone left content if not overwhelmed by the pool of applicants and the final candidates.

After the phone contacts, the race was down to five external long-shots and the two handicapped, internal frontrunners. Two of the seven dropped out, suspicious of process partiality, given there were two in-house candidates. Both did not want to disrupt their current positions to go through a spurious, likely bogus, search. Harrison did not attempt to dissuade those two candidates or any skeptical Committee members with re-assurances the search was fair.

The open faculty meetings with the three external finalists were well-attended. The union leadership officers led the presentation and asked tough and direct questions:

- *We see you don't have a union on your campus. How come?*
- *How do you think you will be able to work with our Faculty Union here?*
- *Do you think faculty should hold a seat on the Board of Trustees?*
- *What would you do if you found that the faculty were underpaid?*
- *How often would you hold faculty meetings and show-up for them?*
- *Will you teach at least one course a semester? Have you ever taught?*
- *How often will you re-organize?*
- *Should Presidents be paid more than faculty?*
- *Do you have tenure at your campus?*
- *How would you handle an intrusive County officer on College governance?*
- *Are you still married?*
- *Do you prefer pizza or tomato pie?*

The Jersey Star published an editorial that November 3rd Sunday, after the Board had whittled the candidates to the Final Five – three external and two internal. The editors listed the five men and praised the College for attracting this array of qualified applicants and conducting an intensive search:

Vice Chairman Harrison saw no need to have open sessions with the two internal candidates. Winters and Kelleher did not protest. They met with the Presidential Search Committee, minus the four employees who were politely excluded. But the sessions were short and the questions shorter. The Trustees ran out of questions to ask after thirty-five minutes.

During their interviews, Kelleher and Winters rehashed and glorified their contributions to the College since becoming Vice Presidents. There was considerable hyperbole in their presentations. Kelleher said, "If not for me, the College would not have received the $2.5 million from Washington." Not to be outdone, Winters said, "If not for me, the College would not have increased its enrollment over the years, and we would not have this outstanding faculty."

Daily Editorial

A New President

The **Jersey Star**

November 3, 1974

We applaud the CJCC Board of Trustees that they conducted a national search and put the two internal candidates through this deliberate process, regardless of who gets the position. Vice Presidents J. Paul Kelleher and Donald L. Winters deserve this consideration.

Whoever gets the appointment will have to work hard to match the legacy of Dr. Greenleaf. He built the college from vast and vacant farmland. These guys now only have to run the place.

Board Chairman Pitman and Vice Chairman Harrison deserve our praise and acknowledgment for the thoroughness of the search process. We just wish the Board had been more inclusive in the membership of the Search Committee and used the process to reach out more to the community.

A member of the media should have been included, we think, or at least briefed after each meeting. We have no idea what went on behind those closed doors. The one external candidate is from Indiana or Iowa.

The new President will have a challenge dealing with the Faculty Union that has gained leverage over the years and with enrollment that continues to grow and demand more and more services. We trust the College can lower the tuition and fees.

We hope that in the years to come, the junior college will become a four-year university, with dorms and fraternities. We trust the new President will lead the institution down that path.

After those campus visits and various meetings, the Presidential Search was down to three finalists. One of the three external candidates had displayed an arrogance that turned off Harrison. Another outside guy had displayed an ignorance of New Jersey that insulted the Board Chairman.

That meant there were just the three remaining candidates, heading neck-and-neck and neck-and-neck toward the finish line.

16

PAST

"And the new President could count on a few more enemies!"

At 44, J. Paul Kelleher was the youngest of the three finalists to be the next President of Central Jersey Community College. Donald L. Winters was 50, and the Iowa outside guy was 52. The Iowa candidate was a Campus Provost, and he had a doctorate in Education from Iowa State University. His campus-based experience, however, was arguably less than Kelleher and Winters who had collegewide responsibilities. Plus, the Iowa college was smaller than CJCC. The Iowa doctorate guy had interviewed well, however, and presented a Five-Point Strategic Plan to the Board to demonstrate he had done his homework. Most of the Trustees did not get why he had done that.

Chuck Harrison, the *Magic Show* guy and Board Vice Chairman, had wanted to compare degrees since one candidate did have the preferred, but not required, doctorate credential.

He called Kelleher to ask how an MBA compared to a doctorate. Kelleher had anticipated that query and had already summoned Roseanne Hart to contact New York University, where he had earned his MBA, to get a written statement.

In the horse race, Winters fell back two-lengths by having a Master's in Education Degree, rather than an academic discipline, although Harrison did not fully comprehend the distinction. Kelleher got even in the race with the Iowa guy regarding their degrees – his two master's degrees matched the other guy's doctorate.

As Interim President, Winters had been performing double-duty as chief academic officer. He had been hesitant to delegate responsibilities in Academic Affairs, even to Dr. Carter. Instead, he stubbornly tried to demonstrate a super-human work ethic to gain an advantage in the presidential race. Winters didn't care to share his decision-making and reveal his true work ethic.

Winters had wanted to show he was incredibly capable, naively and impulsively calculating the position was his to lose. He introduced several well-intended professional development sessions for administrative employees to demonstrate concern for employee well-being. But he witnessed enrollment efficiencies sink, despite overall enrollment growth. Faculty morale dropped too, as several Division Deans and Department Chairmen slacked off their workloads without Winters to coddle them.

Most importantly, Interim President Winters had unwisely let flounder the Title III commitment to building the College Foundation. He did not fill the staff position on the Foundation, let alone raise private funds from solicitations or appeals. He had invited only two businessmen to serve on the not-yet-formed Foundation Board of Directors. One had accepted. The other wanted to know why there was a Foundation.

Kelleher did not exactly rush to help his rival, preferring subversion over fairness. Kelleher never reminded Winters of the Foundation obligation from the Title III grant, and he made sure that Lieber did not either. "Why screw-up an advantage," he asked himself. When the Title III progress reports were due in Washington D.C., Kelleher made sure to let the Board Chairman know that nothing was happening with the Foundation.

When Kelleher observed that a faculty member had been assigned three consecutive sections to teach in the morning that fall semester, contrary to the union contract, he made it a point to encourage that professor to file a grievance. Had Winters focused, or had the Division Dean been awake, the oversight would have been spotted.

Kelleher worked behind the scenes to get the County Commissioner to use his influence to praise Kelleher in one-on-one contacts with several Trustees. It was not that Commissioner Dominic Panichi ridiculed Winters or even disliked Winters as a candidate. Panichi knew he could leverage Kelleher and exchange favors and influence, as he had President Greenleaf. Winters did not grasp or appreciate the political realities of the County. He did not choose to stoop to such depths, or so he told others.

The Iowa doctorate guy with the clever but ungraspable Five-Point Strategic Plan told the Board Chairman he would need to have the maximum salary to leave his current position. Just like that, the selection was down to two internal candidates – Kelleher and Winters. Dr. Iowa forgot that a candidate is wise to negotiate a salary *after* being selected for the position, not before. Dr. Pitman might have granted the amount but not as blackmail that he was the only outside candidate remaining with the advanced degree.

When the full Board of Trustees met to consider whether to grant the position to Donald L. Winters or J. Paul Kelleher, Harrison brought up the issue of the degrees. "I don't like the fact that Winters got his master's from a teaching college. Heck, Towson State College isn't even a university. Kelleher has a true master's from Rutgers right here in New Jersey. Plus, the guy has an MBA from New York University," Harrison argued. "Two masters beat one doctorate."

Harrison was prompted by Kelleher to present the dichotomy on the degrees. Harrison had called J. Paul to ask how he might help him in the process, since he was in Kelleher's corner. Kelleher also prompted *Chuck the Magic Man* to bring up Winters' shortcomings as Interim President. It was not so much that Harrison liked Kelleher as he despised the more academic Winters. He saw Kelleher as a businessman, closer to what he was. And more susceptible to being squeezed.

County Commissioner Panichi's endorsement of Kelleher pushed the Board over the top from the original three-three tie vote, with the Chairman abstaining. Given that the County is responsible for one-third of the budget revenues and has approval authority, having Dominic in Kelleher's corner was paramount, even if complicity was undeniable.

Ironically, it hurt Mr. Winters' case too that Professor Sally Bowens representing the Faculty Union had sent a letter to the Board Chairman endorsing Winters. That did not set well with the Dr. Pitman, who said it showed poor judgment by Winters to have encouraged the endorsement. For Harrison, if the Faculty Union wanted *Coca-Cola*, he would lobby for *Pepsi-Cola* or maybe *7-Up*.

The final vote for the appointment of J. Paul Kelleher as President of Central Jersey Community College was seven in favor and no one against. The decision was to be effective December 1, at a salary of $52,500. Two of the seven Trustees were uncertain, but that did not matter.

As a gesture of appreciation and civility, the Board voted to grant Winters a $5,000 stipend for serving as Interim President. The two Board members who opted out of the Presidential Search process voted against the Winters payment.

Roseanne Hart was not surprised by the Board's vote. She had already started composing the draft press release to go to the *Jersey Star* and other state newspapers:

> *The CJCC Board of Trustees announces the appointment of J. Paul Kelleher as President of the College effective ---------- 1974. The vote of the seven-member Board of Trustees was unanimous and came following a thorough and comprehensive five-month national search.*
>
> *Kelleher has served at the College since 1965 and is 44 years old. His wife, Isabella, is a professor at Atlantic State College and they have two teenage sons, Connor and Ian.*

Board Chairman, Dr. Gerald M. Pitman, spoke on behalf of the Board: "We conducted a national search and then found that the best guy for the job was right here at the College. We were amazed at the number of outstanding applicants for the position, from all over the country, and we had a most difficult time sorting through all these highly qualified and distinguished men."

"Mr. Kelleher has an MBA from New York University and degrees from Rutgers, our State University. He has distinguished himself in his career. J. Paul was instrumental in the College being awarded a two-million-dollar grant from Washington D.C. and settling the last Faculty Union contract."

"Mr. Kelleher will pick up right where Dr. Greenleaf left off and assure a smooth transition. Mr. Kelleher has the full support of the faculty and other staff who were fully represented on the Presidential Search Committee and participated admirably in the process. We appreciate their contributions."

Roseanne quickly set aside her working draft when Chuck Harrison came to her office to announce the Board decision and request that she prepare a press release. She knew what the vote would be. Her thoughts at first went to Donald Winters who would be so disappointed and likely full of vengeance. She knew she would be witnessing a slow-motion train wreck.

Personnel Director Roseanne Hart then reflected on how the MBA versus doctorate letter she had gotten from New York University helped Kelleher land the position. She could now count on a few favors from the President.

Quite a few.

And the new President could count on a few more enemies!

Irish Pooka Spirit

PREVIOUSLY

The College When Kelleher Becomes President

Men as well as rivers grow crooked by following the path of least resistance.
Thomas Jefferson

1

PREVIOUSLY

"This is not a summer baby-sitting service."

Coach Solly ran a summer basketball camp for boys and girls in Pennsylvania's Pocono Mountains, near Wilkes-Barre. Dave Russell, star basketball player at Rutgers University and now a retired pro-All-Star with the Detroit Pistons, owned the youth camp, more as a diversion than a profit center.

In order the attend *Dave Russell's All-Star Basketball Camp*, a young teen had to be invited to the camp or submit a petition. Coach Solly was not about to explain what a basketball was or the difference between a two-handed chest pass and a bounce pass. The young athletes, male or female, had to demonstrate proficiencies and potentials in the sport.

Solly liked to say to recruits, "This is not a summer baby-sitting service." Of course, he and Russell made exceptions if the parents were ready to invest in camp infrastructure by paying a significant surcharge.

Pro basketball's Dave Russell made two or three appearances at the camp each summer, usually unannounced. Solly ran the place, at least the basketball part. Sometimes Russell would bring along an entourage of current and former pro basketball players to stay at his mansion log house and create a flurry of excitement for the campers.

Russell had met Coach Solly through the *Scarlet Knights* basketball coach, Lefty Miller. When the property became available in the Pennsylvania Mountains in 1973, Dave Russell sought out Solly to handle the instructional portion of the camp and do the marketing and administration.

Solly and Russell worked together to design the outdoor basketball courts and indoor kitchen, chuckwagon and the open seating area that easily converted to indoor basketball courts when it rained, or Coach wanted evening drills.

Solly was pals with several pro players and an assortment of ex-college players who had tried out for the pros. A few made off with handsome paydays. He knew Terry Lucas and Maurice Williams who played at Rutgers after Solly graduated and had an unsuccessful try-out with the pros before playing overseas and cashing in there.

In the summers, before starting the camp, Solly had coached workouts for Dwight Taylor who graduated from Princeton and played for the New York Knicks. Solly would periodically share defensive tips with Sean Ellis of St. John's University and Joseph "Birdman" Bryan from LaSalle who played with the Philadelphia Seventy-Sixers. Solly was acclaimed for his knowledge of defenses and of when to switch defenses within a game, even within a possession.

Coach Solly did his promotional work for *Dave Russell's Poconos All-Star Basketball Camp* the rest of the year, usually out of his office at the College and without differentiation regarding his time or job responsibilities. His colleagues were well-aware of the intrusive preoccupation, but only President Kelleher classified the Poconos' obligations as disobedience and dereliction.

Few coaches were as capable as Solly for instruction on basketball fundamentals, especially geared to young teens. However, Coach Solly's competence bordered on ineptitude in management, staff supervision and financial accountability. His concept of tax preparation was dumping the assortment of receipts on his accountant's desk. He restricted his version of order and organization to alphabetical sequencing.

To remedy those shortcomings, Coach Solly partnered with the President's Secretary, Mrs. Edith Reynolds, who proficiently handled the business transactions, bill payments and administrative decision-making. The partnership was quite workable: Russell provided the investment resources and Solly did the teaching. Everything else, Edith handled.

Edith was hired as the President's Secretary when she started. Dr. Greenleaf was the President then, and J. Paul Kelleher was the Vice President of Institutional Support. When Kelleher replaced Greenleaf, he accepted summer camp moonlighting, albeit with reluctance and revulsion.

Mrs. Reynolds received a modest stipend for her administrative contributions to the summer camp, most of which was cash under the table and food supplies. There also were the lovely weekends to be spent in the mountains over the summer. The extra cash was well received, given she and husband Roy had a son at college in Washington D.C., studying to be a lawyer.

Edith could use the Poconos property after the camp closed in the fall with the magnificent autumn colors on display. She could take advantage of the whole place in the early spring as well, when the mountains came alive with deep greens and abundant expectations. She could avail herself of

Russell's colossal log home, basking in the mountains, enjoying the wonders of nature and lolling in the luxury of his million-dollar home, made of solid Western Red Cedar timber brought in from British Columbia.

Unless Russell was in town, Edith and husband Roy could stay in one of the six guest bedrooms at Russell's oversized log house, and enjoy his Ray Charles, Anita Baker and Lou Rawls LP albums. They could play pool and ping-pong in his paneled den that elbowed off the rest of the house. Or they could relax in his movie room with an assortment of drama and comedy videotapes, elongated couches and a popcorn machine purchased from a movie theater. Failing that, they could tranquilize by submerging in his whirlpool bathtub or sweat their cares away in his sauna.

Edith and Roy had had dual family reunions at the basketball camp, including a cook-out in the pit fireplace and half-court pick-up basketball games with the kids, parents and dogs. The kids amused themselves at night in the den with pool and ping-pong, while the parents ate popcorn and watched Clint Eastwood and John Wayne westerns.

Edith had invited J. Paul Kelleher, his wife Izzy and their two sons to spend a weekend at the camp last summer. Izzy gave her a hesitant nod of acceptance, but Coach Solly gave her a look of mystification. The President had no interest in going to a summer camp, especially if doing so would provide Solly with an upper hand.

Izzy and her two sons did make the two-hour drive to the mountains one weekend last summer. The boys were far more interested in skateboarding on the outdoor courts than playing basketball, since there were girl campers who were far more skilled. Izzy had enjoyed the weekend, especially when invited to stay at Russell's mountaintop mini-manor and relax with pro players sitting around at dinner and telling wild stories, some of which were true. She also got a kick out of their flattering but lame attempts at flirtation with an older woman.

They all sat in Russell's man-cave den, progressing through several bottles of *Rolling Rock* beer and David's private label wines, and to increasingly uninhibited revelations. Solly was as entertaining in story-telling and improvisations as the pro basketballers, with an uncanny knack for embellishment and appeal to Izzy's twisted sense of mockery.

Izzy didn't think she would connect with Coach Solly, given all the negative anecdotes told to her by her husband. But she did. She was attracted to him, not in an adulterous or romantic way, but with his banter, wisecracks and all-around joyfulness. He was exceedingly kind to her and generous with compliments. She would have to give more thought the next time J. Paul verbally beat up Coach Solly. She would want to place a different context on the ridicule.

Solly had known Izzy from various campus social events over the years where the spouses were curtly involved or from Commencement and other ceremonies where the program was a command performance for faculty and the President's wife. Solly was not bashful about coming up to her and working his macho charm, whenever he did see her, partly because she was most attractive in ways dissimilar from his wife. Mostly, he wanted to piss-off President Kelleher. The two had somehow connected that weekend at the Poconos basketball camp. The flowing red hair that framed that lingering smile was a striking captivation.

Izzy was not reticent or self-effacing about the unintended rendezvous moments with Solly. She found him engaging in ways J. Paul approximated years ago but had fallen off in recent months. She adored the attention and the boyish, provocative yet respectful, moves to gain her favor. She felt like an innocent school girl being courted. He had a roguish appeal under the jock exterior.

It had been many a year since Izzy had sensed a man was trying to seduce her, emotionally if not physically. It was reassuring to her sexuality to find herself tantalized by a male. She was sufficiently analytical to presuppose that the playful moves were designed to appeal to her, not aggravate her husband or gain an ally. But she could be wrong. She certainly could be naïve.

Coach Solly thrived playing racquetball at the local YMCA indoor courts. He loved his racquetball workouts before going to the office or classroom. He embraced the competitive surge when he played and especially when he won, which was often. Solly relished his acquired skills to smack the ball on angles low to the floor and against the corners rather than rely on finesse shots. He liked to blister the ball low and hard to either side of the court and make his opponents look silly.

A few months ago, Solly had come off the courts dripping in sweat. Then Izzy Kelleher showed up ready to ascend the steps onto the playing surface after the bell rang to signal the next round of play. The two of them eyed each other at the glass door – Solly trying to push the door outward while Izzy blocked the door in a momentary state of bewilderment at seeing the Coach.

Solly enjoyed the light-hearted manner that his conspiring racquetball sportsperson greeted the mornings and her high-spirited approach to life. His wife Marilyn had no interest in racquetball or any sport that involved perspiration. She was usually in a grouchy mood in the morning, which was another reason he left early to commence his exercise regimen.

Solly told Marilyn after the first awkward meeting with Izzy that he had run into her at the YMCA. But he did not share any ensuing moments or conversations he had with the President's wife. Just let it be his version of a schoolboy fantasy, the fool's paradise of a grown man.

Marilyn and Solly had been married for eighteen years and had two teen children, Beth, age 16, and Ben, age 14. Both kids were active in age appropriate basketball, with Beth already playing on the high school varsity as a hyperactive point guard and defensive pain in the butt. Ben was more interested in tennis than basketball, perhaps because he could escape his father's continually unfolding coaching.

Solly reasoned that Izzy had not shared their racquetball encounters at the Y with J. Paul. She probably did not share very much about the weekend spent at the Pocono summer camp with Edith and her husband, owner Russell and several pro basketball titans at Russell's colossus house.

Their friendship had progressed from a few quick minutes over a healthy post-game drink at the YMCA to mutual fondness. Solly had gone from a *Good-Time Charlie* to a kindred soul who listened. In Solly's mind, and even with the hesitation due to her husband being the ultimate boss, Izzy had gone from an attractive red-headed woman, who could use a laugh or two, to a target. He loved that he could mesmerize Izzy and steal her from Kelleher, if only for an hour or two.

Their talk never got around to their respective spouses or their marriages. Neither had designs on escalating the relationship to a physical connection, even though both were enticingly attractive human beings with fanciful curiosities.

That could change. Afterall, Solly's favorite expression was: *Marriage is the number one cause of divorce.*

PREVIOUSLY

"These are only little kisses. Nothing more."

Isabella Brooke Rhode Kelleher had been a member of the National Organization for Women (NOW), since Congress passed the Equal Rights Amendment (ERA) in 1972. New Jersey ratified the ERA that same year. The proposed amendment was still many states shy of the number needed for ratification. Izzy was optimistic the amendment would eventually pass into law.

The reticent states argued ERA would damage a woman's housewife role and lead to female military conscription. There was a contentious national debate over what Feminism was and wasn't. Izzy was secure in her definition as both a mother and a professional woman. She did not understand the confusion or sympathize with dissenters.

Her mother likely would have disagreed, as she was a noble housewife who always had her husband's supper and slippers ready when he came home from work. Her mother was a Master Baker who had not had the opportunity to go to college. She made sure Izzy did. Had mom lived longer, the lady would have challenged the virtues of the proposal and taken on her daughter as to ERA's validity.

The problem Izzy was having with NOW was the deliberate attempt to juxtapose Feminism and Lesbianism. There was a faction of NOW who proffered that recognizing lesbian rights was an attack on Feminism. This division stalled the number of states needed to ratify the ERA and make it a part of the Constitution.

Izzy had endorsed several rallies to support Equal Educational Opportunity, anti-abortion rights and anti-violence against women. She had joined the march in Trenton to bring attention to "Take Back the Night," protesting violence against women. She planned to march in Washington,

D.C. for the ERA whenever that was organized. She would take half of Atlantic State College's faculty with her and a busload of students. Her husband was sympathetic but not about to march in Washington, Trenton or even around the block for any cause.

Izzy Kelleher was with Ella Cosby, a friend and confidant, getting together again after having tried to embrace her inner self and unfold her sexuality. In the interim, Izzy's husband J. Paul had become President of Central Jersey Community College. Some things had changed; some things remained the same.

The two racquetball players had chatted several times by telephone after the breakfast meeting that morning at which Ella tried to explain Lesbianism and address feelings stirring within Izzy's body. Weeks went by before they reconnected. Then months.

It didn't seem like they should get together while the Presidential Search process was underway, and J. Paul was scrambling to come in first in the race to the President's Office. After he got the job, everything was turned upside down in their relationship and at home.

When Izzy and Ella had that initial breakfast after meeting at the YMCA, Izzy found out that Ella was a jewelry maker and presumably a semi-closeted lesbian. She had been surprised by the initial revelation, about the jewelry, but not by the second clarification.

Since then, Izzy had aggressively initiated sex with her husband, hoping to differentiate the feelings and rekindle their passion. It had felt good to climax, although her self-stimulation during the sex relations probably was more causal than the intercourse or J. Paul's amorous overtures.

He had been enormously preoccupied during the Presidential Search process, often cloistering himself in his home office. He wasn't much interested in sex, family, dog, food or sleep. He did retain his interest in the *Marlboro* cigarettes and the *Bushmills* Irish Whiskey. Izzy had understood and given him his space while being supportive. Every night had been a debriefing, telephone marathon, bitch session and a strategy forum.

The two women were having dinner together at Peking Duck House in nearby Fontana just before Valentine's Day in 1975 and just after Kelleher's appointment. They were sitting side-by-side in a cozy booth with a linen tablecloth, folded napkins and attentive service. Izzy selected the Szechuan jumbo shrimp as her entree, while Ella ordered the sweet and sour chicken. Both started the meal with a glass of red wine and orders of Wonton soup.

The restaurant was well-known for its food and its loyal clientele. It was a safe place for two women to meet and have dinner. If anyone Izzy knew saw them, she was having dinner with a friend while J. Paul was at work. This was her friend from playing racquetball at the YMCA. That would be all the introduction necessary.

Since the day she had met Ella Cosby and shared omelets, Izzy had mostly avoided looking at women in the locker room. But she did want to continue the conversation with Ella rather than activate any impulses or fantasies. She had read some notes from the studies by the Masters and Johnson research team on sexuality, including homosexuality. Izzy had intellectualized distinctions between heterosexual and lesbian women and her feelings.

Ella started the awkward conversation, "So how's it going as the President's wife, Izzy? Are people treating you any differently? I haven't played much racquetball lately since I hurt my leg."

Izzy didn't want to talk about her husband and his new position at the College. She had not yet come to grips with her role as official and anointed Presidential Spouse. As CJCC's First Lady, she knew her role was to bake cookies, smile and defer to her husband at social events. She could wear church clothes on campus, but homemaker dresses were preferred. The role would challenge her NOW position. She was not looking forward to years of swallowing her thoughts and hiding her values.

J. Paul did not want her to sacrifice anything in her career. "Izzy just show up at the damn political events and don't piss-off anyone," he had said several times after the appointment. "You have your teaching position and the boys. If the jerks at the College or Board members want something else, they can go to hell."

Sensing Izzy's unease and hesitation, Ella spoke first. "Izzy, I know you have questions, and with your intelligence, I feel comfortable sharing with you. Let me try."

"Like most heterosexual relationships there's a difference between casual sex and committed relationships. Committed lesbian ladies have a relaxed understanding of their partner's sexual needs than most straight couples. This may be perception, but then again, it's easier to understand one's own sex and pleasures than the opposite one's."

"For sure, committed lesbian couples devote an extraordinary amount of time to sexual play," she continued. "There's repeated stimulation of the breasts, but that is after much touching and kissing. Most men travel to the woman's breasts within 30 seconds of initiating sex, as you may have noticed."

Izzy couldn't help but smile, and then she interjected. "Men don't usually wait that long from my experience. But then there were not very many men before Pauly and none since. He's Irish to the core. I should know. Besides, Ella, I've learned that there are only three types of Irish men who cannot understand us females: the young men, the old guys and then those middle-aged ones."

After a gleeful laugh, Ella resumed her explanations. "Men are the bumblers in lovemaking. They tend to hurry sex and massage the female genitals in a straightforward manner, gung-ho in technique. But most women are too bashful or conscientious of societal norms to be candid, even with their male partners."

"Yes, I can see that," Izzy noted. "We place the burden of sexual performance on the man. He must figure out what we want. Dads and the teen peer groups don't tend to cover that part of sex education. We just know that the guy wants his genitals massaged and then go inside, move vigorously and come quickly. That's pretty easy."

"That's often true," Ella replied. "But lesbians do not have the burden of deciphering the opposite sex. They communicate better and are more aware of the level of their partner's sexual excitement and fulfillment."

"That's what you've found in your female lovers, Ella?" Izzy asked. She was sure she knew the answer, even if she had misstated the question.

"Izzy let's get our dinners as take out and head over to my townhouse," Ella said. "I can show you some of my jewelry, and we can relax with another glass of wine and finish our meals. I only live a few miles from here."

"I would like that," Izzy affirmed although she was a bit hesitant, not knowing if the focus of the relocation would be jewelry or intimacy. "I've wanted to see your creative work since we met that day at the Y. We can cancel the soup and head out as soon as the orders can be boxed."

If Izzy misunderstood the intent and gravity of the invitation, she would deal with that later. Besides, she was hungry.

Ella Cosby's townhouse was a two-story, two-bedroom unit that shared an elongated wall with a neighbor and had a covered parking space and access to a kidney-shaped swimming pool and clubhouse. They entered the unit and went to the kitchen where Ella had a round table with two chairs in the adjacent breakfast nook. She placed the takeout dinners on porcelain plates, along with silverware, and discarded the carry-out boxes and plastic forks.

While eating, they discussed Izzy's teaching at Atlantic State College and work with her colleagues in the English Department. Izzy shared how she had met her husband and how she was adjusting as the spouse of a College President.

"I'm naturally extroverted, so meeting people in various situations is comfortable for me, even the highly political times," Izzy began. "I just don't enjoy the way people at the College avoid saying much of anything about my husband. It's as if they are in terror he might find out and hold the comment against them."

"Pauly does have a temper, but he's not vindictive," Izzy continued. "He bullies some, but that's his Irish heritage. He does enjoy chaos, or more accurately he thrives on chaos. Friction too. He'll change the organization, move departments, like checkerboard pieces, just to stir the mix, just to piss off people. But he has his reasons too."

The two ladies finished eating their Chinese dinners. Izzy asked again about seeing the jewelry.

"Let me show you some of my work, although more recent stuff is at the lab. Let's go to my bedroom, and I can show you," Ella said as she pushed aside the dishes, grabbed her glass of red wine and led Izzy up the stairs. "There's excellent lighting and a wonderful mirror over my dresser. We can show off my pieces and your good looks."

As they headed up the stairs, Izzy turned her head to survey the living area below. "Very nice layout. I see your bold tastes in the artwork, especially the colors and textures in the abstracts."

"Thank you, my dear" Ella, responded. "I have a few friends who paint, and I try to honor them by purchasing their pieces. At least the ones I like. Visual patterns and textures are essential for me in art compositions, my jewelry and my choice of art."

Ella went to the dresser and started to lay out pendants, rings and earrings on the edge of the bed, displaying a delightful array of polished stones and settings. Izzy picked out two rings and playfully placed them on her fingers.

"These are wonderful," Izzy gushed. She reached out for Ella's arm and gave it a gentle, affectionate and appreciative clasp. She was excited about the jewelry and amazed at the talents of her friend.

Ella sorted through several other pieces, before selecting one. "This pendant complements either ring you have and would look amazing with your flowing hair and facial color," she said. "I favor this Lapis pendant with the cabochon-cut stone for you."

Ella took the blue jewelry piece, as Izzy turned around to enable Ella to fasten the necklace. She pulled aside Izzy's auburn hair and faced the large dresser mirror. Ella secured the delicate pendant and allowed her fingers to caress Izzy's neck lightly. Ella kept her fingers on Izzy's long neck, lingering and softly running her fingers along the profile, while Izzy stared at herself and Ella in the mirror.

Izzy's eyes moved from contemplating the pendant to Ella's eyes, as Ella admiringly gazed at her neck. She looked up and peeked around Izzy's head to see Izzy focused on her with a look of affection mixed with ambiguity. Ella smiled and gently kissed the elongated back of her neck, two little kisses, each one fluttering and hovering like a hummingbird.

She pivoted Izzy, so they now faced each other, their eyes affixed to each other, a few inches apart. Ella touched the jewelry piece as it rested near Izzy's collarbone permeating her with unquestionable loveliness.

Ella gently kissed her lips with deliberate pauses in between. She spoke softly, "Izzy, just relax. These are only little kisses. Nothing more. Truly."

Indeed, the kisses Ella offered to her friend were meant to be exploratory. The tenderness highlighted the moment itself, rather than serving as a prelude to further intimacy.

Izzy savored the attention. She delighted in the intrigue and the gentleness of the connections, more than the physical sensation or seductive temptations.

She gleefully accepted the stunning and intriguing pendant, suddenly transformed into a stunning and intriguing gift. "I need to pay you for this pendant," Izzy pleaded. "It's just beautiful."

Izzy had her first kiss by a woman and felt she might embrace the confusion and clutch the sensations.

PREVIOUSLY

"Get that damn rat down!"

A solid four-member administrative team conducted negotiations with the Faculty Union in 1976: Mr. Bill Fishman, Vice President of Administrative Affairs, Miss Roseanne Hart, Personnel Director, Dr. Thomas Dandridge, Vice President of Institutional Support and Mr. Eugene Wildwood, Lead Programmer in the Computer Center.

Fishman chaired the team and yet ran every topic and issue by President Kelleher including meeting dates, times and refreshment choices. This was the first round of faculty negotiations with Mr. Kelleher as President. He was not about to let any detail slip by him.

If Bill Fishman was *Starsky*, then Roseanne Hart would gladly assume the role of *Hutch*. If roles got reversed, she would morph into *Starsky* from the TV series. She would play the tough-as-nails Personnel Director in one bargaining session. Then she'd chitchat and schmooze faculty at the next meeting, as if she had suddenly defected.

The President of the Faculty Union for her second term was Miss Sally Bowens, Associate Professor of Business. Sally had been re-elected in 1975 without opposition. She had been on the bargaining team three years ago, and her colleagues credited her with holding the line and gaining a handsome raise. That contract included a modest reduction in weekly classroom contact hours and required office hours.

However, the Union had given up a faculty prerogative to teach back-to-back-to-back class sections on given days and thus end up with one or two days a week without teaching commitments. A modest percentage of her faculty colleagues were still angry over that concession – those who preferred stacking classes even if their teaching suffered due to stale lectures and fatigued discussions.

Sally was cunning and not against pursuing any strategy or tactic to affirm her case. More accurately, she was shifty and borderline unscrupulous. She got along fine with President Kelleher outside of the prolonged negotiation months. She stood toe-to-toe with him when it came to foul-mouthed humor and provocative insults. They were like boxers who got along fine until the public weigh-in before the big fight with the cameras and press. They each had a cameo role to play before a live audience, and they relished confrontation.

Professor Bowens was tall and lean with highlighted auburn hair, pulled back by two plastic combs aligned with the sides of her head. She dressed mostly in business suits with skirts hemmed just above the knee to accent her shapely legs. The look was highly professional, demonstrably feminine and subtly provocative.

Like the President's wife, Sally had been active in the Women's Liberation movement of the late 1960's, marching in both Washington, D.C. and Trenton. She joined the National Organization for Women (NOW) a year after it was founded in 1966 but cooled on membership when the organization grew divided. She advocated Equal Rights but with the preservation and advancement of Feminism.

Professor Bowens was disturbed that some NOW leaders were maliciously characterized, and she got angry when men would argue against equality. "This is not about women wanting to be men or wanting to blur distinctions between femininity and masculinity," she was fond of saying. "This is about rights and opportunities."

She was not bashful about expressing her views on campus either. Given that there was such a small number of female professors and professional staff members and mostly uninterested males, her audience was modest and passive.

Miss Bowens was dating Ralph Hughes, a math instructor. Ralph explained Sally's Feminism by declaring, "If we go up to a door, she expects the first person there to open it, not necessarily me. If we go to dinner, we alternate who picks up the check. Woe is me if I hold out her chair at a restaurant without asking her if I may do so, or assume I always drive on a date. It makes perfect sense, once you grasp the language."

Sally felt empowered by Ralph's support, not only for her teaching and Feminism but for her sparring matches with Kelleher, Fishman and Hart. Hughes was superb at crunching data and finding analytical flaws in the Administration's reports and proposals. If he couldn't find a flaw, he would manufacture one.

Ralph was also above-average tall. He was skinny rather than lean. Ralph always wore long-sleeve starched shirts and a bow tie. He was aligned on the Introverted scale and willingly balanced Sally's hyper-Extroverted personality.

Ralph would think before he spoke; Sally would speak first and think as she went along.

Hughes had been attracted to Sally Bowens three years ago when they paired in that go-round of contract negotiations under President Greenleaf. He had been hesitant to pursue a romantic engagement, even a date. That is until Sally sat in his office one day, revealing the length of her legs and showing even more charm. Sally had suggested they go out for a beer after classes. Ralph blundered "Yes, sure" as an answer and then proudly chased Sally until she caught him.

They also paired up on the disco dance floor, where Sally liked to whirl under the spinning disco ball in her sequined jumpsuit. Ralph liked to show off his latest moves with Sally, both on the dance floor and in the back seat of her Pontiac.

Ralph was humble and meek in a highly attractive way – to Sally. To others, he was someone who would be undistinguishable in a crowd of two. They were comfortable in their non-marital commitment, honoring the relationship, including the carnal duties. But they maintained separate identities, apartments and bank accounts.

Ralph kept a toothbrush and spare set of clothes in his truck. Even when he and Sally had sleepovers, he was not to leave any hint of having been there that night. She did let him use her toothpaste, and she honored his choice of pillows.

Neither Bowens nor Hughes were afraid of the Board of Trustees or impressed with their gyrations about what to bargain. Sally showed little fondness for President Kelleher and prided herself on being able to play to his male insecurities. Neither was the Faculty Union President spooked by rats or by other two-legged rodents. Sally equated most men with the varmints and held Kelleher in that regard at least while negotiations were underway.

But this year, on that Monday morning of *D-Day Week*, October 1976, President Kelleher would be surprised when he pulled into his reserved parking space behind the Administration Building. There high in the morning sky was a giant, inflated grey rat, tethered to a rope tied to the top of the building and facing the main student parking lot.

The helium-filled, *King-Kong*-sized rodent had protruding teeth and a long, outstretched, wagging tail. The rat's head was crooked – tilted to starboard. The balloon carried no written statement, but the message was abundantly clear. J. Paul was infuriated. The President dismissed his early morning campus jog in favor of a panicked call to Security.

"Tyrone, get that damn rat down from the Administration Building right now," Kelleher barked. "If you can find the son of a bitch who got on top of the building this morning to tie that dopey thing off, I want him fired. And don't give me any free speech bull shit."

Chief of Security, Tyrone Jackson, got the message. But the Chief was not about to sound a campus alarm that there was a rogue rat flying in the sky. He figured he knew who got into the Administration Building, and he might not tattle on the culprit anyway.

By the time J. Paul got his shower in his office bathroom and began his piece-by-piece dressing routine, the phone calls started. First, it was Martha J. Rooney from the local *Jersey Star* crossing over from sports coverage to handle the newspaper's contact with the President on the sky-high rat. Martha loved her job especially when she could confront an authority figure and elevate that person's blood pressure.

"Mr. Kelleher," Martha said when the phone was answered, more as a statement than a question. Martha did not appreciate the respectful title of President. She was not a fan of how Kelleher had arrived at the position. Greenleaf had taken her to lunch at least once a year. The new President had yet to invite her to lunch or anything. Plus, Kelleher had canceled the office subscription to the *Jersey Star*. The reporter took delight in referring to him as "Mr." and not as "Dr.," as President Greenleaf had been, and in avoiding the deferential "President" title.

"Yes, this is President Kelleher," J. Paul stated, having swallowed hard that the media was now on his case over the high-flying rat. He knew Martha J. Rooney was at the other end of the phone, but he was damned if he would acknowledge her.

Disguising her questions as an interview, Miss Rooney had begun her interrogation: "Mr. Kelleher, I have to ask you how you liked the helium mouse up in the sky this morning. I assume you saw it since it was tied to the Administration Building, and you usually arrive early in the morning for your jog."

Kelleher took a sip of coffee he had retrieved from the Hamilton Bakery before driving to work, along with a custard-filled donut, thinking he would enjoy them after his habitual run. He was in no hurry to respond to Rooney or eat the donut. "Damn right I saw the blessed thing, and it was totally inappropriate. It was a rat, Rooney, not a version of *Mickey Mouse!*" After he said it, he knew the *Mickey Mouse* reference would be the newspaper headline the next morning.

"Martha, rats are symbols of disease, poverty and depravity," Kelleher continued. "Rats are an omen of a person being trapped, if you've read George Orwell's 1984 book. None of that represents the life of our faculty or staff. You know I was an English Lit major for my baccalaureate. Have you read Orwell's book?" Kelleher asked, anticipating she had not and wanting to stick it to her.

The young newspaper lady knew he was testing her. She reverted to her questions. "Were you impressed with the balloon? Did the Faculty Union put the rat up in the sky? Did you get any calls yet from Board members? Think it will impact negotiations?"

Martha paused for a weighted moment and then added, "Of course, I read 1984 in college. I did a paper on Orwell. Got an A."

"Damn right it will," Kelleher said, dismissing her 1984 admission. "If the faculty wanted to piss me off and draw a line in the sand, this worked. Until we investigate and find out who was on the roof and tied off that balloon, negotiations are canceled."

Kelleher was in no mood for further conversation with the newspaper reporter or anyone for that matter. He ended the phone call with a polite but curt, "Do take care, Martha." Then he hung-up the phone and scowled out the window as Security slowly lowered the high-flying rodent to the ground outside his office before an audience of hysterical faculty and curious students.

Kelleher had a change of heart the next morning after the *Jersey Star* had a half-page photo of the floating rat with the endearing headline of *College Negotiations Hit Rock Bottom. Kelleher says that's not Mickey Mouse.* Rooney's story was the lead feature on the *Star's* front page, not relegated to the Sports Section.

The President knew Board Chairman Pitman would not appreciate the coverage and that the bargaining table might be shut down. He also knew that Pitman and Vice Chairman Harrison would be angrier than he was about the publicity and the flying symbolism.

J. Paul would have to differentiate the sticky points from the stickier points. He'd have to have to settle with the Faculty Union before fall class registration began in three week. Or, as threatened, he would delay the process for months. Just maybe, he could use this to his advantage in negotiations.

J. Paul had Edith call *Starsky* and *Hutch* to his office and asked what could be done to bring closure. "How far are we apart now in salary percentage," he questioned.

Speaking ever so slowly but gaining momentum as the words came to her, Personnel Director Hart offered. "Sir, the damn union is threatening to strike again. Likely some Board member will want you to cave on the contract now, while Harrison wants the faculty to take a bigger pay cut. Shall we pursue or stonewall negotiations for a while?" Roseanne asked. "It does not seem likely that we could reach agreement before classes start."

"Screw them. Stall it. I want to know who's responsible for that god damn helium rat in the sky," Kelleher barked.

PREVIOUSLY

"Oh Candace, have you seen them yet?"

Women at Central Jersey Community College were mostly in supportive clerical positions or hired as Counselors, Librarians or in Admissions. At no time was sex segregation more evident on campus than at noon. That's when guys would pile into cars and head to local diners for lunch, while most females would stay in their offices for coverage and then go two-by-two to the Staff Lounge to commiserate and eat their noontime food brought from home.

Other than Union President Sally Bowens, there was a handful of female faculty who taught Business courses, Biology, English and Nursing. The Department Chairman of Health Technologies, Helen Gray, was a woman. The position was considered as faculty, not administrative, because department colleagues elected the person. All other Department Chairmen were males. Roseanne Hart as Personnel Director was the lone female administrator.

The disparity was no secret. It was considered normative, even typical for a college or school. No one questioned the institutional sexism of that nomenclature or that organizational fact. The proper word was *Chairman*, even when applied to a woman.

Changes in the workplace came slowly and few happened in the mid-1970's. Equal Opportunity was slowly evolving from law and the courts into a reality in employment, pay, promotions and other personnel matters. It was a race of turtles to see who could come in last.

According to Section 501 of the College's *Collective Bargaining Agreement for Career Employees,* there were five clerical position classifications: Secretary I, II and III, and Administrative Secretary and President's Secretary. The demarcations were mostly based on years of service, not training, skills or education. Everyone knew who the highly competent female support employees were, as well as the *Hangers-On.* Everyone knew the

Matronly – those who were lauded because of their affinity to shelter, shield and blindly support their male supervisors.

The President's Secretary – Edith Reynolds – was classified as the sole position at that fifth level. Edith excelled in her post and everyone agreed she did. She would know what President Greenleaf, and then President Kelleher, would do and want before they did, like *Radar O'Reilly* on TV's MASH.

Edith had mastered the art of signature, such that President Kelleher would routinely dump a pile of papers on her desk and direct her to "sign these please." Fortunately, she was over-the-top honest. No one detected her counterfeit autographs. Few cared.

The job classification for Candace Rodewald was as an Administrative Secretary, but she was known as Office Manager, even though there was no such classification. The engraved title on her desk plate with her name used Office Manager. Howard Tucker, the Computer Center Director, had given her that plate and title as an endearing birthday present. From that point, no one dared refer to Rodewald as a secretary.

The Candace and Edith positions were the only Exempt Career Employees. That meant they were not subject to the Career Employee contract, although their pay and benefits were. Both had access to sensitive information and considered their exception as an honor, even though there was no monetary benefit. They would not be permitted to join the Union in any protests or work stoppage, or they would face termination. They would be strangled if they shared sensitive information pertinent to negotiations.

Candace had a fancy *IBM Correcting Selectric III* typewriter with an interchangeable golf ball of typeface and a carriage that remained stationary as the elements magically traversed the page. The carriage also contained a small spool of correction tape, with the spool changed independently of the ribbon cartridge.

Candace only used the fancy office machine at the end of the month when she typed Howard's monthly report. Most months, she merely replaced the prior month's efficiency statistics with the current month's efforts. White-out helped. It was good enough.

Most secretaries had to take dictation as well as have high-level typing skills, producing at least 65 words per minute without errors. Candidates were tested for their typing proficiency before being hired, even if the position had no typing to do. Shapely candidates usually could get a reprieve on the typing proficiency.

If Candace had ever mastered one-on-one dictation, that skill had deteriorated long ago. There was a *Dictaphone* machine on her desk. Other than gathering dust, the equipment had no purpose in her workday.

Howard never learned how to use the modern office equipment even though Kelleher got the set in 1975 after he became President and demanded he use it. Kelleher reasoned the dictation equipment would increase efficiency for the key administrators. Yet, all it did was add semi-decorative, conversational dust collectors to Howard's credenza and Candace's desk.

Howard Tucker rarely sent interoffice memos or letters that Candace needed to type. He preferred jotting notes on the back of stiff 80-column IBM computer punch cards. Howard always had a cluster of the punch cards in his shirt pocket. He was the one person in the freezing Computer Center who had sufficient body fat to ward off the chilly temperatures without long sleeves. The IBM paper products were the calling cards of his profession, and the Programmers had the same shirt-pocket placement of IBM cards.

Howard's position as an Exempt Administrator meant his office would have the latest computer equipment and technology innovations. That was true for the entire Computer Center. Gene's rank was also as an Exempt Administrator, in the event Howard was unavailable or quit. That meant the office would be even higher up on the interoffice food chain.

Candace's position meant she could have whatever she wanted. But the high-tech *Dictaphone* and *IBM Selectric* were mostly decorative. So too, was the office-to-office intercom system. When Howard needed someone to come to his office, he yelled, and his voice carried over the sound of the machines. Even so, the Programmers passed along the message like a water brigade.

Gene Wildwood, as Lead Programmer, liked to tease Candace about the dormant dictating equipment and the seldom-used fancy typewriter. Gene knew when to back off his feeble attempts at humor. Candace knew that when Gene made such reference, it was not as an insult. Gene was her mischievous ally. She realized Gene melted in her presence. She just smiled when he would occasionally stutter. Gene was like a 7th grade boy trying to converse with the cutest 8th grade girl in the school.

Sooner or later, Candace got whatever she wanted. Like Edith, she had graduated from CJCC with an Associate in Applied Science (AAS) degree in Office Management and was only three credit hours shy of a second degree – Computer Technology. Then she would have the same, or higher proficiency, credentials than half the fleet of Programmers.

When she completed the degree after next semester, and an opening occurred in the Computer Center, she would apply. Woe to anyone who deprived her of that promotion. Gene had already assured her of the opportunity even though he would have to clear it with Tucker and Kelleher.

Candace's husband of five years, Bob, was a salesman for an auto parts manufacturer. Most of their family members and friends were convinced that Bob had *outkicked his coverage* in landing Candace as girlfriend, let alone as wife. He had appealed to Candace at the right time, as she had tired of dating handsome men without much apparent character or substance. Bob was exceedingly sweet and gentle in his courtship. He was a nice-looking guy and diligent in his work. Candace was in another league in intelligence, class and motivation.

Bob had been devout in his commitment when courting this lady. But his devotion could come across now as maudlin and boring. He was out of town at least one night a week, usually two, leaving his sensuous partner to ponder what was misplaced in her life and marriage.

Candace had had two long-term lovers before Bob. She had saved herself when she started getting serious with Bob, avoiding intimacy and preaching chastity when her new beau maneuvered to go home from second or third base. Bob had been patient and respectful of Candace's wishes. After marriage, the husband had been like the lead lion who had beaten off all suitors in the pride and now was enraptured with his conquest.

Their sexual intimacy had tapered to a sporadic drip the past year, as Candace had set up a few passion roadblocks. Plus, traveling Bob was finding it less and less necessary and desirable to check-in with his wife, when on the road or at home. He found other outlets for physical and sexual tensions. Candace got fatigued easily and became more self-reliant for her desires. She tired of Bob's misplaced amorous moves and clumsy pillow talk.

Candace had only met Gene's wife, Alice, a teacher, once at a reception held last June after Commencement. She had expected Gene would be paired with a prettier gal. Alice was short, compact perhaps, like a Chevy Corvair rather than a Camaro. Candace reasoned that Alice had probably been trim and petite when younger. Not anymore. Not after years grabbing ice cream sandwiches at lunch and Fudgsicles after the kindergarten classroom emptied of the munchkin brats.

Anyone would know instantly by Alice's appearance and manner of speaking, that she captained an elementary school class. Candace surmised that Gene's meekness and occasional stuttering had prevented him from pursuing a more attractive mate. He likely fell for Miss Alice's tribal chief demeanor and comforting disposition when they met. The couple just did not seem properly paired now. She had wanted kids of her own. That did not happen, and the classroom kids became her surrogates.

Since earning his degree and working in the Computer Center, aka *Meat Locker*, Gene had gained a great deal of confidence. Like some men, Gene got more dapper and handsome as the years progressed. Candace could see the changes just in the last year. She was impressed with him and intrigued by the thought of seeing him outside of the office.

There were still times when Gene would stutter, not on every word or phrase, but mostly in situations. He detested being on the telephone and knew his tendency to stutter was accentuated on the telephone. Why, he did not understand.

Gene was a serious amateur runner and liked to jog after work on the abandoned railroad tracks near his house and then on the circumference of the Winsor Country Club. He had accumulated an impressive collection of orphaned golf balls, gathered as he ran.

He would bounce a found golf ball on the asphalt road while running, thereby jogging intermittently so he could retrieve the golf ball as he catapulted it high into the air and before it bounced again. He had finished the *Jersey Shore* and *Philadelphia 76* marathons in under 5 hours.

Gene did not play golf or even pursue *Putt-Putt Golf*. He just collected stray golf balls. It was a good day when he found one. It was an exceptional day when he could pocket two or more.

As Lead Programmer, Gene made it a point to offer a sophomoric joke to Candace every day or so. "Heh, Mrs. Rodewald, how many Computer Programmers does it take to change a light bulb? None. That's a hardware problem."

Gene would also hum a song or two and offer lyrics that were not part of the original soundtrack. Elton John was a favorite because no one knew or understood the lyrics anyway. Gene never stuttered when he sang. He just didn't always sing on key or get the words right.

Candace smiled charmingly every time Gene would put on sunglasses and feint playing a whimsical piano while singing a modified Elton John standard:

> *Oh Candace, have you seen them yet?*
> *Bennie and the Jersey Jets.*
> *Oh, Candace lady, she's pretty keen,*
> *So, weird and wonderful,*
> *She's got sandy hair, tight jeans and a mohair suit.*
> *Oh, yeah, Bennie and the Jersey Jets.*

Gene did a slightly better job with the lyrics and melody for John Denver's *Sunshine on My Shoulder*, serenading the lady while strumming an imaginary guitar:

> *Sunshine on your shoulder makes me happy,*
> *Sunshine in your eyes makes me cry,*
> *Sunshine on your face looks so lovely,*
> *Sunshine almost always makes me sigh.*
> *And sigh, and sigh and sigh.*
> *Bye, bye.*

Candace was also impressed that Gene remembered her birthday with an exceptional bottle of Italian Chianti *Classico*, the one cloaked with a straw basket. Besides enjoying the medium-bodied *vino* with a delicate nutty, floral aroma, she liked to put colorful candles in the empty basket bottle and let the melted wax drip down in intriguing patterns.

Sometimes, Gene would just bring over a bottle of the wine to celebrate the New Year on January 1, the new fiscal year on July 1 or the Chinese and Jewish New Years. He would also drop off a bottle on Labor Day, Groundhog Day, Secretaries Day or days that began with the letter "F."

Husband Bob drank wine on sale from the A & P grocery and never asked where his wife got the Chianti. He would typically forget their anniversary and be out of town on her birthday.

At Valentine's Day last year and again this year, Gene had a bouquet of flowers delivered to Candace's office with the card denoting that the sender Cupid was anonymous. Candace had her suspicions of who sent the flowers, especially since she knew Bob was not romantic in that way. When others mistakenly complimented Candace on receiving a florist visit from her husband, she would just smile. It was her secret. It was Gene's as well, except he had sent flowers to his wife too.

When he wasn't singing, Gene was worried about Howard's drinking and not at all misled or amused with the desk-top *Dixie Cup* pretense. Gene had shut Howard's office door more than a few times to conduct an inquisition to affirm that Howard needed to stop drinking at work and quit the paper cup charade.

It was not unusual for faculty and staff to drink alcohol on campus, even store it in their offices. They might take a drink during the day or at the end of the day. However, there was a campus preference to drink liquor out of glasses rather than Howard's paper cups.

Every staff party unapologetically served hard liquor as a budget item under Miscellaneous Expenses or as augmented by bottles contributed by discerning employees – or by employees looking to watch their colleagues embarrass themselves.

PREVIOUSLY

"But I'm just a social drinker."

The annual Faculty and Staff Christmas Party, held in the Student Union, was highly anticipated and notorious. Assorted liquors, wines and beers were consumed in large quantity. Booze was the main ingredient in the party punch bowl. Given this was a college, employees knew there would never be a monetary holiday cash bonus, so they welcomed the legendary end-of-semester, increasingly uninhibited Christmas Party.

The December 1974 party had gotten a little out of hand. Some people cheered for J. Paul Kelleher's appointment as President. Others grieved that Vice President Winters, or anyone else, was not appointed. Most just enjoyed the catered food from Tuscany Italian Market including zucchini sticks, Sicilian rice balls, fried ravioli, mozzarella in carrozza, potato croquettes and prosciutto balls along with the bottomless punch bowl.

The liquor made the guys more aggressive toward the ladies and made their teasing more suggestive. It made their jokes funnier to themselves, if not to others.

The 1975 Christmas Party had been considerably more mellow and subdued, not because the punch bowl went un-spiked or the food came from a less expensive caterer. Kelleher's way of doing business and his organizational changes were unsettling to faculty, and many of them were still resentful that Winters had failed to earn the appointment.

The 1976 Christmas Party had been back to a time to let it all out, as faculty and staff were becoming accustomed, and thereby increasingly immune, to Kelleher's annual reorganizations. The punch bowl was spiked, but most employees preferred the array of gin, vodka and bourbon bottles or the Chardonnay and Merlot wine. Heavy on the liquor. Light on the mixers.

Employee holidays were negotiated in the bargaining process.

Twelve-month employees – non-teaching faculty – could look forward to being off from the day after the Christmas Party to the day after New Year's Day. Faculty usually had non-work days from the moment they turned in semester grades, until the day after New Year's. They still came to the party.

Former President Greenleaf had occasionally ignored the negotiated contracts and announced another day the College would close. Kelleher denied any extension. He felt all benefits were to be negotiated – none were given away. What he gained in contract adherence, he may have lost in employee morale.

However, President Kelleher had to fight off Vice Chairman Harrison's ill-conceived plea to *shorten* the December holiday leave period for faculty. They had too much time off in his mind.

Candace Rodewald didn't drink much hard liquor, for many reasons. She did favor the Italian Chianti with pasta and occasionally dipped into the punch-bowl libation at the Christmas Party. She chose not to have a bottle of anything in her desk drawer in the Computer Center.

Her passion was growing Jersey Tomatoes in her backyard garden. She had cultivated a large crop each year which she canned and bottled in quart Ball Mason jars. Her crops were stake grown and ripened and then picked when soft and luscious. She had been an early convert to the Ramapo version developed at Rutgers several years earlier. Her passion may have been boring to others; not to Candace.

If Candace's passion was growing and canning tomatoes, husband Bob's was cutting and stacking firewood. He had a prolonged competition with his two neighbors – who could cut and stack the highest and broadest pile of fireplace wood. For the past two years, Bob had come in a woeful third place. He was determined to win the stacking prize this year. When he would go off on his sales trips, he would spend time gathering limbs from forests and load the trunk of his car.

Candace had nothing to do with the firewood pile contest and was not impressed with her husband's woodpiles. Bob didn't even like tomatoes.

Gene Wildwood knew President Kelleher or Dr. Dandridge, sooner or later, would zero-in and disclose Howard Tucker's gin drinking-in-the-office habit. The rest of the Computer Programmers were respectful but told stories on Howard's drinking, often fabricating his condition. The underground rumor network joked about Howard's breath and his unsuccessful ruse to hide same with coffee, breath mints and *Diet Coke*.

Candace Rodewald was empathetic with Howard because her mother was a confessed alcoholic. Mother had been divorced for fourteen years and not able to fill the void when her husband abandoned her and the kids. Candace and her brothers had conducted an intervention with mom, sitting her down with no means of escape and carting her off to a clinic. Mom had reluctantly consented to attend Alcoholics Anonymous meetings. That was months ago. Now, to her credit, mom wouldn't miss her AA colleagues and mentors for anything. But Candace's teen years were tough.

Candace had regularly attended Adult Children of Alcoholics (ACA) meetings to address her demons and conflicting emotions about her mother. She had embraced the range of feelings – guilt, embarrassment, anger, depression, confusion – and coped with her anxiety by taking on the reversal role of responsible parent to her mother. Candace went through ACA's parallel *Twelve-Step Program*, while mom remained a committed, day-by-day sober lady.

Howard had been resistant to any conversation about his drinking, AA or *Dixie Cups*. The man would wail and remonstrate any intervention, no matter how confidential or well-intended, no matter who confronted him.

Howard could not internalize the threat to his career that the bottles of gin were presenting. True to his misguided manhood, he always thought he could control his drinking. He had a familiar refrain, "I appreciate what you're telling me, Gene, but I'm just a social drinker. I'm not hurting anyone."

Candace asked Gene if they could meet for lunch one day off-campus and talk about Howard. She trusted Gene and sensed he was equally frustrated with Howard and bound and determined to help in some way. Howard's drinking was increasingly a liability for the office, not just for the man and his career.

"I'm not *su-su*-sure what to do with Howard," Gene said as he folded the corner of a Margherita pizza slice and cradled it into his mouth a day later at Frank's Tomato Pies. "He won't listen to *re-re*-reason. He just does not accept his drinking as a problem, even a distraction. His wife, *Gla-Gla*-Gloria, drinks, you know. Perhaps not as much. The times I've spoken to her, she's poo-pooed any alcoholic label for Howard. Like many spouses, I guess, Gloria is an enabler. She's not going to take on her husband over his drinking."

Candace had ordered an antipasto salad but appealed to Gene for a bite of his pizza. Her mouth engulfed the tip end of the wedge with passion and animation, owing to her Italian roots and appetite. She chewed the pizza and added, "My guess is that Gloria has the addiction like Howard. From my ACA meetings, it's typical for spouses to share the booze, not just enable."

Gene put the slice remnant back on the plate and looked sternly at his dining companion. "Candace, do you recall that week about a month ago when Howard mysteriously used a week's leave?"

"Yes, I do," Candace responded. "I knew it was other than a vacation. He plans way ahead of time to be out of the office, and we had a back-up of jobs to process that week. This was sudden. He didn't tell me what he'd done during the week when he got back to the office."

"Well, that week away was required," Gene broke in. "Howard told me. He was supposed to use that time to get his act together and give up drinking at the office. Of course, Kelleher is about as sympathetic with something like this as a vulture is warm-hearted about his prey. Taking that leave was not voluntary."

"Good ol' J. Paul likes to drink, but the guy handles his liquor, if not his language when he drinks," Candace added somewhat conciliatorily. "Remember, he's Irish. My brothers and I got mom to accept her alcoholism through the AA meetings. Do you think one of us might strong-arm Howard to a meeting, or find a person affiliated with AA to counsel him?"

Candace had not waited for an answer. She probably was not looking for one.

Instead, she reached across the table, not to grab another pizza wedge, but to envelope Gene's hand, with her hands on top and bottom. It was a spontaneous gesture of trust and tenderness. To Gene, her soft hand now embracing his was stunning and astonishing. Many a time, he had wanted to grab her hand or caress her shoulder, especially of late. He had failed to stop imagining her in a warm embrace lying next to him in bed. Or dreaming of her in lingerie.

Gene reveled in feeling her hands warmly and affectionately embracing his. His eyes followed her arm to her shoulder and then to her face, focusing on her expressive and suggestively seductive green eyes.

The delicate moment was interrupted when Gene and Candace broke their tender grip, simultaneously looking around the restaurant to see if anyone they knew had seen them. Having stilled that fear, they glanced back at each other with a look of amusement for having tested their sentry skills. They realized there would be other more intimate moments beyond holding hands in a diner.

Howard's drinking problem would have to wait awhile!

PREVIOUSLY

"It was a crooked process from day one."

Despite David Lieber's prowess for grant writing, especially the monumental Title III one, David went in and out of the dog house when J. Paul became President. But it was now fall 1976 and time for preparation of a follow-up or second federal grant proposal.

The College had survived the 1976 U.S. Bicentennial and the July 4th tributes. New Jersey had operated a special Bicentennial Lottery in which the winner had received $1,776 per week for twenty years. People had painted mailboxes and fire hydrants red, white and blue, as patriotism and nostalgia swept the nation.

In celebration, the College purchased 50 flagpoles and American flags to place on the perimeter campus road. Two busloads of students and faculty members had gone to Philadelphia on Tuesday, July 6th, as organized by Global Travel. The group had gone to see Queen Elizabeth present the Bicentennial Bell on behalf of the British people and to enjoy Philly cheesesteak sandwiches.

While he preferred not, J. Paul would have no choice but to appoint David Lieber to head the *Dirty Half-Dozen* again to write the Title III grant. He was not happy about the pressure to do so, and he wanted to make a change. He knew the omission would aggravate Lieber. That was the point. Besides, change was good, even if his motivations were sly.

People had been hired in 1973 for twelve positions funded by Title III. If the second installment were not successful for 1977 re-funding, all would receive pink slips at the end of that fiscal year. Such was the fate of being on soft money.

J. Paul Kelleher, as President, operated somewhat incongruously with Proper Management Principles, as taught in a doctoral program or his MBA. David Lieber operated irreconcilably out of bounds. Also, J. Paul did not like that David was more of a star on campus than he was. Lieber was perpetually a braggart and consistently neglectful in paying homage to Kelleher. If there had been a non-biased assessment, they were both equally responsible for the grant's success.

Unlike President Greenleaf, President Kelleher had offered no toast and no promises to the persons on the second submission Title III task force, when he called them together to give them the charge. He advised the appointees that he had cleared their participation with the respective Vice President and had the blessing of the President's Cabinet. However, he had never even asked the Vice Presidents for their support.

Kelleher rejected Lieber as Chairman and named his Vice President replacement, Dr. Thomas Dandridge instead. That decision relegated Lieber to a mere task force member. He reasoned before the team that Dandridge was new and brought a variety of other ideas and concepts to consider when preparing the proposal. Kelleher also knew it would be a two for one: piss off Lieber and Winters with the same move.

Kelleher added Dr. Vernon Carter, the popular Dean of Science & Mathematics, who had a Ph.D. in Higher Education. To the faculty, Carter's appointment looked like the President wanted to take advantage of the Ph.D. and the ideas he would offer. To the shrewd, Carter's appointment was another dig at his past rival for President, Donald Winters.

Kelleher knew Carter was the undisclosed protégé of Vice President Winters. He wanted to use the work on the Title III task force to loosen, if not break apart, that bond. In the event Winters were to leave, Kelleher wanted to see Dr. Carter in action as a preliminary bout to serving as a possible VP replacement.

The task force was now a seven-member *Bakers' Half Dozen* with seven members. The remaining four were the holdovers from the 1972 submission: Ralph Hughes, faculty; Richard Spurling, Lead Accountant; Frank Richards, Counselor; and Donna Phelan, Resource Librarian and, again, the loan female.

When the second grant submission was still in the conceptual stage, President Kelleher called for Lieber to come to his office and receive multiple lashes. David had overstepped his boundaries by contacting a Board member about equipment needs in the Learning Labs. That was to be the focus on the capital funding portion of the second grant, along with the Media Center productions.

In J. Paul's *Official President's Manual of Acceptable and Not-So Acceptable Practices,* of which there was only the one copy, he devoted a full chapter to one policy – "No one, other than the President, ever contacts a Trustee."

It did not take very long before the two compatriot adversaries were shouting obscenities in the President's Office. Edith Reynolds closed the door just as Kelleher began his assault.

"You son-of-a-bitch. How dare you contact a Board member to ask what he would want to see in the Title III grant," President Kelleher said with an arrogant tone and a demonstrable raising of his arms. "Sure, as hell, we can't have Board members being intrusive in administrative matters. When the time is right, I, and I alone, will present the overview and budget to the Board for their consideration and approval. Not you, damn it!"

"I get it, Mr. President, but I ran into Chuck Harrison at the hardware store last Saturday," Lieber responded somewhat apologetically but more defensively. "He asked me how the grant was coming along. I mentioned we were looking at the latest innovations in Learning Lab programming. Unfortunately, Harrison does not believe in resources to help faculty. He laughed and said he would challenge spending money on equipment for faculty."

Kelleher was not impressed. "I'll handle the prick Harrison," he said. "Everyone knows he dislikes faculty. That's about as ridiculous as a Major League manager disliking the concept of starting pitchers. Or a bartender choosing to dislike ice."

Kelleher was pleased with his metaphors. Lieber held back an insincere laugh.

"You just write the damn grant," the President said, now back on track. "And reduce the equipment money for the Media Production Center. We need to get the faculty more seed money to pursue innovations. And we need to generate better planning techniques, especially for managing our instruction. We have to get Winters to abandon his archaic seat-of-the-pants ways and accept what computers can provide."

Lieber knew when to leave the President's Office. It was now. He bowed humbly for show and headed for the door, the scolding over and normality returning. Kelleher stopped him just as he grabbed the door knob to exit.

"Lieber," the President yelled. "Slow down on the poppycock and crap for the grant submission, or I'll have to overhaul and recalibrate my *Bull Shit Gauge*! I calibrated it for the last grant, but that's as high as it can go!"

David Lieber was not amused. His dislike was morphing into hatred.

Vice President Donald L. Winters withdrew from the discussions about what the focus on the second Title III federal grant submission should be. He had cooled on Media Production even though several faculty members were being trained on alternative media and were enthusiastic to have the opportunity. The problem was that after the first Title III grant monies were exhausted, the College would have to pick up the entire cost.

Winters had cooled on a great many things. It was one thing that he was overlooked in the battle to become President, having served as Interim. It was worse that J. Paul Kelleher had gotten the job, not someone else. Not anyone else.

Had the Board selected a candidate from another community college with outstanding credentials, that would have been acceptable to Winters. But to lose the Presidency due to political intrusion and slimy tactics was overwhelmingly humiliating and shameful. Two years later, he had yet to recover.

Winters and Dr. Vernon Carter had had several private conversations about what they deemed the tragedy of the Presidential Search. "Donald, I'm so sorry, the Board went in a different direction. It's unusual for a Board *not* to go with the academic vice president," Carter said. "That's especially true for your years of service and having had Greenleaf's blessing."

"Vernon, it's me who's sorry," Winters affirmed. "I should not have given you any illusion that I might become President, and that you then might assume this VP position. I should have appointed you as the Interim Vice President so I could have concentrated on the President position. That was arrogant of me – thinking I could do both jobs well, or maybe I was just being insecure. You might have done a better job than me as the VP."

"It was a crooked process from day one, most of the faculty understand that," Dr. Carter continued. "Kelleher played the Board like a drum and got help from the County Commissioner and others who called Board members. *Magic Man* Harrison did not help your cause either. He just doesn't like academic types. What a pain in the ass!"

"That was part of it, but I misplayed the game," Winters offered. "I wasn't impressive in what I did during the time as Interim President. I let some critical things slip in Academic Affairs. Kelleher played up the lack of progress with the Foundation. I just hope you'll stay and not look for another opportunity, at least for a while, at least until I retire."

Winters was not done with his self-analysis. "Only having that master's degree hurt me, too. I've had several opportunities these many years to purse a doctorate. I could have taken a specialty set of graduate courses from Rutgers. It just didn't work out the way it might have, the way it should have been. Anyone but Kelleher. That bastard." Winters paused for several moments, preparing to share something with Dr. Carter that had been deeply troublesome. "I really don't understand why Greenleaf's confidence in me didn't make a difference. He said he would lobby the Board for my appointment. He wanted to honor my loyalty."

"No wonder you're still upset," Carter said.

The *Dirty Bakers Half Dozen* team took only two months to complete the second Title III proposal. Lieber took a back seat to both Dr. Dandridge and

Dr. Carter in conceptualizing the grant request and justifications. Lieber again did most of the writing via "cutting and pasting."

Kelleher had the entire President's Cabinet endorse the grant's goals and objectives. The emphasis would be on Learning Lab materials, Academic Skills and Faculty Professional Development, along with some peripheral equipment for the Computer Center. He included a replacement accounting software package and a computer-based simulation model to manage classroom efficiency.

Harrison balked at getting more instructional materials for faculty, but he was a fog horn in the distance as far as the rest of the Board of Trustees was considered. The fact that Lieber had had the discussion with Chuck Harrison at the hardware store and that Kelleher thus learned of Harrison's objection, served as a forewarning. Kelleher had anticipated the now inevitable rejection from Harrison and beat it down before it could gain momentum.

He and Lieber were back on good terms. For a short while anyway.

PREVIOUSLY

"I best keep neutral throughout this whole process."

Tyrone Jackson had gotten along with J. Paul Kelleher when he was a Security Guard and Kelleher was a Vice President. Jackson got along with Kelleher when Dr. Greenleaf promoted him in 1974 to Chief of Campus Security just before Greenleaf left the College for St. Louis. Jackson did his job and got along well enough, six months later, when Kelleher became President.

President Kelleher could have replaced Tyrone Jackson. He could have restructured the position in his initial or subsequent reorganizations. But he knew that would cause complications, especially with the County Commissioner obligated to what Jackson had contributed to the drug crackdown. Jackson was not anti-Kelleher. He just valued competence more than loyalty, autonomy more than subservience.

Many African-American men and women had let their hair grow into an Afro-textured style during the Black Power Movement, and still in the 60's and early 70's. Some had adopted the hairstyle to accentuate African culture and make a political statement against segregation and token integration. Others wore the style to speak for Black Power and nationalism and to challenge mainstream norms.

After his military discharge, Tyrone Jackson had decided to wear his hair in the Afro style, as a symbol of pride. There were no written rules against same for employees at the Fort Dix Federal Penitentiary, just scornful looks. He let the Afro grow to make himself appear taller and more ominous to prisoners. He wore heavy work boots with steel toes and elevated insole inserts for the same reason. Inmate intimidation was a good thing, if you were a Prison Guard.

When Jackson retired from the Fort Dix Federal Penitentiary, he trimmed his Afro and gave up his steel-toed boots. He shaved his bushy mustache but let his bushy eyebrows alone. He knew he would be entering the dominant culture where being out-of-step with societal norms might cost him a job or even an interview.

Discrimination was prevalent, especially in the workforce. It was illegal and mildly unfashionable to discriminate. All but the most ignorant and hardened organizations took pains to be fair-minded. Yet, Jackson knew most institutions were not fair, and he was leery about those that appeared to be nondiscriminatory and probably were not.

Fort Dix had not been an exception to the societal rule, at least in the treatment of guards. After a few years on the force, Tyrone had filed an official grievance against the prison for what he claimed was harassment because of his race. He felt he had been denied a promotion.

The Grievance Committee of the Security Guard Union had supported his allegations, although not unanimously. However, the Warden had overturned the Union. The Warden chose to treat the complaint as a mere disagreement regarding working conditions, rather than a formal complaint. In his public statement, the Warden said:

> We regret the circumstances under which Mr. Tyrone Jackson felt it was necessary to file a formal complaint. Working day-to-day and week-to-week as a Prison Guard in the Fort Dix Federal Penitentiary is very demanding and stressful. The prisoners need to be under constant surveillance, and there are few moments when a Prison Guard can relax, much less turn his head. As we mature as an institution, we go through some growing pains, as does society, regarding race relations and proper protocol.
>
> I certainly respect Mr. Jackson's integrity and consider him a highly qualified and valued employee. Yet we would have preferred that he worked through his concerns with his supervisor, rather than file as a Union grievance.
>
> I've spoken to all parties involved, and we have amended several in-house rules for Prison Guards. I am confident those changes will be responsive and that we need not process Mr. Jackson's petition as a formal grievance.

Jackson's grievance petition had been championed by his fellow guards, including the white ones. They all felt the Prison Guards were under-appreciated, under-paid, under-benefitted and over-supervised. His official complaint did result in several improvements, and Tyrone kept his Afro hairstyle slightly more trimmed.

Jackson received a promotion and a modest raise one month later. He sent a thank-you letter to the Warden.

The denial affirmed in Jackson's mind then and later that non-racial discrimination had a long way to go. When he got the job at Central Jersey Community College, he knew he would have to align his convictions with those of the organization and its Warden, the College President. Institutional racism was subtle but widely prevalent and largely a cultural norm.

Tyrone had stayed neutral during CJCC's Presidential Search process that fall 1974, and he had avoided all intrusive questions by Board members. He was one of the minority employees who felt Kelleher had a chance, as most had their bets placed on Winters. After all, Winters had been with the College longer, had Dr. Greenleaf's confidence and most importantly, had been chief academic officer. Kelleher was a more recent hire, was not in Academic Affairs and was distant from most faculty.

The eight Security Guards had decided to hold a lottery, with a winner take all regarding who would be selected President. Seven of the guards had chosen Winters. Only one had Kelleher. Had the Board named Winters as President, the seven would have won $80, and the winner would be able to claim the entire prize. The seven drew the days of the week, with the winner to be the guy who had picked the day of the week the Board made the decision. Wednesday won. But the Kelleher guy got the entire $80 prize.

Jackson had been invited to join in the lottery but had told his men that would be a bad idea. "I best keep neutral throughout this whole process. Should Winters get it, and I showed favoritism to Kelleher, I might be ridiculed. If Kelleher gets it, and I'd selected Winters, I might be demoted. And if the outside guy gets the Board vote, I might be out of a job entirely."

As President, it was critical in Kelleher's mind to have the Security Chief's unswerving loyalty to the College, but even more so to him. But Tyrone had had his fill of reciprocal favors as a Prison Guard and was not about to buy into an oath of undiscerning allegiance. He was not about to cozy up without seeing the road ahead and going down it carefully. He would have to know the rewards.

President Kelleher certainly tried. He tried a great deal to get Jackson to be his best buddy and do his bidding.

First came invitations to lunch, which lasted longer than the lunch hour and concentrated on J. Paul's life and experiences. Tyrone just kept mental notes and then created a written President's File when he got back to campus. He made it a point to count how many martinis Kelleher slurped over lunch and how often he criticized Winters and members of the Board of Trustees.

Tyrone accepted a few meal alms and then sporadically declined with a convenient but deceiving excuse. It wasn't so much the free lunches, as it was the feeling he was being paraded into the restaurants with his Security Guard uniform, black face and closely cropped Afro under the cap. He knew the payback would come sooner, not later.

The Security Guards were becoming watchful of collusion. One crass guy tried to make a joke by referring to Jackson as trying to brown-nose the President. Fortunately for him, his colleagues dissuaded him from sharing the joke with the Chief.

There were some other strings-attached rewards for Jackson. He received comped tickets to see the *Knicks* in New York and the *Harlem Globetrotters* in Philadelphia. Kelleher also got Tyrone and his daughter two treasured tickets to ride the chartered bus with Global Travel to see *The Jacksons* perform in Philadelphia. His daughter Crystal was thrilled. Tyrone knew he would probably pay for that benefit down the crooked road.

The chartered bus ride to Philly from Abington was tolerably quiet on the way there, as the riders enjoyed the views. But the bus was filled with imitative *Jackson Five* songsters on the return trip. Tyrone mercilessly imitated a falsetto for "I'll be There." Crystal starred from the front seat in the higher-pitched vocalizations.

The Security Chief walked a flimsy tightrope between due deference to Kelleher's position of authority and unwavering subservience to the person. He liked to think he was incorruptible but saw nothing wrong with getting a few favors to benefit his daughter, the Nursing student. If things went sour, he still had his fallback monthly retirement income from the consolidated Marines and federal penitentiary years.

After his divorce, Jackson swore off women for a year. There were a few single women in his apartment complex who were attractive and offered to cook him dinner. Being that they were white, he was hesitant and avoided them in the hallways. He did not want the apartment superintendent calling the College President to complain.

There were a couple of ladies of color on the nightly custodial crew who gave him suggestive glances. He could have asked one or both out on a date. After all, they spent extra time cleaning the Security Office. But he respected that it was wise not to mess with the women where he worked.

When Kelleher would pointedly bug Jackson about his love life, Tyrone had offered a stock response. "Mr. President, thanks for asking," he had said. "I was married for sixteen years. That was enough. I enjoy spending time with my daughter, Crystal. Besides I like my own cooking, and most women would not care about my career choice or find my bushy eyebrows attractive."

President Kelleher was never satisfied. "Come now, a big, handsome guy like you must be getting some from someplace. A fellow like you must have a place where you can get laid. Come on, you can tell me, Jackson."

Security Chief Jackson had taken a Criminal Law course at Atlantic State College in the Spring 1976 semester. He spent time with a group of students who studied together and critiqued each other's papers. A study date turned into a date-date. That turned into a highly amorous connection. Suddenly, Tyrone was in an ongoing romance with a slightly younger Puerto Rican lady who was a Deputy Sheriff for Monroe County.

Blanca Diaz' parents had immigrated to New York City with baby Blanca and her older brother. Both parents got janitorial jobs, with her mother working at a Bronx barrios law firm that specialized in criminal cases. Blanca preferred the police end of the legal business. As a teen, she loved to hear her mother tell stories about the law firm and the prosecutions, especially the criminal ones.

As if inevitable, Diaz had later completed CJCC's Criminal Justice program. She was only a few credits shy of a baccalaureate from Atlantic State College when she met Jackson. She didn't see any conflict of interest in dating the College's Chief of Security. Jackson didn't care if there was a perceived conflict of interest in his dating the Deputy Sheriff.

Miss Diaz was infatuating and very expressive as a person. She had short brown hair much like a Beatle, the British singing kind. She favored her pudgy nose and inviting smile when she clenched her lips. She was highly competitive as an officer and a non-apologetic sports buff.

Tyrone and Blanca enjoyed going to bars and listening to the jazz sounds at Club Abyss. Blanca was fascinated with Tyrone's cooking, especially his Italian eggplant lasagna and his soul food, oven-baked ribs and spiced potato salad. His daughter, Crystal, was thrilled that her father was dating and keeping an active social life, not just watching football games. Tyrone was thrilled he was back in the sack.

Neither Blanca or Tyrone was looking for a long-term relationship or even a mid-term relationship. Chief Jackson was not looking to find an alternative rebuttal to Kelleher's prejudicial questioning regarding sex. He hoped he could keep his secret from the nosy President and not have his Deputy Sheriff lady friend be fodder for teasing and torment.

Tyrone Jackson was at home that mid-August morning in 1976, sipping his coffee when he got the unexpected telephone call. It was President Kelleher screaming about a helium-filled rat balloon flying gracefully but menacingly above the Administration Building. This was still summer, several weeks after the U.S. Bicentennial Celebration and only a few weeks before the hectic fall registration, when lines of students would form in the Fieldhouse and computer printouts would warn of class closings.

The New York Yankees were doing well at mid-season, and the Summer Olympics were underway in Montreal. Chief Jackson was looking forward to a quiet day, so he could leave campus early and catch a baseball game and the Olympics, channel switching to his heart's content. He had planned to pick-up plates of Italian pencil pasta and tomato gravy from Villa Maria and snuggle with Blanca on the couch. He knew they would not fight over who controlled the channel switching. They might just tangle on seconds of the pasta.

The high-flying rat tethered to the Administration Building had other ideas that morning. So, did J. Paul. The President wanted the "damn rat," as he referred to it, taken down immediately from the building. Then he wanted to know who the person was who got on top of the Administration Building without being seen earlier that morning or the previous night to tie the thing down.

Tyrone Jackson got the message. The Chief of Security grabbed his coffee mug and headed out the door, laughing so hard he almost spilled hot coffee on his uniform. He hurried to the campus, not so much because of the President's urgent order, but because he had to see this flying rodent.

He hoped he could keep a straight face when the colossal inquisition began of Sally Bowens and Ralph Hughes of the Faculty Union.

But he didn't care if he could not.

PREVIOUSLY

"Eventually even the most thick-headed guy gets it."

The Physical Education & Athletics Department was not too thrilled with President's Kelleher's last reorganization. The one in April 1976 had split up the Physical Education teaching end from the Athletics end. Kelleher wanted to piss-off nemesis Winters on the one hand and provide for greater scrutiny of Coach Solly and all other sports on the other hand.

Physical Education stayed with Donald L. Winters in Academic Affairs; Athletics slid over to Institutional Support under Dr. Thomas Dandridge who had been the Vice President for about a year, in Kelleher's former position.

That meant a matrix form of management or dual supervisors. Kelleher reasoned that confusion breeds focus. Winters reasoned that confusion causes resentment.

Alan Fox reported to Dean Lieber, under Vice President Winters, for Physical Education courses, scheduling, programs and everything academic. Fox then reported to Vice President Dandridge for Athletics. There were two budgets, two sets of capital equipment and two sets of challenges. Faculty and staff employees got used to asking Fox which hat he was wearing when they went over assignments or when they went to lunch. Fox was not amused.

While Alan Fox sometimes got confused, Rebecca Campbell, the Administrative Secretary, ended up with dual half-time, schizophrenic jobs. She had had to fend unwanted advances from Alan Fox for several weeks when she was initially hired. That was until she threatened to complain to Personnel and kick him in the crotch. Fox had backed off, but those failed attempts were always in the back of her mind.

After receiving her diploma from Abington Area High, Rebecca had moved to Rochester, New York to get away from her mother. She had lived with her aunt and taken an entry job with Eastman Kodak.

She left Monroe County because her mother was oppressive, overbearing and not appreciative of what a free spirit she had for a daughter. When Rebecca was in diapers, her father had died in a warehouse fire at a printing company. Mother had worked at the same company until the cancer spread, and she needed daily care.

The Kodak job was clerical at first. Rebecca would type, file, answer phones and complete whatever assignments came her way. She took business courses at Rochester Community College and made an annual compulsory trip back to Abington to spend time with her mother. Gradually her responsibilities at Kodak grew, as did her salary and confidence, and as her animosity toward her mother lessened.

Rebecca dated a few guys while living in Rochester, but nothing serious. When asked by fellow Kodak employees about her love life, she would remind them, "I know more about what I don't like in a man than what I do like. Let's leave it at that!"

She had lived and worked in Rochester for seven years, before returning to Abington when mother became bed-ridden with cancer.

Rebecca was still a free spirit, but at 25 she was also a matured young lady confident in her skills and embracing her mother from a different perspective. She moved into the house, where she had been raised as a kid and nursed her dying mother. Her mother died peacefully a few months later. "Mom never recovered," she told the funeral gathering. "But she talked to me with her loving eyes, fully accepting me as a woman and honoring me as her daughter. Her eyes told me."

The secretary position for Physical Education & Athletics had opened at the College in February 1975, shortly after Rebecca moved back to Abington. She applied for and got the job. The fact that Rebecca had starred in basketball for the Abington Area High School *Wildcats* helped the cause. References from the high school coach and principal made quite an impression on Fox, as did the daily lobbying by Coach Solly. He wanted someone in the position who had played sports.

But Rebecca had not anticipated the dual assignment a year later. "What exactly is Matrix Management anyway," she routinely asked her boss, Department Chairman Alan Fox *aka* Athletic Director Alan Fox.

"How the hell do I know," barked Fox. "The guy's nuts. This place would be so much better off if Kelleher would go away. He needs to be placed on permanent suspension. Maybe he will."

Rebecca Campbell had been highly gifted as an athlete. She was also gifted as a young lady in appearance and form. She loved to wear bell bottoms and took much of her apparel concepts from the Cher half of the *Sonny and Cher* duo. She borrowed Cher's bangs and liked to use a flat iron to straighten her hair. Her flowing brunette hair, deep brown eyes and endless legs were captivating to men, and she was highly skilled in dealing with infatuated males and envious females. She had had considerable practice at both.

She had been highly selective in the guys she dated in Rochester and now back in Abington. She had a well-rehearsed and often reiterated expression was: *Only well-educated men with upwardly mobile careers need apply.* But her tastes in men were deeper and more profound than that.

Rebecca loved to tease her male colleagues in the PE Department/Athletics Office about their apparel choices, especially their over-indulgence in the popular polyester leisure suits. Alan Fox was particularly fond of the ones that featured side vents on the jacket, contrasting fabric for the wide collars and too-tight pants.

Fox would augment that look with a solid color, open-neck shirt with a wide butterfly collar overlaying the jacket and exposing the upper portion of his hairy chest. Rebecca often teased him, "Hey boss, good thing you take that suit jacket off in your office and not here. The shirt was blinding me!"

It became a habit for Alan Fox to approach Rebecca when he had a new leisure suit and ask for her opinion. She would inevitably adjust the wide shirt collar to lay flat on the wide jacket collar, while maintaining an arm's length distance. She would always button the jacket to hide the chest hair.

Coach Solly refused to adopt the leisure suit fashion trend, either for work or play. He preferred tracksuits made of synthetic fabric, featuring a full-length zipper for the jacket. He wore a t-shirt under the jacket in spring and summer and a turtleneck in the fall and winter.

Solly was obsessively fond of wearing a gold chain around his neck with the Star of David to celebrate his Jewish heritage. The only time he took off the necklace was to play racquetball or if he joined his colleagues or students for a pick-up basketball game in the College gym. That included making love to his wife, Marilyn, as the necklace would dangle over her face when in the missionary position or rest on his chest if she was on top.

Some people called them warm-up suits, but Solly preferred tracksuit. He wore one all the time, even in the classroom. He had at least fifteen tracksuits in various colors, including five in velour, set apart for formal occasions, Christmas parties and speaking engagements.

Rebecca would diligently strive to get Solly's goat. "Hey, Coach, tell me you don't wear a tracksuit to the synagogue. Oh, that's right," she would hasten to add. "You prefer to worship basketball gods, especially the ones who watches over the defense."

But Solly always had a retort. "Miss Campbell, when you played high school basketball, didn't they play with six girls on a team? You do know that society did not think women could run full court. And I'm pretty sure your uniforms were farmer denim jeans."

Solly would make a clothing exception on game day, and perhaps at the synagogue, when he would wear a long sleeve white shirt and team colors of a forest green tie with thin gold diagonal stripes.

He chose a dress shirt and tie for the games in case some Division I coach might be in the stands scouting one of his players or, optimistically, checking him out for a position. He wanted to look more fashionable for the public and classy for the coach.

The coach's players would have a silent wager as to how long into the game it would take for him to unfasten the shirt collar and yank off the necktie. The length of time was directly proportional to how well the team played. He did make it to the second half of a few games, before the tie went flying. That is, when the team could do little wrong on offense and defense. The earliest the tie was ditched was once when the team lost the ball out of bounds on the tip-off to start the game.

Rebecca took classes at the College, over the lunch hour and one night a week, working toward an Associate in Arts Degree. She intended to transfer to Atlantic State College and complete a baccalaureate. No one doubted she would succeed.

In the meantime, she enjoyed her social life, especially with the former three-sport star guy from her high school who became a lawyer in the firm that handled the College and the County. His name was Jack Kula, with the Triano, Orr and Kula law firm in Abington.

This Jack was not the Kula in the firm name. That was his father, but the son would make partner eventually. Kula was moving upward quickly in status and salary, with Rebecca as a devoted fan and career advocate.

Miss Campbell was particularly fond of the law firm's parties, especially the fancy, dress-up ones with dancing to a live band. She also liked the dress-down, casual picnics. Rebecca could disco in a sexy dress, flowing skirt or blue jeans. She would absorb the attention as she captured the dance floor, no matter the dance partner or the song.

The flattering loose skirt that moved with her body contributed to the spectacle.

Her dance moves drove Kula's colleagues wild, especially the jealous interns and the older guys who had already made Partner.

But mostly, Rebecca focused on Jack, her job and her reverse harem of guys in Physical Education and Athletics. They all required continual attention, steady ego reinforcement and periodic put-downs.

The male harem reminded her of when she was in the seventh grade at an awkward, hormone-crazy boy and girl party. The kids played Spin the Bottle back then, usually with an empty *Pepsi* bottle. Except that in this adult game many years later, she would contemplate spinning a bottle only to have all these bigger boys begging for tender loving care, not kisses.

In her mind, male creatures were the same – as boys or as men. There was no difference. When she was first hired, she was fair game for all the over-sexed males in the office, those on the courts and those in their offices. "How did you handle those guys, Rebecca," Jack asked. "All those guys, and you being an attractive, young female. What did you do?"

"At first, I just looked at them with disdain," Rebecca responded with a look of appreciation that her love cared this much. "They thought they were being cute or funny. Most had no idea their comments were repulsive and insulting. When I did get harassed, I'd pretend I didn't hear and ask him to repeat it, then repeat it again. I found the more they said something sexist, the sillier they sounded. Eventually even the most thick-headed guy got it."

"Fox was probably a bit slow to catch on," boyfriend Jack responded.

"Indeed," Rebecca said. "He likes to tell me, even today, that he doesn't have a girlfriend but knows many women who would be mad at him for saying that. What a pity."

Often, Rebecca would look over the all-male crew of the dual departments and admit to herself that she, as the lone female, was the well-cast extra in an all-male film. Other than her boss, Alan Fox, no one from the all-male cast had hit on her or touched her other than in a playful and respectful manner. But then she excelled in drawing the line and in flaunting flattering stories and awe-inspiring photos of her Prince Charming boyfriend, attorney Jack.

That didn't mean the guys didn't think about making a pass. They just appreciated what a marvelous addition she was to the Department and how well she took care of them.

And true, they thought about what their wives might say.

PREVIOUSLY

"We plan to have bake sales and raffles."

The *Roaring Raiders* had tied New York's Suffix Community College as the opposing team missed its shot and lost the rebound. This was the Regional NJCAA Men's Basketball Championship final held March 17, 1977. There were only seven seconds left in the contest. The *Raiders* had the ball with a chance to win the game if they could score.

Many, perhaps most, coaches would have called an immediate time-out to set up a winning play. Not Coach Solly. He chose to rely on principles he had taught his players. Instead, he emphatically motioned them to push the ball aggressively up the court, rather than enable the New York team to challenge the inbounds pass and set their defense.

The result was a time-elapsing lay-up basket by the *Raiders'* 6'10" center, Mike Evans, and a two-point win. With it, came the right to go to the National NJCAA Championship games.

The National Junior College Athletic Association (NJCAA) dates to 1937, in response to the National Collegiate Athletic Association (NCAA) rejecting a proposal to incorporate junior colleges within NCAA rules and privileges. The first ever event held exclusively for junior and community colleges was a track and field competition in 1940.

In 1948, the NJCAA added Men's Basketball as a regionally competitive sport and elevated it to a National Championship in the early 1970's. Central Jersey Community College had been to the regional finals the past two years, but not yet played for the National trophy. This was the year they would, with J. Paul Kelleher as President, if they could afford the trip.

Most two-year colleges had abandoned the pejorative and seemingly inferior word "Junior" as part of the institution's name. The preferred choice was to replace "Junior" with "Community" to reflect the geographical and local focus. Community implied a concentration on the local populace and a forthright mission, not something less than a university.

The NJCAA had retained the "Junior" moniker as a testament to the heritage or its stubborn revelation as something less than the NCAA (National Collegiate Athletic Association). Besides, NCCAA (National Community College Athletic Association) would appear as a misspelling of the NCAA. Preserving the "J" meant preserving the distinction, even if a notch below the university league.

The National Championship in Men's Basketball was a sixteen-team event held in a round-robin format in Hutchinson, Kansas, the NJCAA home office. The participating teams had to assume costs for travel, housing and food to compete in the event. There were no ceremonial checks or shoe endorsements to pay the way. There was no television coverage. The athletics budget did not include funds for a national tournament.

During the post-game media interview after the Regional Championship, Coach Solly decided to establish a full-court-press, when asked about going to the Nationals. "It's a tremendous honor to win this Regional game and be invited to play for the National Championship in Kansas," exclaimed the Coach. "This team provides such positive news for the College. It's embarrassing we don't get the support we deserve from the administration. These kids sacrifice so much to represent our College. They are fine examples of student-ath-*ah*-letes."

"Coach Solly, you mean you will have to pay your way to Kansas, pay for your meals and hotels," said Martha J. Rooney, Sports Columnist for the *Jersey Star*. The *Star* was a tabloid-sized newspaper, with a regional audience and a penchant for digging into stories and for occasional sensationalism and frequent hyperbole.

Martha Rooney was an African-American woman in her mid-twenties with a deceiving but captivating smile. She graduated from Howard University, a Historically Black College located in Washington D.C., having majored in Journalism. Young Rooney had been active on the school newspaper, preferring investigative columns, most of which zeroed-in on administrative issues at Howard, real or fabricated.

While she was in college, the Watergate Scandal was a national focus, especially for journalism students. The Watergate Hotel break-in by operatives associated with President Richard Nixon had led to his disgraced resignation in August 1974. Her idols were Bob Woodward and Carl Bernstein, the *Washington Post* reporters who investigated the story and broke the national coverup news. From that point on, Rooney was suspicious and distrustful of any figure of authority and always digging for a juicy angle.

Rooney interviewed Solly, partly out of surprise they had won and more so out of a cunning desire to egg him on for more outbursts. She knew that was an easy errand. He would provide a dandy quote for the top of the Sports Section in tomorrow's edition.

"Yes, we pay our way. I guess we'll plan to have bake sales and raffles," Coach Solly said mockingly. "Maybe the faculty will kick in a few bucks, or maybe we just won't be able to go to Kansas. That would be terrible for these kids."

"Coach Solly, why won't you ask President Kelleher to fund the trip?" Rooney proposed, delighted in energizing more animosity for her readers.

"Only if he invites me to meet with him. He didn't come to the game, or any last weekend either, or send me a good luck card," said Solly. "The President is not fond of sports, but he does like his fine arts program, even if the campus concerts lose money quicker than we do."

To be sure, Coach Solly was invited by President Kelleher to visit his office to discuss the team and the Kansas invitation. The telephone summons arrived about 9:15 AM the next morning, while the campus was inundated with copies of the morning's *Jersey Star* being passed around like glamour photos of Christie Brinkley and Robert Redford.

The scorching headline was *Central wins regions. College may not fund trip to National Championship.* Rooney's topic sentence was: *Coach Solly says what a shame the College does not support the team and these kids. We'll have bake sales and raffles.*

Many faculty members lamented the fate of Coach Solly after the article came out. Most just howled at the anticipated prospect of Solly and the President going one-on-one over basketball funding and newspaper coverage.

Some employees placed bets on whether there would be any college funds set aside for the National Tournament. Most wagers, however, were on how long Solly would last in the verbally pugilistic encounter, with Solly receiving a variety of time handicaps. The high bet was that it would last 20 minutes; the low, more popular bet, was 5 minutes.

About 10:30 AM, the President's Secretary Edith Reynolds ushered Solly into the now sequestered office. She smiled and shook his hand. "Congratulations on the Regional Championship and the invitation to the National Finals," Edith said with exuberance, yet softly so no one else might hear. "What a marvelous achievement. We're proud of your team. The game yesterday was fun to watch."

After the covert moment, Edith diplomatically escorted Coach Solly into the office. She invited him to sit in one of the two burnt-orange office armchairs in front of the President's desk. Her eyes fixated on the left one, knowing that J. Paul sharpened his attack when the mark sat in the right chair.

President Kelleher was not at his desk. Solly situated himself in the uncomfortable chair not knowing how long he would be expected to wait. He did not know the President was sparring before the mirror in his Executive Bathroom, much as a boxer would be punching a workout bag. J. Paul was shadow-boxing with anticipated words, not punches. He wanted them to be as lethal.

He could hear Edith and Solly in the office and knew the waiting would piss off Solly – that was the point. He wanted to irk his adversary into a shouting match, assuming Solly would land the first verbal punch. Then he would land the haymaker.

"I'll be damned if I can let you go to Kansas when you sling mud at the College and attack me in the press," bellowed President Kelleher, his teeth clenched together and not cradling a cigarette. There was no assumption or allusion of a welcoming gesture or any tactic to mollify the tension. "What the hell's wrong with you?"

"Now wait a minute," Coach Solly retorted but with reserved composure. "I bring you a nationally recognized program, and we help mature our players as students. Other colleges have budgets set aside for tournament play and never get there. We win and yet there are no funds to play."

"Your players trashed an apartment. They barely get through their classes," Kelleher challenged. "Even with a winning team you seldom get enough spectators and fans to fill half the bleachers, let alone pay expenses. Then you have that basketball camp in the Poconos you work on all during the year, in your office, when the College pays you."

Coach Solly ignored the Poconos accusation. "We disciplined those players," he barked. "They paid the charges for the apartment. We've been through that already. You just don't like me because I get more positive press than you do."

"The landlord called my office to complain," snapped the President. "Good thing it only happened that one time or the apartment dorm thing you do would be finished. Your dreams of being a National Championship coach and hired to a Division I position would also die."

More initially irked by the accusations about his camp, Coach Solly then took on the *barely get through their classes* indictment. "Sir, you can't say the players don't get through their classes. Most graduate, and at a higher percentage than non ath-*ah*-letes." Coach Solly preferred to add a *"ah"* in the middle of the word "athlete" to make it a demonstrable extra syllable.

"We have four players this year with promises of a basketball scholarship to a university when they complete their associate degree in the Spring," Solly professed. "They're on track to do so."

Solly's retort in the President's Office about faculty respect had elevated J. Paul's blood pressure and exasperation. "Dammit, don't you tell me who faculty trust and do not," an infuriated President howled. "Edith has never encroached on her job responsibilities with the College to run your camp. There's no good reason you should either."

"Sir, I put in tons of hours for this College and if, occasionally, I work on my camp, so be it," Solly said, attempting now to reduce both the decibels and the span of the President's tension. He knew nothing would be accomplished if the meeting continued down a path of contemptible allegations, especially since he knew that J. Paul was correct – he did spend much of his office time working on the camp, even if Edith did not.

President Kelleher knew he was basing his anti-academic achievement of these students on hearsay rather than research. It upset him that he had given Solly the opening. It gave Solly an advantage in the match, much like exposing one's king in a game of checkers. So, he chose another one. "Solly, the word is athlete, not ath-*ah*-lete. There is no third syllable in the middle."

The telephone on the President's desk rang abruptly, startling the two pugilistic opponents, much like a lighted firecracker exploding after being tossed in the middle of a family picnic. Kelleher was annoyed at the interruption, as it deflected his growing sparring advantage. Solly was suspiciously amused.

Most of the time, Edith would receive and screen all telephone calls, buzzing her boss through the intercom to see if he wanted to be interrupted. Typically, he would tell her, "Just tell 'em I'm in a meeting." Her goal was to grab the phone after one isolated ring. At most two rings. Never three.

But Edith had left her obligatory station, feigning a need to use the Ladies Room down the end of the hallway, about the time the yelling reached the outer office. She wanted to be elsewhere. As she trekked to the restroom, the sound of the two combatants faded from her ears but not her mind. There had been shouting matches in the past, but not this elevated.

Kelleher impetuously yanked the receiver from the base after the third ring, as if any more would trigger an explosion. "This is J. Paul Kelleher," said the President, his eyes conspicuously directed at the campus through the east window rather than at the telephone or the basketball coach.

Kelleher spoke into the receiver impetuously. "Likely it will be a while, Izzy, before I can leave the office," J. Paul said, lowering the tone and volume of his voice while not camouflaging his distress – with the call, the caller or the Coach. "Yes, I know we have that dinner with your English department tonight. Someone's in my office right now. I can't talk."

His wife was well-aware of her husband's hostile attitude toward the Coach. She liked Solly, liked him more than her husband could sense, but she was not sure why. If asked to take sides, Izzy would lean 90 degrees toward the Coach, at least on the funding of basketball. She was aware of her spouse's unrestrained Irish temper and that her husband of sixteen intermittently blissful and partially tormented years could, and usually did, escalate the situation. She knew how to appease his ego while accomplishing precisely the outcomes she would want from any one-on-one argument.

She knew her husband was meeting with Solly in his office about this time. She had reasoned that an unsolicited and uncustomary phone call might change the mood and provide momentary breathing space. If the call happened to come in the middle of the confrontational session, she could appeal to J. Paul's sanity and encourage a peaceful resolution. If, however, the call was received after an abbreviated and abruptly ended meeting, she could appeal to his insanity and give him hell for being so loathsome.

Izzy spoke into the telephone with a semi-rehearsed narrative, relying on her years of chummy conversations with her husband. "Must be Coach Solly in your office. Now Pauly, you must consider what's best for the College and the community. Not how much you despise this guy and dislike basketball. Just because you didn't play sports doesn't mean they do not have a respected, legitimate place in a college, including a community college. It's not every year a college, university, private college or junior college competes for a National Championship. Be nice. Remember, Pauly, you did tell me you'd have to give him some financial support if only to appease a few Board members or Freeholders. Don't go all Irish here!"

Izzy understood that Solly could not hear her side of the telephone conversation. Nevertheless, she understood he would grasp the intent of her call. He would probably liken it to a time-out in a basketball game when the opposing team had just gone on a ten-point run.

"OK, see you later. I'll call from the office when I leave," J. Paul said as he calmly but suspiciously relocated the telephone into its cradle. The termination of the phone conversation was not with a loving thought to his wife and certainly not with an apology to the person in the room. Kelleher was still annoyed that this *Callus-Interruptus* had occurred. But he quickly regained his form and took back the advantage.

"Isn't it true that the NJCAA people provide meals for the students in the tournament at the gym where you play the games," Kelleher offered. "I presume they have a listing of motels available for the teams at reasonable rates," Kelleher proclaimed, thereby defusing the tension and escalating accusations. The kids can share rooms. Coaches can too. Get three to a room at least."

Edith had already called Hutchinson to find out exactly what the College could expect in expenses. Kelleher liked to have the advantage of knowing the facts before he jumped into a debate.

"Assuming so, then you have to find money for the motels and the bus transportation," Kelleher continued without looking for an answer. He had played his hand and knew no one could beat his cards.

"Yes and no," Solly noted, emboldened by the time-out phone conversation and knowing Izzy had called for that purpose. "Yes, food is available during the games for the kids in what amounts to sandwich meats – bologna, ham, turkey – as well as cheeses and fruits. They're not meals in the sense of breakfast, lunch, dinner. We'd need to provide breakfasts and dinners a few of the nights anyway, assuming we play on and don't get knocked out in an early round."

Solly had to continue needling the President. "Of course, we could ask the students to stuff apples, oranges and sandwiches into their shorts and call that dinner," he wisecracked and then wished he had not.

"I think the kids could pay for their breakfasts, or you and the other coaches and parents could handle that," Kelleher proposed, ignoring the not-so-wise crack. "I'll give you $2,500 to go toward transportation and rooms. You'll need to get sponsors to handle the rest. I do not want you to have any pity-me bake sales, where you bemoan around campus or with your players and their parents that you had to raise money."

The President paused to be sure Solly was listening. "And I don't want to see a poor-me attitude and the how-cheap-can-Kelleher-be in the damn newspaper. No martyrs here. I don't want any crap from you about this. None whosoever. You must keep receipts and maintain a ledger."

Kelleher swallowed and then lit up one of his treasured *Marlboro* cigarettes. He knew what he would be saying next was beyond what he had planned to do. "If the Athletic Director approves, you may take up to $500 from your departmental budget, but only if you can guarantee there will be no end-of-year deficit. Hear me, Solly, no moaning and groaning about having to generate other funds. No bitching that other colleges seem to find the money to pay for their teams to compete in the tournament."

Coach Solly's first thought was to raise the ante to $5,000, but then he had entered the room and the jousting match just hoping to have the President consent to send the team to Kansas. So, this was nearly a slam dunk, even if he had lowered the height of the basket rim from ten feet to the more makeable Biddy-Basketball eight feet. He could go to the National Tournament. He would get his chance to earn a National Championship and maybe then a coaching position at a Division I university.

Solly reasoned to himself that he would ask Edith to make phone calls. He would hit-up Dave Russell, an established millionaire, for some cash. Having the coach of his Pocono basketball camp be in a National Championship would merit a donation. Or, he could tell Russell they'd raise the tuition and fees for the camp next summer, given that the camp's coach had played for a National Championship.

"That will work, Mr. President," Solly said after a deliberate pause. He still needed time to sort out the contingencies in his mind and hold back the thoughts in his head, one of which was that he might come out ahead on the money.

If President Kelleher was expecting an impassioned thank you, he was not going to get it from Coach Solly. Instead, Solly rose from the chair by pushing up his body with his arms until he was suspended in the air, his butt several inches from the seat and his feet still on the carpet. He paused in that state of numbed submission, hovering above the chair as if he might want to fall back down and prolong negotiations.

Coach Solly sighed, stood up, gave a mock salute and headed for the door. He opened the door and looked back with a grimacing grin. He felt like a little boy leaving the Principal's Office who had gotten away with some peevish and cantankerous prank! He had gotten his money.

He had gotten the President's wife to intrude. His game plan was taking shape.

PREVIOUSLY

"Lady, where'd you get all of those cutie marks?"

When Dominic Panichi's Office Assistant retired late in 1976, the County Commissioner had decided to give County public servants the promotional opportunity. The search was a crooked charade, so he could hire Samantha Bartell and get away with it. Equal Opportunity be damned. He had planned for the appointment over several months knowing the vacancy was going to occur.

The County Commissioner recognized the Bartell surname had been altered from Bartelli, but he never pressed her on the variation. Dominic's father, the retired inveterate County Commissioner, knew the Bartelli family and that Samantha's father, Daniel, formerly known as Daniele, had initiated the surname change.

Panichi had his retiring Office Assistant handle the replacement search, but he made it clear who was to receive the appointment. There was no Search Committee. Just an internal search. A bogus search was hardly the worst assignment the retiree had had to accomplish over the years working with Panichi at the County.

There was a mini-parade of ambitious County employees seeking the advancement opportunity. They may have just wanted to experience an interview and see the Commissioner's office. Most people knew Panichi had a candidate in mind and accepted that was the way things worked in Monroe County.

Commissioner Panichi interviewed the one recommended candidate for the position. He hired Samantha just after Thanksgiving that year, and just as promptly changed the title to that of Office Manager and added $1,200 to the annual salary.

Samantha Bartell was all he hoped she would be, fulfilling the job description and managing his office. She was engaging and popular with all department heads and other County employees. Panichi was able to delegate additional tasks to Samantha that were beyond the abilities and ambitions of his former assistant.

The Senior Panichi knew that the Poppi Daniele Bartelli was a loyal contributor to the syndicate a couple of generations ago. He recognized that an Italian does not abandon his, or her, heritage. Junior Panichi didn't care how Samantha spelled or pronounced her last name.

What Dominic Panichi did not include in his plans for Samantha, was that he would fall in love with her, or that his new Office Manager would fall for him. Miss Bartell was remarkably attracted to Dominic because he met her prerequisites. He was influential, positioned in authority and sufficiently handsome. He was of short but confident stature with broad shoulders and warm hands. Most importantly, Dominic treated her with respect, demonstrating a keen pattern of being comfortable with highly capable women.

Most men at the office, and even at her parents' hospital, classified women as only appropriate for support office roles. Men judged women managers as bitchy when they were strong and tough. Her boss saw Samantha as powerful and heroic. The keys to Samantha's heart were Panichi's genuine characteristics of honor and dignity for the Office Manager as a person and a woman.

Samantha had been to the sunny Jersey Shore that Spring on a warm weekend. She told her boss, the County Commissioner, about having been approached by a little boy. "The kid, probably 4 or 5, looked at me as I was sitting by the water," she explained. "The little guy was walking past with his mom. He stopped and kept staring at my face. The boy finally spoke: *Lady, where'd you get all of those cutie marks?*"

Samantha said she must have looked like she had swallowed a canary or perhaps the cat. "I just laughed at the kid while his mother smiled and tugged him along. So, I guess I have to accept all these cutie marks on my face."

For the first time in her 29 years, thanks to a little boy by the ocean, Samantha embraced the predominant cluster of freckles on her nose. A month later, she had ditched the thick-rimmed glasses for contact lenses.

The County Commissioner was charmed and touched by the story of her freckles. He was dreadfully charmed and thoroughly enchanted with the story-teller. When he smelled Samantha's perfume or brushed against her body, even unintentionally, all kinds of things elevated in his head and body. His eyelids closed halfway. His mouth spread into a broad grin, and his mood soared.

Dominic did not remember ever being this much in love or feeling this much passion. He started dating Cecilia, who later became his wife, in high school, although the two families – Panichi and Gambrelli – were close for generations. The two Italian family offspring were born months apart, and before they entered kindergarten, they were suitably engaged. They got married when Dominic finished his senior year at Rutgers. Five months after the formal wedding they had a baby girl.

Three months earlier Dominic and Cecilia had married in a quiet ceremony before the Circuit Court Judge during lunchtime, with the two fathers and no mothers present. They were *Couple Number Two* of three couples in the noon marriage queue that day. The Court Reporter usually ate her sandwich during the vows, as she'd heard the purported commitments many times before, even believing some of the happy couples. But with the Panichi and Gambrelli patriarchs in the ceremony, she was all smiles and meticulously steadfast in her duty, if suspect of the sincerity of the vows.

The wedding reception after the formal Roman Catholic Wedding was chaotically memorable and could have been a script for a humorous off-Broadway play – *Dom and Cecilia's Very, Very Italian Wedding.* The bridesmaids were chased around the room and under the tables by the groomsmen, while Uncle Bernardo danced to the folklore tunes played by the *Lou Pettinelli Band* and pinched every woman who relented to be his partner and most of those who did not.

Aunt Adele's red dress showed too much leg, and Cousin Angelo abandoned his formal tux in favor of showing off his sleeveless underwear shirt and tattoos. The Priest stood guard over the punch bowl and blessed everyone who added more vodka to the brew.

Cecilia's mother did not have to practice being the overbearing and under-appreciated mother. She feigned that she could not discern how many months her daughter was pregnant. Cecilia wore an oversized but flattering snow-white, not off-white, wedding dress that proudly displayed her ample cleavage. The bride spent more time at the buffet than with her guests. Dominic spent his time working the crowd and gearing up for his upcoming re-election.

If the wedding had taken place two generations earlier, it would have been labeled an Arranged Marriage. The marriage of Dominic and Cecilia was merely *assisted* in focus and *expedited* in function, relying upon parental influence and youthful guilt to cement the relationship and the vows.

Samantha was something entirely different for Dominic. Feelings were unleashed he did not know he had. Many of those feelings were outside of his amorous, physical desires.

The intimate connection started one later-than-normal evening at the office a couple months after she had started the job. Dominic had ordered a pepperoni pizza, so he and Samantha could finish the budget. The freckles seemed to pop off Samantha's nose like stars aglow in the sky. They cast a bewitching spell on the boss. Panichi fixated on her. It wasn't the late night or the tomato pie. The spell was more magical.

While she worked at her desk, Dominic came up behind her and impulsively reached his arms around her shoulders. He reached down to her arms and rested his face in her hair. "I did not intend for this to happen," he said. "I don't know where it's going, but I can't hide these feelings any longer."

"Samantha, alright if I kiss you," he stammered. Not waiting for an answer, Dominic reached his head around to the front of Samantha's face and awkwardly but lightly kissed her lips. Then he pulled her chair to the side, caressed her head softly in his fingers and kissed each of the freckles on her nose one-by-one, pausing after each kiss to look into her eyes.

Their working relationship was never the same.

Cutie Marks became Dominic's favorite salutation of endearment for his new love, although not in the office and not within hearing distance of any County building. It was their secret bonding as if they had each purposely and adolescently pricked a finger and put the two fingers together as a tender blood-union. Cutie Marks coupled the two of them.

Dominic and Samantha had several sensual rendezvous over the next month at a local motel, *Sleep EaZZy*, managed by Dominic's cousin. The place had a backdoor entrance to assure secrecy. When they met there in the early afternoon, before or after an out-of-office meeting, the motel guests were still traveling and not around to see them when they arrived separately. When they met late at night, after work, the motel guests were all asleep when they arrived simultaneously.

Samantha had moved to a one-bedroom flat above Dottie's Hair Salon near downtown Abington. Her parents bought her the furniture, with her mother acting as interior designer and father as big pockets. But they were incredibly proud of their daughter. She may not have gone into medicine, and there would be no surgeries.

Instead, Samantha had a wonderful career in Public Administration ahead of her. And there would be no late-night emergency surgery phone calls. No suicide threats from desperate patients.

Dominic and Samantha's clandestine romance was sincere, compelling and persuasive. Dominic's wife was unaware of the relationship and had never met Samantha. Samantha was in love and convinced that the marriage was over anyway and that the love he felt for her obscured any remaining feelings for his wife.

Dominic was trying to figure out what to do next. He could not let Samantha go, but he could not bring dishonor to his family or Cecilia's family, the Gambrelli's. He did not want to hurt his wife or young daughter Carmelo.

It was time, past time, to talk to the Senior Dominic. "Father, please understand, I've fallen in love with another woman and do not know what to do," he said after they had sat down at the pub, ordered a couple of beers and exchanged pleasantries with the bartender and several customers.

"Is she married, son?" the father questioned. "Does she feel the same way?"

"No, she's single, never married, but she works in the office," young Dominic offered. "We have not talked about any commitment, but we are in love like I've never felt before. I'm so sorry for the family, but what do I do?"

Dominic, the elder one, gulped the beer, seemingly biting into the liquid. Then he said, "Must be the Bartelli gal. Can't say I'm too surprised. She's the good-looking gal in your office with the freckles, curly hair and compact body. I should have suspected something. All us Panichi's have a bit of a roving eye. It must be the Italian heritage or just our good looks."

Freckles are Irish camouflage.

Irish Leprechaun

Dominic was somewhat surprised that his father would comment on Samantha's hair and body. He could not recall any moment that his father had commented on Cecilia's looks or figure. He kept listening.

"Ya know, son," his father began. "Our two families have been linked before. My father was part of the same bootlegging as the senior Bartelli guy, Daniel's father and Samantha's grandfather. They were rivals for the attention of the Big Kahuna and worked side-by-side for years. Then father got a job in County government and left cigarette trafficking behind."

Dominic looked his son straight in the eye as he spoke. "Both families pushed you and Cecilia into a relationship and then into marriage. Frankly, son, I've never seen the sparkle in your eyes for Cecilia the way I've always had for your mom. For that, I'm truly sorry. However, that cannot be an excuse for falling in love. Dominic, your mother must not know."

The waiter interrupted the elder Dominic's thoughts by placing an antipasto salad, Italian bread, olive oil and two plates on the table. The predecessor County Commissioner picked up a fork and stabbed a piece of prosciutto. He paused and left the Italian meat on the platter with the fork intact.

"If this were an affair, we could probably work through it," senior Panichi explained. "You would not be the first in our family to have fooled around, although most have done so with call girls or one-night stands. Falling in love, truly being in love, is another matter. If we don't handle this discretely and properly, it can bring great dishonor to our families."

"We may both dislike the bootlegging side of our ancestry, and it's now two generations removed," he said. "We both owe an awful lot to the Panichi family – to the legacy we proudly inherited. This Bartelli babe owes much to her family as well, even if she and her father chose to drop a letter in the name."

Senior Dominic finished the beer with a long guzzle, set the empty beer mug back on the table and scowled. He looked his son in the eyes and proclaimed, without expecting disagreement. "Son, the first thing you need to do is find her another position, another job. Get her the hell out of your office, out of the building, out of County government. Get that done, and we can talk some more. I will not say anything to your mother, now or ever. She's a woman and would not understand."

"But father, she's a marvelous employee, just terrific," young Dominic asserted without even implying a contrary opinion. "I'll never be able to replace her."

"Son, you'll find her a good position somewhere else in the community. You'll hire another Office Manager. That must be done. If you decide to continue to see her, it must be within the bounds of discretion. Let's see what your relationship is in four or five months. If your feelings have deepened, we can take the next step. Understand, if we get to that point of ending your marriage, you'll have to look at an overly fair, even sacrificial settlement with Cecilia. She will get Carmelo. The best you can hope for is reasonable visitation of your daughter."

The next morning Dominic picked up the telephone in his office and called his Irish consort, President J. Paul Kelleher. "Mr. President, you free for breakfast tomorrow?"

11

PREVIOUSLY

"Others need not apply."

J. Paul Kelleher had breakfast with the County Commissioner the day after Panichi had called wanting to meet. After hearing the soap opera situational drama about Panichi's affair with the Samantha Bartell gal, Kelleher had agreed to find a position for her at the College.

"I really will be beholden to you if you can find her a good job at the College, J. Paul. She's a marvelous employee and has served as my Office Manager, working with everyone in the County offices. She has as much aptitude as anyone I've ever known and more moxie too. You would be getting an excellent person."

"Do you think she'd be able to kick-start our Foundation, working out of my office," Kelleher asked, knowing the answer would be favorable. It would have been for most any duties he could have identified. He knew Panichi was desperate.

"She has lots of contacts," Panichi quickly affirmed. "If part of the job is to solicit businesses, you have your gal. She comes from high society – her father is head of Psychiatry at St. Anthony and her mother's an Oral Surgeon. If you need Board members for the Foundation, no one will reject her invitation to serve. No one. No one will reject her appeal for funds either. I'll donate the first day she starts."

Kelleher had taken his time that morning to finish up the scrambled eggs, pork sausage and potato pancakes at the Original Pancake House. He was contemplating the future payback he would receive from Panichi, as they bartered favors back and forth like a ping pong game. It would have to be something spectacular. He sipped his coffee, knowing now he had the upper hand and likely a damn good gal to go to work.

Having another person in the office might help too with relieving the headaches he was having. They seemed to be getting worse.

Kelleher boldly decided to re-direct the conversation. "What are your intentions regarding continuing the relationship?" he asked. "Have you told your wife you're in love with another woman?"

Panichi smiled sheepishly before Kelleher continued. "I assume you won't show up on campus in her office, and we can keep this romance out of the *Jersey Star's* gossip column."

President Kelleher punched the intercom button and told Mrs. Reynolds to have David Lieber come to his office now or at least before lunch. There was little emotion in Kelleher's voice. Usually the President's Secretary could tell immediately if he was happy, annoyed, upset or over the top angry.

Mrs. Reynolds reflected briefly on the President's request before asking, "Is he in trouble again? Should I warn him and call Security?"

"Just see if the goofy ass is available to talk about the Title III grant. You don't need to call Security or a priest or an ambulance," J. Paul barked, annoyed that he had to explain himself.

"Sit down David, chair on the right, please. Want some coffee?" Kelleher said as he motioned to Dean Lieber who arrived twenty minutes after being summoned. David was out of breath, having trotted across campus to the Administration Building. Kelleher was acting uncharacteristically courteous, so Lieber was particularly worried.

"Do we still have that one professional position left with Title III because that Counselor resigned last week?" J. Paul asked. "If I remember correctly, there are two years left on the funding for that position."

Lieber took the diner coffee mug from Edith. He sipped the brew cautiously, trying to gain time to collect his response. The position had been designated as a Counselor in the Learning Resources Center under Lieber. He had no idea what the President might have in mind for the slot. He probably would not like it.

Then Lieber spoke, "Yes, sir, the position is vacant. We've not placed the ad in the *Chronicle* or the *Jersey Star*. Personnel is doing its thing and being sure it's slotted properly. We don't want to have any screw-ups in the classification and job announcement. Washington would not like that. May I ask what you want to do with the position?"

President Kelleher looked relieved but pleased with himself that he would know there was this vacant position. Then he continued, trying to answer Lieber yet being evasive. "I want to get the Foundation going and create a position that reports to me and addresses administrative work in my office. The new administration position will be half-time on the Foundation and half-time as Executive Assistant to the President."

Kelleher knew David would not be overjoyed at the prospect of losing a counselor and control of the vacant position. However, he knew there was a Milestone in the grant about kick-starting the Foundation to provide an alternative source of revenues for scholarships, capital equipment and professional development.

President Greenleaf had initiated the CJCC Foundation just before he left for St. Louis, but it had floundered under Winters during his Interim President months. The Board of Trustees bought into the concept initially but never expressed a desire to get involved. None of the Trustees had ever made a monetary contribution to the Foundation or any other private appeal, including bake sales by Future Farmers and the Honor Society's appeal to provide Christmas toys for low income kids.

The Board's collective wisdom was that they were owed for time spent as Trustees. Consequently, they expected comped tickets for all plays, lectures, concerts and athletic events, even though they rarely attended. Kelleher knew he would have to address that with the Trustees – how could the Foundation expect faculty and staff, and even community members, to contribute to an Annual Fund if the Board did not?

With no one assigned, the Foundation had been dormant since Kelleher had assumed the presidency. By creating this position now and placing someone accountable to manage, he could elevate the organization. He wanted to make a statement of the importance of private gift support.

What little monies were in the Foundation had come from two ill-conceived alumni solicitations by the Student Activities Coordinator under Vice President Purdy. In Kelleher's mind, a car wash would have generated more revenue. He had agreed for Purdy to lead the Foundation. That had not been successful, and Kelleher had regretted that decision.

Purdy's model was to rely on alumni. Kelleher was skeptical that a community college could raise private support dollars from its alumni. He reasoned that associate degree students would be more loyal to the transfer institution, the one where they earned the baccalaureate, not to CJCC. Appeals, so far, had proven his point.

Kelleher was also dubious about using a Foundation led by business leaders to generate funds to support intercollegiate athletics. Yet, athletics needed to be funded by private dollars or, alternatively, by the Student Activities Fee. If J. Paul got a Foundation going, he could see Coach Solly pounding on his door to offer scholarships to tall kids who could jump and shorter ones who could dribble with either hand.

Kelleher needed the Title III personnel slot. He needed it now. His decision to use a vacant grant-funded position for that purpose, and to hire the woman he wanted, was cagey if circumspect. He had to finagle the budget and barter a little more with Lieber. He had owed the County Commissioner due to Dominic Panichi's phone calls to Board members during the Presidential Search. This was payback and then some.

David Lieber knew this was a done deal. He decided to go along rather than provoke an outburst and an argument he would only lose. He could say to himself: *My time to destroy Kelleher will come later. But it will come.*

"That could work, sir," David asserted, barely hiding his animosity. "Do you want me to draft a job description and an announcement, so that we can get underway with the recruitment?"

"No, I'll get with Roseanne and let Personnel do the work. I want to get this position filled quickly. We've farted around with the Foundation enough. Winters ignored it, and Purdy hasn't done shit. Someone needs to be in charge. We'll advertise on the weekend and see what candidates we get. I see this as a mid-level administrative position, but Miss Hart will do the job evaluation."

Dean Lieber could read between the lines – the President already had the candidate in mind. There would be no formal search process. "Others need not apply'" he told himself.

PREVIOUSLY

"What did I get myself into?"

Roseanne Hart had her doubts about the legitimacy of an internal-only job search that also included folks from other County agencies. It appeared to be a mixed message. She knew better.

"Let it go," she told herself. She did and placed the Help Wanted announcement for Sunday's edition of the *Jersey Star*. Applications were due in eight days. There was no Job Description, and the Job Classification was yet to be done.

Roseanne made a wager with herself when she saw the ad in newsprint – how long it would take for the Vice Presidents to react to the ad. She figured an hour at most. She couldn't wait to get to the office on Monday.

When the four Vice Presidents saw the ad, and came to work on Monday morning, they fixated on the phrases *Interfaces with the Vice Presidents* and *for direct access to the President's time and agenda.*

It took less than five minutes before the phones were ringing like tumbling dominoes. Academic Vice President Donald Winters called Administrative Vice President Bill Fishman who called Student Vice President Jonathan Purdy who then called Institutional Support Vice President Thomas Dandridge – who called his wife.

Dandridge, as low man on the totem pole, had spent much of Sunday evening shaking his head and looking at himself in the mirror. "What did I get myself into?"

Samantha Bartell enjoyed her new flat, the privacy of it and particularly the location above Dottie's Beauty Parlor. She could not imagine having privacy with her lover, Dominic Panichi, had she still been living with her parents. The beauty of it was that no one was in the building after 5:05 PM. The business closed its doors at 5 PM, and staff vacated as if there was a bomb scare or a major sale at Macy's.

E. Timothy Lightfield, Ph.D.

HELP WANTED – PROFESSIONAL   The **Jersey Star**
                                                      March 6, 1977

Executive Assistant to the President, Central Jersey Community College
Abington, New Jersey
Reports directly to the President and handles a range of duties for the office.
Interfaces with the Vice Presidents and staff.
Serves on President's Cabinet.
Provides gatekeeper role, creating win-win situations for direct access to President's time and agenda.
Follows-up on incoming issues and concerns.
Handles confidential and sensitive information.
College Foundation:
Position also responsible for directing the College Foundation, generating private funds and managing the Board of Directors.
Minimum Qualifications:
        Bachelor's degree, graduate coursework
        Two years comparable experience in public administration
        One letter of recommendation
        Good communications skills
Application:
        Send a letter of interest and resume to:
        Miss Roseanne Hart
        Director of Personnel, CJCC
        101 Crosstown Drive, Abington, NJ 07700

Application Deadline: March 14, 1977

Had she been living in an apartment complex, her neighbors would have been most suspicious of the highly recognizable County Commissioner repeatedly visiting at, and uniformly being escorted into, the apartment.

The rear entrance and shadowed steps to the second-floor location provided privacy and cover for a certain regular visitor from the County Commissioner's office. Dominic and Samantha could be alone, together.

At the next President's Cabinet meeting, the three veteran Vice Presidents ganged up on Kelleher. Rather, they tried to do so. They had seen the Executive Assistant ad and demanded an explanation of what *interfaces* meant.

"Are you saying, J. Paul, that we report to this Executive Assistant?"

Winters began. "I for one, really, truly object. Why do we need this guy on the President's Cabinet?"

Purdy added, "So this Executive Assistant person will grant us access to you and your office. We must go through this guy to get to you?"

Fishman protested, too. "I've been here the longest, and you can't have someone else decide the priority of my work and triage our reports. I bet this guy can't even read a bookkeeping ledger. And I certainly don't want some young punk going through my financial reports."

Dr. Dandridge just let his counterparts raise the temperature of Kelleher's outrage. He knew that when J. Paul started chain-smoking and fidgeting with his *Cross* pen, the boiling process had begun. He was right. Twirling the pen was a bad sign, more revealing than body language or a flare shot into the sky.

Kelleher took a puff of the *Marlboro* and held his cigarette vertically, to prevent an ever-lengthening ash from falling on the mahogany conference table. He knew his inevitable eruption was coming. He had no intention of stifling it. The ash probably would fall about the same time as his patience expired.

Both did.

J. Paul brushed the cigarette ash aside and onto the floor as someone might robustly sweep leaves off a porch. He did not brush aside his annoyance or his temper.

"Now wait a minute gentlemen, just one damn minute," the President began. "I need to spend more and more time in the political arena, State and County. And the Board needs more nursing every year. You know that, assholes. Now, with Title III, we must get a true Foundation going. We sat on this for two years while Winters pissed on it and Purdy played alumni games."

The four Vice Presidents fidgeted in assorted ways as the President continued to attack and admonish them.

"That all means less time for me on campus," Kelleher barked. "That's less time for me to fiddle with you and your juvenile egos. I need someone to sort out office priorities, insulate me where necessary and take the lead on private donors. Grow up!"

"Besides, it will be a *she* not a *he*!"

PREVIOUSLY

"Can you start tomorrow?"

Miss Samantha Bartell had been to meet with Roseanne Hart in the Personnel Office at the College. Bartell was one of the six applicants. Roseanne was the sole member of the one-person Search Committee. Nevertheless, she grilled young Bartell.

"What makes you think you can work with a man like President Kelleher?" Hart leveled after directing the applicant to a seat in her office.

Then she unloaded more loaded questions: "How will you handle the four Vice Presidents when they want to go against you, which will happen frequently? What do you know about the mission of a community college? What similarities do you see in working with the Board of Chosen Freeholders and working with the College's Board of Trustees?"

Roseanne waited in each case for Samantha Bartell to respond to the questions, but she knew it didn't matter what the young lady said. She would be recommended to the President by the unanimous vote of the solitary member Search Committee.

However, Personnel Director Hart could not be more impressed with Samantha's command of the interview. Hart was surprisingly overwhelmed.

Hart reasoned that had there been a typical seven-person Search Committee and ten times the number of applicants, Miss Bartell would have still emerged as the leading candidate.

Hart ended the mock interrogation with a forewarning to the Bartell woman. "President Kelleher has a reputation of making crude jokes and using profanity. He's very bright and immensely dedicated to this College, but he can intimidate people and fall into chauvinist habits when it comes to interacting with women. Best be aware."

President Kelleher took Samantha to lunch at the Golden Acres Country

Club across town, as planned. He anticipated, from his conversations with County Commissioner Panichi and after perusing her resume, that Miss Bartell would be competent and impressive. He did not anticipate being blown away by her poise and savvy. Or being clobbered by her charm.

"Samantha," Kelleher began the conversation, ignoring any more formal reference to Miss Bartell, "I recommend the *Chef's Choice* fish entrée. I will have a Martini. You're most welcome to join me."

Samantha never drank before the evening, but she reasoned that the invitation by President Kelleher was some sort of litmus test. "Thank you, whatever wine you prefer with the fish would be fine with me."

"You understand that you're going to have two jobs – assisting me in my agenda, interfacing with the four Vice Presidents and interceding when necessary. Plus, you must get the College Foundation running well. I do expect considerable progress in both arenas. However, if you're pushed and shoved, the Executive Assistant is the more important role. Don't forget that."

With a huge smile and glimmer of sarcasm, Samantha responded. "Mr. Panichi speaks highly of you, sir, and considers you a worthy adversary, in the sense of a successful administrator in Monroe County. But, I expect he'll be taking a back seat to you, and I intend to see that happens. That includes getting a successful Foundation off the ground and seeing you heralded as conquering hero."

Kelleher looked at Miss Bartell with inquisitiveness before he asked: "Samantha, is it true you were born on March 17, Saint Patrick's Day? Is it possible that your deep Italian roots are obscured by your Irish birthday?"

Miss Bartell responded with a smile, "Sir, it just means I have some Irish in me and that green is my favorite color. I'm also very fond of corned beef and cabbage."

The pair of *Chef's Choices* were served, giving the President a couple of minutes to think of a suitable response to what he had just heard.

He did not need to ponder long. He simply said, "Samantha, you're hired. Can you start tomorrow?"

Samantha Bartell and Dominic Panichi, her ex-boss but current lover, met for a glass of wine at her apartment above the hair salon after he had left work early that same day. She had taken two weeks of vacation leave from the County job to apply for and pursue the career path with Central Jersey Community College. Now she would start work tomorrow.

She had understood the reasons why Dominic told her they would have to find her a new job and abandon the County position. They could not work together in the same office any longer. They both cried and vowed they would build on their romance and their love. They would continue to seek communion with each other, no matter what.

Samantha had reached the same conclusion with respect to her position in the County Commissioner's office. However, she had not anticipated that Dominic could pull off a transition to CJCC, working directly for the President and at a higher salary. And do that with one telephone call. More and more, she understood how things worked in Monroe County. How they had always worked.

"I like the job very much, but it will be a challenge working with those four bigot Vice Presidents" Samantha said, her voice trembling. She placed the wine glass on the coffee table in her living room as if to free her hands and mind to what she would say next. "They're not used to working with a woman, but they will have to learn quickly. I will too, if I'm going to survive."

Samantha paused long enough to sip the aged California Cabernet that Dominic poured as a refill. Looking at the wine glass and with resolve, she forged ahead, "I intend to enforce the will of Kelleher."

"Let me pose a toast to Cutie Marks," Dominic offered. "To be sure, you'll enforce the will of Samantha."

Kelleher called a special meeting of the President's Cabinet to introduce Samantha Bartell to the Vice Presidents. The four hardened males wanted so badly to dislike the person and to cast her as the ugly and stupid villain. After all, she was a woman, an unknown entity in an undefined position, reporting directly to an unrelenting, unreasonable CEO.

They did not want more change. They were still reeling from the 1976 reorganization last year. Besides, as Winters had proclaimed, "Bartell's twenty years younger than the youngest of us. She's a baby for God's sake!"

President Kelleher had given considerable thought to how he wanted to present the change in reporting, given the new position of Executive Assistant to the President.

He lit up a cigarette and began abruptly. "Gentlemen understand you all report to me, but now there is dotted line to my Executive Assistant. I'll handle your evaluations and your assignments. I'll approve or toss-out your recommendations. But know I'll be seeking assessments of you from Miss Bartell. She will have the authority to discern what gets on my desk, gets on my agenda, gets on my calendar and gets in my face. She will determine what goes back to you for further work or reconsideration, especially on your Board items. That's the way it will be."

There was silence in the room except for Samantha adjusting her seated position, uncrossing her legs, moving her hands from the table to her lap and turning toward Kelleher. Her challenge was to keep a straight face and not look shocked.

Part of her wanted to crawl under the conference table. Another part wanted to let out a loud cheer for woman-kind. Still another part wished

Dominic had been there to witness Kelleher's statement and photograph the sorrowful expressions of the four Vice Presidents. She thought to herself: *They look like little boys left on the sidelines when the Little League Team was picked.*

At first, she thought it would have been better to be out of the room when her boss leveled the Vice Presidents, maybe even out of the building or across town. But no, she needed to hear this too. She needed to understand where he would be coming from and the level of support for this new position.

The President had affirmed her role and how he wanted her to operate. She had read the abbreviated job description and much of the Board Policy Manual. However, this was a new position and she had doubts: *Would he clarify her job to his lieutenants? Would he remain firm when she did something Winters did not like, or Fishman thought was above her pay grade? What if the Vice Presidents took their complaints to the Trustees? What if she couldn't find the Ladies Room? What if these guys let all of the air out of her tires?*

Those were serious questions. Samantha needed to learn if there were any sacred cows, or in this case sacred bulls, among these four stubborn males on the President's Cabinet.

The once-upon-a-time Interim President Winters spoke as if Samantha was not in the room and certainly not within the inner leadership circle. That was a mistake picked up by everyone in the room, especially Kelleher. Winters jumped into the muddy, turbulent water with both feet. "I'm sure I speak for the others when I say this will take getting used to. No doubt Miss Bartell is reasonably competent, but she's never worked at a college, let alone at this level. A County office is not a college. We can all appreciate that. Besides you already have a Secretary."

Kelleher now elevated his remarks, "I'll be damned. What the hell do you think this is all about. It's time you guys understood that I'll do things my way. Get used to it. I did not ask for your opinion on this position or the appointment of Miss Bartell. I am not asking for your opinion now. This is not an item you vote on."

Kelleher started to fidget with his *Cross* pen, the infamous signal he was infuriated. He continued with his statement, smoke coming out of his ears as well as the end of his *Marlboro*.

"Gentlemen, if you don't like it, there's the door. Don't let it hit you in the ass on the way out!"

14

PREVIOUSLY

"We don't often get to see you in a dress and heels."

Gene Wildwood was incredibly nervous, but he found the courage to dial Candace Rodewald's home phone on Saturday morning. This was after the birthday party the Computer Center held for Howard Tucker in the *Meat Locker* that Friday evening.

Neither Gene's wife, Alice, or Candace's husband, Bob, came to the party, but for different excuses. Wife Alice was reading a book she had to finish and was exhausted from teaching little kids all week. She was falling asleep between pages. Husband Bob had a sales road trip to Philadelphia he had to pursue. He was packing to leave in the morning.

Neither Gene or Candace cared that their respective spouse chose not to come to Howard's party.

Howard's birthday celebration had gone well. He was touched by the gathering, even if President Kelleher and Vice President Dandridge did not come. No one knew if they had been invited.

Howard's wife Gloria was surprised by the attention paid to her husband. She had played along with the ruse that Howard had to work late on a priority project that Gene said had to be run. She showed up on campus about the time the Programmers jumped out of Gene's office and screamed in Howard's face before mutilating a rendition of the *Birthday Song*.

Howard opened the gifts, including two *Beefeater* Gin fifths and two tickets to the new Broadway Play, *A Chorus Line*. Candace was responsible for the Broadway tickets, not the gin. She knew her colleagues bought the liquor, justifying same by their choice of *Beefeaters* as a better brand than Howard drank in the paper cups.

"Guys, thanks for the bottles. Good stuff." Howard exclaimed, trying to be nonchalant with the gift concept and the half-century birth bash. "Of course, the Broadway tickets too," throwing out the gift of the pricey tickets as a lame attempt at humor. "Guess I'll share the gifts with Gloria." He knew full well his wife only drank vodka and was not a fan of musicals.

There were also several gag gifts in honor of Howard's 50th birthday – a bottle of prune juice, a package of *Poligrip* denture glue and a t-shirt with the message – *It's Official, I'm now 50 and a Geezer.* They gave him a mug – *In dog years, I'm dead* – and a necktie which included two images of skull and crossbones and the words *50th Birthday.*

As the party wound down and people started to leave, Gene sat in his office mulling over the events and contemplating a boring weekend. He might just come to the office on Saturday and get overtime. It had not been a particularly good week for Gene, as the Programmers had a hard time concentrating on anything other than the party planning and who would get Howard's gin and the gag gifts.

Candace grabbed her coat to head home but looked around for Gene. She peeked in and saw Gene was alone in his office. Howard saw her and asked her to lock up, not realizing Gene was still in the *Meat Locker.* "I'll be glad to, and congratulations on your birthday," she yelled as he pushed open the door. Then under her breath said, "I wish the guys had found some other gift than the gin." She knew the bottle would not last the weekend.

When Candace walked into his office, Gene looked up. He was startled but mesmerized by the lady standing there with her coat over her arm and a smile on her face. He was momentarily stunned by how alluring she was, especially in a dress and heels. "Heh, nice *pa-pa*-arty," he offered and now annoyed with himself for stuttering. "Did you have fun? Sorry, *Ba-Ba*-Bob could not make it, but an office party is pretty much for the office I guess."

Gene rose from his desk chair to come to the front of the desk where Candace was standing. He stood there, his mind spinning from the party beverages or given the woman standing before him.

Candace chose to interrupt the silence. "Howard and Gloria have left, so have the others. No one else is here. You OK, Gene? You seem a bit mellow, and you kept to yourself at the party."

"Just trying to decide if I want to come to work tomorrow or hang around the house. We need to catch-up on the backlog of jobs. You looked more *be-be*-beautiful than ever this evening and after working all day. Wish I could think of a joke to tell you, but I'm out of humor for now."

Candace laid her coat on the chair and strolled to where Gene was standing, inching herself closer to her colleague with infant steps. She did not take her dazzling green eyes off his face.

She was a couple of inches taller than Gene, given she had switched to high heels for the party. It didn't bother Gene at all that he had to look up at Candace.

As far as Candace was concerned, It was another sign of the man's confidence and being content with himself. Her shapely legs, however, did bother him.

"We don't often get to see you in a dress and heels," Gene offered. He tried but failed to avoid running his eyes up and down her body, but she did not mind the momentary gawking.

"Gene, you're stuttering," Candace shared. "Nervous perhaps? Don't be. That was a nice party."

Gene reached out to hold Candace's hands as Candace leaned forward, paused for a moment and then kissed Gene lightly on the lips. She kept looking into his eyes as she hovered millimeters away from his lips. The second kiss was much longer and involved tongue touching and deep breathing.

Candace spoke first, still hovering near his face. "If you want to call me tomorrow, I'll be home. Bob leaves early in the morning and doesn't get back from Philly until Sunday afternoon, more likely Monday."

The next morning, at 10:00 on Saturday at his office, Gene indeed did call Candace. He was nervous and had to re-dial when he messed up the exchange digits. He had told Alice he was going to get in some overtime, but he knew he had another mission that morning.

"Hello, this is Candace," the honeyed voice said, giving great relief to Gene who thought perhaps Bob had not left for Philadelphia, and a man would answer. If so, he would have hung up the phone in a New York City second, even though he was living in New Jersey.

"Good morning pretty lady. This is Gene. I'm at the office catching up on a few things and wanted to give you a call. Didn't know how late you sleep on Saturday."

Candace compulsively spoke as if she had already known what she would say no matter what salutation Gene might have made or question he might have asked. "I've been up for an hour or so, but if I make a fresh pot of coffee would you go by the bakery? Maybe get some donuts and come by for a while."

She waited for an answer but broke the silence again. "I like cream-filled ones with chocolate frosting if they have some left. If not, surprise me."

About 30 minutes later, Gene sheepishly rang the doorbell of Candace's condo. She had not needed to give him her address or directions. He knew exactly where she lived. Like a smitten schoolboy he had driven by her condo unit several times in the past months. On the way to her house this morning, Gene was singing Carly Simon's *Anticipation*. He even got the lyrics correct.

Gene told himself that none of the neighbors would be concerned that a fellow worker from the College would be at Candace's doorstep with husband Bob out of town. He had grabbed a sport coat to wear, figuring that made him look more business-like.

But then how would the neighbors know this stranger was a fellow worker or anyone else, not some guy invited to this lady's house and maybe her bedroom? He held the bag of donuts high above his waist as if they were a passport for all to see and verify his honorable intentions. He should have brought his briefcase as another prop or pretended he was selling insurance or hawking encyclopedias.

Candace opened the door. She stood behind the door and motioned for Gene to enter. Only her head and right arm were visible to her visitor, or to her neighbors. Her smile was all the invitation Gene needed to pull open the door.

The condo unit inside was a few years old and decorated about the way Gene would have imagined – lots of colors, classy furniture and tasteful, joyful paintings, even if prints of originals. He could smell the brewed coffee, but that was way in the background compared to the perfume scent coming from Candace standing behind the door and now facing him as she closed the door.

Candace grabbed the bag of bakery goodies and stood there in a yellow cotton flowing, full-length robe which covered a matching knee-length, yellow nightgown. Gene was not much for details at this moment, but he did see the fields of buttercup flowers floating along on patterns and the ruffled floral lace collar and hems.

He could not mistake that while she had buttoned the robe, the flowing garment did not hide the curvaceous figure of the Computer Center's only female employee. Flannel pajamas and a parka would not have concealed those curves.

Candace pulled one of the chocolate-covered, cream-filled donuts from the bakery bag. She took a generous but sexy bite out of it before putting the remnant donut portion in Gene's mouth. "Take a bite, so we're even. Then I can taste the chocolate on your breath when we kiss."

"Gene, please come in," Candace said assuredly. "Make yourself comfortable. Thank you for coming. Relax and please don't stutter. There's no hurry. We have plenty of time if you want to sit awhile. Or, we can skip the rest of the donuts and let the coffee cool for now. Every woman gets more passionate after a bite of chocolate."

"Whatever you say," Gene responded, his excitement building up within his mind and within his manhood.

Candace started for the back of the house, imploring Gene to follow her, as she grabbed another donut. They came to the guest bedroom, and Candace stopped in the doorway. She undid the buttons on her yellow, buttercup flower robe, letting it slide without encumbrance off her shoulders and fall softly toward the floor. Gene impulsively caught the lounging attire in mid-air and placed it gently on the end of the bed.

"Nice save," said Candace, impressed and amused that her chivalrous male guest would rescue her gown from inevitable ruination had it landed on the floor.

"Hope it's alright with you if we use our guest bedroom," Candace said as if worried her partner for the morning would object. "Bob has a waterbed in our bedroom, and I hate when it sloshes. He says it helps his bad back. I think he likes the gurgling noise. Reminds him of his childhood at the lake."

"Whatever room you prefer," Gene said. "Heck, I'm just a guest here this morning."

Gene had only known sex with, let alone making love to, one woman – his wife. He was petrified about his upcoming debut performance. Questions kept popping up in his mind: *What would she want me to do? Can I avoid a premature explosion? Would she want to make love or have erotic, even bawdy sex? How many lovers had she had before Bob or others since she was married? How long would it take her to recognize I have not had many lovers? Should I have worn a different shirt?*

Candace sat down on the edge of the bed and motioned for Gene to sit next to her. She crossed her legs which meant that her upper thigh was exposed. She put her hand on his knee and began caressing his thigh. She kissed him on the cheek and then deeply on his lips.

Gene matched her move for move, trying to keep up. His hand found her upper thigh. Her skin was smooth and warm. He heard her sigh. He did fine in these preliminary petting and kissing maneuvers and explorations. *Way to go*, he told himself. *Maybe I can do this after all.*

Gene touched her breasts through the nightie and then slid his hand under the fabric to feel the soft skin and fondle her braless *Gum Drop* nipples. His breathing leaped as she raised her nightgown over her head and he saw her fully naked.

The problem was when he amorously rolled on top of her. Then, Gene did not do so fine. The auspicious debut performance came to an agonizing premature climax for him, just after he had lowered his pants and Candace slid down his boxer shorts.

He moved to her side, his arms still around her. Embarrassed, he used his underwear as a substitute towel.

"I'm so sorry Candace. I wanted to hold-off, but that wasn't possible," Gene said apologetically. "I've only been with one woman my whole life, and you are way beyond my imagination in beauty and class. I've fantasized about this moment but never thought it could or would happen. Now that reality kicked in. You're naked on the bed, and I blow it!"

Candace responded immediately, "Gene, it's alright. Just hold me longer, please. Everything's fine. Don't worry or apologize. Let your hands and mind roam my body. Touch me, indulge me, please. There's no reason to apologize. I'll guide you to my pleasure."

After several minutes of agonizing bliss, Gene pulled up his pants, stuffing his soiled boxers into his pants pocket. Candace sat up, then stood while her hand rested on Gene's shoulder. She floated across the hall to the bathroom where she retrieved her red flannel bath robe, all the while sensing Gene's eyes fixated on her.

They held hands and walked back to the kitchen, with Candace leading the way. "Let's have that coffee and finish the donuts," she announced. "Stay a while longer, Gene, please."

Gene stayed, as requested, and not because of the coffee and donuts. The pair of Computer Center staff members talked about the College, Howard Tucker, President Kelleher and computer peripherals. The only topic they avoided was the previous effort at sexual intimacy in her bedroom and Gene's inauspicious release.

A half hour later, Gene felt it was time to leave and head home. He had apologized three more times.

His ruse of working at the office would expire any minute now. An alarm went off in his head. It was as if he had illegally parked his car for an errand, only to speculate he needed to get back to his car because he had envisioned a traffic cop about to ticket him.

"Gene, before you leave let me say a few things," Candace said. "I'm very attracted to a man of your character and spirit. I find you vulnerable, as when you occasionally stutter or confuse song lyrics. That's a turn on for me. It truly is. My marriage is my marriage, and what it is I can't very well explain. I hope we can be more than colleagues, more than friends who meet like this every so often. I respect you have to work out your marital situation on your own, and I hope you'll want to see me again, outside the Meat Locker."

Gene started for the door and stopped in front of it before responding. "I so want to see you again, do better in the bedroom and offer you something more romantic than donuts."

Candace smiled and reached for Gene's arm, "You got it. Next time we can share a few glasses of Chianti and skip the chocolate donuts. The wine might make you pace yourself, but then it might make me even more horny." She kissed him again before cradling his chin in her two hands. "You'll have to decide," she offered.

Gene thought for a moment but not entirely about what Candace had said. Then he asked, "Do you remember that movie a few years ago starring Natalie Wood and Dyan Cannon. It was called *Bob and Carol and Ted and Alice*? Remember, they all ended up in the same bed together."

"Oh sure, I remember the film," Candace said quickly. "It was hilarious and pretty heavy on the intimacy and nudity stuff, but from my perspective the movie starred Elliott Gould and Robert Culp."

"Yeah, I *ga-ga*-guess so," Gene said. "I'm a guy. I only remember the two dazzling dames. But here's my idea. How 'bout if we set aside Bob and Alice – my Alice and your Bob. Instead, you be *Carol*. I'll be *Ted*. Then let's just take it from there. It can even be our little joke. That OK with you, *Carol?*"

"Sure *Ted*" she continued with a glimmer of playfulness sweeping over her face. "For a moment I feared you were going to suggest a foursome. But, before you go, let me finish what I was trying to say."

Gene, AKA *Ted*, did not know if this would be a lecture taken from a chapter in 1972's *The Joy of Sex* or a sendoff theological passage from the Old Testament.

"First, next time we make love, stay next to me and cuddle afterward," Candace offered. "No matter how long you take to come. I'd like to bask in the afterglow of sex with you. Please know how satisfied I was with your touch today. Having you caress me slowly as you did was intense and wonderful."

"Second," she started to speak but could not hold back a broad smile. "Gene, from now on when I enter the room at work, it would be best if you would stay behind your desk, put your hands on the top of the desk and not stand up. Know what I mean?"

Gene laughed, checked that his shirt was buttoned correctly and that his fly was closed before he started to open the door. Candace pulled him back, grabbed his hands and drew him close. They hugged. She massaged his neck, as his hands tenderly slid down her back before settling on her hips.

After they pulled apart, Gene opened the door just far enough so that he could squeeze through the opening. He waved goodbye and said loudly without emotion, "Thank you, Mrs. Rodewald. It was nice meeting with you."

Gene continued walking down the front porch stairs of her condo, trying to give his best Thespian impression of nonchalance and disinterest for the benefit of nosy neighbors. Candace stood at the door with a mischievous grin. "Mr. Wildwood, I forgot to tell you something. Please come back for a second."

Gene hurried back and looked at her as if something was truly wrong. Maybe now she would honestly tell him what a lousy lover he was, and she never wanted to see him again.

At the same time, he glanced around to see if anyone was out at this time on Saturday and would see him at the door or Candace in her robe.

Gene stood in the doorway, but away from the door, so inquisitive folks might not wonder what happened to the donuts. Candace giggled as she whispered to her Saturday morning visitor. "*Ted*, I forgot to tell you something. You really should buy a pair or two of Jockey briefs rather than wearing the boxers at work. They might hide your bulge a bit more!"

PREVIOUSLY

"Oh, I'll address this guy. You can bet on that!"

Coach Solly was despondent. His *Roaring Raiders* had come close, only to lose the National Championship to the Iowa team. Guard Lenny Robinson had twisted his ankle badly and could not play in the second half. The *Roaring Raiders* rallied around Mike Evans, the tall and talented center, rebounding and scoring as if trying out for a pro team and a lucrative contract.

The CJCC team had kept the game close but lost by six points. The Iowa boys made crucial free throws as the pace became increasingly frantic. They probably were the better team, at least on this day. Yet even with Robinson on the bench, CJCC made the outcome in doubt until the clock expired. Solly's team did not lose. They just ran out of time.

While the *Raiders* had the best player on the court in the 6'10" Evans, Iowa had two forwards headed for Iowa State and an exceptionally speedy freshman guard recruited by Wichita State. Most observers, as well as Martha J. Rooney and her *Jersey Star* columns, had Central Jersey as the underdog. Solly liked the underdog role. He did not much like the game's final score.

The support money President Kelleher had provided for the 1977 tournament, along with donations generated by Edith Reynolds, had been sufficient. The team bus had a flat tire traveling through Illinois. Solly had paid the bill out of gratitude that the delay did not keep them from arriving in Kansas for their first game. He'd worry about being reimbursed another day.

Dave Russell, owner the Poconos summer basketball camp, had loaned Solly $500. He had said that if the team was in the championship game Solly would not have to pay the money back. Solly made sure that everyone at the meetings knew he was Russell's partner with the camp and had no intentions of paying back the money.

Solly's mind wandered on the long ride home, feeling for his players in this time of agony and contemplating another bus break-down. He was celebrating on the inside for the offer coming from Southern New Mexico State University and its head coach, Ray Kropp. Kropp had been interviewing for an Assistant Coach in charge of the defense, and Solly was handicapped as the favorite. This was his big opportunity.

Solly felt terribly for his kids, especially coming so far in the tournament. The box score would have the results, but it would not reflect that CJCC played the last half without its star guard. Coach had made some terrific connections while in Kansas and contacted a couple of players who might find their way to New Jersey to play for him next year if he was still in the Garden State.

Solly was not the coach when the College began its athletic program, so he had nothing to do with the mascot name of the *Roaring Raiders*. Given that his coaching prowess was based on solid and changing defenses, raiders was a terrific name. He taught his players to rob opponents of their shots, dribbles and rebounds. Some opposing coaches thought his players mastered the art of mugging, not robbing. Usually, the refs did not agree.

The team colors were scarlet red and oxford blue, not the forest green and purple. He chose uniforms that emphasized red, as it could be associated with Courage, Force and Passion. He posted those three words on the dressing room walls along with corny motivational expressions. The oxford blue was more of a trim color to coincide with the blue of the American flag.

Solly's wife, Marilyn, knew about the potential move to the West. Alan Fox, his Athletic Director, and Rebecca Campbell, the Department Secretary did too. But most people at the College knew it was just a matter of time, and a few more state championships, before Solly bolted to Division I. That is, unless his obstreperous behaviors and disrespectful mouth kept disqualifying him.

He had shared the coaching prospect with Izzy Kelleher when they met at the Y's racquetball courts for a fresh squeezed orange juice the day after the team's return from Kansas. Izzy had embraced him in genuine excitement. "Solly, how wonderful. Being the basketball coach here with my husband as President has not been easy. Now you have a chance to go to university and coach. You'll be at a top conference. I'm thrilled for you."

Solly had not told his two teens. Not yet anyway. He was not certain how they would take it. Ben would be fine with the move, and indeed with the warmer weather. Daughter Beth would not be so happy. She was already on the varsity and would now have to try out for another school in another state.

Marilyn said if he got the job, she and the kids might stay in Abington over the summer and fall and make a gradual move to New Mexico. Beth had another year of high school, and Marilyn might decide to stay so their daughter could graduate with her class. Solly and young Ben would get an apartment near the University campus after school closed, so Ben could start school and Solly could begin to evaluate players and fine-tune the defense.

Solly was to get a telephone call at home from Coach Kropp on Sunday evening, confirming the appointment and salary. Then on Monday he could tell Fox he'd be leaving and tell President Kelleher to shove it. He was overwhelmed with anticipation of telling Kelleher what he could do with the coaching job. That would be the dominant Rooney story. The loss of the National Championship was already old news for the *Jersey Star*.

On Sunday evening and into that night, the phone did not ring. Solly had prepared a prime rib from Aaron's Butcher Shop and invited Fox and a date to the house for a celebratory dinner, along with Rebecca Campbell from the office. The medium-rare Prime Rib was superb, but the mood deteriorated as the evening wore on. The celebratory nature turned into anguish. The anguish into alarm. The alarm into a sleepless night.

Just after 11 AM on Monday, Rebecca flagged down Solly who was shooting baskets by himself in the gym. He had a phone call from Coach Kropp of Southern New Mexico State. She could tell there was anxiety in Coach Kropp's voice and not due to the time difference. She crossed her fingers that the news would be good. Her intuition and Kropp's hesitation belied something different.

"Coach Ray, great to hear from you," Solly began with quivering in his normally strong voice. "Everything all right? I was waiting for your call last night, and I've been looking at the film you sent me about the team."

"Hey, Coach," the other Coach said, trying to be upbeat but pausing to recall the words he had rehearsed Sunday evening and again this morning. "Solly, I'm afraid I can't offer you the position. I'm so sorry, but I'm getting pressured at this end. We have a former player who has the support of the AD and President, and I have to go with that guy for my coaching staff."

Solly felt like he was on an airplane that instantaneously lost altitude, leaving him out of breath and in cold sweats. "I don't understand, Coach. I don't."

"Solly it wasn't just that," the Coach began again. "Our AD got a call from the President of your College. Kelleher. Isn't that his name?"

Kropp did not wait for an answer but kept explaining. "This guy was calling to endorse your hiring, or so he said. But we got the impression your President was pressing us to hire you, get you out of his hair. How do you think he found out about it?"

"Beats me," Solly said and then he thought about it for a minute. "Kelleher has spies who tell him things. Our Personnel bitch probably told him."

"Well," Coach Kropp continued. "The AD chose to share the call with our President about the same time as he got a call from the Chairman of our Athletics Foundation about the former player here. So, end of story."

"Wow," Solly lamented. "So, J. Paul was trying to get me out of here, and just after we came in second for the National Championship. Pretty crappy."

"I know you were already starting to pack to make the move," Kropp said. "You would have done a great job. But I had to halt the process. I am sorry. Anything I can do?"

Coach Kropp waited for a response. When there was none, he continued. "Solly, you didn't tell anyone yet, I hope. Let me call some coaches in the conference. There may be other openings."

Coach Solly did not know if he was madder at Coach Kropp for backing down from an oral agreement or at Kelleher for screwing up the opportunity. He had to ask a few questions. "Coach, did his call make that much of a difference? What really happened?"

"I'd have to say it screwed things up," Kropp answered. "The AD here would not have needed to share the call with our President. The damn paperwork was in front of him to sign. He called me into his office just after the call and lamented that he'd have to tell President Simon. Your guy's probably a prick, especially if he does not appreciate what a marvelous coach you are. I don't know what he holds against you, but it's something you'll need to address if you apply for other Division I jobs. It was bad timing. His call gave our AD and President an opening."

Coach Solly cursed his fate and started to construct an offensive play in his mind, but not for the basketball team. He politely thanked Kropp for the call, and ever so faintly said to the phone, as much as to Kropp, "Oh, I'll address this guy. You can bet on that!"

16

PREVIOUSLY

"There would not be a second fling."

Professor Nancy Wiegand had served as Chairman of the Search Committee when Dr. Vernon Carter was hired as Dean of Science & Mathematics in 1974. She had an outstanding reputation for being student-oriented, while holding high standards in her teaching and grading. All her classes were popular.

Mrs. Wiegand had begun her employment with the College in 1972 and was immediately dumped into the Faculty Credentials Committee for the 1973 Middle States Association Reaffirmation of Accreditation. That meant reviewing all materials filed on each faculty member and stored in Personnel. That meant going through every transcript to assure the copies on file were properly affirmed by the awarding undergraduate and graduate institutions for each degree and each current employee.

Professor Wiegand was 26 years old when hired. She was relatively small of height, with dazzling blue eyes and long, loose curls framing her pixie face. She had a slightly crooked nose, owing to a face plant on a ski trip and a resulting deviated septum. She was an intermediate skier, but a mogul got the best of her on the *Devils' Elbow* run at Pennsylvania's Seven Springs Ski Resort. Her face plant was a thing of beauty to everyone except her.

Nancy was highly personable and not bashful about demonstrating her affable and gregarious personality in the classroom, on committees or in the hallways. It took her less than a month at the College before practically all administrators, most of whom were males, knew who she was and drooled to have opportunities to interact with her. She was fun to be around.

Nancy was from the western suburbs of Chicago, having graduated from Illinois State University with bachelor's and master's degrees in Psychology. Founded as a teacher education institution named Illinois State Normal, the University had flourished in recent decades.

Wiegand had finished her coursework for the Ph.D. but decided she Wanted to get on with a career and set aside completion of a dissertation for a year or two. Her topic dealt with the relationship between the *Quantity and Quality of Scientific Output by Psychologists* and *Professional Recognition*. She intended to identify and track the publication patterns of two-hundred licensed Psychologists. She had her Dissertation Prospectus approved but had not started to collect data and was in no hurry to do so.

Nancy and her husband, Greg, were both from Chicago and met at Illinois State when she was a junior and he an entering freshman. They had gotten married while she was completing her master's.

Greg was not much of a student and dropped out after his junior year to go into the food enterprise, working at a McDonald's fast food restaurant. His father had been a pioneer in the business, turning an initial $10,000 investment into a multi-unit enterprise and an impressive income. Greg had had to work his way through the organization to be qualified to manage a unit and be awarded his own franchise. He was currently an Assistant Manager and waiting for his opportunity.

The young couple had decided to postpone having children until Nancy's career path was resolved and Greg got his franchise store. For Nancy, the question had been: Did she want to teach college or hang out a shingle for a clinical practice? The gap in their education and the dissimilarity of their career choices created some marital strain, but nothing alarming. Children were on deferral until both careers got settled. Regardless of their differences, their Midwest roots kept them connected; their love kept them faithful.

David Lieber, Dean of Instructional Resources and a major contributor to the Title III federal grant, saw Professor Wiegand as a faculty star. She had participated in the professional development programs on campus and in Washington, D.C. on how to create media programming. She took to it like a dog to a bone.

Wiegand had developed experimental teaching media, taking advantage of CJCC's Title III media production equipment. She was designing, writing, screenwriting and directing videotapes for use in the popular PSY 101 course – *Introduction to Psychology.*

Lieber knew the teaching materials would have an enormous impact on student learning. He also saw a marketable product where he, more than Wiegand, could profit. He had his eye on a New York artist whose work would be a marvelous addition to his home gallery and future retirement account.

Nancy Wiegand had other intrusions in her life and complications for her time. Alan Fox was also developing media materials for the classroom due to the grant funding. His project was for teaching Physical Education that was required of most majors and a popular elective for the rest. Besides being proficient in his work, Fox was a charming bachelor. Alan did not hesitate to make moves on Nancy, even though she was married. His ego would not let him pass up hitting on her.

One evening that Spring 1977, Fox decided to make an all-for-it move on his colleague. He walked over to where she was editing tape. "Nancy, how 'bout joining me for a drink when we finish up tonight. I could use a beer or two. I'm buying. Pizza as well, if you like. I'll get you home in an hour or two. We can go over our notes, if you want, and relax."

The woman knew at once that Fox was interested in more than notes on their media work, but she was ready to put a toe in the water with Mr. Fox, perhaps her whole foot. He was persistent, and she liked that, or so she thought. She did not find the leisure suits attractive, but she could tell he was brawny and buff. He was educated, like her, and she liked that too. Tonight, at least, she was vulnerable. Besides, she reasoned, she could draw the line if things got physical.

Alan Fox had his smooth moves and ladies' man lines down pat. "We can listen to some Henry Mancini, and I can take a closer look at your script." They both knew what he had in mind by looking at her *script*. He and Nancy ended up that night back at his apartment otherwise identified as a Wolf's Lair.

By the time the evening was over, Fox had indeed taken a closer look at Nancy's body, not a *script*. He had pressed his flesh against hers, smoothly writhing from side-to-side. Nancy had honestly never experienced a man with such sensorial and polished moves. She was enthralled by the sex, if not necessarily the man. He touched her and kissed her in places like no man ever had and spent far more time focused on her body and pleasure than his own.

She told herself it was wrong to be there, naked on the couch but for that night it was right.

Nancy was relaxed from the wine and exhausted from the day. She fell asleep on the couch, while Fox left the room to change and make coffee. Fox covered her body with a blanket but not before taking his Polaroid Camera and snapping several candid shots. The machination of the camera caused her to stir, but he got what he had wanted. The Psychology professor had been a lovely, if unknowing, naked model for the shameless photographic session.

When Nancy got home later, much later, that night, Greg was waiting for her in the living room. So was their dog. Both man and dog jumped up, the husband

Each petal on the Shamrock brings forth a crooked act.

Irish Leprechaun

giving her a big hug before saying, "Honey, I'm so sorry you needed to work late on this media thing. I wish you had called, but I made dinner and saved you some. Anything I can do to help you relax?"

161

Greg waited for his wife to process his questions, but he could not wait any longer. "Babe, I've got terrific news."

Nancy felt culpable, but the emotion quickly passed. She focused on keeping the Fox rendezvous secret, acting as if she had been working all night and preparing her mind for this announcement. "Greg, everything's fine," she said. "Sorry to be so late. I love you, dear. I want to shower first. Then we can talk."

Greg followed her into the bathroom and watched as she peeled off her clothes, revealing the seductive curves and exquisitely creamy skin. Nancy dropped her clothes to the floor, less like a subtle striptease than a sober jettison of the garments and her unfaithfulness.

Greg followed her into the shower, pajamas and all. He grabbed a washcloth and bar of soap, as she laughed out loud. "Here, let me scrub your back and shoulders," he commanded. "That should help."

The effort to wash her back soon lapsed into washing her bare butt, until she turned her head seeking a kiss. Greg obliged, and he moved his arms around from her back to gently roam across her soapy breasts. His wet pajamas fell, revealing his erection. That part of his anatomy became an innocent soaped-up frankfurter pressed against her hotdog bun buttocks.

They wasted a lot of hot water in the shower. Neither minded. Their soapy bodies lubricated their lust and their love. The shampoo washed away most of Nancy's guilt.

"So, Greg, what's the great news," Nancy said, as she finished toweling off and slipped into her bathrobe. She watched her satisfied husband tie the string on his replacement pajama bottoms. She had had lustful sex with a guy earlier in the evening. Now she had made love with her husband. The latter was so much more enjoyable and gratifying than the former.

"The deal on the new McDonald's unit outside of town on the interstate came through," Greg blurted, his eyes fixed on his wife. "The location is terrific. Dad worked out the financials and agreed to lend us some of the franchise capital we need. I just need to attend a couple more seminars in Chicago and decide on the design features and construction details."

Greg let his announcement float in the air for several seconds as he basked in his adoring wife's face. Then he continued to tell her the whole story. "We have the entire northcentral Jersey region. The Abington guy did not want to expand. That means if there's a market study to add stores, we get first option. We can put roots down in the area. And, my love, we can continue our lineage."

Nancy had anticipated that they eventually would receive the franchise award, especially since Greg's father had been an early-on investor. But indeed, this was terrific news. All her husband had wanted. He had been through the ringer with interviews and background checks and training to be a manager and owner. She could continue to teach and perhaps take on some responsibility with the restaurant operation if she wanted. She could even finish her doctorate. The new McDonald's would be state-of-the-art, highly popular and amazingly profitable.

But she was curious, "What do you mean by putting down roots and continuing our lineage?"

"I mean, we can look to buy a house or even build one – whatever you want," Greg said. "We can have a garden in the back yard, a garage and a ping-pong table in the basement. Nancy, we can start a family. No hurry mind you. I want you to be ready, too. But I feel a huge weight's been lifted off my head. Being able to follow in my father's footsteps with my own franchise is a wonderful feeling. Owning and operating these restaurants can be a family business for generations. This is work I really enjoy, and I'll be my own boss."

Nancy could not hide her tears. She knew her husband would think they were celebrating his career and the restaurant to be. They were mostly in anguish and sorrow over her earlier evening escapade.

Greg put his arms around his wife. "How 'bout we celebrate over the weekend. Let's take in a fancy dinner and a play in New Hope. Let me take you to Macy's and get you a new outfit. Better yet, some new lingerie."

Nancy felt all warm inside and knew there would not be any more time spent in Fox's apartment or his car or anyplace else. She would defiantly and unequivocally end the affair. The sex might have been good, but her marriage was now even more important to her. She told herself: *There would not be a second fling.*

163

PREVIOUSLY

"Here's what you will do for me."

David Lieber was pleased, jubilant really, with the equipment purchased for faculty use in the Media Center through Title III. Eight faculty, some in pairs, were working on various projects in Mathematics, Nursing, Physical Education, History and Psychology. Nancy Wiegand's Psychology project was so outstanding that the U.S. Department of Education wanted the College to negotiate the product as Intellectual Property even before it was completed.

As the Dean of Instructional Resources, David Lieber sought to identify a media company interested in the materials. He had approached Wiegand about partnering with him on the venture. "I know you have created these materials, Nancy," Lieber told her. "Let me handle the negotiation portion, so you don't have to. You can trust me."

David Lieber was inwardly elated with the gifts he had received from Media Visual Equipment, Inc. out of New York. First, he was presented with a case of elegant red wine, delivered to his door with the note *Compliments of MVE, Inc.* He thought about reporting the gift to the College and to the Title III folks in Washington, D.C. He decided the wine was not to be shared.

There was nothing crooked about a case of wine to enjoy, he reasoned. After all, he did work together with the company in making the orders, and MVE had won the competitive bid. What was the harm?

A few weeks later, Lieber received tickets to the Broadway Play, *Annie*, and a gift certificate for a prime-cut sirloin steak dinner for two at Gallagher's, the New York City place where aged steaks were shown in a front window meat cooler. No need to acknowledge that gift or look differently at the Kodak home movie camera that appeared on his doorstep another day.

David did get nervous and suspicious, when an insured package from MVE arrived in the mail. Upon opening, he found $250 in cash and a note:

> *David, we so much appreciate that the College awarded us the contract for the Media Center equipment. What a privilege and honor to work with you and your faculty in ordering and setting up the production equipment.*
>
> *We at Media Visual Equipment, Inc. have put in another bid on the second wave of equipment and just want you to know how much we appreciate your business.*
>
> *We'd very much like to negotiate the contract to mass produce the Psychology course materials you have prepared. We can assure you a profitable percentage of the revenues. More to come!*

David pondered the *More to come* expression. He thought to himself: *Did that mean more gifts for him, more equipment for the College or more press? Was the focus on a proposal for the Intellectual Property project in Psychology that Wiegand was generating from the Title III grant? Or did it mean more problems and more complications for him?*

Nevertheless, Lieber figured there was no point in reporting the cash received in the mail. Besides faculty would be determining the winning company for the second round of funding. He really couldn't influence that selection much. Or, could he? He'd be sure that Wiegand got a piece of the contract. A piece. Maybe a bottle of the wine too. One bottle.

Alan Fox was not pleased when he got to the Media Center the next afternoon. Unexpectedly, he found that Nancy Wiegand, his passionate one-night-stand class-act woman, had turned into a distant figure and a frozen, not even cold, fish. There was an imaginary but impenetrable wall around her now.

"I'm embarrassed and so ashamed about what happened last night," Wiegand moaned. "Alan, I can't, I just won't let that happen again. I have too much to lose. I do love my husband, and if he knew I'd cheated on him, he'd be devastated. I can't let that happen. You got to let it go. I'm not going to screw up his dream or our marriage. I want children, raise a family and concentrate on my career. I don't want to play around. Please understand."

It wasn't like Fox figured now he'd have to enter a monastery or cloister himself in his office. Not likely. There were too many women in the town and so many more eligible ones in his classes. But he did not like to lose a conquest. It was as if he was deep sea fishing, caught a trophy red snapper and then watched in agony as the gorgeous creature jumped back into the ocean.

"Not so fast, lady," Alan pronounced. "I'm not letting you off the hook, especially since you're married. No intention whatsoever. None. Sorry."

Nancy did not look amused or ready to cave, but she did not know what this ex-one-nighter had in mind. "What do you want?"

"I get it, and I have no intention of pursuing a woman who doesn't want sex with me," Fox blurted. "There are many other fine ladies who adore my talents, and even more women who don't know it yet." Fox looked at Nancy with a suspicious grin and said, "No, the sex won't happen again with me, you can bank on that."

A week later, Professor Wiegand got a phone call from Alan Fox, inviting her to meet him in the Student Union for coffee later that morning. There was an isolated Faculty Lounge, but he figured the Student Union would be less conspicuous, as few faculty or staff took a break there.

Nancy was hesitant to meet with Fox at all. But she could handle this meeting and a time of reckoning. Besides she had two, almost three, degrees in Psychology and knew all the research. She could handle this. *No problem*, she told herself.

"I bought you a cup of coffee, as you like, even added some cream," Fox said as he invited Nancy to sit in one of the plastic-metal seats at the table. "This won't take long, Nancy. I trust you're doing alright. Haven't seen you working at the Media Center lately. You know, we still have work to do for the grant."

Nancy took a spoon and stirred the cup nervously, but she had little intention of drinking the coffee. "As far as the Media Center, I told Lieber I wanted to back off a bit in production and concentrate on script writing. Don't take it personally. With my husband now owning a restaurant, I want to carve out time to contribute to the business and help him. Lieber will get media staff to complete production of the PSY 101 stuff."

Fox was not impressed or dissuaded from his objective. "Well isn't that sweet. Lady, I don't give a shit about the Media Center or any working relationship with you. There are plenty of chicks around here and more coming each semester."

Fox looked around the Student Center and saw only students, sitting at the tables or walking past at high speed on the way to class. The coast was clear for him to make his proposition.

"Here's what you will do for me," he began. "There's nothing you need to do now, not until the end of the semester. Then it's something easy for you. It's not illegal or anything and doesn't involve money or sex."

Nancy looked like she had been caught in a net, a big, thick enveloping net. She did not know if she could escape. Her anger and her shame were building.

Fox continued, "Nancy, there are a few student-athletes who from time-to-time need a little help with their grades. You understand. Only a few."

"Wait a minute," Nancy yelled. Then she realized some students at the tables had turned to see who was making the outburst. With a smile to camouflage her agony and at a reduced decibel level, she affirmed, "Alan, I am not about to give away grades, if that's what you're asking me to do. You can't want me to do that."

"No, no, not that at all," answered Fox. "It won't be very many students and only those enrolled in your *Intro to Psych* course. All I want you to do is raise a D grade to a C, a grade of a C to a B and a B grade to an A for a handful of students each semester in your class.

"What the hell do you mean?" Wiegand asked defiantly. "What are you asking me to . . ."

Fox cut her off. "Take it easy, sweetheart. You see, often students are on the border with the grades anyway, you know that. So, giving the higher grade is not crazy. No one will know but you. It'll just help those few students who need to raise their GPA to keep their eligibility and graduate."

Nancy wrestled with the concept. "Alan, I would never do this. How dare you!"

"Oh, don't worry, you'll be able to do this. In fact, you'll do it willingly," Fox said, pausing to be sure she was listening before he dropped the bomb. "Nancy, I have some lovely Polaroid photos of you that are *Playboy* worthy and pretty convincing of your sexuality. And, truly, you have my word that it will only be a few students each semester and only in the one class. I promise. Do this for a year, two at most, and I will give you the photos to destroy."

Nancy knew this would make her a little crooked, but only a little. No big deal. Just how revealing were the photos? She must have been asleep when he took them.

But, she thought, here's the big question: *Do I have the courage to reject his proposal? What if Greg were to see the photos? Can I call his bluff? How naked was I?*

PREVIOUSLY

"Be ready to duck!"

Samantha Bartell was not a fan of parties, especially those held by a team of lawyers who had contracts to serve County offices, including the College. But Samantha needed to build an alliance with the attorneys and staff at the Triano, Orr and Kula Law firm. She needed to keep up the pretense of having had only a working relationship with County Commissioner Dominic Panichi.

This attorney firm party was a picnic, a classy, catered event with Philadelphia cheese-steak sandwiches, *Rolling Rock* and *Heineken* beer, German potato salad and five different flavors of ice cream, including peppermint candy, founding partner Triano's favorite.

Lawyers, especially from this firm, were not fond of make-your-own-sandwich buffets, cook-your-own wieners or shared buckets of fried chicken. They despised covered dish dinners and needed to presume the firm could afford a swanky affair with hired crews serving plates, refilling drinks and taking out the garbage.

Samantha grabbed a cold *Rolling Rock* and headed for a seat on one of the cushioned lounge chairs arranged in staggered groups adjacent to the volleyball playing area. She was wearing double-knit slacks with a matching plaid jacket and platform heels. All male eyes in the crowd were affixed to her, as she walked with a spirited gait. Most of the female eyes were checking her out as well.

She was about to sit down when she spotted Jack Kula, the College's attorney, and caught his eye. Kula started to move toward her, and Samantha reciprocated toward him, while noticing an attractive young lady following him, as if tethered to his hip.

"Samantha, so glad you decided to come," Jack offered as a greeting. "We need some better volleyball players, so you might get asked to pick a side. Go with *Kula Clowns* if given a choice. We have Bob Kamen on our side, and he's the tallest attorney in the County."

The lawyer remembered his manners and changed the focus. "Do you know Rebecca Campbell from the College," he asked. "She works in the Physical Education Department or is it the Athletics Department," he said with a hint that he might be on to some confusing information.

"Actually, I work for both departments," Rebecca quickly clarified with a chuckle.

"We met at the reception President Kelleher held for me," Samantha interjected, finally placing who the young lady was at the College and with what office. "You work with the coaches and Alan Fox, Department Chairman of Physical Education. You must have your hands full with him, those jock coaches and student-athletes. I admire the success of our programs both on and off the playing fields, and especially what Coach Solly has accomplished in basketball."

"Looks like you've mastered the art of stroking people with compliments," Kula countered. "From years of working with the College, if anyone has her hands full these days it's you, young lady, with those four jerk Vice Presidents and a President who is so fond of change, bombshells and bloodshed. Kelleher doesn't just stir the pot. He turns up the heat and causes it to boil over."

Samantha saw an opportunity to correct a misconception. "The Vice Presidents are highly qualified and enormously productive," she said. "As for President Kelleher, he's easily the brightest person I've ever worked with. He's amazing at pulling rabbits out of a hat. I so admire the way he sees the big picture, the whole picture before he acts."

"As I said, you're good at passing around the praise, even for those who may not deserve it," attorney Jack parried. "I wish you well, but from what I hear you're taking the place by storm."

"Now who's loading on the compliments," Rebecca interjected.

Samantha wanted to change the subject. "You seem a bit young to have your name as a partner and all. I'm impressed."

"Here we go again with the compliments," Jack said. "The Kula name in the firm title is my father, not me. I still have a few years ahead of me to make Partner. Dad started the firm and retired a couple of years ago, though he still does tax work for clients he's had over the years."

Rebecca quickly added, "Jack's modest. He's on a fast-track to partnership and is practically assured of that honor and, to be sure, that income."

Jack was prepared for action in his athletic shorts and Brooks running shoes, so he could star in the volleyball game. His normal business garb was a dark, tailored shirt with a white, pale blue or yellow Gant button-down shirt and Bass Weejun loafers. Kula chose to make his fashion statement with his ties, particularly those that howled and screamed in paisley and broad rep-striped patterns. Yellow, red and purple were his colors of choice.

His mother would hand-sew ties for him, often employing colors and patterns far more suitable for draperies than neckties. She started making them when her son was in Law School. She kept making them even though he could afford the whole collection of ties at K-Mart, even at Brooks Brothers.

The son would wear mom's hand-made ties only when she would be around to see him in his attorney work clothes. Otherwise, they'd be toward the back of his closet. He could not bring himself to tell her to stop making the darn things.

Jack Kula's daily mission was to walk into a room and have the person or persons comment on his colorful, patterned tie, even before greeting him. Most would snicker, shield their eyes from the glare and intentionally avoid a comment. Jack found his ties were a marvelous ice-breaker, and he was comfortable in his appearance and confident of his demeanor.

His colleagues made it a point to gift him overly hideous neckties and bowties, knowing Jack would wear each in the halls of the law office – at least once. He kept a more modest collection of neckwear in his office to exchange if he had to attend a client meeting or a conservative appearance was required.

The much-anticipated, but overly promoted, office volleyball game was about to start. Jack paid his respects to the two ladies, grabbed a good luck kiss from Rebecca and a swig of beer before heading for the makeshift court on the grass field.

There were seven attorneys or clerks on one side. Seven on the other. All male. Jack was the most athletic in the bunch, having starred in baseball, basketball and football at Abington Area High and intramurals at college. But he had inherited the same competitive spirit wrapped in an unwilling and inflexible anti-team resolve.

"These guys have a real problem with their volleyball teams," Rebecca began. "You see there are fourteen players on the court but only the one volleyball. They mean well, but they have no concept of teamwork. It's all about the individual star."

"They all seem like they want to win," offered Samantha, watching the fourteen proxy athletes, respectively, smack the ball into the net or over it and out-of-bounds while grunting with each effort. It reminded her of *Tarzan* pounding his chest as he went from tree to tree in the jungle.

"True, they surely want to win. Each one must win. However, each guy wants to be the star, the stud who spikes the ball for the game-winner and whose photo makes the cover of *Sports Illustrated*."

"Most were the top of their class in law school," Rebecca continued.

"These guys reject basic volleyball strategy – setting-up teammates. They spike the ball from the front line, the back line, or from any line, including the out-of-bounds line. It's rare it ever takes more than two whacks to get the ball back, although not necessarily over the net. Usually, the ball ends up in the food line on a fly or in our face. It's best to stand way back to watch. Be ready to duck!"

"Our women's volleyball coach at the College would go nuts trying to discipline these guys," Rebecca continued. "Ironically, they want to win ever-so badly but not if it means sharing the glory or setting up a teammate. Their egos are considerably bigger than the dumb volleyball."

"Competition is highly individualized in a law firm," Samantha added. "I guess that's why they choose that career. On second thought, perhaps law schools have a required course on the subject: LAW 411. It would be called *Lawyers Always Win*. Those who fail the course, are kicked out."

"How did you like working with the County?" Rebecca asked, once they stopped laughing at their own monologue humor. "Weren't you in the County Commissioner's office?"

"Yes, for the better part of a year, but then this opportunity at the College opened. Mr. Panichi encouraged me to go for it," Samantha advised. She was being exceptionally careful with the words she used, sticking to the script she, Dominic and Kelleher had prepared for these moments.

Later that week, Miss Bartell gave Miss Campbell a call in the middle of the morning. "Rebecca, good morning, this is Samantha. How's your day going so far? Got time for lunch today? My treat. You pick the place. I'll come by and pick you up."

The two ladies bonded almost immediately, sipping tall iced tea from straws in apparent unison, and before they had ordered a corned beef sandwich from the Hightstown Diner. They decided to get one sandwich and one house salad and split the two orders. The corned beef monster was known to be piled high and higher and to defy anyone from being physically able to take a bite of the whole thing.

"How long have you and Jack been dating," Samantha asked her new friend. "I just love his ties, the louder the better, I guess. What a wonderful sign of confidence."

"You jest, Samantha," Rebecca interrupted. "The ties have become his signature fashion statement. I tease him that his necktie preference may keep him from becoming Partner."

"We've been going out for several months now," Rebecca finally said. "We knew of each other in high school. He was a big deal senior. I was a lowly sophomore. You know how that goes. He flirted with me a couple of times, as he did most of the girls, even though he denies it now. He asked me for a dance once at the Senior Prom though I wasn't his date and it was a fast dance. Some other guy cut in before the song finished. The song was *Respect*, by Aretha, if you can believe that. Most of the underclass girls had a crush on him. No, probably all of them."

They laughed at her recall of high school days and the last decade's Rock and Roll classics. Then Rebecca continued. "After high school, I lived for several years in upstate New York before coming back to the area. Had some mother issues, but she died a while ago, and we were at peace. As fate would have it, Jack and I saw each other at this diner one morning. He came over to my table, bringing his coffee and sliding into the booth. Jack asked me out, and here we are."

"What about you? Are you seeing anyone special, Samantha?" Rebecca asked. "As attractive as you are, you must have guys panting in the halls trying to chase you down. Although some might be intimidated by your position, working for the President."

Samantha gave the question, and particularly her answer, some thought. She hesitated to share, even though she had connected with Rebecca. She thought about the rehearsed response to the question, knowing people would be curious or, more likely, nosy. But Samantha decided to skip that one and take a chance to share the truth with Rebecca. She really needed a soul mate.

"Can I count on your confidence, Rebecca?" Samantha pleaded. "I want to share, but this is difficult for me and incredibly personal."

Rebecca put down the half of the sandwich she was nibbling and leaned forward over the table. She looked Samantha in the eyes, smiled and simply said, "Absolutely. I can keep a secret, truly I can."

Samantha sighed, took in a fresh breath of air and blurted, "I'm deeply in love with a married man."

PREVIOUSLY

"Then she took him on."

The President's Secretary, Edith Reynolds, had worked for Dr. Robert Greenleaf for nine years and J. Paul Kelleher now for over two. Describing Greenleaf as laid-back and low-key was akin to saying a turtle runs slowly. But the former President was a hero to Edith. She had cried for days when he departed for St. Louis, in 1974. He had selected her from a slew of candidates. "Best decision I ever made," he told most everyone.

Greenleaf asked Edith to come with him, knowing she would not, given husband Roy's job and her son entering his junior year in high school. He asked her, anyway, knowing Kelleher would be furious.

If President Greenleaf was a turtle, President Kelleher was a barracuda, rapidly paced and with sharp, intimidating teeth, a ferocious attitude and slippery scales. Edith had found the changed work pace fascinating. She did not like the infamous Kelleher outbursts, the occasional foul language and the propensity to challenge people who opposed him. Like the barracuda, Kelleher had few predators, or at least few that cared to show themselves.

Now there was a new boss lady in town, a likely new associate boss, in the person of Samantha Bartell. Bartell was the newly-appointed Executive Assistant to the President and, like Edith, she reported to Kelleher. Some of Edith's responsibilities had shifted to Samantha to be handled at a different level.

Kelleher had told Dean Lieber to relocate the two Planning Associates, funded by Title III and who shared the office at the far end of the hall. He wanted Samantha to be on the same second floor as his office and near the Board Room. Then Kelleher directed that Richard Spurling, Lead Accountant for Vice President Bill Fishman and veteran of the Title III team, move into that vacant, smaller and more distant office.

Those domino moves enabled Samantha to have the office next to the Board Room. Kelleher's dictatorial game of *Musical Chairs* was not lost on the rest of the folks in the Administration Building. Neither was the new office furniture and a posh desk chair that made their way to the Executive Assistant's new office.

The four Vice Presidents were not keen on Miss Bartell's role or her existence. They did not much care what office space she occupied or that she got new furniture. Had there been an option they would have preferred an office at the other end of the campus in a temporary trailer. Better yet, they'd place her desk in the middle of the highway.

Fishman caught Kelleher in the hall one morning while the College's maintenance crew was pretending to be Mayflower Van Line employees, hauling furniture back and forth. "J. Paul, don't you think it might be just as well to put Miss Bartell in the former Title III office at the end of the hall? Let's leave Richard where he is next to my office suite. He's been in that office for seven years."

Fishman had not put up much of a protest. He would readily admit that his half-hearted argument was more to show he backed the irritated Spurling than contemplating reversal of Kelleher's decision. He was right. The President ignored him and kept walking to his office while his voice drifted, the words echoing in the hallway, "Hell no, Bill. Hell no!"

Fishman watched as Kelleher continued down the hall. Then he said to himself, *Just wait, Mr. President. You'll get yours. We'll see to that!*

Edith had always had a tough challenge when preparing the Monthly Agenda Packet that would go to each member of the Board of Trustees. Inevitably, the four Vice Presidents would wait until, or after, the last minute before submitting their written Monthly Reports. Often, they would have spelling and grammar mistakes even in the Board Action Items prepared for the President's signature.

Edith was hesitant to point out errors to these four astute male members of the President's Cabinet, given she was, in their minds, a lowly female in a lowly clerical position. When the Executive Assistant came on board, Samantha now was to review the entire Board Agenda Packet before presenting it to the President for final approval and distribution each month. Edith thought that was terrific.

Samantha had no hesitation in sending recommendations, memos and reports back to the respective Vice President if she found a spelling or grammatical error or a poorly worded sentence. If the logic of the memo escaped her, she was quick to tell the offending VP to redo his manuscript.

Miss Bartell demanded their Monthly Reports get to her a full day earlier. That had been the accepted but ignored practice. Not anymore.

The culprit VP might test Bartell or might complain. He soon learned that if he raised the issue with the President, Samantha would win the skirmish and likely the war. Better just to do the job right or redo it. Better to lay in the weeds for an opportunity to browbeat and embarrass the young lady later. There would be ways to retaliate.

Edith gave Samantha all the credit for the behavior modifications. Not only was the everyday work better but Kelleher's daylong disposition was as well. Edith took charge to point out discrepancies, knowing Samantha would support her.

Edith controlled the President's calendar, and now Samantha coordinated it. Miss Bartell would make notations in red ink to signify *High Importance* within each division folder. She would use green ink notes for items she judged as of *Modest Importance*. And she would apply blue ink for *Who Cares Really* and for *Read It at Home If You Ever Have the Time*. Kelleher eventually got to all the items, but the blue ones piled up for cursory reads on weekends or got pushed into the vertical file – the wastebasket.

The *High Importance* items were read that evening, if not over quiet time in the office, and usually while sipping some Irish Whiskey after most everyone else had left for the day.

Each Vice President would have to check with Samantha before he could get on Kelleher's agenda, even though Edith kept the President's working calendar. It didn't take Samantha long to be able to rate the relative urgency of each petition. If Dandridge had to see the President, she pretty much could accept he needed to. If Fishman wanted time with Kelleher, and it was about the budget, he would get it that day; if not about the budget, much later in the week.

"That bastard," Fishman spurted at Spurling one morning over coffee. "He has me waiting to see him until the bitch in the skirt blesses my agenda. Can't take this much longer."

"There are ways to handle this, Bill," responded Spurling. "I can get with some of my organization contacts and see what can be done, if you want."

If Purdy pressed her for a meeting with Kelleher, she could usually ignore it. Student Affairs had earned the lowest priority for the President's time.

Then there was Donald L. Winters. He was selective and didn't want to meet with Kelleher at any time, even for his pre-scheduled monthly meeting in preparation for the Board agenda. Winters loathed having to make his request to an Executive Assistant, a woman, worse even a young woman, and wait for a supreme ruling from her.

When Winters petitioned Samantha to meet with the President, she chose to comply. Samantha had dismissed the notion that Winters was just playing her. She internalized that his spite for her position was genuine and his growing animosity unmistakable. So, she tried to meet him halfway except when he crept into ignorant, disturbing chauvinism or tried to bully her.

Then she took him on.

PREVIOUSLY

"Let me check my calendar."

The Winters-Bartell relationship worsened when Samantha Bartell began work with Gene Wildwood in the Computer Center to install a software program she obtained through Title III. The innovative software program enabled the College to run various models for class enrollments and faculty assignment distributions. One could then input variables to see the consequences of simulated decisions.

As a crusty, long-time academic vice president, Winters was of the tenacious opinion that adjunct faculty should be employed and deployed on a *Supply Side* model. That is, if he had adjuncts in History, he would assign them to individual sections, even if other faculty staffing combinations might be more efficient.

The computer simulation model enabled *Demand Side* economics. Samantha could determine an optimum percentage of adjunct versus full-time faculty in each discipline, each course array within a discipline and each department, unit and division. That analytical capability was unheard of and monumental.

Winters wanted to rely on his experience and professional judgment, and that of his Division Deans, to make faculty assignments and determine section/course maximum and minimum enrollments. That was how he had operated since his appointment in 1962. Samantha's model enabled staff to determine optimum configurations, not rely on historical guesses, however experienced.

Dr. Dandridge loved what the model enabled as well as the empirical analyses when the computer programming was added. Samantha knew her work had solidified her acceptance by one Vice President and hardened the mounting hatred of another. She had no interest in keeping score, and Kelleher had no sympathy for score-keeping.

President J. Paul Kelleher praised her work with the simulation efficiency model too, thereby further wounding Winters' deteriorating pride. Edith marveled at how Samantha handled herself in the meetings of the President's Cabinet. Samantha did not get a vote. She did not need one. Her arguments for or against a decision were cogent, researched and persuasive. During a debate, she could take and hold a position on a par with any Vice President.

More importantly, when Samantha Bartell spoke, Kelleher listened. He might well ignore the other arguments while puffing on his *Marlboros* and fiddling with his *Cross* pen.

Besides, everyone knew votes in the Cabinet meetings did not mean much. President Kelleher would overrule the decision, or support it, when back in his office, and Samantha had access to Kelleher anytime she wanted. She just had to get a nod of approval from Edith that the President was in his office and then a slight knock on his door.

Samantha Bartell was becoming used to Kelleher's manner of getting dressed each day. She became less and less embarrassed that he'd have his shirt untucked and his pants on but his fly unzipped. She reasoned that his shoe-shining habit was a way to focus his mind. He never shined his shoes when he was alone, or at least she had never caught him doing so. She wondered if he ever did.

Winters became more belligerent with each meeting, but he was also becoming more defeated and more crushed with each decision. He had begun to jump on his Vice President colleagues for not supporting his adverse arguments and criticisms. After all, he was the granddaddy administrator and expected filial piety to include respect for the eldest VP.

It seemed that if Kelleher wanted to go to the right, Winters preferred going left. If Winters chose black, Kelleher adopted white. Life was falling hard on him, like raindrops in a storm splattering the bare heads of pedestrians. Winters had no umbrella or way to gain cover from the storm. He could not let go that he had lost the presidency.

Vice Presidents Fishman, Purdy and Dandridge were beginning to understand the new mode of operation and that a retreat or reversion was not likely. Winters had no desire to understand. He hardly cared anymore, at least on the outside. On the inside, there was a scheme taking shape.

Samantha had not habitually smoked until she started working at the College and had to endure the President's incessant nicotine habit. Out of self-defense, nerves or as a strategic move to bind with J. Paul, she started to smoke *Virginia Slims 120 Lights*.

Virginia Slims was the *You've come a long way baby* cigarette for women, marketed just a few years previously and patterned after *Benson & Hedges*. The smoke was narrower and longer than the standard king-sized version and with a more elegant appearance that caught the attention of women. The pack was fashionable, with a glossy white background and bold vertical line piping. The ads featured classy and stylishly dressed women, not cowboys riding horses in the snow or a camel standing in the sand with pyramids and palm trees.

Kelleher mocked her *Virginia Slim* cigarettes as the same brand his wife, Izzy, smoked and as too skinny. He held up his filtered manly-man *Marlboros* as the ultimate smoke.

Like his Italian pals, who gathered once a month for an Italian men-only roasted chicken dinner, Dominic Panichi, Samantha's hush-hush lover, smoked an occasional cigar. Dominic was not thrilled with Samantha's *Virginia Slims* behavior modification but figured he was part of the reason for the new habit. Samantha did not object to the Men-Only Dinner or the custom of downing a few straight shots of 80-proof *Italian Strega*. She thought the whole thing was akin to a fraternity party without dates.

Samantha had remembered that her father and grandfather went to those roast chicken, Italian booze and fat cigar dinners, too. She had understood that drinking the liqueur in the tall, thin-throated yellow bottle with its seventy-odd herbs was an Italian rite of passage.

Grandfather had said the high-proof drink aided digestion. Samantha would ask, "Well what did you eat that you needed help with the digestion?" She didn't expect an answer. She never got one.

Edith Reynolds knew Samantha had previously worked at the County Offices, and for the County Commissioner. She was unaware of any personal relationship between Panichi and Bartell. She would occasionally hear hall gossip, but she was not inclined to lend any credence to same, on any matter or person. Confidentiality was the hallmark of her job and her personality.

Dominic and Samantha rarely phoned each other at the offices and never met for lunch. It was hard, but Dominic refrained from his reference to Samantha as Cutie Marks. Every time he thought about her, those adorable freckles came to mind.

When the County Commissioner and the Executive Assistant to the President did have a meeting, it was strictly within the confines of College-County business. There were no flirtations or lingering sweet-talk conversations. In the privacy of their respective residences, there were plenty of cold showers and frequent tears.

Dominic's County office usually cleared out by 5:30 PM. Typically, Samantha closed the President's Office about the same time. If Kelleher worked late, he didn't know she was camped out in her office on a personal call. The departure disparity created a tolerable time in which she could safely call her love before he left to go home each evening. Unless, he was able to stop by her apartment on the way home.

Samantha always had a bogus, if semi-legitimate, back up justification for calling the County, if, by chance, someone else answered the Commissioner's phone. "Oh hello, this is the President's Office at Central Jersey Community College. President Kelleher would like to get on the Commissioner's calendar."

The deceptive conversations and evasive games were beginning to be intolerable. Something would have to be done.

Edith Reynolds continued her administrative work for *Dave Russell's All-Star Basketball Camp* in the Poconos. She loved the focus on young male and female athletes and appreciated the extra money. But she really enjoyed the benefit of taking her family to the mountains several weekends during the year to stay at Russell's log construction mini-mansion.

She had told Samantha she'd invite her for a weekend in late summer or fall. "Let me check my calendar – thanks for the invite," was Samantha's rehearsed response. She'd have to pick a weekend when Dominic could not get away and going to the Poconos with friends would beat staying at home alone.

Samantha had known Kelleher was not pleased that Edith worked with Coach Solly. He was less than thrilled with the basketball camp and annoyed with the man. Weekends were precious times for her, trying to balance a clandestine relationship. She could count on a few hours of private, alone time with Dominic without undercover maneuvers to avoid the neighbors and every other Monroe County citizen.

The invitation to the Poconos cemented the feeling that she and Edith were mutually supportive and developing a close office alliance. Everyone saw it and appreciated it, except the four cynics from the President's Cabinet.

PREVIOUSLY

"Of course, that would be conditional on coming by my apartment one evening."

Alan Fox had served in Vietnam as an Army helicopter pilot. The U.S. started using helicopters in warfare during World War II, but choppers were heavily relied upon in Vietnam. They transported personnel throughout the war zone and provided firepower. Fox's work was to resupply troops on the ground and evacuate wounded Americans and South Vietnamese. He was co-pilot on the UH-1 Iroquois helicopter, commonly known as a *Huey*.

Like many other military personnel, Fox met and socialized with South Vietnamese women in brothels and as casual relationships. Thousands of American servicemen fathered children with Vietnamese women during the long Southeast Asian war. These children faced enormous discrimination in their home country and severe complications in attempting to unite with their American fathers.

Fox had met Ngoc Anh in Saigon where she had worked as a waitress and a self-dependent, short-order-cook at a military club. Ngoc Anh was slim, flawlessly pretty and pertly feminine, with long black hair. She would wear her hair in a bun at work and softly draped over her shoulders when she wasn't working.

Anh was looking for a soulmate to enjoy life together and to cuddle passionately as the war wore down. Fox was looking for an escape from the war and to cuddle carnally as the days grew longer and the war persisted.

Miss Anh was an exceptional cook. Had she been a man, she would have been a chef. She and Fox spent evenings, when the pilot was on leave, sampling her native cuisine and delving into American recipes. She dismissed sex with Fox for a while, except for heavy petting and oral pleasures. But Fox was robust, persistent and seductive. Then their physical desires became insatiable.

Shortly before his discharge, Anh got pregnant. The out-of-wedlock child was immediately accepted and surprisingly embraced by Anh's extended family, despite the social ridicule.

Alan Fox was a young man, only 21 when he started his *Huey* helicopter duty. He was 23 when his term of duty ended in 1969, and the Army discharged him. His departure coincided with the war's decline and major troop withdrawals ordered by President Richard Nixon.

When Fox returned to the U.S., he found little sympathy and less support from his neighbors in Toledo where he had grown up and where his parents lived. Many people associated servicemen with war atrocities including revelations about civilian rapes and killings.

Fox used his GI Bill benefits and enrolled at the University of Toledo to complete the bachelor's degree he had started before being drafted. With his eligible military credits, he then completed a master's in Physical Education.

While still living in Toledo, Fox had tried to return to Vietnam or bring Ngoc Anh and the child to the U.S. He was not successful. He chose not to marry her.

Miss Anh received child support from Fox for several years. She stopped returning his letters when he quit trying to reunite them and immersed himself in other female escapades. The payments dwindled in both amount and timeliness.

To escape the indignity and growing outrage from his Vietnamese war service and the guilt of his fatherhood, Fox had moved to Trenton, New Jersey. He had gotten a position at Hightstown Community College as an instructor in Physical Education and as coach of the men's and women's tennis and soccer teams.

In 1975, the Athletics Director position had opened at Central Jersey Community College. Fox got the job, partly due to recognition of his military background, the advanced degree and his willingness to teach Physical Education courses and manage athletics too.

Alan Fox had three passions, with sports being a distant third to his first two choices. He cherished his 1974 Chevrolet Custom Coupe Impala, including a 350-cubic inch V-8 engine, rear fender skirts, dual exhaust and grillwork. He added radial tires to the yellow machine and dubbed his prize possession as his *Yellow Hornet*. The two-door sports coupe cost him $3,519 and was kept highly polished and unmistakably cool.

Fox's first passion was, undoubtedly, women. Having distanced himself from his Vietnamese mistress and mother of his child, he liked to frequent bars, dressed in his leisure suits complemented by the gold chain and wide collar shirts. He was not much interested in casual encounters. Rather, Fox coveted the energy he absorbed from charming women and practicing his macho moves and chick flirtation skills.

In college, Fox had polished his finesse on coeds and on the younger female instructors – the former to score, the latter to tease. Many a young female college student received her introduction to sex from the womanizer. His dorm roommate marveled at Fox's stamina. When asked about his amorous adventures, Fox would say, "I can't leave flowering buds to some awkward, pimply teenage guy and risk the girl being traumatized for life."

To be sure, the second passion – the Chevy Impala – was connected to his first one. Fox's *Yellow Hornet* was heralded by him as a visible sign of his macho persona and conquest. Had he been in the Wild, Wild West he would have had notches in the fender, rather than his gun, to signify his scores.

Fox liked to drive the classy car around the road circling the CJCC campus, revving his engine and downshifting. He would let his left arm hang out of the window, no matter what the weather. He maintained a collection of 8-track cartridges to play in the car, rotating Captain & Tennille, Frankie Valli and Neil Sedaka hits until the magnetic tape got jammed or failed to rewind.

He kept a similar stash in his apartment with high fidelity amplification. He had arranged the 8-tracks by mood, not by performer – Relaxation, Temptation, Inducement, Seduction and Final Conquest. The stash was next to his favorite lava lamp, a blue one, that rotated.

His colleagues in the Physical Education & Athletics Department teased him about being a bachelor and having a hot car to chase the ladies. When they would comment, his response was, "You ain't just woofing."

Alan had flirted with Rebecca Campbell when she was hired. She had repelled him. Fox stopped hitting on her but did not cease his chauvinistic cracks. He once said to a colleague that she was built like a brick house. Rebecca elbowed him sharply in the stomach on her way out the door that day.

When Rebecca started to date attorney Jack Kula, Fox's dreadful endeavors stopped immediately. Partly that was due to this impressive man now in Rebecca's life. Partly it was due to Fox's revelation regarding other ladies to pursue. There was a more fertile source for his amorous pursuits, his wandering eyes and roving hands.

While Fox enjoyed the intimacy, what appealed to him most was the conquest. If he did not score with a woman, he merely re-evaluated his techniques. He thought like a door-to-door *Fuller Brush* salesman who accepts rejection as merely a closer step to a successful sale.

Unlike most universities, community colleges have varied ages of students, both male and female. The institutions appeal to women other than 18-year-old gals who enroll straight from high school. More commonly, a community college has classes dominated by women in their mid-to-late twenties, thirties and older. Many have children; some have grandchildren. These women have had jobs, careers and varied experiences in higher education.

Many CJCC students were single moms trying to get an education in pursuit of a higher quality of life. Consequently, Alan Fox's playing field was not the gym, swimming pool or athletic grounds. His conquering field was no longer local bars, bowling alleys and dancing joints. The targets were the many returning-to-college females in the classes he taught.

Some of the female students were guilelessly vulnerable to his looks and swagger. Others relented to his repeated banter about getting together after class and taking a ride in his yellow Camaro. His neatly trimmed mustache, long sideburns and over-the-ears dark hair were dashing.

Single ladies, and even a few married ones, could not help being attracted to a good-looking professor who showed romance potential. Every class he taught for each new semester provided a pool of conceivable, gullible partners.

Fox found that some women in his classes were looking for indiscriminate romance. They could separate sexual intimacy from emotional connection. The counterculture left over from the 1960's had proffered promiscuity without social or legal restraints, even within marriage. Still, those women were a challenge to separate from the flock, lasso and corral. Fox thrived on the challenge, fully aware of his leverage.

Based on the mid-1960's Civil Rights legislation, instances of sexual harassment in the workplace were fully directed at employment and job advancement. The law did not address males pressuring females through unwanted sexual advances in college classrooms or faculty offices.

There was no normative standard for how a male professor might choose to act and proposition female students. There were no policies within colleges regarding what leverage he might employ to hit on the women. CJCC had no policy restricting, let alone defining, appropriate classroom behavior.

That would come many years later. For now, Fox was free to pursue his intimidating onslaught on women.

Alan Fox taught the *Introduction to Physical Education* and the *Personal Fitness & Conditioning* courses. Each class attracted 40 or more students, with over 50% being women of various ages. Fox used subtle come-on techniques early in the semester.

As the semester wore on and grade anxiety grew, Fox branched out to more overt invitations for dates. He had mastered the art of seduction, knowing when to back off a woman and when to press onward.

"Miss Jones," Fox would say, changing the name to fit the lady but with the same approach, "I think you'd benefit from direct tutoring. I'd be glad to provide some help for you. We can meet in my office after 5 PM and study for a while. Then we can go and have a drink or two, relax and get to know each other better. How does that sound?"

As the semester neared an end, with term papers to be graded and final exams yet administered, the approach would change. "Miss Smith, I see you have a solid B average going into the final exam. If you do well on your final, I might be able to give you an A for your grade. You'd like that. Perhaps there's a way I can help you prepare and maybe even provide some hints as to the exam questions. Of course, that would be conditional on coming by my apartment one evening. Then we can get to know each other better."

Fox's appeal, even with his ill-favored leisure suits, as well as his degree, position, car and gallant prowess, landed him at least one encounter per class, per semester. He might even have a couple of former students left over from the prior semester he could continue to chase.

Fox was hero-worshiped by most students, male and female. He thought of himself as a macho deity, put on this earth to befriend and indulge women and be an exemplary role model for men.

His colleagues were aware that Fox dated students, but they chose not to interfere. After all, Fox was not married, and the women were adults. He never hit on the young, right-out-of-high-school ones or those much older than he was. If the woman wore a wedding ring, that did not necessarily preclude his maneuvers, unless accompanied by the stern statement, "Mr. Fox, I'm very happily married."

Given his well-deserved reputation, the coaches decided never to sit on the couch in Fox's office, as did some of the student-athletes. They knew his posted office-hours took on a different meaning if the lights were out in the room.

For female students, Fox's pressured invitations were considered a huge compliment and an opportunity for a relationship – something to be valued and appreciated. If the vulnerable young woman summarily rejected the suggestion, she could be assured of the lower grade, no matter how well she did on the term paper and final.

Athletics Director Alan Fox fancied himself as a lady's man. He employed every amorous technique in the book once he corralled a woman into his office or his apartment. If she resisted, he would try another move. If that one failed, he would try another. But if she continued to resist or attempted to leave, Fox would be forceful in demanding at least an oral sexual favor. If a student accepted Fox's invitation, she knew sexual intimacy was the expectation.

Alan Fox never approached what could be called rape or forcible sexual relations. He was careful to assure any act was consensual, more or less, though he would pressure the students by his grade intimidation and overbearing presence.

But he was not subtle, either. "You sure you don't want to stay a little longer? Your final exam's coming in a few weeks."

PREVIOUSLY

"I give a damn what the faculty think of me."

Izzy Kelleher was firm in confronting her husband, J. Paul. "Our son simply wants to go with another first name. He does not like Ian and wants to be called Jim. His buddies make fun of his name. Don't try to convince him that Ian is a wonderful Irish name. You can't take on the kid's peer group."

They were seated in the den, finishing up their morning coffee and dueling with smoke from J. Paul's manly *Marlboro* cigarettes versus Izzy's sleek *Virginia Slims*. The *Marlboro Man* put out a more extensive fog. The *Slims* woman had a more rapid cadence.

"It's just a phase the kid's going through," argued her husband. "Just because his buddies are all Mike, Bob, Joe, Dave or Bill does not mean Ian has to have a similarly monotonous or shallow name. Ian was my grandfather's name. It's a damn honor for him. The name means *God is Gracious*. That's special, Izzy. Just like his brother, Connor."

"While we're at it," Izzy continued with intentional interruption. "Why did you call the guy at New Mexico University and kill the opportunity for Coach Solly to go there? What a lousy thing to do. How did you even know he was under consideration? You may not care for the guy, and I know you dislike college athletics, but this was his big chance."

A chagrined J. Paul explained. "Roseanne told me. I want to know whenever she comes across an employee seeking a job at another college. I called to support his move, not screw it up. And it's Southern New Mexico State. Big deal. I poured accolades on the guy for his coaching. Hell, you know I would want him to leave so that we can decide the future of Intercollegiate Athletics here."

"Bull shit," Izzy said. "The AD and coach were together in wanting to give the position to Solly. You got your retribution. Instead of honoring him for his coaching and getting the College to the final championship game, you pulled the rug out from under him. You yanked it all the way out."

"Bull shit is right," J. Paul responded. "Izzy, I don't think they were honest with Solly. The AD wanted this former player to get the job. My guess is that their coach caved and didn't have the balls to be honest with Solly."

The confrontation had now escalated to a combination of yelling and badgering. J. Paul walked from the den into the master bedroom, with Izzy trailing him, her arms swinging defiantly.

"Why the hell do you care, anyway?" the husband yelled, the queen-sized bed acting as a barrier to heightened verbal or physical collisions. "You see him at the YMCA, you told me, and at some College functions, but since when are you in his corner? How did you even know he didn't get the coaching job? I sure didn't know until Roseanne told me."

Ignoring the accusation, the wife countered. "Just because you're President does not mean you can't care about people. Why do you want chaos on the campus and among staff?"

"I give a damn what the faculty think of me. Being President is not a popularity contest, Izzy. I stir things up on campus because that motivates people, gets them out of their comfort zone. God knows how complacent they've been in the past. Winters hasn't done anything constructive in years. Lieber copies one proposal and submits it to a different funding source, with the crap thick enough to scrape. Then he gets kickbacks from the lab equipment company. God knows what else!"

Izzy got tired of standing. She sat down on the edge of the bed, her arms folded to ward off more of her husband's outbursts.

"Izzy, if Solly didn't get the offer, then someone at that university is not telling the truth. Someone wanted the other guy to get the job. If I am blamed for him not getting the coaching job, so be it. But it was not me."

"My Computer Center Director is a drunk." J. Paul continued. "My Board Vice Chairman hates faculty, and the County Commissioner wants more favors. Solly works on his summer camp most of the year and gets his players through class by cheating. And as for the faculty, and Sally Bowens, let them fly helium rats all they want. That's all in-line with my job description. All comes with the territory. Somedays it feels like I'm trying to drink from a firehose or piss into a hurricane."

J. Paul coughed again, this time in a repeated manner. "Besides," he said. "I can't get rid of this damn cough and these shitty headaches. My arm tingles too. Yesterday, I almost fell in the office I got so dizzy from the headaches. Am I getting that old now? Are the *Marlboros* finally getting to me?"

Kelleher walked toward the bedroom windows and looked out over the backyard where Cerberus was patrolling. Then he turned back to look at his wife to continue listing bad behaviors.

"I found out Lieber has been accepting payments and gifts," J. Paul said. "They're like bribes – Broadway tickets, wine, photography stuff – from the company that outfitted the Media Center with Title III funds. He must think I'm stupid. What would you want me to do with that information?"

Izzy was empathetic with her husband's plight regarding his health. She sensed the headaches were not a result of smoking. He would occasionally slur words and have trouble sleeping. But she was not sympathetic to him about the staff and their alleged transgressions. She thought a moment and then foretold, "Everyone cheats if the stakes are high enough."

The momentary silence and standoff were disturbed by a muted knock at the door. "You guys OK," said Ian. The interruption did not solve any disagreement or lighten the mood. It did force a timeout.

They opened the door, and Ian ran into the room. Tears were rolling down his face. "Mom, dad, I don't want you fighting over my stupid name," Ian whimpered.

At dinner, when it was dessert time, J. Paul went to the pantry rather than accept the fresh bakery blueberry pie. There had not been much conversation at dinner. The tension was hanging in the air. Kelleher seized a can of *Dole* pineapple slices from the pantry shelf, returned to the table and slowly opened the can with a hand-cranking opener.

Izzy, Connor and Ian had gotten used to this maneuver and the crude manner Kelleher chose to devour the sugary pineapple slices, holding up a circular slice on a fork and biting off pieces.

Izzy had to say something. "We have a delicious pie from the bakery. Why in the hell do you choose canned pineapple? And why do you eat the stuff right out of the can? Can't you put them in a damn dish?"

"I don't know why I need to apologize for eating canned pineapple," her husband barked. "Life's little pleasures, you know. When's the last time you baked a pie?"

Izzy got up from the table and walked to the screened porch, noticeably upset. It was not Ian's name or Solly's fouled-up coaching position. It was not the overly sweet pineapple slices being eaten by her husband out of a tin can or even his insensitive comment about her baking skills.

It was feathery kisses by Ella that had her flustered and confused. She had not pulled away when Ella held her momentarily. She did not resent the gentle stroking of her arms or the touch of Ella's hands as she caressed her neck and shoulders.

Yet, Izzy had not returned the look of seduction and had appreciated that Ella chose to unwind the affection.

"Izzy this is marvelous," Ella had said softly. "You're so lovely and sweet. But, you need to be ready for intimacy. You need to have thought it through and be fully comfortable. It's not my intent to rush things, let alone mess up a friendship. I don't believe in quickie interludes. Certainly not any pressure. Give it more time, much more time. Be sure, Izzy, that it's right for you."

Izzy left the porch. She wandered out to the yard only to have Cerberus dash over to her side, tail wagging and tongue flopping. She retrieved her floral cigarette case and pulled out another *Virginia Slims*.

Izzy had concluded she was not going to respond to her sensitive feelings about lesbian expression. She had other thoughts: *Could I avoid acting on my thoughts about marriage? Could I continue being married? What would it take to turn things around? Was it his fault or my problem?*

Izzy bent down and stroked the German Shepherd. "Cerberus, I'm pretty sure I prefer men, male touch and hardness over female warmth and tenderness. Pauly is one of a few men I've been with. Sometimes that attraction seeps away. We need to get our relationship back on track or go separate ways. He's a good man, Cerberus. But to tell you're the truth, I'm not sure I need a man. But, I do need my dog."

J. Paul opened the door into the yard and ambled toward his wife and his dog, "You alright?" he asked. "I don't know what to say about the pineapple. It was dumb of me to mock you for not baking the pie. Who cares? When was the last time I baked anything? You cooked a fine dinner. You always do, Izzy. I don't know how you do all you do, plus put up with me."

Izzy stood up and faced her husband. "Pauly, it's not about baking a pie. We have more of a roommate arrangement these days than a marriage. You know that as well as I do. You're more and more wrapped up in the College, while I have other interests – my teaching, my colleagues, the boys, racquetball. More and more, we make love out of habit, the few times a month we do have sex."

J. Paul was a little bewildered. He had not expected a full-frontal assault in the middle of the backyard. His coughing continued to the point where he cleared some phlegm, spitting on the ground and convulsing momentarily until his throat cleared.

Izzy was not finished. "We catch up on weekends but with abbreviated news highlights, frequent weather updates and newsy bulletins on the boys – not meaningful conversations. These are bites of our lives. We only have our boys, this house, our dog and smoking in common anymore. When was the last time we went away together, with or without the boys?"

Izzy could see in her husband's eyes that he was paying attention. "Pauly, we've each talked about a divorce, just at different times and different points.

We may need to talk about it at the same time, now that the boys are older and could probably handle it. But that's not what I really want."

Izzy got that out of her system and looked concerned, as she was worried about her husband's health. "That cough's getting worse," she said. "I can see you suffering from the headaches. You need to cut back on the cigarettes and see Dr. Feldman. Don't be a stubborn Irishman. Do it for the boys, if not for yourself or me. See what it is."

"Is that what you want, Izzy," the frustrated and begrudged husband asked, trying to sound compassionate when he felt ambushed. "A separation or divorce, I mean? I sure don't. How about we go away someplace for a while? The two of us. A long weekend. Maybe New York or Philly."

"Pauly, I don't know if getting away is the answer," Izzy stated. "I know you're not feeling well lately but this has to stop."

J. Paul looked at his wife as if there were doom in her eyes. "Shall I just go away?" he said.

"We have to dig down into our relationship and reconstitute it," Izzy replied. "Perhaps we should get marriage counseling. Maybe talk with Reverend Bender."

"I've been thinking Izzy and hope you agree," J. Paul proclaimed as if he had suddenly switched to a new TV channel. "We should let Ian go with the name Jim. It will be good for him. After all, I never liked and never used my first name, Jacob. Few people even know what the J. stands for. Why shouldn't Ian adopt a preferred name."

There was a long moment of silence. Cerberus had dropped to the ground and started to whimper for lack of attention. Izzy turned her head away, closing her eyes and finally putting the *Virginia Slims* cigarette to her lips as she fumbled in her pocket for her lighter. She lit the smoke and inhaled deeply.

The silence was broken when J. Paul asked, "Are you sleeping with that damn basketball coach?"

Izzy turned away just before her husband asked a follow-up question, "Are you jumping the bones of that lesbian gal from the Y?"

PREVIOUSLY

"I think they're going to fire me."

Gene Wildwood walked meekly into the Computer Center on Monday morning. He was running late. This was two days after he had visited Candace at her townhouse offering donuts and passion in exchange for coffee and her yellow nightgown with the buttercup flowers and floral lace.

He dashed from the parking lot along the walkway and up the stairs to the second floor *Meat Locker*. Slightly out of breath, he looked at the lady in the green sweater behind the desk and greeted her. "Sorry I'm a bit late this morning, Candace. Traffic was bad. How was your weekend?"

"Not a problem," Candace responded. "Howard got here early, and everyone else is doing their thing from what I can tell. No fires to put out. No angry calls from Kelleher or Dandridge. My weekend was fine, at least Saturday. Bob didn't get back home until late Sunday, but he had a productive trip apparently."

Gene went closer to the desk and lowered his voice to a whisper. "Candace, or should I say *Carol*, I really enjoyed our time together. You're amazing. Again, I apologize for my early response, way too early, but that doesn't take away from how fantastic you were. Hopefully, I can make it up to you."

Candace looked up at Gene. She smiled as if to say, *No harm, no foul.* As Gene reached for the door to his office and the behemoth computer, she interrupted him, "I'd love that to happen. Let's see how the week goes, *Ted*."

Gene pulled open the door and signaled with a bow that he was grateful. He couldn't help but notice her nipples protruding again from the snug fitting sweater. The gum drops were showing – they bothered him even more than usual. Then he said, "By the way, *Carol*, I went shopping yesterday. Got a few pair of those *Jockey* briefs."

Gene chuckled at his attempt at morning humor and his good fortune to know this lovely woman. He waved at the Programmers and peeked into Howard Tucker's office. Normally the door would be ajar. Open enough, so people would know he was there. Closed sufficiently to hide his habit. Today the door was wide open, and Howard was seated behind his desk.

The Computer Center Director gestured for Gene to come in. "Let me get a cup of coffee first," Gene said. "I'll be right there, Howard." He could not help noticing that Howard did not look well. The guy's hands were shaking. He was sweating even in the frigid *Meat Locker* temperature.

After he had coffee in hand, Gene ventured into Howard's office and took a seat, his attention fixed on his boss.

"Hey Gene," Howard offered, visibly trembling but trying to remain stoic. "Did you have a good weekend? You and Alice go anyplace?"

"What's going on, Howard?" Gene asked, coming to grips that Howard was not acting normal and something had happened or was about to happen.

"I just got a call from Roseanne Hart. She said she needed to come over and see me. She wanted to be sure I was in the office. When I asked her what for, she hung up the phone on me."

"Well, so what," Gene responded, trying to sound unalarmed when he wasn't. "What's the big deal?"

"I think they're going to fire me," Howard divulged. "They already had me take that forced leave last month."

"Then chew up a few more of those peppermint candies and throw those damn *Dixie Cups* in the trash," Gene bellowed as he turned to face the door and heard the approaching sets of footsteps.

Personnel Director Hart and Attorney Jack Kula were walking in step toward the door. They were on a mission. They were not smiling.

"Good morning, Howard," Roseanne said. "Gene, would you excuse us, please. We need to talk with Howard."

Gene walked from the office, closing the door ever so slowly, while offering a hopeful but worried smile in the direction of his boss.

"Can I get both of you a cup of coffee," Howard offered, more to break the mood than to be hospitable. It was like providing the executioner a sandwich before he pulled the rope to hang the accused from the gallows.

"Mr. Tucker, I think you know Jack Kula, our attorney with Triano, Orr and Kula," Miss Hart began, dismissing the coffee invitation and getting right to the business at hand. "Dr. Dandridge is out of town and thus could not be here. Mr. Kula and I are here to deliver this Letter of Termination to you. You are welcome to read it, of course, and ask us questions if you like."

The letter was signed, "J. Paul Kelleher, President" and dated that day. It began with the phrase of *I regret to inform you* and stated that Mr. Tucker was to be *relieved of duty* as Computer Center Director:

This action was necessary due to your repeated violation of the College's moral turpitude provision and your expression of depravity on campus with repeated use of alcohol, thereby revoking your license as a computer professional.

This College cannot tolerate such behavior from one of its employees, let alone a high-level administrator.

This letter of termination will be placed in the Confidential Section of your Personnel File and made available to others only upon written request to, and approved by, the President or by you. The remainder of the file will be available to anyone asking for a history of your performance at the College, should you choose to seek other employment now or in the future.

I have regretfully reached the conclusion that said action was and is in the best interests of the College. I wish you well in all your future endeavors.

Kula looked at Howard as he was reviewing the letter. When Howard had read the entire document, Kula continued. "Mr. Tucker, it will be necessary for you to vacate this office. We will allow you 30 minutes to retrieve your personal belongings. A Security Guard will stand by the door to enable privacy and escort you from the office and the campus after you have collected your things."

Kula opened his folder and read the following information, after first acknowledging for the record that Howard Tucker was present and Miss Hart a witness:

Be advised, you have the right to request an appeal hearing before the President of the College about these allegations and your termination. You may bring an attorney to the meeting at your expense and if you so choose.

You will be paid through the end of this month. In addition, you are entitled to receive payment for all accrued and unused vacation days and up to one-half of all unused sick leave days. We calculate you have 12 days remaining of unused vacation days, and one-half of the accumulated 20 sick days would amount to an additional 10 leave days. Therefore, you have accumulated 22 days as of this date, for which you will be properly compensated.

Furthermore, given that you are previously vested in the employee retirement system for the State of New Jersey, given your past years of employment, you are entitled to receive full retirement benefits upon reaching retirement age. Alternatively, you may choose to receive all or a portion of the cash value of the plan before retirement. Personnel will assist you in determining said amounts and clarifying your options.

Looking up from the document, and handing over a copy, Mr. Kula addressed Howard as if in a court of law. "Do you, Howard Tucker, understand the contents of the letter from the President and of this document which I have read and now henceforth provide a copy to you for your record?"

Howard Tucker's mind was on the end of the President's letter where he stated that he had "regretfully reached the conclusion that said action was in the *best interests* of the College." How could termination of a long-term employee be in the *best interests* of anyone, he thought.

Howard jumped back into reality, his eyes watering and staring at the small stack of *Dixie Cups* balanced on the corner of his desk. Ironically, he had filled his coffee cup with drinking water from the breakroom water cooler. Today was another of the many days in which he vowed no more gin. Or at least not this early.

"Yes, Mr. Kula, I understand, even though I think this is grossly unfair and unwarranted. The production of this Computer Center is what should be weighed and what I've accomplished as Director."

With tears in his eyes, already red from a hangover, Howard said, "Mr. Kula, can I resign instead? Can I have that option to avoid this termination?"

Kula was prepared for such an inquiry. "Mr. Tucker, you have worked for this College for many years. President Kelleher has given me his approval to enable you to resign from your position, assuming you choose to do so at this moment and without lingering."

Howard looked at Roseanne who was reaching for a second document. She handed it to Mr. Tucker and said, "Howard this is a draft of a Letter of Resignation, if you want to sign this. Or, if you choose, you can write your letter, but you will need to do so in the next several minutes."

Howard, feeling ashamed and betrayed, took the letter, read it over quickly and signed it. He knew he was far better off to resign than be fired. Kelleher's scary termination letter would not go into his personnel file.

But Howard had a question for the pair he had to blurt out. "Since when is drinking a reason to fire someone? Lots of people have booze in their offices, including the President."

Attorney Kula jumped to beat Hart to a reply. "Mr. Tucker, we all know your drinking is beyond excessive and a topic for conversation across the campus. You were advised to quit drinking and given time to change. Your past evaluation also advised you to change your behaviors. You were adequately warned."

Truly not looking for any response, Jack Kula said in his best *attorney-doesn't-give-a-shit* voice. "Miss Hart and I will leave you now. A Security Guard will be here momentarily to escort you to your car. Thank you, sir, and best wishes to you in the future. Should you desire to see Miss Hart, you may do so after today and given that it is now best for you to leave the campus."

Everything had come to a halt in the *Meat Locker*. The mainframe computer was spinning, but no input programs were in place. The Programmers were huddled together whispering opinions of what was going on in Howard's office. Gene and Candace were confabbing in the outer office and not about their Saturday morning donut and nightgown adventure or the misadventures of *Bob and Carol and Ted and Alice.*

Kula and Hart walked out of the Computer Center, motioning for Gene to come outside in the hall with them. Roseanne pulled Gene to the side and filled him in on the termination. "Gene, Dr. Dandridge will be calling you within the hour, so please anticipate his call," she said. "As you know he's in Washington, D.C. on Title III business and could not be present for this meeting. President Kelleher did not want to wait."

Gene could feel his heart pounding, his breathing shortened. "I don't understand. Who decided to fire him, Roseanne? Why now, for heaven's sake? Was it the booze?"

The Personnel Director ignored the questions and kept speaking. "Howard was directed to leave the office. I ask that you assure he leaves promptly and without staff interference. A Security Guard will escort Howard to his car. Understand, Mr. Tucker chose to resign his position effective immediately. He asked to avoid being fired. That was his choice."

Kula and Hart departed, heading back to the President's Office in the Administration Building to provide a Tenth-Inning report for Kelleher. Gene went back into the outer office where Candace was in a state of shock seeing the Security Guard march through the doorway and continue to Howard's office.

About an hour after Howard had left the Computer Center, head down and heavy briefcase in hand, Gene's phone rang. It was Dr. Thomas Dandridge, the Vice President of Institutional Support. Gene barked "hello" into the receiver, and Dandridge got the message: Gene was an angry, maybe vindictive man right now.

After a moment of uncomfortable salutation, Dr. Dandridge spoke. "Gene, I am sorry I could not be there today. The President made this decision regarding Howard on Friday after seeking counsel from the College Attorney. This action, while difficult for you, is made in the College's best interest. We can hope, in the long run, the decision is best for Howard, too. He was wise to resign and keep his record with the College clean and his retirement intact. No one wants negative evaluative comments in their personnel file."

Gene kept the receiver pressed against his ear while biting his tongue, as Dandridge continued.

"For the time being, I'm authorized to tell you that the President would like you to serve as Coordinator of the Computer Center. As part of the President's latest reorganization, we are not replacing the Director position but instead will have a Coordinator and appoint you to that job. That will free-up a full-time position. The President wants to go with an evening Programmer, a new position, to work in the evenings. I will assume some of the Director responsibilities. You are asked to take over some, too, and be the new Coordinator. There will be a modest salary increase for you in this new role."

Dandridge continued with his formal statement. "Mr. Wildwood, at this time, you are asked not to share this communication with anyone on staff. When I return to campus, we can fully discuss the ramifications. Should you decide not to take the Coordinator position, you would be reassigned as a Programmer, and another person will be identified or hired as Coordinator. Understand, there will no longer be a Lead Programmer position."

Gene quit biting his tongue. Instead he dropped his head into his right hand, massaging his temples. "Yes, sir, I appreciate the call. I'll call your Secretary and get on your calendar for when you get back, if that's all right."

Dandridge was about to end the conversation when he remembered another point of the call. "Gene, leave the Director's office as it is unless there are papers in there you need for work. Kindly work out of your office for now. But do verify for me that there's nothing amiss in the Director's office, papers are not missing, files are where they should be, that sort of thing."

Gene acknowledged that he understood, hung up the telephone and looked at the room filled with Candace and the others. All had been trying to discern the half of the conversation they did not hear, the part with Dandridge talking.

"Sorry, folks, Dr. Dandridge asked me to respect the confidentially of the phone call, but I'm Acting Director for the time being. Howard has resigned under pressure from Kelleher and directed to leave the campus."

Gene specifically chose not to clarify that Howard chose to resign rather than be terminated. He ignored the Coordinator title in favor of the Acting Director title for himself.

The Programmers mumbled as they departed, while Candace held back until all were gone. She was alone with Gene in the *Meat Locker*.

"You may not believe this", Gene started. "They want me to be the Coordinator and do away with the Director position. We get a new Programmer position, and I'll get a raise. Sounds crazy to me. Not sure if I get the Director's office and his parking space or not. If I tell them no, they'll find someone else to be Coordinator."

Candace vowed her silence. She looked at Gene with concern and now realized she was entirely entangled in Gene's world and his interpretation of the events that had just taken place.

She reached for Gene's hand and squeezed it with both of hers. Then with a look of having figured this all out, she said, "Coordinator, no Director and a new Programmer. Must be another one of Kelleher's late-night nightmares he turns into a reorganization."

"Candace," Gene stated with conviction. "Despite the risks, we need to take care of this."

PREVIOUSLY

"Kicking the can down the road was a damn good strategy."

Negotiations with the Faculty Union began fall 1976, with the contract to expire May 30, 1977. But no one, especially the Union leadership and the College President, expected the contract to be renegotiated by the deadline.

Board Vice Chairman Chuck Harrison was hoping the contract would never be resolved, unless the faculty agreed to a salary reduction or hell froze over.

The flying helium rat tethered to the Administration Building had come down the day after it was put up. Really, the morning after the night before. No one was ever found guilty of, or even charged with, having gained access to the roof of the Administration Building on a night with a waning crescent moon.

Dispassionate minds were amazed that one or more faculty members or hired mercenaries found a way to get helium tanks on a truck to the parking lot. That clandestine maneuver would have enabled a hose to connect to the monster balloon to inflate it. The astonishment continued as to how the culprits got the end of the rope affixed to the plastic blimp and up to the roof. And to have accomplished all that without being seen or heard.

Campus Security swore they saw nothing out of the ordinary that night or during the early hours of the morning after. Tyrone Jackson vouched for his Security Guards. So, did the Abington Area police and the County Sheriff's office as well as the National Guard, the U.S. Coast Guard and the Jersey Shore's Life Guard Association. The conspiracy was safe.

The *Jersey Star* newspaper was flooded with Letters to the Editor about the flying rat that week of August 1976. Some blasted the College for frittering away time that should have been spent on teaching. Others torched the

Faculty Union for spending funds on frivolity. Some questioned how the effort had eluded Security and called for armed guards to be posted at night.

Others blamed President Kelleher for the lack of a sense of humor. The Faculty Union marveled at the enormous size of the rat and lobbied for its inclusion in next fall's *Mummers Parade* in Philadelphia.

The impact of the flying rat was that negotiations were put on hold for eight months. This provided time for the President, Personnel Director, Vice President of Administrative Services and members of the Board of Trustees to calm down, recompose and line up their blockade.

It also provided a much-needed period for the Faculty Union leaders, all faculty and most staff of the College to stop snickering and making rat jokes:

> *What did one lab rat say to the other? Hey, I've got the president so well-trained that every time I push the buzzer, he brings me a snack.*
> *What did the rat say to the other rat after he broke his tooth? Guess you must have had hard cheese.*
> *What did the 50-pound rat say to the cat? Here kitty, kitty.*
> *What do you call a rat as big as the Administration Building? Ah, you call him sir.*

Bill Fishman had called Sally Bowens and Ralph Hughes on Tuesday, May 3, 1977 and invited them to join him and Dr. Thomas Dandridge for lunch at the Golden Acres Country Club the next day. The President had a comped membership at the Club. He didn't play golf or tennis or swim, or even play bridge, but he loved being able to charge food orders and entertain folks.

Fishman's invitation made it clear this lunch was not a negotiation session and that the rest of the Administrative Team would not be present.

Early on, Vice President Fishman chose to set the record straight. "Sally, Ralph, President Kelleher appreciates that you would join Dr. Dandridge and me today for lunch. The purpose is to acknowledge the legitimacy of the Faculty Union and request that we return to negotiations as soon as possible, with the intent to complete a contract by June 30."

Sally Bowens was somewhat alarmed. "Mr. Fishman, you know most faculty are away for the summer," she clarified. "But we're willing to get back to the table, even if a contract can't be officially ratified until they return in August. Understand, too, the Union will not make it a contract issue to reveal if we were involved and, if so, and how the helium rat found its way to the roof of the Administration Building."

Even Fishman had to laugh at that one. He chose to ignore sharing that piece of the bargaining discussion with President Kelleher. The rat was not on the bargaining table.

Roseanne Hart knew about the union reconciliation lunch at Golden Acres Country Club, but she settled for a turkey sandwich in her office. She might have been invited, but that would have meant three from the Administration versus two from the Faculty Union. Kelleher did not want uneven odds.

Roseanne's sandwich-eating that day was abruptly interrupted by a telephone call from the Sheriff's Office.

The officer on the other end was Deputy Sheriff Blanca Diaz, who spoke mechanically but soberly announced, "Miss Hart, I regret to inform you that one of your employees, Mr. Howard Tucker, was in a car accident earlier today. I'm sorry to tell you, he died."

Deputy Sheriff Blanca paused to allow the notice to sink in, and then continued, "Mr. Tucker was driving on US 206 and veered off the road, crashing head-on into a tree. There were no skid marks. Since the brakes were not applied, we can assume he lost control of the vehicle or deliberately crashed at high speed. It would appear he had been drinking. He died from the injuries sustained. Probably instantly."

Besides salary, and with health insurance set aside, the key issues for the Faculty Union were governance and Intellectual Property. The faculty enjoyed significant authority over their classrooms and labs, due to Academic Freedom. In virtually every other administrative decision or policy matter, however, the faculty were consigned to an advisory role. President Kelleher was willing to up the ante on a salary increase but not to abandon his or the Board's powers.

Secondly, with Title III money, several faculty members had created and developed classroom materials, known as Intellectual Property. The faculty argued there was danger that the Board would claim proprietary rights over everything – from patents to scripts to recorded lectures.

The Faculty Union wanted to enumerate the types of scholarly course materials that would automatically remain the author's sole property. They wanted language that if the Intellectual Property had commercial potential, a specific contract needed to be negotiated and properly approved, including the exact nature of ownership. The Administration countered that the faculty were under College employment and were receiving a salary as compensation. Thus, the argument went, anything faculty created belonged to the College.

President Kelleher had supreme confidence in himself, especially in negotiations. He would keep asking questions and ignoring answers until he got the one he wanted. Thus, on any Collective Bargaining topic that arose he would define the correct response and identify the parameters of the debate.

He had wanted to transition to a managed health care program as the College's Medical Insurance Plan. That meant faculty would give up the right to choose a doctor in favor of physicians in the plan's network. He would still allow the Blue Cross option but with a higher premium. Had there been more time to reach closure, he would have persisted. Given the timeframe, all the parties agreed to defer any change in medical insurance until the next contract.

"Kicking the can down the road was a damn good strategy," Kelleher argued before Chairman Pitman, when asked why he had abandoned an insurance change.

Besides, Kelleher had other decisions to make, and he made them.

When David Lieber received praise that the College had won the first Title III grant, Kelleher had replaced him in the subsequent proposal process. When Winters protested before the President's Cabinet to the hiring of Samantha Bartell as Executive Assistant, Kelleher reduced his span of control. Then he announced that Bill Fishman, not Donald Winters, would be Acting President when Kelleher was officially out of town or unable to work.

When Jonathan Purdy, Vice President of Student Affairs, had announced intentions to purchase a new television set for the Student Center, Kelleher had given him a call. "Jonathan, I've checked this out," he began. "Go ahead and buy the Sylvania 25-inch color console from Sears. You can purchase it for no more than $700 and place it in the inside corner of the Student Center lounge. Along the north wall."

Purdy listened and responded, "Oh, sure. That's fine." He had asked the Student Government to survey students and recommend a purchase. He would now let them know there was no longer a need for the group. "Sorry student leaders, but the President chose the TV and its location for you."

When informed of Howard Tucker's death, President Kelleher told Mrs. Reynolds that he wanted to be alone in his office. He gazed out the window for a while and then picked up his telephone.

The President phoned Howard's wife to share his grief and express his condolences. She was not aware that her husband had resigned or that the College would have fired him. She was also not aware that there was an empty gin bottle on the floor of the car that had smashed into the tree.

Kelleher decided there was no need to clarify why her husband had left work early that day or had a bottle in the car. Kelleher did not regret his approval of Dr. Dandridge's recommendation to terminate Howard Tucker. He did regret the College did not do more to help the guy.

The Computer Center staff, particularly Gene and Candace, were livid when they heard the news of Howard's death. They blamed Kelleher. They blamed Dandridge. They blamed Hart and Attorney Kula.

Mostly, they blamed themselves.

"We should have banned the booze from his office," Candace blurted out while the tears cascaded down her face. "We should have dragged him to go with my mother to an AA meeting. Damn it anyway!"

"It would not have done any good," Gene responded. "Every day when I would see him in his office with those damn *Dixie Cups,* I would tell him he needed to quit the booze. Every day his answer was the same: *Hell, I quit drinking every morning.*"

"But then you know what he would say back? *And I start again every afternoon.*"

PREVIOUSLY

"I don't like these symptoms and your vitals. Don't like them at all."

J. Paul Kelleher explained his coughing, slurs and headaches to Dr. Reuben Feldman, the doctor he had been going to for years. The family physician practiced out of his home, in a basement remodeled into a clinic.

The CJCC President decided it was past time to pay his doctor a visit. He had made a mid-day appointment with Dr. Feldman early in June while negotiations were still underway. Kelleher was aware that Feldman's wife, Deborah was co-owner of Global Travel. After all, he had directed that the College do its travel business through Global ever since he became President.

"J. Paul, you've been having these symptoms for several months, and they're getting *worser* rather than better," said Dr. Feldman, trying to elicit humor with the butchering of the comparative word. "Why do men tend put off seeing a doctor? Never fails."

"Sorry, doc. But with faculty negotiations, the start of the semester and a crazy Board, I've put off doing most anything except my work," responded Kelleher with a sheepish frown.

"Which reminds me, you should know that Global Travel does a superb job with our corporate travel," Kelleher interjected. "The records for the College are precise and promptly submitted each month. The agency's co-owner, Katherine, is the wife of one of my Deans, Dr. Vernon Carter, as you know. I thought those invitations Deborah was giving me for deals on cruises were because I was such a good guy."

"You should really take advantage of more of them," Dr. Feldman encouraged.

"J. Paul, small talk aside, it's time for focus and honesty," said the doctor, extracting his stethoscope from his ears and sitting down in the chair next to the examining table. "I don't like these symptoms and your vitals. Don't like them at all."

Dr. Feldman was slow to conduct the exam but quick to pitch a proposal. "J. Paul, there's this fairly new body scanning procedure modern hospitals are now using. It's called an MRI or Magnetic Resonance Imaging. The remarkable machine enables us to look inside your brain using radio waves. There's no injection of fluids, no pain or discomfort. You just lie there quiet and still, while the MRI does its thing."

"Never heard of it," came Kelleher's reaction. "Sounds like it might be radioactive. Do I wear a lead vest?"

Feldman continued, while ignoring Kelleher's failed attempt at lightening the mood. "The MRI is experimental for now. The manufacturing company won't have the product for wide marketing for another couple of years. But St. Anthony Hospital got one owing to its cancer specialization."

There it was, the "C" word, uttered by Dr. Feldman as if it were an incidental and innocuous concept. It was anything but, to Feldman and Feldman's patient.

"Yes, J. Paul, there's a distinct possibility you have a growth on the brain. If we find it, we can look at treatment. Still your symptoms may have nothing to do with cancer. Or, it could be benign. I'm going to call Dr. David Charles who works out of the hospital. He's a Clinical Pathologist, in addition to an MD, and schedule you for the MRI for first thing in the morning."

After hearing the MRI and the implied "C" word, President Kelleher coughed and coughed again, habitually reaching for a cigarette. It was as ridiculous as an obese person reaching for a chocolate, cream-filled doughnut when told to go on a diet.

He paused for a moment and looked Dr. Feldman squarely in the eyes. "Reuben, we've known each other for many years," he said. "You treated my son's broken leg. Now I'm going to ask you to do me a favor, and you must promise. I do not want you speaking to anyone about this potential for cancer, other than this Dr. Charles. Do not tell your wife or anyone with the College. Do not tell Izzy about this. If Dr. Charles finds something in my brain, we can talk further. Do I have your promise? I don't want Izzy to get worried or the Board to get all excited about my illness, especially since nothing has been determined."

The MRI came back positive, meaning there was cancer in the brain of President J. Paul Kelleher. It had been spreading. Dr. David Charles was solidly convinced from the review of symptoms and his examination that there was a malignant growth. The MRI showed the location and just how invasive the cancer had become.

Dr. Charles was a licensed Clinical Pathologist who understood diseases.

He had interned at the Nittany Medical Center at Penn State University, where his clinical training emphasized image analysis, molecular diagnosis, biochemistry and changes in diseases, especially cancer. Dr. Feldman was well-aware of Dr. Charles' specialization.

"Mr. Kelleher, this tumor is malignant," Dr. Charles advised his patient. "There is no easy way to say that or to sugar-coat the truth. As a primary brain tumor, the cancer originated in the brain itself rather than elsewhere in the body before spreading to the brain. The cells have grown out of control. I'm so very sorry."

J. Paul Kelleher was not appreciably surprised by the doctor's diagnosis. The symptoms had been increasing in intensity, the past two or three weeks, especially the headaches and dizziness. Occasionally he had memory lapses and slurred speech.

"What is your prognosis, Dr. Charles? How long do I have?" Kelleher asked, knowing the answers would be grim. The alternatives few.

"I truly wish things could be different. It could be a year, but more likely six or seven months," Dr. Charles said. "You will experience increased pain, relentless pain and severe headaches, excruciating headaches. You can expect blurred or double vision and problems with your balance. Chemotherapy could defer the timeframe by one or two months, perhaps, but there's no way of knowing. Surgery at this point, even taking a biopsy, would not be productive or worth the risk."

"Will I be able to continue working? Will there be a time when I'll need to be hospitalized?" Kelleher asked the questions, with tears coming to his eyes and throbbing to his head.

Dr. Carter saw that Kelleher was tearful, but he had to complete his explanation. "As the tumor increases and spreads within your brain, you will experience poor concentration, difficulty in thinking and frequent struggles with verbal expression, in addition to the headaches. Most likely, when that comes, it will be unbearable to work, certainly without painkillers several times a day. Each of us has a level of pain we can tolerate before breaking down. Yours might be a much higher threshold than someone else with the same type of cancer."

Dr. Charles did not want to project an image as the Grim Reaper, but he needed to be forthright. "Mr. Kelleher, the science is far from perfect, and I could be wrong. It might not enlarge as quickly as I envision. I will take your MRI and symptoms to our Radiologist at the hospital and get another opinion. The MRI is relatively new but the imagery has been overwhelmingly valuable and definitive."

"I don't want the Chemo, an operation or any treatment,'" Kelleher bewailed. "Nothing. Absolutely nothing. I want to work as long as I can and pursue my life as I have been, until the end."

"I can prescribe Morphine injections for the pain," continued Dr. Charles. "You can inject yourself using a hypodermic needle under my authority and oversight. You can control the amount you take according to your symptoms and pain levels. Aspirin and Tylenol won't help much longer. Let's see how your symptoms persist over the next several weeks."

The doctor knew that, in this case, watching the symptoms to see if they would change positively would be like watching a person jump out of an airplane without a parachute and expecting to land without harm.

"The Morphine comes in small vials and does not need refrigeration," Charles added. "You need to store them in a darkened, dry place. I'll show you how to inject yourself. Morphine is a narcotic, as you know, and can be habit-forming."

Dr. Charles saw that Kelleher's expression had not changed at all, so he continued. "J. Paul, there is no other option for the pain, at least now. I'm not worried about your injections becoming a *long-term habit* for you. You're the best person to judge your pain and administer the meds as necessary."

"Thank you, Doctor," Kelleher said, having absorbed all he could. "However, given the degree of cancer, I need not worry about a *long-term habit*."

J. Paul Kelleher looked around the room as if gathering strength in the process. "Dr., I need time to process this, but I want you to promise me something. Understand, I do not want you to tell Dr. Feldman about the cancer. It may seem strange, but I don't want you to tell my wife or anyone else about it. This must be our secret, at least for now."

"You may change your mind as the symptoms persist, especially with the tormenting pain," Dr. Charles cautioned. "You're going to need support and comfort from others as you become more convalescent. In the end, you will need hospitalization and a steady drip-drop of Morphine intravenously. You should tell your wife and bring any necessary order to your affairs. If you don't tell her now, you'll have to most certainly within a few months. The shock to her then might be worse. Regardless, she will notice the changes and grow worried and intolerant of your excuses."

"Besides, as the pain worsens you can expect to pass out," the doctor added. "Your wife needs to know why and what to do. Someone in your office, too."

"My wife or some poor nurse or Candy Striper will have to wipe my ass and empty my bedpan," Kelleher said out of exasperation and defeat. "Is that what you're telling me? And I'll have a needle up my prick."

J. Paul ignored his own questions and continued to speak. "I hear you, Dr.

Charles, but this is what I want. I will deal with this illness myself. As I need refills on the vials, I can get them from you. Correct? And, what's the worst that can happen – I deprive cancer of taking my life a little longer."

"J. Paul, time becomes the issue for you," Dr. Charles interjected. "Time will dictate where and how you spend your final weeks. Knowing that, think about what gives you the most pleasure? Maybe take a vacation somewhere you've always wanted to go. Maybe there are out-of-town family members you'll want to see. Maybe go on a cruise with your wife or take a scenic trip to . . ."

"Doc, that's not me," Kelleher said interrupting. "I get the most pleasure from my sons and that I've had a pretty damn good marriage to a lovely, highly intelligent woman. My parents are dead. What I want is to accomplish what I can at the College and spend what time I have left on the goals set when I took the job almost three years ago. That's why this must remain our secret. You must promise me."

Dr. Charles paused to look into Kelleher's eyes again. He had been with patients with similar diagnosis and who knew they did not have many months to live. Most of them wanted to continue the life they had, not do something else.

"I truly understand, J. Paul," the doctor said. "I cannot promise to keep this from Dr. Feldman, but I will agree not to contact him myself. If he calls me and inquires as to the MRI and your diagnosis, I will share the tumor results with him. I can't promise he won't share that information with others. But, I will tell Reuben that you do not want that to occur. That's the best I can do."

Kelleher was not entirely satisfied, but he nodded acknowledgement. The MD and the College President shook hands in agreement. Their physical and emotional connection lasted longer than might be expected and was incredibly sincere.

Then Dr. David Charles spoke, breaking the silence. "You'll need to use the pharmacy here at the hospital to get your Morphine vials and needles."

PREVIOUSLY

"He's a master at his craft, which also included hitting on me."

Roseanne Hart had closed her office door and asked to be alone. She sat at her desk looking over her checking account. The bottom line was not good. She knew why.

Her Saturday trips to Monmouth Park Racetrack to play the horses was creating a significant financial hole. When she won, she had a fantastic high that overwhelmed the remorse when she lost, which was more prevalent.

When she was a kid, Roseanne's father had visited the tracks often and came home with winnings, usually. Like her dad, Roseanne was addicted to racing – the horses, jockeys, colors, smells – and to the betting. She had tried harness racing at Freehold but could not get into the handicapping the way she could at Monmouth Park and the sensational thoroughbreds.

The Personnel Director had begun with innocent wagers of a few dollars. She had long since graduated into sizable bets in a failed attempt to escalate the highs. She would get a rush on the act of betting, mostly waging $10 on two different Exacta combination tickets. She would do so five or six times in an afternoon.

When she took a weekend off from the races for another commitment, she found herself incredibly irritable. She would fixate on getting back into action the next *Those we love go away. Most, but not all, are missed at the end.*

Irish Leprechaun

Saturday. She was hooked. She knew it. Society and the medical profession both thought gambling was a compulsion, a craving. But, the horse betting had to be something more than that for Roseanne.

She did not care for playing cards – Poker, Blackjack, Canasta or Hearts – or wagering on them. She preferred the sanctity and isolation of selecting race winners to sitting with strangers waiting for a slick card dealer to make or break the bet. She thought the one-armed bandit slot machines were silly and could hurt her right arm. And roulette was just dumb.

It took skill to play the horses. Thoroughbred racing tested her prowess. When she didn't win, she would admonish herself and promise to do better the next time. Usually, she didn't. When she went on a hot streak or even a lukewarm streak, she picked up the pace and glorified her skills.

Roseanne had gone through her savings to gain more available cash and pay debts. When she hit desperation, she started to claim travel expense reimbursements that were false. She had submitted manufactured receipts for about $500 for each of the past three months. She had been both sly and careful. So far, no one had picked up on her crooked ways.

Roseanne sought out the *Gamblers Anonymous* chapter in Trenton, avoiding any Abington connection. Given that the Trenton group was all males, eyeing her suspiciously, she opted out after one meeting. Her Sunday morning church remorse, grounded in prayer, was increasingly insincere and shameless.

Gambling on ponies at the track was the first thing she thought about in the morning and the last thing before she went to bed. In between, there were thoughts about Kelleher and the precarious position she was in with her finances and her job.

When the New Jersey Lottery came into being in 1975, Hart liked to bet the *Pick-3*, usually with a pair of bets. One number was 0909, her month and day of birth. The other would be a hunch. She had not had a winning ticket. She rationalized that If she lost, the next time her preferred numbers would win. She bet the lottery because it was fun, not because she believed that the State revenues would go to education or she would ever win anything.

The ponies sent her down the black hole, not the lottery.

Samantha Bartell knew it would be a challenge to generate private donations to the new CJCC Foundation. Jack Kula had prepared the Articles of Incorporation such that the entity was separate from, and not under, governance by the College's Board of Trustees. The basic structure and organization were in place. The operation was not. There was no Mission or Core Values. There was no Case Statement for why anyone would donate to the organization.

Bartell turned to her lover and former boss, the County Commissioner. "Dominic, I am stuck," she began. "Most colleges rely on alumni to generate private dollars. That doesn't work for us. Our alumni are short-termers. Most have their allegiance to the baccalaureate institution, not where they received their stepping-stone Associate degree."

"I went to grad school with Bill Surterre, a guy who was the Foundation

Director at Lollins College in Florida," Dominic began. "He's now President of CAFE – Council for Advancement and Funding of Education. I'll call him. Perhaps you can go see him, get some ideas and find examples of successful community college appeals."

The CAFE offices were in Washington D.C., near the U.S. Department of Education. Samantha grabbed the Metro one morning and headed south.

Bill Surterre graciously ushered Samantha into his office. He knew the lady had once worked in the County with Dominic; he did not know she was his lover.

"I was at Dominic and Cecilia's wedding," he cackled. "I still wake up nights with the shivers when I think about all the crazy stuff that went on that day. One groomsman was literally under the table where the bridesmaids were sitting. The expressions on their faces were priceless and not because of what they were eating. Dominic's uncle was sloshed and pinching every behind in the place. It's a wonder their marriage survived that day, let alone the past five years."

"It looked like Dom and Cecilia didn't want to be there," he added apologetically.

Samantha had no interest in learning more about the wedding or how lasting Dominic's marriage was.

CAFE's Surterre began the conversation with a direct question. "Samantha, do you like to raise money?"

"Honestly, no, I don't," Samantha responded without much thought.

"That's your problem, right there," said the non-profit executive. "You need to change your paradigm about raising gift support. Can you do that?"

Samantha shook her head, but not confidently or convincingly.

"A paradigm is a frame of reference," Surterre began. "For many years we thought the earth was flat. Then we changed our paradigm. Until Copernicus, we thought the earth was the center of the universe. Same with raising money."

"Consider this, please," Surterre continued. "Suppose you have money invested in an equity fund, some stocks, and they are doing well. Wouldn't you want to share that information with another person? Wouldn't that exceptional investment excite you?"

"Of course," Bartell responded.

"Now if the purpose and mission of that company, of that stock fund, appealed to you, wouldn't that encourage you to invest more," he added.

"Of course."

"Think of cultivating and soliciting private gifts as the same paradigm," Surterre said. "You want others to share in the gifting investment to your College. You want to create a positive gifting experience such that people want to give, choose to give again and want others to give. But you must affirm that the organization is well-managed. You need to demonstrate there are positive outcomes from the donations. That means hard facts and meaningful anecdotes – testimonies from students who have benefitted and gone on to successful careers. People whose lives were changed. That should be easy to accomplish. You are a college. You change lives every day, I expect."

The CAFE executive looked at his visitor and smiled. "According to the paradigm you've had, you're seeking a handout, not a gift investment. You reluctantly stick out your hand and hope someone passing by feels bad enough or guilty enough to give you something. That doesn't work. Guilt doesn't work."

Samantha was beginning to get the picture. This guy was good.

Surterre continued his explanation. "Samantha, the paradigm you need is one that you are so excited, so confident about what happens to the gift that you can't wait to share the great news."

"I like that," Samantha declared. "Sharing the great news of how CJCC changes lives and how a gift truly makes a difference."

"Yes, but that means too that you have the systems in place for the gifting."

"Like what, Bill?" Samantha asked.

"Systems to properly receive and be accountable for ongoing donations. Systems to honor donors and demonstrate proper stewardship. Systems to assure relevant recognition. You can copy or borrow those systems from most any successful non-profit. But you need them to cultivate a donor, move them from an annual gift to a legacy gift. You do that first. These must be fully and properly developed."

"I get it," Samantha responded. "Even if we have a wonderful mission and convincing testimony, we can't expect people to give and give again if we fail to assure proper stewardship."

"Bill, what about fund raising events, bake sales and raffles? Can those be successful in raising dollars? That's all we've done so far. We plan to have a golf outing next spring and probably a dinner dance later this fall."

"Those events are productive, in many cases, in generating contacts, reaching new people and elevating awareness. Most non-profits, unfortunately, spend all that time on events and run away from stewardship and the systems necessary. Events can be fun, but they eat resources and have low cost-benefit reward."

"Then why have them?"

Surterre smiled and then added. "Use events to build contacts, start friendships. Show off the mission. Then you make your appeals. You must move people up the ladder of giving. Maximize the interactions."

Bill Surterre decided there had been more than enough talk about paradigms, foundations, stewardship, generating donations and creating systems. "Samantha, let me take you to lunch. We can have a cocktail, relax and talk some more," he offered. "There's a great place right around the corner." The guy was intrigued by the prospect of being with this attractive, single woman and having her fan his ego as well as his libido over cocktails.

When Samantha Bartell got back to Abington, Dominic came to her apartment before he headed home. "Well, how did it go," Panichi asked.

"Very well," Samantha responded. "I have so much work to do but a far better understanding of how to generate private gifts. I'm excited. We can make it happen. I know what the President needs to do also. He'll be good at this."

Samantha went to the couch where Dominic was seated. She put her hands on his shoulders as she sat down on his lap. "Thank you so much for telling me about the guy and arranging for me to meet with him."

"That's great. You're more than welcome," Dominic said as he kissed his love, lingering in the embrace. He was contemplating taking the moment and Samantha's gratitude into the bedroom.

He paused and then asked, "How did you like Bill?"

"Bill was a wealth of useful information," Samantha offered, trying to find the proper words to describe the time at lunch earlier that day.

"He's a master at his craft, which also included hitting on me."

PREVIOUSLY

"You'll regret this young lady. No one runs away from me."

At the end of the Spring 1977 semester, just before final exams, a student named Betty Greer had accepted an invitation to come to Alan Fox's apartment one evening. Her professor had ordered take-out lasagna to go with a bottle of red wine. The Athletics Director had flirted with her a few times at the end of his class and walked her down the hall several more.

Miss Greer welcomed the attention. After her brutal divorce a year ago, she chose to focus on her young son. Consequently, she spent little time in social situations with a man, and never as the date of a professional, eligible male.

They shared a couple of joints of pot in his apartment that evening. The marijuana was a remnant from Fox's military days. Occasionally he would smoke a joint to ease the lingering migraines. On this night, Fox pressed student Greer for sexual favors when the pot ran out and his manipulations failed to produce the desired result.

Betty Greer had come willingly to his apartment trap and enjoyed the food, wine and attention. But the attention was soon elevated.

After dinner, in response to his groping hands and wrap-around hugs, Betty told him. "Alan, I'm flattered you invited me here. Truly, thank you for dinner and the wine. Please understand, though, I'm not ready for sex."

She had looked at Fox with pleading eyes. "Can't we just enjoy our wine and talk for now? I haven't been with a man for a while. This makes me uncomfortable. Please understand."

Fox was not about to let this bewitching, thirty-something chick out of his apartment without at least heavy petting and seeing her partially, if not entirely, naked. He persisted, grabbing her shoulder. "Young lady, I've not yet completed the grade report for the semester. Do you want to take a chance you won't get an A in my course? Come on now, a man's needs must be satisfied. And we did spend time tonight on what the final will cover."

Betty had pushed Fox away, snatched-up her purse and hurried out the door. Fox briefly followed her down the pathway, yelling, "You'll regret this young lady. No one runs away from me."

Student Greer marched in a daze toward town alone that evening after abandoning Fox's apartment. She hailed a taxi to take her home, where she threw herself on her bed, crying over her situation and cursing men.

After the final exam and the grades came out, Betty Greer saw she got a C in the course. She was devastated.

Betty Greer was mature and strong, but she knew the deck was stacked against her. She was a young female student. He was an older, tenured faculty member. He and he alone controlled her grade. And he was a male.

Nevertheless, she wanted to talk with someone about Fox's behavior and her term grade. She felt intimidated by what he had done. She had wrestled with whether to pursue what had happened or live with it the rest of her life.

Greer decided to contact Miss Roseanne Hart, the lady in the Personnel Office. She was not sure Hart was the proper official. Nevertheless, she scheduled a meeting in mid-August, the earliest Hart was available to her, or any student, due to her negotiations, vacation plans and reluctance to meet with students.

"So, Miss Greer, what can I do for you," queried Hart when they met. "You wanted to see me about Mr. Fox, our Athletic Director and a faculty member."

Betty Greer told Hart about Fox's trade-off expectation – an A grade for sex. She shared that even though she had done well on the final and had a solid B average to that point, she got a C in the class.

"When Mr. Fox posted the class grades, I went to see him in his office," Miss Greer said apologetically. "He told me he had to take into consideration other factors and decided to grade the class on a curve. He was defensive and not interested in explaining what he meant or why the lower grade."

Personnel Director Hart listened intently and then summarized the situation. "I can appreciate that you might have gotten this impression from Mr. Fox while you were in his apartment. However, Betty, since you're an adult and accepted his invitation, there's nothing I can do. I did talk to Mr. Fox in anticipation of our meeting. He said you did poorly on the exam and didn't grasp the material."

"As for what happened, he said you got tired at his apartment," Hart continued. "While he offered to take you home, you decided to walk. Most likely, Miss Greer, you were mistaken on the grade and, as you said, he did not pursue you after you left his apartment. You were a willing participant up until the time you left."

Seeing the student swell up with tears, Miss Hart put a semi-sympathetic arm around her and continued. "Betty, the faculty have total control of the grades they assign. Many faculty choose to grade based on a curve. If Mr. Fox stated such in his class syllabus, then he had the right to grade accordingly. Whether your refusal of his alleged romantic advances contributed to your grade, we can never know. I doubt it."

The Personnel Director knew she had been unduly harsh. "Miss Greer, you may not understand, but there's no policy against faculty seeing students outside of class or dating students. There is no language for that. None at all. I'm sorry."

In July, President Kelleher called a meeting of Dr. Thomas Dandridge who oversaw Athletics, Vice President Donald Winters who oversaw Physical Education, Personnel Director Hart and Athletics Director Fox. Dandridge and Winters had no clue as to why they were called to a meeting in the Board Room. Edith would not tell them anything.

Hart was unsure of the purpose until she saw Alan Fox sitting at the table. Fox figured the meeting had to do with another reorganization, perhaps to reconnect Athletics and Physical Education. He was wrong.

President Kelleher walked into the gathering, discarding any attempt at social graces. "Roseanne, gentlemen, a young female student named Betty Greer recently visited my wife and me at our house. She was very upset. Miss Greer happens to be the older sister of the teen who babysat for our sons on several occasions. Betty detailed an incident that took place at Mr. Fox's apartment in which he made unwanted advances to her in a failed effort to gain sexual favor. This student had to fight him off to get out of his place. Furthermore, Miss Greer had a solid B grade going into finals but got a C for the course."

Alan Fox was beside himself and boldly interrupted the President. "Mr. Kelleher, I assure you, I made no such proposition to this young lady. We may have had too much wine, and I may have touched her shoulder, but I never attacked her, I never took advantage of her. When I sought intimacy, she had the option of turning me down. As for the grade, I chose to grade the class on a curve this semester. Betty fell just below a B for the term. Not my fault."

Kelleher ignored Fox except for directing a glare which silently communicated: *Don't speak again unless asked to do so. Don't say another word.*

Kelleher picked out a *Marlboro* and lit up. He needed the cigarette as much to calm his nerves as to interrupt any thought Fox might have had to speak.

The President looked back at Alan Fox. "Mr. Fox, I believe Miss Greer, totally. You may have thought you were giving the young lady an option – have sex with you or not. But, you were placing her in a huge and dangerous predicament."

The President then turned to Vice President Winters. "Donald, are you aware that Miss Greer is not the first? There are others too? Yes, Mr. Fox here has been pursuing ladies in his classes and threatening their grades if they did not yield to his advances? Are you aware, Winters, that he's manipulated his grade reports as much as he's manipulated these students? And that this has been going on for several semesters?"

"No," Winters responded defiantly. He was the Vice President of Academic Affairs. He knew more about teaching, grading and faculty behaviors than Kelleher did or ever would, so his response was definitive.

"Kelleher, you should know, there's no rule against faculty dating students," he began. "Understand, the Vice President does not review faculty grade reports. Our Department Chairmen don't either. We cannot challenge Mr. Fox on his classroom behaviors. That's his business. The women in his classes may be young or younger than he is, but they are still considered adults and responsible for their own behaviors."

Kelleher looked sternly at Winters, after taking another puff of his cigarette. "I figured that might be your reply, so I had Miss Bartell make some contacts. She spoke with several young ladies from his two classes this past semester. They told her how he had tried to manipulate some students and intimidate them. A couple students affirmed that Mr. Fox had invited females to meet in his office or come to his apartment or take a ride in his car for sexual favors."

President Kelleher could see the tension rising in Winters. He did not need advanced sensors to recognize the anger. Yet, he continued with his attack. "That's not all, Miss Bartell also analyzed his grade reports. Miss Greer had as high or higher GPA in the class than other students who got B grades and even A's. Curve or no curve."

Kelleher took still another puff, tapping the dangling ash onto the overflowing glass ashtray on the table before he bore down on his former rival for the presidency.

"Winters, you are to conduct a review of grade records for Miss Greer in Mr. Fox's class and make the appropriate correction to her grade. You will inspect his course syllabus to determine if, indeed, Mr. Fox grades on a curve. You will immediately cause a review of grade reports for all classes Mr. Fox has taught. If you find discrepancies, you are to assure corrections are made and student grade changes are registered."

Winters tried to interrupt Kelleher. The President waived him off. "Winters don't defend him and don't argue. This is on you as much as Fox. And don't you dare call this a matter of Academic Freedom. That's bull shit. You know it."

Alan Fox knew he had been had, but he was not about to end the skirmish without at least one more plea, even if he was only digging the hole he was in deeper. "Kelleher wait just a minute. You had no right to go into my grade records. That's private property. How I determine grades is my business. Besides, how does this Bartell woman know what a grading curve is?"

Fox immediately regretted he had said anything. He had grasped that Winters was no help in appealing for tolerance, leniency or the privacy of records. Winters was expressing his own animosity and couldn't care less about Fox and his romantic escapades.

The President brazenly ignored Winters and Fox. He turned instead to Personnel Director Hart. "Roseanne, I understand you spoke with Miss Greer but said there was nothing she or the College could do. Poppycock. You are to draft an official Letter of Reprimand for Mr. Fox according to the Faculty Union Contract. State this man's misbehaviors, without mentioning his name, in interacting with female students in his classes, threatening grades and making them dependent on sex. I will review the letter myself, and if it's not strong enough, I will revise it. You understand?"

Kelleher did not wait for an answer but continued his directive. "Miss Hart, you will then meet with the Union Leadership and advise them on why the letter is being sent. If the Union protests, send them to see me. After you've told them what happened, add Mr. Fox's name to the letter and send it to him Certified Mail with copies for his file and to Winters, Kula and me. You got that?"

President Kelleher dismissed everyone from the meeting except for Roseanne Hart. Fox stormed out into the hall and confronted Winters, much like a convicted prisoner might hang on to a guard in hopes of keeping him from going to his cell. Winters turned his back to his faculty member and headed down the hall.

Hart was pleased to have more time to discern exactly what Kelleher wanted her to do. After all, this was the first time the College had discussed faculty dating, much less acceptable classroom sexually-related behaviors. She wrestled with her thoughts: *I simply ignored Betty Greer when she came to my office several weeks ago. No, I had believed Fox, not the student. Just because he was on the faculty. How many other Miss Greer's were there?* The Personnel Director had felt powerless anyway. She vowed that would never happen again.

Roseanne's facial expression betrayed how delighted she was with the assignment, but she wanted clarity on faculty-student sexual encounters. "Mr. Kelleher is there anything you want me to do concerning male faculty dating students and intimidating them?"

"I'm not sure what we can do," Kelleher said. "See what Jack Kula says. Convene a meeting with Sally Bowens and Kula. Explain what took place here, without mentioning names. Have Kula research what colleges and universities are doing about this issue relative to Civil Rights. Come up with a Board Policy on harassment or intimidation or classroom abuse, however you want to frame it. Get it done. I don't want this to get bogged down or become a negotiations issue or be anything that . . ."

The President stopped in mid-sentence and then resumed the directive. "On second thought, set up a meeting – you, me, Kula – before you address the Union part of this. I want to pick his brain on what we can do outside of the contract. Include Samantha as well. Not Winters."

Roseanne reached deeply within herself and made a request of the President. "Sir, if all right, may I contact Purdy and get his thoughts about designating someone in Student Affairs who would be available for these girls – to help them figure out what to do. To be their advocate, especially when it comes to believing them and taking on male professors accused."

The President looked at Hart and smiled. He could sense her anguish at not believing Betty Greer. "Roseanne, that may be the best idea you've had since negotiations. Tell the Purdy jerk that the designee needs to be a female, a professional person who can stand up to a man and his Department Chairman. Get the name of the person Purdy selects and her contact information and put it in the Student Handbook. If Purdy objects, or if he stalls, have him come see me."

Kelleher's final thought was direct and straightforward. "Do I make myself clear?" It was not a question.

"Absolutely, sir," Rosanne Hart responded. "Men like that give all men a bad name. We'll want to give this student advocacy thing a name. What shall we call it?"

PREVIOUSLY

"You got to trust me. You got to trust someone."

Negotiations with the Faculty Union finally concluded the end of July 1977, about two months after the contract had expired and two weeks before fall registration. Sally Bowen and Ralph Hughes, as leaders of the faculty, had arrived at an agreed-upon 3.25% salary increase. That closure did not satisfy faculty or please Board members.

The bargaining table had also established language on Intellectual Property. Those faculty who developed the learning materials via the federal grant would receive a minimum of 25% of any royalty from the production and sales.

There was no movement on College governance or medical insurance. There was no change to class size parameters or any agreement to provide a larger office for the Faculty Union.

President Kelleher had made it a contract issue to prohibit the Faculty Union from desecrating the campus with protest signs. That included flying rats, mice, bats, birds or flying anything. That concession moved the percent from 2.95% to the agreed-upon 3.25%.

Section 501.2 of the bargaining contract now read, "No bulletins, no buttons, no banners and no balloons." Placards and handbills were still permissible, so Sally was delighted. She did not have to reveal where the remnant flying balloon was being stashed or who had hoisted it from the Administration Building.

The President's coughing had not eased up, or the nausea or the headaches, even though Kelleher went from three to two cigarette packs a day. The smoking helped take his mind off the headaches but tormented his throat and lungs. The coughing didn't seem to have much to do with the smoking, let alone the slurred speech or constant headaches.

Classes would start soon. Enrollments were going to be up again. The parking lots would be full. The newly hired faculty would find their way to the Library, Faculty Lounge and the Faculty-Only bathrooms. Students would locate their classrooms, purchase their textbooks and maybe find the Library.

The Student Government Association had completed a clever plan to start a shuttle service wherein an incoming car would wait at the end of the walkway. When a student would come out and head for the parking lot, the driver would pick up that student and take him or her to their car. That driver would grab the vacant parking space. Of course, the shuttle system would only be necessary at peak class times or as an ingenious way for guys to meet coeds.

The College was hiring an extra cafeteria worker to meet the service demand of the additional students. Faculty were back in their offices, planning for the term, content if not overjoyed at the new Union Contract they had just approved.

The Board of Trustees had approved the new, three-year contract with the Faculty Union. Vice Chairman Chuck Harrison was the only naysayer. He would only have been content if the faculty had accepted a salary reduction.

"We gave away the store again," Chuck, the magic shop owner, had protested at the Board meeting. He wanted to affirm that his defiant vote be recorded in the minutes. "Besides, we did not raise their deductibles for insurance and gave them this *Unintelligent Properties* provision, whatever that is."

Kelleher had interrupted. "Excuse me sir, but that's Intellectual Property. It has to do with media materials such as videos that the faculty develop and how we share royalties. With Title III, we had to resolve how to handle these projects. The contract still leaves the door open for negotiations, with the company to produce and sell the materials our faculty develop."

Chairman Pitman had come to the defense of his Vice Chairman. "Next time we need to be tough with the faculty, Kelleher. We can't continue to give them raises. Maybe we should introduce sections in the next contract to charge them for parking and have them punch a timeclock, like people do in real jobs."

Kelleher knew that his Board Chairman was serious, but the snickers from a couple of other Trustees made him smile too.

Ignoring the Chairman's suggestion, Kelleher continued. "The good news, gentlemen, is that we start negotiations with the Career Employees Union in the fall. I know we all can't wait."

Samantha Bartell and Rebecca Campbell had much in common. They both were involved in growing romances, albeit one with a married man. Both were bright, local ladies on upwardly mobile career paths.

The colleagues had dinner together at least once a week, usually at each other's apartment. Samantha would attempt Scottish recipes while Rebecca would go Italian. Each tried, with mixed success, to honor the other's heritage. When they ran out of recipes, they grilled hamburgers or broiled skin-on chicken breasts. Heavy on the garlic.

Desserts always involved chocolate. Always. Usually brownies or chocolate cake. If there wasn't time to bake, they would have chocolate ice cream topped with chocolate frosting and chocolate sprinkles.

After they had devoured most of the chocolate cream pie she'd made that day, Rebecca ventured where she had never gone before with a direct question. "Samantha, who's this married man? You know you can trust me. Come on. Tell me."

Samantha waved the question off, but her friend persisted. "If you share, you can ask me a highly personal question, too. You got to trust me. You got to trust someone."

"He's the Commissioner, the County Commissioner," Samantha blurted, as easily as if it were an innocent admission. "You've heard of Dominic Panichi?"

"I've never met the man, but Jack's had dealings with him. His firm represents the Commissioner's office too. What's the marital situation? Dare I ask?"

"I know I love him," Samantha said without hesitation. "I believe him when he tells me he's hopelessly in love with me. Not his wife. We decided to give it a year and see where we are then. It's been a few months, and we are only more deeply in love."

Rebecca interrupted and said without much forethought, "Oh, is that how you came to get the position in Kelleher's office?"

Samantha responded immediately and defensively. "I got the job, Rebecca, because I was best qualified, but Dominic did speak to Kelleher about me. Dominic and I thought it would be too tempting and too precarious for both of us for me to continue working in his office."

Rebecca started to scrape the chocolate pie plate with her fingers to grab the last morsels. "I'm sorry. I apologize for that crack. It must be a challenge to find time together and be alone. Your apartment is neat and quiet, but you can't go out on the town or anything. Ouch."

Then Rebecca remembered that she had access to a key, a key to a gorgeous house in the mountains, thanks to Coach Solly.

"Samantha, how would you like a weekend in the mountains, courtesy of Dave Russell, the former All-Pro with the Detroit Pistons? He has a wonderful log house near the basketball camp Coach Solly runs for him. Technically, it's a log cabin, but that sounds as absurd as calling a *Chris Craft* yacht a dingy. Solly's given me access to the key for most any weekend. Jack and I have been there a couple of times. It's private, quiet and, most importantly away from this crazy town. Visitors pack the Poconos in the summer, but now that schools are open again, the camp's closed. Most of the locals are raking leaves, preparing for the winter or heading to Florida."

"Is this weekend too soon to take you up on your offer," Samantha jokingly asked. "Not sure what excuse Dominic can make, but I'll beg him to make an exceptional one. We need time together, whenever we can make it work. The thought of alone time in the mountains sounds glorious."

"Hey, why not the four of us go up there? There must be seven or eight bedrooms. I kid you not. Jack can be trusted. I know it. Hey, it might be a relief for Mr. Panichi to have a confidant, too."

"And, Samantha, Jack's an attorney who handles divorce cases."

Edith Reynolds got on the telephone with Coach Solly to share the good news about the fiscal audit of Russell's basketball camp. Solly knew the only reason the camp venture was profitable, or still in business, was Edith. He had recovered from his disappointment in not getting the university position. However, he was no less upset with his fate, no less angry at Kelleher for his interference and no less determined to get revenge.

Coach Solly was still trying to process his conversation with the President's wife regarding her seemingly marital misery and her husband's health. Solly was fond of Izzy, to be sure, but they had agreed and re-agreed that theirs was an arm's length friendship, not a prelude to a physical encounter. There was an attraction between them, but both had too much to lose to venture into intimacy. Neither one wanted that.

"Edith, if you aren't doing anything one of these weekends, invite Izzy and her boys to go with you to Russell's place for the weekend. She could use a break, and I know you love it up there this time of year. Bring your dog."

When Edith called, Izzy was delighted with the invitation to go to the Poconos for a weekend. "This would be great for me," Izzy said, unable to hide her excitement. "We can meet you and Roy there or drive together. I'll get some steaks and wine for us, and we can grill burgers for the boys."

"Roy will opt out, Izzy," Edith shared. "He's not a fan of the mountains. Roy's a Jersey Shore person. And with me gone, my favorite husband can immerse himself in baseball, basketball, football and beer. I'll check the calendar. We can stop at Italian Peoples for bakery treats on the way up. Their cheese Danish is to die for."

Izzy had another thought. "Edith, I have a gal friend who I play racquetball with at the YMCA. Ella is a Dental Lab Technician who also does lovely fashion jewelry. May I invite her to join us? I can ask her to bring along some of her jewelry designs. That will be fun."

Izzy gratefully ended the conversation, "I really, really need this! Thank you."

PREVIOUSLY

"There's something really crooked about all this."

Central Jersey Community College was in line to receive $5.2 million from the General Assembly for a capital project to expand the Library. The outdated building was constructed in 1960 and was one of the few campus structures under-modernized and under-sized for the mid-1970's.

President J. Paul Kelleher had had a capital proposal in Trenton before the General Assembly for two years, patiently waiting in line for funding, while raising hell behind the scenes. Universities drank robustly from the capital construction trough before community colleges could sip anything.

Several business leaders on the College's slowly blossoming Foundation Board had traveled to the capital and made strategic phone calls. The *Jersey Star* had published a *Daily Editorial*, drafted by Martha J. Rooney, in support of the project.

Kelleher had gained the support of the Chamber of Commerce to petition the General Assembly to fund the design and construction and even prioritize it over several university capital projects. Chamber officers and the County Commissioner, Dominic Panichi, had traveled to Trenton on three occasions to speak to the Legislative Delegation.

President Kelleher had announced receipt of the funding at a reception for community and business leaders at the Country Club and to celebrate the award. Board Chairman Pitman thanked all the leaders present and gave a sterling toast, noting how supportive the Board was. However, he ignored Kelleher's heroic efforts to round-up the votes and orchestrate the onslaught of advocates to Trenton. He also ignored the ignorant editorial comment about the College becoming a four-year institution.

Daily Editorial   The **Jersey Star**

CJCC's Library   **July 13, 1977**

We thoroughly support the expansion of the Library at CJCC and applaud the President and the Board of Trustees for their initiative and perseverance in seeking the state funding. The $5.2 million construction award would be a significant achievement. Congratulations to Board Chairman, Dr. Pitman, for leading the charge.

We also recognize the efforts of our Chamber of Commerce to be sure our General Assembly knows and appreciates how much CJCC contributes to the local economy and to the growth of businesses in the area. All these men took time from their work to go to Trenton and lobby for the capital funds.

Despite the occasional political missteps by the Board and the President' Kelleher's wrongheadedness in faculty negotiations, the community benefits greatly from the CJCC. The faculty and students, for generations to come, will benefit from this newly expanded and state-of-the-art Library and all of the books.

The Editorial Board hopes the expanded Library will be funded as a first step to making CJCC a four-year college or university and have bachelor and graduate programs along with dorms, fraternities and real intercollegiate athletics.

We hope students will take advantage of this new building and study occasionally.

We understand there are three final architect companies to design the building, including a local firm. We haven't yet been able to ascertain their names. We'll find that out at the next Board meeting or rely on our sources.

Central Jersey Community College had to identify an architectural firm to design the Library expansion and supervise construction. They advertised the Library project according to the State's prescribed competitive process.

Twelve firms submitted written responses to the College's Request for Proposal (RFP), addressing each of the required elements in a ten-page submission.

Vice President Bill Fishman had reduced the number to five highly qualified New Jersey architectural firms. Each of the five had proven track records and extensive experience in the design of university and college buildings, including libraries.

Fishman had invited the five firms to prepare and submit tentative design concepts and come to the campus to make 40-minute presentations before Kelleher, the Dean of Instructional Resources, David Lieber, and himself. Lieber's Division included the Library. Winters was not invited. Samantha Bartell was to be present too.

The presentations provided an overview of the building design, based on the College's program plan, and identified the names and credentials of the assigned architectural team. Each firm fielded questions for another 15 minutes.

Kelleher and Fishman agreed on the two firms best prepared and most experienced to complete the architectural design: Princeton Architectural Group and Landtag and Associates. The Princeton Group had been the principal architect for the design and construction of the comprehensive campus. The firm had received a design award for the project. Lantag had very impressive references and projects for Princeton and Trenton State.

Lieber had suggested that they include a local firm in the mix with the two others, but he did not provide a rationale. Kelleher ignored the proposal.

Then Kelleher got a telephone call from the Board Chairman, Dr. Gerald Pitman. "Morning J. Paul," Pitman said cheerfully. "I trust your day's going well. Say, I wanted to talk with you about the architect business. You mentioned in your Board memo that you and Fishman were down to two, but I want you to add another firm."

Somewhat stunned because of the petition to compromise the prescribed process, Kelleher asked for an explanation.

"We need to include a local firm," Pitman announced. "Harrison and I will introduce a motion to include Zelinski, Corradetti & Greco along with the two firms you propose. You know these guys. They've done several corporate projects in the area."

Flabbergasted but being political, and sensing something a bit crooked was to happen, Kelleher responded. "Gerald, the State has an explicit process we must follow on architect selection. Besides, Zelinski has never done an educational building for a college or a school in New Jersey. They gave no example of such in their proposal. If we stray from the requirements, we could see the money pushed back another year. We could lose the funding for having violated the process."

"Perhaps," Pitman countered not conceding anything. "Zelinski submitted a response to the original RFP. You said so. Therefore, they met the initial requirement. That should be good enough for Trenton. How difficult can it be to design a library – shelf spaces, labs, some cubicles, book storage, bathrooms and a few offices? They don't have to get the job. Just include them in the firms for the Board to consider. That's all."

Kelleher tried another approach. "Dr. Pitman, the State will still review the process and look for a rationale why we included them. Not sure being a local firm is a valid criterion. What about other Board members? Won't they be suspicious when you amend the motion to include Zelinski?"

"You just let me handle that. I appreciate you doing this," Dr. Pitman declared. "Besides, I've already told the press," as he hung up the phone.

Kelleher summoned Bill Fishman to his office, along with Samantha Bartell. He sat them in the two burnt orange chairs. "Son-of-a-bitch, we have a problem. The Board Chairman and *Magic Man* Harrison want to include a local firm with the final two architects for the Library. He insisted, even when I told him the State would be suspicious and might cancel the funding."

"Which firm, President Kelleher," Samantha asked, getting the words out just before Fishman asked the same question.

"Zelinski, Corradetti & Greco. They responded to the RFP but would be way over their heads in this project."

"Let me make a few phone calls and see what I can find out from my County contacts," Samantha offered while looking at Kelleher and rolling her eyes to add to the message. "It might be good to contact Jack Kula for the legal implications of what we would be doing. I can do that too, if you want. Getting Kula involved might be enough to scare the rest of the Board, if not the idiot Chairman and Vice Chairman."

"This stinks," Kelleher blurted. "There's something really crooked about this. Why would Pitman give a damn about this firm? Does he have a relative who works there or something? Did they offer to build him a new house?"

Samantha waited until Fishman left the President's Office before making her phone call to the County Commissioner, Dominic Panichi, her clandestine lover. She wanted to make the call while Kelleher was in the room in case he had specifics in mind.

Panichi was surprised to get a call in the middle of the day from Samantha, but he presumed it was business. "Let me check and get back to you," Panichi said. "I'll get the records and contact Zelinski myself. He won't lie to me." Then he whispered, "Take care babe, eh, Cutie Marks."

Monroe County enabled private donations of any amounts to go to political parties but not to individual Board candidates or Board members for community colleges, public schools or county parks. The reasoning was that if an individual received the donation, there would be distinct *quid-pro-quo* expectations.

The County Board of Elections recorded all political donations. Panichi discovered that poppa Zelinski, the founder of the architectural firm, was to make a $5,000 gift to Dr. Pitman. That was more than crooked; it was illegal.

Kelleher met Pitman at his office after his last few patients had left for the day. He came armed with combat information and a threat. "Gerald, I know Zelinski himself made a $5,000 gift to you in the form of a political donation. That would be illegal."

Pitman did not back down from his demand that Zelinski, Corradetti &

Greco be among the finalists for award of the architectural bid. He planned to have Harrison introduce an amendment to the motion and add Zelinski. Pitman was still resolute to add the local firm. After all, he was the Board Chairman. The President answered to him.

Before the vote to approve the Princeton Architectural Group at the following meeting of the Board of Trustees, on September 14th, and before Pitman could entertain an amendment from Chuck Harrison, Kelleher called for an Executive Session. Away from public scrutiny and off-the-record, he could advise the full Board about the illegal gift and the likely consequences of including the local firm in the motion. Attorney Jack Kula was invited to the meeting, too.

Pitman explained his reasons for wanting the local firm included. "They do a lot of work in our community, and we need to support local agencies. They're generous in the pro-bono work for parks and recreation. I don't see the harm in including them, and we can still go with one of the other two firms. That is, if necessary."

Attorney Jack Kula took the floor in the private Executive Session, as had been rehearsed. "Gentlemen, I regret to say there is the possibility that a representative of that firm made a cash donation to someone on the Board. That would be a violation of the law. If you as Board members approve the amendment for inclusion of the firm, I'll be forced to reveal the person's or persons' names and submit an Ethics Violation to the County."

Pitman did not wait for any further disclosure, and Harrison looked like he was totally bewildered. The Chairman cried out, "It was me, and the money has nothing to do with my feeling that we include this firm in the final group. Why in the hell did you get involved, Kula? That's not your job or what we pay you for."

Kelleher had had enough. He stood up and moved behind his chair to gain an advantage. "Gentleman, I know first-hand that the deal was to include Zelinski in the final group, or they'd remove the money set up with the bank. Don't blame Mr. Kula."

The President looked ominously at Pitman. "To be prudent and fair, let's ignore the fact that what took place was illegal and could result in prosecution. If the Board chooses to let the amendment to include the Zelinski firm die for lack of a second, we can let this pass. The public meeting will never reveal that the issue came up at all."

There was nothing that the President could say that would lessen Pitman's outrage. He didn't try.

PREVIOUSLY

"I'll be working to get two more votes and kick your ass out of that office."

After the September 14th Board meeting had finally ended, J. Paul Kelleher, Samantha Bartell and Bill Fishman were hanging around the President's Office. They commiserated about the meeting and shared glasses of Irish Whiskey. The other folks had left, some in bewilderment as to what had taken place in the public session and what had happened during the closed Executive Session. Most were just glad the meeting was over. They could go home.

Samantha chose the stale Merlot wine rather than the whiskey. Kelleher took a healthy gulp from his glass, put it down, took off his shoes and started to buff them. Then he started coughing.

The phone rang, startling them. It was almost 11 PM, and Kelleher knew it was Izzy or, more likely, the Board Chairman. He put down the shoe shine brush and sat upright in his monster chair.

"Kelleher, you got me tonight," Dr. Pitman began. "Know you now have an enemy, and I do not forget easily, if ever. You're one son of a bitch. You could have just included Zelinski and not brought in Kula to rattle the other Board members with the legal bull shit."

The President motioned for his two colleagues to be quiet. He wanted them to remain in the room just as witnesses and in case Pitman got angry and threatened him.

"Sir, I appreciate what you tried to do, and I take you at your word that it was for the right reasons. But it would have been illegal. A Board member cannot accept monetary contributions in any manner."

Kelleher was hoping that the Board Chairman was at least listening. He did not expect Pitman to change his mind.

Kelleher decided to continue this slippery slope. "My effort, sir, was to enable consideration of the Library architect to be in private, in Executive

Session, without the Press and to avoid what could have been a public reprimand. I wanted to be sure the Board understood the ramifications of what you and Harrison would be doing, but in a private session."

Pitman was not impressed. Not at all. Kelleher's explanation only served to take him from annoyed to infuriated.

"Kelleher," Pitman began, "You know I gave you a pass a year ago when you moved that guy from the campus to the off-campus job center. That was Representative Ridgeway's nephew, and he was upset. Called me several times. You didn't know, but when I told you, you said you could not move the guy back to the campus."

"Dr. Pitman," President Kelleher offered, "Bruce was creating problems in the Adult Ed office, and I wanted to give him another opportunity to succeed. He kept his salary. His evaluations were weak. Would you have preferred I fire the guy?"

The Board Chairman was not satisfied. "Kelleher, I would have preferred you left him alone. But no, you had to flex your muscles. I could have had your ass then. Instead, I let it go even though Billy reminds me of it every time I see him at Rotary or church and every time I . . ."

J. Paul stopped Pitman in mid-sentence. "As per Board Policy, I have full authority to reassign personnel. I only need to bring terminations to the Board. Besides, Bruce has responded well to his new assignment. And the gal who replaced him here is a star. All came out ahead."

"Understand, Kelleher," the Board Chairman started. "You have two votes on the Board against you. I'll be working to get two more votes and kick your ass out of that office. You can count on that. We all know how you schemed and manipulated the Board into selecting you as President. Greenleaf certainly screwed Winters. He'd be in that fancy leather chair now, or the Iowa blockhead would be."

Kelleher unintentionally interrupted their exchange with several coughing bursts. He choked them down, so he would not vomit. He sipped

This President innocently walked alone in his office late last night, after most everyone else had left the building. Well, most everyone. Big mistake when you're Irish. Now he's probably going on a wild ride.

Irish Pooka Spirit

once again on the Irish Whiskey, momentarily soothing his throat but not helping his headaches. The cancer was creating physical problems and was on his mind all day.

Samantha Bartell and Bill Fishman could not hear what Pitman was saying. They heard enough to know tension had escalated. Fishman wished he had left before the telephone call. Bartell wished she could punch Pitman in the nose.

Dr. Pitman had one more question that had been bugging him. "Kelleher, how in the hell did you get Jack Kula to contact Zelinski, and how did Kula get him to admit the money?"

Izzy Kelleher and Coach Solly stayed longer than usual at the racquetball courts after they had each showered and dressed. Solly could tell his friend was weary and hurting. "What is it, Izzy? Can I help some way?"

They sat in the lounge facing the racquetball courts where privacy was at a minimum. Speaking loudly was the norm, with all the activity noise.

Izzy struggled with whether she should share her secrets. She was desperate and decided to swallow caution. "It's my husband. It's J. Paul. We've had an unusual number of silly arguments lately."

"Beyond that, I'm deeply worried about him, his health," she lamented. "His coughing is almost incessant, even after he cut back on smoking. He complains of headaches, and he slurs his words sometimes. I'm an English Lit major, not Psychology, but I think he's registering signs of a personality disorder. I'm not a doctor, but he's getting sicker."

"What do you mean," Solly asked, as mystified by the discussion of Kelleher's health as by the marital struggles, but insidiously wanting to hear more of both.

"My husband often makes others angry. He doesn't feel bad when he hurts others, so long as the cause is right. You know that. The man gets moody at home after a day at the College and sits in his brown leather recliner. Increasingly, he seems to have a crappy perspective on life, and he's at the office all the time lately, including weekends. He almost fell down the stairs the other day, and he lost his balance coming in the door another day."

"Maybe it's the booze," Solly volunteered. "He's Irish, and he likes his whiskey and wine, from what you've told me. That's the story according to the College's underground rumor bulletin."

"No, I don't think so," Izzy said. "The last six months, J. Paul and I are more like roommates than husband and wife. The marriage license hangs over our heads like a sword ready to decapitate us if we suggest a separation, especially with the boys. He wanted to know if I was sleeping with you."

"That bastard," Solly said, not realizing until too late that everyone at the courts could hear his shout. Outwardly, Solly was visibly upset; internally he was thrilled. His plan for vengeance and retribution was getting closer. "Why don't you leave the guy?"

"We've had too many times together," Izzy replied. "Good times. Tough times. Maybe even more in-between times. But all that matters."

Izzy looked around the lounge, not recognizing anyone.

"I really don't know what to do about him," Izzy said convincingly.

"I do," Solly responded without expression.

J. Paul sat in his living room recliner with his feet up as he read the *Wall Street Journal* after working at the office that Sunday morning. His ashtray was overflowing with cigarette butts, so he had started to flick his ashes into the empty *7-Up* bottle he had finished. He never liked to have stray ashes. He had been reading the same article about the stock market for twenty minutes.

The first part of 1977 had been brutal for financial investments. Stock averages had wobbled and steadily worked their way down. J. Paul was particularly concerned about his Pfizer investment, as he wanted to leave that stock in the hands of his sons when he died. Pfizer was a good selection when he had made the initial investment. He was a fan given they invested heavily in research and development.

Kelleher had always enjoyed playing the stock market, even as a young man. His dad had given him $100 when he turned 16 so he could pick a few stocks and make investments. He placed half of the nest-egg in Western Insurance, Inc. and the other half in a new brats n' beer franchise restaurant venture based in Florida.

The investment and stock manipulation interest did not exactly coincide with his degrees in English Literature. The financial work did help explain why he ended up with the MBA degree. He had a decent portfolio set aside and had made prudent choices.

His thought that afternoon was about how he was going to handle the growing resistance among the Board Chairman and Vice Chairman to his recommendations and his leadership. In hindsight, he could have just let the motion to add the local architectural firm happen. Pitman would have been pleased, and Harrison would have claimed a victory. Who knows what Pitman was going to do with the $5,000 anyway?

He knew there was no way Zelinski, Corradetti & Greco would have gotten the contract, even if the Board had coalesced on a vote. He was sure the State's Capital Development Board would have raised a red flag as soon as they saw that name with the other two firms. Had he let the architect thing go through, chances were good the project would have been delayed for months. Maybe put on permanent hold. And when the *Jersey Star* finally found out what had transpired, the College would have been dragged through the mud.

Kelleher was also troubled by the growing realization that the Board Chairman had mentioned how they had done business with his predecessor, Dr. Greenleaf. He had underestimated the amount of pressure on his position to do business according to the good ol' boy network.

His head was throbbing. His throat was no better. He had taken the dosage of Morphine when he was at the office and had hidden another vial in his briefcase in the event he could not tolerate the pain. He still had a few pain pills left over from Connor's surgery. The pain was dreadful, but he was managing.

J. Paul finished the *Wall Street Journal* article as Connor and Ian came into the room, with worried looks. "Dad, you seem to be getting sicker, coughing more," Connor said. "Mom says your headaches are no better. What's wrong?"

J. Paul was not sure what to say. He decided to change the subject. "Boys, I know your memories of your grandparents, Daideo and Mamo, are few. They died when you were young. I think of them often these days. We're coming up to what would have been their 50th Wedding Anniversary had they lived. They were married young. That's what people did in the 1920's and 30's. Remember, Daideo had the meat market. He loved to grind fresh chuck even when you were little shavers. You boys would nibble on the raw ground chuck while standing in the cooler."

"I remember that," Connor said. "He liked to cook a lot also, especially sauces and make pork sausage. How did he get the meat into those skinny tube things?"

"I thought Mamo was the cook in the family," offered Ian. "She always baked the coffee cake, some with nuts and raisins, some with apricots. And she had all that melted sugar as frosting."

"They each married their Best Friend," Kelleher offered. "I did too, even though I don't tell that to mom very often. You guys know she's my Best Friend and in a world where it's hard to find friends. Any friends."

Kelleher saw worry in his sons' eyes. "I'm OK, guys," he proclaimed, more to soothe them than to clarify his condition. "I'm just working too hard these days and dealing with some struggles with members of the Board of Trustees."

"Are they gonna fire you, dad," Ian asked. "Are you not going to have a job anymore? Will we have to move?"

"No chance, son. I have a multi-year contract," Kelleher explained. "They would have to pay me for another two and a half years. They won't do that. Be assured they won't. If they did, wow, we could have a big party or take a fancy trip."

"I just want you not to have any more headaches," Connor said. "To get back to your running, even though Ian and I make fun of the way you run."

Kelleher put down his paper. He put his arms around his sons and cuddled them to his chest. "Connor, Ian," their father said. "When I was your age, I remember Daideo telling me he may not have been the best father in the world, but he was the best he could be. I hope you guys think of me that way."

"I probably don't tell you enough," the father lamented. "Dads screw up lots of things, but no dad was ever prouder of his sons than I am of you guys.

Your intelligence comes from your mom. Your good looks too. We know that. Your persistence probably comes from me. Some would say, stubbornness. I hope that's something to remember me by."

Kelleher cradled both his boys, one in each arm. He thought for a minute and then continued. "Guys, it's corny to say that life's a journey, but it is most of the time. You got to keep moving forward. Learn from the past but spend your time in the present. It's also important not to give up or give in, even when you feel like you're all alone and things are all piled-up around you."

Kelleher looked away from his sons and thought a moment about what he wanted to say next.

"Boys, before you came into the room, I was reading the paper but mostly rehashing in my mind what happened at Wednesday's Board Meeting. I could have ignored something that was wrong that night, really wrong. Instead, I chose to do the correct thing. That upset some others. They got mad. That's gonna happen."

"I was sitting here in my chair," he said. "I was rehashing the other night and thinking perhaps I should have just gone along with the bad decision. Then you guys show up. Just by being here, you remind me as to why we need to be strong. Why we need to try to do the right thing, even at a cost."

"Thanks for worrying about me," Kelleher said. "These headaches will go away soon. I'll be much better then. Maybe I'll go for a run tomorrow. Care to join me?"

Irish Banshee

PRESENT

The College After the Death of President Kelleher

No public man can be just a little crooked.
Herbert Hoover

.

PRESENT

"It's him. It's President Kelleher. He must have collapsed."

The clock on Edith Reynolds' desk read a few minutes before 10 AM on Thursday, October 20th. She had not heard from President Kelleher. His absence was most unusual. The door from the Board Room to his office was ajar, but that was not unusual. Often, he would do his morning run and then go the back way to the Executive Bathroom to shower.

She saw no signs of him having been in the office that morning, getting dressed and leaving the office for a meeting or for more bakery rolls. The room was dark when she had opened the door about 8:45 AM after she got to the office. If he weren't at an appointment, Kelleher would be at his desk pouring through papers and the Division folders, smoking his *Marlboros* and enjoying his morning coffee in that preferred cup and saucer.

Kelleher was scheduled to hold a President's Cabinet meeting at 10 AM which he always did the morning after a Board meeting. That enabled the lead administrators to ruminate over the previous evening, let off steam and get their marching orders. It was Samantha Bartell's job to make the working list of topics, but each Vice President was to do the same for his set of responsibilities.

The Board Meeting the evening before had been tense and disruptive, as a perilous follow up to the weird September 14th Board Meeting and the award of the Library architect bid. Board Chairman Gerald Pitman had fumed and done his best to stare down President Kelleher and anyone else who spoke from the administration. Harrison looked distant the entire evening. His mind was elsewhere, and likely not planning his latest magic trick.

The Board had returned to the Open Meeting that September night, a month ago. After that fateful Executive Session, the Board had voted 5 to 0 in the public session to award the bid to the Princeton Architectural Group.

Chairman Pitman said nothing. Vice Chairman Harrison abstained from the vote without giving a reason.

Mr. Zelinski of the Zelinski, Corradetti & Greco architectural group had withdrawn the $5,000 payment to Dr. Pitman when his firm was not included in the award finalists. Few people knew that, as Kelleher wanted.

Dr. Pitman had vowed revenge against Kelleher. If he had been in a game of Poker, Old Maid or 52-Card Pick-Up, his expression would have betrayed him. He just had not quite figured out what the retribution would be or when he would spring it. He would have Kelleher gone before the new year, one way or another.

No one was going to embarrass him before his colleagues, much less threaten to expose him, dirty linen and all. That was a month ago.

The three Vice Presidents and Samantha Bartell had assembled in the Board Room awaiting the President that October 20th morning. Since Dandridge was in Washington, D.C., Gene Wildwood was his surrogate and in attendance too.

Kelleher was occasionally late, presenting a grand entrance. Other than Bartell, they were all disinterested when Edith came in and said the President had not yet arrived. Winters proposed they give Kelleher ten minutes before heading back to their offices. The ten minutes passed, and another five, before they left the room, coffee mugs and notebooks in hand, having wasted a chunk of the early morning.

Samantha strolled over to Edith's outer office and peeked into Kelleher's office from the doorway. She noticed his desk chair was pushed off to the left side of the desk, rather than anchored in the center. She could hear Kelleher's farcical preference, ringing in her ears: *I like to put my chair in the middle to confuse those damn Board members as to whether I'm a Democrat or a Republican.*

Then his words rang in her ear a second time. He would often tell her: *I have this big chair, Samantha, so I can push it toward anyone coming after me and escape out the back door.*

Samantha called for Edith to come into the office. "There's something different about this place, this morning. Do you feel it? I don't think President Kelleher got to the office today, even though his car is parked in the President's space."

"Several of us stayed after the meeting," Samantha offered. "We rehashed the verbal contest and praised the work of Professor Wiegand. Some left. Others stayed in the Board Room or went into Kelleher's office and drank his Irish Whiskey. A few stayed longer. Some drank more than others. I left after nursing a glass of wine. Maybe someone drove him home? Lord knows, the guy deserved to sleep in."

As Edith maneuvered to the right of the behemoth desk, she observed the President's daily calendar. It was still on Wednesday, the day before. Then she saw the outreached, white-shirted arm with the cigarette butt dangling from the extended fingers.

"Oh, my God," she shrieked. "It's him. It's President Kelleher. He's on the floor. He must have collapsed."

Samantha hurried to the spot where Kelleher lay behind his desk. The bottom half of his body remained partially hidden, as if he had tried to crawl backward, as one might seek refuge from a storm or a Florida lobster would retreat into a safe hole. "Is he alive?" she howled, more curious than distraught, more fearful than anguished.

Edith had backed up several steps from the prone body until she hit the wall, holding her hands to her face, crying and shaking unrestrained. "No, I don't think so. He may have been here all night. You touch him. I can't. I just can't! I think that's the same tie he wore at the meeting last night. Oh my God!"

Bill Fishman wandered into the office, still curious as to why Kelleher had uncommonly missed the Cabinet meeting. Fishman wanted to salute him for standing up to the Board Chairman the previous night, yet he had secretly hoped the President would have been beaten up and crushed at the meeting.

"What's wrong, Edith?" Fishman asked, rushing over to where the President's Secretary was standing. Edith held her hands over her mouth, the shaking having transitioned to a quiver. Her eyes remained transfixed on the lifeless body of her boss.

"I think he's dead. He hasn't moved, and he looks so pale, so ashen," Edith said. "He can't be dead."

Samantha touched President Kelleher's face lightly with two fingers. It was cold and clammy. "I'll call Security and get some help, an ambulance, police, something," she cried. "Edith's in no condition to move, let alone summon an ambulance or talk to the police."

When he got the call, Tyrone Jackson rushed over in his security cruiser. He stopped long enough to grab his walkie-talkie and Campus Security baseball cap.

When he got to the Administration Building, observing employees had already lined the hall and staircase with murmurs of assorted impressions on what was happening:

- 1st Observer: *Edith's in tears. Kelleher must have scolded her again and then ran away.*
- 2nd Observer: *Fishman went into the office but didn't come out. He's on the phone now. They're probably trying to track down Kelleher. Must be something broke there. Too bad it wasn't him.*

- 3rd Observer: *No, they say it's the President on the floor. He must have fainted or else he's hung over.*
- 4th Observer: *Is he dressed? Does he have pants on?*
- 5th Observer: *Where are his shoes?*

Security Chief Jackson parted the employee spectators as if he had practiced parting the sea after reading in the Bible how Moses did it. He shed the random observations, too, as he took the stairs two at a time to the second floor and dashed down the hall to the President's Office. He could hear the ambulance sirens closing fast. Jackson had contacted the Sheriff's Office immediately after he had gotten the call from Samantha. They were on the way.

Jackson talked quickly when he saw what was happening in the President's Office. "That's the President on the floor. Don't touch anything. Let me check his body. Who found him?"

Jackson bent down and noticed the polished pair of black shoes sitting perpendicular to the body as if placed there to complete a symmetrical composition. He did not find a pulse, and he did not see any blood or visible signs of trauma. Except for the telling vital signs, the man could be sleeping, albeit uncomfortably on the floor.

With a professional calm of a man who had been at war both with the U.S. Marines and in a Federal Penitentiary, Jackson spoke confidently. "Mr. Fishman, would you kindly stand by the outer door. Please escort the Marine Medics to this office and see if you can clear the halls. Get someone to help you." The former Marine had forgotten for the moment that he was not still in the military.

Upon arrival, the two emergency team members entered the office and quickly engulfed the body. The first one to the body started to measure the vital signs. The second moved people away from the body.

The ambulance folks confirmed that Kelleher was dead, to Edith's wails, Samantha's stunned silence and Fishman's smirk.

Chief Jackson looked again at the body and kneeled on the floor next to the attendant. He gently placed his hand over Kelleher's eyes, closing them peacefully. "Rest in peace, President Kelleher. Thank you, sir, for being our leader."

The hallway observer contingent quickly converged on the gossip that the President was dead. From there, the rumor mill spread across the campus and into classrooms, faculty offices, ball fields and employee lounges. Some faculty scattered to their offices to call their spouses, siblings, neighbors and bowling buddies about what had happened.

Samantha called Winters, Purdy and Wildwood and asked them to come immediately to Fishman's office. By the time the group had re-gathered, Deputy Sheriff Blanca Diaz had arrived and secured the area, including the Board Room. So, they stood in the hall.

Chief Jackson nudged the inquisitive staff away from the office door and commanded they go back to their workstations. He winked at Diaz. His expression was that this was going to be a long day. Be ready for anything.

Diaz wore her Deputy Sheriff uniform, complete with dark blue slacks and sky-blue shirt with the emblem seal of Monroe County Sheriff's Office over the left shirt pocket. She preferred her date-night fashion when she met off-duty with Chief Jackson, but this was indeed official business. The plain slacks and oversized uniform shirt did not hide her feminine figure or defer Jackson's imagination.

Diaz designated the area as a Crime Scene, although no one knew if a crime had been committed or what crime. Diaz barked orders to clear space around the body, so she could document the scene. Chief Jackson did her bidding, holding back his thoughts as to how fetching his girlfriend looked in a power position.

The President had a five-o'clock shadow, suggesting he had spent the night in the office. Diaz turned the President's body on his side. She noted there were no visible signs of assault and no blood. There was nothing near the body that could be labeled a murder weapon.

The Deputy Sheriff took multiple photos of the body and the five-o'clock shadow, the paired shoes, the desk chair, the extended right arm and the *Marlboro* cigarette butt. She cordoned off the whole room, the huge desk serving as an imposing blockade. Diaz took photos all around the body, the hallway and bathroom, along with the credenza and desk.

Something about the perpendicular pair of shoes bothered her. They had to have been purposely positioned. She knew the shoes would bother the Sheriff, so she took additional photos of them from several angles.

Diaz took close-ups, medium range shots and overview photos, all the while being sure to incorporate various vantage points. The photos would be processed later in the day and presented to the Sheriff as evidence of something, someone or nothing. Diaz had imagined herself one day being an acclaimed professional Crime Scene photographer with a classy array of expensive equipment. Not today.

Diaz' forensic training came to the front as she moved on hands and knees slowly across the floor, closely examining the expensive Persian rug under and near the body, inch by inch. Tweezers and evidence bags were in her hand. She cocked her head slightly to one side to transform the perspective, still not sure this was a Crime Scene where a crime had been committed.

It was her job, her passion, to document evidence at the scene. She had to do so in a scientific manner and then process and store the collected materials for lab examination.

"Did anyone call Izzy yet," Edith asked the Cabinet members who were remained huddled in Fishman's office staring into space. Each guy was mumbling to himself in purposefully indistinguishable words.

"Let me do it, Edith," Samantha said as she left the room to go back to her office for privacy and without waiting for a response. But first, she dialed the office phone of the County Commissioner, Dominic Panichi, out of duty or partiality.

"Let me speak with the Commissioner," stated Samantha in her best rendition of an authoritative man. "This is President Kelleher's office at CJCC. I need to speak with him immediately. Thank you."

"This is Panichi," Dominic answered, not sure who would be calling from the President's Office but hoping it was Samantha with a plan on how they might see each other at end of day.

"Dominic, President Kelleher is dead," the shaken lady said, pausing long enough for the words to sink in. "Edith and I found him behind his desk and on the floor of his office this morning. Deputy Diaz is here now, along with the ambulance people and Security Chief Jackson. Sheriff Clough is on the way. Dominic, there are no visible signs of foul play or anything, and neither Jackson or Diaz is about to speculate. I just wanted you to know. I'm not sure what happens now. I must go, Dominic. I volunteered to contact Izzy. She doesn't know yet."

Samantha looked to see if the coast was clear before she ended the conversation with the words, "I love you. Take care of yourself."

Samantha dialed the Kelleher home number, but there was no answer. So, she called Izzy's office at Atlantic State.

"He must never have come home last night," a shaken and desolate Izzy spoke into the receiver. "He always comes in late after a Board Meeting. He likes to blow-off steam at the office or sometimes at Old Heidelberg, so I was in my bed in my room last night before he would have gotten home."

Izzy took a moment to compose herself and continued to confide in Samantha. "I checked his bedroom when I got up, but figured he'd left early. The bed was made but he usually makes his bed before he heads out anyway. Sometimes he leaves me a note in the kitchen, but there was nothing this morning."

"Seems likely then that Mr. Kelleher never made it home last night," Samantha concluded out-loud. "Mrs. Kelleher, I am so sorry. He was good to me. He trusted me. And I enjoyed working for him."

Izzy thought of her boys and what she would tell them. She started to grab her purse and head for the office door, so she could drive to their school.

But she had more questions.

"Samantha, tell me how you found him? Did he have a heart attack, a stroke or was it an accident? Had he been drinking last night? Pauly's been moody, even distant lately. The coughing's gotten worse. He's complained of headaches too. I know he's not been well the past month or two, but he hides any illness and pain. He avoids the doctor. Tells me nothing."

Then realizing what she had said about the bedroom, Izzy quickly figured an explanation was due. "Samantha, J. Paul and I have been sleeping in separate bedrooms for two months. And not just because he's been sick."

The folks at the Title III office in Washington D.C. would now review the CJCC recommendation to award the Library contract to the Princeton Architectural Group. Vice President Dandridge had accompanied the proposal, taking the dawn Metroliner the Thursday after the October Board meeting. He personally walked the document into the administrative offices on Maryland Avenue.

Dr. Dandridge and Dean Lieber had made impressive presentations at the October 19th Board Meeting on what was included in the new Title III proposal. Psychology Professor Nancy Wiegand had demonstrated her media materials to scattered applause from Board members as well as folded arms and grimaced faces from Chairman Pitman and Vice Chairman Harrison.

Dandridge carried the signed paper in a locked briefcase that never left his hand. The cloak and dagger intrigue could have been a scene from an Alfred Hitchcock espionage movie. The only thing missing would have been a metal chain from his wrist affixed to the briefcase and having the villains waiting for him to get off the train, so they could relieve him of his burden, wrist and all.

Thomas Dandridge was unaware that President Kelleher was lying dead on the floor in his office. Apparently.

PRESENT

"This is my uniform for what I do. Why change?"

Arthur Clough was the appointed Monroe County Sheriff, having succeeded Clarence Jones who did not get along well with the County Commissioner and the Freeholders. Mr. Jones left after less than two years. No one missed him.

Clough's surname was lineage French and was pronounced correctly like the word *clue* or to rhyme with *blew, stew* and *true*. Usually, people who saw the name would pronounce it to rhyme with *plow* or *cow*. If he introduced himself as "Sheriff Clough," they would assume the spelling was C-L-U-E or perhaps C-L-E-W.

He corrected people once. Then he expected them to adhere to the proper pronunciation and spelling. Most did not.

Clough had taken the Monroe County position after the Board of Chosen Freeholders had held an emergency election to fill the vacancy. He had been Sheriff of neighboring Carroll County and sought the promotion and modest salary increase.

Blanca Diaz had also been a candidate for County Sheriff, but the Freeholders were not ready for a female as the Sheriff. They thought they were progressive to have consented to a woman as a Deputy. Diaz was disappointed but did not hold that against her new boss. She knew from his resume and reputation, she could learn a great deal for him. She was not ambitious enough to leave the area.

Arthur Clough had served Carroll County well for fifteen years. He had distinguished himself in several solved cases, including a hold up of a Dairy Queen and an armed robbery of an ACE Hardware store. He had tracked down and arrested the culprits for attempted homicide in a notorious cold case involving the murder of a judge. Little did Clough know that only six months into the new Monroe County job, he'd confront the sensational potential homicide, natural death or suicide of a College President. He'd have to establish a Crime Scene in a College President's office. What are the odds of that happening?

The President's Office had been cordoned-off with no one allowed in the room without explicit permission. Deputy Sheriff Blanca Diaz guarded the door to the office and Board Room as if she were a bank security guard with millions of dollars in the vault.

Diaz had then completed an initial sweep of the Crime Scene but was mindful the Sheriff would do his thing and overlap, if not duplicate, much of what she had done. Diaz dusted for fingerprints. She searched for carpet fibers and signs of blood or contusions. The officer took dozens upon dozens of photos with the official camera and the Polaroid Clough had wanted, so he would have Crime Scene prints more quickly.

The body was beginning to get stiff and thus meet the definition of a *stiff*, as the Coroner would say. Rigor mortis, or hardening of the body, was setting in, but the body was still movable and flexible. That meant Kelleher had died as late as midnight on Wednesday evening or as recently as a couple of hours ago this Thursday morning.

The office was cold, very cold. Kelleher wanted the AC cranked up, even in mid-October. He got warm easily, and he also liked to see his colleagues shiver a bit in the burnt orange chairs, first from the cold temperature and then from his interrogation. The Computer Center staff joked that his office was the mini-*Meat Locker*.

Clough's mind momentarily drifted to the reputation of Al Capone's Chicago mafia years and how the victim would end up in the cold, cold water of Lake Michigan wearing cement shoes.

Clough knew that had the room been at a more normal temperature, the rigor mortis would have been more advanced. The alcohol in Kelleher's system might have insulated the body some, he speculated. Time of death was not a major factor anyway. He knew that. Not in this case. The President had died early or later this morning, a span of eight hours at most.

Edith Reynolds had decided to lay down on the hard couch in Fishman's office. She had to get away from the Crime Scene, knowing J. Paul's body was still lying there. Her mind was fixated on seeing the body of her boss on the floor.

Samantha had called each of the Board members. Chairman Pitman wanted to call an Emergency Board Meeting to designate an Interim President. Samantha said it would be better to wait until the Sheriff came and clarified procedures.

When asked by Chuck Harrison if Kelleher had been murdered or had a heart attack, Samantha responded as Tyrone Jackson had advised. "Tell anyone and everyone who asks that you do not know and would not know until after the Sheriff completes his examinations."

When Board Vice Chairman Harrison persisted, raising his voice on the phone and demanding an answer, Samantha gave him an earful. "Mr. Harrison, the President of this College has just died. We do not know any details. Most of us here are in mourning, trying to balance our shock with respect for the family and the position. Sir, I sincerely urge you to do the same."

The silence on the other end of the phone was only interrupted by the click of the receiver being placed back in the handset by Harrison.

Sheriff Arthur Clough was tired when he got out of the car and headed up the path to the Administration Building that Thursday morning. He functioned best in the morning, but only after his second cup of coffee.

Tyrone Jackson was waiting for him at the door. They had met previously, and Clough knew Jackson was dating his Deputy Sheriff. He didn't see any conflict.

The Sheriff was pushing 50 years old. Some days he looked like he was closer to 60. Clough wore a shabby, tan waterproof bucket hat that covered his balding head. He would wear an oversized baseball cap when he fished in Lake Carroll, which had not been often in this new job, serving a pretty crooked county.

The particular attire and disheveled look were intended to create a visual disturbance for suspects, criminals, reporters, lawyers and others. He had slightly crooked teeth, and unappealing teeth stains, owing to years of smoking and the absence of braces when a teen.

Clough was less than thrilled to hear of Kelleher's demise. He knew this bizarre death of a College President was guaranteed to suck up his time. This death and the ensuing investigation were not going to be good for his fishing plans.

The Sheriff's hefty frame had gone considerably soft in recent years, due to an overinvestment in TV cop shows and an overindulgence in barbeque brisket, cheesy potato skins and *Rolling Rock* beer. His favorite boob-tube shows were Rockford Files, Quincy M.E. and Police Woman. The Sheriff was fond of the way Jack Klugman solved cases as a Medical Examiner when no one else could.

Clough prided himself on his ability to solve television crimes before the heroes did. Occasionally, he would pick-up tips on examining a body. In his mind, however, he could have shown *Dr. Quincy* a thing or two and avoided getting punched regularly or hit over the head as *Jim Rockford* did. He found Angie Dickinson's *Pepper Anderson* character entirely unrealistic, but what man cared. The blond actress was so attractive.

Despite the worn-out hat and tousled appearance, the Sheriff was highly committed to order in his life, like J. Paul Kelleher. Clough woke precisely at 6:15 AM, without an alarm clock. He brewed one cup of black coffee and ate one medium bowl of steel cut oatmeal before heading to the campus. There he would have his second cup of coffee, now decaffeinated.

Clough's former wife had gone nuts with his demand for sameness and order. She had given up offering alternative breakfast options and, two years ago, given up on the marriage in favor of her sanity.

The Sheriff had sworn off women and was at peace with that decision, at least for now. He was comfortable with his order and habits and wasn't about to pursue breaking in another human as a life partner. However, if Miss Dickinson showed up one day to solve a crime, he would ask her out.

Arthur Clough only wore dark gray slacks with a pinpoint-oxford, light-blue shirt and a black tie. His preference was to include a wheat-color corduroy sports coat, with leather elbow patches. He had two of the same blazers in his wardrobe and alternated them, depending on which one looked more crinkled. That was the one he wore this Thursday.

When asked about why no variation, his response was simple. "This is my uniform for what I do. Why change?" He would wear a starched white shirt version when a more official event required same. In the evening, Clough might add a dark brown corduroy blazer, absent the elbow patches, or even a charcoal gray suit, discarding the rumpled work image for an impressive, casual image. In the fall and winter, he might wear the same blue shirt for two days, letting it air out for a day in between.

If the weather was cold, Clough would don a Navy-blue pea coat, rather than the corduroy sports coat. He had purchased the pea coat from a fellow military guy who served in the Navy. But the hat and apparel stayed the same, no matter the season, the weather or the audience.

When he saw the body of Kelleher, and with Security Chief Jackson at his side, Sheriff Arthur Clough asked if College employees were routinely fingerprinted.

"No, sir," was Jackson's answer. "But I see no reason we can't require that now if you want to check fingerprints you find near the body with people here at the College. Pretty sure Board member prints are on file at the County office."

"That's exactly what I intend to do. I expect Deputy Diaz arranged for that to occur, so keep the Crime Scene free of contamination. No one should be permitted to enter this office or the Board Room. Hopefully, if there was foul play, we find some near the body where employees and others would not normally be touching."

Clough then noticed the hallway leading to the back entrance to the

Board Room. He started to walk in that direction, pausing at a door off the hallway. "That's the Executive Bathroom," said Jackson. "No one supposed to use it but the President."

The door was locked. "Cordon off this room, also," he said. "Who knows what details might be in there. Probably stuff in a cabinet. Miss Diaz will conduct a proper assessment of the bathroom and check for fingerprints."

He entered the Board Room and abruptly halted, causing Mr. Jackson to bump into him as if he had been tailgating.

"Is this where the Board Meeting was held last night, Tyrone?" the Sheriff questioned. "Does anything look unusual to you in this room? Were you at the meeting yourself?"

Jackson was a bit startled by the questions. "Yes, I did attend the meeting. Usually do. President Kelleher wants me to be present in case an unruly student has a bitch, or a Board member or employee gets out of hand. Toward the end of the meeting last night, there was a strange reference regarding the architect bid from last month's meeting. Other than that, the meeting was tolerably standard. Dull, I mean. A faculty member made a presentation that seemed to bore a couple of Trustees. Nothing new about that."

"Chief, please make a list of people who had contact with Mr. Kelleher yesterday and last night. Include everyone in attendance at the Board Meeting. You can help, too, by adding notations as to the position and nature of the contact each person would have had with the President."

"Yes, sir, I'll take care of it," Jackson said, his strict Marine training kicking back in for the moment.

"Oh, feel free to call on Deputy Sheriff Diaz to work with you, but only in a professional manner, if you get my intention. Nice you two can spend time together off-duty."

In Monroe County, the Coroner was, in fact, the elected Sheriff. Thus, Arthur Clough had another role – inspect the body and, as may be necessary, conduct a post-mortem examination. He had authority to order analyses and autopsies and make the final ruling on the death. He was licensed and certified.

The County Coroner did not have to be a physician or have a medical degree. His role was to affirm the person's identity and ascertain that the deceased did or did not die through foul play. If there was a discrepancy, or he needed specific tests, he could refer the case to the designated local medical doctor, who served as the County's Clinical Pathologist.

The Sheriff was still hesitant to call the President's Office a Crime Scene. He had no idea if a crime had been committed. But that was the proper label for now.

As he was entering his Sheriff's patrol car, Clough had another request of Security Chief Jackson. "Chief, I assume the President had a car. Where is it parked and is there a report on its movement over the night?"

Jackson pointed to a parking lot behind the Administration Building where the higher-end administrators had reserved spaces. There at the far end was the car used by the President. "The President's car is leased by the College and given to him to drive for personal and professional use. He turns in a mileage report every six months, and we gas-up and maintain the vehicle. I expect your Deputy Officer will want to examine the car."

"If the lease is in the College's name, we do not need the widow's permission or a Court Order," Clough said. "Verify that with the College Attorney. Keep an eye on the vehicle until we can complete an examination of it. It's something to check, although I doubt it will reveal much of anything."

Then he said to himself, "This is going to be a great deal of work. Bummer."

PRESENT

"Did anyone have a grudge? Just about everyone."

Early the next morning, Friday, Izzy Kelleher came to the County Morgue to identify the body and affirm it was her husband. There was no doubt it was J. Paul Kelleher. Several witnesses had verified that fact. However, Arthur Clough preferred having a family member view the body in the morgue while he observed the person.

On the Coroner's order, Kelleher's body had been transported to the morgue on Thursday afternoon to be kept in cold storage. Clough would be deliberate with the preliminary examination of the body, probably stretching his focus into late afternoon. He would process the notes taken by the Deputy Sheriff at the scene of the death and verify pertinent points with the corpse.

"Mrs. Kelleher, mind if I ask you a few questions," he stated, once she had completed the miserable task at hand. Unlike some people who see a corpse, especially of a loved one, Izzy was not overwrought and did not vomit, choke or hyperventilate. She had had the previous night to process her husband's death, helped by two packs of *Virginia Slims* and a bottle of Chardonnay. She had received hugs from her sons, licks from Cerberus and assorted hot and cold casseroles from neighbors.

"No, that's fine, Sheriff, whatever you need to ask," Izzy said and then volunteered more information before he raised a question. "You're in charge. But, as I told Miss Bartell when she called me yesterday, I was in bed Wednesday night. I didn't realize until Samantha called the next morning that Pauly had not come home, that he was dead in his office. Wait, that's not right, I'm sorry. I thought he likely got up early that morning and went to the campus, where he showered. He has more clothes in that closet than at home. I guess it should be he had more clothes there. Wow. The realization is still not fully accepted – my husband is dead."

"So, you didn't miss him Wednesday night or yesterday morning?" Clough asked. "What about your kids?"

"No, not really. Our mornings are hectic. The boys are big enough to fend for themselves at breakfast. Connor and Ian hardly even check in with us, before they dash out to catch the bus."

"Tell me what he liked to do, to eat, what he did for fun, Mrs. Kelleher. What were his dislikes."

"He liked to read, mostly non-fiction, and he kept track of Broadway Plays. He didn't like elevator music and shag carpets, if that tells you anything. What he liked to eat? Well, he hated cucumbers and corn on the cob, to be sure. Yet, he loved Kosher pickles and *Karmekorn*. Go figure. He also liked Kielbasa, German potato salad and anything Chinese except chopped suey."

"So," Cloud responded. "He was an Equal Opportunity Ethnic Eater."

Izzy smiled at Clough's attempt at humor. Yet, she knew his description was quite accurate. "Yes, he loved Irish and Italian cooking too, just not what I prepared."

Trying to catch her off-guard, the Sheriff quickly interrupted. "And how were things between you and Mr. Kelleher? Mind telling me where you were last night and what time you went to bed? I have to ask."

"I don't mind, but I'm a little surprised at the question," Izzy said. "I was home all night and probably went to sleep about 10 o'clock or so. I usually read for a while in my room. The kids were home. Their lights were out about 9."

"Excuse me but wouldn't you normally hear him come into the house or at least into your bedroom, use the bathroom," Clough kept probing. "Wouldn't you know when he got into bed, at whatever hour it might have been? It seems like you'd be expecting that, even if asleep, especially given that it was a Board Meeting."

"Take this as you prefer, Sheriff, but my husband and I have had separate bedrooms the past couple of months," Izzy replied somewhat embarrassed. "Yes, our marriage has been shaky of late. Nothing bad. No, I did not miss him coming to bed. To be sure I love him, he's the caring father of our kids. I would never hurt him. I'm sorry I didn't know that he never came home. But he's been coughing a lot and getting up several times during the night. He offered to sleep in our guest room. He insisted on it."

Mrs. Kelleher paused to contemplate her next words. "That will haunt me for a long time. I could have called Samantha or Edith and asked them to check on him. But I didn't know."

"If that's all, may I leave," Izzy said, feeling worn and tired. "I have the boys in the car and am taking them to the mountains on Saturday to get away for the weekend. They don't need all this right now."

"Just one more thing, Mrs. Kelleher," said Clough working on his annoyance strategy of interrogation. "Do you know if Mr. Kelleher had been sick or suffering from any pain before he died?"

"Not sure about that, Sheriff," Izzy said. "The coughing has been more intense, and he spit-up phlegm a few times. The headaches increased, and he may have been drinking more. My husband was private about his health. That was part of his independent world, off the record to everyone, including his family. That it, sir?"

"We covered a lot," the Sheriff said. "I appreciate it, Mrs. Kelleher."

"Oh, one more thing," Clough proposed, sensing the widow was losing her patience. A rattled suspect can divulge things they might not otherwise. "I assume your husband had his share of enemies, what with tough decisions, personnel, budget cuts and all at a college. Lots of pressure. Did anyone have a grudge?"

"Just about everyone," Izzy quickly said and headed for the door before turning back and leaving him with a final thought. "How's that sound?"

Arthur Clough felt it was premature to sign the Death Certificate until he could ascertain and double check the cause of death. He could only speculate, at this point, on the cause. He was not about to rush judgment. He knew he would need to question several people at the College and order toxicological tests by the County Pathologist, mainly since there were no signs of trauma.

The story of J. Paul Kelleher's death was the *Jersey Star's* frontpage feature that same Friday, the morning after the day his body was discovered. There was a half-page photo of the corpse being transported into the ambulance and another of Sheriff Clough standing watch. The reporter, Martha J. Rooney, referred to the death as "suspicious" without a conclusion on suicide or murder and absent any justification for her gossipy conclusion. She had ruled out a natural death, most likely to help sell newspapers.

Like a foreboding Hitchcock short story, a *Jersey Star* editorial the week before had been about co-mingling of the County Sheriff and Coroner positions. The Editor cited anecdotal research from five New Jersey counties that had "progressed" to an elected Sheriff position as distinct from an appointed Sheriff and had a designated licensed physician as the Medical Examiner.

The Monroe County Board of Chosen Freeholders and the County Commissioner were not moved by the editorial or by the paper's position. Sheriff Clough had not read the newspaper that morning, or any morning.

As Coroner, Arthur Clough had the authority to call for an official Inquest and to summon witnesses. He could hold a Court Hearing in which he would act as the Inquisitor, with or without a jury to rule on verdicts. He would decide whether the death would be officially ruled an accident, suicide, homicide or due to natural causes.

He held in reserve the possibility of scheduling an Inquest. If there was to be an indictment, then a jury could be called. Often the Inquest served to sort things out, to be followed by calling for a Grand Jury to rule for prosecution, if the conclusion was murder and the District Attorney was involved.

Coroner Arthur Clough conducted the initial post-mortem examination without prior knowledge that Kelleher was suffering from a cancerous brain tumor. Like *Dr. Quincy*, Clough embraced the concept that the body held the clues to the cause of death. There would not be a need for a complete corpse dissection. He knew that would require Mrs. Kelleher's approval. He was confident he could arrive at the right and proper conclusion by interviewing key people and, as necessary, calling witnesses to testify under oath.

There were needle marks on Kelleher's right and left arms, on the underside of each elbow. The marks had been camouflaged by the long-sleeve shirt while the body was in the President's Office. Clough could not discern at that point what medicine or drug had been induced through the hypodermic needles or whether such was causative to the death.

Coroner Clough had distinguished a slight bruise on the scalp but no other physical signs of trauma. There had been no signs of a struggle. There was no vomit, but it was easy to discern the stench of alcohol on his breath and a remnant of the whiskey in a glass left on the desk.

He concluded, unofficially, that Kelleher had died of a natural heart attack or, more likely from an induced and over-dosed ingestion of drugs due to complications. But it would be premature to arrive at a full diagnosis and speculate as to whether the drugs were consequential, self-induced or a direct result of *interference* by others, as he liked to call it.

Clough kept thinking about the pair of polished shoes resting perfectly perpendicular to the prone body behind the desk. He had concluded that they had to have been purposely positioned, not haphazardly removed from his feet by Kelleher himself or by the person or persons who *interfered*.

He had wondered whether the outstretched arm was a natural manner a person might fall to the floor. More likely, it was positioned by others or less likely by Kelleher himself. What was the message being sent? He did not know yet. He would.

Clough's concentration on the corpse was interrupted by a phone call taken by Deputy Sheriff Diaz. At first, he did not want to take the call, that is until he was told that it was Dr. David Charles.

"Good morning, Arthur, guess you're busy at work," greeted Dr. Charles. "I wanted to let you know that I was the specialist doctor that Mr. Kelleher sought out three months ago and upon referral from his regular MD."

Clough was indeed surprised. Dr. Charles was the designated Clinical

Pathologist who would conduct the toxicological analyses, should he decide to order them for the body.

"Whoa, no kidding," Clough said into the phone. "Anything you can tell me about his health, about why he would seek you out?"

"Dr. Reuben Feldman was his MD," Dr. Charles advised. "Reuben's been a family physician in the area for twenty years. Probably more. His wife, Deborah, co-owns Global Travel. Reuben referred Kelleher to me for an examination. He'd been having headaches and dizzy spells. The symptoms were suggestive of a tumor in the brain."

"At my insistence, he had an MRI," Dr. Charles continued. "The MRI detected a highly malignant type of brain tumor. He had all the symptoms when I prescribed the scan, including headaches, nausea, dizziness and partial memory loss. The symptoms had become more acute. Kelleher was a heavy smoker and drank more than most people. Irish Whiskey from what he told me. Kelleher was high strung and had a remarkably stressful job as College President. All those factors would not have helped – likely they contributed to the cancer. We know for sure he was dying."

"What else can you tell me, Dr. Charles," asked the Sheriff. "How long did he have to live? What kind of tumor was it?"

"He had six, seven months, when first diagnosed. That's what I told him when I delivered the morbid news. The size and location of the tumor made it inoperable. The rate of growth would have made chemotherapy useless too. He was resigned to his death and seemed to accept that fate. Kelleher was highly intelligent, perhaps borderline genius, but seemingly short on emotions and empathy, or else he'd trained himself that way."

"One thing more," offered Dr. Charles. "It was a bit strange that his wife never accompanied him to the MRI or any follow-up sessions I had with him. He insisted I not tell her or anyone else about his condition. I would not understand why a person would want that kept from their spouse, but I do not know the status of their marriage or what was happening in Kelleher's mind. I don't think she knew, Arthur."

"That does seem strange," replied Clough.

"I asked him why, and he shrugged off an explanation. But I did tell him I'd honor his request. You're the only person with whom I've shared his diagnosis, other than the surgeon who agreed with me that the tumor was too advanced for any intervention. Dr. Feldman called a few weeks ago, and I told him about the cancer. Feldman has not contacted me since the death, but he probably knows about it and defers to me as Kelleher's last attending physician."

Clough was familiar with the cancer and wanted to know what sort of pain-killing medication Dr. Charles had prescribed.

"I gave him doses of Morphine meds, so he could inject himself when the pain increased," Dr. Charles offered. "He did contact me regularly and routinely over the period before he died when he needed additional medications, additional vials of the pain reliever. The amount of Morphine prescribed was tolerable and was arresting his pain, according to my examinations and our discussions."

Dr. Charles knew he was talking with a medical person who understood all he was saying. He was respectful. "As you know, Arthur, everyone's different in their tolerance or acceptance of pain. Kelleher was much tougher than he looked. He took the cancer as a given and did not curse his illness, at least in my presence. He just wanted to keep on working at the College until he couldn't anymore."

"That explains the needle marks on his arms," Clough stated. "You confirmed what I suspected. No doubt we will validate that when you do your tests. David, I've not finished my examination of the body, but I'll want you to do some toxicology analyses before I pronounce the official Cause of Death. It will likely be a few more days before I finish here and release the body."

The Coroner paused for a moment, to assure Dr. Charles had understood. "That OK with you? It will be critical to ascertain the levels of the Morphine and any other substances in his body, including the level of alcohol."

"Sure, that's fine," Dr. Charles replied. "But Arthur, let me share another comment that Kelleher made to me the last time he was in my office. He said he was never into sports. Yet he marveled at how a truly great player would get tackled on the football field. Clobbered is the word he used. The great player would get up after every hit, maybe slowly, but get up and be ready for the next play. He so admired that."

"That may be why he didn't want anyone to know," Clough responded. "He did not want people to notice he was sick, that he was dying. He wanted to stay in the game and take on the next play."

"Have you reached any preliminary observations on the cause of death," Dr. Charles asked.

"Not really. Still possible this was a suicide, given the cancer, or even a homicide, given he had plenty of enemies. It could well be accidental, given he may have taken too much Morphine and it mixed with the whiskey. I'll need to interview several people and likely call for an Inquest before this is over. My investigation into the death itself may take precedence over determining cause of death. Your toxicology report will be critical, and your testimony at an Inquest too."

"See you at an Inquest?" Dr. Charles asked his colleague.

"If not before," Clough said, as he hung up the phone.

PRESENT

"May there be no reorganizations where you're going, no union negotiations and no Board of Trustees."

Izzy Kelleher felt it was appropriate to have a Memorial Service for her husband, especially since she would have to delay burial given the Coroner's post-mortem examination. That could take two weeks, longer, if the Coroner could not make a definitive determination without holding an official Inquest.

With assistance from Edith and Samantha, Mrs. Kelleher held the event at the College's Little Theatre on Friday afternoon at 4 PM, when there were few classes underway and just before the weekend. Staff were to be released from work an hour earlier than normal to participate. However, attendance was not required, so most people just left for home.

The Little Theatre, used for plays and lectures, held 200 people. The public auditorium held 1,200. The fieldhouse would hold 2,200 people, albeit mostly in bleachers and with squeezed butts. She opted for the small venue, accepting that this would not be a rousing event and a must for people to attend. She was right!

The weather that Friday in central New Jersey was chilly, windy and gray, with turbulent clouds. A typical fall day. The weather reminded Izzy of the day she buried her mother and how everyone was entertained watching the wind toss aside ladies' hats and piled-on hairdos and unravel men with comb-overs. Maybe it was natural to have a cloudy, windy day when a person was memorialized or buried.

There would not be a body in repose for the service. The Coroner held the corpse at the County Morgue and would for some time. The official Cause of Death had not been determined and certainly not whether Mr. Kelleher's death was from natural causes, foul play, an accident or a product of taking his life.

Those who attended Friday afternoon were grateful to get inside the building and out of the elements. The wind was blowing dust in their faces and throwing papers and leaves all over campus.

The faculty who stayed were not pleased to end their day with a lame tribute to dead President J. Paul Kelleher, especially with the uncertainty as to how he died. The President got blamed for whatever was considered weak or wrong with the Union's Bargaining Contract. The fact that the President took on the Board to argue in support of many of the faculty wants and concerns was unheeded.

Some employees wanted to get an early start on the evening commute, pick up kids at school and complete a few chores. Most were looking for an excuse to skip the ceremony. Those who came did so out of a sense of duty, compassion for the family and curiosity on who would say what and how the widow would react.

Izzy had labored over the direction the Memorial Service should take and who should speak. Her husband had not left her notes on what he might have wanted. They had wills, a trust for the boys and life insurance policies. All good. But they had not talked about funeral or Memorial Service protocol or preferences. J. Paul was young at 47 to think about death, and they never discussed it. They figured they had plenty of time when they were old or at least older.

Some people contend that a funeral or Memorial Service should be directed at the grieving family and friends, not the dead person. Izzy wasn't so sure. She was grieving. After all, Pauly was her life partner for sixteen years, even if the last few months had been troublesome.

Connor and Ian were old enough to understand dying but not the death of their father. They cringed over the front-page newspaper coverage. They agonized over their dad being found in his office. People around them were hesitant about what to say to the boys, given the unsettled circumstances. Izzy opted for them to stay at home with her sister rather than appear on campus.

After the night when his parents had argued in the bedroom, Ian had dropped his petition to rename himself. The younger Kelleher boy returned to the name Ian, embracing his father's Irish heritage. With his father dead, he cried aloud that he had ever wanted to use a different name.

Neither Izzy or J. Paul was a regular attendee at Ewing Presbyterian Church where they were members and mailed a monthly offering. Reverend John Bender seemed like the reasonable choice to guide the service. He had conducted confirmation training and related ceremonies for the two boys. Izzy wanted the Memorial Service to be respectful of all faiths, more secular than sacred, more pensive than maudlin. Upbeat not downbeat.

J. Paul had grown-up Roman Catholic as a diligent Irish kid. He bragged in adulthood that he had outgrown the orthodoxy without surrendering the methods of Catholicism – subtle blend of bribery, guilt provocation and Skinner's Behaviorism.

Izzy grew up Baptist. Both she and J. Paul had to confront their parents about dating each other, given the divergent religions. Neither had received the blessings of their parents to date. Certainly not to marry. That had soured the couple on organized religion, and they became protective of what beliefs they retained.

The couple decided on Presbyterian – for them and for the boys. The decision was not a result of any logical inducement, ranking of Christian denominations or comparing theologies and social policies. Rather, they liked the way Ewing Presbyterian Church looked with its gray sandstone façade and oak trees on the exterior and its grand wooden pews, red seat cushions and the prow of a ship as the pulpit on the interior.

Izzy had arrived at a personal observation she would often repeat. "The boys survived this religious mystification by ignoring their parents rather than attempting to reconcile our disparate advice and fumbled theological information."

"There are faculty and staff of all faiths and some of no faiths," Izzy advised Reverend Bender. "Pauly would not want to offend anyone. One of his most difficult tasks was coming up with a joke to tell at Convocation or to Rotary and Kiwanis Clubs, that would be non-offensive to a diverse community. As I recall, Pauly said he had five jokes he could tell reasonably well in public. The last thing he'd want to do is disparage any religion, denomination or non-religion for this service."

The widow Izzy asked County Commissioner Dominic Panichi, Board Chairman Gerald Pitman, Union President Sally Bowens and administrator Gene Wildwood to offer remarks. Interim President Bill Fishman would call the assembly to order, offer a brief statement and introduce Reverend Bender. At the end, after all remarks, Reverend Bender would invite anyone from the audience to speak. Fishman would stand at his side to assure all comments were appropriate and timely.

Panichi praised Kelleher as an "incredible leader" and "one of the smartest and most savvy administrators" he had ever known, thereby unleashing groans from a few folks. Vice President Donald Winters, Kelleher's rival for the presidency three years earlier, dropped his head into his hands over the superlatives. He still blamed politics and Kelleher for not getting the position.

Board Chairman Pitman did not show for the Memorial Service. Fishman offered a convenient if totally fabricated excuse. "I understand Dr. Pitman had a dental emergency and couldn't make it this afternoon," he said. "Something about a tooth extraction. For the patient, not for Dr. Pitman. I'm sure I speak for the entire Board of Trustees when I say how distraught they are about J. Paul's death. They had worked together well the past couple of years."

Instead of groans, there were snickers from several people seated in the theatre. Most people could not discern if Fishman was serious or making an absurd joke. Plenty of heads swiveled to look around to spot any Board members. There were three in the audience. One was a former Trustee.

Professor Sally Bowens was judicious and compassionate in her remarks. She praised Kelleher for his leadership. If people had expected an arsenal of insults, they were disappointed.

However, she did attempt sarcastic levity in her concluding remarks. "We all know President Kelleher was not pleased when he came to work that October day a year ago, to find a balloon mouse flying from the Administration Building. No one knew how that air-filled *Mickey Mouse* relative got up in the sky. Certainly, those of us in the Faculty Union still have no idea how that could have happened. The Sheriff, State Police, FBI and Marines were called in to conduct investigations, without success."

The previous groans and snickers turned into bursts of laughter as Bowens continued. "*Rattus Norvegicus* is the scientific term for a brown rat. As educators, we should all be aware of that nomenclature. Nevertheless, in celebration of President Kelleher's legacy, I am here to announce how the *Rattus Norvegicus* got tied to the roof."

With a huge smile and a wink as she left the podium, Sally admitted, "It was not the Faculty Union but the Support Staff Union that flew the helium that morning."

Gene Wildwood was next to speak. He approached the podium with a wave of laughter, given the balloon rat allegation. The laughter gave him a few moments to come up with an off-the-cuff retort. "President Kelleher, we mourn your death, on this day," he said. "We respect your contributions to our College. Izzy, we mourn for you, Connor and Ian and trust you'll find comfort in the days ahead. As for the helium rat, the proof is where that deflated balloon is now."

Wildwood praised the President for the Title III federal grant and for dedicating resources to the Computer Center. Then, as he exited the podium, Gene finished his remarks, "By the way, I have it on record that the flying rat balloon is stored in the garage of one Ralph Hughes. FBI agents are on their way."

Reverend Bender had no idea why the people were laughing, but he smiled as if he did. He asked if anyone wanted to make additional reflections.

Mrs. Edith Reynolds stood and asked if she could speak. "I've had the privilege of working with President Kelleher for three years. I'm going to miss him dearly, including his language and occasional flare-ups with Coach Solly, Dean Lieber, Miss Hart, the Union leaders, Commissioner Panichi, members of the Board of Chosen Freeholders and the four Vice Presidents, among others."

The President's Secretary continued, after waiting for the chuckles to subside. "I'm not sure if I can handle going into his office and not seeing him shining his shoes. I offer this toast of pretend Irish Whiskey to J. Paul." She held up a water glass for all to see and offered aloud: "To J. Paul Kelleher. May you rest in peace. Thank you for your dedicated services to this College, to our students and to Monroe County."

An unidentified faculty member in the back who had stood for the toast, added to what Edith had said. "May there be no reorganizations where you're going, no union negotiations and no Board of Trustees."

The widow Izzy was smiling too. She felt confident that her husband would have enjoyed the humor, including the jokes at his expense.

Once the audience settled down, and to everyone's amazement, Coach Solly stood to speak. He looked directly at Mrs. Kelleher when he spoke. "Izzy, we regret that J. Paul Kelleher has gone. We care for you and your family. If you need anything, please come to us."

Then, redirecting his eyes to those around him, he continued with a tell-tale grin. "Edith, I too will miss the wonderful conversations I've had with our President, but I know his impressive legacy will include our athletic program, and especially our men's basketball team."

When the hoots and howls subsided, Solly surprised everyone with an announcement. "Ladies and gentlemen, Mr. Fox, Miss Campbell and our coaches have approached Bartell to establish a Foundation scholarship in the name of J. Paul Kelleher. We have pledged to raise $10,000 to initiate this fund."

There was a murmur of applause, more out of shock than of understanding what had just happened.

"We already have $2,500 from Jack Kula of the Triano, Orr and Kula law firm for the scholarship fund," Solly added. "We expect the Board of Trustees to seek donations, too. Well, maybe not. However, if you would like to contribute, see Samantha Bartell."

Coach Solly then looked at Mrs. Kelleher, who was shaking her head out of confusion. "Izzy, we hope you and your sons are pleased," he said. "This is to honor your husband and out of respect for your family and admiration for you."

There was a hush over the audience as Coach Solly sat down and everyone turned to see Mrs. Kelleher seated in the front row. She was solemn but had no tears in her eyes. She was touched but also observant enough to know most people saw the sentiment Solly had for her. That could be an issue down the road.

To be sure, one County Sheriff saw it.

5

PRESENT

"Not sure he would have the balls to murder the guy."

Arthur Clough, the County Sheriff, was seated in the back row of the Little Theatre at the Memorial Service for President J. Paul Kelleher. He sat with his ears alert to the speakers while his thoughts focusing on the audience: *Who were these people who came out for a called service at the end of a Friday? Was the murderer or murderers here? Who was a conspirator? Who might be accomplices? Was there a murder? Why was no one crying? Who's that guy who came in so late?*

Sheriff Arthur Clough knew that if the President had been murdered, the guilty party or parties were most likely in the audience that day. He, she or they may even have been a speaker. Killers liked to return to the scene of the crime or in this case, stay around the scene of the crime. They delude themselves that they got away with the crime.

Clough sat next to Security Chief Jackson who pointed out persons who had repeated contacts with the President. Jackson focused on those who had grievances and resentment or had groused with Kelleher on more than one occasion – Coach Solly, Vice President Winters, Dean Lieber, Alan Fox, Roseanne Hart and Bill Fishman, among others.

Clough looked to the opposite side of the auditorium and saw Dr. David Charles watching the service too. He pointed out a young-looking man seated next to Fishman. "That's Richard Spurling," said Jackson in a whisper. "He's the Lead Accountant in the Business Office. Don't know much about him. He keeps to himself but doesn't wear a green eyeshade visor," Tyrone said, trying to lighten the moment.

"Spurling made a big deal out of Kelleher moving him out of his office," Jackson said. "He hated him for that. The moving guys showed up at his office door one morning and started to move furniture. Spurling's got some questionable connections in the County from what I hear. But our job is not to investigate employees. If so, I'd need to quadruple the number of Security Guards and pack more firearms."

Clough ignored the attempts at humor, choosing instead to scan a few more faces. "If he deals with money, he may be involved," he said. "What do you know about the Athletics Director, Alan Fox? He sure likes those leisure suits and apparently thinks he's stylish. Does he pursue the ladies? He did not seem pleased that Solly had made the announcement on a scholarship."

"He and Rebecca, the good-looking Department Secretary, are close but not in a romantic way," Jackson said. "She's nuts over Jack Kula, the College Attorney, in case you didn't know. Fox is a bit repulsive, if you ask me. Yes, he has more than one eye out for ladies, including the young ones in his classes."

Jackson leaned closer to the Sheriff and held a hand over his mouth to camouflage his words as if a spy was running around the place. "Fox's been a bit more subdued in recent weeks, as I see him in the halls or coming out of classrooms. Kelleher told me they spoke, but he didn't tell me the nature of their conversation. He did ask me to keep an eye on him."

"The guy that gets me, though, is Winters," Jackson continued. "He screws up when appointed as Interim President, and Kelleher wallops him. Then he disengages from everything. Checks-out. The guy needs to retire, if you ask me, or find another job. Now he's probably pissed Fishman was made Interim President and not him. He despised Kelleher."

"Do you think he'll try again to be President, with Kelleher gone?" asked the Sheriff. "He got the balls to go another round?"

"Who knows, but I doubt it," said the Security Chief. "He didn't have the backbone the first time. Many people would disagree, but the Board's not that disconnected in what's happening. They know he's withdrawn and not a good candidate for the position he has, let alone as a president. Even faculty have backed off the guy."

"What about this Dean Lieber guy?" the Sheriff asked. "Is he here today?"

"No, I don't see him," Jackson responded after glancing around the theater. "Lieber has lots of irons in the fire and may be out of town again. He would have reasons to see Kelleher gone. If angry or pressed, I suspect he could do anything."

"What about that tall, thin guy sitting next to Sally Bowens," Clough asked. "He's either very close to her or would seriously want to be. Who's he?"

"That's Ralph Hughes," Jackson replied. "Guess you can tell by the body language that he has the hots for Bowens. She does have a nice ass. Sally teaches Business and heads the Faculty Union. Ralph teaches Mathematics, but his claim to fame is that he's Sally's numbers cruncher. He's well-regarded for tilting the numbers to favor faculty during negotiations. Sally likes to tell people that Ralph knows his numbers. That means when she asks Ralph what's 2 plus 2, his answer is *whatever you want it to be*."

"Does he have a temper too," Clough asked while he scanned the crowd for more suspicious faces.

Jackson didn't hesitate to answer: "Sir, anyone who can juggle numbers probably has a conscience that can endure a murder."

Clough had moved on to another person, but Jackson continued his description of Hughes. "Ralph's the quiet one. Sally's the loud, extroverted one. He and Sally are an item as of a year or two. He got on the Faculty Union team just to get close to her, or so the rumor goes. Guess it worked. They don't live together, at least not yet. They can be quite devious."

"The widow Kelleher seems awfully calm, given she just lost her husband yesterday, and we don't know for sure how he died," Clough said. "An awful lot of women would be a wreck. She's not even wearing dark glasses."

"That's her nature, from what I have seen of her and regardless of setting," countered Jackson. "She's a tenured professor at Atlantic State College and overly intelligent in a grand and remarkable way. Not sure their marriage was 100%, although whose is? Mine sure wasn't. I hear you struck out in your marriage, too."

Jackson thought for a moment before he spoke. "Kelleher would be a tough guy to be married to. Before he became President, you should know, he liked to tease some of the women, harmlessly for the most part. He would joke with them in the halls or stick his head into their offices unannounced and ask them if they were horny. But he was selective regarding whom he approached. He knew the ones who would laugh, even if they did not like what he said, and those who would have thrown something at him."

"Did Kelleher or his wife fool around," the Sheriff asked casually, as if the question had little consequence.

"No, at least he didn't," Jackson responded, leaving the question hanging with respect to the wife.

"I understand Kelleher had a dirty mouth, liked to swear in meetings," said Clough more as a statement to be challenged.

"Yes," Jackson said. "J. Paul often used foul language even around women. He practiced *Equal Opportunity Vulgarity*. It didn't matter to him who was in the room. Kelleher needled the ladies, but to my knowledge he never made an improper advancement. Come to think of it, I doubt he ever made a proper advancement either."

"Who is that group of women sitting in the row behind widow Kelleher?" Clough asked, wanting to re-focus on the people in the audience before they all left.

"Don't know. I guess they may be Izzy's colleagues from Atlantic State,"

Jackson responded. "They are not with the College. Or if they are, they were just hired."

"Who's the black guy sitting next to Winters and the black lady next to him? They work here too?" Clough persisted.

"That's Dr. Carter, Vernon Carter," Tyrone answered. "He's the Dean of Sciences or something like that. Titles change a lot here. The pretty lady is his wife. She co-owns Global Travel in town with Dr. Feldman's wife. I expect you know Feldman and his wife, Deborah. Everyone does. Carter was tight with Winters, when he was Interim. Winters brought him in after the former dean got fired for a bogus resume. Rumor has it he told Vernon he could be the new Vice President of Academic Affairs when he, Winters, became President."

"That didn't work out too well, did it," Clough responded.

"Not even close. Vernon has a doctorate from Penn State," the Security Chief added. "He has a science background. Good guy, talented. The others, especially Lieber, resent him because he's good and works beyond the minimum."

"Does he have a motive," Clough asked.

"I would think he could be in cahoots with Winters," Jackson offered. "If that's what you're asking. Lieber could be too. Of course, race is still an issue here, as with most colleges, most organizations, most counties, most cities, most schoolyards. I heard that when he came for the on-campus interviews, the Search Committee had no idea he was not another white male."

"I doubt race was a factor in Kelleher's death if it was homicide," said Clough. "Everything else is on the table. I'll just keep poking around until I finish my preliminary report and get the toxicology data and can be sure how Kelleher died."

"Yeah, race was not an issue with Kelleher," Jackson volunteered. "After all, he kept me on as Security Chief when he could easily have put someone else in the position. He did try to butter me up though. Tried a great deal. Lunches, gifts. He wanted me to be beholden to him. He paid for that stuff out of his pocket. I checked. I made notes but never had to think about compromising anything. If I were a white male or a purple zombie, he would have tried to butter me up."

"What did he want from you, Jackson?" the Sheriff asked.

"Much of it was a test, to see when I would draw the line. Beyond that," Jackson explained, "Kelleher wanted to see the overnight registry we keep in our office. That's where we list strange or suspicious matters from our random drives around campus and walks in the buildings. Kelleher started that a few days after the helium balloon incident, probably to make sure we were on our toes. He was pissed that we had made no entry for that night. But, Arthur, Kelleher was far less crooked than a bunch of others here."

"Say, Jackson," the Sheriff started to ask. "What are these notes you keep? Would you share them with me? They could be useful in my investigation."

"Well, much of it is just my hunches, my sleuthing around stuff," Chief Jackson answered. "Some are notes from meetings. I put that stuff on paper, so I'd have a record if I'm ever boxed by someone for something I did or didn't do. I learned to do that when I was with the federal pen, especially with the warden there. With Kelleher, I didn't want him saying one thing about our lunches when my memory was something else. But I never had that sort of a problem with J. Paul. Never. He just wanted me to do my job, and it was his way of testing me on my integrity."

Jackson had left the Sheriff's question about seeing his notes without a reply, hoping that Clough would forget. He did not.

"So Chief, would you let me see your notes?" Clough re-asked.

"I'm embarrassed by some of them," Jackson said. "There are some comments on my staff and some on faculty that are a bit personal. How 'bout if I go through it first and pass on anything and everything pertinent to your investigation. I promise I will be thorough."

"Tyrone, you're admitting you have some passionate, mushy comments in there about one Deputy Diaz," the Sheriff surmised. "You want to censor them before I read those. Am I correct?"

Izzy Kelleher stood alone in a reception line at the back of the Little Theatre, as the participants filed out when the Memorial Service ended. Some passed respectfully through the door where she was standing to greet them. Most eased out unseen via the other two exits.

Within a few minutes the widow was overcome with anguish for her husband's death. More so, she agonized over having to absorb the death jargon and insensitive condolences from those who stood in line to say something:

> *Sorry for your loss.*
> *He will be missed.*
> *We were so shocked.*
> *He seemed so healthy.*
> *Your husband's in a better place.*
> *There's a reason for everything.*
> *God must have wanted J. Paul to be with him.*
> *I know how you feel.*
> *I lost a cousin last month.*
> *You plan to stay in town?*
> *Need anything?*
> *I'm a widow too.*

Do you like macaroni casseroles?
God doesn't give us more than we can handle.
How are you coping?
I knew someone who also got killed in his office. Imagine that.
How are the boys? What are their names again?
I wish I had the right words. Just know I care.
My thoughts and prayers are with you.
I am always just a phone call away.
I'll bring over a mac and cheese covered dish. From a box though.

Izzy got tired saying her stock response to each such question – *Thank you for coming.* So, she came up with a surrogate – *Thank you for joining us* – and began to alternate the retorts.

The best response was to Mrs. Helen Gray, Chairman of the Nursing Department. Gray pleaded, "Mrs. Kelleher, if you sell your house, Walter and I would love to make you an offer."

To which, the widow Kelleher responded, "Oh, sorry, Helen, my boys and I don't plan to move anytime soon. But when we do, be assured you and Walter will be the first persons we contact."

Mrs. Kelleher turned away and mumbled to herself, "When pigs fly, you bitch."

PRESENT

"We all have secrets, some of them may even be a little bit crooked."

The drive took a little over two hours for the two loaded cars on Saturday morning, two days after the body of President Kelleher was discovered in his office. Both cars were headed to Dave Russell's luxurious log cabin mansion in the Pocono Mountains.

This log cabin was not built by Daniel Boone, not with the high-end imported materials, multiple fireplaces, a loft with custom-crafted bunk beds, exposed beams and carved wood entry door. In this case, rustic and elegant were not an oxymoron.

Rebecca Campbell, Jack Kula, Samantha Bartell and Dominic Panichi were silent and solemn at first, driving together in the one car. They warily shared observations about Kelleher's Memorial Service and sympathies for his widow, Izzy. They would arrive by 11 AM, in time for a brisk walk and lunch in town.

The mood quickly switched as anticipation increased for seeing the mountains and Russell's mansion. The laughter peaked as they told tales about the law firm's ludicrous volleyball game and joked about the upcoming attorney basketball season.

The Triano, Orr and Kula law firm were holding a contest to pick the firm's team name for basketball. A few wanted to go with traditional names like *Lions*, *Tigers*, *Chiefs* or for a change of pace, *Teddy Bears*. The other finalists had been *Bricklayers*, *Big Subpoenas*, *Judges* and *Hung Juries*.

Liti-Gators was chosen, with an image of a toothy, guiltless alligator. Eventually, the four folks in the car came up with more alternatives – *Narcissistic Barmen*, *Spirit de corps*, *Disunity* and the favorite, *Egomaniacs*.

"You may not think we grasped the concept of teamwork when it came to volleyball," Kula shared, holding back his laughter. "However, once you see us play basketball, you will know where the term *one-on-one* originated!"

Edith Reynolds drove the Pocono-bound station wagon with passengers Izzy Kelleher, sons Connor and Ian and Cerberus, the family dog. Izzy's friend, Ella Cosby, met them at the YMCA parking lot and climbed into the front seat next to Edith.

After the experience of dealing with sympathizing relatives and nosy neighbors, the Kelleher boys were sleepy. It was after 10 AM on that Saturday when they hit the road, and the boys fell asleep almost immediately. The trio of women spoke in whispers, as much for the content as the volume.

Edith and Izzy were looking forward to an escape weekend, transitioning from the agony of processing the death of boss and husband, J. Paul Kelleher.

"So, Ella, I hear you have a jewelry business and make some wonderful pieces." Edith said. "Is that one of your pieces Izzy's wearing?"

Izzy jumped up and waved her necklace, so Edith could see it more clearly from the front seat. "This Lapis pendant is one of Ella's creations. The dark blue stone is the Lapis."

Ella had to interrupt, "Izzy, I didn't tell you earlier, but the Lapis or Lapis-Lazuli stone is said to relieve anger and negative thoughts, and ease frustrations. The word means Blue Stone. It takes polishing very well. It's a birthstone for Pisces. Izzy's birthday is March 17. She told me."

"Yes, it's St. Paddy's Day," Izzy said with a smile. "That's why J. Paul proposed to me. He still thinks I'm Irish." There was silence in the car as everyone processed that the widow had used the present tense to refer to her husband.

"Well," Izzy broke the silence. "I guess he went to his death still thinking that I'm Irish or predestined to marry one. But then green is my favorite color."

Edith's eyes and mind were on the road ahead. Her intuition suggested this Izzy and Ella friendship was more than platonic girl talk. She understood the necklace to be more than a sweet gift. But she chose not to look sideways.

Rebecca steered Jack's four-door 1976 BMW into the winding driveway at the side of the log mansion. She pulled to the back of the house in front of the three-car garage. She opened the back door with the key and then raised the middle garage door with the automatic opener.

She pulled the Beemer into the garage, as much to show off how comfortable she was with the whole place as to reveal the display of motorcycles, bikes and sporting equipment. There were about a dozen basketballs harnessed in a wire mesh cage, and cases of soda, beer, paper towels and toilet paper stacked on shelves.

Dave Russell's swanky cabin mansion had seven bedrooms – the expansive master bedroom, four more on the second floor and a fun and games bedroom off the first-floor den. The seventh was a loft accessed via a spiral staircase off the second floor, with rustic bunk beds, a pinball machine and a telescope.

Rebecca Campbell and Jack Kula gave Samantha and Dominic first choice. They grabbed the second story room overlooking the mountains with a walk-in shower. Jack and Rebecca selected the first-floor one that opened onto the massive wooden deck and the Jacuzzi hot tub.

The regulation pool table in the den was balanced by a dart board encased in a cabinet and a marbleized *Wurlitzer* jukebox. Blue lights lit up when playing one of the two-hundred 45 RPM records in the collection. There was a wet bar, commercial refrigerator, dishwasher and ice-maker. A previously tapped, eight-gallon, stainless-steel keg of beer was housed in its own refrigerated cooler, adjacent to cases of soft drinks and mixers.

"Time for a short hike," Rebecca shouted. "Grab a jacket. Let's head to the mountains. We can have lunch at that greasy hamburger place on the edge of town and then walk back to the car. Let's go guys!"

An hour or so later, or about thirty minutes past noon, Edith pulled her orange 1970 Volvo station wagon into the driveway. The car emptied quickly. The boys were excited now, if sluggish from the late-night confusions and morning nap. Izzy watched them for signs of despair and sorrow from having their father yanked from their lives.

Edith led the group down the second-floor hallway where the bedrooms were aligned. "Choose any one of these you want but omit the master bedroom on this floor. That's where Dave sleeps, usually not alone, with or without his wife. Check it out later, especially the extra-long mattress and the sunken shower and tub. He can close the blinds and turn on music right from his night stand. Don't ask me how I know. Not what you might think."

The door to the first bedroom was closed, so Ella, Edith and Izzy grabbed the next three. The one with the view of the stream behind the house was Edith's favorite. "There's a cool bedroom in the upstairs loft," Edith said to Connor and Ian. "Go and take your bags there. Have fun."

"Dyno-mite," declared Ian, in his best Jimmy Walker imitation.

After unloading their suitcases and inspecting the hall bathroom, with its two sinks, walk-in shower and separate tiled bathtub, the three ladies caught up with the boys in the first-floor den. Connor and Ian were arguing over a game of pool and how far they should open the sliding glass door to the deck. They were unusually argumentative, harboring anger cloaked in anguish over dad's death.

Izzy saw them and enveloped both in her arms, crying for them and her husband's death. "We'll make it, guys. Your father would want us to be strong.

Let's do our best to enjoy this fall weekend and being with Edith and Ella in the mountains. Pretty neat to see such a huge house and owned by a professional basketball player."

Izzy knew she was not very convincing, but she offered another appeal. "We can have fun. Edith said there is a brook with running water a half mile from the house."

They had picked up subs at the sandwich shop in town. Edith set the table with the turkey and roast beef heroes plus the chips and soft drinks she had brought. Hunger kicked in, and Izzy and the boys headed for the food. Edith and Ella headed for a bottle of chilled Pinot Grigio they found in the refrigerator.

The earlier-arrived hikers had now returned, a little tired but stuffed from the greasy burgers, fries and old-fashioned malted milkshakes. They piled out of Jack's BMW and headed single-file for the front door. "Hey, I think someone else is here," exclaimed Jack as he saw the heavy wooden door ajar. "Did I leave the front door open when we left?"

Izzy was the first to hear footsteps coming down the hall from the front door. She looked at Edith for an explanation. "Must be one of Russell's basketball buddies up for the weekend, too," Edith volunteered. "I'll go see. Not to worry. There's a ton of room."

Before she could rise from the table, Dominic and Jack descended from the kitchen and were entering the den, followed closely by Samantha and Rebecca. Connor and Ian looked worried, as much about having four more adults as not knowing who they were.

Ella initially looked with alarm at the intruders. Then she smiled in anticipation of more good times. The two pairs were dressed in hiking clothes and baseball caps, and the two guys each carried two bottles of wine. "Well, hi there," she said, "I guess there's more than one key to this house."

Cerberus looked up from his early afternoon nap and decided the group looked friendly enough. The German Shepherd need not go on guard duty.

Edith and Izzy reacted differently than Ella, once they had realized who was standing in the room and with whom. "Oh, hi, Samantha, Jack," Edith said, trying to get the lineup correct. "Rebecca, Mr. Panichi, hello to you. Or is it Samantha and the County Commissioner and Rebecca and the College's attorney?"

"Guess Coach Solly had multiple reservations, or we screwed up," Rebecca volunteered to replace the awkwardness. "Nice to see you all. Are these your boys, Mrs. Kelleher?"

Rebecca paused for a moment and added, "I'm with Jack. We've been dating for several months. Not much of a secret. Samantha can introduce Dominic."

Edith was quick to jump at the embarrassment. "Samantha, no need to introduce Mr. Panichi or anything. We all know him. This has been a weird week. Meeting you all here in the Poconos, I suppose, and sharing a house together for a weekend is pretty normal."

"Dominic, thanks for coming yesterday and offering remarks on Pauly's behalf," Izzy added, wanting to send a message that all was good with her. "Boys go out and shoot some baskets. Take your sandwiches and Cerberus and have a picnic."

For the next hour, the conversation was a round-table ebb and flow. One person would ask a problematic, penetrating question. Then another would throw out a frivolous follow-up inquiry to lighten the mood:

> *So, how long have you two been dating?*
> > *What's your favorite wine?*
> *Does Mr. Kula share legal cases with you?*
> > *I hear they use real ice cream when they make those milkshakes.*
> *Did you date Mr. Panichi when you worked for the County?*
> > *How was the drive from the city?*
> *I thought you were dating Alan Fox, the Athletic Director?*
> > *Have you seen the sports equipment in the garage?*
> *Was President Kelleher aware you were seeing the County Commissioner?*
> > *It sure is a lovely weekend, don't you think?*
> *Had he been drinking at the Board Meeting?*
> > *How does everyone like their steaks?*
> *What was Kelleher doing in his office that late at night?*
> > *Have you looked at the wine collection in the den?*
> *How many people turned out for the Memorial Service yesterday?*
> > *Did you know one can close the blinds and turn on music right from the bed in the master suite?*

They cooked the prime New York strip steaks on the fancy outdoor propane grill and roasted acorn squash in Russell's ultra-modern *Thermador* range. The oven itself was spotless, owing to superior cleaning and likely, sparse baking. Dominic made a pitcher of Margaritas topped with lime slices. He expertly poured the concoction into wide-mouthed salt edged-glasses.

Jack swallowed a hearty gulp of his Margarita while standing in the corner of the backyard deck talking with Izzy. "Izzy, may I ask a question? None of my business, but I am a lawyer after all. It's in my blood."

"Ask away. If I don't like the question, we can just finish our drinks, for now," Izzy said with a glimmer and wink of an eye.

"Izzy, did J. Paul leave any note or letter at home or the office? He seemed to have been coughing more lately, so had he been sick or something?"

Izzy sipped her drink and twirled the glass around to expose another area of salt on the rim before taking a second gulp. Then she answered. "Hey, that's two questions, Kula. But no, there was nothing, no note or letter. That seems odd to me, too, if he did take his own life. The Sheriff has not said for sure. Guess we don't know. I don't think he did."

"Not trying to be farcical, but Pauly was an English major, well actually, English Literature," Izzy added. "The guy loved to write. Now that I think of it, that would have been a good time to write prose or a poem in iambic pentameter. The verse could have simulated a heartbeat. Or he could have written his obituary. Now I have to do that."

They both suppressed laughter and looked at each other, managing grins. Jack spoke first. "J. Paul would have liked that reference, but he might have added a few foul words to go with the poetic verse." He thought to himself: *Sometimes humor is a substitute for grief.*

The two laughed openly now. Izzy could tell why Rebecca was in love with this guy, despite him being a lawyer. Jack could not help but embrace how fortunate J. Paul had been to be married to this beautiful woman, despite being a redheaded, English Literature professor.

Samantha and Dominic had taken their drinks for a walk toward the meadow in front of the mountain vista. "Do you think Izzy or Edith is upset with you or me?" Dominic asked. "They haven't said anything to me directly, at least not yet."

"There's too much going on in Izzy's life now, and she has the boys to consider," said Samantha. "Edith's a trooper. I was remiss in not sharing our relationship with her sooner. She may have known anyway. She is quiet but very perceptive. Besides, what's up with the Ella babe?"

"Said she was a racquetball friend," Dominic countered. "We all have secrets, some of them may even be a little bit crooked. Regardless, this Ella must be a good friend to accompany Izzy this weekend, after all she's been through."

Everyone headed for the bedrooms at the same time after eight-ball pool and two more bottles of wine. That is except for Samantha and Dominic. They stayed on the patio deck in the moonlight. All the couples refrained from any PDA (Public Displays of Affection) while gathered together. But now alone, the married man and the unmarried woman held hands and took turns tenderly rubbing each other's shoulders.

"Are you comfortable with what happened today?" Samantha asked. "I'm sorry. I had no idea the others would be here, too."

Dominic hugged the lady and kissed her on the forehead. "Hey, it's fine.

This was bound to happen sooner or later," he said. "We can trust them to be discreet, and we sure are blessed to have this time together. Except I don't like having to lie to my wife. I told her it was a convention I wanted me to go to, last minute. She did not seem to care."

Izzy put the boys down to sleep in the paneled loft after settling a minor argument on who got the top bunk. She cradled her sons in her arm, one by one. No one cried, but all were sad and somber.

A little after midnight, Izzy was still staring at the ceiling with the light drifting into the shadows of her sky blue-walled bedroom. A faint knock came at the door. The door slowly opened to reveal Ella in her flannel pajamas peering into the room.

"Ella, that you?" Izzy whispered. "Come in. I'm awake, pretty much. Rough day. Did I tell you how much I appreciate you'd come and be with us? I sure love my necklace. Samantha commented on it earlier this evening, too."

Ella went to the side of the bed and sat on the edge, while Izzy spooned a pillow as she snuggled under the covers. "Anything I can do, lady? Turn over. I'll give you a back scratch. That'll help you relax."

Izzy rolled over as Ella pulled back the top covers. She began a side-by-side and up-and-down motion with both hands scratching and then massaging Izzy's back.

"Thanks. That feels great." Izzy sighed, laying quietly, almost drifting into sleep. "I so appreciate we can be good friends and share experiences, even ones as horrible as a husband's death," Izzy whispered to Ella, who stopped the massage as Izzy fluffed the pillow, turned on her side and pulled up the covers.

"Pauly was not the perfect husband," Izzy whispered. "Clearly, I was never the perfect wife, but I did love the man, and we didn't believe in perfection. I loved him a lot. It's hard, maybe harder because we did have tension in the relationship the past few months. I will miss him, not only for the boys but for me, too. He was much sicker than I thought. He was too proud to share. Why didn't he tell me how sick he was? That's just not fair, not fair at all."

Izzy rolled back over on her side and closed her eyes. Ella stayed sitting on the edge of the bed until her troubled lady friend fell asleep, her arm resting on Izzy's shoulder. Consoling Izzy and soothing herself. Then Ella quietly left the room and headed back to her bed, where she lay for quite a while before finally falling asleep.

Izzy rose from a deep sleep at sunrise. She had to authenticate in her mind where she was and what day it was. It had been a refreshing sleep with the window open and a brisk breeze providing a marvelous tonic.

The widow glided down the stairs awake but still in a daze and found the kitchen. She located the *Mr. Coffee* drip-coffee machine and made a pot before heading to the front porch and the white rocking chairs.

The birds were busy chirping. The morning sun came dappling in through the rustling leaves. She could smell the forest and the coffee percolating in the kitchen.

It was a perfect time to cry.

PRESENT

"Was your animosity enough to consider killing him?"

On Monday morning, the following week, Edith Reynolds and Rebecca Campbell thanked Coach Solly profusely for the Poconos weekend retreat. Rebecca had mentioned earlier that Jack had joined them. She did not tell him that Samantha had brought a male friend who happened to be the County Commissioner.

Edith noted over the phone that Izzy's two sons had accompanied her. "My husband declined the invitation, Solly, so he could watch football." Edith chose not to mention the single, female racquetball friend Izzy brought along. Fortunately, the basketball coach did not ask if anyone else had come or been there.

"How did Izzy handle the weekend, what with J. Paul's suicide, Friday's Memorial Service and all?" Solly asked Edith.

Edith jumped on Solly's question. "No one said anything about suicide. Where did you hear that? It seems remote given there was no suicide letter at the office. I can't bear to think that someone murdered the guy. He had enemies but . . ."

Solly cut her off mid-sentence. "Enemies are one thing. People who want to kill you is something else. Izzy's strong. She'll survive this, no matter what the outcome. The suicide just seems more logical."

"Hey Edith," Solly said trusting he had her attention. "You think it'd be all right if I were to call Izzy or stopped by her house sometime?"

Just then there was a firm knock on his office door. "Edith, I'll need to get back to you. Someone's at the damn door. I have a class to prepare for in an hour," Solly said. He simultaneously hung up the receiver and abruptly spoke, "Yes, come in."

It was Arthur Clough, the Sheriff and Coroner all rolled up into one, looking slovenly as was his modus operandi.

Clough was on target and in full mode. His game was in progress. He had found that his interrogated prey liked to think they had a superiority over him. He let them have the decided advantage in outward appearance and lulled them into misjudging him, while he ran over them in foxy astuteness.

"Coach, sorry to bother you, but I have a few questions to ask, if I may," said the sly, snoopy cop. "I'm Arthur Clough, C-L-O-U-G-H, pronounced *clue*, the County Sheriff. I'm investigating the death of President Kelleher."

"I guess I have a few minutes, but I have a class shortly," offered an off-guard and inconvenienced Solly. "Monday mornings are hectic, so what do you want? Hey, didn't I see you at the service on Friday afternoon at the College?"

"Yes, I was there," said Clough. "Horrible thing that your President has died. From what I gather, though, you weren't a big fan."

"He was a real prick when it came to basketball. We have a winning program. Kelleher ignored it and didn't appreciate athletics. Thought athletes were bums."

"He wouldn't grant you funds for the National Championship games in Kansas. That right?"

"Oh, he finally did, $2,000. We made up the difference in donations and a bake sale," offered the Coach. "The bus needed a tire change on the way. I paid for that. All the other teams had decent budgets. Not us. Clough, I need to get to class. Anything else you want to know?"

Choosing not to wait for another opening, Clough continued his line of questioning. "I hear Kelleher screwed up your promotion to a university to be an assistant coach. That must have upset you."

"Am I under suspicion or something, Sheriff? Just because I didn't like the man, may even have detested him, doesn't mean I'd do anything to the guy. Kill him? Besides, I thought it was suicide or a bad heart or something. Are you telling me you think it was murder?"

"Premature to comment," Clough said calmly. "I like touching all the bases, one at a time."

Clough offered a fishing metaphor to substitute for the baseball one. "You can catch a big fish without making a splash with just a piece of string, a sharp hook and inviting bait."

"So, the hint this was murder was the inviting bait?" Solly said, as he gathered his class textbook and headed for the office door. "Not very nice."

"Ah, just one more thing," the Sheriff said, casually blocking the exit. "Any truth to the rumor that you see Izzy Kelleher on a social basis and Kelleher found out about it?"

Solly impolitely shoved the Sheriff to one side and plowed through the door. "Sorry, Clough, my teaching comes first. As for Mrs. Kelleher, we both play racquetball at the Y and sometimes run into each other. I see her at various College events. That's all, I'm married with two kids and plan to keep it that way. She's married, too. Well, now she's a widow with two teenage boys. Check you later."

As Coach Solly hurried down the hall, he yelled back at the Sheriff, "Go cast your fishing pole someplace else."

David Lieber, Dean of Instructional Resources, sat in his office that same Monday morning, contemplating several pieces of artwork going for auction in Philadelphia the end of the month. His mind was not really focused on the art or the reports on his desk. He decided to make a call.

"Hello, Donald, this is David," said Lieber. "How's your day going so far?"

"What can I do for you, David" said Winters. "I hear that Sheriff is running around campus poking his head into people's business and making hints that Kelleher's death was not suicide or an accident. For all I know, he's on his way to see me. He come to you yet?"

"Donald, I could use a good alibi for late Wednesday evening after the Board Meeting, when the bastard Kelleher died," Lieber blurted, catching Winters aghast. He knew he could enlist Winters to the scheme.

"What are you talking about? Where were you that you need an alibi?" said the still confused Winters.

"I thought you could help me. I was at the Board Meeting for the Media Center thing, but I stayed longer than you did, enough to see Kelleher dig into the liquor he keeps in his office. As you know, Pitman and nut-case Harrison didn't want to spend the grant money on equipment for the faculty, and people were pissed off. I left but ended up at a bar and didn't leave there until the 2 AM closing."

"Well that's still a decent alibi, assuming the bartender could confirm, or other customers saw you. Which bar was it? Did you get smashed?"

"Donald, it was a stripper bar, a girlie joint outside of town. The drinks were flowing, and I was being nice to the ladies, trying to drown my anger. I wanted an escape. My wife would not understand. This Clough fellow might not either."

Lieber then sprung the purpose of his call. "Can we say we ended up at Murphy's Pub for a couple of beers and then went home about 1 AM," Lieber asked, more like a plea than a proposal.

Donald Winters was correct. Sheriff Clough was in his outer office looking around and waiting. Winters' secretary figured she had stalled long enough and used the desk intercom to alert her boss of the bizarre visitor.

"Well, of course, send the Sheriff in," said Winters so that Lieber could hear. He gingerly laid down the phone receiver and straightened the papers on his desk.

"Good morning, sir, we met briefly. I'm Arthur Clough, the County Sheriff. I just want to ask you a few questions as I try to figure all this out. Not easy for me. I usually don't have such a high-profile case in a county like Monroe."

Winters looked over Clough's appearance without being offensive. He could not help noticing the wrinkled light blue shirt and rumpled hat. The Sheriff was inside the building and a Vice President's office, yet he kept that hat on his head.

"Looks like a lot of people, you included, did not care much for the former President," Clough said.

"Hate might be a better choice of words, Sheriff," Winters clarified. "Maybe despise. People loathed the guy."

"Enough to murder him?" Clough asked.

"Probably. If you're asking if I had reason to murder him, then the answer is *yes*. Hypothetically," Winters quickly differentiated. "If I could piss on his grave, I'd consider that my gift to the College. How's that."

"You know we have a Faculty Union?" Winters continued. "Well, we have seven unresolved formal grievances this year, more that we've had in the past four years."

"Could be that some faculty need to be disturbed, shoved a little or a lot out of their easy life," Clough offered. "Perhaps you needed a nudge out of complacency."

"Complacency," Winters echoed. "Is that what you think this is about? Look, last Spring, Kelleher sent out a collegewide memo about faculty cuts and financial exigencies. He said he needed a minimum 15% overall budget cut, including staffing, health insurance, supplies. We were already preparing the new budget, and then we had to revise our projections drastically. We weren't told why."

"Look," an angry Winters continued. "Kelleher does this every April, as if it's an exercise, a medicine we have to swallow like cod liver oil. Except this doesn't make us better or stronger. Then like the previous year, he thanks us and says to submit the normal budget. We never implemented the cuts. All that work. All that agony."

"Perhaps he wanted the budget managers to spend more time with their accounts," Clough tried again. "Maybe he wanted you to begin with zero budgets and then affirm what you needed funds for. Did the Deans re-think what was important for their Divisions?"

"I screwed up as Interim President," Winters said defiantly, ignoring Clough's question. "That's my fault. But Kelleher played the Board and the politics. I didn't pay attention to the details of political machinations and tried to be both Vice President and President at the same time. Kelleher screwed me. I deserved to be President. I still do. Greenleaf promised me, and he championed me to the Board. That should have been the turning point."

Clough let Winters continue to rant, looking for signs of rage that might have provoked an assault or well-conceived plan to destroy the President. "Mr. Kelleher pulled your power base away from you," Clough added. "Must have been tough. Seems like quite a nasty guy."

"I hated Kelleher, if that's what this is about. Am I sad he's dead? No. Hell no. Hell no!"

Winters tried to restrain his anger, but he forged ahead. "Sheriff, at some point in life, we must face the reality of our existence. If we were made for better things or better things were to be in our lives, that would have happened. Know what I mean? I'm adjusting to lower expectations of myself. Lesser dreams. Take that as you want, but I'm glad he's dead."

Roseanne Hart knew she was in for it when Bill Fishman called midafternoon on Monday. He told her to meet him after work. Fishman's tone was serious. He did not give her an opportunity to come up with an excuse to bow out. "I'll meet you at 6 PM at the bar at Old Heidelberg. Don't be late."

Fishman was sitting at the bar, halfway through a frothy German beer when Roseanne mounted the stool next to him. He had already ordered her a draft.

"Good evening, Bill," Roseanne said. "Have a good day?"

"Roseanne," Fishman began without giving Roseanne time to grab the beer mug let alone take a drink. "I believe in being frank, especially when it comes to money. I know you've been padding your travel expenses to pocket the money. Right now, it amounts to almost $1,500." Remembering the 1970 Apollo 13 space command, Fishman concluded by saying, "Houston, we have a problem."

Roseanne tried to look normal and unimpressed, but she was scared. "Anyone else know about this, Bill?" she asked, her trembling voice giving away her panic.

"Spurling showed me the records last week, but I asked him to keep the details to himself and find a way to cover the discrepancies," Fishman said.

He placed his hand on Roseanne's opposite shoulder and lightly stroked her neck with his fingers. "He's good at hiding crooked numbers. We both are. Did it for Greenleaf and do it now, although Kelleher didn't realize it or care much."

Bill Fishman had been Vice President of Administrative Affairs, in charge of finances, almost since day one, rising from Lead Accountant when the founding VP died of a heart condition that first year. Fishman knew every nook and cranny where funds were spent, invested, stored, concealed and buried.

He was 50-something with a slightly expanded waistline. He had thinning salt and pepper hair, considerably more salt, and a similarly endowed mustache. His sideburns were carefully sculpted in a crescent shape that stretched to his chin. His wife had left him after their youngest daughter went off to college and there was no more reason to stay together. Now single, he ate what and when he wanted, and it showed.

Fishman may have lost interest in his weight and appearance and given up on style. But that did not mean he had lost interest in women. But after twenty years of marriage, he was out of the dating game. Why shop for new clothes or worry about thinning hair if not looking for companionship? Why worry about your weight?

"What's going on with you, Roseanne, that you suddenly need money?" Fishman's arm dropped from her shoulder to the back of the bar stool.

"I enjoy gambling, Bill, the horses at Monmouth Park Track. I've tried to quit, even cut back, but it's such a high for me," said Roseanne, abruptly appreciating that her colleague was affectionately sympathetic rather than antagonistically judgmental. She was not sure why. Her emotions were stampeding with no corral in sight.

"Roseanne, I think we can handle the money thing, but you know if reported, this could mean your job and prosecution," Fishman told her. He was more matter-of-fact than accusatory. "These are public funds, lady."

"Could you do something?" Roseanne moaned. "Bill that'd be great. I promise not to falsify records anymore. Promise. I can cut out the horses. But what about Spurling? Can you trust him to be discreet?"

"Let me worry about Richard," Fishman responded. "He's not squeaky clean by any means. I have leverage on the guy. He's cooked the books for many a Mafia business."

"Roseanne," Fishman said lingering on her name and with a pregnant pause to signify something major was to follow. "You're an attractive, middle-aged woman. To use today's language, you're a foxy lady. How 'bout we have dinner one night and get to know each other a bit more? I'll treat you well."

Fishman paused so his invitation would sink in, and he would be surrounded by the new logic of his attraction. "Would you be willing to do that?" he said, somewhat expecting rejection and hoping for at least acquiescence.

"Sure, Bill," her smile at his depiction of her as foxy, turning into a muddled laugh. "I've been called a few things in my life, especially by the Faculty Union, but this may be the first time I've been called foxy. I'll have dinner with you. To use another expression, do you intend to jump my bones?"

"Not sure how to answer that, lady," the VP said. "Yes, and you might slap me. No, I'd need to slap myself. I'm a guy, after all, getting older and putting on some weight. We're both single and not getting younger. My divorce was over five years ago. It's way past time to have some fun, treat a lady well."

"That would be fine, Bill," Roseanne responded knowingly. "I could use a good time, and honestly, I haven't been with a man for a while."

"There's one more thing, Roseanne, if I may," he said, not waiting for her to grant him a second request from the generous Genie Bottle. "I need an alibi for where I was the night Kelleher died, especially if that Sheriff character rules it a homicide. I thought you could tell him I was with you, having coffee at your house after the Board Meeting. That be acceptable to you? Just a bit of a fib, our little secret. Harmless, especially since we're seeing each other now."

Roseanne had to agree to the deception, but she couldn't help wondering why her new faithful companion would need an alibi. She was still wondering why he would so easily forgive her financial transgressions. Then it came to her: *Maybe the two are linked. He really needs an alibi. What is this guy capable of? What do I do now? What is really going on here?*

"Shall we eat," Bill Fishman said to his date for the evening. "Another beer, or do you want to move to wine?"

"Say Bill," Roseanne said with a hint that she was about the ask a burning question. "Have you ever thought about dying your hair?"

The funeral for Howard Tucker had been held at the Forest Lawn Memorial Gardens outside of Abington. The Programmers had served as Pall Bearers, and Gene had made brief, compassionate remarks at the site before the casket was lowered into the grave. No one mentioned or gave much thought to the fact that Howard had died while drinking. No one said he had lost control of his car and was unable to correct his path of destruction.

Dr. Dandridge and Miss Hart had positioned themselves together at the gravesite. The *Meat Market* staff directed projectiles of disgust and blame at them. Gene and Candace had stood together on the opposite side, unable to look at the two administrators or anyone else. Alice, Gene's spouse, had offered to come to the funeral, but Gene said he preferred to go alone. Bob, Candace's spouse, was away on another sales tour, but Candace would not have wanted him to come either.

Gloria, the widow Tucker, had opted from having guests toss dirt on top of the casket as it was lowered. She freaked at the concept of her husband lying under the earth. She had decided to hold the funeral service at the gravesite. Howard's wife did not want a parade of autos going from a church to the cemetery. That would only serve to remind her of how her husband had died.

They had expected a more substantial number and array of faculty and staff from the College to show up for Howard's ceremony. The trauma of a dead colleague had squashed much of the sentiment. Employees knew Howard, but most did not have any interaction with him. Everyone needed a break.

Gene Wildwood had bowed out of a romantic rendezvous that past Saturday, even though Candace's husband was out of town again. His wife, Alice, had gone to spend the weekend with her mother in Harrisburg. Kelleher's sudden and mysterious death had taken the wind out of Gene's prurient passion. Guilt replaced passion, but he hoped it was momentary. The last thing he wanted to do was disappoint Candace.

They had connected a few times, going back to the Computer Center in the evening to work. Gene put the time in for overtime pay, and Candace came for overtime help with her class homework. Gene was more than willing to assist. He appreciated how responsive she was when they finished the work and turned off the lights.

Gene wanted desperately to apologize to Candace that he did not come over to her house that Saturday afternoon. Candace had decided to come in late on Monday, after the weekend, so Gene had had to postpone his regret and remorse.

She arrived just after noon, and Gene asked Candace to join him in the hallway outside the Computer Center.

"I'm truly sorry, Candace, but with Kelleher's death, I'm still feeling guilty over Howard's death – what I might have done differently to save him from getting drunk. I have no misgivings about us or guilt about Alice. My shame is Howard's destiny with that tree."

"As long as it's not remorse over our relationship or shame about something you know about why Kelleher's dead," Candace quickly offered.

"Not hardly," Gene responded. "But I do need to share something with you about Kelleher, though it was only a few weeks ago I found out about it."

"Sure, what is it?"

Gene took a fresh breath of air before speaking. "Kelleher called me into his office and asked about the software package Bartell acquired to simulate and manage class size. I noticed there was a small, ring-bound notebook on his desk. He was writing in it when Edith pushed open the door to his office. When I came in, he quickly set it aside."

"I didn't pay much attention to it," Gene continued. "But he got up to take a leak in his bathroom. I peeked and saw he had written notes that day on Harrison, the Board Vice Chairman. There were notations on Hughes, the Union guy too. The journal was alphabetical with dividers, so these guys were under letter *H*. I quickly flipped to the letter *W*. There was a notation by me, *Wildwood*. It said you and I were in the Computer Center after hours with the lights off."

"How did he know that? Does he have a spy or something?" Candace frantically asked, becoming more and more alarmed that their romantic rendezvous was no secret.

"I thought I was tempting fate, so I didn't look at the notebook any further. He didn't close the bathroom door, as I heard him peeing into the toilet. When the peeing stopped, I flipped the book and jumped back in my seat. Kelleher didn't say anything to me when he came out, other than about the efficiency classroom ratings."

Gene got nervous, and his stuttering started to interfere with his speech. "I saw him in the *ha-ha*-hall last week, a *da*-day before the Board Meeting. He told me you are one fine looking chick. Built like a brick house, he said. Too bad you're married, or maybe not."

"That pissed me off. I thought he was just his obnoxious self. No, it was his way of telling me he was on to us screwing around. I guess Security had made a *no-no*-notation in their overnight register, seeing us together with the illusion of working late. Kelleher sees that record book every day or two. It just fed his narcissistic voyeurism."

Candace looked like she had seen a ghost – not *Casper the Friendly* one. "Gene, this is not good. If Kelleher knows about us and has written about us in the damn notebook, what happens if someone finds it? I'm screwed."

"Not much we can do about it now," Gene stated straightforwardly. "The guy's dead and the office is still a Crime Scene, as far as I know anyway."

"Gene, we have to do something, find that notebook," Candace responded, sounding both desperate and determined. "Maybe I can find a way inside the office one of these early mornings. Just so that Sheriff doesn't find the thing."

"I haven't heard anyone else mention it," Gene offered, trying to calm his hush-hush lover. "I'll call Edith and find out if the Sheriff has it. Kelleher may have kept it someplace other than his office, but I doubt it."

"Candace," Gene continued now remembering why he had called Candace. "If Kelleher's death is ruled a homicide, and that's the prevailing campus opinion. That gives me the other reason to call you today."

"What, what is it?" Candace asked, with considerable trepidation.

"I know we're innocent, but it'd be best for us to agree on our alibis. Let's agree that we met up at the Computer Center to catch up on some jobs after leaving the meeting. We cover each other. Security has a record we've worked late together before. I don't care if they speculate on what we were doing."

"But Gene," Candace said, "I was home with Bob. He'd be my alibi. Where were you?"

"Candace," Gene confessed, "I was at the Board Meeting. Kelleher wanted to acknowledge before the Board what Samantha and I did on the course efficiency stuff. The trouble is, I was one of the last to leave after the meeting. That's sure to come out. He invited me and others into his office for a drink, and some of us stayed longer than we should. I thought I might ask him about the notebook."

Professor Sally Bowens was gathering her notes and erasing the blackboard at the end of class Monday afternoon when she saw a man standing in her path to the doorway. Her students were filing past him, screening the guy's appearance with their eyes and shaking their heads as they walked. Some snickered. Others banged into the wall with their attention so diverted.

Bowens fidgeted with her lecture papers and tried to look surprised when the man approached her. She struggled to avoid mocking him, as the guy kept checking out the classroom as if he'd never been in one. He had an unlit cigar stuck in his mouth and a floppy hat. She thought the cigar might be glued to his lips. She wondered if she should call Security. The guy looked menacing.

"Professor Bowens, I'm Arthur Clough," said the Sheriff. "I'm working on the death of President Kelleher. Do you have a minute to answer some questions for my report, and as I complete my Coroner's examination of the body?"

"What do questions of me have to do with an examination of Kelleher's dead body," Sally Bowens said, in an impugning manner.

"Thanks for asking," replied Clough. "My questions may help me determine if he died of natural causes."

"Miss Bowens, you battled with Kelleher repeatedly over the years. No doubt things got hot from time to time," Clough offered without giving Bowens an opportunity to reply until he had overwhelmed her.

"This incident with the helium balloon was more than a nuisance to President Kelleher and stalled negotiations for months," Clough continued. "You must have been furious. You had faculty breathing down your neck to get the Union bargaining agreement done. It took several months after the contract was up before there was a settlement. That about right?"

Bowens checked her watch and the wall clock to gain time, to prioritize her best answers. "Stalls in negotiations are normal," she began. "No big deal. Kelleher relished conflict. After-the-fact, it might not have been the best tactic to fly that balloon, but you got to admit it was funny. Got the College on the front page of the local paper. Probably helped enrollment. But the helium-filled *Mickey Mouse* pushed Kelleher too far. He came at me with both barrels. Chief Jackson tried to get me to confess who got on the roof to fly the thing."

"But you refused to relinquish the culprit, or did you not know?" Clough persisted.

"I knew. Jackson knew that I knew. He thought the prank was harmless and Kelleher had no sense of humor. When negotiations were put on hold, Kelleher never asked Jackson again about any investigation or how it got in the sky."

"Was your animosity enough to consider killing him?" Clough blurted.

Sally Bowens ignored the Sheriff and headed toward the rear classroom door, books and papers under her arms, a purse dangling from her shoulder.

"Sorry," said Bowens. "But I have another class in another building and need to stop by the Ladies Room first, if that's OK with you. We can talk some other day."

"Oh, sure, Professor. I wouldn't want to impede your students from learning."

"However, just one more thing," said Clough, tossing out more bait to get a reaction as Bowens sped up her gait. "Were you with Professor Hughes the evening the President died?"

PRESENT

"Sounds like a pretty good motive for murder."

Sheriff Arthur Clough was not pleased to have this death on his personal police plate and forced to devote so much time to its resolution. The fact that the *Jersey Star* carried a frontpage story on the case in every issue made it even more unbearable. The bizarre murder, suicide, ordinary or extraordinary death was guaranteed to suck up his time for weeks.

Clough liked being called "sir" around the County Sheriff's Office and on the scene. It might be formal, but it reminded others he was boss. Being early to appointments was another style mannerism. He found distinct advantages to being early, particularly in catching people unprepared. His pretense of being pesky was a maneuver to agitate them to give up clues, say or do something they would later regret.

He loved the word *clue,* especially since people could not pronounce his surname *Clough* as they should. His French ancestors had insisted on the surname respect after emigrating to New York's Castle Garden Port in 1855. They had arrived in a wooden schooner after forty-three days at sea, crammed together with the other 200 passengers in steerage below deck, with meager food and water.

The Sheriff relied on his intuition, but he didn't like that reference. He held that his mind-skill was just the accumulation of his experiences and everything he knew. Clough had long ago concluded that people possess a subconscious tendency to lie. For most folks, the tendency lay dormant. For others, it surfaced without hesitation. If Clough could get a suspect to blink, it would tell him something, betraying lies.

"The face, especially eyes, betray inner turmoil," he would say.

The Sheriff thought of himself as having a political Watergate Scandal with every investigation, even though he had never had one. The 1972 White

House coverup of the office break-in and eventual discovery of the "dirty tricks" to impede the FBI, had inspired him to adopt creative investigatory deception and assume the worst. Any obstruction of justice was a red flag to Clough.

Clough had completed a preliminary review of the body on Saturday in his dual role. The results had been conclusive that the cause of death was an overdosed ingestion of Morphine. Nevertheless, he was not about to share that information with anyone other than Dr. Charles, who would complete the toxicology analysis and add to the puzzle of how the College President died.

He preferred to conduct his interviews now. The dissection and subsequent inspection of the corpse could wait while he gathered more facts and surely more distorted and fake answers. Those notes would drive the direction of his investigation, along with the Inquest. He felt a formal courtroom inquisition was inevitable. It was well within his authority to call and preside over. It would be his starring moment.

Clough had to gather a few more lies and add those to his files before he would reveal that there would be an Inquest. Those same people would need to stand up to his questioning under oath and penalty of perjury prosecution.

Thanks to Security Chief Jackson, the Sheriff had an extensive list of persons who might well blink and provide him with information on the death. He wanted to give those persons time to sweat by subjecting them to tough questions before pressing them again under oath. Most would not expect a knock on their door and would be shocked to see him standing there, rumpled and looking out of sorts, but ready to go to work.

The Sheriff had called Samantha Bartell on Tuesday morning and asked if she would meet him for coffee in the Student Lounge in the Student Center. He knew she would not be surprised by a visit from him. He knew she had worked for the County Commissioner. *Everything is fine at the end. But first, wait for the end.* *Irish Leprechaun*

He wanted others in the College to see him talking to her and have that connection spread around campus.

He was halfway finished drinking the cup of coffee he had severely weakened by a milk overdose, when the Executive Assistant to the President showed up. She took a seat next to him at the table near the front windows. Samantha declined coffee, opting instead for a large *Tab* with ice. It was closer to the noon hour and to the re-energizing, sugary soft drink than to the early morning caffeine wake-up brew.

"Samantha, if I may, can we agree on one thing before we start," the Sheriff began the interview. "I won't ever call you Sam, if you never call me Art."

"I appreciate your request and will honor it, sir," Samantha responded. "Given this investigation and the unresolved death of my boss, I'd prefer you address me as Miss Bartell."

Clough held back a chuckle. The lady was sharp. He could see she was trying to disarm him even before he had a chance to disarm her. He made a mental note that this was a formidable witness and an intriguing potential suspect or, perhaps, a promising ally.

"Miss Bartell how are you taking the sudden death of your boss, President Kelleher?" Clough asked, casting out just another chunk of bait.

"I liked working for the guy. I really did. He was so smart and ran rings around the Vice Presidents, the union folks, Trustees and especially the politicians. Truth is, though, I'm worried about my job. Kelleher created this position in his office, and part of my charge was to press and irritate the Vice Presidents – with goodwill and a smile."

The position is being funded out of the Title III grant, and that can't go on forever."

"With Bill Fishman as Interim President, does that mean your job's in jeopardy?"

"Not now at least," Samantha said. "Fishman told me to keep doing what I was doing and that he had specific orders by the Board Chairman that this interim period was to calm the waters. Not do anything. He's to serve as caretaker. Period. Fishman had to agree he would not be a candidate for the President position when the investigation ended, and the Board started another search process."

"Fishman wanted to look at the four folders I keep for the President and that are usually on his desk," Samantha continued. "I told him the office was still a Crime Scene, and I would not touch them until you or Chief Jackson approved. Bill seemed pretty focused on seeing those files and going through the desk."

"You're right, Miss Bartell," the Sheriff clarified. The files are the property of the investigation now. Leave them untouched. The desk too."

His curiosity peaked, the Sheriff added, "What do they contain, Miss Bartell?"

"There's a folder for each of the four divisions," she responded. "They contain notes on assignments, memos, reports and the like President Kelleher used to track progress. There are colors on some items inside to signify the degree to which I thought the matter was a relative priority. The blue, or low priority items, he'd look at when he got home or never. Green would be something he should address. Those marked with the dreaded red were intended to get his attention ASAP."

"Kelleher wanted you to do that, I presume," said Clough.

"Yes, that's what he wanted."

"Did the Vice Presidents know you had authority to do that, essentially prioritize their work before the CEO," Clough asked.

"They knew, and they didn't like it. The guys were not happy Kelleher had each of them approach me before they could see him. That riled them good, as they had been able to wander into Greenleaf's office whenever they felt like it. Dr. Greenleaf had an open-door policy – if the door's open, come in. If closed, knock first. Kelleher was not keen on interruptions."

"Would you have any reason to harm the President, Miss Bartell?"

"He would yell at me sometimes, but I got plenty of that with the County, and I appreciated his intentions. I never understood all he was doing, and there were days when he was self-absorbed and mysterious, especially the past month or so. But if not for him, I would not have this job. Executive Assistant is a long way from a County Clerk, Mr. Clough. This position was made for me, so I don't see any logical or illogical reason I'd want to see Mr. Kelleher gone."

"I'll accept that," the Sheriff said. "Who do you think might have had the motivation or some reason to see Kelleher dead?"

"Mr. Clough, you must know that Donald Winters hated the man. After the presidential search, Kelleher picked on him even when he was down. He wanted the guy to do things. The Computer Center people were upset, given that Howard Tucker, the Director, was fired and then got drunk and rammed his car into a tree. David Lieber and Coach Solly were in and out of Kelleher's doghouse. The other Vice Presidents were too, except for Dr. Dandridge. There were others."

Samantha paused to twirl the straw and sip on her *Tab* soda and continued her inventory of suspects. "Dr. Carter was pissed at Kelleher for the way he felt he treated Winters. Vernon had ambitions that Kelleher's appointment squashed. J. Paul ripped up Alan Fox, the Athletics Director, for screwing around with students and screwing with their grades too. That was recently. Even Roseanne Hart got hit by Kelleher from time to time. He relied on her but kept her at attention most of the time. He wanted her to be more authoritarian, more directing."

Samantha took another sip, so she could consider more names. "The Faculty Union people, Sally Bowens and Ralph Hughes, had reason, perhaps. Kelleher put them down hard, and it was more than the flying rat. Others too. I'd not want to implicate the Board Chairman or Vice Chairman, but they were livid about the architect decision and other stuff. They are real oddballs. Why they are Board members is beyond me."

"Quite a list," Clough said. "Board members too? That surprises me."

Clough was far from surprised, but he hoped it would be a tease, a stepping-stone to further reveals.

"Edith told me some Board members have had hanky-panky goings-on at conventions," Samantha added.

"Tell me more about that. I'll get with Edith later."

"Well, every year, several Board members, certainly Pitman and Harrison, go to the annual conference of the Association of Junior and Community College Trustees. They mostly play around – skip the seminars and meetings. They do attend the Gala Trustees Recognition Dinner at the end. The one with an open bar and shrimp cocktails."

"A boondoggle," said Clough. "But that sounds more like an ethical problem, or is there more?"

"There's more. Edith told me about Nashville last year. The Vice Chairman brought his girlfriend rather than his wife, if you get my drift. The College pays for everything – air, hotel, food – for the Trustee and his wife. Ironically though, Edith tells me Dr. Greenleaf thought nothing about it. Guess it's been going on for years. Kelleher told Chuck Harrison it was wrong and could not support it. Harrison and Pitman jumped all over Kelleher for that. They reasoned that a guest is a guest. Spouse or not. They felt entitled to spend College money on those trips."

"Surely not because they work so hard as Board members," Clough said. "Misuse of public funds constitutes a fraud, Miss Bartell. Could be a motive. Does Dominic know about it, or did they not use County funds? Did no one at the College look to report this malfeasance?"

"Sorry, I have no idea," Samantha admitted. "Fishman would know, probably Richard Spurling too. Spurling does all the proofing of the books and tracks every dollar and most every penny. President Kelleher was becoming aware of areas and decisions where Dr. Greenleaf had looked the other way. Some of those Board members thought Kelleher would do the same when they made him President."

"It took Kelleher two years to figure out that there was a conspiracy in the finances," Clough said. "He didn't know Greenleaf had bought into the deception? It was all that well hidden?"

Samantha Bartell nodded her head.

"Sounds like a good motive for murder," Clough offered.

Samantha Bartell nodded her head again.

"Miss Bartell, what about County Commissioner Panichi?" Clough asked. "Did he and Kelleher get along, have any problems?"

"I would not have any idea about that. Don't know. I worked at the County for Mr. Panichi for several months. He was good to me. They talked on the phone once or twice a week and had lunch at the Country Club every so often. I hardly see Mr. Panichi now. Did see him with Kelleher at the office a few times," Samantha said with a straight face that would foul a lie-detector machine.

"You worked for Panichi less than a year before you applied for the job with Kelleher," Clough said. "That seems pretty ambitious, or didn't you like the job? Was he upset that you left the County?"

"No. No. Not at all. He encouraged me to apply. I liked working for Dominic," replied Samantha, wishing she had referred to her former boss by his surname.

"You want me to believe you don't know much about our County Commissioner, Miss Bartell," the Sheriff said as he began to reel in the catch. "You're telling me you don't see the County Commissioner very often? Is that what you want to tell me?"

Samantha did not nod her head now. She knew she had been had. All her honesty was down the drain with lies about Panichi.

"Miss Bartell, that's the first lie you've told me," the Sheriff said. "The hell, you don't know. The hell, you don't see the guy. I understand you and Panichi know each other very well indeed, and in the Biblical sense of knowing. Not a big deal for me, even though he's married. What is, is that you lied. Care to revise your answer? Care to tell me how you got this job at the College?"

The ploy was working. He was now the one disarming suspects.

PRESENT

"That makes it look more like murder, don't you think?"

Izzy Kelleher and Coach Solly were meeting for breakfast at the Hightstown Diner after YMCA racquetball on Wednesday morning, a week after J. Paul Kelleher was found dead in his office. They had not played long. They preferred to prolong their time together afterward, rather than bouncing a ball around the court. Izzy needed to bang the stupid rubber sphere off the wall a few times. Maybe bang an opponent too.

Izzy and Solly got out of their respective cars, rendezvoused at the entry door and exchanged pecks on the cheek intended to miss their respective marks.

Solly picked out a corner booth meant for a party of six but now to serve the two of them. The waitress poured hot coffee for them. Solly ignored the menu and ordered the famous Philly Breakfast Special – two scrambled eggs, rye toast and *Scrapple.* Izzy ordered a toasted English muffin and orange marmalade.

With the waitress still standing over them, Izzy said, "Solly, do you really eat *Scrapple*? You do know it's made of pork odds and ends, mostly ends. Besides, you're Jewish!"

The waitress walked off with a big smile on her face, perhaps her first pleasant expression of the day. The place was full of hustling and bustling people; however, smiles and tips had been sporadic.

"Hey, you have to eat this shit if you were raised in Philly or Pittsburgh," Solly replied with a sheepish look conveying his partial embarrassment. "Why do you think they serve *Scrapple* at this diner, Izzy? Don't you want more to eat than an English muffin? You been eating well enough lately?"

Izzy was having a difficult time coming to grips with her husband's death and whether it would be judged as murder, suicide or from natural causes.

The more days went by without an official finding in her husband's death, the more stress and agony she felt. It had been a week since his death, five days since she had identified the body of her husband at County Morgue.

"Solly," the widow moaned, "I'm so damn tired of people asking me about the death. The dumb questions: *So how did J. Paul die? Did they really find his body in his office on the floor? How are the boys taking the death? What are you planning to do now? You must be so horrified?*"

Coach Solly tried to console his friend. "Izzy, I know you're a fan of movies. Remember in *Rocky* when Sly Stallone talks about how hard life hits us. He says how hard a boxer gets hit in the ring but keeps moving forward. How one chooses not to quit. That has to be you."

Izzy smiled at Solly's attempt to encapsulate the popular movie. "Funny, but J. Paul's version of that same movie was different. We saw it together. On the way home, his version was more like: *It's not how you take a hit. It's how fast and how hard you hit first and put 'em down, so they can't hit you at all.*"

"That sounds like him," Solly admitted. "But he barked more than he bit. More than he hit. If he'd hit me, he'd see what put 'em down is."

"Maybe. Maybe not." Izzy began. "J. Paul asked me whether I was sleeping with you or Ella Cosby, my friend from the Y. I didn't answer. I was upset with him. I don't know how he knew about Ella. I'm not sleeping with her either."

"The strange thing is," Izzy added, "I mostly feel apathy now, not sorrow. Disdain not grief. Feelings I don't understand. Damn it. All my emotions have been hollowed out, except I know I loved him. We went through a lot together. That's hard to forget or let go of. Son-of-a-bitch!"

"Hey, girls shouldn't curse," Solly exclaimed.

"Let's change the subject," he said. "How are the boys doing? Anything I can do? Maybe take them to a movie and grab pizza with my kids?"

"I'll curse if I want to," Izzy retorted. "At least I don't eat shit for breakfast. Since when do you judge speech? And the proper word is women, not girls."

"You forget, the boys and I were in the Poconos this past weekend at Dave Russell's cabin," she continued. "Then Rebecca, Jack and others showed up. It got awkward. We all got along fine but left Sunday morning."

"Would you have left him, had he not died, Izzy," asked Solly, getting back on target.

"No. Marriage is about working things out," Izzy offered as an abrupt philosophy. "It's not a sprint, but a marathon. It's not even a race. You have to pace everything."

"Have you noticed, it's divorced people who say that," Solly interjected. "Izzy, have you given thought to what you plan to do now?"

Izzy had not thought about that question at all. "Guess, for the time being, I'll stay here," she offered. "Things won't change much. It'll be tough on the boys, but they're older now. They'll get past it, though I do worry about them, especially Ian. How they compensate for losing their father. I'll look for a shrink, a child specialist, probably a male one. We are good financially. Pauly saw to that."

"You have your job and friends here too. You got the YMCA, racquetball and fresh fruit juice. And where can you find a better diner, one that has orange marmalade and serves *Scrapple*?"

"The boys are not into sports," she said. "They have friends, but teen boys can be cruel to each other. Our sons have never found comfort in a book. Go figure. The offspring of two English majors are determined to be as unlike their parents as they can. With their dad gone, not sure what they'll want to be like now."

"Izzy, I've not met Ella, but if she's a friend of yours, that's fine," Solly said as he finished his breakfast and looked for more coffee.

"She and I get together every so often to share," Izzy replied. "Her jewelry is quite lovely. Sometimes it's just good to have another female for conversation and sharing, without any agenda. I have colleagues from work and a few other friends, but most are couple friends. The others are awfully judgmental. They hesitate how to act toward a widow, especially with the jury out on how the husband died."

Solly decided to change the subject again. "Izzy, there's a campus rumor that J. Paul kept a notebook on people and suspicious things. Maybe to give him leverage. A Security Guard I know says he routinely checked the overnight logs. If he did keep notes, I'm there a few times. There may well be a whole chapter devoted to me. Did you ever hear of that? Perhaps he logged into it at home?"

"There was nothing in his briefcase" Izzy shared. "Edith and Samantha were the first to see his body on the floor. The Sheriff hasn't said anything to me about it, and they probably checked every square inch of Pauly's office. His desk too."

Solly looked away from Izzy. Then he said, "If there was a notebook, and it's gone, that makes it look more like murder, don't you think?"

"Since when did you become *Perry Mason*?" Izzy said. Still, she thought to herself: *Since when do you have something to hide? What are you not telling me?*

Dr. Vernon Carter, Dean of Science & Mathematics, and his wife, Katherine, co-owner of Global Travel, were on a chartered bus to Philadelphia and a Diana Ross concert. It was a rare mid-week evening concert, one of the first performances since the *Supremes* broke up.

"Reserved seats on the fifth row," Vernon said, loud enough for folks in other seats to hear. "Date night with my classy wife. What a great concept. You're still the best-looking woman at Global Travel."

Katherine playfully slapped her husband on the arm and said, "What do you mean, still?"

Carter had been visited by Sheriff Clough earlier that day. He was still processing the questions and attempting to resolve Clough's intent. Clough had revealed only a blank stare on what or who killed Kelleher. Carter thought to himself: *Was the Sheriff now convinced Kelleher had been murdered? Was he a suspect? What about Winters? He would be a more logical suspect, as would Lieber, Pitman, Sally Bowens, Solly and others he could inventory. Did he really trust me?*

Then he said to his wife, "You know, the Sheriff may be unkempt and wrinkled on the outside, but he's smooth and cunning on the inside."

"Katherine, most everyone on campus knew Kelleher smoked too much," Vernon added, now having his wife's attention. "His health was poor. He drank, probably to excess. He'd been coughing in meetings I attended. Winters said there were times he'd cough-up mucus and try to hide it. There were rumors Kelleher fainted one morning and was popping *Bayer* aspirins for his headaches like someone would down chocolate *M&M's*."

"Clough did share that there were no telltale signs of violence, no blood or bruises on the body. But he didn't rule out anything. My guess, Kelleher died of a heart condition. Then again, there might have been something serious with his lungs due to the smoking."

"I'm worried about Donald, though," Vernon emphasized. "Security said his car was there in the parking lot long after the Board Meeting ended that night."

"You think he might have done something," Katherine asked. "Maybe he got mad and confronted Kelleher. Lord knows he had reasons to be pissed at the guy. But is he capable of murder, whether planned or spontaneous?"

"Maybe not," Vernon responded. "But he and Lieber might."

Vernon gazed out the window at the stream of passing cars, before changing the topic. "Honey, do you remember David Charles? I took two chemistry classes with him at Drexel when I was working on my masters? He went to med school at Penn State and interned at Nittany Medical. We got together on campus a few times for coffee. Anyway, David ended up here in Monroe County as an MD specializing in Clinical Pathology. Small world."

"You did talk about the guy a few times," Katherine said as the bus entered the outskirts of Philadelphia and traffic picked up.

"I didn't know until today. Clough told me he was going to order a toxicology report, and it would be done by Dr. David Charles. I told him I knew David from grad school. David was top notch. Very bright guy. Monroe County doesn't employ a Medical Examiner, and Clough is Coroner as well as the Sheriff. That's how things work here."

"Clough farms out toxicology and other analyses to specialists, who are credentialed for that sort of thing," Vernon said. "He can obtain whatever analyses he needs. He examines the body and determines if and what further tests are necessary. He alone has authority to execute the Death Certificate."

"The Sheriff said he'd mention me to Dr. Charles, so I expect I'll be getting a phone call from him," Vernon shared. "The fact Clough needs a toxicology report suggests drugs were involved. He wasn't about to volunteer any information to me about his post-mortem exam. But he seemed to trust me, especially when we discussed the science of it all. The death could still be suicide, murder or just natural causes."

"Vernon, you know the College has been doing its travel business with us for the past couple of years. Is that something the Sheriff would want to see?"

"I expect so," Vernon said. "Winters told me that some Board members charge expenses over the per diem limit and get away with it. He says one Board member brings along a lady friend, and the others look the other way. You would have a record of the lady's travel."

"What's so bad about that? Aren't they allowed to bring their spouse," Katherine said to make a point.

Vernon smiled, kissed his wife on the forehead and added, "Yes, dear, but the guy is married. And the lady friend he brings is not his spouse!"

PRESENT

"Maybe he'd still be alive."

Deputy Sheriff Blanca Diaz had completed her Crime Scene investigation late on Tuesday. She had emptied the contents of the wastebasket in the President's Office and gone through drawers and cabinets in the desk and credenza. The photos she had taken were in the lab and were laid out at the Sheriff's Office to reflect where the body was relative to every other place and space.

She had given the *Polaroids* to the Sheriff that same day. He would use them until the lab processed the photos taken at the scene with the official, state-of-the-art camera. Clough liked to have a set as soon as possible. He kept them for reference in his binder or the side-pocket of his corduroy coat.

He would pull-out the photos, even at inopportune times, to study them anew. Clough felt the image would eventually reveal something critical to the investigation. It was like a fortune teller reading tea leaves, knowing ultimately the images provide powerful insights.

Clough knew if he studied the photos repeatedly enough, he would be getting that much closer to a key detail. It was just a matter of time, and Clough was deliberate and patient.

Diaz had taken the glass on the credenza to the lab for fingerprinting. But most likely, it would only reflect Kelleher's prints and the Irish Whiskey consumed.

There had been six retrievable fingerprints on the desk chair next to the body. The prints were sent to the FBI to examine with their new reader. The prints were initially matched to the nightly cleaning crew who had volunteered to be fingerprinted, as did Edith Reynolds, Bartell and Fishman.

There was one print that stood alone, however, and for which a match could not be placed. All were smudged, owing to the uneven leather surface of the chair. It would be a challenge to match the undistorted images with prints taken under controlled conditions.

The County Sheriff would have to decide the extent he would want other staff and Board Members to submit to being fingerprinted – to identify that one print. Deputy Diaz figured he would want prints from Izzy and other family members. But she was not counting on the stray set to reveal much. Besides, who would question a wife's fingerprints on her husband's office chair?

The door to the Executive Bathroom had been locked. It had taken a phone call by Deputy Diaz to her friend and lover, Security Chief Jackson, to approve access the room. She could have broken through the door with her hip, but then evidence might have been compromised. There was no hurry.

"Tyrone how long had Kelleher kept his bathroom door locked?" she asked. "Check the records with the custodial crew, please."

"I was in there a few times," Tyrone offered. "We would be in meetings in the Board Room and during a break, the guys would head to his bathroom. The women would go down the hall to the Ladies Room. I doubt a female ever set foot in that space. He kept the door closed."

Edith had told Diaz that Kelleher kept the door locked and did not allow maintenance or cleaning crews to enter the bathroom the past three months. She had not asked him why. Knowing Kelleher, Edith was confident the bathroom was clean, unlike what it would have been had her husband, Roy, been the one with private access.

The President's private bathroom did not appear to add any information to the puzzle as to how he had died. For a bathroom used daily and exclusively by an adult male, without a custodial crew scrubbing the sink, toilet and shower, the room was spic and span. Diaz had to laugh when she looked in the cabinet under the sink and found two boxes of the Procter & Gamble cleaning product along with *Bab-O*, a toilet-bowl brush and several terry-cloth rags. Her apartment should be so clean.

The towel rack held two white bath towels each monogrammed with *JPH*. If Kelleher had used the bathroom the night he died, he left no remnant of a bodily function. Diaz took photos anyway, and with both cameras. *Clough would want the Polaroids right away.*

The Deputy Sheriff wondered if President Kelleher had cleaned his toilet and sink as often as he polished his shoes. She knew that those shoes, left perpendicularly behind the desk, were still on the Sheriff's mind.

There had been no evidence of foul play or anything else in the President's car. No empty bottles or tell-tale meds tossed under the seats. No misplaced underwear or stale food in the back seat. No blood traces anywhere.

The car's interior was clean and tidy, including a stand-alone ashtray for

Kelleher's cigarette butts. The standard ashtray in the car was not ever used, or else it had been scrubbed.

The past weekend had put a hold on the investigation and completion of the Crime Scene processing, as had the locked Executive Bathroom. Typically, the initial process would take two-three days. In this case, it was the middle of the day on Wednesday, a week later, before the area could be released.

Edith and Samantha looked over the office one more time after the barriers were removed and the space could be visited. There was something therapeutically restorative for her when Clough released the office as a Crime Scene.

As soon as she got approval from the Sheriff, and with the Chief Jackson's permission, Edith Reynolds arranged for a thorough cleaning of the President's Office.

"It's going to be very difficult for me to come into this office, at least for a while," Edith said. "I just look behind that desk and see his body on the rug, his arm raised above his head with that cigarette. I sometimes feel like one of those threatening Irish Leprechauns is hiding somewhere, ready to attack me."

Samantha walked around the desk to the get a better angle on the place where Kelleher's dead body was found. "I understand," she said. "I just wish I had stayed later that night of the Board Meeting. Maybe he'd still be alive."

Edith chose not to rely on the campus janitorial workers. Instead, she contracted with an outside professional firm to swarm the property with its truck that day, unloading crew, supplies and machines. The attack squad was directed to scrub, scour, shampoo, deodorize and sanitize everything, and then redo the effort.

The industrial-strength disinfectants and antiseptics assured that all germs and bacteria, much less any aura of death, had been eliminated. Even the Irish Ghosts that lingered in the room were sanitized.

> Whatever you do.
> Whatever you don't do.
> Don't upset a Leprechaun.,
> Especially when he is drinking.
> *Irish Leprechaun*

The furniture was highly polished, along with all items on the credenza and the desk, including the ashtray, pen set, desk blotter, cigarette lighter and photos. Mrs. Kelleher was not ready to enter the office and remove any personal effects. Edith was not ready to remove anything.

After the Sheriff had completed his examination, the President's Secretary had returned the four division folders to their proper place on the right side of the leather-edged desk blotter. She had extracted a few documents to pass on to Interim President Fishman.

Reynolds ceremoniously replaced the brilliant glass *Waterford* Shamrock paperweight on top of the folders, taking pride that the glass piece was spotless. Exactly as Mr. Kelleher wanted it. Indeed, everything else was too!

Edith looked around and deliberately breathed in the sanitized smells, now monopolizing the air. She adjusted the Shamrock to be squared with the folders and thought to herself: *President Kelleher would want everything returned to its rightful place. How he loved this glass paperweight. How many hours did he spend in this office going through reports, writing memos and dictating letters to me. And he was a sick man, fighting cancer.*

She felt like she had had a scrub-down bath herself.

Edith had placed Kelleher's polished shoes back in the closet with the other shoes. These were the ones conspicuously positioned under the desk when his body was found. She could see the President sitting back in his desk chair, a red paisley necktie around his neck but not yet tied. He would be waxing his shoes with another layer of *Kiwi* spit-shine. Then, the next day if not sooner, he would be shining the shoes again.

She did not see any need to have the professional crew apply its magic to the Executive Bathroom or the Board Room. There had been no dead body in those rooms.

There were still toiletry items in the bathroom that had belonged to Kelleher. Edith would wait until Mrs. Kelleher gathered or discarded those items or told her what to do with them. She could not wait for same in the President's Office.

PRESENT

"Looks like we have what we're looking for."

Sheriff Clough listened to the tape recording of the last Board Meeting and the September meeting, too. There was no recording of the Board's Executive Session to address the architect selection, so he called Jack Kula.

Kula told him about the pressure put on Kelleher by the Board Chairman and Vice Chairman to include the local firm, Zelinski, Corradetti & Greco. He told him that the two had been prepared to offer an amendment to the recommendation in the public session.

"The President met with Pitman, Harrison, Fishman and me before the meeting and explained the State process for architect selection," Kula said. "That didn't matter to Pitman. J. Paul asked me to check it out. I found out that old man Zelinski had promised $5,000 to the Board Chairman if his firm got in the final grouping. Zelinski didn't necessarily want the bid. He just wanted the firm to be in the newspaper and listed as a finalist along with the other more prestigious, recognized and far more experienced firms."

"What does that do for Zelinski?" Clough asked, priming Kula for more information.

"It means a lot to have your firm selected in the final two or three firms for a project as major as this Library," Kula replied. "It gets a foot in the door for another school project and promotes a legitimacy of corporate prestige."

As he drove to the College on Thursday morning, Arthur Clough was going over the conversation he'd had with Kula. He wanted to conduct a walk-through and tidy-up some Crime Scene irregularities. He visualized what the end of the September Board Meeting must have been, especially with Pitman arguing to hire a local, far less qualified firm. The money bribe never came out publicly. *Pretty smart of Kelleher*, he thought.

In his mind, and on his notepad, Clough had recorded that this would be a bribe of a public official, likely a felony. He observed that Pitman was stupid not to realize the embarrassment and potential prosecution Kelleher had avoided.

Clough wandered back to the President's Office early on that Thursday morning after enjoying his second cup of coffee. He would take down any leftover Crime Scene signs as part of his walkaround, but the doors were all locked. Edith had taken the rest of that week off, deciding not to be present when the Sheriff conducted the last of the death business in the office.

Samantha Bartell was at her desk, but she heard the Sheriff approach. She rose quickly to open the door to the outer office and then the President's Office. "Sheriff Clough," she remarked as she switched on the fluorescent lights, "Edith had a commercial cleaning crew come in here yesterday to do a heavy-duty number on this office. Top to bottom. It smells like someone dropped a bottle of *Lysol*. But the place is cleaner than it ever was. Everything got steam cleaned, polished and sanitized. The drapes are still at the cleaners being pressure washed, I think."

Samantha followed the Sheriff into the office. "Most of the files and materials, as well as Mr. Kelleher's personal items, are still in place. Mrs. Kelleher's in no hurry to come by. Who'd blame her? Edith put the four division files back on the desk with the Shamrock glass paperweight. You said it was fine for me to go through the files and his desk. So, I did."

The *J. Paul Kelleher, President* nameplate was on the desk, seemingly as a tombstone, more than an adornment. According to the *Polaroids*, nothing had been displaced or replaced. His frozen-in-time memory told Clough the same thing.

Fishman had been admonished not to make plans to move into the vacant office as Interim President – ever. Indeed, some people might never want to have that office.

The Sheriff thought it strange, maybe suspicious, that widow Kelleher had not come by to pick-up her husband's personal things, including photographs of herself, the sons and the dog. The array of liquor was still in the credenza along with two full *Marlboro* cartons.

Samantha had gone through Kelleher's desk and file drawers, sorting out anything that needed to be passed on to Fishman. She set aside numerous files that the next President could peruse if he ever got bored. Kelleher was not a saver type, except things that were important to him.

The office appeared to be frozen in time. The desk calendar was still open to Wednesday, October 19th, now over a week later. The desk chair had been restored to its favored center position.

Clough walked behind the desk and noticed that the perpendicularly placed Kelleher shoes were not there. "Do you know where the shoes went, Samantha?" he asked, more out of curiosity than a need to track them down.

"Edith put them in the bathroom – there in the closet. The cleaning people would have bathed them in *Lysol*, too, had she left them on the floor. She did not have the *Mr. Clean* staff touch the bathroom. Kelleher kept it clean, and she figured the regular custodial could go in there one of these days. I don't think the door is locked anymore, if you need to go in there."

The shoes were still crucial to Clough, given they had been so illogically perpendicular to the prone body. The shoes were like a persistent pebble in the Sheriff's shoe. He kept asking himself: *Were the shoes a signal? But what was the message? Did he shine them that night? Who put them under the desk? Could he figure it out?*

Clough proceeded down the hall to the Board Room, pushing aside the desk chair so he could pass and trying to push aside the shoes in his mind to focus on other things.

He paused at the door to the Executive Bathroom, which he felt still held a key to the investigation. Diaz had not found anything out of the ordinary in the room and only Kelleher's fingerprints.

The medicine cabinet held *Bayer aspirin, Tylenol, Palmolive* shave cream, *Gillette* razor, *Mennen* deodorant, *Colgate* toothpaste and *Scope* mouthwash. It looked like nothing had been touched. There was the unopened bottle of *Old Spice* aftershave next to the sink. There was a bottle of *Johnson's Baby Shampoo* in the shower along with a bar of some soap.

The adjacent closet next to the shower was still packed with Kelleher's long sleeve shirts, suits and shoes. His infamous shoe-shining kit was prominently placed on the counter next to the sink and close to the door. The shoe-shining rag was draped over the box. The intriguing shoes were on the closet floor next to two pairs of *Johnston & Murphy* wingtips, but they were all aligned against the back of the closet wall.

There was no ashtray anywhere in the bathroom or stale cigarette air, meaning Kelleher chose not to light up there. The bathroom was a private sanctuary, an inviolable retreat. That much was becoming clear.

The bathroom was orderly and clean, almost too tidy, too spotless. That suggested Kelleher had ratcheted his hygiene habits, given no one else would be cleaning the place. But Diaz had not found anything. His thoughts circulated: *Why would Kelleher lock the bathroom door? Why would he want to preserve his privacy before he went to his desk and died? Or did the killer decide to close the bathroom door? How come we have not found any traces of his medications?*

The explanation would likely have to do with the cancer and the Morphine, he thought. *But if so, where was the stuff? Where would he hide it if he had even chosen to conceal the vials, the hypodermics?*

Clough closed the bathroom door and urinated into the toilet. He pulled up his zipper and pivoted to the left to go to the sink. Clough washed his hands and slapped cold water on his worn face, much as his father had told him to do so whenever he was tired or felt ill. He reached for a couple of the paper towels that were neatly but cumbersomely stacked to his right on the counter.

Then the Sheriff looked past his image in the mirror above the sink. He saw the paper towel dispenser behind him in the reflection. *Why would Kelleher have a stack of paper towels on the crowded sink space when there's a functioning towel dispenser so handy?*

The white, metal paper towel dispenser looked off-kilter, askew from level in the mirror's reflection. The Sheriff did an about-face, like a soldier on parade. The dispenser was off-level but not much. His thoughts were concentrated. *For a man who preferred detail and order, it seemed like something Kelleher would have had repaired. There were paper towels protruding from the dispenser, so why have a stack on the sink?*

Clough pulled out a paper towel and a second one. Then a third. He felt the box shift, ever so slightly. That irregularity bothered him. It would not be a problem for most people, but he identified with the order that had enveloped the President.

The Sheriff used his penknife to twist the flimsy lock that held the stacked paper towels and opened the compartment. Several hypodermic needles and a collection of small drug vials rested on a makeshift shelf. He looked closer – the vials held Morphine.

The unused needles were on one side of the shelf, lined up like a picket fence on a short stack of paper hand towels. Several apparently used needles and a like number of empty vials were clustered in a small bowl on the right side.

"Bingo," said Clough aloud. "Looks like we have what we're looking for. The man had cancer and knew he was going to die. He wanted privacy to the end, concealing his illness, yet . . ." Clough's voice and mind trailed off, and he did not complete the sentence.

Kelleher had hidden his cancer and closed off the Executive Bathroom, so he could have a secret place to store and conceal his meds. He disguised his pain. He hid his treatments and preserved his private sanctuary.

Clough made a mental note to have Diaz check Kelleher's set of keys. He was sure she'd find a small penknife on the chain. He wanted to be sure Diaz dusted the towel dispenser on the inside for fingerprints. But he suspected there would only be the deceased President's prints.

The Sheriff made another mental note to contact Chief Jackson and have the Executive Bathroom secured as a Crime Scene. No, on the way out, he would see Miss Bartell and have her contact Security.

Then Clough finished his thought. *We still don't know if Kelleher administered an overdose intentionally or accidentally, mixing a lethal dosage with the alcohol. Or, did someone help him die?*

PRESENT

"We expect a retraction."

Because of Alan Fox's threats, Professor Nancy Wiegand had reluctantly and ashamedly changed six grades from that Spring semester in her *Introduction to Psychology* course. Fox had given her the student names after the final exam and before she was to submit grade rosters to the Registrar.

She had changed the grades of four students from D's to C's and two from C's to B's. Rather than doctor the respective grades, however, Wiegand had contacted each student after the final and given them an extra-credit assignment. That meant having to change the grades after the term was over and after the grade roster was submitted. Faculty grade changes for logical reasons were not unusual. Grade changes for extortion were extraordinary.

From those one-one-one student meetings, Professor Wiegand had concluded that none of the six students, all on the soccer team, knew Fox had made this arrangement to improve their grades. None were overtly complicit in the fraudulent grade caper. That soothed her battered conscience – a little.

She had to figure out how to identify the students before the end of this fall semester. She didn't want to be told the student names at final exams. However, with the death of President Kelleher a couple weeks ago, she did not feel secure with her situation. She had no idea if the President had ever done anything with the information she had provided him on Alan Fox.

Wiegand had been unprepared for the call from President Kelleher back in June, asking to meet with her in his office that afternoon. He was noticeably irritated and told her he had suspicions Fox was threatening female students in his classes.

Kelleher wanted to know if she, Nancy Wiegand, had any awareness about that. Perhaps she had overheard Fox when working in the Media Center? Perhaps students had confided in her? Kelleher had insisted she keep the content of the private meeting to herself, at least for the time being. He had pulled a notebook from his desk and wrote something in it.

He had asked her to spy on the guy. She was reluctant to do so, given the naked *Polaroid* shots Fox had taken of her. She had found herself walking a tightrope, precariously suspended between Fox's blackmail black hole and Kelleher's persistent petitions for her to tattle.

Edith and Samantha had gotten curious as to why Kelleher had been meeting behind closed doors with the Psychology professor. He seldom met with faculty alone. The two ladies weren't the only overly curious ones. Kelleher had a reputation for teasing women, and Wiegand had a reputation for being beautiful.

Martha J. Rooney, she of *Jersey Star*'s Sports Section, had been assigned by her editor to handle follow-up stories on the death of President Kelleher. She had interviewed Edith and Samantha and had a feature story on them as the first persons to see the body. Sheriff Clough had declined to meet with her, deferring all media requests to Deputy Sheriff Blanca Diaz.

An earlier story had concentrated on the September Board Meeting and what Rooney identified as "lingering animosity" between the Board Chairman and the President. It didn't take a clairvoyant prophet to reach that conclusion. The scowls and petulant questioning gave the tension away.

Rooney erringly surmised that Board members did not want to expand the Library. She made that mistake the focus of her story, along with her false observation that some Trustees were still ticked-off over Title III grant money going toward media equipment.

President Kelleher had wanted to scold her for publishing false information. But he wanted to preserve the integrity of what had transpired in the Executive Session and not embarrass the Board Chairman, especially via a newspaper headline.

Samantha Bartell had chosen to called Rooney herself to defend the College's honor. "Miss Rooney, had you checked your notes you would have remembered that the Board voted 5-0 in favor of the recommended architect for the Library project. That vote didn't jibe with your story. Perhaps Dr. Pitman and Mr. Harrison had reasons for abstaining, but a 5-0 vote is still considered unanimous. We expect a retraction."

Rooney was quiet for the moment and then said, "You must be kidding."

Sheriff Clough was sympathetic about the plight of newspaper people trying to get their stories. He just didn't like the way some writers chose to embellish and twist facts. He had been burned two times previously and was never going to give another reporter an opportunity to singe him. Since Rooney had mostly done sports features, he had not had much connection with her. He wasn't about to start now.

Since Kelleher's death, Miss Rooney had camped out on campus. She was prying rumors, fabrications and innuendos, distinguishing real and not-so-real scandals from faculty and staff.

Reporter Rooney had emphasized a variety of questions she put to CJCC staff during her times on campus:

What did they think of the death of Kelleher?

Did they think the President was murdered?

Who was on Kelleher's shit list and might have a motive?

Who met with Kelleher the days before he died?

Was Vice President Winters still as mad about Kelleher as he had been?

Did Kelleher find out who raised the helium rat from the building?

Was Security Chief Jackson dating the Deputy Sheriff?

Which people hung around at the end of the Board Meeting that night?

Was there a problem in Kelleher's marriage?

How much did Kelleher drink?

Did Wiegand's husband find out about the meetings with Kelleher?

Why did Mrs. Reynolds have the President's Office steam cleaned?

Reporter Rooney would make up answers to questions. She was a huge fan of the *National Inquirer* which had recently moved from New York to Lantana, Florida. She did not appreciate the paper's relocation, as that made it more of a challenge to be hired, to achieve her career goal.

The faculty teased Miss Rooney as being hard-headed and far from mild-mannered reporter *Clark Kent* of Superman fame or the firebrand *Lois Lane*. Rooney laughed it off and was more preoccupied with why Professor Wiegand had come and gone from Kelleher's office on several occasions. She decided to confront Wiegand on campus on Thursday.

"Mrs. Wiegand," Rooney asked, "I understand that before he died, you met many times with the President in his office with the door closed. I have some questions:

Why would a professor need to see the President so often and in secret?

What was the nature of your meetings?

Was he dressed when you met with him?

Were you and Kelleher having a relationship outside of the College?

Was he drinking?

Was your husband aware of these many meetings?

Doesn't your husband work at McDonald's?

Wiegand was extremely flustered to have the reporter in her office asking questions, regardless of the content, let alone ones about the nature of her meetings and relationships. The more Wiegand tried to respond professionally and affably, the more suspicious Rooney got and the more notes she took in her spiral journal. Rooney interpreted Wiegand's fidgeting and apparent nervousness as hiding the truth. The lady was hiding the truth, just not the truth Rooney thought it was.

"We met a few times, certainly not many times, Miss Rooney," Wiegand finally said. "It was all highly professional. Mr. Kelleher routinely met with faculty in his office. There was no relationship as you want to infer. He was interested in the media work I was doing for my psych course."

Rooney's byline story in Friday morning's *Jersey Star* accused Nancy Wiegand of having something to hide, including the possibility of an affair with the President. It did not help Wiegand's marital affinity that the article mentioned her husband's forthcoming McDonald's franchise, as if the two news items were connected in some crooked manner.

Greg Wiegand trusted his wife, but he, too, wondered why she had been spending time in the President's office at the campus. She had never told him that she had met with the President at all.

Sheriff Arthur Clough wondered too, at least enough to knock on Professor Wiegand's office door later that same Friday morning. She was not there, so he decided to wander the halls. Her schedule, posted on the office door, noted her class would be over in ten minutes.

Nancy Wiegand noticed Clough meandering the hall and quickly deduced he was there to see her. She put on her game face and scoured the area to see who might witness her being with the Sheriff. She unlocked her office door, after politely greeting her visitor.

"Mrs. Wiegand," Sheriff Clough began, "I did not have you on my list of persons to interview before I concluded my investigation. I am not a fan of journalists, especially ones who write gossip rather than facts. But what was the nature of your relationship with Kelleher? Edith Reynolds did verify that you had met with him four times in the weeks before his death."

Nancy swallowed hard. She knew it was time to clarify what the meetings were about before the speculation and conjecture got out of hand. "Mr. Clough, the President was aware that Alan Fox, the Athletic Director, was pursuing female students from his classes and pressing them into sexual favors. Since I worked in the Media Center on my Psychology Title III project, where Fox also worked on his materials, Kelleher wanted me to see if I could get him to talk about his behaviors."

"Were you able to provide any evidence of that to Kelleher?" the Sheriff asked.

"I knew from my own experiences with the man that he likes to chase skirts and leverage sex. I had no knowledge of him approaching students, but I would not be shocked, either," Nancy admitted.

She hesitated before continuing. "Sheriff, I understand the importance of your investigation. But sir, I need to share something very personal with you. Can I count on your confidence?"

"I cannot promise until I know the nature of your admission, Mrs. Wiegand," the Sheriff responded. "If your situation is not pertinent, I will keep the information to myself. That's the best I can do."

Wiegand started to cry and grabbed a tissue from the Kleenex box in a desk drawer. "I'm not proud that I succumbed to his advances, his charms, one night. But it was just the one night."

"I doubt you were the only member of the faculty to have spent time in his place," Clough said, seeing her tears were genuine. Clough had a hard, seemingly impervious exterior, but a woman in tears got to him. And he was able to separate phony tears from real ones.

"There's more," Wiegand sobbed. "While at his apartment that night, I dozed off on his couch, and he took *Polaroids* of me, naked. He threatened to share those with my husband. I told Fox the day after that I did not want to continue seeing him. That's when he showed me the photos. He was angry and told me that if I wanted to keep the photos secret, I'd have to raise the grades of some students in my course at the end of each semester. He wanted me to raise a D to a C, a C to a B. That's pretty bad."

"Sheriff, I raised the grade for six students this past semester. But at least I had them do an extra credit assignment. Fox hasn't yet told me which students would be in my class this semester and for whom I'd need to raise their grade."

"I think I can keep this our secret, Mrs. Wiegand. However, while I'm disgusted, I don't see a way to prosecute the creep for this. That's an academic issue. You were a willing participant in the relationship even though he took photos of you, photos you did not know that he had. Again, he's rotten."

The Sheriff tried to think of the best way to frame what he wanted to say next to the desperate woman.

"Nancy, if I may, from my experience, those photos will end up on your husband's doorstep sooner or later," he blurted. "You won't want to hear this, but it would be best to tell him what happened and work to strengthen your marriage. You don't want your husband to be one of the last to find out you slept with Fox and that he took pictures of you."

Clough started to head toward the office door to leave. "Nancy, if your husband loves you like I figure he does, he'll forgive you," he said. "If he's the guy you think he is, he'll get it. He'll deal with it. It might take a while, but the alternative of not telling him would be far worse."

They both took a collective breath. Wiegand grabbed another tissue and listened, while the Sheriff had one more comment.

"Hustling students is a serious issue but probably little to do with the death of Kelleher. But I need to ask. Did the President have evidence of Fox hustling students for sex? Do you know if he confronted Fox with this information? Did he intend to fire or discipline Fox in some way?"

Arthur Clough waited for a response from the professor. He had one more comment before he left her office. "That's something I will need to consider. That, Mrs. Wiegand, is a motive for murder."

PRESENT

"You can't lie. We don't put people in concrete boots anymore."

Cecilia, Dominic Panichi's wife, had been aware her husband had a roving eye. He fit the Italian male stereotype. Her father had had the same optical condition, as did her older brother and uncle.

Mrs. Panichi had arrived at the assumption that this *Romeo-rapport* was a male thing, bolstered by heritage, testosterone, Sophia Loren and Gina Lollobrigida. But until recently, she had reasoned that Dominic's penchant for other women was from afar, more fanciful and harmless than intimate.

Dominic had been in a recent pattern of coming home late at least two nights a week. On the weekends, he would announce that he needed to go to the office or elsewhere in the County for hours. Then when he got home, and she asked him how much he got done, he changed the subject or headed to the refrigerator for a beer. Sometimes she heard him on the downstairs phone after they had gone to bed.

Cecilia was typically exhausted each weekday from teaching and herding her middle school, overly-hormonal kids. Thus, she did not mind solitary time away from her husband or, frankly, most any human. Their daughter, Carmelo, demanded attention, but Dominic devoted himself to her when he was home. The grandparents were only too thrilled to be asked to babysit while Cecilia did errands or napped.

The Italian lady loved to cook. She thought nothing of canning multiple batches of Italian gravy, made from a famous family recipe. She knew Dominic was passionate about her cooking – anything Italian, anything Old School. He drooled at the thought she'd prepare pasta e fagioli, chicken piccata or tomato tortellini.

Dominic liked to spoon his wife at night while in bed, as much out of habit as being amorous. Occasionally, his hands would roam and caress parts of

314

her body, including the erogenous ones. She could feel his excitement. But instead of pursuing sex, he would apologize, kiss her on the neck and turn his back. That made her think: *Was he just too tired or was he on a guilt trip? Am I getting fat?*

Cecilia had been horrified when she and Dominic were dating, and she found out she was pregnant. The last thing she wanted was to box Dominic into marriage. He felt the same way. This was the first man she had slept with. The last one, too.

The marital role model of her parents was not something to emulate. Besides having a skirt-chasing penchant, her father was often cruel to her mother. The only other prototypical marriages were those on the television that either were soap operas where everyone slept with everyone or syrupy versions of *Walt Disney* fairytales.

In movies, the wife checks her husband's shirts to see if there's lipstick on the collar or the smell of perfume. Cecilia was not about to spy on Dominic. If he was cheating on her, she could accept that, provided he eventually came home. After all, she had the wedding ring on her finger and their daughter in the next room.

Cecilia would remain married to Dominic. The guy was a good man. He continued to support the family, spend time with Carmelo and show affection. She would look for more roving-eye signs and see if he continued to spoon her at night.

Dominic met again with his father, the Panichi family patriarch. They had dinner Friday evening at Toscano Ristorante, a family Italian restaurant in Chambersville. They didn't need menus. They were delighted to partake in whatever Italian delicacy Chef Salvatore prepared for the evening. But they always had an appetizer of the pencil points and marinara sauce along with whole roasted garlic.

It was not unusual for father and son Dominic to meet, and it was a family tradition to have dinner at Toscano's. The former and current Monroe County Commissioners would vary where they had lunch. It was important to spread the wealth and touch base with constituents. But when it was time for dinner, it would be Toscano's.

The place had been a residence for four Italian generations. Salvatore and his wife had re-oriented the house to a fine-dining establishment. When his mother passed, Salvatore moved into his parents' house and delicately placed his father into a nursing home.

The former living and dining spaces now served as the main dining rooms. They had transformed the first-floor bedroom into an intimate banquet room and carved out another entry into the kitchen. The rezoning of the property from residential to commercial was handled according to tradition – under the table.

"Father, I'm still seeing Samantha. My love for her has grown and matured," the junior Dominic shared with the senior one. "We see each other a couple days each week. The time we talk and share intimately is wonderful. I had no idea a man could feel this way about a woman. I don't know what else to say. I am deeply in love with her and can't see any way I can let her go."

The father pushed his pencil points around on the plate, soaking up more of the luscious sauce, while he reflected on what his son had said. "I'm proud you took my advice and got her out of your office at County. Getting her a position with the College was beyond what I could have anticipated. You said she was a talented worker, but you must have had some connection with Kelleher. Whatever. That was well done!"

"That's part of the problem now," Dominic offered. "With President Kelleher dead, we're not sure what will happen to her position. She pissed-off the four Vice Presidents to do what Kelleher wanted. Now he's gone."

Dominic spread a garlic clove on the Italian bread and took a bite. The topic they were discussing was enormously important. So was eating, if you have Italian roots.

"Sheriff Clough is pestering everyone as part of his investigation," Dominic said. "He hasn't ruled out homicide. Why did we hire that guy anyway? It would have been better to have another screwball in the position. This guy thinks he's the second coming of detective *Columbo* and *ME Quincy* rolled into one guy. He even told me that once."

"I have to ask, son. Did you and Samantha have anything, anything at all, to do with his death," a suddenly worried father implored of his son.

"Absolutely not," Dominic said, alarmed at the question. "Why would Samantha do that? Why would I for that matter? J. Paul had nothing on me, and he thought Samantha walked on water. Kelleher knew about me and Samantha, of course, but he kept that to himself. Didn't even tell his secretary or his wife."

"Do you have an opinion on who might have killed the guy?" the family patriarch asked immediately.

"From what I've picked up from my contacts, Kelleher was dying from some terminal disease. My guess is cancer or a heart attack. Dr. David Charles, who does the toxicology analyses, has the body now and is conducting the tests. Clough will probably hold an Inquest and call a bunch of people as witnesses to testify. Probably Samantha. Likely, me too."

Chef Salvatore came to the table holding two plates of veal marsala with mushrooms. The waiter tied a paper bib around each Panichi. The chef stood at attention while they lavished praise on the exquisite dish set before them.

"This looks wonderful. Thank you so much," said the senior Panichi.

"Buon appetito," said the Chef as he bowed and left his Italian friends with their sumptuous dinner. The dutiful waiter followed him into the kitchen, reasonably assured he had done a good job with the exceptional guests.

"The problem with the Inquest is that Clough is aware of our relationship. He trapped Samantha in a lie about knowing me and may have to bring that up at the Inquest. She'll have to be truthful. Hell, he'll likely call me as a witness, since he may see a connection with her getting the job and Kelleher's death."

"That doesn't make sense to me," senior Dominic said as he simultaneously took a forkful of the veal, while wiping his mouth of excess sauce and looking down at the paper bib the waiter had knowingly placed on him earlier.

Senior Dominic only had to use a fork to cut the tender veal. He took another bite, chewing the delicacy slowly. "You can't lie," he said to his son. "We don't put people in concrete boots anymore. If you still feel as you do about this Samantha gal, we best get ahead of the curve. We need to figure a course of action before Clough calls, and you and your young lady friend testify. Before all this becomes public."

"Son, your mother's very fond of Cecilia. After all, she's the mother of our granddaughter, our dearest Carmelo. We're both close to her parents. We've known the Gambrelli family since way before you and their daughter were born. They'll be heartbroken and beyond angry if they find out you were fooling around. Dominic, I don't want your mother to find out from that damn newspaper."

Dominic, the son, understood everything Dominic, his father, said.

PRESENT

"We simply frame and construct what becomes the new truth."

On Saturday, Dr. Gerald Pitman decided to meet with Board Vice Chairman, Chuck *"House of Magic"* Harrison. They both knew that Sheriff Clough was going to call them to testify at the Inquest into the death of President J. Paul Kelleher. Indeed, Pitman had learned from a County Freeholder who heard it from an assistant for the District Attorney that the Inquest was scheduled.

"What do you think the tone of the Sheriff's damn Inquest will be," Pitman asked of his colleague. "He questioned me last week about the two Board meetings, especially the one the night Kelleher died. I was careful what I said. He didn't push me."

Harrison corrected Pitman. "Gerald, you ass, he'll be wearing his Coroner hat at the Inquest. He can ask us anything, especially since we're under oath. If he asks us about the architect, we'll have to admit Zelinski's payment. You'll be screwed because you agreed to it. I'll be screwed because I knew what you were doing and why."

"No," replied Pitman. "Where we got screwed was appointing Kelleher as President. We thought he'd be a pussycat. The bastard fought us after we crowned him President. Winters is a weakling. He would have gone along with whatever games we were playing. What a mistake to make him Interim, even for six months."

"Understand, Pitman," Harrison said with his index finger pointed directly at the Board Chairman, as if a play pistol. "I do not plan to pull a rabbit out of my magic hat. If we agree now on what we will both say, we probably can escape this guy."

"But only if we agree," Harrison continued. "You just say the money was to be a donation to the College Foundation for scholarships. I'll say the same thing with a straight face. That's honorable. Fortunately, Kelleher kept the disclosure of Zelinski's money confined to the Executive Session. Asshole did us a favor."

"Don't worry. I can lie under oath," Pitman replied, pushing Harrison's finger away. "We were going to split that cash. Trouble is, Kula knows about it. And what if they talk to old man Zelinski about the money?"

"It's Kula's word against ours," Harrison concluded. "We can handle that."

The *Magic Man's* eyes brightened as if he had suddenly discovered a new magic trick. "Speaking of assholes, it's time to contact Representative Ridgeway. I've funded Billy's stupid elections, and I've never asked him for much. I'll get him to lean on Panichi and tell Clough to back off. I can make him see that if he doesn't bail out us on this one, I'll tell about how he gets jobs and promotions for his relatives. Billy likes to go to Newark occasionally and visit a special house – the one with red curtains, black glass windows and plenty of soft couches and fluffy cushions. I'll bring that up too!"

"I'm still worried," said Dr. Pitman. "We're public officials. The publicity can hurt us, maybe force us to resign."

"You are a stupid bastard," fumed Harrison. "If we tell the same story, same narrative, that becomes the truth. The paper will print that. Since when does the reckless *Jersey Star* search for the truth? No, sir. We simply frame and construct what becomes the new truth. Together, we form an unmatched pair, Mr. Chairman, a highly formidable force. Clough can't penetrate that."

"Remember, it's not lying," Harrison continued. "We would not be committing perjury or anything. No, no. We are redefining what took place. Its honestly reinventing history. That, Mr. Chairman, is not lying."

Pitman's mind wandered from his concern about avoiding the truth at the Inquest to what might be exposed on who killed the President. Pitman was clear that he was a prime candidate, owing to the Zelinski fiasco and his vocalized threats to Kelleher.

But he figured Harrison was a contender. A better contender. He thought to himself: *The hothead had all sorts of tricks he could put into play to disguise a murder. Smoke and mirrors would do it. I just need to get him to say something incriminating under oath. Clough can do that. I just need to stay cool. He was with Kelleher after me.*

Pitman knew Harrison had started a momentum among the Trustees to terminate Kelleher's contract. It could have been a momentum for murder too. The President had signed a contract the Board could rescind only for cause. However, there was nothing in the agreement that disallowed spurious and contrived accusations.

Pitman now had misgivings that he had induced David Lieber to be a whistle-blower and surreptitiously report Kelleher decisions that could be read as crooked. He had just needed a suspicious action, so he could force Kelleher to resign.

Lieber had passed along questionable reorganization decisions and vague insinuations about pestering women and demeaning the Faculty Union. That was nothing Pitman could have used. Now, Kelleher's death might expose his alliance with Lieber.

Coach Solly went to the YMCA on Saturday. He usually avoided the weekends because they were crowded times, and it was difficult to find an open court. But his son and daughter were driving him nuts. Solly was troubled about Izzy and her dead husband. Besides he had received a subpoena from the Coroner to appear at the Inquest to be held at the County Courthouse.

Solly finished his game, having won all three of them. He showered, trying to wash away the week's symbolic grime. He headed for the exit but saw Izzy Kelleher playing racquetball with her lady friend, Ella Cosby. He watched for a while and quickly surmised that the younger player was the far superior athlete and competitor. The Cosby gal might even give him a challenge, given her youth.

Izzy and Ella paid no attention to Solly as he sat, sipping on a *Dr. Pepper* from the refreshment bar. He took a pass on the fresh juice today. He wanted the caffeine and sugar fix. It was good to relax and play spectator for a while. Solly found himself silently coaching Izzy on how she could score more points and make the game closer. His telepathic coaching was not working on his unaware mentee.

Red-haired Izzy seemed to be handling the death of her husband reasonably well. He knew his wife, Marilyn, would be a total wreck if he, Solly, had died.

Play ended. The two perspiring ladies headed off the court. Izzy saw Solly, and her face showed surprise and a bit of anguish.

She was like a frenzied and flustered little girl whose matinee hero just walked into the room. "Solly, how are you doing? You remember Ella," she said. "I'm sorry I haven't called, but there have been issues with Pauly's death, and the Sheriff keeps asking me these damn questions. He's been to the house three times. I appreciate he's thorough, but enough already. He must have a miniature Encyclopedia of questions tucked in his back pocket. I'm back to teaching, and there's been a lot of catch-ups. Plus, I have to deal with sympathy expressions from students and colleagues, and unsolicited donations of mac and cheese casseroles."

"You two did pretty well on the court," Coach Solly told them. "Ella, you must have played competitively someplace. That's pretty damn good for a girl!"

Ella took a moment to process what had been said – the compliment portion and the sexist comment. "Well, thank you," she politely responded. "Coming from you, that's real praise. Izzy, I'm going to shower. I'll meet you in the lockers. I know you two have things to talk about. I'm glad we could play this morning. Get you back in the game."

"Thanks, Ella," Izzy said extending her racquet as a gesture of solidarity, not unlike two fencers raising their swords in honor after a match.

Izzy turned to Solly with tears beginning to swell her eyes. "Solly, I was surprised about the scholarship to honor J. Paul. The contribution from Kula is a great gesture. We will make a gift and keep track of how the fund grows. I'll solicit family members and others and get them to dig into their pockets."

Solly chose to ignore the comments about the Foundation. "Listen, Izzy, I asked if you'd look around the house and see if you could find the notebook he kept. I figured he must have brought it home occasionally, maybe left it there the night he was killed. No one's found it."

"No, have not seen it," Izzy responded, while lingering on Solly's *he was killed* observation. "I did see him writing in a notebook a couple of times in the weeks before he died. He said he was jotting thoughts on projects underway at the College. I never thought much about it. What does it matter?"

"Well, if the Sheriff concludes Kelleher's death was a homicide, it could matter a great deal. There might well be clues for Clough in the thing. Hey, that was clever of me. Get it, *c-l-u-e-s for Clough*. His name's French, but I wonder if he changed the pronunciation to fit his career choice."

"If a notebook existed, it was in his office," Izzy advised. "His briefcase was empty. I've not gone to his office. Not yet. I'm not ready for that."

"Maybe you could go to the office and see if you can find it," Solly asked.

Izzy looked surprised by Solly's invitation to become a sleuth for him. "Solly, I heard Edith had the place steamed cleaned one night – by a Marine battalion. Fishman was told emphatically not to go into or use the room. Edith keeps the office locked. She's still terrified to go in there. I'm just not ready to go to the office."

Izzy looked at Solly's face and could tell that anything other than a clandestine maneuver by her to get into the office would be unacceptable. Several thoughts raced through her mind: *Why was this notebook so important? What had Solly done that would be in the damn thing? Did he really want me to sneak into the office and scrounge around for it under the guise of getting Pauly's personal items? What did this guy do that would be so incriminating? Why did he think that Ella was that much better than me at racquetball? She's just younger!*

"No, that's OK," Solly responded, sensing he had pressed too far. This was still the guy's grieving widow. But he had to know what she thought. If the widow would lie for him. If she'd be on his side.

Izzy began to tear again. It was from the agony of learning, after-the-fact, that her husband had been dealing with cancer, causing him to hide the truth from her.

"I've had trouble sleeping, knowing the man I was married to for fifteen years, and still loved, was suffering so badly," Izzy muttered. "By sleeping in separate bedrooms, the past couple of months, I didn't get as close to him as I would, had we still shared a bed and master bath. I don't think anyone knew about the cancer."

"Does the Sheriff know about this notebook or journal, Solly?" Izzy asked.

"I'd be surprised if he did not," Solly responded. "The guy may look like he just got of bed, but he's sharp. In fact, I may toss these track suits I wear and adopt a fashion statement of gray slacks and a blue shirt. Maybe find a droopy hat and a rumpled corduroy coat in my size. No cigar though."

"When the Inquest is over, Solly, let's go to lunch," Izzy said. "Better yet, let's take the boys and go to the Poconos for a weekend with your kids, Marilyn too."

"That would be fun, except there's snow up there already," Solly said. "Not now. Not with this stuff hanging over my head. The Inquest will tell us whether someone prematurely ended his life. Somebody may be in jail by then."

As he walked away, Coach Solly told himself he had an ally. Her husband, the President, was dead. She was even more vulnerable. The rules of the game had changed. Just what he wanted.

Roseanne Hart invited Bill Fishman to go to church with her on Sunday morning and then to her house for a breakfast of homemade sour cream pancakes and pork sausage. She drew some stares as the two strolled down the aisle to a pew in the middle of the congregation. As far as she knew though, she was the only person from the College to attend this Lutheran Church.

Hart wasn't fond of the sermon that morning, or for that matter, those of the past several weeks. She despised pretend Christians who cherry-picked Bible passages to accommodate narrow-mindedness. Or those who sang the hymns and never bothered to follow the messages within the lyrics.

Normally, Roseanne sang with the church choir, but with the happenings at the College, she had skipped practice. The choir director had a rule: *Miss practice and sit with the congregation on Sunday.* She preferred to sit with Bill anyway.

"Thanks for coming with me to church this morning," Roseanne said. She was dressed in a royal blue shirtdress with a whirl of pleats and self-tie belt on the waist, giving a new dimension to the attire and her middle-aged figure. "Bill," she whispered, "I am happy for the first time in several years and not so dependent on the damn horses running around the track. I promise we can still go out, even if you never set foot in this church again."

The pastor's sermon focused on the first of the Ten Commandments. He described Moses coming down the mountain to deliver the slates. As they walked out of the service and approached Fishman's Ford Fairlane, she questioned him, demonstrating her wry sense of humor and testing his. Bill, you ever wondered why God only presented Ten Commandments? We could have used several more, don't you think," Roseanne offered and then quickly answered her leading question. "Perhaps Moses couldn't carry the other heavy slates down the mountain? He should have made a second trip or borrowed a wheelbarrow!"

Fishman was beginning to be glad he and Spurling had uncovered the travel records and had decided not to report the situation. Being with Roseanne made him stand up straighter and push back from the mashed potatoes and gravy. He had abandoned his barber in favor of a hair stylist.

When they got in the car, Roseanne resumed the conversation they'd started before it was time to enter the church. "So, Bill, do you think Kelleher committed suicide or someone decided to take him out?"

Without waiting for an answer, Hart continued. She was on a roll. "I think it's down to Alan Fox, Winters and David Lieber, with Coach Solly a dark horse handicap, if you excuse my track metaphor. But you can't count out Pitman and Harrison either."

"Did you know that before he died, Kelleher had me check on faculty at Columbia County Community College. He wanted to see a listing of full-time instructors, but he didn't tell me why. Something about Ralph Hughes, the Faculty Union guy."

"No one else knows too, but Kelleher had me check on what life insurance Howard Tucker had and how the family was doing," Hart added. "He had me send his wife, Gloria, a cashier's check for $1,000. All the money came from him, as far as I know. However, he told me to tell her it came from the Employee Bereavement Fund."

"There's no such thing," Fishman said, surprised as much by this phantom fund as the amount gifted to Mrs. Tucker.

"Ya know, Roseanne," said Fishman, "I'm beginning to dislike Kelleher a little less as a dead person than when he was alive, reorganizing every other month and scrutinizing my fiscal reports."

"Don't get syrupy with me," Roseanne said. "Save that for the pancakes I'm making for you at my house."

She thought about what she had said and then offered a great incentive for Bill. "Let's get going. I want to have plenty of time after brunch for other sweet treats."

PRESENT

"If that happens, if you screw up, you can get the hell out of town."

Dominic's father went to the County Office on Monday, two days before the Inquest. He arrived with a purpose. Senior Dominic greeted the receptionist and walked, unannounced, past her into his son's office. Whatever young Dominic was doing, or with whomever he was meeting, would be interrupted and dismissed immediately. This could not wait.

"Dominic, we have to talk, right now," implored the father waving his hands in the air. "I've figured a way out of this mess. The sooner we talk and act, the better for all concerned."

"Dad, good to see you," Dominic said, trying to regain his composure after having his father make such a pronouncement. "Have a seat and tell me what you've done. Want a cup of coffee or something? We probably have a Danish left over from this morning."

Dominic knew his father was ready to burst, but he had to tell him something first. "I received a subpoena from the Coroner to appear in Court for the Inquest hearing, Wednesday. Samantha did not get one. Clough's questions for me will focus on my relationship and dealings with Kelleher – not Samantha. I wanted you to know."

"No. No coffee. No Danish!" senior Dominic replied, obviously agitated. "We can talk about food and the Inquest later – when I finish."

Now that he had his son's complete attention, he continued. "Listen, do you realize divorce in Italy has only been possible since 1970. It remains complicated, but it's now recognized in our homeland. That means we have our opening to pursue a divorce here in New Jersey. If divorce were still banned in the Old Country, your mother and Cecilia's parents would never accept a divorce for you and your wife."

The family patriarch wanted to pat himself on the back, but he decided to continue with his explanation. "Son, that cultural change makes divorce possible, even acceptable for the family. However, be that as it may, I have pursued yet another angle that's better. Much better."

"Dad, I'm so sorry to be putting you through this," Dominic said with his eyes swelling with shame for himself and pride for his father. "I truly love Samantha. You know that. But, I don't want to hurt Cecilia or the family. I don't want our child to be messed up by this either. I didn't want to burden you."

"For God's sake, let me finish," his father interrupted. "We need to act. Sooner the better. The Roman Catholic Church, as you know, is not keen on divorce. However, they recognize annulments. There are only a few justifications, but we have one that'll work for you and Cecilia. Father Francis agrees. We argue that your marriage was performed solely as a means of legitimizing the child who was in Cecilia's womb at the time, our precious Carmelo."

Dominic was alarmed by the word *legitimizing*. "Father, not legitimizing my daughter? I can't do something that would hurt Carmelo. Nothing's worth that. Nothing. I would jump off a cliff before I'd allow that."

"No, calm down. It means the marriage itself had a defect," Dominic explained. "Simply put, there was a defect in the marital contract. This annulment wouldn't affect the legitimacy of the child's birth. I would never go along if that was the outcome, or even implied, for Carmelo."

The senior Dominic waited for his son to sit back down and breathe awhile before continuing. "Now normally, it takes a year before an annulment can be granted. However, Father Francis will push for it to be done in two months. You would still have to get a legal divorce. We'd have to seek dispensation before the Parish Priests or maybe the Tribunal, but Father Francis would be supportive. He's of the opinion he can convince the Bishop to waive Tribunal review and rule himself. That would really speed things up."

Dominic noticed the smile slowly developing on his son's face. "Lord knows how generous we've been to Saint Joseph's Cathedral, even though we don't go much and skip confession except for holidays. Having the marriage officially annulled by the Bishop would be crucial to your mother's perception and thoughts. For our famiglia and for Cecilia's too, especially the old Italiano ones."

"You don't think Cecilia's parents would protest?" Dominic asked.

"I don't think so," the father responded. "I'll speak to her dad privately. Me and Mr. Gambrelli go way back. I can convince him to be calm and let this happen. If not, I can pressure him to shut the hell up. The church annulment saves them embarrassment and ridicule. We know plenty of other people in the Parish, so getting support from members will be easy. No one will contest. Most are Italian anyway. Hell, most families have been through a divorce of some sort, for whatever reason."

"Jack Kula can serve as your advocate," Dominic added. "Jack can read the petition before the Bishop and as necessary before the Priest Tribunal. He can argue the marriage was never a true marriage. The Bishop knows Jack's father, if not him. We have that going for us, too. Jack's not Italian, unfortunately, but he's well thought of in the community, and he's Catholic. That helps."

"Dad, Jack Kula already knows that I'm seeing Samantha," Dominic shared. "We had an awkward moment when we went to the mountains. He likes Samantha. Kula's not the only one who knows about us. Rebecca Campbell and Edith Reynolds, also from the College, were at the same place that weekend when we all showed up. Oh, and Mrs. Kelleher too."

"That's gonna happen, but you need to ask them to respect your privacy," Dominic wailed in an irritated tone. "If the word gets out too far, my plan could be ruined. Do what you must to be sure about that. I mean it."

He looked in his son's eyes and continued. "Understand, Dominic, the mother is almost always given custody of the children in a divorce, with agreed-upon access for the father. We would be wise strategically to have Jack protest mildly and then relent without prejudice. Kula can have a private confab with Cecilia's attorney and with her family to figure that out behind the scenes. We can't have anything contested in public."

"According to Father Francis, once Carmelo reaches age, she can decide which parent she wants to live with," the senior Dominic added. "We can worry about that then."

"Son, we just want this to go smoothly. That means not contesting the child, giving her the house and agreeing to pay overly reasonable alimony and child support. All that and how you conduct yourself over the next few years will be considered by the Court. Officially, the Roman Catholic Church would grant you and Cecilia a dispensation and award a *Decree of Nullity*."

"What about the divorce? Do we wait on that?" Dominic asked.

"No, you pursue that simultaneously, simply based on incompatibility. You just need one person, in this case you, to believe in the incompatibility. You would not get into infidelity, abuse or anything. Nor would she. Just two people who married in a rush because of the pregnancy, and pressed by their families to get married. But five, six years later, you realize you have disparate interests and values. All you really have together is the kid. The Court will divide the property based on what it deems fair and equitable, not a fifty-fifty split. Cecilia has a decent job and a good salary at the hospital from what you told me. That helps."

Senior Dominic went over and put his right arm around the shoulders of his son before continuing. "This divorce will be expensive to you. Make no mistake. But your Samantha has a salary too. And you're young. You can handle it. I'd argue you fight to retain your retirement account. Let Cecilia keep hers. She has insurance through the hospital. You keep Carmelo on your County plan or switch, as Cecilia wants. We know the lady can be highly emotional, but she's not stupid. She'll get an attorney, a damn good one. We need to start with an honorable proposal, and you need to be forthright. Don't put Carmelo in the middle. You will lose."

"If I must," Dominic's father added with a sneer, "I can convince the judge to understand, to be fair, maybe even bend in your direction. He won't go crooked on the settlement. Let me worry about the judge."

"Father, this could happen in the next two or three months, couldn't it," Dominic concluded. He was exuberant and considerably overcome with the scenario and the specifics his father had constructed.

"Yes, you still need to cool it with the lady, not be seen in public," Dominic warned. He placed his hands upon his son's shoulders to reinforce his point. "Keep the circle very tight of those who know about your relationship. You can decide based on Kula's advice if you should tell Cecilia your lady's name and when."

Senior Dominic was not done. "You must move out of your house and establish a separate residence until the annulment happens, the divorce goes through and you marry Samantha. I will not stand for you sharing an apartment with her, or a house, a trailer, motel room or backyard tent. Shacking up, they call it. You can't do that while you're still married, while your annulment and divorce are proceeding. Get your own place. I don't care where. Sleep in you damn office if you have to. You understand me, son? We've got a damn fine way to get this done, so don't screw it up by having the whole County wake up on a Sunday morning and read in the newspaper that the married County Commissioner is shacking up with this other woman."

Dominic's head nodded up and down, enthusiastically, as it were a buoy on rough seas slapped by waves.

"Understand me, son," emphasized the father. "If that happens, if you screw up, you can get the hell out of town. Go hide out in Alaska. I won't be able to help anymore. You must promise. So too, must this lady you're sleeping with."

Dominic took his son's arm tenderly and squeezed his neck from behind for emphasis. He was pleased he had remembered. "Son, I have one more thing that will greatly advance your mother's sanity and my longevity in this life."

"What's that?," the son responded, eagerly waiting for the guidance.

"Not now, but as soon as you two are married, get her pregnant. Have a child. That will ease any pain your mother has and affirm to her that you're in love. Nothing heals an Italian mother's loss of pride than another grandchild."

The senior Dominic smiled and continued. "Better yet, Dominic, make it a son. Then have a second child, another son!"

Dominic placed his hands on those of his father, still resting on his shoulders. "Father, I am so relieved," he said. "I'll get with Kula right away. I do have one more thing to ask you to do."

"What's that?" the father asked, expecting to be angry now.

"I'd like you to meet my Samantha."

16

PRESENT

"The Sheriff's on the warpath to find out if it was a murder and if so, who the hell killed the guy."

On Monday morning, David Lieber, Dean of Instructional Resources, decided to call his contact at Media Visual Equipment, Inc. He didn't fret about the gifted case of wine or the camera received from MVE. He did not worry about the comped tickets for the New York City splurge, including dinner and theatre. The cash, however, could be incriminating.

The Inquest was only two days away. Who knows what questions Arthur Clough would have for him? He had received the subpoena to appear. He would have to testify and under oath. He would have to figure out how to avoid the truth.

David Lieber was regretting he had agreed to be an informant for the Board Chairman. Pitman had called it a *whistleblower*; Lieber knew it was a *weasel*. He had approached Lieber two days after the fateful September Board Meeting when the Board approved the Library architect, albeit not without public agony, private consternation and the two abstentions.

Pitman had promised Lieber a salary increase, once they got Kelleher out of office and put in a more receptive person as President. It was an offer Lieber did not want to pursue, except he might be able to use it to leverage concessions, especially if Kelleher got fired.

He reasoned the Board Chairman would not stop if he, Lieber, refused the invitation. He'd find someone else. Better to know who the informant was. Pitman would have kept bugging him until Lieber had something worthy of blackmailing Kelleher.

Lieber's thoughts had been logical: *If the President received gifts from MVE, he'd have a deceit worthy of recounting. If he could embarrass the President, he'd be sitting pretty. Should he tell the newspaper reporter about Wiegand and*

Kelleher again? Why was the guy staying in his office every night until at least 7 PM? Why had he stopped jogging around the campus in the morning?

That was before Kelleher's death. He wasn't sure what Pitman would want now.

When they met, Sheriff Clough had not asked him about any of the MVE gifts, but Lieber wasn't about to push his luck. If it came up at the Inquest, it could be seen as a motive for murder.

Winters had agreed to the alibi as to where Lieber was after the Board meeting. He was in good shape there. People would undoubtedly believe the Vice President of Academic Affairs. He had that covered. Having Winters vouch for him on a bogus alibi was better than a sound one.

It would be a lie, however, if Clough asked him which bar he went to after the Board Meeting and how long he stayed. But it had been several weeks now, and Lieber told himself he could convince himself that he had forgotten the stupid name. Let Winters drop the name of the place, under oath, not him.

The gifts had been sent by MVE's Vice President of External Relations, Barry Buckman, who supervised equipment sales. Buckman had been to the CJCC campus for a signing ceremony. He had not met Kelleher or Winters. Lieber had preferred to insulate them from the guy. Buckman had only met a few professors, including Wiegand, Fox and Mrs. Gray from Nursing. All three had media projects underway.

Lieber phoned MVE and found Buckman in his office. Buckman was pleased to hear from his CJCC contact, especially since the company now had a second round of equipment on order. "David, my man, how are you doing? Say, is that Ann Wiegand babe still cranking out the psych materials using our wonderful equipment? Is she married?"

"Barry, we need to talk, and it's Nancy Wiegand," Lieber proclaimed. "I appreciate the money that appeared in the mail one day, but I need to figure something else out before someone learns you sent it. You know our President died on October 20th. The Sheriff's on the warpath to find out if it was a murder and if so, who the hell killed the guy. I don't want to leave a trail to me."

Lieber paused for just a moment before adding, "Barry, she's happily married."

"Too bad," said the MVE man. "Doesn't hurt to ask. What do you have in mind? What can I do, David? What's up, man? Did you take the guy out?"

"Shut up and listen. Hear me out, "Lieber barked. "First, did anyone from MVE send gifts to others here at the College?" He was unsure if he wanted an answer or what the desired answer would be.

"David, David, David," the executive responded. "MVE just likes to honor our clients. No big deal. We sent tickets to some Broadway play to your Dean.

Winter, I think's his name. Or maybe it's Summer. Can't be Fall or Spring. But that was some time ago. Nobody else."

Lieber began to think his phone call was a waste of time.

Then Barry Buckman spoke again. "Oops, we sent Broadway tickets to your President. Dr. Keller, I think is his name. Is he related to Helen Keller? Hope he's not blind too. Anyway, he sent them back with a gracious note about not wanting to go to jail. Guy has some sense of humor."

"Thank you," Lieber remarked, feeling somewhat relieved but more stressed. "Winters, not Winter, is fine, Barry. He's the Vice President. I'm the Dean. Leave it at that though, please. No more gifts to anyone until this   Malarkey is Irish for bull shit. investigation of the President's death   *Irish Leprechaun* is behind us."

"Wait, have you sent a gift or anything to faculty here?" Lieber asked.

"No gifts, I can recall," Buckman admitted. "However, David, I did send the pretty Ann Wiegand gal a room key to a Washington D. C. hotel. But don't worry, the hotel is discreet. Can you dig it!"

When there was no laughter coming from Lieber, Buckman quickly pulled back. "Just kidding, David. No need for a heart attack."

"No more gifts. Got it. What else?" Buckman asked, knowing that if there was a first from David, there would eventually be at least a second.

"You need to send me someplace for a day or two to do something for you," Lieber answered, trying to sound like he had it figured out when he didn't.

"Send me to some college and let the $250 you sent be an advance for trip expenses and a modest honorarium. That way I'm just letting you reimburse me for going to a school and sharing what we're accomplishing. We might even get Title III to bless us for this effort. I'll make the charges more than the $250, and you can reimburse me in a company check for the remainder."

"Far out. That can work, Lieber," said Buckman. "We do send representatives to institutions considering media purchases. I can write and back-date a letter inviting you to do this. Better yet, I'll date the invitation before this Dr. Kellen, died."

"Barry, his name is Kelleher, not Kellen," Lieber corrected. "He's dead and he didn't have a doctorate. If you screwed up his name while he was alive, you'd hear from him."

Clearly, David had had enough. His attitude had shifted from indulgence to mocking despair. Now he was just plain surly.

"The letter and all will work well, Barry. Thanks. That's enough!" Lieber said brusquely. He was relieved. He could look forward to getting out of town for a couple of days. His plan was taking shape, now that he had his ass covered on the gifts and especially the money. He was burying the incriminating evidence.

"Hey, David," Buckman added before Lieber could hang up. "Make sure you stay in a high-class hotel and have a steak and martini dinner. If you can talk the babe, Ann Wiegand, to come with you, I may just choose to come along. That a deal?"

PRESENT

"Have you ever had a crime where there were so many suspect pairings?"

Deputy Sheriff Blanca Diaz knocked on Sheriff Clough's office door Monday afternoon, just before her shift was over. She respected this guy so much, especially his integrity and resolve. He may look like he just got out of bed, having slept with his clothes on, but her boss was shrewd. She knew Arthur Clough was preparing for the Inquest and that Wednesday would be a show. Quite a show.

The guy was psychic the way he could absorb himself in the victim, becoming the dead person, at least in spirit. He could adopt the person's self. Then he would use that connection to reveal insights and facts about the case.

The past couple of weeks had been indicative of his super-perceptive and concentrative powers. She marveled at his ability to capture details and then assemble them into a logical picture that made total sense.

"Hey, come on in, Blanca," the Sheriff said when his Deputy opened the door and poked her head into the room. "Before you head home, if you can spare a few minutes, let's compare notes. Your processing of the Crime Scene was textbook. Well done."

"If I can help in any way, sure," Diaz offered. Clough would not be asking his Deputy to share her thoughts if he did not regard her highly. "But, sir, I missed that towel dispenser thing in Kelleher's bathroom. You, sir, discovered his hiding place for the syringes and Morphine."

"Miss Diaz," Clough began with a smile on his face. "You know I like being called sir when we are on the scene. It reminds me and everyone else that I'm the boss. But in this office, at the end of the day, call me Arthur or Sheriff, please. And as far as the hypodermics, that was a detail. I knew he had to have the meds stored someplace, and the locked bathroom suggested he was hiding or concealing something. The guy was a control person. Order was paramount for him. He and I are alike in that way. Other ways as well."

"Sir, or Sheriff, I mean," Diaz answered, embracing respect for her boss. "Is there anything I can do tonight or tomorrow for the case? There were only Kelleher's prints on the paper towel thing. The one print on the chair we couldn't identify was that of a younger person, likely one of his two sons. We couldn't find anything in his desk or the credenza that might help us determine who killed Kelleher."

"I checked out the desk, too," Clough said. "Kelleher didn't have a lot of papers in it. There were a few files and notepads, some cigarettes. He passed on most of his papers – documents, contracts, letters – to Edith, for her to catalog and file. Guess the prior President had bought that huge desk as a gigantic work space. Kelleher used it as a gigantic fortification. Ironic, he would die behind it."

"Kelleher certainly had some odd quirks," Diaz said. "Imagine shining your shoes every day, sometimes more than once a day, to say nothing about getting dressed in your office while meeting with people."

"Those damn shoes still bother me," confessed the Sheriff, as he retrieved the *Polaroid* photo Diaz had taken. "That's bugged me ever since the first time I saw them, side-by-side, perfectly perpendicular to the desk. I asked Edith. She said that after Kelleher finished shining his shoes, he'd wear the things. He never set them down or put them back in the closet or under the desk. They went back on his feet. That was the point. No, the shoes were deliberately placed. Why, I don't know yet. But I will!"

"Perhaps, he had just finished wearing them that night and wanted to relax his feet," Diaz offered. "You said he always liked order, so placing them side-by-side might make sense."

"Likely not as perfectly centered and straight as these shoes were," Clough said conclusively.

"Miss Diaz, did you understand Mr. Kelleher kept a private notebook?" Clough asked. "Edith Reynolds said he did, although he kept it hidden even from her. She never asked him about it. I wonder where that journal is now. The widow was not aware of where he kept it, and I believe her. Most folks on campus said they had no knowledge of it. Some were lying. The face betrays the inner turmoil."

"Whoever killed him probably came for that notebook," Diaz volunteered. "Either because they knew there was something in there about him or her, or they wanted the details about others."

"Say, who does Chief Jackson think committed the murder?" the Sheriff asked. He knew full well that on at least one of their semi-intimate moments, they discussed the case. More likely, every night.

"Tyrone leans toward the Lieber-Winters pairing," Diaz offered. "Winters has been over-the-top obnoxious in expressing his hatred, and Lieber seems to have a lot of crooked irons in the fire, if that's a decent metaphor. Winters hired the Carter guy, and they're tight, too. But the two Union faculty, Hughes and Bowens, are a close second. They just seem to have lots of secrets. Dr. Dandridge, the guy who took Kelleher's VP position, and Lieber were working on the federal grant – $2.5 million is an incentive for murder. They may have spent grant monies to their benefit."

"What about the Board Chairman and Vice Chairman," Clough asked, adding another pairing to the suspect pool. "And then there's Athletic Director Fox along with his buddy, the basketball coach. Another curious tandem. Accomplices, perhaps."

"There's no doubt Pitman was furious about the architect thing," the Deputy Sheriff added. "He and Harrison thought they controlled Kelleher when they made him President, and then found out not so true. I'm not aware of Fox's role in this thing, but the guy seems shady. Good looking, but shady."

"Did you have a conversation with Mr. Jackson about Bill Fishman and this accounting guy, Spurling," the Sheriff asked, as a leading question.

Diaz paused for a moment, counting the potential culprit pairs in her mind and then demonstrably on her fingers for Clough to see. "Have you ever had a crime where there were so many suspect pairings? Like *Batman and Robin*, *Lone Ranger and Tonto*, *Bonnie and Clyde*, *Archie and Jughead*. But no, Tyrone didn't say much about the two finance guys."

"I like the *Jughead* pairing," Clough said laughing. "We have a bunch of those running around!"

Diaz had to finish her thought. "The fact the Board made Fishman Interim President, by itself, makes him a top suspect for me. Anything that Board does, if it comes from Pitman and Harrison, is suspicious and has a stench."

Diaz reconfigured her hand into a pointing figure for emphasis. "How the heck does a person get on a Board of Trustees in this state."

"The local State Assembly Representatives make the recommendations that are rubber stamped by the Freeholders," Clough responded. "Most get the support of the State reps by making campaign contributions and drumming up votes."

"Do you know, Blanca, that only two of the seven CJCC Trustees went to college? Pitman is the only one with a degree. That's like having a hospital medical board largely composed of people who are not doctors or nurses, just folks who had a first-aid Boy Scout merit badge or played doctor as kids."

"They don't all need to be college graduates, but to have only two is ridiculous," Diaz continued. "No wonder they just follow Pitman's lead and let Harrison run around without a tether to honesty or principle."

"What about the computer guy, Gene Wildwood, and Candace – the pretty one who controls what gets done in the Computer Center," Clough asked. They seem chummy to me. The two were thoroughly pissed that Kelleher fired their Director, and then the guy gets drunk and rams a tree. Security says they spend time alone in the Computer Center in the evenings."

The Sheriff switched momentarily into his other role. "I can tell you, as the Coroner, that Tucker's body was broken into pieces like a China plate smashed against a wall. The alcohol in his body was off the charts."

"Tyrone says that when a man and a woman stay late and work in the office, they are either scheming or screwing. In this case, he's pretty sure it's screwing." Diaz thought some more before adding. "The Personnel lady, Hart, spent a lot of time with Kelleher. He wanted her to tell him everything about everyone. That could be a motive too. Maybe he found out something about her."

"Assuming you do rule it murder, Sheriff, you'll get the guy, or perhaps the pair of murderers. You'll use that intuition or your subconscious brain and figure it out."

"It's odd. Very odd," Clough offered. "The suspects do appear to be in pairs, kind of like Noah's Ark. They pair-off, two-by-two. Except these are humans, not animals, and they are plotting murder together, not escaping some damn flood."

The Sheriff, who would morph into the Coroner on Wednesday, looked at Deputy Diaz as he sat on the edge of his desk. She stood before him. "Blanca, did you ever see Shot in the Dark, the movie with Peter Sellers and Elke Sommer? Must be about ten years old now. If not, go rent the video from *Blockbusters* and view it on company time."

Diaz shook her head from side to side, giving Clough an opening. "In this hilarious movie Sellers plays Inspector *Jacques Clouseau*, a French cop. He wears a soiled trench coat, the kind with the belt and wide collars, and bungles his way around a case like a presumed fool. He solves the baffling cases in the end, much to the agony and chagrin of the Chief of Police. *Clouseau*, while fumbling around and being distracted, demonstrates a marvelous intuitive sense."

Recalling the farcical plot and goofy characters, the Sheriff continued. "A famous movie quote from the guy is something like: *I believe everything, and I believe nothing. I suspect everyone, and I suspect no one.* All the clues point to the blond Elke Sommer character who is the maid in this French mansion. She's caught with the murder weapon in her hand, not once but twice. But Sellers has no part of that. He knows she did not commit the murder."

Clough could tell he really had Diaz' attention, so he laughed in anticipation of what he would say next. "Eventually, Sellers diligently lists the case facts on a chalkboard, all of which conclusively point to the maid as the killer. Then he makes a profound statement to his deputy: *Nothing matters but the facts. Without facts, the science of criminal investigation is nothing more than a guessing game.*"

The Sheriff snickered before continuing. "Then *Clouseau* proceeds to ignore the facts, all of which point to the beautiful maid as the murderer. He releases her from custody. Then in the big finale, a grand scene, the Sellers character confronts the beautiful maid and everyone in the household."

"So, the blond maid did do it," Diaz said. "He was probably just overwhelmed with her looks and sexy voice. Can't fault the man for that."

"No, no, everyone in the mansion committed that murder and several other murders as well," Clough corrected. "Not the maid. *Clouseau* had it right. All the others were having affairs with each other. The beautiful blond maid was the only one in the place who was guiltless."

"Maybe, that's what we have with this murder," Diaz concluded. "The culprits paired off, two-by-two, and everyone murdered the President. If that's true, the most likely candidate is the one who looks most guilty. Or, perhaps the beautiful blond lady."

PRESENT

"You knew this would happen, sooner or later."

Sally Bowens and Ralph Hughes were talking behind the closed doors of the Faculty Union office at end of the day, Monday. The room was on the second floor of the Library and was arguably the smallest office space on campus.

The Faculty Union Contract stipulated the Administration was to identify and provide an office. However, the contract did not say how large or how small the room was to be, or where it was to be located. President Kelleher was not about to be generous. He thrived on showing he was more astute than the faculty team when it came to negotiations. If they wanted a bigger office, they should have bargained for it.

"Did you hear Edith Reynolds had the President's Office professionally deep-cleaned – walls, carpet, windows, furniture and all," Sally told Ralph. "Apparently the effort was so complete and powerful that the place no longer smells of stale cigarette butts and shoe polish. The joke was that the industrial crew used a hot water pressure-washer, a gallon of *Clorox* and a case of *Q-Tips* cotton swabs. Some said the rug shampoo machine ran on diesel fuel."

Ralph found this description exceedingly funny, as he collapsed into the sole chair in the cramped space. Sally was not finished. "The covert operations crew did this industrial cleaning overnight, one day last week. Then they disappeared. Maybe they slid back up the chimney like Santa Claus! Amazing."

Sally's long sleeve blouse was unbuttoned at the neckline just enough to expose some cleavage, as she sat on a corner of the desk. Her sleek hair was pulled back. She was trying to look natural, but she was most alluring. In Ralph's mind, Sally could wear a potato sack and be alluring.

There was a four-drawer, battleship gray metal filing cabinet, a trash can and a Smith-Corona electric typewriter and phone on the matching metal desk. There were no papers in sight, no books or anything to suggest it was anything more than a storage room without the storage.

Ralph was tired from his teaching that day. Monday was a challenge. The instructor had to finish teaching two 90-minute Intermediate Algebra morning classes and a Statistics class. Then he had to drive to Central Jersey Community College for a slate of three afternoon classes. Such was his routine on Mondays and Wednesdays.

But he was not too tired to notice Sally's semi-sheer blouse or the angle view of her breasts. Sally caught his stare and gave him a demeaning smirk, as she pushed together the lapels of the blouse as if that would redirect his stare. "You really think now is a good time to get all jacked up? I know this would not be the first time we had sex in this godforsaken office, but this won't be a time it happens, Ralph. Dream on."

Ralph knew he was busted. He didn't care. "Sally come on," he said. "It's been a long day, and I'm a virile guy after all. Let's go back to your house and spend some time together. I really could use a beer and some hugs. And maybe a chance to see what's under that blouse."

Sally cut him off before he had time to make the invitation sound any more, or any less, appealing. "Ralph, have you heard anything about the bungling Sheriff Clough running around campus, interrupting faculty and others and asking incriminating questions? He found his way to my office and was stubborn about leaving. He likes to ask a final question and then ask another final question."

Ralph was surprised to hear his colleague and lover use *bungling* to describe the Sheriff. He pouted, his manhood crushed by the change of subject matter and hoping his sophomoric smirk might get the romance back on track.

He shook his head and said, "My dear, that guy knows exactly what he's doing. The droopy hat, the unlit cigar stub, plain tie, even plainer gray pants and tan corduroy coat, along with the annoying questions, are part of his trap. Don't get caught."

"He just aggravates me no end," Sally said. "I have no idea why he would question me, but he's zeroing in that Kelleher was murdered."

"Can I change the subject, not go back to your blouse?" Ralph asked humbly. "Do you know any more about the journal Kelleher kept on people and things at the College, including people and places? From what I hear, it included reports from Security on campus happenings, people screwing around one way or another. Stuff missing. Like money. You name it. Who knows. But, for sure, there would be dirt."

Sally looked annoyed that Ralph had changed the subject again. She wasn't done with her criticism of the Sheriff. But she relented. "Edith

Reynolds blabbed to me that he had something of a journal or a notebook. He would hide it when people came into his office, probably in his desk. Lieber mentioned it to me once too."

"I sure would like to get my hands on that book," Ralph said, much like a hormone-crazy teen boy anticipated getting his hands on the latest *Playboy* issue.

"Sally, what did you do after I left here on that Wednesday evening," he continued, promptly changing the subject again.

"I left about 11 PM, as I recall," Sally said. "About the same time as you. I came straight home. You know that. Why would you ask?"

Sally paused as if some thought bubbles suddenly appeared over her head like a cartoon drawing. One bubble said: *Did you go back to the Board Meeting after we left this office?* A second had: *Did you confront Kelleher and then do something stupid?* But the third said: *This guy is pretty stupid!*

"Yes, I did go back to Board Room," Hughes admitted. "I wanted to ask Kelleher what he was doing by having someone contact Columbia Community College, asking for a listing of faculty who teach there. I wanted to jump ahead and just tell him I have a brother who works there and see if that would satisfy him. Get him off track."

"You knew this would happen, sooner or later, Ralph," Sally said. "You can't work two full-time teaching jobs in the same state and get away with it. So, what did Kelleher say?"

"I've *gotten away with it*, to use your terms, for over two years now, pulling in two salaries," Ralph said, feeling like he had been cornered with no escape. We both enjoy the extra money."

"By the time I got back to the Board Meeting after we fooled around here, the meeting was over. Still, several people were hanging around like always happens after a Board Meeting."

"A few people were waiting for Kelleher to open the mini-bar in his office. They didn't have to wait long. The prick Kelleher headed for the office and into his Irish Whiskey as soon as the press lady left. He looked like he needed a drug fix the way he stampeded to his office and was coughing. Kelleher closed the door and then reappeared with a bottle in one hand, a glass in the other and a cheesy smile on his ashen face."

"Sally," Ralph said, "I sure would like to get my hands on that notebook. Wonder where he hid the thing."

"Ralph," Sally interjected as she crossed her legs and leaned back on the desk, "I thought you wanted to get your hands on my blouse."

Izzy Kelleher said goodnight to her sons. They looked so much older these days. Connor was genuinely intrigued by girls and asking sex questions, most of which were embarrassing. Ian still was of the mindset that the female species was icky. Connor would be getting his driver's license in a few months. Pauly had promised to teach him. Now that woeful assignment would fall to her.

She was now hoping that Connor would not remember his Sweet Sixteen birthday, as well as ignore the fact that he could get his learner's permit and start to drive. She also hoped that she could find a letter from her late husband or, better yet, a love poem that he wrote for her.

Her husband would not be there to witness and explain to Ian what was happening when he got his first wet dream one night. She and J. Paul had laughed hysterically when two years ago, the elder son, Connor, had woken up in the middle of the night and come to their bedroom pounding wildly on the door. Izzy remembered Ian shouting, "Mom, dad, I think I just became a man!"

Izzy retreated to the living room and a glass of Chardonnay she had poured earlier. She sat on the couch with her legs stretched out. She gazed at the chocolate-brown leather recliner where her husband would spend most nights reading, watching television and going through the day's inconsequential office mail.

She thought about the day years ago when she had driven the boys to school, only to run over a squirrel who was slow to scamper across the road. This was not the first squirrel that had decided to play chicken with the car and dash to the other side of the street. This was the first one to crunch beneath her wheels.

Connor had laughed so hard he fell out of the car when they got to school. Ian did not speak to her the rest of the day and held a private ceremony in the backyard after retrieving the squashed, furry carcass at the end of school that day.

In just two days, the Inquest would begin, with her husband's death as the sole focus. She would be front and center while Arthur Clough would swear-in people she knew and then grill them. She knew most of the witnesses but not enough to predict what truths they would reveal and what lies they might tell.

Her husband had upset plenty of people at the College and from the community. There were various motives to commit murder, including ones she had, if she was honest with herself. Her thoughts wandered: *Had Clough narrowed the list of suspects to pull off a Perry Mason and expose the culprit at the Inquest? Would the partial autopsy reveal how J. Paul died? What about the toxicology reports? Would they find any other drugs than the Morphine? Had she trusted people who had more than a grudge against her husband? Should she include herself in the list of suspects?*

If it was suicide, why had J. Paul not left a note? She told herself: *Pauly was a writer for God's sake. He'd written two masters theses, several grants, a multitude of reports and a host of correspondence and memos. He'd authored* short stories and written poems when they were dating and again when each son was born. Could Pauly decide to end it all and not say goodbye to his wife, to his sons? Perhaps the Irish Whiskey or the Morphine screwed up his mind, and he could not think straight? Perhaps she just hadn't found the letter yet?

Ella Cosby, her jewelry-creating YMCA friend, said she would like to come to the Inquest. Izzy said sure. She could use whatever moral support she could gather. Some of her female professor colleagues from Atlantic State asked to come too. She had asked Edith and Samantha to sit with her, thus creating a small cheering squad.

Samantha Bartell had received a subpoena to testify, but Clough had told her he would only call her to witness if her statement was necessary to trap someone. Still, any testimony could be awkward for her, especially if her relationship with the County Commissioner was revealed.

Clough had told the widow he would not call her to witness, but if desired, she could ask him to ask a witness a specific question. That would present a great advantage to her. Right now, Izzy did not know what line of inquiry she might take.

Izzy grabbed the pad of paper and the pencil she had placed on the coffee table to capture any queries she would want to pursue. Or the names of those to question herself.

So far, the pad was blank.

19

PRESENT

"Maybe one of those Irish Ghosts will speak to me."

Arthur Clough was in his office, preparing for the Inquest to begin in a day. He couldn't sleep any longer and was at his desk with his coffee just after 6:15 AM on Tuesday.

As the Monroe County Coroner, Clough had had the Clerk of the Court send subpoenas to his list of potential witnesses a week ago. He did not plan to call everyone subpoenaed to provide testimony, but he wanted to keep all options open.

Usually, he would take another week or two before calling for an Inquest. But he did not have uncertainty as to what caused the death, and he wanted to complete the Death Certificate. He knew exactly *what* caused the death of President J. Paul Kelleher, and he knew the approximate time of death.

The Sheriff-Coroner was still not convinced J. Paul died of his own doings, accidentally or on purpose, or from the hands of another or others. Kelleher had a few people who disliked him, several more who detested him and a couple who admitted hatred. But, he thought, if dislike, detest and hatred were lone criteria for murder, he and most of the people he knew would be dead too.

The Sheriff had found the hypodermic syringes and the Morphine vials in the towel dispenser in Kelleher's off-limits Executive Bathroom. There was no way to match the needle marks to any of the hypodermics, but as the Clinical Pathologist confirmed, there was no doubt a Morphine overdose, complicated by alcohol, brought about the man's death. Death would have likely occurred shortly after the last injection or injections.

If it had been murder, the culprit could have found the Morphine in the bathroom or seen Kelleher about to relieve his pain. Or, the murderer might have acquired Morphine from another source and made the injection in Kelleher's arm. Clough knew it was possible to purchase Morphine from Canada. If so, the person or persons likely would have taken the used syringes and vials. It could be done quickly. It would be easy to do the injection, especially if Kelleher was drowsy or blacked-out from the alcohol. The President might not even have known he had received the fatal dosage.

As an alternative theory, Clough postulated that Kelleher gave himself an injection in the bathroom. Then he had placed the used syringe and vial in the towel dispenser and gone into the office to pass out, unaware the dosage would relieve the pain and end his life. Or was quite aware that it would.

Clough was confident he could wield the Inquest in such a way that the correct truth would come out. The murderer would confess or box himself or herself to the point that a confession was only a luxury to prosecution. Or, as might be the outcome, he could confirm Kelleher's accidental death or his intentional taking of his own life.

Clough was comfortable with the person-pairing couple theory he and Diaz had talked about. Yet, he did not discard the alternate that it was one person, not a tandem two, who committed the murder.

The Coroner was making a list of questions he wanted to ask the witnesses. He would surprise several of them with his inquiry. To do that, he might identify misdeeds, misdemeanors, indiscretions and felonies by these witnesses. All the focus was to get at that final question – just how did Kelleher die and who was involved?

Having indulged in *Hardy Boys* novels as a kid and in Criminology and Social Psychology textbooks as an adult, Clough had concluded there are two kinds of liars. There are the ones who adhere to the truth, veering off-sides slightly. In their minds, they are still telling the truth, well most of it. They reveal the truth disingenuously.

Then there's the type who reinvent reality. These people form a made-up version that becomes so ingrained in their mind, that they are not actually lying. They manipulate the truth and re-rationalize their devious behavior. These, Clough held, were the most dangerous ones.

He could see several of the witnesses who would testify in the morning who were the second type.

Arthur Clough finished his second cup of coffee and was reviewing his notes. Still not comfortable with the investigation, he decided to take one more look in the President's Office. He could use the driving time to re-consider his witness questions in his mind. He left his office and drove out to the campus that Tuesday morning, a day before the Inquest was scheduled.

The Sheriff did not expect anyone to be there this early, so he stopped by the Security Office to have someone meet him at the Administration Building and unlock the area. But when he got to the President's Office, there was

Edith Reynolds at her desk, typing a report in between wiping tears from her eyes with a handkerchief.

She was startled when Clough walked in the doorway at 7:30 that morning but relieved, even excited, to see him. She jumped out of her chair and ran over to him, as a young daughter might respond to her hero dad coming home from work.

"Sheriff, I'm so pleased to see you," she said, as she kissed him on the cheek and embraced him in a semi-bear hug. Semi because she could not reach her arms completely around the guy. "The lack of closure, of knowing exactly how Mr. Kelleher died, is driving me nuts. Anything I can do at the Inquest, ask away. I've racked my mind trying to think of something I may have missed that you'd find helpful."

Clough was touched that this classy, professional lady would give him a little kiss and a big hug. In his profession, he didn't get many of either. He hadn't thought much about his wife or his years of marriage, but her absence the past two years had left him devoid of female friendship and physical contact. It didn't take all his analytical skills as a detective to conclude Edith's husband was a fortunate man.

"Edith, let me into the President's Office again, please," asked the Sheriff. "I want to look around. In my profession, revisiting the Crime Scene can provide fresh perspectives. So, I want to envision the moment he died and see if something clicks in my mind. Or maybe one of those Irish Ghosts will speak to me."

"Sure, I'll get my keys," Edith said as she pulled her leather purse from the bottom drawer of her desk after unlocking it with a key she kept on a rabbit's foot in the top drawer. Ever since there had been a series of three stolen pocketbooks on campus, Security had told ladies to place their belongings in a locked desk drawer and not on the floor under the desk.

Edith opened the door. The lingering cleaning fumes caught her square in the face. "Sorry Sheriff, but I had the office deep-cleaned from top to bottom, wall to wall," Edith confessed. "They may have overdone it. I was only in here one time since they did the cleaning. Since then, I locked the door. The fumes will knock you out."

"It's fine, Edith. I can appreciate your zealousness. And the bleach vapors can clean my sinuses and open my pores."

They both looked around the office, first with just the natural light coming from the windows and then with the overhead fluorescent lights at full blast.

Edith saw the four manila folders stacked on top of each other. "Sheriff, I put the folders back on the desk after Deputy Diaz returned them. Samantha went through them to pull anything that needed to be addressed. But that's all. No one else has seen them to my knowledge."

The President's Secretary stopped abruptly. She looked like she had witnessed a ghost, the kind that comes on Halloween to a haunted house, not the *Friendly Casper Ghost* variety.

"Sheriff," she exclaimed, "I know I put that big crystal Shamrock paperweight back on top of the folders, in the center, just the way Mr. Kelleher wanted it. That Shamrock was a lucky charm to him, something his grandfather gave him, as I recall. Samantha will tell you how important it was for Kelleher to have that *Waterford* paperweight in its proper place. Someone was in here and moved it. I'm sure of it."

> We Irish Spirits are real even if not on the same physical plane as humans. We'll determine soon whether J. Paul spends eternity prowling the streets or roaming the graveyard. Be forewarned. Don't insult Irish honor.
>
> *The Irish Banshee*

The expensive paperweight had not been stolen. Instead, it was resting on the desk far to the right of the stack of folders. Edith was not done. "Sheriff, I know I made sure after the super-cleaning that the desk chair was back in the true center of his desk, just the way Mr. Kelleher wanted it. Now, it's positioned way to the left, closer to the hallway that goes to the bathroom and Board Room. Someone moved that too."

"Are you sure, Edith," Clough asked, knowing full well that this lady was certain. Someone had been in the office since the cleaning and without authority to be there. It was as if *Momma Bear* witnessed that *Goldilocks* had sat in one of the living room chairs.

Clough calmly asked Edith for a piece of typing paper which he then slid under the crystal paperweight by using his pen to lift the object. He held the elegant glass object to the light, to examine closely. Then he laid it back down.

"Hard to tell for certain with the naked eye," he said. "But there are fingerprints on the crystal. I'll get Deputy Diaz in here right away to dust the paperweight, chair and desk area for fingerprints. I'm confident we'll find ones we can use. The office cleaning means the prints were left recently. Thank the crew for me. Tell 'em, nice work."

Clough was feeling a burst of adrenaline and an awakening of his senses. "Edith," he said, "I need to have you witness that I found the paperweight in this condition. You may be called upon at the Inquest to affirm this. If the person who came in here has his or her prints on file, we can identify who was in this office. It would appear the person moved the desk chair to be able to get into Kelleher's desk, obviously looking for something in the drawers or those folders. Our visitor was in a hurry and not a professional. Perhaps he or she left a clue from that night Kelleher died?"

Edith looked bewildered and disturbed. She took it as a personal insult that someone would violate the sanctity of the office. Now she wondered if she'd have to have it cleaned all over again. Bring back the SOS pads and the Q-tips cotton swabs.

"Mr. Clough, there's nothing much in that desk," she affirmed. "As you know, Mr. Kelleher had me file most everything. Samantha went through the desk, so did Miss Diaz. Frankly, if the desk was only to serve as storage or a cache for personal possessions, a child's kindergarten version would have been sufficient for President Kelleher."

Clough reached into his pocket and dragged out the photos he had stored for reference. By now the *Polaroids* were crinkled and creased. He sifted through them and picked out two photos of the polished shoes resting perpendicular to the desk. The shoes were perfectly placed together. Even the shoe strings were pulled tight and then laid across the respective shoe, but not tied. There was no way they were just deposited there like an athlete taking off his or her shoes and tossing them toward the locker before heading for the showers.

"Edith, the shoes point to something, something on, inside or under that huge desk," Clough said. I know it. Let me go through the drawers again."

Clough reached for his handkerchief and ever so gently opened each drawer with his pencil and the piece of cloth. The person who had been in the office would have accessed the desk drawers via the handles. Clough was able to massage the opening slowly without contaminating the surface areas.

There were three drawers in the desk positioned above where the pair of shoes had rested. The top one held two unused cartons of *Marlboro* cigarettes and an open box of wooden safety matches. The drawer beneath that one held two legal-sized pads of paper and a half-empty box of unsharpened No. 2 pencils. The third one, at the bottom, was the deepest drawer. It held a paperback version of *Webster's Dictionary* and a similar paperback version of *Roget's Thesaurus*.

When Edith saw the two books, she said, "Mr. Kelleher prided himself on always using the correct and best words. He usually had those two references on his desk when he was writing. They were both heavily used. He bought a set for Samantha and told her to use them. It's kind of funny, but he would not want to be interrupted when he was writing. He did not want others to know that a Rutgers English major relied on these tools. I guess they're keepsakes for Mrs. Kelleher now, if she wants them."

Clough saw that the two books were aligned in the same direction as the shoes – perpendicular to the desk. But otherwise, the drawer was empty. Like the shoes, they were not haphazardly deposited in the drawer. They were strategically placed. Kelleher may not have carefully positioned them when he was using them. They were now, just like the shoes.

"Mrs. Reynolds, were these two books moved at all during the cleaning or when Samantha went through the desk?," the Sheriff asked. "It's very important for me to know if they remain as Kelleher left them."

"The cleaning people were told not to go through the desk," she replied. "And Samantha knew where to look for any work papers. She would not have bothered with his cigarettes, pencils or these reference books. I'm sure of that. We were leaving those things for Mrs. Kelleher when she finally came by. Miss Diaz may have moved them, but I doubt it."

"Here look at this photo," Clough asked. "The two books are perfectly aligned, same as they are now. No one moved them. The person who broke into the office did not move them either."

Clough picked-up the *Webster's Dictionary* and the *Roget's Thesaurus* with a *Kleenex* and his handkerchief and sat down in one of the burnt-orange chairs on the other side of the desk. Edith stood looking over his shoulder so that she could take a closer look at each book herself. He thumbed through the pages and saw underlined words here and there, with some words crossed out. Three pages in the dictionary were dog-eared, with an encircled, not underlined or crossed-out, word on each page. Similarly, there were three dog-eared pages in the *Thesaurus* with a word encircled on each of those pages.

The three words in the paperback dictionary were in alphabetical order: *Bottom, Drawer* and *Fake*, while the three *Thesaurus* words were *Hidden, Journal* and *Righteousness*. It didn't take all of Clough's deductive reasoning skills to conclude Kelleher meant the six words as a message.

Clough went back to the desk and that bottom drawer. With the two paperbacks out of the drawer, Clough felt around and noted a gap in the back. It felt about a fourth of an inch wide. He placed his hand on the wooden bottom and pushed it to the back via his handkerchief, so that now the space was at the front of the drawer. He remembered that a penknife enabled him to open the towel dispenser. He decided to try his luck the same way here.

"This is a false bottom drawer, Edith," the Sheriff said. "Let me see what happens when I slide the bottom and lift it out. My hunch is that something is hidden underneath. That's what Kelleher was telling us."

Clough's penknife was sufficient to enable him to slide up and then lift out the bottom of the drawer, revealing a notebook – President Kelleher's private journal.

"Oh, my God," Edith screamed. "That's his notebook. I only saw it a few times, as hard as that may be to believe. But that's it. See those alpha indexes on the side. He had it hidden in his desk, out of sight, amazing. Do you think he wanted you to find it?"

"I do not doubt that, Edith," Clough said. "The shoes were the directional key, and the paperbacks were the clues to where the journal was hidden. Wow. I will take this notebook now. Edith, you're my witness as to where the notebook was, here in this office in this hidden drawer. That's what the intruder, perhaps the killer, who moved the paperweight and desk chair was looking for. But he didn't find it. It was here all the time."

"Kelleher knew something was going to happen that night, so he left us a clue," the Sheriff summarized.

"I expect the doggone journal has a ton of clever and juicy Kelleher observations," said Edith. "Maybe a few tattletale notes as well. Sheriff, can you use this at the Inquest to find out who killed Mr. Kelleher?"

Before the Sheriff could respond, Edith moaned. "Oh no, is this a Crime Scene again? Do you think I should have the office steam-cleaned one more time?"

PRESENT

"That doesn't add up, and this Sheriff is very good at math."

County Commissioner Dominic Panichi called Samantha Bartell from his office just before he left to go home. He was working late Tuesday. He knew he would be out of the office for the Inquest the next day. He had received Arthur Clough's subpoena to appear.

"Hey, Cutie Marks," Panichi said as he heard Samantha answer the phone. "I wanted to call to wish you well tomorrow. Not sure what will happen, but are you doing all right?"

"As well as could be expected," replied Samantha. "That's given that my secret love may be exposed at this Inquest for all the world to know. In case you didn't already know, Dominic, that's you."

There was a pause at Dominic's end of the telephone before he replied. "Samantha, I spoke with Clough. He wants me to testify about the architect thing, the $5,000. But he said he'd try to avoid the personal questions. He must get the payoff thing on the record, so he can attack Pitman and Harrison, especially if either chooses to lie on the witness stand. What they did, or tried to do, must come out. They could face prosecution. And that might flush-out other secrets."

"Who else do you think must be sweating it out tonight," Samantha asked, but answered herself. "I imagine Winters is in for a rough time. He's made no secret of how he felt about President Kelleher. I would not want to be Alan Fox either, given what Kelleher had me divulge about him and female students. Not sure his classroom sexual adventures would be a motive for murder, but he may end up standing in line for unemployment or behind bars."

"What do you want to do, what do we say, if it does come out at the hearing that we're lovers," Dominic interrupted. "If that happens, I know I will have to call my father, even before I talk to Cecilia. He will be furious. So too will most everyone else in New Jersey whose last name is Panichi or Gambrelli. For that matter, for anyone with an Italian surname."

"Don't worry about me, Dominic" Samantha said. "I will get plenty of crap from others at the College, and my folks will be upset, but that's nothing compared to you."

"Don't underestimate how people will react, especially with a new Presidential Search getting underway at the College," Panichi added.

"Samantha," Dominic continued after pausing for several moments. "Please know and believe that nothing that comes out, nothing that happens as aftershock tomorrow, will change my love. Nothing will distract my intense feelings for you. Nothing can change my desire to be with you for the rest of my life. I almost want it to come out, so we can again be honest with others, with the world. We won't have to continue secretive phone calls, sneak behind closed doors or rely on a rendezvous in the Poconos."

If the telephone had been visual and not just audio communication, the County Commissioner would have seen the tears roll down Samantha's cheeks.

Tyrone Jackson, Chief of Campus Security, and Blanca Diaz, the Deputy Sheriff of Monroe County were having a late dinner on Tuesday at Diaz's apartment. Diaz had configured a crock pot of Cuban chicken and yellow rice that had cooked much of the afternoon. The exceptional dish contained baby peas, onions, yellow rice, peppers and chicken thighs. Tyrone was sipping a *Rolling Rock* beer right from the bottle, as Blanca proudly served him.

"Blanca, this looks fabulous, but you're Puerto Rican," Tyrone proclaimed. "Why do you make Cuban chicken?"

"When I was a kid, mom found ways to stretch meals. We had rice with most every meal. Cuban chicken is made with various parts of the bird. She mostly made it with chicken wings and backs. My version celebrates her culinary skills but with meaty thighs. The Puerto Rican version has lots of garlic, cumin and paprika. It is served with beer and plenty of water to put out the fire."

"Blanca, you could serve me the wings and backs, even chicken necks and feet. I'd still be overwhelmed with your recipes and want seconds," Tyrone said.

"Who do you think got into Kelleher's office," Tyrone asked, switching roles from lover to Security Chief, while taking a robust bite of the flavory chicken dish.

"We're pretty sure the person did not have a key," Blanca responded. "The door to the Board Room from the hall was unlocked, as it usually is, because many groups use that room. The person got into the President's

Office via the access door in the Board Room. It's a push-button that's locked from the inside. Someone, who knew what he was doing, picked the door knob in the Board Room, probably with a paper clip or nail file. There were scratches. The Board Room gave him access and privacy – time to work on the lock."

"Well, whoever got into the office was looking for that journal," concluded Tyrone. "To my knowledge, this is the first time there's ever been a break-in to an office or any room on campus. Those locks are easy to pick."

Changing the subject back to who got into the office, Jackson said, "We know from our Security logs that Gene Wildwood and Candace Rodewald occasionally stay late at the Computer Center, or what we call the *Meat Locker*, because it's so damn cold in there. The lights were out a few times when they were still there. In fact, they were there after the Board Meeting the night Kelleher was killed. And I don't think it would take Sherlock Holmes to figure out that they were into hanky-panky, not programming."

"I don't see that as a motive to kill someone or even break into an office," the Deputy Sheriff responded. "Hughes and Sally Bowens spend a lot of time together in that tiny second floor Union office in the Library. Pretty sure there is more than contract negotiations going on there, too. They despised Kelleher, perhaps because he usually out-smarted them."

"Besides," Blanca added, "I'm not sure it was a murder."

"You have to consider how relatively easy it would have been to kill the guy, what with the Morphine injections and the alcohol," Jackson said. "The guy could have been slumped over in that desk chair or sprawled out on the carpet. He might have passed out. Someone saw the vials and decided to compound the dosage."

"You have a point there," Blanca conceded. "You know, from the reports we got, Winters was still on campus late that night. Not sure where Lieber was, but they say they were together at a bar consoling themselves. That doesn't add up, and this Sheriff is very good at math. I doubt many middle-aged married guys go to a bar that late in the middle of the week unless they have something to celebrate or hide."

"The Sheriff said that Coach Solly was quite angry, even belligerent," Diaz added. "He hated Kelleher, so why in the world would he announce a scholarship in the guy's name? Makes no sense."

"Hell, if I know," said the Security Chief. "The guy has his demons and is known as highly manipulative. He'll be something on the witness stand."

"*Magic Man* Harrison told the Sheriff he was with Pitman after the Board Meeting," Diaz offered. "That sounds awfully convenient to me. They were both super pissed at Kelleher and hiding something."

Diaz cleared the plates from the table before continuing. "Mr. Clough had me expedite the results from the fingerprints I got in the President's Office this morning. The one on the glass paperweight and two from the desk drawers. I should have the results in the morning, assuming the person's prints are on file with the FBI. Since this person was no rookie on picking locks, chances are good his prints are with the FBI."

Jackson got up from the table to grab another beer from the refrigerator. "I suppose Clough is plowing through that journal now and making notes on what to ask people at the Inquest," he said.

"Tomorrow will be a most interesting day, to say the least," the Deputy Sheriff said. If the witnesses veer from the truth or think about lying, Clough will jump all over them."

"I plan to be there and grab a front row seat," Jackson proclaimed. "I did not get a subpoena, but Clough wants me there and said he'd call me to testify if needed. He's not going to sequester me with the others. That's good. I am looking forward to watching my sweetheart in action."

Tyrone set his beer down and put his arm around his girlfriend. "Blanca," he said, "I had to give Arthur my office file with notes that I keep. He may want me to say in court what I wrote. He said if he did, he'd censor the romantic parts about you."

Blanca turned to face Tyrone and put her hands to cradle his face lovingly. "My sweet, tomorrow is a big day. You'd better get there early. And don't worry. It's an adult audience. They can handle a little romance stuff."

353

THE INQUEST

The Official Inquest Into the President's Death

The integrity of the upright will guide them,
but the crookedness of the treacherous will destroy them.
Hebrews 11:4
New American Standard Bible

THE INQUEST – SESSION 1

You see through love, and that deludes your sight,
as what is straight seems crooked through the water.
John Dryden

The Coroner, Arthur Clough, called the gathering together at 10:05 AM on Wednesday, November 16, 1977. The Inquest was held at the Monroe County Courthouse in Courtroom II, the smaller of the two spaces. There were about 50 people there, with most assembled in the gallery section. Seventeen had received a subpoena to be testify. Others had come out of curiosity or as gapers, as if driving by an accident on the Interstate, looking to see how bad the crash was or, in this case, would be.

Some, like Tyrone Jackson and Jack Kula, were there in deference to the deceased President and to serve the Coroner. Others, like Candace Rodewald, Samantha Bartell and Nancy Wiegand, were afraid of what might be said under oath and in open court about their romantic alliances and awkward affairs.

The room itself was composed of wood panels, flooring and railings in front of two wooden attorney tables tarnished by repeated use. The building was 42 years old and, while well-maintained, looked tired and overworked. There was nothing that could be done with the Courtroom without extensive renovation, unless a judge would choose to cover the wood and adorn the panels with vibrant, light-colored paint. Then a decade later, the prevailing judge probably would order the ugly paint removed and the natural wood restored.

Mr. Clough stood in front of the eight-foot long bench, where the judge would normally preside, and behind the wooden table where the prosecuting attorney would be stationed. Deputy Sheriff Blanca Diaz and Mr. Phil Smith, the appointed Court Attorney, flanked him. The Court Reporter, Mrs. Vicki Parkinson, sat adjacent to the bench on her innocuous stool, preparing to put her shorthand skills to work with the phonetic stenotype machine. Clough placed his briefcase and a binder with forensic results and interview notes on the table, so that he could reference it from time to time. He would do so often.

Seated at the other wooden table customarily occupied by the defense attorney was Clinical Pathologist Dr. David Charles, College Attorney Jack Kula and Security Chief Tyrone Jackson. They were present to testify because of their positions and had not received subpoenas. There was an empty seat nearest the aisle in the unlikely event Deputy Diaz would sit in it. Most likely, she would stand throughout the process or be on the move, shuttling witnesses and observing the audience.

Izzy Kelleher sat at the end of that row of chairs, with Edith Reynolds, Samantha Bartell, Ella Cosby, Rebecca Campbell, Nancy Wiegand and Dr. Rueben Feldman and his wife, Deborah aligned in the first row of the gallery just behind the bar that separated the areas. They were all considered guests of the Court, having been asked by the Coroner to attend and contribute to the proceedings as might be necessary.

The jury box was empty and would remain so for the duration of the Inquest. There were no empty chairs in the gallery, but the overflow was not permitted to sit in the jury box.

Eight people were held from entering the Courtroom due to the packed gallery. They were advised by Deputy Diaz that they could enter the Courtroom once the subpoenaed witnesses were excused and isolated in the Jury Room. That would free up at least 17 seats in the gallery.

Martha J. Rooney of the *Jersey Star* got a seat in the front row just behind the prosecution table where Mr. Clough was situated. Miss Diaz had received petitions from reporters with Newark's *Ledger-Star* and the *Trenton Daily* to be present. The two media representatives were in the gallery. She was not sure where they had decided to sit.

Mrs. Wiegand shuddered at the thought she might be asked to testify if Alan Fox did. She would have to admit to having had sex and lying naked with the guy and how he blackmailed her. Nancy had not received a subpoena to testify. She did not know, but she was relieved – somewhat. She stared at Rebecca Campbell, admiring her loveliness and poise. Her mind wandered: *I wonder how much Rebecca knows about the escapades of her boss, and if his lies will shock her. As attractive as she is, there's no way Fox hasn't made a play on her. He probably got slammed. How come I didn't slam him? Oh Greg, I hope you can forgive me. I hope one day I can forgive myself.*

The Sheriff had discarded his slovenly garb of the elbow-patched corduroy blazer, blue shirt and gray slacks. Clough wore his charcoal gray suit and left his hat and cigar remnant in his car. Blanca had gone motherly and insisted he wear a white shirt. The Deputy had given him a new burgundy tie with blue diagonal stripes for the occasion. Clough was too overweight to look good, but he did have a dramatic presence. If the proceedings had been televised, he would have filled the TV screen.

Arthur Clough had decided to honor J. Paul Kelleher that morning and spit polish his own black shoes. They needed a good shine. Any kind of a shine. The Sheriff had gone through a *Metamorphosis*, not unlike author Franz Kafka, at least in appearance. But he did not awake as *Gregor Samsa*, a cockroach or a related bug. He was now Coroner Clough, looking reasonably sharp and notably intimidating.

Clough grabbed the judge's walnut gavel, pounded it twice on the matching wooden sound block and began his remarks. "Ladies and gentlemen, thank you for coming today. My name is Arthur Clough, spelled C-L-O-U-G-H. You pronounce my surname as in *"crew"* or *"blue"* or *"flew."* You may prefer to address me as *Mr. Coroner*."

"I am duly appointed by the Monroe County Board of Chosen Freeholders to this official position as County Coroner. Though not particularly common, it's not unusual to have the County Sheriff also serve as Coroner. While I am not a doctor, I am trained in methods of forensics and certified as a Licensed Coroner. Both positions are law enforcement officers. I have full authority to seek medical and pathological analyses by qualified physicians in the County or elsewhere. In the words of Dr. Quincy from the television show: *You are entering the fantastic world of forensic medicine.* Actually, I added the word fantastic because it is that."

"Understand too, that as Monroe County Sheriff I have full authority to conduct the investigation into Mr. Kelleher's death. I also have the right and responsibility to apply my investigation to this Inquest and the testimonies of witnesses."

"Many of you received a subpoena and therefore are not present of your own choice. Please know how important your witness will be today. We have a very important function. My responsibility is to assure that our official business is accomplished and to conduct the Inquest according to proper protocol."

"My role is to convene this assembly, administer the oath to each witness and conduct the proceedings. I do not serve as judge, prosecutor or Grand Jury. My charge as Coroner is to seek and differentiate reliable and valid witness information contributed today and make the determinations applicable to complete the Death Certificate."

Clough pointed to the persons standing next to him and introduced each one. "Next to me, on your right, is Mr. Phil Smith, flanked to his left by Deputy Sheriff Blanca Diaz. Mr. Smith is the appointed Court Attorney for this Inquest today. He will be called upon, as necessary, to identify or explain a point of law, as requested by a witness or by me. He will determine whether the inquiry from a witness is appropriate after considering any objection raised by me."

"Miss Diaz will retrieve and accompany each witness to the stand and assure proper decorum throughout this process. Any disruption of these proceedings will be dealt with immediately and subject to investigation and prosecution, as appropriate."

"Next to the Deputy Sheriff is our Court Reporter, Mrs. Vicki Parkinson. We thank you, Vicki, for being here and for your professional transcription. Make no mistake, this is an official session of the New Jersey County of Monroe, with the standing and constitution of any Court of Law."

Clough paused for several moments, more to re-set the mood and elevate attention to the proceedings than to disturb the flow of the agenda. He continued with his opening remarks. "We have three functions today to complete the Death Certificate. The first is identification of the body of the person found dead on the scene in the President's Office of Central Jersey Community College on the morning of Thursday, October 20, 1977."

"To that end, positive identification was made on Friday, October 21, 1977 at the County Morgue that the deceased person was indeed Mr. Jacob Paul Kelleher, commonly known as J. Paul Kelleher of 183 Country Lane, Lawrence, New Jersey. At approximately 10:10 AM, Mrs. Isabelle Brooke Rhodes Kelleher, spouse of the deceased and of the same address, confirmed the identification of Mr. Kelleher."

"Before I clarify the other two functions of this Inquest, let me recognize Mrs. Kelleher. Mrs. Kelleher, the Court expresses its extreme grief and sincere sorrow for the loss of your husband. J. Paul leaves behind two young sons, Connor Allen Kelleher, age 15, and Ian Sullivan Kelleher, age 13. We extend our profound condolences to them for the tragic loss of their father. No child should ever lose a parent, a father, this soon and this tragically."

"Ladies and gentlemen, this Inquest is intended to bring closure for, and to, the family of Mr. J. Paul Kelleher so the Death Certificate can be properly executed. We need to establish the official Cause of Death and determine, based on that cause, whether the deceased expired due to one of the following:

(a) *Death by natural cause, primarily attributed to illness or affliction.*
(b) *Death by accident.*
(c) *Death by misadventure of his own hands intentionally or unintentionally.*
(d) *Death by the hands of one or more other persons.*

The Coroner waited for the courtroom murmurs to subside. People were trying to differentiate in their own minds the four causes and pick the one they favored.

Then he resumed his statement: "This is not a court of prosecution and judgment. Should the death be determined as homicide, the witness or witnesses exposed as allegedly responsible for same shall be subject to further investigation and prosecution, as well as full protection of the Court. That is, this Inquest shall not serve as a Court of Law pertinent to prosecution. Culpability shall be reviewed and resolved by decision of the District Attorney's office, not here today. I trust that is clear to everyone."

"Similarly, if consequent to this Inquest, a witness under oath commits perjury, the prosecution of that offense shall be outside of this hearing and resolved by the District Attorney. I trust that is understood."

"Deputy Sheriff Diaz will administer the oath under the supervision of Mr. Smith. To save time, she will administer it once to all of you scheduled to witness. When you take the witness stand, I will remind you that you are under oath and have pledged to tell the truth. I trust you will take me very seriously. There is no room for exceptions."

"My duty today is comparable to an orchestra conductor. As the Coroner in Monroe County, I bring together the different parts of an investigation, like an orchestra. Instead of a string section, brass, percussion, etc., I conduct autopsies, forensic photography, odontology, Crime Scene analyses and related functions. I wield my baton as the conductor would do, so each witness adds to our knowledge of this death. The intent is to produce music – the truthful ballad of the deceased J. Paul Kelleher."

"In a few minutes, all of you who received a subpoena to appear today will be escorted to a secure Jury Room. There you will be detained until you are called one-by-one to come back into this Courtroom to testify. There will be another representative of the Sheriff's Office to escort each witness and assure no one leaves the Jury Room without proper authorization."

"Once you have completed your testimony, you may remain in this Courtroom, unless I rule otherwise. If you choose to leave this room, you are to promptly exit the building, unless permission is granted otherwise. Please understand, you may not return to the Courthouse or this Courtroom until the Inquest is complete. Before or after your testimony, you are not to have any physical or verbal contact with other witnesses regarding testimony. Violation may result in fine or prosecution. You may talk to one another but not about anything that does or might impact this Inquest. Be sure you understand what I have said."

"There are some of you here today who received a subpoena, but whom I may choose to exclude from giving testimony. Nevertheless, you are to remain in the Jury Room for the entire proceeding. I may need further information from you pertaining to this gathering during the Inquest, or I may later see no need for your witness today."

"As for those of you in the Courtroom who are here on your own, you are to obey this same protocol. You are free to leave, but you will not be permitted to return. You are not to have contact with the witnesses. Failure to do so will result in immediate expulsion from the Courtroom. Violation may result in fine and even prosecution."

"Only I will ask questions of the witnesses, unless permission is granted by me for another person to do so. An example of a proper request would be one that might come from Mrs. Kelleher as the deceased's spouse."

Clough looked directly at Mrs. Kelleher and saw her looking back at him. Then he continued. "Mrs. Kelleher, if during the testimony, you have a question of a witness, you may address me and explain the question you would like to ask. I will grant permission for you to address the witness or ask you to withdraw the request. Or, I may choose to ask the witness the question myself."

Clough scanned the audience to see if anyone looked clueless as to what was about to transpire. Winters' face betrayed a scowl of disgust. Alan Fox shrugged his shoulders as if bored by everything. Sally Bowens was whispering something to Ralph Hughes that Clough could not overhear. Martha Rooney, of the *Jersey Star*, was surveying the room to find a potential *National Inquirer* story.

The Coroner looked again at the audience. "I now ask every witness who received a subpoena to appear today to come and position themselves at the front of this Courtroom. Deputy Diaz will administer the witness oath."

Clough waited for all 17 subpoenaed witnesses to come to the front of the room before he spoke to Miss Diaz, who was standing next to him. "Deputy Sheriff Diaz kindly read the witness oath to these people who stand before me."

Diaz turned to face the sober people now lined up and rubbing shoulders. She looked down the row of witnesses to assure she had everyone's attention. Only then did she begin the ritual by reading the oath in a booming and highly authoritative voice: "Please listen and respond to this statement:

Do you solemnly swear, that the testimony you are about to give in this Inquest today is the truth, the whole truth and nothing but the truth, so help you, God?"

Clough listened to the chorus and then said, "Let the record show that everyone said *yes*. Thank you. I now ask you, one-by-one, if you shall commit to the truth here today consequent to rebuke and punishment, if it is determined you did not speak the truth. You are to raise your right hand and answer that question."

"Miss Diaz, you have the listing of witnesses," Clough proclaimed. "Please call each person in alphabetical order. Wait for an oral answer to the question posed before you read the next person's name."

Deputy Sheriff Diaz faced the line of witnesses and looked to Mr. Clough to nod for her to proceed. She paused and called out the first name: *Miss Sarah Bowens.*

Miss Bowens was surprised to be the first name called. She had not realized that no one with an A surname was in the group. She bashfully, but promptly, raised her hand and responded with an emphatic *yes* to the question.

Miss Diaz continued through the list of witnesses, the last one being Donald Winters. Winters raised his hand slowly, more out of protest to being there than to affirm the witness oath. "Yes, ma'am," he said. "I was hoping you'd skip me. But since you're asking, I commit to speaking the truth, even though I choose not to be here."

The Coroner ignored the comment, filing it away for future reference when Winters would be called to testify. He then spoke directly to the Deputy Sheriff. "Miss Diaz kindly escort all witnesses to the Jury Room where they shall be under the supervision of the Court Officer, Mr. Harold Drefus, who is standing by the exit."

Then Clough addressed the line-up of witnesses. "Ladies and gentlemen let me state again that after you have testified or during this period before your testimony, I admonish you not to discuss this Inquest with any other witness. Mr. Drefus will tend to your physical needs, and we have provided refreshments for you. Miss Diaz will come to the Jury Room to accompany you in the order I prescribe and for you to complete your testimony. Do any of you have a question before you depart this Courtroom?"

Clough looked over the array of people, before continuing, as if his stare would seal the deal on truthful testimony. "Hearing none, please follow Miss Diaz and Mr. Drefus to the Jury Room. Do so in silence and single file."

Clough's eyes tracked each witness, as everyone formed a single file and passed by him on the way to the exit. Some began to fidget and squirm over the prospect of being stuck in a room all day. There were many other things they could be doing. Some wished they could be anywhere else for that afternoon, certainly back at work. Some would have preferred to be at the dentist having a tooth pulled. Others would have traded that day for the times they waited in lines for gas during the 1973 shortage when oil prices surged and fuel rationing was the norm.

Mr. Clough waited for the single-file parade of witnesses to march out of the Courtroom and the double doors had swung closed. He paused to collect his thoughts and rehearse, in his mind, his next comments. The departure of the witnesses left many seats unoccupied. Most were immediately filled by the overflow attendees.

"Regarding the official Cause of Death, let me now summarize my examination. Based on my authority and given the permission of Mrs. Kelleher, the initial post mortem examination at the County Morgue was restricted to the external organs, arms, legs, torso and face. There was nothing in my examination of the body at that time to suggest we would need to complete an all-encompassing autopsy. There was no physical trauma evidenced to suggest a wider scope of analysis. Given that a deceased person loses about two degrees of body temperature per hour, I calculated Mr. Kelleher died between 1 and 3 AM on Thursday, October 20, 1977."

Clough again paused to survey people in attendance. He focused on those few who seemed more preoccupied. Then he continued. "There were evident signs of the use of a hypodermic syringe in both arms, indicating drug usage. There was no other evidence of disturbance of the body. It would not be possible to ascertain to what extent the injections had occurred within a timeframe before his death. However, there is every reason to conclude that the injections had been made within the past eight to ten hours before death."

"Before I completed my preliminary examination, I was contacted by Dr. David Charles, a medical doctor specializing in Clinical Pathology at St. Anthony Hospital. Dr. Charles told me that Mr. Kelleher was a patient before and at the time of his death. He had examined Mr. Kelleher after referral from Dr. Reuben Feldman, the family physician and Kelleher's primary doctor. Dr. Feldman had conducted preliminary tests and believed further tests were necessary to confirm a diagnosis."

"On June 13, 1977, Dr. Carter conducted an MRI – Magnetic Resonance Imagery. An MRI is a new diagnostic tool available at a small but growing number of hospitals. It uses a magnetic field and pulses radio wave energy to make photos of organs inside the body, such as the brain. The MRI enabled affirmation of Dr. Feldman's initial observation and Dr. Charles' diagnosis that Mr. Kelleher had an advanced form of cancer in his brain. The MRI showed that President Kelleher had a major growth."

"In a moment," Clough said sternly, "I will ask Dr. David Charles to take the stand, before other witnesses, so he may confirm the cancer and the use of pain medications. Dr. Charles was asked to identify the presence or absence of natural disease and other microscopic findings and to interpret toxicology on body tissues and fluids."

Clough knew his next statements would offend some people for their directness and unqualified language. He pressed on.

"Dr. Charles was asked to determine the chemical cause of overdoses, poisonings or other cases involving potential toxic agents, as well as conduct his examination of physical trauma. Tissue specimens and samples from the throat, liver, lungs and brain were taken and made into slides for examination under the microscope. Dr. Charles was asked to conduct a toxicology analysis of the body, especially given the ingestion of one or more drugs before or at the time of death."

Clough found Dr. Charles where he was sitting. "Dr. Charles, please come to the witness stand and testify under the oath of your medical profession as well as of this official Inquest."

Dr. Charles rose from his seat, checked that his red rep necktie was pulled all the way to his neck, acknowledged Mr. Clough with a nod and confidently took the seat at the witness stand. He was a professional, used to being asked to testify in court.

Coroner	Dr. Charles, I have shared your credentials as a medical doctor and clinician. But tell us about your medical training.
Dr. Charles	My undergraduate study was at Drexel University where I earned a Bachelor of Science in Biology and Chemistry. Essentially, I was a Pre-Med major. I did my graduate work at Penn State University and interned at the Nittany Medical Center, specializing in Clinical Pathology.
Coroner	Thank you and thank you for being here.
Dr. Charles	You are most welcome. Mr. Clough, may I take a moment to address Mrs. Kelleher?
Coroner	Yes, please do so.

Dr. Charles stood up and faced the widow Kelleher as he spoke. "Mrs. Kelleher, Izzy, I am so sorry about your husband's death. I hope that this Inquest and the findings from today will offer you some peace." He then returned to his seat.

Coroner	Dr. Charles, you were Mr. Kelleher's doctor who told him of his cancer? Is that true?
Dr. Charles	Yes, I diagnosed the cancer.
Coroner	Dr. Charles, tell us the basis of your examination and your conclusions regarding the deceased.
Dr. Charles	Mr. Kelleher had an aggressive form of cancer in his brain, as validated by the MRI and confirmed by a Radiologist at the hospital who studied the MRI images. The tumor caused pressure and severe fluid build-up.

There was a collective hush among those in attendance at the Coroner's pronouncement that President Kelleher had suffered from brain cancer. Clough let the outburst subside before he motioned for Dr. Charles to continue.

Coroner	Dr. Charles, how serious was the cancer?
Dr. Charles	I concluded the cancer would overwhelm his brain within six months. No longer than a year. There was no benefit to surgery, and Mr. Kelleher did not want to pursue chemotherapy. I affirmed that the benefit of drug intervention would probably not outweigh the loss of what quality of life he would have at that point.
Coroner	How did President Kelleher take the news, your diagnosis?
Dr. Charles	He took the information quite well. He was stoic when we talked about it. But you should know that he asked me not to tell anyone about the condition, including his wife and his family physician, Dr. Reuben Feldman.
Coroner	Dr. Charles, if you did not have the MRI equipment and were not able to complete the MRI scan, would that have made a difference in the diagnosis?
Dr. Charles	All of the symptoms would have continued and worsened. Obviously. In my opinion, given the extent of the cancer and the amazingly fast spread, a delayed diagnosis would not have made a difference.
Coroner	Please continue describing his reaction in dealing with the tumor.
Dr. Charles	I told President Kelleher I'd prescribe Morphine in doses of 2 to 3 mg. to manage the pain. He could take it via hypodermic injections from vials of the drug that would be available at, and only through, our St. Anthony's pharmacy. He could acquire the medicine on a weekly basis, upon my authority and only when the pain got beyond his level of tolerance. Mr. Kelleher would manage the doses according to the level of his pain and could refill based on my assessment and decision. He needed to keep the medicine at room temperature and dry.
Coroner	Did Mr. Kelleher have a particularly high or low tolerance for pain?

Dr. Charles	Yes, he did – high. For a somewhat frail man, who did not look healthy, he was strong of will. Each of us has a different threshold of pain. Mr. Kelleher's was assuredly high, given the tumor was already advanced. He was taking the Morphine injections in less than the doses prescribed. With the regularity of his dosages, which he began toward the end of July, he could slowly develop a dependency. Given his pain tolerance and desire to continue to work, I expect Mr. Kelleher paced himself. The last thing he would have wanted was to become so dependent on the pain-killer that he would have to stop working, stop thinking.
Coroner	What about the dosage itself?
Dr. Charles	Each vial contained 3 mg. Mr. Kelleher's desire to be alert, to keep working, affirms he was using the dosage needed to relieve the pain. President Kelleher would retain the vial each time he used the hypodermic needle, each time he gave himself an injection.
Coroner	You made that decision on the vials?
Dr. Charles	I did, Mr. Clough. Mr. Kelleher would return the empty glass vials and used syringes. In that way, I'd know the amounts and judge his conscientiousness. He was very diligent. These were single dosage vials because of the potential for bacteria growth. His prescription would be renewed, and we would talk about how the pain relief was working. Given that each dosage would last about 6 - 8 hours, he would probably take the drug three or four times a day. More, in the latter stages probably. That's what he told me. I'm confident that was accurate and consistent.
Coroner	Dr. Charles, do you know if Mr. Kelleher ever told his wife about the cancer? And if he told anyone else about his condition?
Dr. Charles	No, I do not think he told his wife or anyone else, unless he had a confidant whom he trusted.
Coroner	Not even his wife? Can you explain that from a medical perspective?

367

Dr. Charles	Mr. Coroner, President Kelleher disclosed to me he wanted to complete several projects at the College, while he had his health. That's how he would prefer to spend his remaining months of life. I told him he'd want to share all of this with his wife at some point, especially since the pain would become extreme, and he'd require care and hospitalization. J. Paul did not say he wouldn't. He did not say he planned to do so, either.
Coroner	What about Dr. Feldman who had referred Mr. Kelleher?
Dr. Charles	I did eventually tell Dr. Feldman about the tumor. Reuben called me about two weeks after I had conducted the MRI and told President Kelleher about the advanced state of the cancer. I had told Kelleher I would share the diagnosis with Dr. Feldman, if Reuben contacted me. When I told Reuben, I passed along Mr. Kelleher's desires that he, Dr. Feldman, not tell anyone else.

Mr. Clough glanced across the room to where Dr. Reuben Feldman was sitting next to his wife, Deborah. Dr. Feldman acknowledged the statement by Dr. Charles, nodding his head in polite affirmation.

Coroner	Dr. Feldman told me he honored his patient's desires and did not tell anyone of Mr. Kelleher's condition. Let that be the statement of record.
Dr. Charles	Yes, I believe that to be true. Mr. Kelleher wanted to keep his illness private.
Coroner	My investigation after the death revealed the only other person who knew of Mr. Kelleher's condition was Dr. Thomas Dandridge, also of the College. Dr. Dandridge was subpoenaed and will testify. Dr. Dandridge told me Mr. Kelleher shared his terminal condition two months before he was found dead and did so over lunch at that country club he likes. President Kelleher said he needed to share the information with someone else, given the tension at the College and his ever-increasing symptoms. Dr. Dandridge had to promise he would not tell anyone.

Dr. Charles	Having said that, Mr. Coroner, President Kelleher would have exhibited symptoms which would cause people to be curious and suspicious that his health was suffering. But he did not want others to know. He was insistent that I tell no one.
Coroner	Thank you. Dr. Charles, please continue telling us about your examination of the body and your lab reports.
Dr. Charles	There was significant alcohol in the body at the time of death. That suggests the Morphine was released quickly in the body. As you know, that leads to breathing problems and threatens loss of life. There was evidence of significant nicotine in the system due to heavy smoking. Ironically, the smoking probably gave him some degree of pain separation during those weeks before he died.
Coroner	Tell us about the partial autopsy.
Dr. Charles	Given my knowledge of the brain tumor, and as we discussed, I made an incision in the back of the skull and separated the scalp from the underlying skull. I removed the top of the skull with a vibrating saw and exposed the full brain within the cranial vault where I could see the tumor and the extent to which it was pushing on the skull. I apologize if this is too much detail, but I think this is what you want for the record.

The doctor's vivid description of the autopsy was both unsettling and irritating, and the Coroner waited until people quieted. The mood was as if someone had repeatedly scraped a giant blackboard with their fingernails.

Coroner	Please, continue.
Dr. Charles	Because of the alcohol and the cigarette use, I inspected the liver and the throat. There was no apparent damage to the lungs. There was the beginning of inflammation with the potential for throat cancer had the patient lived. The liver was normal.
Coroner	That's significant, given that the deceased smoked several packs a day.

369

Dr. Charles	It's unusual for a heavy smoker, but not rare. Mr. Coroner, after the partial autopsy, I replaced the extracted organs into the body and closed the incisions. Based on your approval, I released and turned over the body to the Hirsh Funeral Home for embalming and dressing, as per Mrs. Kelleher's desires. Hirsch Funeral is holding the body pending your completion of the Death Certificate. Hirsch will complete funeral arrangements and body cremation, as per Mrs. Kelleher's desires.
Coroner	That's correct and why I wanted to have this Inquest as soon as reasonable. Please continue Dr. Charles. What are the symptoms of the cancer that Mr. Kelleher would have had?
Dr. Charles	Certainly. As the tumor grew, President Kelleher would have experienced memory loss and nausea. He would have had balance and reflex issues. The cigarettes, while temporarily masking pain, would not have helped those symptoms, either. The repeated use of Morphine eventually would induce respiratory depression as well as constipation and drowsiness. There would have been a significant reduction in his blood pressure, and he would fall into a stupor and severe loss of memory near the end of his life. It's not likely he had a convulsion at death since there were no fluids in his mouth or on the rug.
Coroner	Tell us about that last meeting with Mr. Kelleher.
Dr. Charles	Certainly. I met with President Kelleher for what was the last time on September 29th. That was about three months after the initial diagnosis and about three weeks before his death. Mr. Kelleher said he was losing his appetite and having difficulty swallowing. Funny, but he told me how he got relief from eating canned *Dole* pineapples. He said he would do so in the evening and eat them straight out of the can at the kitchen table or sitting in his backyard. We laughed at that.
Coroner	Is that unusual, for a patient to get some relief from something he or she chose to eat?

Dr. Charles	Not really. The sugar relief from the pineapple slices probably was physiological, but even the act of getting the can, opening it and eating the slices would have been somewhat therapeutic. The routine was probably important to him.
Coroner	Please continue, Dr. Charles.
Dr. Charles	By the time of death, a little over four months after my initial examination and my pronouncement of the terminal cancer, the moderate pain would have transitioned to acute pain. As I've said, Mr. Kelleher likely would have been in that quarter of cancer patients who experience a high threshold of pain. The use of alcohol, occasionally to excess, likely came at some cost to his overall health and may have contributed to the death. There's no way to establish that. The alcohol did not cause the death or yield any notable organ malfunctioning.
Coroner	Dr. Charles, please tell me about the toxicology reports you completed.
Dr. Charles	My toxicological analysis revealed the patient died of an inordinately high amount of the Morphine drug in his system, likely advanced due to the high presence of alcohol. There is no way to discern the amount of Morphine ingested by the hypodermic syringes and whether or not the fatal amount was administered by the deceased or by the hands of another person or persons.
Coroner	Explain the Morphine reaction.
Dr. Charles	The condition emanated from a high dosage of the Morphine. The drug injection produces respiratory depression by action on the brain stem itself. An inordinate amount may result in respiratory arrest and death within a brief period.
Coroner	Thank you, Dr. Charles. You may step down.

After Dr. Charles had returned to his seat next to Dr. Feldman, the Coroner looked at his yellow, legal-size notepad he had placed on the table. He ran his index finger down one of the pages. He coughed to clear his throat and to highlight that he was about to speak with great command and authority.

"If I may have your attention. Let me then summarize my findings regarding the Cause of Death and following my physical examination of the body, the tests conducted by Dr. Charles and his testimony today:

> *Based upon my post-mortem examination, the focused partial-autopsy of the brain and other crucial organs, as conducted by Dr. David Charles and as properly verified by Dr. Charles' toxicological studies, we can conclude, with assurance, that the Cause of Death was respiratory depression and subsequent heart failure."*

Arthur Clough was confident of his conclusion regarding the Cause of Death. But he knew that the work of the Inquest was just starting. The remainder of the day would be incredibly significant.

He began to speak again. "We still must determine whether a repeated dosage was self-induced, accidentally or intentionally, or the result of foul play. The witnesses called to testify, consequent to my questions and investigation of the death, shall enable us to determine that matter."

Mr. Clough waited for the murmurs to subside before he stood at attention and continued. "Ladies and gentlemen, I would now ask that we recess this Inquest for fifteen minutes. Be back in this room before the allotted time has passed so we may commence the Inquest immediately. The restrooms are to the right of this Courtroom, and there are water fountains. If you must make a phone call, there are five pay phones to the left, but I caution you to be here before the fifteen minutes. If you have any questions or concerns, see me during this break."

Mr. Clough knew no one would dare approach him with a question, let alone a concern. Something was gratifying, almost spiritual, about being in the center of an official Inquest. He thrived on being in total command. He knew what would transpire in the next hours and that no one else in the whole world did. Clough did not know all the answers to his questions, but he certainly anticipated what would trip-up his witnesses.

Clough went over to Mrs. Kelleher who sat between Edith Reynolds and Samantha Bartell, as if they were guarding her. Samantha was nervous because Dominic Panichi, the County Commissioner and her married lover, was in the group of witnesses in the secluded Jury Room, while she was not.

Samantha looked at Izzy and asked, "Mrs. Kelleher, is there anything I can get you? There's coffee in the lounge, and I can find a soda."

Clough looked directly at Izzy, ignoring Samantha's efforts at hospitality. The President's wife was crying, with the tears rolling down her face as rain falls on a windowpane. "Izzy, as I told you privately yesterday, Dr. Charles and I are convinced your husband died of the excessive dosages of Morphine compounded by the alcohol and declining health. I trust his presentation was not too graphic. I had to set the stage for the Cause of Death. You do understand? Your husband didn't want others to know about his condition. We may never know exactly why. Had he lived a little longer, he may have come to you and shared his condition."

Clough tried his best to console the woman. He was glad he had decided to take the break in testimony.

Izzy looked at Clough, then at Edith and Samantha. Her tears overwhelmed her for a moment as she uttered in broken sobs, "I didn't know the *Dole* pineapple slices were such a relief to him."

Then she broke into a subdued smile and managed to say with a muffled voice, "At least he could have taken the slices out of the god damn can!"

THE INQUEST – SESSION 2

The best way to show that a stick is crooked is not to argue about it or to spend time denouncing it, but to lay a straight stick alongside it.
Dwight L. Moody

Fifteen minutes later, at 11:15 AM, the Monroe County Coroner, Arthur Clough, tapped his gavel on the judge's bench and told everyone to take a seat. "I would like to proceed with questioning witnesses. Deputy Sheriff Diaz, kindly ask Mrs. Candace Rodewald to leave the Jury Room and come here to testify."

There was a collective hush among those seated in the Courtroom, reacting to the announcement that Rodewald would be the first witness. People were thinking: *Why call her first? Why call her at all? What did she do? Doesn't she work in the Computer Center? Isn't she that lovely young lady. Do you think she killed Kelleher? Must have been a torrid love affair. Why is a woman the first person to testify?*

While Diaz was retrieving Rodewald, Clough reminded the gathering that if they left the room, they would not be able to return. He also told them again the role of the Court Attorney, Phil Smith.

Candace Rodewald looked unnerved, more like frightened, as she walked into the Courtroom followed closely by Deputy Diaz. Husband Bob was away on another sales trip. She was alone. The Computer Center employee caught everyone's eyes with her stylish appearance. She was wearing exaggerated bell-bottoms, or Palazzo pants, and an autumn-orange, long-sleeve, cowl-neck sweater. Mrs. Rodewald also was wearing platform boots that made her two inches taller. However, no one was looking at her feet.

As Candace Rodewald took the witness stand, trying to appear calm and undisturbed, Clough began his questioning.

| Coroner | Mrs. Rodewald, please recall you took the witness oath. Therefore, you are obligated to tell the truth in this Inquest. Failure to do so may result in charges |

	of perjury. Mrs. Rodewald, for the record, you are Office Manager of the Computer Center. You've been with the College for about three years. Correct?
Mrs. Rodewald	Three years, yes. My job classification is Secretary III. But everyone refers to me as the Office Manager. I don't type, take dictation or file a great deal. But I have a responsible job and a heavy workload. Frankly, the place would fall apart without me. I do not do computer programming or run jobs, but I'm taking courses toward my AAS degree. I understand the technical processes. All of them.
Coroner	Thank you for that clarification. I'm sure you are an asset to the Computer Center. Mrs. Rodewald, you were upset with President Kelleher and Dr. Dandridge when they decided to fire your boss, Howard Tucker, and then he died in a car accident. Correct?
Mrs. Rodewald	Yes. Except Howard quit his position under the threat of termination. He was not fired. We thought it was cruel to do that to Howard, after all the years he worked for the College. We managed to get the work done, so what's the big deal if the guy drank?
Coroner	You said *we*, Mrs. Rodewald. Who is that?
Mrs. Rodewald	Mr. Wildwood, me and most of the Programmers.
Coroner	Mr. Wildwood, you say. That's Gene Wildwood. Are you and Mr. Wildwood friends as well as work colleagues.
Mrs. Rodewald	True, we are friends. He's helped me with my Programming class. We work well together. We were united in our concern for Howard as well. Gene's been there for me as a woman in a man's world with the computers, the programming, the wandering male eyes and hands.
Coroner	Aren't you and Mr. Wildwood more than friends?
Mrs. Rodewald	Not sure I understand the question.
Coroner	Were you having a relationship with Gene Wildwood outside of the office?
Mrs. Rodewald	I'd rather not say.

Clough ambled over to the table and reached into his briefcase to pull out the Waterford crystal Shamrock paperweight. He held it up to the witness to examine and to the audience for emphasis.

Coroner	Mrs. Rodewald, do you know what this is?
Mrs. Rodewald	Yes, it's the paperweight Mr. Kelleher had in his office. I think it was a gift to him from his father or grandfather when he got his first job or something. Mr. Kelleher's Irish, you know.
Coroner	I think everyone in Monroe County knows Mr. Kelleher was Irish. But to the point, you have been in Mr. Kelleher's office?
Mrs. Rodewald	Yes sir, a couple of times.
Coroner	Have you been in Mr. Kelleher's office in the past week?
Mrs. Rodewald	The office was a Crime Scene. May still be.
Coroner	Mrs. Rodewald, do you follow baseball? If so, you know a batter has three strikes and must hit the ball fair before the count reaches three strikes, or he's out. Mrs. Rodewald, we know you were in this office a few days ago. You see, when you were there, you left a beautiful thumbprint on this crystal paperweight, and the FBI found a match to you in their files. Now you have one strike. Two to go.

Clough retrieved a paper from his briefcase along with a worn, alpha-indexed, blue notebook. He then walked back to the witness stand, frowning at Rodewald.

Have you seen a crock of Shamrocks lying around anyplace?

Irish Leprechaun

Coroner	I don't want to embarrass you further, but the copy of the police record here shows you were arrested for shoplifting as a high school senior. When you were about a year older, you were caught and held again. This time you stole a watch from a jeweler. You were below the age limit for the shoplifting but not for theft of the watch. The police took your fingerprints and a mug shot.

Mrs. Rodewald	Yes, that's true. I'm ashamed, but those were tough years for me. I really needed the money. I sincerely apologize for that, but it was a long time ago.
Coroner	Mrs. Rodewald were you aware that President Kelleher kept a notebook about the College – random observations he would make every so often. Isn't that why you broke into the President's Office – to find that journal?
Mrs. Rodewald	I heard rumors about the notebook. That's all.
Coroner	Now you have two strikes, Mrs. Rodewald. You not only knew about it, but that's why you broke into the office and went through his desk? Fingerprints don't lie. You do understand, I have the authority to charge you with perjury and ask the District Attorney to prosecute. The penalty would be a fine and time in community service. If you continue to lie to me, to this Court, I will likely recommend time in the County Jail.
Mrs. Rodewald	Please don't do that.
Coroner	Let's try again. Why did you want to find that notebook? Be careful what you say. You don't need three strikes. Then you're out.
Mrs. Rodewald	Yes, sir. Gene told me he was in Mr. Kelleher's office one day and saw him writing in that. Gene got a chance to see it when Kelleher left the room. He saw there were notes on people in the file, including him. He said Mr. Kelleher probably had a notation that me and Gene were together in the Computer Center late one evening. I was hoping I could find it and tear-out pages that mentioned Gene and me. I shouldn't have done that, but I thought Mr. Kelleher was going to recommend me for the vacant Programmer position. I wanted to see if he had left a note in the files on his desk. That was irresponsible. Stupid too.
Coroner	Would you like to hear what President Kelleher had to say about you in his notes?
Mrs. Rodewald	Only if you must. I take it you found it, Mr. Clough. That must be what you have in your hand.

Coroner	Yes, it is. Let me read portions to you. You won't be embarrassed in the way you thought you would. There were five notations alphabetically under R for Rodewald. Let me read them:
	The first one says: *Candace is a delightful young lady. Should be praised for continuing her education. When Programmer opens, make sure she gets every opportunity. Time for a female pro staff member.*
	On another day, Mr. Kelleher had this entry: *She's helped Gene come out of his complex. Stuttering less. He exudes confidence. Make a fine couple. They're married tho.*
	Then this third reference: *Both were horrified Howard crashed his car. The gin bottle did him in. Enabled his drinking. Should have intervened earlier.*
Coroner	Were you aware of any of this, Mrs. Rodewald?
Mrs. Rodewald	No sir. I just had hoped he did not mention Gene and me.
Coroner	I didn't think so. Let me continue. Here's his fourth note: *Terrible Howard died. Could not do anything. Tell Roseanne to check-out current programs to help employees with alcohol. We must accept it as a disease and not as a weakness. Damn it. We need an Alcoholics Anonymous chapter on campus for the community?*
Mrs. Rodewald	Wow! This makes sense, given what my mother has gone through as an alcoholic.
Coroner	Let me finish. Finally, on the day before he died, he wrote: *Send check to Foundation – for Howard's wife. Start bereavement fund for faculty and staff through Foundation.*

Candace had her head in her hands, sobbing. Clough looked at her and offered her a tissue from the box on the judge's bench. He liked to keep some handy for such moments.

Coroner	Mrs. Rodewald, did you, or did you not, pick the lock from the Board Room to the President's Office and enter the office with the intent to find the President's notebook?

| Mrs. Rodewald | Yes sir, I did. I am truly sorry. The door from the hall into the Board Room was unlocked early last Thursday morning, and I manipulated the office door. I was worried about what he might have said in it about me. I'm sorry he died. I guess he was decent about me. And yes, Gene and I were having a relationship, but it is over. We are both ashamed. |
| Coroner | Thank you for the truth. Mrs. Rodewald, thank you for your witness. You are excused. I ask you to stay in the Courtroom. I do not at this time consider you involved in the death of Mr. Kelleher. However, that may change with the testimony of others. And your perjury makes you suspect to further scrutiny. |

Deputy Diaz walked over to the witness stand and assisted Candace Rodewald in getting up and walking to a chair in the back of the room. Candace sat down as she heard the Coroner advise her, "Mrs. Rodewald, remember, you still have two strikes."

The Coroner smiled slyly and then announced, "Deputy Diaz, please ask Dr. Thomas Dandridge to join us and testify."

As with the initial witness, those gathered looked at each other, wondering why the Vice President of Institutional Support would be called to the Courtroom. *Why would Clough call this guy? What did he do? What kind of doctor is he? Didn't he replace Kelleher as Vice President? He's too young to be a Vice President? Was he having an affair? I think he's the one who fired the Computer Center Director. Was he making a move on Rodewald too? With Kelleher gone, won't he be up for President next? Is he really a doctor?*

Thomas Dandridge took the witness stand and waited for the first question from the Coroner. He was confident and assured, even though this was the first time he had ever been a witness.

| Coroner | Dr. Dandridge, let me remind you, you are under oath. Sir, in March 1975, you replaced Mr. Kelleher when he was named President. He seemingly had confidence in you, as he made you Chairman of the federal grant initiative and the Administrative Team for faculty negotiations. But you were the one who recommended the firing of Mr. Howard Tucker. |
| Dr. Dandridge | That's correct, Mr. Clough. We did give Mr. Tucker the opportunity to resign, which we didn't have to |

	do. That enabled him to retain his retirement and keep his personnel record clean.
Coroner	Would you have fired Mr. Tucker on your own or was that a directive from the President?
Dr. Dandridge	We'd advised Mr. Tucker a month ago to take a week's paid leave of absence and seek help for his drinking. We were drawing a line in the sand. That was made explicit, and a written record was made of the meeting and the expectation. When he came came back to the College after the week, he met with Miss Hart and me. Howard agreed he would discontinue drinking in his office. We clarified that this was his last chance. But yes, Mr. Clough, I was resolute that we had to act. We could not continue to have him lead the Computer Center in that condition. There's too much at stake with the information and the investment we have in the equipment and files.
Coroner	What happened after that?
Dr. Dandridge	I went to his office, unannounced, one day and saw he was continuing to drink out of those stupid paper cups, as if that masked his actions. And that was despite saying he'd stop. I met with the President and told him that I recommended we terminate Howard's contract.
Coroner	So, it was on your initiative that he was fired, or then allowed to resign?
Dr. Dandridge	Yes, that's true. I discussed it with Miss Hart, too, and she was supportive, given the reputation Mr. Tucker was getting around the campus. Some of the faculty and staff were mocking the guy. I heard some the computer staff started to drink coffee and sodas out of paper *Dixie Cups*. We decided we couldn't wait longer.
Coroner	Why did you not deliver the news to Mr. Tucker?
Dr. Dandridge	Unfortunately, I had to be out of town on Title III business, so Roseanne and our College Attorney, Jack Kula, were the ones to tell Howard. That probably was best anyway. If Mr. Tucker wanted to complain or challenge what happened, he could make an appointment and talk to me later. He did not

	contact me, at least not before he had the accident. So, no, we did not speak again. I wish we had, even though I don't think it would have made a difference. I didn't know him very well.
Coroner	Thank you, Dr. Dandridge. You told me when we talked in your office that Mr. Kelleher confided in you that he had cancer and was dying. Please share that time you met with the President.
Dr. Dandridge	Mr. Kelleher had invited me to lunch two, no, now three months ago. He hardly touched his food, a Reuben, same as I had. We've had lunch at the club before, and he devoured that sandwich. I asked him if he felt alright. He ignored the question and said he wanted to share something with me in complete confidence. Mr. Kelleher told me about the cancer and that he had four, maybe five months to live. He said he was tolerating the pain but knew it would be unbearable eventually. Then he might have to take leave of his work with the College. He made me promise not to tell anyone, including my wife.
Coroner	Why do you think he told you, Dr. Dandridge?
Dr. Dandridge	Mr. Coroner, he said he wanted someone to know at the College in the event he passed out in a meeting or had an accident. He told me his cancer doctor was Dr. David Charles. He explicitly said he had not told his wife or anyone in his office. He said he'd do so when the time came for him to step aside or hospitalization was imminent.
Coroner	But apparently he never told his wife or others?
Dr, Dandridge	I guess not. Mr. Kelleher wanted to handle things his way and not be the subject of anyone's pity party.
Coroner	Anything else he told you.
Dr. Dandridge	Only that he encouraged me to apply for the President's position when he died and to do anything to be sure Winters or Fishman did not get the position. I did not take him seriously. At least not then.
Coroner	Did he say he was taking Morphine for the pain?

Dr. Dandridge	No, he did not. He said he was handling the pain on whatever meds he had. But that was a couple of months before he died.
Coroner	Dr. Dandridge, were you aware Mr. Kelleher was keeping a private notebook in his office that included observations about people and goings on at the College?
Dr. Dandridge	No, I was not. He was always fair with me in getting back to me on my questions and requests. Miss Bartell is an asset for that, though the other guys dislike her. When we met in his office, we'd go through the papers in the folder he kept on his desk, but I never saw any personal journal or saw him write in a notebook or anything. I'm not at all surprised that Mr. Kelleher kept something like this. Wow, the guy kept a personal journal. Of course, he would. He kept track of details and, of course, he was a writer. His memos were works of art, in terms of classic writing style, word choice, grammar. He kept a dictionary and a *Thesaurus* in his desk.
Coroner	He was that particular?
Dr. Dandridge	Yes, he was. Sometimes in the middle of a meeting or a conversation, he'd stop and look up a word in the paperback dictionary. And if one of us used the wrong word, he'd tell us about it. Gave me the same pocket dictionary that first Christmas, after I was hired, along with a great bottle of wine and a *Cross* pen.
Coroner	Based on the conversations you had with Mr. Kelleher about his health, do you think his death was an accident, intentional or murder?
Dr. Dandridge	As you know, Mr. Clough, I was in Washington, D.C. the day his body was discovered. I didn't find out about it until after lunch when I phoned my office and was told. I left immediately, but even then, I did not tell anyone about the cancer. I told the folks at DOE – Department of Education – but not about the cancer. In answer to your question, sir, I assume he died of the cancer, at least I did when I heard of his death that morning. He was determined to live out his life.

Coroner	Did he show signs of the disease?
Dr. Dandridge	There were times in various meetings, it looked like he was suffering, especially those two-three weeks before he did die. He'd get some inquisitive stares from others, but I'd just look away and presume no big deal.
Coroner	Did you and President Kelleher discuss his health and the cancer again?
Dr. Dandridge	No, we did not ever talk again about the cancer. The times we met after that and before he died, I asked him about his health. He said he was fine and changed the subject immediately. His look said *don't ask me that again*. So, I didn't.
Coroner	When we met in your office, you told me about the stages of accepting one's death. Please share that again here.
Dr. Dandridge	Certainly. As a grad student, I studied the Sociology and Psychology of death. Studies show that most people go through stages during the living-dying interval. That includes *Denial, Anger, Depression,* etc. Most eventually get to the level of *Acceptance* of their imminent death. If you ask me, President Kelleher never processed those earlier reactions and was fully at the *Acceptance* stage. Skipped to that. He wanted his remaining living times to be irretrievably unchanged.
Coroner	Dr. Dandridge, what might be the significance if indeed Mr. Kelleher did pass over or ignore the normal reactions?
Dr. Dandridge	I would think it wouldn't affect his dying, just his overall outlook. That may be why he did not want to tell others. His anger may have been inside. Repressed perhaps. He was a very private man.
Coroner	Did you see him vent any anger during those last few weeks? Release it somehow?
Dr. Dandridge	No, I did not. We do that in various ways, sir.
Coroner	Thank you, Dr. Dandridge. You are excused, and you may step down. I do not consider you a suspect or complicit in Mr. Kelleher's death. You may remain in the Courtroom, as you desire, for the rest of the

proceedings or leave. If you go, you cannot come back to this Courtroom. You may not have conversations with the remaining witnesses.

Dr. Dandridge got up and started to step off the witness stand. He stopped when Clough held up his arms to signal he had another question and motioned Dandridge back to his seat. There were a few giggles in the room. They had heard this *one more thing* bit before. Clough smiled briefly, then continued his investigation.

Coroner	Sorry. One more thing. In your mind, is there anything you might have done differently, knowing now that Mr. Kelleher had the cancer and died?
Dr. Dandridge	Mr. Clough, I gave that matter considerable thought before he died and even more now that he's dead. I could have found someone else on campus, Miss Bartell or Edith, and said something. I don't know if that would have helped. Perhaps. Understand, President Kelleher was defiant in wanting to stay with the job to the end. He would have been furious if I'd told anyone.
Coroner	Nothing you could have done?
Dr. Dandridge	There were things I wished I could have done, like kick the collective butts of the Board Chairman and that ignorant Vice Chairman. The man's dying, and those two jerks are bickering about an architect. I wish I could have somehow made things easier for J. Paul. That was not to be. Perhaps I should have contacted his physician to see if he had some advice for me on observing President Kelleher at work. I knew his family was under the care of Dr. Feldman. So am I and so is my family. I should have let Dr. Feldman know I was aware of the cancer. I am sorry, yes.
Coroner	Thank you, Dr. Dandridge.

Dr. Dandridge started to rise, looking relieved that his time in the hot seat was over. He had been in a courtroom before, when he had received a speeding ticket, but not as a witness. He hesitated long enough for the Coroner to motioned him to sit back down.

Coroner	Ah, just one more thing. Dr. Dandridge, why do you think Mr. Kelleher had such a tough time with the rest of the President's Cabinet? The other VP's.
Dr. Dandridge	Oh, I don't know. They're old-timers, not used to change. They wanted *changes*, if you will, but not *to change*. Make sense? They got used to a certain pattern with his predecessor, Greenleaf. President Kelleher was one who liked to manage by chaos, shake things up. But the place needed it. Still does. I'm convinced that's why he reorganized once a year. That made some of the people packs break apart and then establish new relations. It brought fresh eyes to the same challenges.
Coroner	But it upset people, didn't it?
Dr. Dandridge	Sure did. The other Vice Presidents got upset when he would require them to revisit their budgets in the spring. *Zero-Based Budgeting*, Mr. Kelleher called it. Others called it *Nonsense Budgeting*. Fishman said it was *Piss-Off Budgeting*. But it made us rethink our needs and priorities and assure a greater cost-accountability. I think our President Kelleher thought of it as administrative cod liver oil. Tastes horrible and hard to swallow but effort was most healthful.
Coroner	Do you plan to follow in his footsteps?
Dr. Dandridge	I may never become a college president. Not sure I want to be after this, after those Board meetings. But if I were to be appointed one day, I'd mimic his leadership and reorganize every so often. Well, perhaps not quite as often.
Coroner	Thank you, again, Dr. Dandridge. The Court does appreciate your candor. I wish you well in your career, wherever it takes you.

Dandridge made it out of the witness stand this time and went to the back of the Courtroom, taking a seat next to Candace Rodewald. He patted her hand that was resting on the armchair, intending to provide a degree of comfort to the red-eyed and ashamed woman. He didn't say anything, but his look was one of concern.

The Coroner looked again at the Deputy Sheriff. "Miss Diaz, please gather Mr. Ralph Hughes from the Jury Room and ask him to join us."

Then Arthur Clough announced: "If you would like to stand for a quick stretch, that would be fine. When I do call for order, please comply quickly. We have a lot to accomplish."

Once again there was a wave of murmurs cascading over the audience with questions and comments: *Isn't this the guy who runs the Faculty Union? He's that skinny fellow. Why does he always wear a bow tie? Doesn't he have a thing for Sally Bowens. Gene Wildwood said at the Memorial Service that he has the plastic balloon rat. Could he have killed Kelleher because of that flying thing? Doesn't he teach math? I hated my arithmetic classes in school.*

Professor Ralph Hughes walked with an assured gait into the room and up to the witness stand. He stood before the Coroner, as Clough raised his left arm to signal silence and pounded the gavel twice, bringing the Courtroom to order.

Mr. Hughes was dressed in his signature butterfly bow tie, this one bright blue in color and tied somewhat asymmetrical. He disdained the pre-tied version with the adjustable strap.

When his students would ask why he wore a bow tie, Hughes gave two reasons: "First, bow ties don't get caught in the car door or soak up gravy or ketchup when I eat. They don't flop around or blow up in your face. I don't have to wear a bib when I eat barbecue ribs. Secondly, wearing a bow tie says you're classy, like wearing a tuxedo every day. Women love it. Most men are jealous they can't tie one properly. Want me to show you how?"

Hughes took the seat on the witness stand. He wished Sally Bowens would have been in the Courtroom, so he could have gauged her reactions and smiled back. But now he'd be testifying before she would that day.

Coroner	Mr. Hughes, be reminded you are under oath to tell the truth here today. You are an Assistant Professor of Mathematics, and you've been with the College for three years. You also have served on the negotiating team for the Faculty Union. Is all that correct, sir?
Mr. Hughes	That's correct. I teach math. Also, I crunch numbers for the Union, according to whatever Miss Bowens requests for analysis and support our positions.
Coroner	You mentioned Professor Bowens. When we spoke on campus, you indicated you have a personal relationship with her as well as the professional one at the College. How would you describe your relationship?

Mr. Hughes	Not sure it's anyone else's business, but Sally and I are close. I'm very fond of her. If you're trying to get me to say I love her, yes, I do. No big deal. Is your next question going to be whether I was the one who got the helium rat balloon on the top of the Administration Building last summer?
Coroner	I did not mean to upset you, but it may be highly consequential to this Inquest to establish that you have a personal relationship with the Union President. It's not important who got the inflated rat up on the air, unless that person lies about it to this Court. It is important if the negotiations caused friction that might have resulted in murder.

There was a mix of hushed comments from the audience, most of whom were aware of the flying rat but astonished to hear the word murder for the first time. Mr. Hughes did not flinch at the word. Clough had wanted the word to permeate the room and stir emotions.

Coroner	Mr. Hughes, let's start again. Please keep in mind, I ask the questions. You do not ask questions. If you have an inquiry about a legal matter, I can ask Mr. Smith. Other than that, you are to respond to my questions only. We are here to uncover the truth. That's why you are a witness today. Mr. Hughes, please give us your full name.
Mr. Hughes	Ralph Hughes. Ralph E. Hughes. I don't have a nickname. Just Ralph.
Coroner	What does the E in your name stand for, sir?
Mr. Hughes	My middle name is Edward, but I only use the initial.
Coroner	Are you any relation to Professor R. Edward Hughes who teaches at Columbia Community College, west of here? There's a notation in Mr. Kelleher's journal that he was checking on the names of faculty at Columbia. Those with the Hughes surname.
Mr. Hughes	That's cool. Must be a coincidence. Why does this matter anyway? What's that got to do with old man Kelleher's death?

Coroner	Mr. Hughes, I warned you about not asking the questions. That's my job. Do it again, and I will have the court issue a citation through the District Attorney. I will decide what is relevant in this Inquest. Let me continue with the questions.
Mr. Hughes	Go ahead. Do what you gotta do.
Coroner	Thank you. The Mr. R. Edward Hughes at Columbia Community College also teaches math. He goes by Edward, his middle name. We checked. His course schedule includes four 90-minutes classes, taught in a row on Monday and then the same four on Wednesday. Then on Friday, he teaches a course via the Electro-Writer machine to Trenton State Prison. That leaves him free in all day Tuesday and Thursday. No classes those days.

The Coroner stopped speaking for a moment as he recalled his interview with Roseanne Hart. Then he refocused on the witness.

Coroner	Mr. Hughes, Miss Roseanne Hart tells me such is not permitted at CJCC according to the contract. One cannot stack classes, more than two consecutive classes in a row, without prior approval of the Dean. She says that in the past and before the contract was changed, a small handful of faculty arranged their schedules to have no classes at least one day a week. Guess that freed them to go to the Jersey Shore or work another job and make more money. Now is that something faculty does at Columbia Community College, Mr. Hughes?
Mr. Hughes	I wouldn't know about that. We have a substantial teaching load, and the Union did not want faculty to teach three or more courses in a row and be exhausted, so their teaching would suffer, and student learning deteriorate.
Coroner	Have you ever taught three or four sections or classes in a row on the same morning or afternoon? If so, how did it work out for you?
Mr. Hughes	I may have done that when I was first hired at CJCC. Not since. You get weary by the third class, and you

	can forget where you left off with one class and began with the next one. We only did that when the administration made us do so.
Coroner	Mr. Lieber, we tend to verify the alibis witnesses provide, especially those who we consider a suspect should there be foul play. The chances are that if a witness lies about his or her alibi, that person will lie on other matters. Like you are now about the contract. Indeed, Miss Hart told me, and Mr. confirmed that the President instigated the language change in the faculty contract. I can have her testify to that point. She's in this Courtroom. According to Miss Hart, you and Miss Bowens argued against that change and only relented when President Kelleher upped the percent salary increase to reach consensus.
Mr. Hughes	That is not the way I remember it. Not so. We have wanted that change for the last two negotiation cycles. Besides if we got more money out of the deal we were doing a good job.
Coroner	The Faculty Union wanted that change? And Mr. Kelleher refused to change the contract?

Clough stopped his questioning abruptly and looked Mr. Hughes squarely in the eyes, as he moved closer to the witness stand. He knew he had to make his point emphatically if this witness was to comply. He wanted to be sure Hughes could not defend his words later by saying he was never adequately advised.

Coroner	Remember, Mr. Hughes, you remain under oath. You do understand that, do you not?
Mr. Hughes	Of course. But if I need to correct you, I need to do that. We put that article in the Union Contract because the faculty wanted that provision. We do not like being made to teach three, let alone four, sections consecutively. Can you imagine teaching classes three straight hours, let alone four, with no break? Talk about getting stale or going crazy.
Coroner	From what we know, Mr. Hughes, you have had plenty of practice doing just that. I'm still not sure

	you are grasping the concept that you are subject to a perjury conviction, as well as misleading us in your testimony. But, let's get back to Columbia Community College and this other math guy who teaches there.
Mr. Hughes	I don't see why.
Coroner	Your CJCC teaching schedule does not include classes on Monday, Wednesday and Friday before 2 PM. You have three 90-minute classes on Tuesday and Thursday, two in the morning and one in the afternoon. And then one evening class. Is that correct?
Mr. Hughes	Yeah. So, what?
Coroner	I also note that this Columbia professor lists his home address as 703 Walnut. Do you happen to know who lives at that address, Mr. Hughes?
Mr. Hughes	I have no idea. Why are you asking me these questions? I teach at this College, CJCC. What does any of this have to do with Kelleher's murder?
Coroner	We have not established that Mr. Kelleher's death was a homicide. Mr. Hughes, once again you are not to ask the questions. I've warned you repeatedly, so I will recommend to the District Attorney that you be held in contempt.
Mr. Hughes	Wait a minute! Just because I asked you why you were asking me these questions?
Coroner	Oh no, Mr. Hughes, because you've committed perjury by lying on the witness stand under oath. You see, I know that math instructor Mr. R. Edward Hughes at Columbia and math instructor Mr. Ralph E. Hughes who teaches at Central Jersey are the same person. The very same person. And I also know, as you do, that your sister lives at that 703 Walnut Street address. You've been using that address for two years. Records show you've paid your sister her monthly mortgage for that address. That means you have committed perjury, big time.
Mr. Hughes	How in the hell did you know about this?
Coroner	Yes, that's still another question you have no authority to ask. But, obliging as I am, I can tell you that there was a notation in Mr. Kelleher's notebook

	to check on faculty names at Columbia. Miss Hart was to visit there, but she didn't get to do that before Mr. Kelleher died. My Deputy, Miss Diaz, made the inquiry yesterday. We added it up. You see, Mr. Hughes, I can do math, as good as you. You are in a great deal of trouble. Your course schedule adds up to a lie. And, in your case, there will likely be a subtraction of your employment. How's that for mathematics?
Mr. Hughes	Okay, I had two teaching positions. I took care of my classes. No one got hurt. So, what?
Coroner	In your mind perhaps, but the records indicate, as per your Columbia department chairman, that you maxed-out leave days and did not put in the required office hours. You are also notorious for skipping your student advisement conferences and dodging committee assignments. Columbia allows stacked classes but only in an emergency. Mr. Hughes, your chairman there didn't know you were also teaching at CJCC. That is against their policy and State Board Rules. We checked.
Mr. Hughes	I can explain all that.
Coroner	Your chairman was also unaware you had moved one of your sections from the afternoon to that morning schedule on your own. He said they would initiate termination and legal proceedings against you as soon as we complete this Inquest and your testimony is on record. Now, it's on the record.
Mr. Hughes	Wait a minute. I don't think you have the authority to question me regarding my contract at another college if indeed I do have one, which I am not admitting to.

The Coroner turned and faced Mr. Phil Smith, the Court Attorney and posed a question. "Attorney Smith, Mr. Hughes here has raised the question regarding his alleged faculty contract with Columbia Community College. Our Ralph Edward Hughes likes to raise questions, but this is a good one. One he may regret. He questions that I have a basis to raise the legitimacy of same as part of this Inquest. Could you provide a legal opinion on this matter?"

Attorney Smith rose from his chair and took a deep breath. "Mr. Coroner, this is an Inquest regarding a person's death. Any questions relative to that line of pursuit are appropriate, if asked by you. As for the question itself, we have heard Mr. Hughes allude to his double-contract with a public agency. That puts him in a prosecutable position. Mr. Hughes might be wise to consider his Fifth Amendment rights, even though he's not on trial here. However, he cannot refuse or ignore your questions, or he can be found in contempt. It's a fine line for someone who has admitted to a false statement under oath and for which there is now a record of deceit."

Attorney Phil Smith looked at Mr. Hughes and then fixed his eyes back on the Coroner. "Mr. Clough, I am quite certain New Jersey does not permit state employees to hold two full-time salaried positions when both are on the public payroll. From what I have heard here this morning, it is apparent Mr. Hughes did not seek or receive approvals from either institution or anyone with the State Board."

Coroner	Thank you, Mr. Smith. We can leave that line of questioning for now, at least. It will be something for the District Attorney and others to pursue. Instead, let me ask you, Mr. Ralph E. Hughes and Mr. R. Edward Hughes, about the night Mr. Kelleher died. I understand you were at the Board Meeting. Is that correct?
Mr. Hughes	Yes, I was there, but I went to the Union office in the Library after it ended. Sally, Miss Bowens, and I had some Union work to do. We always gather back at the office to share thoughts on the Board Meeting and make some phone calls.
Coroner	You did not come back to the Board Room after the meeting?
Mr. Hughes	No, sir.
Coroner	Our records indicate that, indeed, you were there in his office on that evening.
Mr. Hughes	Mr. Clough, you didn't ask me if I went to his office, only if I was there in the Board Room.
Coroner	That's a truly remarkable answer. Now that we have established that you were in his office, who else was in the Board Room after the meeting ended, Mr. Hughes?
Mr. Hughes	I don't remember. I think the County Commissioner was there, along with Fishman.

Coroner	Mr. Hughes, you do realize that we will be having Miss Bowens testify at some point today?
Mr. Hughes	That's fine. She'll back me up on my whereabouts and the teaching stuff.
Coroner	Did you, or Miss Bowens, have reason to want to see President Kelleher dead?
Mr. Hughes	Not really. You can ask her.
Coroner	Sir, do you know about the drug Morphine?
Mr. Hughes	It's a pain killer. Right? It's a narcotic that can be habit-forming from what I am told. I've never used it, if that's what you're asking.
Coroner	How is it administered?
Mr. Hughes	Injections or I think, intravenously in a hospital.
Coroner	Have you ever purchased Morphine or tried to do so?
Mr. Hughes	Why the hell would I do that?
Coroner	Just answer the question, please.
Mr. Hughes	No. Why do you ask?

The Coroner surveyed Hughes' face looking for signs of stress that would suggest he was not telling the truth. The instructor had been twitching in his chair for most of the testimony.

Coroner	Mr. Hughes, as for Mr. Kelleher's death, you remain a prime suspect, if indeed the man was murdered. However, I do not want to proceed with additional questions now.
Mr. Hughes	Am I done, now? I can finally leave.
Coroner	Deputy Sheriff Diaz and Mr. Smith will escort you to the District Attorney's office. He can determine the next course of action. You will not be permitted back into this Courtroom. You are to remain in seclusion with the D.A. for the remainder of this Inquest so that I may call upon you later, if necessary.
Mr. Hughes	Are you saying that I may need a lawyer of my own?
Coroner	There you go again, asking the questions. Mr. Hughes, you are dismissed under the custody of the Deputy Sheriff. Have a nice afternoon.

The Coroner watched as Mr. Ralph Hughes, alias Mr. Edward Hughes, was led out of the Courtroom, with Attorney Smith walking in front and Deputy Diaz walking behind him. Mr. Clough waited until they had left the room and the door had fully closed before making a statement.

"Ladies and gentlemen, I have repeatedly advised the witnesses to tell the truth and respond to my questions. What Mr. Hughes has done is beyond lying under oath. He will be arrested and probably arraigned. He likely will be fired from both jobs and mandated to pay back a significant portion of his dual salaries. I do not choose to make an example of him, but it was necessary to get his testimony about the dual full-time jobs on the record. Plus, we needed to establish he was in the President's Office, on October 19th, at the end of the Board Meeting."

Clough looked at his wristwatch and then at the Courtroom wall clock, thereby confirming the time. He looked back at the people gathered. "It's now 11:45, or just 15 minutes before noon," he said. "Accordingly, we will recess until 12:45 PM, so I can go to the D.A.'s office and make sure the proper allegations are levied regarding Mr. Hughes. I ask you to take this lunch recess but remain in the building. Do not leave the Courthouse unless you don't plan to return."

"There's a small luncheonette in the basement floor. You can find premade sandwiches and salads. I can vouch for the tuna fish and the red Jell-O. I think it's cherry, but I'm not certain of that. Let's just call the flavor red."

THE INQUEST – SESSION 3

Don't show your inferiority by climbing a stunted tree,
show your superiority by climbing the longest and crooked one.
Michael Bassey Johnson

Arthur Clough walked back into Courtroom II at 12:35 PM, having accomplished what he wanted regarding Ralph Hughes and his lies. As Clough walked to the front of the room, he announced, "Let us return our attention to this Inquest and the death of Mr. Kelleher."

When he reached the front of the judge's bench, he pounded the gavel to settle the audience.

"Ladies and gentlemen," he announced in a robust voice. "I apologize for the delay, but it was necessary for me to accompany Mr. Hughes to the District Attorney's office. Miss Diaz has been advised to bring in the next witness to testify. Thank you for your patience. My goal is to complete the testimony and make my determination regarding Mr. Kelleher's death before the end of the day. We shall see."

There was a momentary hush when the County Commissioner, Mr. Dominic Panichi, strolled into the Courtroom accompanied by Deputy Diaz. Then there was the familiar buzz of questions and comments as Panichi walked to the front of the room: *Oh, bet he's got plenty of skeletons in his closet. Can you really trust an Italian in a county job? Who paid for the nice suit? Why is he testifying for the College? Does the Sheriff report to him as County Commissioner? Does the Coroner also? I bet Panichi did something illegal with Kelleher? Don't you think old man Panichi did a better job? I thought the guy was taller.*

The County Commissioner confidently took a seat at the witness stand, as Clough gestured for him to do. Panichi could not avoid a glance at Samantha Bartell. Her head was down, in prayer or communion that the next several minutes would pass quickly and uneventfully.

Dominic Panichi was dressed in a black suit, white shirt and black tie. This was his uniform when he was in his legal mode, when he was in court. Panichi considered black to be an elegant color, and a black suit his armor. He

395

preferred blue and grey suits, colorful ties and pin stripe shirts at the office. Not in a courtroom. Certainly not today.

Coroner	Mr. Panichi, thank you for being here. I wanted to get you to witness early in the process, so that you could get on with your day. But we had testimony we had to get into the record first, sir. Thank you for your patience.
Mr. Panichi	Not a problem, Mr. Coroner. I have set aside my entire day to witness and be a part of these proceedings. That is the least I can do for the deceased, for President Kelleher and his family. Thank you for what you do, Arthur.
Coroner	I would like to focus on the issue of the architect selection for the College's Library expansion project. How and why did you get involved in this matter?
Mr. Panichi	I got a telephone call from President Kelleher that a member of the Board of Trustees was planning to include an unqualified local firm to be in the final selection. He said the maneuver was after the formal process had eliminated that firm from the final two. I said I'd make some calls and see what I might discover. I did that as a favor to Mr. Kelleher, who was being boxed. I suspected it was an illegal act, so I needed to check it out anyway.
Coroner	Did you make those calls?
Mr. Panichi	Yes. I found out that Alfred Zelinski, the founder of Zelinski, Corradetti & Greco, had approached a Board member about including his firm. This is a reputable architectural group but not for a project of this size and complexity. Moreover, I found out that Mr. Zelinski himself told the person he'd set aside $5,000 if he would get his firm in the final group.
Coroner	How did you find that out, Mr. Panichi?
Mr. Panichi	I went to see Alfred. I know him well through my dad. He told me all about it, although at first, he declined to address the matter at all. Zelinski confessed to offering the money to a Board member when I assured him we could dismiss what had happened without embarrassment to him and his firm. I didn't

	know then that the matter would be part of an Inquest after the President's death.
Coroner	What did Mr. Kelleher do?
Mr. Panichi	When I shared that information with Mr. Kelleher, he confronted the Board member on the $5,000. He decided to avoid public awareness of the payment.
Coroner	You do not refer to this person by name. Who was this Board member, Mr. Panichi?
Mr. Panichi	I'd hoped to avoid mentioning this person's name in public and avoid public scrutiny. Since you ask, and I'm under oath, it was the Board Chairman, Dr. Gerald Pitman. His intention may have been honorable, that is to include a local firm. But the money made the transaction undoubtedly unethical and potentially illegal.
Coroner	Thank you. As I understand, you were at the Board Meeting the night of October 19th when Mr. Kelleher died. Why were you there that evening? Do you usually attend the meetings?
Mr. Panichi	I anticipated a confrontation at the Board Meeting over the hostility created by this architect decision. You did not have to be clairvoyant to see the tension that night. The guy on the Board who does the opening prayer laid it on longer than usual, but I guess he didn't hit the right notes. His prayer didn't seem to make a difference.

Panichi's comment caused a few spectators to bow their heads in prayer or in wonderment at what might have taken place at the Board Meeting.

Coroner	Please continue, Mr. Panichi.
Mr. Panichi	Sure. When the Board Meeting ended, Chuck Harrison said something to President Kelleher and followed him into his office, I guess to tell him whatever else he wanted to share. Then he left the Board Room along with Dr. Pitman. The rest of the Board had already gone home. The two of them talked in the hall for a while. I decided to stay after the meeting and see how Mr. Kelleher was.
Coroner	Did Mr. Kelleher tell you what happened?

397

Mr. Panichi	Yes. President Kelleher told me that night that Harrison said he should get his resume in order. He said Harrison told him he and Pitman only needed one more Board member to have enough votes to oust him or force his resignation.
Coroner	Did you happen to observe what Mr. Kelleher's reactions were, how he seemed to be?
Mr. Panichi	He was upset and coughing a great deal, more than usual, even with his smoking. For sure, more than the last time we met. Anyway, President Kelleher went into his office and closed the door. He came out a few minutes later with a bottle in his hand. He'd started drinking.
Coroner	Were you aware that President Kelleher was dying of cancer and taking Morphine for the pain?
Mr. Panichi	No, I was not. How awful, but it makes sense as I look back. Mr. Coroner, J. Paul and I didn't meet regularly. Occasionally he'd come to a Board of Chosen Freeholders' meeting to report on the College, and we'd have lunch every couple of months. He always invited me to the campus Christmas parties, and I usually came to be cordial and share holiday greetings. Mostly I came due to the outstanding food and liquor served.
Coroner	Had you seen him before that night, that is, recently?
Mr. Panichi	Before that Board Meeting, I'd not seen him for two, maybe three weeks. We spoke on the phone, as we usually do, a week or so earlier. A couple of people at the College told me he was coughing more and occasionally slurred his speech and appeared dizzy. Most blamed that on the smoking and poor health.
Coroner	Was one of those people Samantha Bartell, Executive Assistant to Mr. Kelleher?
Mr. Panichi	Yes, it was. As you know, Miss Bartell worked for me at the County before the position opened at the College. We remain in contact. But Edith Reynolds also told me she was concerned about the President's health.

Clough glanced across the room to where Miss Bartell, Mrs. Reynolds and Mrs. Kelleher were sitting. Samantha looked back at him fearfully, pleading with her eyes that the next question not be: *Are you having an affair with Samantha?* It wasn't. Clough saw no reason to make the Courtroom a soap opera episode.

Coroner	Let's move on, Mr. Panichi. I need to get your statement on the record, so please share the phone call you had with State Representative Billy Ridgeway.
Mr. Panichi	Mr. Clough, as I reluctantly told you in my office, Representative Ridgeway wanted me to get you to back off your investigation. He argued you were spending too much time on what was clearly a natural death. He said the media attention was terrible for the College and not good for the Board of Trustees.
Coroner	What did you tell Representative Ridgeway?
Mr. Panichi	I told Billy you were under contract. One could not just fire you. And any pressure on you during the investigation and just before the Inquest would be stupid. Then I asked him why he was getting involved.
Coroner	What did he say?
Mr. Panichi	Not much, but I pressed him. Mr. Ridgeway told me that Chuck Harrison, the Board's Vice Chairman, had contacted him, complaining about the investigation and asking for a favor. Harrison was worried you were exposing other issues with the College, including some political ones. He asked Billy Ridgeway to use his authority and connections with some of the Freeholders to cancel the Inquest.
Coroner	Well, thank you very much, Commissioner Panichi. We can leave it at that, for now. From what you've told me previously and now have on public record, there is reason for me to conduct a further investigation of Mr. Ridgeway's dealings and communications, but not as part of this Inquest. I will do that subsequently.

Clough reached for Panichi's hand to shake as the Commissioner stepped off the witness stand. "Ladies and gentlemen, everyone in this room owes

Mr. Panichi gratitude for taking the high road. But know that I would not have caved to Representative Ridgeway, the Freeholders, Governor Byrne or President Carter. I do not cave. I was All-State in high school as a linebacker, plus I was a Marine. *Semper Fi.* I'm a tough SOB."

Clough looked at the Court Reporter and smiled a gesture of appreciation and relief that she was capturing this testimony. Then he addressed the audience. "It's not unusual for an Inquest to unearth issues or areas in need of further investigation including possible misdemeanors and felonies. Having crooked dealings on public record helps in the follow-up."

Coroner	One more thing, Mr. Panichi. Did you have any reason why you would have wanted Mr. Kelleher dead?
Mr. Panichi	No. Not at all. I had made phone calls on his behalf during the presidential selection. That's how much I thought of the man. To be sure, I admired that he took on some Board members. Lord knows how some of them got to be Trustees. A few people told me he was doing an exceptional job, trying to move the College forward and addressing lingering problems. Not everyone, certainly. Some didn't want changes or challenges. The rumors at County offices were that some staff had arrangements with the prior President, Greenleaf, that were to their personal benefit. That was not the pattern with Kelleher. We had begun to work together on a few County issues – drugs, spousal abuse and illiteracy.
Coroner	Would one of those people be Miss Bartell, Mr. Panichi? Is she one of those who said he was doing an admirable job?

Mr. Panichi nodded his head, while thinking he spoke too much of this woman and gave away that his relationship with Miss Bartell was more than professional. But then, most of his thoughts were about her. Part of him wanted the truth told. That part said he was tired of the secrecy and hiding in shadows. The other part wanted to keep it a hush-hush until he found the words to tell his mother and his wife.

The annulment petition was underway with the church. It was time to share with Cecilia that he would be seeking an annulment and pursuing a divorce. She would be hurt certainly but probably not surprised. Maybe not hurt that much. Regardless, with what had happened today, there was now an urgency to tell her.

Father Dominic had already talked to the Bishop at Saint Joseph's Cathedral. He had affirmed that the annulment petition would not have to be heard before the full Priest Tribunal. Young Panichi had not yet spoken to Jack Kula about serving as an advocate, but the wheels had been greased. Nothing like a little Italian heritage and a pledge to the capital fund to make things happen. Besides, Kula already knew about the relationship.

Dominic's thoughts drifted away from the Inquest: *I best speak to Samantha after the hearing, call my father and then meet with Cecilia. Tomorrow, I'll talk with Kula and have somebody at the office look for an apartment in town for me. I think I'll ask dad to join me when I tell mom. I must face little Carmelo. I better meet with my accountant too. Wonder if she'll want my car? My golf clubs?*

The Coroner saw that Mr. Panichi was no longer attentive to his questions.

Coroner	Mr. Panichi, are you alright?
Mr. Panichi	Yes, sorry, I lost my focus. Yes, Miss Bartell speaks highly of President Kelleher. Attorney Jack Kula was impressed, at least from what he's told me. Mrs. Reynolds always complimented him. Frankly, Mr. Clough, the Board did too until the architect thing. I expect most still do, if they had the balls to go up against Pitman and Harrison.

Clough looked over his notes and made his usual comment. "Sorry, I have one more thing." There was a murmur of laughter in the audience. Clough smiled at his statement and the humor of it. "Just one more thing," he repeated.

Coroner	As I understand from Mr. Kula, Mr. Zelinski's promise of a payment to Dr. Pitman was confined to the Executive Session. Thus, it never was made part of a public record that evening. Since the money offer was withdrawn, does that technically mean there was no payoff?
Mr. Panichi	Yes, that would have been the case. There might have been an ethical violation but not anything my office or the Board of Chosen Freeholders could legally hold against the Board member or pursue with Zelinski. But that changed with this Inquest. The matter is public now. As angry as Pitman and Harrison were at Mr. Kelleher, the President's clever

	manipulation of Zelinski's proposed payment had saved those two from public embarrassment.
Coroner	And if the payoff had been made public, there would be a difference?
Mr. Panichi	Absolutely. Keeping the matter confined to the Executive Session, where votes aren't taken. Ironic isn't it, Mr. Clough, that the President's death has caused these dealings to become public and subject to an investigation and legal scrutiny.
Coroner	The District Attorney will make that determination with or without the influence of any Freeholders.

While the Coroner directed his last remarks to Mr. Panichi, his intent was for the entire audience to see and appreciate the irony, too. Everyone in the room heard him. All knew there would be subsequent investigations, even if the outcomes were not certain.

"Mr. Panichi, you may step down," said the Coroner. "Your relationships with others at the College are not of concern to this Inquest. I admire you for using stepping-stones to cross the river with some of your answers, but I do not see you as involved or complicit in Mr. Kelleher's death."

"I would expect the President held you in high esteem, especially since you chose to gravitate to his side on this stubborn architect decision. You may leave the Courtroom, but I ask you not to betray my confidence. Do not speak to anyone regarding your testimony today, including Miss Bartell, Mrs. Reynolds and Mrs. Kelleher. If you leave, you are not to return until the proceedings are complete."

"Sir, if alright with you," Panichi said to Clough with a sincere expression, "I prefer to remain in the Courtroom and hear the rest of testimony, the medical findings and your conclusion regarding Mr. Kelleher's death. I'll take a seat in the back of the room and avoid any conversation about what is occurring today. Thank you, Mr. Clough."

Clough shook the hand of Dominic Panichi as he stepped down from the witness stand and headed for the back of the room. He noted that Panichi's eye contact with Samantha, Mrs. Reynolds and Mrs. Kelleher did not reveal which one of the three women was his lover. Indeed, this man was a good politician, well-trained and on the top of his game or blessed with unusual instincts.

Clough found his Deputy Sheriff with his eyes and called to her. "Miss Diaz, please ask Mr. Donald Winters to join us and serve as a witness."

Clough went to his binder and flipped through a few pages, as random whispering traversed the room: *Oh boy, this should be good. Do you think Winters will cooperate? Look at how angry he was just being sworn in. He may have the best motive for killing Kelleher. I heard he was the last to leave the Board Room that night. You know he could have been the President. Perhaps then he'd be dead and not Kelleher? Is there a mandatory retirement age in New Jersey?*

A few minutes later, Donald Winters walked through the door ahead of Miss Diaz, as if he was a highly experienced prizefighter on his way to a big payoff bout in the center ring. Clough cut in front of him, so Winters had to stop in his tracks and face the intimidating Coroner. "Mr. Winters, please take the stand. I remind you, you are under oath, under penalty of perjury."

"I get it," Winters said. "Some others may lie in this Courtroom and on this witness stand. Not me."

Coroner	Mr. Donald L. Winters, you are the Vice President of Academic Affairs at the College. How long have you been in that position, sir?
Mr. Winters	Almost twelve years. I was hired to teach History and then became a Dean before being appointed as chief academic officer under Dr. Greenleaf.
Coroner	You were the Interim President for several months after Dr. Greenleaf left to take the position in Missouri. That correct?
Mr. Winters	Yes, about six months. As you know and probably want me to say, I was a candidate for President. The Board got political and chose Kelleher, against the wishes of the faculty, I might add.
Coroner	You told me in your office you hated President Kelleher. That's a strong word. Mind telling us why?
Mr. Winters	He stole the position from me by convincing Board members he was the stronger candidate because he had a Master's from Rutgers and another from NYU. I only have one graduate degree, and it's from a teacher's college, not high and mighty Rutgers. Harrison, maybe others, thought a teacher's college wasn't a real university.
Coroner	Was that all?
Mr. Winters	Hell, no. Kelleher also made it a big deal that we had not made much progress on the Foundation while I was Interim. There were a couple of faculty grievances I think he instigated.

The only real whiskey is good ol' Irish Whiskey.
Irish Leprechaun

403

	But since you asked, after he became the CJCC President he hammered me with his repeated tinkering with the organization, especially Academic Affairs. Then he hires that little woman as Assistant President, just to piss me off. None of that should have happened. None of that would have happened had I been chosen. Greenleaf supported me. That's why the Board put me as Interim. I had it.
Coroner	That certainly puts your anger in perspective. Sorry, but I'm confused, Mr. Winters. My discussions with several Board members led me to understand that Greenleaf did not endorse you for President.
Mr. Winters	Oh, that can't be.
Coroner	I'm afraid it is. From what I gathered during my investigations, former President Greenleaf proposed that the Board make you Interim to see you screw up. That's the exact phrase Dr. Pitman used – *screw up.* I'm sure he'll affirm that later today when he testifies.
Mr. Winters	I can't believe that.
Coroner	I am sorry, but Dr. Greenleaf told Dr. Pitman he thought you were weak, and your faults and lapses would show up even during the short period you were in office. The only reason he felt you should be Interim is because of your years of service. He didn't want Kelleher to get the position either. Greenleaf argued that the Board should look for an external candidate.
Mr. Winters	That crooked son-of-a-bitch. Bastard Greenleaf two-faced me.
Coroner	Yes, that seems to have been the case. Most Board members thought the guy from Iowa with the doctorate would get the position. A couple wanted to dig deeper into the original pool of applicants. But they could not come up with a justification that would hold water.
Mr. Winters	No one had the balls to tell me to my face. The ones that spoke to me after the appointment said Kelleher had made it a political process.
Coroner	Let's move on. I'm sorry you had to find out this way, but it does speak to your resentment and anger.

Mr. Winters	Glad you can understand. Who the hell can you trust anymore?
Coroner	Let's back up, Mr. Winters. By saying *that woman*, do you mean Miss Bartell? I believe her title is that of Executive Assistant to the President, not the Assistant President. Is some of your anger a result of having Miss Bartell in this position? Is some due to President Kelleher's leadership or decision style, which was quite different than Dr. Greenleaf?
Mr. Winters	Whatever, as far as her title. I don't like having to go through another person to get to the President and especially some young thing, barely out of graduate school with a bunch of freckles on her nose.
Coroner	Sounds like you have some issues there too, Mr. Winters.
Mr. Winters	You're a guy. You certainly get it. Bartell hasn't figured out yet that her role is to make the coffee, takes notes and be a good girl.

The Coroner paused to look at Mrs. Kelleher along with Miss Bartell and Mrs. Reynolds, who were seated together. Both were seemingly shocked by what Winters had said and that he was so visibly angry. They looked as if they were eating dinner at a fancy restaurant and the waiter decided to yank the table cloth out from under their plates.

Coroner	Let's move on. You were at the October 19th Board Meeting. You told me earlier you remained for a while after the meeting adjourned. Why did you stay after that meeting and how would you describe Mr. Kelleher's disposition, his demeanor at that point?
Mr. Winters	Most Cabinet officers hang around after a Board Meeting. When the weather is fairly decent, we congregate on the balcony off the Board Room. The space there is narrow. No chairs. No places to sit. But the air is fresh. The smokers can smoke and the second-floor balcony looks over that end of the campus. But that night, it was cold. If anyone was on the balcony, I did not see him or her.
Coroner	Are you saying that someone could have been on the balcony that night?

Mr. Winters	Yes, I suppose so. But it was very cold. I left shortly after congratulating Mrs. Wiegand for her media presentation and saying goodnight to folks. I hate going to the Board Meetings, so I take off for home as soon as the theatrics are finished.

Mr. Clough walked back to the table where he had his folder next to his yellow pad. He pulled out a separate set of papers. He ran his finger down one of the pages to a section he had marked. When he had found it, he returned his attention to the witness and resumed the questioning.

Coroner	I made notes on the Campus Security report that evening. It says your car was in the administration parking lot considerably after the Board Meeting ended. In fact, they noted the Board Room lights had been turned off about midnight and were off in the President's Office around 1 AM. Were you still on campus? How would you explain that your car was still there, sir?
Mr. Winters	Simple. I went with Dean Lieber that night to a bar off campus and had a couple of beers. Lieber drove. I got my car later, sometime after midnight, maybe 12:30 or so. Well, so what? I don't see how that matters.
Coroner	Mr. Winters, what was the name of the bar where you and Mr. Lieber went after the meeting?
Mr. Winters	If you must know, it was Murphy's Pub. A great little Irish bar on the northside. A couple of beers soothed our souls. We certainly weren't drunk, if you thought you were going there, Clough.
Coroner	That's good. Mr. Winters, we have not yet had Mr. Lieber testify, so we'll verify your alibi when he gets on the witness stand. But what about President Kelleher's demeanor at the end of the Board meeting? You did not answer that part of the question earlier.
Mr. Winters	Kelleher went into his office, his private sanctuary. He closed the door and came back out with a bottle of Irish Whiskey in one hand, a glass in the other. That's when I left. He did rub his forehead a few

	times during the meeting and seemed to be in pain. But then our cursed Board Meetings can do that to anyone. Bring pain, I mean. You could tell by the way he squeezed his forehead. I never pay that much attention to him. Didn't that night either.
Coroner	Who was in the Board Room when you left, Mr. Winters?
Mr. Winters	For God's sake, Clough, I didn't take notes. I didn't make a roll call or have a secretary take names or get people to sign in. What would you have wanted me to do? Mrs. Reynolds usually takes the minutes. Ask her.
Coroner	Just do the best you can and leave out the attitude.
Mr. Winters	If you want. I probably will overlook someone, but it was Lieber, Panichi, Dandridge and the Bartell girl. Harrison and Pitman were hanging around in the hall outside the Board Room. I don't know if they went back into the room or left the building. Gene Wildwood was there. Not sure why. Hart may have been there as well. That woman likes to show others how important she is. I find that amusing.
Coroner	Why was everyone there at the end of the meeting? Being that late, one would think they'd want to get home.
Mr. Winters	Kelleher started a warped tradition several months after he became President – stay after the Board Meeting and have a drink. Socialize, I guess. Big deal. Now that I think of it, Fishman was still there. He always hangs around, like a mongrel looking for scraps. Pretty sure Purdy left before I did. The Press, or what this County classifies as such, might have still been there. The snoopy Rooney girl likes to gather idle gossip, then embellish it in her articles. That good enough?
Coroner	President Kelleher suffered from cancer and was taking Morphine for the pain? Did you ever see him use a syringe to inject the painkiller?
Mr. Winters	He did, huh? Most of us knew something was different. You could tell something was not right with his health. He stopped his morning runs around

	the campus. He cut back on his meetings, although I just thought he was being a prick. I don't think I met with him in his office the last month or so. Edith asked me once or twice what I thought about his health. I told her that I really didn't care. Never saw him shoot-up. Never saw him shirtless to see his arms for needle marks either. Guess that explains things a bit.
Coroner	You are not exactly eliminating yourself as a suspect, Mr. Winters, if indeed Mr. Kelleher was murdered. Is that how you want to leave this testimony today?
Mr. Winters	I didn't kill him. I would probably defend anyone who did murder the guy, with apologies to his wife and children. But I didn't do it. It's your job to find the guilty party, Mr. Sheriff or Mr. Coroner, whichever title you prefer. Not mine. Am I done now? You sure ask lots of stupid questions.
Coroner	You remain a prime suspect, Mr. Winters. Nothing you've said today suggests otherwise. I question your answer about leaving the campus at that late hour to go to a bar with Mr. Lieber, but we'll see what transpires. You may step down. You are to remain in this Courtroom and not leave. I may call you back to the witness stand later in the day.
Mr. Winters	Thought you just said he had cancer, a brain tumor? So why are you looking for suspects?
Coroner	Because it had not yet been determined the manner in which he died, and death via homicide is a consideration. That's why we are here today.

Donald Winters glowered at Cough as he stepped down. He held his gaze on the Coroner for several seconds. Arthur Clough held his deadpan face, intentionally. Most everyone in the room saw the scowl and shook their collective heads at the testimony Winters had just given.

Clough looked again at Deputy Diaz. "Please ask Miss Sally Bowens to come and witness before this Inquest." He then saw Winters who had stopped and was talking with Katherine Carter, wife of Dr. Vernon Carter. Clough looked up and said, "Mr. Winters, you are not to converse with anyone in this room while testimony is underway. I think I made that clear. Please take a seat, or I will recommend you for contempt."

As Deputy Diaz left the Courtroom to call upon the witness from the Jury Room, the audience was abuzz: *Wait 'til Sally hears what her boyfriend said? Think she'll support his alibi? She's a tough lady. Doesn't she teach Business courses, Typing 101 probably. She may have to rat on the guy who raised the rat balloon. I'm surprised the faculty have a woman as its leader. Must not have been a male interested in the position. Let's see how she negotiates this Coroner. Like most women, I guess she relies a lot on looks. Bet she eats up this Clough guy!*

Clough again started to look through the notes he had assembled in his binder, setting them aside as soon as Deputy Diaz and Sally Bowens entered the room. He could feel the close quarters of the crowded courtroom.

Sally Bowens was dressed in a tailored blue suit with a classy, bold-print blouse. While she preferred a mini-skirt for the freedom and trend-setting it represented, she had chosen a maxi-skirt for today's performance. The stylish tweed skirt draped to ankle length and revealed a slit along the left leg to above the knee. As the Union President approached the witness stand, the skirt swished with her movements like a high fashion model sashaying along the runway.

Coroner	Miss Bowens, thank you for your witness today. Please tell us your full name and position at the College.
Miss Bowens	My name is Sarah Ann Bowens. I am Associate Professor of Business and President of the CJCC Faculty Union. Most people know me as Sally, though, not Sarah.
Coroner	Thank you, Miss Bowens. Please remember that you took the oath to tell the truth. May I assume you understand that?
Miss Bowens	Yeah, I get that. I'm under oath.
Coroner	Now Miss Bowens, your colleague, Mr. Ralph Hughes, testified before this Inquest earlier that he was with you the night of the Board Meeting when Mr. Kelleher died. Mr. Hughes testified that you both were in the Faculty Union Office after the meeting. Did either you or Mr. Hughes go back to the Board Room or the President's Office later?
Miss Bowens	No, I went home. Ralph apparently went by the Board Room for a moment or two before joining me at my house. I think he went back because he wanted to congratulate Nancy Wiegand on her presentation and see if there was any further dispute about the architect selection. We had a glass of wine. Then he left to go to his place.

Coroner	Why did he think that, about the architect I mean?
Miss Bowens	Ralph believed Kelleher had done something underhanded with the selection process, given the Board Chairman and Harrison wanted to include another architect. He knew they were upset about something. Ralph loves the drama. Absolutely loves it. Not me.
Coroner	Thank you. Miss Bowens, are you aware there's a Professor Hughes who teaches at the Columbia Community College? He teaches mathematics, too, in fact.
Miss Bowens	No, I'm not familiar with such a person at Columbia. Hughes is a common name, so I guess, I'm not surprised. Ralph has a sister who lives in that area. You probably are confused.
Coroner	Would it surprise you if I told you that your Ralph Hughes is the same person who's on the full-time faculty at Columbia Community College teaching math? As President of the Faculty Union, wouldn't you be horrified to find that a member of your Union was doing such a thing: holding down two full-time teaching positions? Deceiving everyone?
Miss Bowens	Yes. I mean, no. Let me back up, Mr. Clough, and clarify. I may have misunderstood your question.
Coroner	By all means, try again.
Miss Bowens	I did not know Ralph was teaching at both colleges. If it is true, that's Columbia's problem, not mine. Not ours. You should ask Columbia's Union person or their Personnel Office guy. But, it would not be possible.
Coroner	It is if you teach multiple sections in a row on those days.
Miss Bowens	I suppose so.
Coroner	Has Professor Hughes done that at CJCC? That is, teach multiple classes in a row.
Miss Bowens	No. We have a section in our Bargaining Contract that addresses what we have termed stacked or back-to-back course sections. Mr. Hughes does not teach more than two sections or classes in a row on

	any morning or any afternoon for us. He teaches one evening class each week too, at least he does this semester. That's how Mr. Hughes covers his math teaching load of four classes, 12 credit hours a week. He gets a one-course reduction because of the Union work. I get two courses reduced: 6 credits.
Coroner	Thank you for the information. Whether it's legal to stack classes at CJCC is hardly the point. Do you think it's also according to College policy to employ a faculty member under false pretense?

Clough walked to the table and retrieved the President's private, and formerly hidden, notebook. He thumbed through several pages, so the witness would grasp that this notebook was quite comprehensive. He then held it up for Miss Bowens to see.

Coroner	Miss Bowens, see what I am holding here? This is a notebook President Kelleher kept in his office to record his observations. Are you aware of this journal? Before you answer, know that due to Kelleher's notation in this regarding Mr. Hughes, Deputy Sheriff Diaz found out about the dual positions. Mr. Winters may not have been aware the Mr. Hughes was teaching at another college. Miss Hart was not either. Mr. Kelleher became aware.
Miss Bowens	There were rumors that Kelleher kept a secret notebook, but he never mentioned it to me. I never saw him write in anything like that or saw it in his possession.
Coroner	Mr. Hughes will be properly disciplined by Columbia Community College and likely through the District Attorney's office. You may be called to testify for that case, and your testimony here will also become part of the investigation.

The Coroner looked for a reaction from the witness. Bowens was indifferent, as if she knew she was above incrimination and insulated from censure. She hardly flinched.

Coroner	Let's go back to that October 19th Board Meeting. Miss Bowens, do you want to rethink your answers about your whereabouts the night Kelleher died? Get it correct this time?
Miss Bowens	I guess, I'd better. I just got confused. Ralph and I left the gloomy Board Room together, which was just after adjournment. I went home shortly after that. Ralph told me later he did go back to the Board Meeting and that he was aware Kelleher had been phoning Columbia asking about faculty named Hughes. Ralph asked me if I would agree that we went back to my house together.
Coroner	He asked you to lie under oath here today?
Miss Bowens	Yes, but that's why I've changed my testimony. It seems you found out about Ralph. I have no intention of going down with him, or anyone. As I said, I only found out about that teaching thing recently. Honestly. How terrible of him to do that.
Coroner	Honestly? Strange he never told you, or you weren't curious. Didn't you wonder where he was for most of every Monday and Wednesday when he wasn't on your campus?
Miss Bowens	Not really. I don't keep track of faculty comings and goings. Including his. That's not in my job description. Besides, I have my own classes to teach and office hours to keep, plus all the hours spent for the Union.
Coroner	Had this court not uncovered Mr. Hughes' deception regarding his dual faculty positions, would you have recanted? Would you have lied to this Inquest and provided a false alibi?
Miss Bowens	I'd rather not speculate on what I might have done. I have now told you the truth, and I resent that you could badger me in my testimony.
Coroner	Miss Bowens, I have full authority to question all witnesses subpoenaed here today. I am trying to get at the truth, and you have already admitted you initially attempted to mislead this Inquest. I will review the transcript of your testimony later and in the immediate company of the District Attorney.

He will discern if there is a legal basis for charging you with perjury. The Monroe County D.A. does not usually forgive such transgressions. In case you are not aware, perjury is giving false testimony during an official proceeding of the Court, which includes this Inquest.

Clough paused to see if the witness had understood his authority and how close she was to a citation. Her body language suggested he had gotten her attention and that her answers now might be more responsive.

Coroner	Now Miss Bowens, I will continue my questioning. Do you understand?
Miss Bowens	I'm sorry, Mr. Clough. I'm worried now about Ralph and what might happen to him.
Coroner	Aren't you also worried that, in fact, he might be guilty of murdering the College President? He lied to this body under oath, and he lied to you. You would be wise to use utmost care with your responses unless you want the D.A. to bring charges against you as an alleged accomplice.

Mr. Clough watched as Miss Bowens started to cry, although the gallery was mixed as to whether the emotion was genuine or a marvelous play-actor performance. In any case, the Coroner was not about to watch her wiggle out of the testimony.

Coroner	Were you aware, Miss Bowens, that Mr. Kelleher was dying of a malignant tumor in his brain and taking Morphine injections as a pain-killer?
Miss Bowens	No, I was not. We finished negotiations in July. He seemed all right then, although he wasn't pleased with some of the Board members who challenged the proposed contract. Did someone kill him?
Coroner	That has yet to be determined. What do you mean about the Board and the proposed Union contract?
Miss Bowens	Not sure. I wasn't in the Executive Session, but when they came out, Harrison was pouting and did not vote on the motion. He made some comment about faculty being coddled and money down the drain for the media equipment.

Coroner	Had you seen much of the President after that?
Miss Bowens	Not really. I hadn't seen him much before he died, except at those Board Meetings. Outside of the negotiations we would only meet once a month, and he cancelled the last two. I guess he was still perturbed from the flying helium rat. Occasionally Kelleher would venture to the Library to read something or get a cup of coffee and chat with students or faculty in the Student Union. I would see him then. We did not have anything other than a professional relationship. Why would I want to?
Coroner	Why do you think, seriously, he cancelled his last two meetings with you?
Miss Bowens	Kelleher was off-campus more this fall semester. At least out of the office, or holed up in it. Word was, he was lobbying for that Library project and working to get the CJCC Foundation to become a solid organization. Hell, for all I know, he was at the Jersey Shore every day or perhaps on a stool at an Irish Pub.
Coroner	You mean that as a joke, I assume.
Miss Bowens	I don't keep try to keep track of faculty or of our administrators. Not the President, either. Besides, Mr. Kelleher was such a private person that I don't suppose he would want to show the emotion of an illness or pain. To my knowledge, he did not. I didn't care for the guy when it came to negotiations, but he was an honorable adversary, perhaps smarter than we were, admittedly more strategic and certainly more politically savvy. I am sorry about the brain tumor. I did not know that at the Memorial Service, and I am sorry, Mrs. Kelleher.
Coroner	Thank you for that assertion. Nevertheless, some people would say you are a prime candidate if, indeed, Mr. Kelleher was murdered. You did not try to hide your animosity. You lied here today. You called the President out on several occasions. You put him down repeatedly in faculty meetings.
Miss Bowens	If he was killed in his office late that Wednesday, I told you I was at home, alone, after leaving the Board Meeting. I will leave it at that. Ralph did not

	come to my house after the Board Meeting. We usually did not see each other during the week unless in the Union pigeonhole office. I didn't kill Kelleher. I'm not about to go down with Hughes over this or anything. I have a career to protect. I told Ralph that they would find out about it eventually. He was careless. I think he's too dopey to figure out a way to kill Kelleher.
Coroner	I guess we are done.
Miss Bowens	I can leave now?
Coroner	Oh, just one more thing. Did the Board Chairman ever contact you about providing him with information on President Kelleher? Information on alleged wrongdoings or anything?
Miss Bowens	No. I avoid all of the Board members, but especially Dr. Pitman.

Clough shook his head in amazement. "Well then, Miss Bowens, you may step down from the witness stand. You should know that Mr. Hughes was escorted to the District Attorney's office and is awaiting arraignment later today. Given that situation, Mr. Hughes can be called back to testify later in these proceedings."

Clough waited to see if there was any reaction from Sally Bowens to the fact that her boyfriend and colleague was in custody. There was none. She was completely impassive.

Then he continued. "If you want to track down Mr. Hughes, I can appreciate that, and you may do so. Since he has already testified and now is in custody, I can hardly prevent you from having a conversation. I would ask you not to leave this building without checking back with Deputy Diaz or with Mr. Dreyfus in the Jury Room. Since your testimony is now a matter of record, I will not object if you choose to discuss what transpired here with Mr. Hughes."

Miss Bowens now looked undeniably shaken, especially for someone as impassive as she had been and who was used to strain from carrying the burden of faculty negotiations. She was still processing in her mind that Ralph was going to face prosecution and could lose one or both teaching positions. Bowens was internalizing that she, the re-elected President of the CJCC Faculty Union, might be charged with perjury, because of her knucklehead boyfriend and colleague.

Several heads turned as Miss Bowens walked out of the room led by

Deputy Sheriff Diaz. Winters looked amazed and Bartell looked disgusted. Mrs. Kelleher stared into space with contempt.

Reporter Rooney gawked with delight. The enterprising reporter was sitting on two juicy frontpage features for tomorrow's *Jersey Star*. In her mind, she could see the first headline now: *CJCC Union President Lies on Witness Stand at Kelleher Inquest.* Then the second one: *CJCC Faculty Member Arrested for Holding Two Teaching Jobs . . . Collects salary at both!* These exclusives could well be picked up by the *National Inquirer,* and they would want her to move to Florida to be on staff as a feature writer.

Clough saw the mood disruption and decided it was a good time to take a break. "Ladies and gentlemen, while Deputy Diaz escorts Miss Bowens to the District Attorney's Office and gets her properly situated, let us take a fifteen-minute recess. I will speak with Miss Diaz to bring forth the next witness immediately after the break. Thank you."

The Courtroom emptied of all attendees except for Donald Winters who lagged, waiting for the Coroner to walk toward the exit door. "Mr. Clough, may I speak to you for a moment, please?"

Clough was not expecting that he would be intercepted by anyone during the break, especially not Vice President Winters. "What do you want to talk to me about, Mr. Winters?"

"I may have *slightly misrepresented* where I was after the Board Meeting," said Winters. "But you probably knew that already. I expect it will be revealed when David Lieber testifies, so let me get ahead of the curve."

"Please be specific, we only have a short time for this break, and I need to see the D.A. and go over my notes," Clough barked. He was not pleased that a person would admit to having lied and then expect him to receive the truth outside of the witness stand. Yet, knowing the truth now would help in questioning Lieber later. And he still had the record of what Winters had said, had lied about, under oath.

"Yes, I understand," Winters said hurriedly. "Mr. Clough, when the Board Meeting was over, I went back to my office. I sat in my office chair for a few minutes, going over the meeting in my mind and feeling sorry for myself. But I fell asleep, and it was after 1 AM when I woke up."

"So, you did not go to a bar, any bar, with Lieber? And you did not have a couple of drafts at Murphy's Pub? Is that now the truth?" asked Clough, quite irked. "Or are you still *slightly misrepresenting* the truth?"

"Yes, Lieber wanted me to tell you that we went out together. He was embarrassed about the drinking establishment that he did go to after the meeting and that he was there alone. I don't know why I told him I would support his lie, but I did. Guess I felt I owed him for being loyal to me. Lieber said he went to some stripper bar. I didn't care for Kelleher, but I realize now he wasn't the reason I did not get the appointment. I should not have made-up that Lieber alibi. I did so out of spite for Kelleher."

"Mr. Winters," Clough said. "I will correct the record when we get back into session, and when I interview Mr. Lieber. I may need to call you back to witness and admit your lie. Your statement only adds to the baggage you claim as someone with a motive to have been involved in the death of President Kelleher."

Clough looked into the eyes of Winters and put his hand on Winters' right forearm, squeezing it hard. "You do understand that your admission now does not rule out or preclude a charge of perjury or contempt? Be certain you understand. I don't want you to *slightly misrepresent* what I have said here."

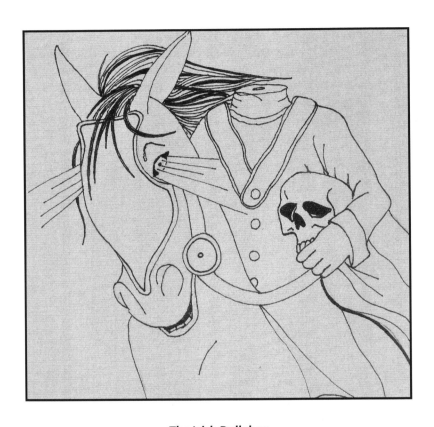

The Irish Dullahan

THE INQUEST – SESSION 4

Criticism of others is thus an oblique form of self-commendation.
We think we make the picture hang straight on our wall by
telling our neighbors that all his pictures are crooked.
Fulton J. Sheen

A few minutes after 2 o'clock, Deputy Sheriff Blanca Diaz stood at the front of the Courtroom with Coach Solly sitting at the witness stand, as the audience filed back into the room and took their seats. Solly fidgeted and squirmed from the moment he sat down. He was used to action, on the basketball and racquetball courts, with his son and daughter and anyplace else he went or things he did.

As people found and took a seat, the mutterings began to drift around the Courtroom: *Where's Coach Solly's track suit? Did he put any money in that new scholarship fund? When's he going to get to be university head coach? Doesn't he run a summer camp for girls somewhere in the mountains? What a shame that he finally got to Kansas for that tournament but then got beat. I think he must be Jewish.*

Clough went over to the witness stand after asking the audience for quiet. He anticipated a fiery set of answers to his questions. Solly had declined his favorite velvet track suit for a grey sportscoat and black slacks. His necktie was loosely knotted with the top shirt button not fastened. The tie looked like a sailboat's mainsail stuck a few feet from the top of the mast.

Coroner	Mr. Solomon, state your full name and position with the College. May I remind you, you are under oath. Be aware that at least two witnesses today have been caught in lies before this Inquest, and the D.A. will review their testimony for perjury.
Mr. Solomon	My name is Nathan Howard Solomon. I am the Head Basketball Coach of the *Roaring Raiders*, our Runner-Up National Championship Basketball team

	this year. Clough, I have been known as Coach Solly for most of my adult life. Call me that. I don't lie.
Coroner	Mr. Solomon, I am more comfortable with your given name for purposes of this Inquest. Let me start the questioning by asking if you disliked Mr. Kelleher. If so, why? And, please characterize your relationship with the widow, Mrs. Kelleher.
Mr. Solomon	That's a whole bunch of questions. Do you always ask so many at one time?
Coroner	Just take them one by one. If you forget, I will remind you.
Mr. Solomon	On the first one, President Kelleher refused to give much attention to my basketball program. He didn't care. My goal was to win a National Championship. I had to do that on my own. We had a minimal budget, and he seldom came to a game. As for Mrs. Kelleher, I see her from time to time at the YMCA where we both play racquetball. We've talked on occasion – in person and on the phone. I'm sorry she now's a widow. Sorry her two boys are without a father. I doubt he was much of that to them.
Coroner	But you started an endowment in Mr. Kelleher's name. Why?
Mr. Solomon	Simple. Pity for his wife, not because of him. Yeah, I disliked Kelleher a hell of a lot. Any coach would detest this guy.
Coroner	Why did you take your complaints to the Press, rather than work through your Athletics Director and Vice President to accommodate the President and address his concerns? Perhaps Mr. Kelleher had reason to be irritated, especially when he reads in the paper that his coach is angry, blasting the College. Wouldn't any President be upset?
Mr. Solomon	I suppose so. I did what I had to do. I don't see why a President would not be 100% supportive of a winning basketball program. 110%.
Coroner	Did Mr. Kelleher recently hurt your chances of getting a university coaching job? A position with much more visibility and higher salary where you would not have to teach as well as coach?

Mr. Solomon	As for the associate head coach job I had out West, I was told miserly Kelleher spoke with the Ath-*ah*-letic Director. That screwed me. He should have left well enough alone. No, he had to intrude.
Coroner	We'll remember to come back to that line of inquiry. Mr. Solomon, was President Kelleher aware of your friendship with his wife? That you were spending time together?
Mr. Solomon	Doesn't matter to me if he was. Izzy told me Kelleher asked if we were having sex. We were not. Neither of us wanted to go down that road. We're both married and working to one degree or another to make those relationships work. But Mrs. Kelleher appreciated the attention I could often send her way, probably because he wasn't giving her much.
Coroner	How do you know that?
Mr. Solomon	I make it my business. The ladies need attention. Lots of it. You probably know that, unless you're not married. Oh, that's right, I understand that you're divorced. So, you wouldn't know. Kelleher misrepresented us. Ours was a mutual connection, a collaboration or an alliance, if you will. I was delighted to be stealing his wife's attention, something he valued like I do basketball, even if we never went to bed or got close to it.

From her seat, Izzy Kelleher cringed at the words collaboration and alliance. Her eyes enlarged with surprise, the kind that hurts. She was thinking of words to use to describe their relationship. Collaboration and alliance would not be among them.

Coroner	President Kelleher's misrepresented you. Is that what you said?
Mr. Solomon	Yes.
Coroner	Were you aware he was terminally ill and taking Morphine injections for the cancer?
Mr. Solomon	On a few occasions, Mrs. Kelleher said she was worried about his health. Didn't matter to me. After the National NJCAA Tournament in Kansas, I hardly saw Kelleher, and those games were back in

	April. After he screwed my chance to be a university basketball coach, I had no desire to meet with him, see him or anything else. It was vindictive. Who the hell cares if he had cancer.
Coroner	Mr. Solomon, you certainly are providing us with your feelings – nothing held back.
Mr. Solomon	No need to hold back now. That's not me.
Coroner	Are you aware that Mr. Kelleher kept a notebook where he made notes about people and lists of things he wanted to accomplish at the College?
Mr. Solomon	No, I was not. I am not. I don't care about that, either.
Coroner	Coach Solomon, let me read a portion of his journal concerning you. This first one was several days after the NJCAA finals in Kansas: *Proud our men's team did so well at the Nationals in Kansas, and for Solly. The guy's a tremendous coach. Too bad his attitude gets in way of his success.*
Mr. Solomon	He should have been proud. So, what?
Coroner	So, what, Mr. Solomon? This note was a week later: *Looks like the Southern NM State AD doing a number on Solly. From his comments, no way Solly gets job. The AD and President want this other guy, former student. Solly will be pissed. The coach there is a damn wimp.*

Mr. Clough paused in his reading and looked up at Mr. Solomon to be sure he was listening and internalizing the notes from Kelleher's journal. He could see that the defiant expression on Solly's face had morphed into anguish and insecurity.

Coroner	Then these are some related notes from this same notebook, this past summer: *Spoke to NYU coach. Remembered him from business classes we took . . . He's checking on assistant coach jobs in conference – teams that may be thrilled to get Solly.* A few days later President Kelleher added: *My NYU guy called. Buffalo U. to contact Solly. Will have an opening . . . guy retiring. 8-team Women's Professional Basketball League is forming. NJ looking for PT coach . . . made to order for Solly. Hope he knows about it.*
Coroner	What is your reaction to these notes, Mr. Solomon?

Mr. Solomon	I did not know he was trying to help me find a university coaching position. I did get a call from Buffalo and was invited to interview. This new women's pro league would be great. I could coach the girls and maybe continue coaching here. Those gals would listen to me and follow my instructions – better than the guys do. But why was Kelleher cynical about my efforts here? For God's sake, we played for the National Championship. Guess Kelleher would have done most anything to get me out of here.
Coroner	Maybe, but not for the reasons you think.
Mr. Solomon	If I believe you, that is. If what you read is right, I was duped by Southern's AD. The bastard lied to Coach Kropp. Guess that would not have been a right situation for me. Maybe Kropp lied too. That sucks. No, Kropp would not lie to me. Kelleher got it wrong. I don't care what he wrote in his damn notebook.

Before continuing, Clough walked slowly to his binder and pulled out a typed document. He looked at Samantha Bartell momentarily before returning his focus to the witness. Miss Bartell had a good idea what line of questioning was coming.

Coroner	Mr. Solomon, Miss Bartell gave me a copy of a memo she received from Mr. Kelleher five weeks before his death. The subject is *Concept Paper for Intercollegiate Athletics at CJCC*. I now enter this document into the public record. Part of her job as Executive Assistant to the President is to direct the College Foundation. Miss Bartell shared the Foundation's mission, as per the original proposal, and it's clear the entity is to address the funding of the athletics program.

The Coroner took the document and walked closer to the witness, standing just a few feet from Solomon.

Coroner	Let me read portions of Kelleher's memo to Miss Bartell and the CJCC Foundation: *In all sincerity, I'm not sure of the role of Intercollegiate Athletics at a public community college.*

I have never been an athlete, as demonstrated by my jogging style. However, I've always marveled at what the human body can accomplish, with sports as the vehicle. My favorite spectator sport is the Olympics where teams play for their country in a variety of competitions.

Dr. Greenleaf hired Coach Solly, and he has done a marvelous job. He got the College media attention when we were a new institution. His success on the basketball court carried over to the public perception of quality in our faculty and classrooms. And, who could imagine our central New Jersey college would win the Regional twice and play for the National Championship?

But I have to question if that's what we should be doing. I do know it's not the role of the President to make that determination. It's not up to the AD or coaches either. It's the role of the Board of Trustees but upon whose analysis and recommendation?

That is why I am entrusting in you the charge to arrive at a comprehensive Mission and Philosophy for Intercollegiate Athletics at CJCC. Please initiate this through our energizing Foundation Board and ask them to make a timely analysis and present their recommendation to the President to take to the Board of Trustees.

You have recently added several well-known leaders of our community to the Foundation Board, and they have embraced the role of a college foundation to provide funds for student scholarships, capital funding and other items not addressed or well-addressed by our State and County budgets or student tuitions.

The Coroner stopped reading the memo and looked at Coach Solly again. The basketball coach did not show any distress or inquisitiveness at what Clough had read aloud. It appeared he was utterly uninterested. There was a glaze that dominated his expression. Clough saw it and shook his head.

Coroner   Mr. Solomon, do I have your attention? Sir, this is an important reference for us to enter into the record, especially given the accusations you've made, and the motive provided by your statements.

Mr. Solomon	Yeah, I'm paying attention. All this bores me. Really does.
Coroner	This Inquest and the death of the College President bore you? Sir, I strongly suggest you focus your attention, no matter how bored and distracted you may be. You may be under suspicion.
Mr. Solomon	Wait. Thought you said he died of cancer?
Coroner	No, I said he had cancer, and he was taking Morphine for the pain. I did not say how he died. That is what we are here to determine.
Mr. Solomon	The guy was a druggie as well as a shitty person. Swell. Hey, how 'bout that.
Coroner	Please watch your language in this Courtroom.
Mr. Solomon	Sorry. I shouldn't have used the word druggie.
Coroner	Let me continue to read excerpts that pertain to you and to get into the record. Try to stay focused:

> *If we are going to continue to compete on a national basis, we will need to set up funded scholarships for student-athletes and perhaps provide housing alternatives and travel budgets. Those dollars will need to come from private donations. Public funds – State, County and student tuition – should support Athletics but not, in my opinion, on a nationally competitive level.*
>
> *I have trouble paying for a team to go to an out-of-state National Tournament with public funds, redirected from faculty salaries, equipment or library books. I am not convinced that a community college can generate significant revenues from ticket and merchandise sales like a university can.*
>
> *Coach Solly belongs at a four-year university with the alumni support and with the resources devoted to championships, probably not a college that competes with local players and without scholarships and out-of-state travel. But he needs to embrace the Mission.*
>
> *Let the Foundation Board consider whether an increase in the Student Activities Fee is justified to fund Intercollegiate Athletics or a portion of same. Let them recommend what sort of private and corporate*

> funds could be generated for ongoing expenses of
> tournaments and perhaps creating an endowment.
>
> Please include Vice President Purdy in the
> discussion and have him add an Athletic Director from
> another college in New Jersey to contribute. Do not
> include our AD in the deliberations.
>
> If I am correct, you have built up the Foundation
> Board to a current membership of twenty. Set up a
> process by which they can address this Mission and
> Philosophy for Intercollegiate Athletics and arrive at a
> policy recommendation.
>
> Be deliberate and inclusive in the discussion,
> knowing that the Board of Trustees and the Board
> of Chosen Freeholders may have concerns, too. I will
> support that recommendation fully before the Board
> of Trustees, whatever the outcome is from this body.

Mr. Clough took a break from reading the Bartell memo to see what
reaction Mr. Solomon was having.

Coroner	Mr. Solomon, is any of this making any sense to you? Do you see what the President was trying to accomplish?
Mr. Solomon	No. Not at all. Say, are you about done?
Coroner	There's just a couple more paragraphs to read:

> If the Foundation Board agrees that CJCC should
> be nationally competitive and generate the private
> resources to accomplish same, and the Board of
> Trustees adopts same as institutional policy, I will be
> the first person to buy a season ticket.
>
> Until then, however, I believe I have a fiduciary
> responsibility to direct public resources to the highest
> priority areas – classroom and lab instruction and
> support services.
>
> Thank you in advance for this marvelous
> contribution. If you have any questions or concerns,
> please let me know.

That's the end of the memo. Now, Mr. Solomon, at
the time Mr. Kelleher wrote this memorandum, he

	knew he had cancer. It's clear he agonized over the conflict of funding Intercollegiate Athletics out of public funds, maybe had for years. But he entrusted the College's Foundation Board with making that determination. They were to wrestle with this topic and arrive at a recommended policy. Any reaction to any of this memo?
Mr. Solomon	We won Regionals three of the past four years. Not twice. Outta sight. Kelleher got that wrong. Sorry, I could not help but correct that for your records. There are other priorities for a College President. So, what? That's why they pay him the big bucks. I'm the coach. I determine how well we play and what kids I get to play here. He challenges this new Foundation to recommend a direction. Screw that. I win. His job is to get me the resources to support what we do. Nothing else. I never heard that he was asking Bartell to do this. What does she know about Intercollegiate Ath-*ah*-letics anyway, let alone a sorry bunch of middle-aged businessmen?
Coroner	Mr. Solomon, having heard what the President was trying to do, does not change your perception of him? What about the fact that he knew he had terminal cancer, yet he wanted to bring resolution into funding the athletics program?
Mr. Solomon	Not really. It's his job to find the money for the basketball team, so I can coach a championship, not mine. Mine is to get players, coach the kids and win games.
Coroner	You know the President had the authority to recommend to the Board of Trustees that they suspend Intercollegiate Athletics or even restrict competition to instate colleges. Even without the Board's approval, Mr. Kelleher could have prohibited recruitment of any out-of-county or out-of-state athletes. Instead, the President kept your program going, even as he was dying. He was asking the Foundation to recommend the overall direction and determine the scope and the degree of competition in the College's best interests. Because you were

geared toward winning, no matter what, he thought it best to find you a position that was consistent with your philosophy. He tried to advance your career. But apparently, you do not see it that way, Mr. Solomon?

Mr. Solomon   No, I don't. Not at all. You deaf? Don't you hear? My job is to coach for success, whatever it takes to win. That's all there is to it. We don't need a dumb-ass Board policy, determined by a bunch of guys who probably were losers on the courts, if they ever played high school or college ball.

Coroner   Let's change the topic. Where were you on the night the President died?

Mr. Solomon   I was at home with my wife and two kids. I wasn't at the idiotic Board Meeting, if that's what you're asking. Kelleher invited me to come to the May Board Meeting to be recognized, but I told him to screw off.

Coroner   Do you believe someone murdered the President? Was his death an accident?

Mr. Solomon   From what you said, he was going to die eventually, sooner not later, so what difference does it make? Be assured, the next President will appreciate our wins. He'll put me on a pedestal.

Coroner   You admittedly despised President Kelleher, yet you stood up at the Memorial Service for him and announced you were starting a scholarship in his name. That doesn't seem to square with your feelings about him.

Mr. Solomon   The lawyer guy, Kula, came up to me just before the thing started and told me about his firm wanting to donate $2,500 for a scholarship. Fox wasn't there. I decided to make the announcement myself.

Coroner   I was at his Memorial Service that Friday. I recall you saying that you, Mr. Fox and others in the Athletics Department started the fund.

Mr. Solomon   I exaggerated. So, what? If the lawyer wants to donate money, why do I care. He needed someone to make the announcement. Why not me? Kula didn't mind. Wasn't even his money.

Coroner	Was this all part of your collaboration with Mrs. Kelleher, the so-called alliance you were forming?
Mr. Solomon	The guy's dead. We'll be getting a new President. I don't need an alliance or anything anymore. And I didn't kill the guy, if you're trying to get me to admit anything.

The Coroner looked over at Mrs. Kelleher. She looked like someone had punched her in the face. "Mrs. Kelleher, are there any questions you would like me to ask Mr. Solomon based on what he has testified so far? We owe you this courtesy."

Izzy Kelleher slid forward in her seat before she spoke. "No, thank you Mr. Clough. I've heard enough. You can never be sure of your friends or their motivations. Let me say, however, before you and these people that this man and I had no alliances. We collaborated on nothing other than racquetball and fruit juice. I am ashamed we did that."

The Coroner then returned his attention to the witness.

Coroner	One last question, Mr. Solomon. Do you have any knowledge of your department colleague, Mr. Alan Fox, applying pressure on students for sexual favors?
Mr. Solomon	What are you asking? Of course not. Even if I had, I'd take his word over that of any coed student any day, any week. That's what teams do. Stick up for each other. He may tease the ladies from time to time. What's the big deal? I tease too. All guys do? Maybe even you, Sheriff.
Coroner	One person's tease is another person's insult and torment. And what about if there were multiple students with the same story, same accusations.
Mr. Solomon	Unless you insist, I would prefer to leave that alone. I don't know anything about that.
Coroner	Mr. Solomon, you may step down from the witness stand. Just one more thing. Do you see any conflict of interest regarding your Pocono basketball camp and your responsibilities with the College? There were notes in President Kelleher's journal that Personnel should develop an ethical statement regarding jobs or obligations that interfere with one's duties at the College during the contract year. Mr. Kelleher

	believed you worked on the camp during your office time at the College. Is that true, sir?
Mr. Solomon	I put in so many hours that I don't count what I work on. I just work, Clough. Is that the last of your one-last-thing questions?

Mr. Clough glared at Coach Solly and motioned for him to leave the witness stand. He looked over at Mrs. Kelleher who was crying, upset over Solly's comments.

As the coach strolled past the row where Izzy was sitting with Edith Reynolds and Samantha Bartell, she stood up and faced the coach. "How could you? I hope you get a university job too, to get you out of my sight. I can't believe I had a friend so incredibly selfish and self-centered. You weren't interested in being a friend. You only wanted to antagonize my husband. Make him resentful, even jealous. We didn't connect on anything except your damn Poconos basketball camp!"

Arthur Clough walked over quickly to Mrs. Kelleher as Edith and Samantha put their arms around her shoulders. Clough said to her, "Are you alright, Mrs. Kelleher? Sorry I had to put you through his testimony. This was the guy I spoke with in his office, and amazingly he kept the same mindset today. I thought it important for you to hear how he felt, in his own words. Miss Bartell came to me with the memo that the President had sent to her about the Foundation. Miss Bartell started to initiate that review with her Board. Hopefully, the next President will see the wisdom in arriving at some rightful closure and presenting the Foundation's recommendation to the Board of Trustees."

The Coroner looked up, as Coach Solly stood in the aisle. "Mr. Solomon, despite your comments here today," Clough said, "I do not see you as complicit in the death of Mr. Kelleher. You were not at the meeting, and you were not aware of the cancer. You are asked to leave this room and the building. Please do so at once!"

Clough returned his attention to the widow Kelleher, who had regained her composure and looked resolute. Izzy looked at the Coroner and said, "I don't think Coach Solly, despite his arrogance and selfishness, had any idea how much my husband tried to support him. I didn't either. I'm ashamed. Solly's been a friend. Someone I could talk to, who would make me laugh. That stopped today. This is the perfect time for the Foundation and Board of Trustees to consider and set forth the scope and direction of Intercollegiate Athletics, especially men's basketball. I'm sorry it took my husband's death to surface this conflict, to discern the fundamental direction. I'll talk with Solly when I calm down. When I get home, I plan to take a long, hot shower and scrub myself clean with soap and a *Brillo* pad."

Deputy Diaz stood next to the Coroner, respectful of the stress Mrs. Kelleher was bearing, especially with Solly's testimony. Then she said to Clough, "Who do you want me to bring to the Inquest now?"

Arthur Clough touched Izzy Kelleher's arm tenderly. He then looked at his Deputy and walked over to his binder. "Thank you, Blanca. Please escort Mr. Wildwood to the Courtroom."

Only those persons near where Clough was standing could discern what he said. But the announcement soon spread, as did the questions and comments: *Isn't he the quiet guy? Think he'll stutter? Given what Rodewald said, he's got some explaining to do. Doesn't his wife teach elementary school someplace? Wonder what those two do in the Computer Center after hours? I hear the computer thing's as big as a house trailer. What's a computer used for anyway?*

Several tense minutes passed before Gene Wildwood entered the room and took his place on the witness stand. He sat at attention, his back straight and hands folded on his lap. Nothing he did clouded his anxiety and nervousness. Clough looked over his notes before he addressed the witness.

Coroner	Mr. Wildwood, thank you for being here today. Let me remind you, as I did the others, you're under oath. Please state your full name and position with the College.
Mr. Wildwood	Yes, sir. My name is Eugene Victor Wildwood. I'm the Acting Director of the College's Computer Center. No, wait. Sorry. My title is Coordinator, not Director. There's been no appointment of a successor to Mr. Tucker. I've assumed many of those duties with Howard's death. There's not been an appointment or search for the Director, and given Kelleher's death, that may take a while longer.
Coroner	Thank you. Do you and your computer colleagues hold Mr. Kelleher responsible for the death of Mr. Tucker?
Mr. Wildwood	We did. We felt he shouldn't have been fired. Made him leave the campus. Escorted him to the parking lot. Took his keys. I was told Dr. Dandridge made the recommendation, but Kelleher pulled the plug.
Coroner	Sounds like a motive for murder?

Mr. Wildwood	The President was murdered? By whom?
Coroner	We have not yet determined how President Kelleher died, but you should know he was suffering with terminal brain cancer these last several months. I was just questioning what motive you might have to commit murder.
Mr. Wildwood	My relationship with Mrs. Rodewald would not be reason enough for me to murder him or anyone.
Coroner	But you were very upset with Mr. Kelleher.
Mr. Wildwood	Yes and no. We bear some of the responsibility. We all knew Howard had a severe drinking problem and drank heavily in the office. We knew he did not address it. Didn't want to. Mrs. Rodewald and I talked about how to deal with it. We all dug into our pockets and chipped in for two bottles of *Beefeaters* for his 50th birthday party. That was stupid. We enabled him. We laughed at him drinking his gin out of those paper cups in his office.
Coroner	Why the paper cups?
Mr. Wildwood	At first, he was hiding it. Then he did it to mock everyone. Several times a day we'd pose the same question: *Say, Howard, who makes you drink?* Each time, of course, he'd say: *No one makes me drink. I volunteer for it.* Was funny then, we thought. Not now. We should have kicked his ass or insisted he get help, not made jokes. Still, Mr. Clough, firing our Howard was not a good answer.
Coroner	That's not easy to admit, Mr. Wildwood. Are you aware President Kelleher had asked Miss Hart to see if the College could initiate some sort of Alcoholics Anonymous chapter and hold meetings for the community? You also may not know, he made a personal contribution to the Foundation to honor Mr. Tucker and initiate an employee bereavement fund. Few people knew.
Mr. Wildwood	No, I was not aware of the alcoholics support business or the donation. Nice of him. He didn't share that with us, so we could have thanked him? Now he's dead. A shame.

Coroner	Tell me, why were you at the October 19ᵗʰ Board Meeting, the evening on which the President died? Please know others have testified you were there at the end of the meeting and lingered afterwards.
Mr. Wildwood	Mr. Coroner, there's a blue notebook on that table. I believe it's the one that belonged to President Kelleher.
Coroner	Yes it is. How did you know that?
Mr. Wildwood	I was in his office several weeks before he died and saw he had made notes in that book. There are alpha-tabs, including the letter W. He wrote something about me and Candace. That's why I was at the Board Meeting. I was hoping to catch Mr. Kelleher in his office before he went home. I wanted to explain our relationship. Or try to. I did not want Candace to be hurt or miss out on that Computer Center position.
Coroner	Did you get to speak with the President?
Mr. Wildwood	Not really. There were others there who seemed determined to see him, and I was low man on a totem pole. Plus, you could see Mr. Kelleher was not feeling well. It had been another rough Board Meeting. I just said I hoped he would support Mrs. Rodewald if she decided to apply for the new computer programming position.
Coroner	Did the President respond when you asked him?
Mr. Wildwood	No. He just looked at me and gave me a half smile as he sipped his drink. But I'm sure he heard me.
Coroner	Were you aware that the President was taking self-administered injections of Morphine for the pain?
Mr. Wildwood	No, I did not. He must have been in a great deal of pain. How terrible.
Coroner	Candace Rodewald has already testified, and she's still in this Courtroom. What you do not know, Mr. Wildwood, is that she admitted in testimony that you were having a relationship outside of the office. She also admitted she broke into the President's Office to try to find this notebook. She was not successful. I found the book earlier this week in a hidden desk

	drawer. Were you aware she had done this – broken into the President's Office?
Mr. Wildwood	Yes. She told me about it the next day. I was surprised she could get into a locked office, but she can accomplish whatever she puts her mind to. She may be very attractive, but she's no airhead. She said she couldn't find it. Candace didn't want others to know about us. We'd hoped to keep the relationship a secret, at least until we figured out where it was going. It started innocently enough. Talking about work, sharing concerns over Howard and where our careers were going. We insulated each other from some of the job stress. We had more of an emotional connection than a physical one, although no one would believe me.
Coroner	This must be hard for you. I think Mr. Kelleher understood – what you did for each other as colleagues, as friends.
Mr. Wildwood	Candace recently told me she wanted to end it. End us. I understood and agreed. Neither of us wanted to screw-up our marriages. It was dumb, but I don't apologize for caring or finding her an attractive, perceptive person. Pretty as she is, Candace is even more glorious on the inside. I'll have to try to explain that to my wife, my parents, Alice's parents. Maybe I can't?

Mr. Clough could see that Wildwood was sincere in his confession. He put his hand on the man's shoulder, momentarily. Then he turned back to the audience as the witness resumed his statement.

Mr. Wildwood	Mr. Clough, Candace was hoping President Kelleher would not keep her from getting the new position because of our office romance. That's the only reason she wanted to see that notebook.
Coroner	Thank you. Now, I want to ask you about the gifts you've received. Allegedly the gifts are tied to the priorities for completing jobs in the Computer Center.
Mr. Wildwood	Gifts? The gifts are bottles of wine, for the most part. It's a *quick pro quo* thing. I advance their job, and

	they acknowledge with favors. I've received a few gift certificates too. Ten bucks, $15 tops.
Coroner	The expression is *quid pro quo*. Don't you think that's a bit crooked? I presume Mr. Tucker was aware of what you were doing?
Mr. Wildwood	If he was, he never mentioned it to me. For all I know, he was getting favors too. He got his gin somewhere.
Coroner	So that's how you conducted your business? From my conversations with some of your users, they feel they have had no choice but to bestow small gifts – favors you call them. That's called extortion.
Mr. Wildwood	Well, if I may, a couple of years ago, I got a Christmas gift from Mr. Lieber when he had a rush job. The word got around. Then I would get a smile, a wink and a gift when people would submit their jobs. It started innocently. Maybe the favors got out of hand. I liked giving a bottle of the Italian wine to Candace. Made her day. Shared a bottle or two with the others as well.
Coroner	Mr. Kelleher was aware of the way you operated with programming jobs and had a couple of staff members willing to confront you and Mr. Tucker.
Mr. Wildwood	I didn't know that he knew anything about it.
Coroner	He did. Mr. Wildwood, you might also care to know, Mr. Kelleher said in his notes that he wanted Mrs. Rodewald to get that Computer Center job. He was going to push it with Dr. Dandridge. He also complimented her that she helped you gain more self-confidence. I will be meeting with Mrs. Rodewald later this week to discuss her testimony and that she lied under oath. I appreciate, Mr. Wildwood, that you did not lie. There have been too many somewhat crooked testimonies so far.

The Coroner turned and looked at Mr. Winters and Mrs. Rodewald to get their visual attention about the perjury charges they would be facing. He returned his attention to Gene Wildwood.

Coroner	Mr. Wildwood you may step away. You are asked to stay in the Courtroom. You are not to have any

	conversation with Mrs. Rodewald until this Inquest is adjourned. Do you understand?
Mr. Wildwood	Yes, sir. I humbly ask you to be benevolent and tolerant about Mrs. Rodewald. She's an excellent employee. If I had kept my knowledge of Mr. Kelleher's notebook to myself, she never would have gone into his office. I deeply regret that. Sometimes when you try to hide something, it only makes it more visible, more conspicuous. I'm sure she had nothing to do with Mr. Kelleher's death.
Coroner	Thank you. Mr. Wildwood, I realize this has been a highly personal admission. The Court does appreciate your honesty. I will take into consideration your comments about Mrs. Rodewald. But she has committed a crime. She entered a locked office in a public building with intent to steal.

Clough looked away and motioned for Deputy Diaz to come to his side. As she approached him, he addressed Gene Wildwood again. "Mr. Wildwood, I do not, at this time, see you as complicit in a crime or contributing to the death of Mr. Kelleher. I will leave it up to the College to determine whether any discipline is in order respecting the gifts you have received to prioritize computer jobs."

The audience in the Courtroom was silent, waiting for a response from Mr. Wildwood. There was pin-drop silence. The Coroner said nothing.

Arthur Clough spoke to his Deputy as Gene Wildwood walked to the back of the Courtroom. "Miss Diaz, please ask Mr. David Lieber to come to the Courtroom to witness next."

Clough looked again at his notes but could not help overhearing the comments people made in the first few rows: *Did you know this Lieber guy has a world class art collection? Well, maybe Jersey class. Wonder what he's hiding. He's always looked suspicious to me. Aren't he and Winters tight? What the heck are Learning Resources? He's written several funded grants for the College. He and Kelleher were like oil and water. Think he will admit to it? How much does he drink you wonder? I hear he's a whiz at writing bull shit.*

The Coroner noticed Donald Winters squirming in his seat when he announced Lieber's name. He also saw *Jersey Star* reporter, Martha J. Rooney, furiously scribbling notes on her pad. He knew this would be a tabloid story in the paper tomorrow. Probably help sell copies on the street.

Clough spoke up, "Miss Rooney, I know you're assigned to cover this

Inquest. Remember that the point of it is to identify the manner Mr. Kelleher died. Not to generate sensationalism. Kindly use some discretion."

David Lieber walked slowly up the aisle in the Courtroom and saw Arthur Clough and Izzy Kelleher engaged in an emotional conversation. He had no idea what the discussion had been, just that Winters, Hughes and others had testified. He paused and waited for Clough to advise him.

Coroner	Mr. Lieber, please take the witness stand. You understand you are under oath. The court will not tolerate false testimony. Please state your name and position with the College.
Mr. Lieber	My name is David Daniel Lieber. I am Dean of Instructional Resources, reporting to Donald L. Winters, Vice President of Academic Affairs.
Coroner	Thank you. We spoke in your office a couple of weeks ago. You told me you felt President Kelleher took credit for some things you did for the College, especially the Title III federal grant. You said Mr. Kelleher was vindictive toward you for supporting Mr. Winters during the Presidential Search and because you were so innovative. That correct?
Mr. Lieber	That would be true. We didn't spend much time together the past three-four months as at other times. Kelleher chose to rely more on Dr. Dandridge for the second Title III, and he distanced himself from me.
Coroner	Previously, you told me where you were the night he died. Would you kindly share that with this court for the record?
Mr. Lieber	I was at the Board Meeting. A couple of faculty members were doing presentations on their Title III media efforts. Also, to be honest, I wanted to see if Board members were going to challenge the purchases. We have a major order for additional equipment from MVE – Media Visual Equipment – out of New York. I wanted to be sure the bids were approved. I stayed after the meeting, long enough to see Mr. Kelleher with his bottle. Then I left. I met Mr. Winters at Murphy's Pub where we like to go after a meeting and unwind some.
Coroner	Mr. Lieber, you do realize Mr. Winters has already testified as to his whereabouts that evening?

Mr. Lieber	Sure. If you say so. I know he left the witness room before I did. Why would I lie about where I was?
Coroner	Sir, the bartender at Murphy's Pub stated to Deputy Diaz that you were not in his bar that evening. He remembers it well because there was a group of guys celebrating a job promotion until they closed the doors. He also validated from a photo that Deputy Diaz shared that Mr. Winters was not in the bar that evening. Do you understand that you and Mr. Winters have committed perjury?
Mr. Lieber	Sorry. Wrong bar. Wrong night. I was at another bar that night after the Board Meeting. I asked Donald to support me because I was embarrassed that it was a different place, and I was there alone. He said he would. There's a difference between a faulty memory and a lie. Didn't want my wife to know.
Coroner	Then would you care to remember better and tell us now which bar this was?
Mr. Lieber	It was the Playhouse Lounge outside of town. I was there from about 11 PM until it closed at 2 AM, Thursday.
Coroner	We don't need to establish what sort of enterprise the Playhouse is, Mr. Lieber. But, it's not possible for you to have been at the bar at 11 PM. The Board Meeting ended at 10:45 PM, as per the Minutes. If you stayed a while, it would be at least 11 PM, probably later, when you left the campus. Care to revise that time?
Mr. Lieber	I do get confused on the time. Sorry. Guess it was closer to midnight when I got there.
Coroner	We have certainly established that your recollection is anything but accurate, Mr. Lieber.

The Coroner went over to the table and picked up President Kelleher's blue notebook. He held it up for the witness to see. Lieber looked at it without expression.

Before I continue with questioning this witness," the Coroner said aloud, "I want to get on the record that Mr. Donald Winters has chosen to recant his statement as to his whereabouts after the Board Meeting. Mr. Lieber, you'll be dismayed, but Mr. Winters told me during the last break he was in his office until after 1 AM. He'd fallen asleep at his desk. That's why his car was in the lot that night when Security made its rounds."

Clough looked to the back of the room where he spotted Winters. "Ladies and gentlemen, Mr. Winters is in the Courtroom. Mr. Winters, you are asked to affirm from where you are standing that I've accurately stated what you told me."

Donald L. Winters, the former Interim President stood up to speak. "Yes, sir, that's accurate. I was not with Mr. Lieber that night."

In response, Clough looked at the Court Reporter and scowled as she smiled, indicating she had documented the statement. Then he said, "Thank you, Mr. Winters but as I said, your apology and change in testimony notwithstanding, you remain under consideration for perjury."

Coroner	Mr. Lieber, do you have anything to say?
Mr. Lieber	I was just embarrassed that I'd gone to a bar, that type of bar. But that does not change the fact that I was not on campus when Mr. Kelleher was murdered.
Coroner	We have not established that there was a homicide. President Kelleher was dying of brain cancer.
Mr. Lieber	Cancer. My God. I did not know that.
Coroner	Maybe so, but you can understand why it might be difficult for this Inquest to believe you.

The Coroner retrieved Mr. Kelleher's notebook and showed it to Mr. Lieber. The Dean did not acknowledge what was in front of him.

Coroner	Let's proceed. With your blank look, I assume you don't know what this is that I'm holding.
Mr. Lieber	How am I supposed to know that?
Coroner	A yes or no answer is sufficient. This is a journal Mr. Kelleher kept in his office. We found it hidden in one of the desk drawers. Mr. Lieber, there are numerous comments in here about you. Without a detailed tabulation, I think you have the most references. Some of President Kelleher's notes are complimentary about your vision and your guidance of faculty to create media-related products. Others are very disturbing, often quite accusatory and borderline incriminating. Would you like me to share some of those?

Mr. Lieber	Not if I have a choice. But I can probably explain whatever it is Kelleher said or had against me.
Coroner	We can give you that opportunity. Let me identify a few. There's a notation almost a year ago that he was approached by the Media Visual Equipment firm out of Rochester, New York, to receive tickets to a Broadway play for him and his wife. He asked the College Attorney to check it out. Mr. Kula found the firm is notorious for client paybacks.
Mr. Lieber	This was not a payback. It was a legitimate gift. Just a simple thank you gift!
Coroner	In your mind perhaps. But the Rochester Police Department is investigating. Mr. Kula gave a legal opinion to the County Commissioner that the play tickets could a bribe and leverage for future favors. Does any of these behaviors sound familiar to you? And you do have new equipment orders from MVE.
Mr. Lieber	Well, I did get some tickets. A few. They sent me a small camera, too, but that's all. MVE's a fine company. This is just their simple way of thanking customers. Some of their staff may get carried away. Their selection for the media equipment purchases had nothing to do with the gifts.
Coroner	So, you would submit to us that there is no connection between the gifts and the renewal of the Colleges' media purchase agreement? And, Mr. Lieber, before you respond, I caution you again, you are under oath. You're on thin ice, sir. So, did you receive a cash payment from them?
Mr. Lieber	They did send me money, but that was a travel reimbursement.
Coroner	Mr. Lieber, you apparently do not realize we have investigative powers and a great amount of hard-nosed persistence. Mr. Kula found that the $250 cash payment sent by courier was not a reimbursement.
Mr. Lieber	But it was. I did a consultant visit for them.
Coroner	The truth is that, after the fact, they tried to hide the money as a consultant fee. However, they could not produce any documentation to support that claim, and the paperwork said something different. Their fiscal agent, when pressed, admitted that it was

	something they regularly do, when courting clients. There was a trail to the cash, and that information, Mr. Lieber, was provided to the police.
Mr. Lieber	Why the police?
Coroner	Since the transaction crossed state lines and involved federal dollars, they have begun their investigation. So, again, you have not told the truth under oath here today.
Mr. Lieber	You're planning to fine me for that? For receiving a couple of gifts? I thought this Inquest was about Kelleher's death. A lousy 250 bucks.
Coroner	The District Attorney determines the penalty for perjury, not me. Mr. Lieber, I don't consider you a prime suspect, should we establish that there was a murder. You relied too much on the President for your ego enhancement, and you were off-campus when the death occurred. Just not the place you said you were or at the time you told us you were there, and likely not for the reason you said.

Lieber stared at the Courtroom ceiling as if a huge weight had been lifted off him and perhaps the heavens had interfered in his favor. He thought he was free from further scrutiny.

Mr. Lieber	Now can I go?
Coroner	I am far from finished, Mr. Lieber. Your testimony has not helped Mr. Winters, and you can expect to hear from the Rochester police, very soon. And I would anticipate the College will pursue disciplinary action. *Shenanigans is Irish for Crookedness. Irish Leprechaun* There is a is a public record of today, and we will send that to the Board of Trustees for consideration. Mr. Lieber, you seem to have perverse ethical standards and unusual definitions of what is crooked behavior.
Mr. Lieber	Sometimes you just must do what you must do. I hustle. That's what I do. Occasionally, I may cross over the line.

Coroner	Did you know that President Kelleher was taking Morphine for the pain of his cancer?
Mr. Lieber	How would I know that?
Coroner	Just answer the question, please.
Mr. Lieber	Except for the smoking and drinking, Kelleher never put anything harmful in his body. That's why he looked so healthy.
Coroner	We can do without the humor. Please answer the question.
Mr. Lieber	Of course, I did not know about the injections.
Coroner	I asked you if you knew he was taking Morphine. I didn't ask you about any injections.
Mr. Lieber	Nice try. That's how one takes Morphine unless in the hospital.
Coroner	You are pretty good with the B.S, Mr. Lieber. I have one more thing about your Media Visual Equipment company. You negotiated a contract with them for the Intellectual Property rights to the Intro to Psychology course materials that Professor Nancy Wiegand has developed. That correct?
Mr. Lieber	Yes, but it's not finalized.
Coroner	That's odd you say that. I have a copy of the signed contract MVE provided. It looks finalized to me. There are signatures. The curious thing is that 20% of the royalties go to the College and 30% to you, according to the language in the Collective Bargaining contract. The company that produces and markets the materials gets 40%. That left 10%, which is to go to Professor Wiegand. Would you explain why the person who wrote, developed and produced the media videos only gets 10%, and you receive almost a third of the royalties?
Mr. Lieber	I must have overlooked that when I hastily signed the agreement. I can correct all of that. But without me, the College would not have the grant, and Wiegand would not have had the opportunity to create classroom materials for publications. Think about that!
Coroner	That's truly an interesting perspective. However, an MVE representative told me the firm was under

	the impression you did most of the work and only included Mrs. Wiegand since it was her discipline. You do understand that if this is all correct, Mr. Lieber, you are guilty of fraud?
Mr. Lieber	There must be a mistake. I don't recall that. MVE must have done that without my knowledge. Are we done now?
Coroner	I have one more set of questions, Mr. Lieber. Dr. Pitman has not yet testified, but when I asked him during my investigation about a couple of matters, he let it slip that he relies on you as his own personal whistleblower. That's the term he used. Whistleblower. Given that relationship, Mr. Lieber, you might not be too worried that the Board will take any action against you.
Mr. Lieber	The Board knows I hustle.
Coroner	Let me clarify something. A whistleblower exposes activity deemed illegal or unethical within an organization. The fraud or corrupt behavior could be a violation of college policy or of ignoring State laws. Whistleblowers take the risk of facing reprisal and retaliation from those who are accused. That sound about right to you, Mr. Lieber?
Mr. Lieber	Well, Pitman would call me once a week or so and try to pry information I might have about Kelleher. He wasn't interested in violations of policy, fraud or corruption. He wanted dirt. Any Kelleher decisions or screw-ups, real or imaginary, he could use against him.
Coroner	By your description of what was expected, you were closer to a snitch than a whistleblower. Pitman had induced you to report anything he could use against the President. You complied. For the record, please give us an example of what you passed along to the Board Chairman?
Mr. Lieber	Well, I told Pitman that Kelleher likely had received gifts from MVE, as Winters and I did. I told him Bartell had been hired without a Search Committee. Of course, I told him Kelleher would drink in his office, although most everyone knew that. I told him

	he kept his bathroom locked for no reason. No one cared about that.
Coroner	What else?
Mr. Lieber	I told him there was a rumor that Coach Solly and Kelleher's wife were having an affair. I said Kelleher might be keeping pot in his bathroom. That's why the door was always locked.
Coroner	So, you passed along rumors. Or was it gossip? Maybe slander?
Mr. Lieber	The rumor mill is pretty accurate at a college. It's very active at this one.
Coroner	What did Dr. Pitman offer you as a payment or reward for these rumors and gossip tidbits?
Mr. Lieber	He didn't get specific. He just said that down the road there'd be appropriate considerations.
Coroner	When did this begin?
Mr. Lieber	My calls to Pitman started before the Board's September meeting when the architect thing was up for vote. I did not know the whole story about that, but Winters told me later what he and Harrison had tried to do about the architect. Last thing I would want is some lightweight architect taking on our new Library. Honestly, I planned to advise Pitman that I no longer would be his weasel. Then ol' Kelleher died. Pitman would have kept bugging me anyway until he had something worthy of blackmail. The guy's evil.

There was a rush of amazement at the second bombshell. First, that Lieber had been the subject of a New York police investigation. Now, that Lieber and Pitman were in cahoots to undermine and threaten the President. If someone had taken a poll, the audience would have been split on which was the more potent shock.

Arthur Clough motioned for David Lieber to leave the witness stand. He signaled the Deputy Sheriff to come to the front and escort Lieber out of the room. Diaz walked up to Clough and said, "Mr. Sheriff, sir, I know you watch cop shows, especially *Streets of San Francisco, Police Woman* and *Hawaii 5-0*. So, isn't this when you tell me *Book'em Dano?*"

As Lieber walked toward the exit, the Coroner discarded the smile on his face to address the audience and speak again. "Ladies and gentlemen,

Mr. Lieber will be escorted by Deputy Diaz to the District Attorney's office. I thought I had made myself clear about the significance of being under oath when testifying. Be assured, however, we will make that point in another Courtroom and before a judge."

"Understand, I will follow-up on the actions of the full Board of Trustees regarding Mr. Lieber's conduct. I will press for appropriate disciplinary action, up to and including termination because of payments received from the MVE company and the self-serving Intellectual Property contract."

Clough turned toward Jack Kula. "Mr. Kula, I will see you receive a copy of Mr. Lieber's testimony, so you can present the case to the Board of Trustees, unless they reject any consideration."

He then turned to look directly at Dominic Panichi. "For the record here today, Mr. Commissioner, please note that I will also present a copy of Mr. Lieber's testimony to you. Mr. Panichi, you will receive a request to present this matter to the Board of Chosen Freeholders regarding consideration of sanctions against the Board and its officers."

The Coroner looked away from Panichi, who was nodding his head, and faced the full room again. He paused before speaking, as he wanted to be very careful about the words he was about to recite.

Then he spoke. "Ladies and gentlemen, as long as I retain my position as Monroe County Sheriff and Coroner, I will review the actions of these public entities. If, in my mind there is not reasonable injunction and proper accountability set forth, I will present the material facts to the State Board of County Colleges and to the Governor's Office. Even if I am fired, there is now a public record that will make its way to the State Board and Governor Byrne should our Freeholders and the Trustees decline to review the testimonies."

The Coroner stood back and peeked at his watch, as much to recess his thoughts as check the time.

Then he said to the audience, "I think it would be wise to take a 20-minute break, as we await Deputy Diaz taking Mr. Lieber down the hall and retrieving our next witness. Deputy, please call Mr. Chuck Harrison to join us here."

THE INQUEST – SESSION 5

If the first button of one's coat is wrongly buttoned,
all the rest will be crooked.
Giordano Bruno

Deputy Blanca Diaz held the door open for Mr. Chuck Harrison at 3:50 PM, knowing full well he would not welcome a woman holding the door for him, not for any man. After he passed through, Diaz said, "You're most welcome." Harrison chose not to acknowledge her. Diaz shook her head in disbelief. She smiled, knowing what was to come.

Harrison walked defiantly to the front of the Courtroom. He saw the Coroner and stood right in his face, giving Arthur Clough a machine-gun rally of scorn. "Where do you want me? I want to get this over with, as soon as possible. I have a business to run. Why couldn't you have called me first? Most of the other witnesses are faculty. They just get excused from their classes. They don't work for a living, like I do. What do you want to know from me? I'm the Board Vice Chairman. This is ridiculous!"

Clough stared back and said, "Mr. Harrison, you need to take a seat on the witness stand. I remind you. You are under oath. There's no exception from that oath just because you are a College Trustee. Which person I call and how I call my witnesses is my business. Mine alone. I strongly advise you to take a seat and change your disposition toward this Inquest. That will not serve you well."

Harrison thought for a moment about verbalizing the rest of what was on his mind. He decided this might not be the most opportune time to do so. As he sat down at the witness stand, he replied, "Well, if that's what you want. Let's get this over with."

Coroner	State your name, your work and your position with the College.
Mr. Harrison	My name is Charles George Harrison. My wife and I own and operate Chuck's House of Magic. I am the

446

	Vice Chairman of the Board of Trustees. You can call me Chuck or *Magic Man*. Most everyone does.
Coroner	I'll address you as Mr. Harrison. Tell us where you were the evening of Wednesday, October 19th, the night the Board of Trustees met.
Mr. Harrison	I was at the meeting of the Trustees that night, of course. I've only missed one meeting in three years. Pretty impressive, if I say so myself. I remember the agenda that night. It included presentations on the media equipment the spoiled faculty get to play with. You're gonna ask me, so I'll beat you to it. I was there at the end of the Board Meeting. I wanted to have a private talk with Kelleher.
Coroner	How long did you stay, sir? Who else was in the Board Room or with the President when you were there?
Mr. Harrison	Pitman and I left when the meeting ended and went out in the outer hall to talk. I don't think I know everyone's name who was there. It was the Lieber guy, Panichi, Fishman and that cute assistant gal, Bartell. Her real surname is Bartelli. Some computer guy was there too. The one who stutters. One or two more. I guess. Hell, I don't know their names. Bill Fishman was there too, kissing ass.
Coroner	Thank you. That's consistent with what others have said. Now, Mr. Harrison, what did you and Dr. Pitman want to talk about with the President after the meeting?
Mr. Harrison	Do I have to? It was a private meeting.
Coroner	Only if you don't want to be in contempt.
Mr. Harrison	If you say so. Pitman said he had his law buddy look at the President's contract. He wanted to see if we could find a loophole, fine print, so we could fire the guy or pressure him to quit. Kelleher went into his office and shut the door. He came back with a bottle in his hand. Kelleher gets upset about the computer guy drinking on the job, and what does our President do? He gets his whiskey in his office. Because he's a big shot. He gets ice from his mini-frig.

447

Coroner	Do you know what Dr. Pitman talked to the President about?
Mr. Harrison	He said he advised Kelleher that his days were numbered. He should get his resume shaped-up and see what jobs are there. He told me he told Kelleher if he left, he'd give him a glowing reference and his retirement. If he resigned. Otherwise, no deal.
Coroner	What triggered your decision to want to remove Mr. Kelleher from office? What did he do?
Mr. Harrison	The bastard challenged us in an Executive Session at the September meeting. He insinuated that if we did not comply, he'd have Kula see if an ethical violation would be in order. Imagine, that guy telling me I was suspect to an ethical violation. Who the hell does he think he is?
Coroner	You do recall that Mr. Kelleher died that night? Is the issue you two had with the now dead President about the architect selection?
Mr. Harrison	Well, that's one for sure. He also argued Title III was an excellent opportunity for the faculty. I thought it was a waste of taxpayer money. Any stupid teacher just needs a blackboard and chalk. They don't need special equipment and time off for worthless professional training. They don't need movies on the subject to show in class. Read the textbook or watch the filmstrip! I never saw any value in any of that audio-visual stuff. The faculty don't need raises every year, either. We coddle them.
Coroner	Did you find a loophole in the President's contract, Mr. Harrison?
Mr. Harrison	Sure did. Pitman said we had it. With the four votes, we could boot him out or dump him in a faculty position. We'd have to pay him the President's salary for the rest of the fiscal year, until the end of June. That would be worth it to get him gone. Good thing he died. Now we don't have to pay, and he's gone. Good thing.

Clough walked away from the witness stand after Harrison's last remark. His thoughts wandered to the process by which the Board of Chosen

Freeholders would choose such a person to be on the Board. He knew there wasn't any process other than cronyism.

The mind of the Coroner wandered: *This guy doesn't have respect for faculty or what they do on a campus and in their classrooms. He just said publicly he was pleased the President was dead. What else will he admit to? Did he really just say college students can just watch filmstrips? Filmstrips.*

Coroner	Did you have the votes on the Board to do that – boot him, as you say, out of his contract?
Mr. Harrison	Pitman was sure he had one vote besides the two of us. So, we only needed one more. Four votes would do it. I was starting to work on that when I got the call that Kelleher was dead.
Coroner	Did you know President Kelleher had terminal cancer and was taking drugs for the pain?
Mr. Harrison	No. No one told me. Too bad.
Coroner	Had Mr. Kelleher not died on October 20th, he would have been dead within three months, maybe sooner. But let me ask you directly. Did you have anything to do with President Kelleher's death? Do you know if Dr. Pitman did?
Mr. Harrison	That's a question I don't have to answer, but you can ask your attorney pal here if I need to. I'm not admitting anything. I have my rights.
Coroner	This is an Inquest into the death of a person. No one's on trial here. We are trying to find out why Mr. Kelleher died – accidentally, on purpose or at the hands of others. You may choose that option, based on not incriminating yourself. However, know I will take that into due consideration in determining whether there should be further investigation into your actions.
Mr. Harrison	Hey Clough, I can pull a rabbit out of a hat. I'm a magician. I can carve a person in half or make someone disappear. I can make a rope stand on its end. So, I can find one more vote to fire the guy. Why would I stoop to killing him? I guess I could have cut him in half and then forgot how to put him back in one piece. Funny, huh? You ever been to my magic store? Lots of costumes and masks, and if you

449

	wander to the back, there's a special room for adults. Mature goodies. You'd like it.
Coroner	No, not really. Your store and its contents are not an issue here. More importantly, were there things you wanted Mr. Kelleher to do that he refused to do, other than this local architect issue?
Mr. Harrison	Well, yeah. Occasionally, we get requests from our local delegation to find a job for this or that person or reassign them from one supervisor. Sometimes it's to encourage a promotion. There are requests from business people, but not that often. I don't see anything wrong with giving a maintenance job to this guy's cousin if that guy's a State Senator and votes on our budget.
Coroner	Did Mr. Kelleher agree with that?
Mr. Harrison	He's stubborn about things. Dr. Greenleaf was far more flexible, more accommodating. Hell, Kelleher likes to pick and choose what he'll do. Not sure why.
Coroner	Mr. Harrison, you continue to speak of Mr. Kelleher like he's still President. He is dead.
Mr. Harrison	Yeah, guess so. But like I said, Greenleaf got this whole campus built and knew he had favors to take care of. Kelleher is, or was, touchy about that stuff. Someone might have decided they'd had enough of the guy. There are ways to take care of problems like that. But they should have just waited for the guy to die from the cancer.
Coroner	Are you saying Kelleher had enemies in the town, outside of the College?
Mr. Harrison	Oh, he pissed off other people, not just Pitman and me – vendors, contractors, a couple Freeholders. One or two from Trenton. Maybe young Panichi, but you have to ask him. I doubt your investigation is encompassing enough to include all those who despised the guy, who won't be at his funeral.
Coroner	Sounds more like you and Dr. Pitman wanted to stir up consternation and create some animosity. My investigation did not turn up any Freeholders who held a grudge. The County Commissioner was

	laudatory about how he felt about the guy. Admired him greatly. But you're entitled to your opinion and your testimony.
Mr. Harrison	Clough, how long have you been Sheriff, lived in this County? Less than a year as I recall. You just don't get it. We get things done here a certain way. You best get on board or you may fall overboard.
Coroner	I just have one more area of questioning.
Mr. Harrison	I'm thrilled.
Coroner	There is documentation that you have gone on College-funded trips as a Trustee and took someone other than your wife. That means, sir, that you have falsified a report and received a benefit to which you were not entitled.
Mr. Harrison	Bull shit. I can take a person, spouse, son, girlfriend, my dog, whomever, if I want. Greenfield didn't care. Suddenly with Kelleher it is wrong to do this. And I don't appreciate that you would bring this up in a public session. What if my wife hears about this? Now I'll have to think of something to tell her. Oh well. Thanks a lot, Clough.

The Coroner suppressed a smile and motioned for Chuck Harrison to exit the Witness Stand. "Mr. Harrison, you are free to exit this Courtroom, but you may not return if you do leave. Most likely, sir, there will be further investigations into your interactions with the College and scrutiny into recent contracts. Be assured, my investigation will encompass a wide range of transgressions, a wider net of crooked behaviors. But I don't think murder is one of your misdeeds. But then I don't think you are a magician who can make this disappear!"

Clough watched as Harrison exited the room. Then he called Deputy Diaz and whispered in her ear. "Deputy, please have Mr. Fishman come and witness before this Inquest."

Clough went over to the Court Reporter, Mrs. Parkinson. He leaned down and said quietly, "I trust you captured those comments from Mr. Harrison. I'll need that to substantiate investigations into Board behaviors."

Vicki Parkinson nodded that she understood, while looking at Clough with chagrin. Her expression showed how mortified she was. "Sir, it never ceases to amaze me what people will say in this Courtroom. It's as if this is their big moment in life to blow out all their feelings. I wonder how many, like Mr.

Harrison, will think back to what they said today and what sank them. Then go and kick themselves?"

"You're so right, Vicki," Clough said gently touching her shoulder. "Harrison implicated Pitman and most of the Board, plus some Freeholders. He will rule this day, I promise. Perhaps not for murder, but certainly for the crooked things he and others have done. And he was non-apologetic about it all. No remorse. No regret. No repentance."

Arthur Clough turned his head as Deputy Diaz led Bill Fishman down the aisle from the back of the Courtroom. Fishman had a look of determination and trepidation, not unlike a soldier walking confidently across a field of battle knowing it was probably laden with exploding mines.

Fishman looked around the audience trying to discern the mood of those folks assembled and whether others had betrayed him. The audience looked away from him, but not without idle chatter: *Is he the latest temporary President? Isn't he a bean counter? What does a business guy know about teaching in a classroom or what a library should look like? Think he'll be the next President? Looks like he lost some weight. Did he get a new haircut or is that a toupee?*

Coroner	Mr. Fishman, please have a seat and tell us your full name and position with the College. Need I remind you, you're under oath.
Mr. Fishman	My name is William Thomas Fishman. I am currently the President of Central Jersey Community College. My position before Kelleher died was Vice President of Administrative Affairs, essentially chief fiscal officer. I held the Lead Accountant position since before the College started holding classes, hired faculty or even had a name.
Coroner	I thought you were named the Interim President, Mr. Fishman?
Mr. Fishman	Whatever. Not sure there's a difference anyway. I do the work.
Coroner	Well, thank you. You've been with the College for almost twenty years. That's impressive. Let me ask what you thought of the appointment of J. Paul Kelleher as President toward the end of 1974? What sort of job was he doing when he died?
Mr. Fishman	I would have preferred the Board stuck with Donald Winters. He and I go way back, but Kelleher proved

	his worthiness and cunning during the search process. Winters fumbled. He dropped the ball on the way to the end zone. Get it? Anyway, the Board might have gone with that one external candidate – the Iowa guy. He pissed off the Board Chairman and showed he was a bigger jerk than Winters.
Coroner	Did you make your preference known to the Board?
Mr. Fishman	Not really. They were in charge, and they weren't seeking opinions. As for the job Kelleher's done, some things he did well. Other things, I would have done differently or not at all.
Coroner	Would you provide examples, please?
Mr. Fishman	Sure. Kelleher liked to move people around on the organization chart and even with their offices. That creates disloyalty. The fool hired the Bartell girl, and none of us on the Cabinet thought that was a good move, especially when she interfered with access to the President. Kelleher played musical chairs with offices and moved my right-hand guy down the hall to make room for this assistant gal. He didn't need to do that. Pissed me off.
Coroner	So that made you angry?
Mr. Fishman	Damn right. Then girl Friday Bartell starts sending our memos and reports back to us. She wants us to correct things. This girl wants me to redo a report because of spelling or what she considers weak sentences and faulty grammar. Can you imagine that? I'm a Vice President for how many years. Then some young thing with a skirt and cute freckles starts critiquing my work. No, I don't think so.
Coroner	That bothered you, Mr. Fishman, that she wanted the Board recommendations and reports submitted without errors?
Mr. Fishman	Who is she to tell me that? I have better things to do than edit and rewrite reports to the President or the Board. But there were many other things too. Kelleher favored Dandridge over Winters and me, perhaps over Jonathan Purdy also, except Purdy's harmless. He doesn't do much. Just runs around

	praising students and trying to get more of them into remedial classes and GDE, or is it GED, when they shouldn't even be in college. Dandridge has a doctorate. Guess that made him special. Big deal. Kelleher put him on the negotiations team, Title III too.
Coroner	Well, we heard a great deal there, Mr. Fishman. It sounds like you have some opinions on things. Did some of that not sit well with Mr. Kelleher? Did you confront him about the reorganizations? Did you question why he had Miss Bartell review your work, critique your reports?
Mr. Fishman	I tried, but he was intent on shaking-up stuff. I could understand the need to do that for some areas of the College: surely most of the lazy Deans, given they've always done things a certain way. He should have left Administrative Affairs alone. He had a hard-on for Bartell. He should have known you can't put a woman in that sort of a high-level position, especially at a college. I asked him not to move Spurling's office, but he ignored me. Just walked away. Didn't even give me an explanation. What happened to the value of seniority, let alone the ranking of job importance. You have a valued Lead Accountant versus a glorified secretary gal new to the place.
Coroner	You have been identified as being on the scene at the end of the October 19th Board Meeting. Please describe what you were doing there.
Mr. Fishman	Hey, the Vice Presidents are expected to be at all meetings. That is unless Kelleher provides written approval, like you must go to your wife's funeral or you're having heart surgery. There are financial things that come up at the meeting, sometimes from left field by a Board member who didn't bother to look at the agenda and who can't read a ledger much less add numbers greater than 10. I detest that when Trustees go over the monthly expenditure report, they focus on the coffee and sandwich purchases for meetings. Then they won't spend any time on fiscal planning or even looking at investments. That

	would piss-off me and Kelleher to no end. That was absurd to watch.
Coroner	Not sure I understand. Please elaborate on the Board and their role.
Mr. Fishman	The Trustees are appointed to their positions in New Jersey, not elected as in some other states. Political appointment of Board members is not the answer, as they morph into mavericks, like Pitman and Harrison. They're supposed to set policy, govern the place. Represent the community. But they prefer to meddle in day-to-day stuff and show off their authority at meetings. From what I hear, elected Boards can be worse. They develop coalitions and party affiliations.
Coroner	But, from what you say, they avoid tracking what they should be paying attention to?
Mr. Fishman	Yeah, I guess that's the good side of how bad they are.
Coroner	You were speaking about the meeting that night.
Mr. Fishman	Sorry. I was there at the end, along with Samantha, Panichi, Roseanne, Lieber, Dandridge, I think, and Purdy. Pitman was there at least until I left. Some were concerned as Kelleher didn't seem well at the meeting. Others, I suppose, were just curious and wanted to be spectators, more like gawkers. They wanted to see him go off the deep end or watch the confrontation with a Trustee or with faculty.
Coroner	You didn't say if Dr. Pitman was there after the meeting had ended. And what do you mean by off the deep end?
Mr. Fishman	Sometimes he would lose it, raise his voice. Maybe even shout. And, as I said, he appeared sick. Pitman was out in the hall with Harrison. Harrison came into the room later, but I think Pitman stayed in the hallway. Harrison was trying to get a moment alone with Kelleher. He seemed pissed. Pitman may have been there also. Now that I think of it, pretty sure he was.
Coroner	What happened then?

Mr. Fishman	J. Paul went into his office, closed the door and came out a couple of minutes later. He sat down at the Board Room table and poured a glass from his bottle. Samantha was the only one who did not drink. Well, she might have had wine. Panichi got chummy with J. Paul, and Harrison left the room. Lieber did too. One of the computer guys was there too. The guy who stutters. Wildwood.
Coroner	It was you, Panichi, Bartell, Hart, Dandridge, Gene Wildwood and Purdy at that point, still in the room with Mr. Kelleher?
Mr. Fishman	Yeah, sounds right. Although, after I left with Dandridge and Purdy, someone else could have come back into the room. It seemed like Kelleher had no plans to head home anytime soon after that meeting. Maybe Pitman stayed. He seemed to be circling like a shark, waiting until just the right moment to attack. Kelleher liked to stay while and unwind from all the shit.

The Coroner tried to picture in his mind the end of the Board Meeting with Kelleher in pain from the cancer. His thoughts took shape: *Was Kelleher buying time at that point? Was he hoping everyone would just leave him alone? Were others waiting until he was alone? Did Kelleher expect to be confronted by Pitman or by Harrison, or both? How mad was he? How mad was Pitman? Why did those others hang around? Maybe he should have used a Take-A-Number system?*

Coroner	Mr. Fishman, let me go in a different direction with my questions. My investigation has uncovered some debatable and shady purchases by you and your accounting guy, Mr. Richard Spurling. This Inquest is not about that, but about how Mr. Kelleher died. However, do you have anything to say about such purchases and contracts?
Mr. Fishman	Not sure which ones you're talking about, Clough. We make a huge number of purchases every year, hell every month. Perhaps we make a mistake here or there. I doubt you found anything. Anything at all.
Coroner	Well, we did. Some relate to purchases from local vendors. Mr. Purdy, the guy you said didn't do much,

is supervising an informal audit with the County CPA. From what the CPA told me yesterday, there are numerous discrepancies. If true, there will be an outside audit as well and other investigations by me as Sheriff. We may get the State Board involved too. Do you still have your doubts?

Mr. Fishman I don't care what dumb ass Purdy says or does. He's a lightweight. Everything we did was within the law. I got more knowledge in my little finger about student aid than he has in his whole body. And who is this stupid CPA? Probably some schmuck. Spurling could do rings around him.

The Coroner shook his head while thinking of Mr. Purdy sitting obediently in the Jury Room. He could only guess what might be going on in Purdy's mind and if he'd ever understood his colleague on the President's Cabinet thought so little of him.

Coroner Rather than take up time at this Inquest, I will save further questioning of you regarding financial transactions for my subsequent investigation. You said you were in the Board Room after the meeting. Where did you go after you left the campus, Mr. Fishman?

Mr. Fishman Miss Hart invited me to her house after the meeting. We had a cup of coffee and talked about Kelleher and how ill he looked. We discussed the Board of Trustees. I joked about the one Board member falling asleep during the meeting. I left Roseanne's place about 12:30 AM. Miss Hart will vouch for me and the time I left her place.

The Coroner gave Fishman one of those *you got to be kidding* looks. He knew Fishman's alibi would fall apart when Hart testified. He could tell when he had a witness who would bend when reminded of her or his oath and those, like Fishman, that preferred to re-create history.

Coroner Let's try this question, since you've brought up Miss Hart. Mr. Fishman, have you covered-up some of Miss Hart's indiscretions or errors regarding false or exaggerated reimbursements for travel?

Mr. Fishman	Spurling pointed out a couple of errors. I brought them to Hart's attention. We excused those. No big deal. It happens with all the paperwork. She paid back the dollars, or most of it. No harm done.
Coroner	No harm done, Mr. Fishman?
Mr. Fishman	Roseanne is pretty good with personnel policies and negotiations, but not so much with numbers. She just added wrong. Doesn't matter much in the big picture. It happens.
Coroner	Are you aware President Kelleher kept a notebook in his desk, which we have since discovered? It has numerous notations about you. Mr. Kelleher noted that you and Mr. Spurling hide some numbers and probably pocket money that belongs to the College. Most of it, he says, is in financial aid, where students don't get the full value of their loan or scholarship.
Mr. Fishman	Couldn't be. Kelleher never said anything to me about that. If he had, I would have shown him documents that validate everything we've done.
Coroner	Mr. Kelleher also made notes that Mr. Spurling works on the side for a couple firms in this County and another in Trenton. Do you know that?
Mr. Fishman	I assure you, Spurling puts in his 40-hour week. If he does some work on the side, that's his own time. I would not know which business firms they might be. He does their work. They pay him. So what?
Coroner	Well, Mr. Fishman, know and be assured that we have contacted the County Commissioner and the IRS folks. They, along with an impartial accounting firm, will be conducting their own audit.
Mr. Fishman	I thought this Inquest was about how Kelleher was murdered. What's all that got to do with your questions about Spurling, our books or Hart's pitiful travel reports?
Coroner	As I said, Mr. Kelleher left these notes. In pursuing what did happen the night he died, I wanted to raise these issues. Mr. Kelleher may have wanted the authorities to find the notebook and expose some of these matters.

Mr. Fishman	Well, I didn't kill him. I don't know about anyone else. Couldn't have been Miss Hart, either. She was with me. I can retire if I get squeezed, so press me all you want. May retire anyway. Don't look forward to breaking in another damn President.
Coroner	Mr. Fishman, were you aware that Mr. Kelleher was suffering from brain cancer? He only had a few more months to live.
Mr. Fishman	Is that what you are telling me now? The cancer got him. How 'bout that.
Coroner	Sir, I did not say that. That determination will come later in this Inquest and after all of our witnesses have testified.
Mr. Fishman	I'm sorry he suffered. Not much sorry he's gone. He should have left me and Richard alone. You should leave us alone too. Board does.
Coroner	Mr. Fishman. You may be excused, sir.

Fishman paused for several moments before rising from his chair. Some thought the pause was to let what he'd said sink in and reflect on what would be investigated. Others thought his hesitation was to hide his facial expression and body language and not betray how incensed he was, or how scared.

The Coroner glanced at Bill Fishman and easily read his emotions. He was pleased this man was upset, likely panicked. Clough looked forward to his subsequent investigation into the College's crooked finances.

Arthur Clough turned and spoke directly to Fishman. "Sir, you may leave the Courtroom or stay as you prefer. I do not intend to call you back to witness. As you know, I issued a subpoena to Richard Spurling to witness. I may call him later to testify. However, your testimony provided ample confirmation that you appear to cook the books. That's a recipe for the District Attorney."

The audience watched every move Bill Fishman made as he left the Courtroom, defiant in his walk, distraught in his mannerism, hate in his face.

Clough knew he had at least two more witnesses to call to testify before he completed his deliberations and made his conclusions public. In his mind, it was a coin toss as to whether to have Dr. Pitman or Miss Hart go first.

The Coroner called Deputy Diaz to his side and said quietly, "Blanca, bring Dr. Pitman to the Courtroom."

"Yes sir," Diaz said. He's getting grouchy. Keeps wanting to leave the Jury Room to make phone calls. Don't worry, we didn't let him leave."

"Deputy, you can tell Mr. Purdy that he can be excused or come into the Courtroom. I wanted to save him in the event that there was denial by Bill Fishman on the student aid question. Do apologize for me."

Diaz stood at attention while Clough looked at his notes before speaking again, hearing what she had said about Pitman but not wanting to disrupt his concentration. "With Purdy being excused, that leaves Miss Hart, whom I plan to call, along with Fox and the numbers guy, Spurling, left in the Jury Room. Spurling and Fox are subject to disciplinary action at the very least. I don't see either as having serious motive or opportunity to murder the President, but we are not done yet. For the time being, have Mr. Dreyfus retain them both. We still have a ways to go."

Dr. Pitman opened the Courtroom door ahead of Deputy Diaz. He walked confidently to the front, giving Clough the evil eye and a silent curse. Diaz followed him and tracked the assembled as they turned their heads in cadence, saw who it was and started to whisper: *Oh, here we go, the Board Chairman. Didn't he retire as dentist years ago after that lawsuit? Bet he's had this place bugged to hear what Harrison said? This guy makes the Godfather look like a babysitter. I wonder how many horseheads he's left around the city? Guy has lots of allies. Think Clough has met his match? The guy should have been removed from the Board years ago.*

Pitman relished the whispers and did not wait to be instructed to go to the witness stand. He went and sat down. The Board Chairman was perturbed and ready to pounce on Clough's first question.

Coroner	Dr. Pitman, thank you for being a witness. Please state your full name and occupation, as well as your position with the College. Be reminded you are under oath. Should you slide from the truth, you will be charged with perjury. Do you understand?
Dr. Pitman	Yeah, sure. Terrific. Get on with it.
Coroner	Thank you. Let the record show Dr. Pitman affirmed his oath. You may proceed.
Dr. Pitman	Terrific. My name is Dr. Gerald Evans Pitman. I've had a dental practice in Abington for thirty years and serve on the CJCC Board of Trustees. For the past eight years I've been Board Chairman. There's a large bust portrait of me in the Board Room, you know. Mr. Clough, you're a public servant, so you get a weekly salary. I'm a professional, a doctor, who provides a highly valued medical service to

this community. My patients do not get taken care of when I'm sitting in a Jury Room for hours rather than attending to them in the dental chair. And I don't get paid.

Coroner   Dr. Pitman, I apologize for calling you to testify this late in the day. I understand, however, that you are semi-retired and see only a few patients a week. Nevertheless, please understand, it was necessary for me to arrange the schedule this way. We needed to establish specific facts, information, testimony before calling you to testify. Plus, you have certain obligations as a Board of Trustees' officer. Surely being a part of an official inquiry into the death of the College President is worth your time.

The Coroner waited for Dr. Pitman to regain his composure, although it was clear that was not going to happen. The Board Chairman remained resolute in his defiance of being there and having to submit to questioning.

Coroner   We've heard testimony today to understand that Mr. Kelleher was dying with a brain tumor and only had months to live. We know he was taking injections of Morphine. He died as a result of that drug. We have not yet reached a conclusion, however, on whether or not his death was simply consequent to a self-administered injection or as a result of interference from others. Were you aware of the cancer and the injections?

Dr. Pitman   As a doctor, I'm not surprised by what you're telling me. That would explain why he was so insolent when I told him I had the votes to fire his ass. How long did he have to live?

Coroner   His doctor told him he had six to seven months when he was diagnosed in June. When he died in October, he may only have had a couple more months before the cancer engulfed his life.

Dr. Pitman   Son-of-a-bitch. Wish I'd known that. I would have handled our things differently.

Coroner   What does that mean?

Dr. Pitman   I don't care to answer that.

461

Coroner	Dr. Pitman, you should know you've been implicated in the death of President J. Paul Kelleher. There is sufficient testimony that you were out to get Mr. Kelleher and crookedly remove him from office. Should we conclude it was murder, and understand we haven't done that yet, we know you were in the Board Room after the October 19th meeting. Thus, you had motive. You had opportunity. Would you care to tell us, from your perspective, why you'd have reason to want to see him dead?
Dr. Pitman	This is ridiculous. I planned to get rid of the guy as President, not kill him. Had I known he was dying, I wouldn't have even talked to him again, as I did that night. The guy was ill, and I'm sorry he died, at least for his wife and family. No one should have to deal with cancer. As a medical professional, I know what that means.
Coroner	What did you talk with him about that night?
Dr. Pitman	I waited in the hall until most everyone else left. Sometimes we go out on the balcony, but it was too cold. Eventually, it was just Hart and me, unless someone came back later. Harrison had seen him earlier, alone, but after we talked, Chuck said he was going home. Roseanne was in the Board Room by herself, biding her time until I split. J. Paul went back to his office with his Irish Whiskey and sat in that throne. I stood over him, looked down at him and told him I had three votes to get him removed. He understood I only needed one more to void his contract.
Coroner	I'm thinking that Mr. Kelleher knew you didn't have the votes, and he was not about to resign and take a faculty position, given his contract. I'm thinking you knew that too and decided you needed another course of action to get rid of him. And, as a doctor, you might have had access to a supply of Morphine and could tell from his symptoms that he was injecting himself with the drug.
Dr. Pitman	Prove it. I had the votes.
Coroner	When you left him, Mr. Kelleher was still alive, even though he was drinking? How much alcohol had he consumed when you saw him?

Dr. Pitman	A couple of glasses, two fingers high each I'd say. He poured a third as I left. The guy could handle his liquor. Must be his Irish ancestry.
Coroner	What did he say when you told him you had the three Board votes?
Dr. Pitman	Just smiled. Didn't say much. Something like, *Do what you gotta do.* I asked him if he wanted to keep his job. He mocked me. I didn't like that. I'm the Chairman. He's just the President, working for us. I gave him the opportunity to do business as we've always done at the College.
Coroner	To do business the way you've always done it? Is that your justification for wanting Mr. Kelleher out of office?
Dr. Pitman	Hey, I looked the other way when Kelleher kicked an employee from the campus to an off-campus job and upset Representative Ridgeway. Billy's a friend of mine. He wouldn't reverse his decision.
Coroner	Why did Representative Ridgeway get involved on a campus personnel matter?
Dr. Pitman	The guy who got moved was Ridgeway's cousin or nephew, one or the other. We don't ignore our political friends.
Coroner	Sir, you are saying that Representative Ridgeway interfered in personnel decisions?
Dr. Pitman	He didn't interfere. He got involved. He spoke up for his relative. Kelleher didn't even know the guy was related to Billy. Pretty dumb don't you think?

Arthur Clough had to take a step back to let Dr. Pitman's testimony sink in. He decided to pursue another topic.

Coroner	Dr. Pitman, the President kept a personal notebook hidden in a drawer in his desk. We found it, thanks to his clues. The journal includes numerous notes about things going on at the campus and people who appear crooked in their behaviors, including you and Mr. Harrison. Care to comment?
Dr. Pitman	I don't give a shit what he wrote. I was the Board Chairman who put that ingrate, that rogue exec, in

	the big fancy, leather chair. Then he embarrasses me before the rest of the Board. He wouldn't do what we asked him to do. Do you not understand Mr. Coroner? He owed me his job for God's sake.
Coroner	Dr. Pitman, I get what you're telling me, but there's a difference between the role of the Board and that of a President.

Again, Clough could see no reaction from Pitman. Clough paused and thought to himself: *The guy could readily show his anger on the outside but disguise what he's thinking on the inside. That takes some practice. Lots of practice. Lots of nerve. I can see how he would intimidate the others on the Board. Probably intimidates his dental patients too. The Tooth Fairy may be too scared to visit his patients!*

Coroner	Is it true you worked out a deal for David Lieber to be an informant for you and pass along anything that might damage the President?
Dr. Pitman	I have no idea what you're talking about.
Coroner	Mr. Lieber has testified to that effect.
Dr. Pitman	I don't care. I didn't hire the guy. Lieber lied to you. He lies a lot. Lies like a rug. Get it?
Coroner	Then I guess it's his word against yours, Dr. Pitman?
Dr. Pitman	I don't care. Listen Mr. Sheriff or Mr. Coroner, whatever your title. If I wanted to get dirt on Kelleher, I can get that most any time and from all sorts of people at the College. Besides, what does it matter if I did?
Coroner	In fact, you were going after any gossip, trying to slander President Kelleher.
Dr. Pitman	If you say so.
Coroner	Let's get back to President Kelleher's notations. He recorded what had happened in the Executive Session at that September meeting. That's been verified by my investigation and by testimony today. What happened is damaging to you and Mr. Harrison. Should the charges prove accurate, you would be subject to censure and even removal from office. But, Dr. Pitman, you don't seem to understand that had you received the $5,000 from the architect

firm, you would have been subject to prosecution. If anything, Mr. Kelleher protected you. He could have exposed your plot in the public meeting. He did not. Kula did not either, at the President's request.

Dr. Pitman — Maybe so, but he should have gone along with it, the local architect I mean. The Zelinski firm wasn't going to get the contract anyway. Zelinski knew that. Kelleher just wanted to show me up. As far as the money goes, I don't know what you're talking about. You'll have to speak to my lawyer about that.

Coroner — I'll do that. Mr. Chairman, shouldn't the Board be above crooked acts, and shouldn't they applaud a President who values integrity?

Dr. Pitman — That's pretty ridiculous. I'm sure Greenleaf would have been fine with the proposal. Integrity is highly relative. How do you think we got the College built? Greased the wheels. Greased them good. That's how it works, Clough. You can't remove me from office. That won't happen. I know too many people here and in Trenton.

Mr. Clough backed away from the witness stand, looked at Attorney Smith who was shaking his head and asked him a question. "Mr. Smith, who has the authority to remove a member of the Board of Trustees in this County? And under what conditions could that happen?"

Mr. Smith rose from his chair and cleared his throat, before addressing the question. "The Board of Chosen Freeholders has the authority to remove a Board member and suspend the Chairman's appointment. The County Commissioner would be able to recommend discharge for several valid reasons. Malfeasance of office is one. A bribe. I don't know if unwarranted threatening of a president would be malfeasance. It certainly would qualify as an impropriety and trigger a public reprimand."

Mr. Clough looked at Pitman for a reaction. All he saw was an impassive and indifferent expression.

Coroner — Dr. Pitman, do you still believe you cannot be removed from the Board as well as from serving as Chairman?

Dr. Pitman — I'm not worried. I have my own guy who'll advise me. Get it tossed. I don't need some low paid public lawyer interpreting anything for me. Go ahead. Try.

465

Coroner	I think we have established what is pertinent to a further investigation.
Dr. Pitman	Maybe in your mind, but look who's on the Board of Chosen Freeholders.
Coroner	College records indicate that Mr. Harrison went on college-paid trips as a Board member and was accompanied by a woman who was not his spouse. That would be against College policy. Yet you've known of this and apparently challenged Mr. Kelleher who objected and said he would not be able to continue reimbursing for someone who's not the guy's wife.
Dr. Pitman	Harrison's wife has a hard time leaving their magic store. Thus, Chuck takes along a female friend. He can make women disappear, so why not make one appear in his hotel room.
Coroner	You are making light of this behavior.
Dr. Pitman	Look Clough, we don't get paid for being on the Board, and we take advantage of any and all perks we can. The College pays for our spouses on trips, so if his wife chooses not to come why not substitute a bimbo and have the College pay?
Coroner	I doubt most people share your logic. But let's move on. Dr. Pitman, did Mr. Harrison come back into the Board Room later, the night Mr. Kelleher died? Did anyone else?
Dr. Pitman	Chuck and I went our separate ways once we got to the parking lot after the meeting. I went home. I can't swear he left the campus. And you certainly wouldn't want me to lie.
Coroner	You said Miss Hart was still in the Board Room when you left. Biding her time was how you phrased it.
Dr. Pitman	If I said it, she was there. She was pretending to sip from a glass but was nervous. Maybe she's your killer? I would not be surprised. Winters may have done it. Fishman played along, but he hated him too. Our spoiled basketball coach was no fan. Or, it might have been some bitch on campus getting revenge for his lousy jokes?
Coroner	Just one more thing. Did Dr. Greenleaf support Mr. Winters in his bid to become President of the

	College? Mr. Winters told us earlier that indeed he had or that's what he had been promised.
Dr. Pitman	Hell no. Greenleaf told us to get an outside person, and not hire Winters or Kelleher. We should have taken his advice.
Coroner	You do realize, sir, based on your testimony today, there will have to be a proper investigation into construction contracts. Conceivably there will need to be an outside audit of capital purchases since you became Board Chairman and Robert Greenleaf was appointed President. We know there are recent purchases that are suspicious, as per Mr. Fishman's testimony. But you just opened the door to a much more expanded set of dubiously crooked financial transactions and potentially illegal acts.
Dr. Pitman	Go ahead, try to prove something. That was a long time ago.
Coroner	Not all of them, sir. If I have my way, Dr. Pitman, you will be removed from the Board of Trustees by the Freeholders for malfeasance. I will also see you are subject to scrutiny by the District Attorney as to illegal activities.

Arthur Clough saw no reaction except the twitching of an eye. So, he told Dr. Pitman, "You may step away from the witness stand and exit this Courtroom. You may stay as you prefer. Be assured you will hear from my office."

Dr. Pitman brushed past the Coroner and rushed down the aisle and out the exit. He did not look at anyone or anything. He snorted, not unlike a raging bull. All eyes were targeted on him, including those of Arthur Clough. Except for the clop-clop of Pitman's shoes, the Courtroom was silent. Most were shocked.

Clough's questioning of the Board Chairman had surfaced enough investigative issues to keep his office and staff occupied for months. But Clough was wondering to what extent members of the Board of Chosen Freeholders were aware of the contract violations, personnel interference and other intrusive matters.

Clough knew the Freeholders put Pitman in office years ago and kept him there. His thoughts turned to himself: *Have I unearthed too many skeletons? There's a good chance Monroe's full-time Sheriff and part-time Coroner is the one to lose his job. I may be among the unemployed. The Freeholders had to know what he's been doing? How deep does this go? The media will carry this stuff. They'll have to do something. Won't the State Board or Governor care? Probably not. Won't the public?*

Clough looked through some other notations in the folder on the table. Deputy Diaz stood diligently by his side. Blanca was not a person who cried at the drop of a hat, even if multiple hats were dropped. She had a hard time remembering when she last shed a tear – at least one that wasn't of joy for Tyrone.

There were tears on her face now, out of respect for her boss. The Inquest and its significance had gotten to her.

The Deputy's words came quickly. "Sheriff, I've held you in the highest regard for your professionalism, dedication and your class. Ever since your appointment. Today, you have added to that by demonstrating incredible integrity. I'm proud to work for you. Martha Rooney may well feature the testimonies of Rodewald, Fishman and Wildwood in tomorrow's *Jersey Star*, given her preference for sensationalism. Instead, she should put a full photo of you and a caption of *Our Most Honorable Sheriff*."

Arthur Clough wanted to hug his Deputy but not in front of a crowd at the Inquest. Instead, he said softly, "Blanca, my job today was to strip a few layers away from what's been going on and determine how Mr. Kelleher died. We are doing well on the former and getting close to the latter."

Clough put his hand on his Deputy's shoulder to signify his appreciation, before telling her, "Let's bring in Miss Hart and wrap up the testimony. Well, maybe."

Deputy Diaz looked surprised, as Richard Spurling and Alan Fox were still waiting in the Jury Room.

Clough continued. "I do not need Spurling and Fox to testify. Not now. But don't dismiss them. Not yet. Let them sweat. Maybe get some religion. In the weeks to come, we'll deal with them. They'll sweat a great deal more. Better yet, ask the D.A. what he wants to do with them now. Whatever he says is fine."

A few minutes later, Roseanne Hart and Deputy Diaz opened the door as a tandem and marched together down the aisle. Hart looked as if she was about to be pushed out of an airplane, absent a parachute. Diaz looked as if she had had more than enough of escorting witnesses to the Courtroom.

The Personnel Director wore a bright red pullover mohair sweater with a mid-length corduroy skirt. She accented the look with a scarf tied loosely around her neck. She would not wear this look to the office or Sunday church. Too stylish. Too dressy.

The buzz started as soon as the Courtroom folks saw Miss Hart in the doorway: *What does Clough have on her? How could a woman oversee Personnel for a college? I think she may go to my church. Isn't she a spinster. Wonder why she never married? Looks like a new hairdo. Different makeup too. I think I see her from time to time at Monmouth, playing the horses.*

Diaz told her she was the final witness of the day. Yet the Personnel Director had no idea what had been said before or how much she'd be bombarded with questions. Hart was sure she was mentioned in prior testimony and perhaps the brunt of a few incriminating statements. She hoped the Coroner agreed with her that truth was a relative term.

Roseanne Hart walked over to Clough and stood before him uneasily, as if a new employee or an entering freshman student waiting apprehensively for her first assignment. Clough smiled and motioned to her to take a seat on the witness stand.

Coroner	Be reminded, Miss Hart, you're under oath. We expect you to tell the truth here today. Now, please state your full name and position with the College.
Miss Hart	Yes, sir. My name is Miss Roseanne Webster Hart. I am the Director of Personnel for Central Jersey Community College. My mother's maiden name was Webster. I'm not married.
Coroner	Thank you. Is it true you are the College's only female administrator?
Miss Hart	No, not any more. We classified Miss Bartell's position as Exempt from the Union and as Administrative in responsibility and given the confidentiality of her responsibilities. I was the first female administrator. That's typical for colleges and universities these days. Things are changing slowly for women. Very slowly. You'll note there are no women on the Board of Trustees. There was one lady when the founding Board was created. She died within a year and, of course, was replaced by a man.
Coroner	You mentioned Miss Bartell. Were you involved in her search and appointment?
Miss Hart	Yes. Mr. Kelleher asked me to classify the position, post the want ad and review applications. He was determined to get the Foundation in gear. He had been to a resource development convention in Chicago about raising private gifts. Mr. Kelleher kept telling me we had to adopt a new paradigm for

469

	generating gifts. Not sure what he meant. Anyway, he came back thoroughly convinced he wanted to jack everything up here.
Coroner	So how did Miss Bartell get the appointment?
Miss Hart	Miss Bartell applied from her County position. By far, she was the most outstanding candidate. She had good skills in office administration and a unique background to address raising private funds and working directly for a CEO. There were not a ton of applicants. Only six as I recall.
Coroner	Why did not have many applicants?
Miss Hart	Probably due to the dual responsibilities and likely apprehension about being asked to work directly for the President. But then we did not advertise nationally for the position and only posted the opening for that week.
Coroner	Please continue describing the search process.
Miss Hart	Usually we have a Search Committee with six or seven members. That group does the work and makes a recommendation of the final two or three candidates to the supervisor who makes the selection. But, not in this case. As a grant-funded position, we can choose to expedite the searches. You see, once Title III runs its course, we may not continue to fund those jobs. They could still be out of work. We did that for a new Library position also – not have a Search Committee. Just me. And as I said, there were few qualified applicants, other than Miss Bartell. Her work with the County, and her degrees, gave her a considerable advantage in the horse race to the position.

The Coroner looked at Roseanne Hart when she compared the search process to a horse race. That probably was not a wise choice, given that her Saturdays were spent at the race track. He saw a gulp form in Hart's throat. He would let the metaphor go.

Miss Hart	Had there been a candidate with like credentials, I don't know if Mr. Kelleher would have looked at him. But that was not the case.

Coroner	Did President Kelleher hire Miss Bartell as a favor to Commissioner Panichi? Is that why she was hired?
Miss Hart	I have no knowledge of that. She had worked for Mr. Panichi. J. Paul Kelleher created the position. Again, Miss Bartell was and is highly qualified and doing a remarkable job. I have no knowledge of that. This position certainly was a promotion for her. She's ambitious, but because she's a female we find that offensive.
Coroner	Just trying to understand what happened. Miss Hart, is Miss Bartell's position one the College might not continue once Title III runs out?
Miss Hart	That's correct. The College is supposed to assume the burden of absorbing the cost for identified grant-funded positions once the grant runs out. But there is some flexibility. We'll see. Of course, we do not know what the feds would do if we simply ignored that requirement due to cost. Someone else would need to take on the Foundation, and a new President might not want to retain this Executive Assistant position. Who knows?

Miss Hart looked over at Samantha Bartell and smiled. In the months that Bartell had worked at the College, Roseanne had developed a high appreciation of the young lady's skills and contributions. Roseanne had forewarned the new employee about the challenges she'd encounter being a woman in a man's playground. But as time went on, she had no doubt the Executive Assistant to the President could handle anything.

Miss Hart	Mr. Coroner, I have tremendous respect for Miss Bartell. She's an excellent employee. I know she's not received well by the Vice Presidents. They are males, men, guys, little boys really. They wear wing tips and pants, not a skirt and heels. You understand? The norm is this double standard. They're not used to women in leadership positions, in any position other than inferior or subservient to them.
Coroner	Subservient?
Miss Hart	Yes. Miss Bartell is a barrier between them and the President, as Mr. Kelleher wanted. If the new

	President asks, I'll tell him Samantha is a trusted, incredibly competent employee. Frankly, Samantha is one of the best employees on campus, male or female. I knew it the moment I interviewed her, and Mr. Kelleher said he had the same experience when they talked. Like me, she works every day to prove herself. Has to.
Coroner	Are you one of the best, Miss Hart?
Miss Hart	I like to think so. But, Personnel has become hugely litigious. Way too many lawyers in the mix now. Too much litigation. The union negotiations can be so controversial, so confrontational, especially with our Board of Trustees. One side wants everything, and the other wants to give nothing. The pressure can be overwhelming. I'm probably in the same boat as Samantha in terms of being unpopular on campus.
Coroner	Why is that?
Miss Hart	That may be because I'm doing my job damn well. Mr. Kelleher thought I was, and I take pride in that. He told me that when I was hired, the Search Committee was split on whether to interview a woman for Personnel Director. Mr. Kelleher heard that and told them to interview me. Had they had a reasonably qualified male, even if less experienced, that guy might have gotten the job. Sometimes, Mr. Clough, even in my own office, I get mistaken for a clerk or secretary, just because I'm a woman. A new employee will come to the office to complete the paperwork and ask me if I can get him a cup of coffee or sharpen a pencil. I'm probably known less on campus for my accomplishments than for my middle-aged ass!
Coroner	I certainly hope not. This next one is a personal question, Miss Hart. Would you comment on your relationship with Bill Fishman? He mentioned it during his testimony regarding where he was the night of the President's death.
Miss Hart	Mr. Fishman and I have recently started dating. Nothing more. Office relationships are not usually the smartest, but we're both single, not so young and

	looking for companionship. There's no Board Policy on employee dating or on nepotism. Regardless, I don't report to Mr. Fishman. No, I report to Dr. Dandridge. Bill has no say in my employment, my salary, raises or evaluations. He has no say in where my office is on campus, whether I even have an office, or when I go to lunch or when I choose to go to the bathroom.
Coroner	Point made. That's all fine. What about his statement that you and he were together after the Board Meeting? Understand Miss Hart, we've had testimony that you were among the last, if not the very last, person to be with Mr. Kelleher the night he died.
Miss Hart	Bill asked me to say that he was with me after we left the Board Meeting. That was not the case, I'm sorry to say. I hope he did not say that. I like Bill, but I cannot lie under oath. I was hoping you would not ask me that question.
Coroner	Sorry, but Mr. Fishman did say you and he were together after the meeting. He also offered that you had falsified some travel records, but such was no big deal. We'll see. However, some of the business contracts he's had in the past could be incriminating. We'll investigate those. He likely covered up several misdeeds other than what you might have done. They were far more serious and more career-destroying. Why did he want you to lie about his whereabouts after the Board Meeting?
Miss Hart	He was worried that since he was there in the Board Room at the end, you'd connect him to the murder. He can be manipulative, I have found out.
Coroner	Manipulative in what way?
Miss Hart	He's good at putting people in a corner in which the only way out is through the crooked door he creates. Off-kilter may be a better description. I'm so sorry about all of this. I did not know. I should have been smarter, especially in my position at the College.
Coroner	Thank you. Let's move on. Dr. Pitman said it was just him and you in Kelleher's office after the Board Meeting. That correct?

Miss Hart	If I can remember correctly, I was talking with President Kelleher in his office. When I left, Dr. Pitman came in. I left the building, so I don't know how long he was there or indeed why he was there. He did not look happy. Harrison had been there earlier, so had Gene Wildwood.
Coroner	Dr. Pitman said he left first and walked out with Mr. Harrison. He said you were still there when he left.
Miss Hart	That's not how I remember it. I was waiting for him to finish his conversation with Mr. Kelleher. I waited for them in the Board Room, respecting their privacy. I could hear Pitman shout but not what words he used.
Coroner	You couldn't hear what they were discussing?
Miss Hart	No, sir. After Dr. Pitman left, somewhat in a huff, I went into the President's Office. We talked for several minutes. President Kelleher was drinking his whiskey, sipping it slowly. It was his second or third glass, but he didn't seem to be enjoying it like he usually does.
Coroner	What else?
Miss Hart	Mr. Kelleher looked to be in pain. Kept rubbing his neck and fingering his temples. He wouldn't say what the shouting was about. Mostly, I was concerned about his health.
Coroner	Miss Hart, you probably don't know, but Mr. Kelleher was suffering from a malignant brain tumor. He was taking injections of Morphine for the pain but only had a couple more months to live when he died.
Miss Hart	Oh, my God. I should have known. He'd lost weight. It showed on his face. He said he hadn't slept well lately and was having difficulty eating because of his throat. He told me he was losing his appetite anyway. Frankly, I thought his health had to do with the smoking, not that he had terminal cancer. How awful. I'm so sorry, Mrs. Kelleher. I wish I'd known. I'm the Personnel Director, I should have pressed him about his health.
Coroner	Did you ever see Mr. Kelleher inject himself with the drug?

Miss Hart	Of course not.
Coroner	Let's get back to the meeting or at the end. When you met with the President, had Dr. Pitman left?
Miss Hart	Dr. Pitman was out in the hall, much to my surprise. He didn't say anything to me, and I do not know if he went back into Mr. Kelleher's office. He may have been waiting there for Mr. Harrison. They were chummy all evening about something. Very distracting to the meeting, to be frank.
Coroner	What else did you and Mr. Kelleher talk about?
Miss Hart	Mr. Kelleher told me he was aware of my gambling. I probably let it slip a few times that I liked the track or used some stupid horse race metaphors. He didn't know about the travel money, or at least said nothing. He looked very pale and drawn.
Coroner	Anything else you two talked about? Anything that would give us a glimpse into his state of mind at that point in the evening?
Miss Hart	Hard to say. There was a sense of resignation, not in what he said or even what we talked about. More in his demeanor. He always kept that bathroom door closed and locked. He never used to do that. Staff could use it if they were in a meeting in the Board Room, or at least the men did. That stopped in June. We all noticed it. Now that I know about the cancer, I presume he didn't want anyone to see his medications. But, the bathroom door was open that night. Others would have noticed that too.
Coroner	Tell us more of your impressions of Mr. Kelleher.
Miss Hart	J. Paul wasn't a very emotional guy. He did not allow his emotions to consume him. He was shrewd. It's been weeks, maybe months since he jogged around campus. That used to be a terrific experience for him early in the morning. Then as others probably told you, after his run he'd shower in that bathroom and finish dressing in his office. I thought it was strange the first couple of times I would be in there or in the Board Room for a meeting. He was never indecent. Certainly not lewd. He'd have his shirt untucked and

	a tie hanging around his neck. Then our President would buff his shoes – polish, shoeshine brush and a rag. I often thought he might soon have a big hold in the toe of the damn shoe from over-polishing or even start a fire due to the friction.
Coroner	That was not how Dr. Greenleaf was?
Miss Hart	Dr. Greenleaf would never be seen in public without a shirt and tie. Greenleaf wore a suit to everything. We used to say behind his back that he probably cut his grass in a three-piece suit. Had he overheard that comment, I imagine he would be flattered, except he had someone else cut his grass.
Coroner	You said the Executive Bathroom door was not closed the evening of the Board Meeting, Miss Hart?
Miss Hart	It was open, at least more open than closed. The light was on too, if that matters. Mr. Kelleher did not go into the bathroom while I was there.
Coroner	Did you finish what you wanted to say during your time with him that evening?
Miss Hart	Yes, except that I told him I admired how he handled the Board on the architect selection and on the purchase agreement for the additional media equipment.
Coroner	What did he say? Did he sound appreciative or what?
Miss Hart	His mind was on Dr. Pitman whom he had just talked with, although not in a worried sense. More out of confidence, as in glad to have gotten that over with. Confrontations did not bother J. Paul. He would not back off from *King Kong* and *Attila the Hun*.
Coroner	Just one more thing, Miss Hart. What time did you leave his office that evening?
Miss Hart	It had to be close to midnight. I asked J. Paul if he was leaving soon. He said as soon as he finished that drink. But the way he was lingering, Mr. Coroner, he might have stayed longer.
Coroner	What do you mean?
Miss Hart	Gee Whiz. I think he was soaking up the satisfaction that he had made it through another Board Meeting while keeping his sanity. You have no idea how crappy

	Board Meetings can be. We have a drink to unwind, to celebrate that we got through another Board Meeting.
Coroner	What then happened?
Miss Hart	The bottle of the *Bushmills* was still on his desk. He hadn't finished the drink in his hand. But Mr. Kelleher was alive after midnight. He didn't look very well, but he was very much alive. As I said, he looked satisfied, relieved, pleased with himself. So sorry the cancer did him in.
Coroner	You may have gotten the wrong impression. Mr. Kelleher had cancer and was taking Morphine. We have not yet determined that he died of cancer. That we have yet to determine.

Arthur Clough looked satisfied with how Hart had described Kelleher in his last few hours before he died early that morning of October 20th. He smiled at her in a genuine sign of appreciation.

"Thank you very much, Miss Hart. I do hope the College can manage compassion for what you did about the travel monies, given your testimony here today. You may leave the witness stand, but I ask you to remain in the Courtroom."

Clough went back to his binder after assisting Roseanne Hart from the stand. She knew her intimate relationship with Bill Fishman had run its course. If Fishman stayed on the job, let alone became President, it would be time to look for another position at another male-dominated organization, likely one far from a racetrack. If he was fired, she'd have to play it by ear.

In her mind she told herself: *Fun while it lasted. But I learned I can be attractive. I'm a good lookin' dame. Not sure I want to work here any longer anyway. Let the new President pick his personnel person.*

The Coroner faced the audience, took a deep breath and said, "Ladies and gentlemen, it's now 4:45 PM. I plan to call a couple of people back to testify after we take a deserved break. We are getting close to the end, believe it or not."

Some of the folks started to stand to leave, but Clough earnestly motioned them to remain seated. "Let me finish, please. At the end, after all the testimony, I will provide the Summation of my findings. At that time, I will rule on the official Cause of Death before adjourning this proceeding. Please be back in this Courtroom in twenty-minutes. I can't promise, but we should be able to complete the Inquest by 6:00 PM, or a few minutes past. Thank you for your patience."

With that statement, everyone stood and slowly made a beeline for the exit, except Roseanne Hart who headed over to where Mrs. Kelleher was now standing.

"Izzy, I'm so sorry I did not stay longer in his office that night," Hart said. "I didn't know about the cancer. I should have stuck around to see what Pitman and Harrison would say or do. And I never should have told Bill Fishman I would support his alibi at the Inquest. If I'd stayed longer, your husband might be alive today."

"Roseanne, you don't need to apologize," Mrs. Kelleher responded. "If indeed my husband was murdered, Mr. Clough now has a good idea of who was there at the end, and who wasn't there. My guess is he already knows who did it. It may be a question of who is the more evil. Who's most evil. There are several candidates."

"There certainly are," echoed Hart.

THE INQUEST – SESSION 6

You never know a line is crooked
unless you have a straight one to put next to it.
Socrates

The Courtroom emptied for the break. Arthur Clough was the last person to leave. He found Dr. David Charles in the lobby and went over to where he was standing with Dr. Carter and Dr. and Mrs. Feldman. "David," he said, "I need you to explain a few things from the witness stand when we get back in there. I'll call you as soon as we return to order. It shouldn't take too long."

Clough motioned for Dr. Charles to move away from the others, so he could speak to him alone along the opposite wall. "David, do you have any change of mind given what the witnesses have admitted and the lies? Any different thoughts from what we talked about?"

"None whatsoever, Arthur," Dr. Charles said. "I'm amazed at much of the testimony. I can better appreciate why President Kelleher wanted to continue working as long as he could. But I'm still troubled he chose not to tell his wife or kids about the cancer. She obviously loved him, and he loved her from what he shared. But he was resolute that no one know about the cancer. Maybe they were not close in a lovey-dovey way or like married couples are portrayed on television, but there were genuine feelings. Sometimes we adults have dubious ways of acting. At least, we husbands do."

Dr. Charles saw Deputy Diaz walking directly toward them from the opposite end of the foyer, but he wanted to complete his comments to Clough. "Arthur, I guess you and your Deputy will be busy for a while investigating perjury and these Courtroom admissions. You'll be like hungry crocodiles when the zebra and wildebeest herds cross the Serengeti River."

"Thank you, David," Clough said, as he too saw Diaz walking toward him. "Let me spend a few minutes with my Deputy and sort my notes before we finish in there. I appreciate that you stayed and can testify further."

"I'm keeping you hopping today, Blanca," Clough said as he noticed she was breathing hard. "All part of my new office exercise program."

"I sure could stand to lose a few pounds, so keep it up," Diaz replied, exaggerating her panting. "Anyone you want me to call now? Hughes, Fishman and others are being held in custody for the time being, as per the District Attorney. Sally Bowens' waiting in the D.A.'s outer office. The D.A. is taking statements from those subject to perjury charges. I did tell Fox he could leave. I know we can't do much about his romantic classroom antics, as disgusting as they are. Was he ever mad. It was a busy morning and afternoon for criminal justice in little Monroe County."

"Blanca," Clough said to his Deputy looking her straight in the eyes, "I plan to call Mr. Jackson to witness and bring back Dr. Charles before I provide the Summation. Don't fret. I just want Tyrone to confirm a few things. I could have done that earlier, but it will be fresher on people's minds to do now. Go and alert Chief Jackson. He'll be a big help to the cause. He knows that."

"Much of what you do is in your presentation, isn't that so, Sheriff?" Diaz asked, knowing full well the answer. "Your skill at throwing witnesses off-balance is remarkable. You must have had a wicked change-up when you were a baseball pitcher in high school. I'm glad I'm on your side."

Clough chuckled for a moment and then said, "I didn't have a change-up. That was my fastball, but I did have a tough curveball. Lots of swings and misses, that is until I screwed up my arm. I like that approach in the Courtroom. Swing and a miss!"

The Coroner continued, "Deputy, an Inquest is a time of discovery – unmasking. Some we uncover. Some we highlight, as if we just discovered it. Make sense?"

Then Clough got philosophical. "The derivative Latin word is *Inquirere*, which means *thing inquired into, asked about or examined*. I know that much thanks to my high school Latin teacher, Mr. O'Connor. The only other thing I can claim to remember from Mr. O'Connor's Latin class is *Romulus and Remus*, those twins raised by a wolf who somehow founded Rome. If pressed, I can conjugate Amo. That's Latin for love."

"I'll try to remember that, Sheriff," Diaz said with a smirk. "Mr. O'Connor would be proud. I took English classes in high school. I mastered Spanish when I was just a kid. Funny? Funny, me. Heh, Mr. Clough, is this a good time to ask for a raise, given all this new investigative work?"

"There's no good time to ask for a raise, but I think you've earned it," said Clough. "Your Crime Scene work was impeccable. If you hadn't made so many photos of those damn shoes and that open desk drawer, I might not have found the false bottom and notebook. In the meantime, I need to figure out a higher-sounding, more laudatory title for you. How does Associate Sheriff or Deputy Chief sound? Colonel or General Sheriff has a nice ring to it. I could support Undersheriff except for the weird connotations that might bring to others. How about Sergeant Major Diaz or Major Sergeant Diaz? Anyway, you decide and let me know. We could go with Corporal Captain, like *Radar O'Reilly* from MASH."

Clough turned to head back to the Courtroom, as Diaz stood, not knowing if the Sheriff was pulling her leg or alerting her to a promotion. She did know her boss was about to put on a show with the final questions and his official Summation.

At 5:15 PM sharp, Deputy Diaz closed the Courtroom doors. She nudged the last three people through the door. Hurriedly, she looked up at Clough to signify he could call the Inquest back in session.

"Ladies and gentlemen," the Corner said, "I call Mr. Tyrone Jackson, the College's Chief of Security, to come to the witness stand. We did not issue Mr. Jackson a subpoena, but he's been most conscientious in working with our office. I asked him to be here. He can add information I'd like in the record."

Tyrone Jackson stood up, buttoned his Security blazer and straightened his tie, not the new one Blanca had given him for his birthday. This had to be the uniform tie. Blanca and his daughter, Crystal, were alike in their desire to sharpen dad's wardrobe. It was a challenge.

Jackson had appreciated the heads-up he'd received from Blanca about testifying. He had understood the Coroner would call upon him at some point in the Inquest. He was ready and knew the line of questioning.

Coroner	Mr. Jackson, please take the oath: *Do you solemnly swear, that the testimony you are about to give in this Inquest is the truth, the whole truth and nothing but the truth, so help you, God?*
Mr. Jackson	Yes, I certainly do, Mr. Clough. It's my privilege to testify in this proceeding.
Coroner	I asked you to bring the Security Log for October 19 through October 20, the night before and the day Mr. Kelleher died in his office. I see you have it, so tell us the routine and your relevant notations.
Mr. Jackson	Yes, sir. We have a drive around the campus during the night – several times. We cover most buildings that way, although not every building each time. We do that every hour or so, altering the pattern. We check the premises on foot every two to three hours between 22:00 and 06:00 hours, sorry 10 PM to 6 AM, on a staggered basis. We make sure every building is locked, every exit door secure. We walk

	the halls in the evening before the third shift comes on duty and check doors. There are two people for our late-night shift. At 06:00, the morning shift starts, and we open the buildings.
Coroner	What about the Board Room?
Mr. Jackson	When the Board of Trustees has a meeting, we do not lock the Administration Building until everyone is out. Our records show the lights were still on in the Board Room at midnight and thereafter. There was still light in the President's Office, but since he has a key to the building, we locked the Administration Building about the 00:30 hour, or 12:30 AM.
Coroner	Is it unusual for Mr. Kelleher to be in his office that late, after a Board Meeting?
Mr. Jackson	Not really. Most days, he leaves the building about 19:00 hours, that is 7 PM. Sometimes later. When there's a Board Meeting, it's much later. It's not unusual for him to be at his office after midnight those nights.
Coroner	Does he always stay that late, 7 PM?
Mr. Jackson	No, that wasn't the case five months ago. Then he left promptly at 6 PM. He told me he liked to get home in time to catch the NBC news. Actually, we had an office wager that he'd leave within five minutes of 18:00 hours each day for a month. Those who bet against that lost money.
Coroner	What about Board Meetings?
Mr. Jackson	Most Board Meetings last until at least 22:30 hours, sorry 10:30 PM. Some closer to 11. Most end up with people lingering in the room, the hallway or the balcony afterwards.
Coroner	What about Mr. Kelleher being alone in his office?
Mr. Jackson	Regarding the morning of October 20, when you said he died, the records say there were lights in the office and Board Room until at least 01:15 hour. The book then shows the light was off on the next drive around at 2:35 AM.
Coroner	Thank you, Mr. Jackson. Based on your records, we can conclude that the lights in the office and

	Board Room were extinguished by Mr. Kelleher or by someone else, between 1:15 and 2:35 AM.
Mr. Jackson	That would be pretty accurate.
Coroner	Mr. Jackson, was the President's car in the parking lot all night?
Mr. Jackson	The log doesn't record that, but I asked the guy who made the drive around that morning. He said the car was there. Likely all night. It's in a highly visible space. The parking lot lights go off just after midnight, but his space is observable because of the street lights. We check cars left in the student and faculty lots after the campus closes. They may be abandoned cars, for one reason or another. Some faculty and staff car-pool, so we don't concentrate much on those lots overnight. A single car or two in that lot would not be suspicious. Oh, that's right, Mr. Winters' car was in his assigned space when the lights went off where he parks. We did not make a note if it was still there in the morning. If there were cars left in the other lots that night, we did not make a note of them.
Coroner	It's not that important. We've already established President Kelleher did not come home that night. He spent the night at the College. He never left. He was dead in his office between the hours of 1 AM and 3 AM, as per Dr. Charles. That coincides with when the lights were on and then off. Are there any other notations from that night relevant to this Inquest?
Mr. Jackson	Not really. The Administrative Building was locked just after midnight. That means Mr. Kelleher and others could still have been in the building. It also means no one could get in after then without the key.
Coroner	Who has the building key?
Mr. Jackson	The only persons with keys to the external locks are Mr. Kelleher, Mr. Fishman, Miss Hart, Dr. Dandridge, Mr. Spurling and Edith Reynolds. Oh, Samantha Bartell has a key now too, as does Gene Wildwood since Mr. Tucker's no longer with us.
Coroner	Do you have any reason to suspect that others have a key?

Mr. Jackson	Well, it would be simple to make a copy. There's no protection against that. The external doors would be hard to pick, and there were no signs of forcible entry. Others could have a key, yes. Our employees sign a form that they will not duplicate keys, but it's impossible to enforce.
Coroner	You were at the Board Meeting that night?
Mr. Jackson	Yes, President Kelleher wanted me at every Board Meeting. I did not know he had cancer and was suffering. I wish I had known.
Coroner	What did you do after the meeting?
Mr. Jackson	I went back to the Security Office after most of those in attendance had left when the meeting adjourned. I signed out and headed home. By the time I left, it was close to midnight. I did not go past the Administration Building, but I did see Mr. Lieber drive out ahead of me. He appeared to be alone in his car.
Coroner	You sure it was him, his car?
Mr. Jackson	Absolutely. He drives a powder blue Cadillac De Ville. Hard to mistake.
Coroner	Anything unusual about that Board Meeting?
Mr. Jackson	Just that Mr. Harrison and Dr. Pitman did a lot of whispering and seemingly mocking what was going on. They were very rude. Everyone noticed it. Mr. Kelleher somehow kept a straight face. Had it been me, I would have thrown something at them!
Coroner	That does it, Mr. Jackson. Once again, thank you for your support in this investigation. You and your staff at the College have demonstrated a high level of professionalism and competence. You may step down.

Tyrone Jackson stepped away from the witness stand and scanned the room to find where Deputy Diaz was standing. She moved around the room. He caught her eyes and affectionate smile as he walked back to where he had been sitting next to Jack Kula.

Arthur Clough decided to clear-up one other matter, so he looked for Jack Kula. "Mr. Kula, would you kindly take the stand? I got what I needed from you during my investigation, but I have another topic brought up earlier. I would like your testimony."

Attorney Kula rose confidently. As an attorney in a Courtroom, he felt as comfortable as a seasoned football coach on the field for a big game or an executive chef preparing exquisite dishes in a commercial restaurant. He took the witness stand, as Mr. Clough stood before him to administer the oath.

Coroner	Mr. Kula, I present the oath: *Do you solemnly swear, that the testimony you are about to give in this Inquest is the truth, the whole truth and nothing but the truth, so help you, God?*
Mr. Kula	Yes, I do. How can I help?
Coroner	Thank you. You are an attorney with the Triano, Orr and Kula law firm and as such you represent the College. Is that correct?
Mr. Kula	Yes sir. Our firm has handled the legal matters for the College since it was founded. I have served as lead person the past six years.
Coroner	First, I want to acknowledge your exceptional contributions to my investigation. Having said that, Mr. Kula, I have one area of questioning.
Mr. Kula	Yes, sir.
Coroner	Chairman Pitman has raised questions about Mr. Kelleher's contract. He said the Board could terminate the President with a simple majority vote. Please affirm that statement or provide testimony to the contrary.
Mr. Kula	I'd be glad to do so. I wrote the contract. Mr. Kelleher had what we call a Rolling Three-Year Contract. Accordingly, at the end of every year, unless the Board decides otherwise by conscious action, the contract adds that third year. If they had taken proper action at the June meeting, the last month of the fiscal year, not to renew his contract, he would have the two remaining years at full salary. If they do not act, the renewal of that third year is automatic.
Coroner	It would need to be a conscious act of the Board – to not renew.
Mr. Kula	Absolutely. He would still be President for these remaining two years at full salary. But, Mr. Kelleher

	could not be dismissed unless by cause, that is moral turpitude.
Coroner	There has to be a specific cause. What's an example of moral turpitude?
Mr. Kula	Turpitude means a vile, corrupt or depraved act, such as assault, forgery, robbery or commission of a heinous crime. Moral turpitude just means that the behavior shocks the public conscience. Stealing money from the College would qualify, as would deliberate falsification of key reports.
Coroner	There is an explicit legal definition for what constitutes a cause?
Mr. Kula	That's correct. What the Board Chairman offered earlier as reasons on why he and Harrison wanted to fire Kelleher – namely the architect selection, those media equipment purchases and reassigning a staff member – would not qualify under that definition.
Coroner	The Board Chairman was wrong about that?
Mr. Kula	Absolutely. Further, and most important to your inquiry, Mr. Coroner, is that the contract includes language that the Board must have a two-thirds majority vote to fire the President, no matter the charge or cause presented. That translates into a minimum of five of the seven members, with the Chairman expected to vote. If the Chairman abstains, they still need five votes in favor.
Coroner	So, contrary to what Dr. Pitman testified and said he told Kelleher, four votes would not get him fired or not renew his contract. And there was no legitimate cause?
Mr. Kula	That's exactly right. Dr. Pitman may not have been aware of the contract. That seems unlikely since he's been Chairman through two Presidents. Plus, I meet with the Trustees at that annual meeting to present the President's contract, which is a legal document. More likely, Pitman tried to pressure Kelleher, intimidate him to resign.
Coroner	Mr. Kelleher would not have resigned?

Mr. Kula	No way Mr. Kelleher would just walk away from his contract. Why would he walk away from the rest of his salary? Even with the cancer.
Coroner	Mr. Kelleher was well-informed about his contract?
Mr. Kula	Be assured, J. Paul Kelleher knew every clause and codicil in his contract. If indeed, Dr. Pitman had that conversation that night in Kelleher's office, as he testified today, Kelleher most assuredly did not flinch. There's no way President Kelleher would bend or panic, given he knew exactly what was in the contract. The President held the cards for whatever game Pitman wanted to play. If Pitman was trying to bluff, he picked the wrong man and the wrong hand. Kelleher had four aces. Pitman didn't even have a pair of deuces. On second thought, he had a pair of *jokers* – Harrison and himself.

Clough turned away to hide his smile at Kula's attempt at humor. He thought: *These guys were jokers all right.*

Coroner	You may be right. I don't play cards much. But to be clear, if the Board had voted at the October meeting to release Mr. Kelleher's contract, they would have had to continue his employment and salary until June 30, 1980. That's over two and a half more years. Correct?
Mr. Kula	That's correct. They could not demand that he vacate the office, let alone walk away from the money he would be owed. There's one other major provision we need to clarify for the record.
Coroner	What's that Mr. Kula?
Mr. Kula	Had the Board approved the termination for cause, the State Board Rules provide that a President is entitled to a hearing before the Board of Chosen Freeholders.
Coroner	Would it be a public meeting, with the Press present?
Mr. Kula	Yes, the Board could go into Executive Session to get legal opinion and reach consensus on their position. But any motion and all votes, even the discussion on

	each motion, would have to be in a public session and a roll-call vote. With the Press in the room, the Board of Trustees would have to present its rationale, its reason for the motion.
Coroner	Why would that be?
Mr. Kula	The justification would have to be substantiated. They simply can't put in the Board minutes that they voted to fire the guy based on his hair color or that he upset someone. His failure to yield in the architect selection would not be justifiable cause.
Coroner	Would the President be able to say anything at the meeting?
Mr. Kula	President Kelleher would be permitted to offer evidence to challenge the justification and provide a defense, including documents that showed the Board had supported him. Can you imagine how the Press would have covered that hearing when the reason for the termination vote was identified as the ridiculous architect selection? Imagine, sir, the embarrassment of the Board members when President Kelleher presents the past three years of documented evaluations? All very positive.
Coroner	So what alternative did the Board have?
Mr. Kula	The only reasonable alternative would have been to buy out his contract. That still takes five votes. That would have generated considerable interest from the *Jersey Star*, too, and cost a great deal of money. I can't see the Board doing that. The amount, depending on when they vote, would be at least $115,000, plus accrued benefits, like his unused leave. The cost would be closer to $150,000.
Coroner	That's a great deal of money.
Mr. Kula	Yes, but Mr. Kelleher could negotiate the release of his contract and demand other benefits such as additional years in the retirement system. Probably continued use of the car too. As you know, he's pretty damn good at negotiating.
Coroner	Is that typical? That the President's entitled to a hearing?

Mr. Kula	Absolutely, except for South Carolina, Alabama and one more state I can't recall. They are *At Will* states. That's a sloppy euphemism for ongoing political intrusiveness and intimidation. In those states, the Board can demand a president hire their relatives or award contracts to buddies or even do something immoral, likely illegal. If he doesn't do what they direct him to do, they just fire the guy. No public hearing. No opportunity for the sorry president to defend himself against the charge and the purported reasons. Plus, there is no public disclosure. Nothing. Those states are protecting cronyism. That's all. Protecting their corrupt will, not the people's will.
Coroner	True. Sounds more like the provision should be called *At Whim*.
Mr. Kula	They tend to hire presidents not based on an exceptional resume or competence but because they know someone and play the same political games. What experienced, credentialed administrative talent would want to be president at a college in those states?
Coroner	Not many.
Mr. Kula	Mr. Clough, here's what the *At Will* really stands for: *We don't want to tell the public why we fired this person, because we can't justify it. But then we don't want to tell the public why we hired him, either.*
Coroner	Does this New Jersey contract provision extend to other employees?
Mr. Kula	Yes, sir. All College employees, all New Jersey County employees, on annual or multi-year contract have the same right. Why should the president be different? It opens the door for meddling, under the ignorant and misguided pretense that the Board should be able to fire anyone. That never serves the public well.
Coroner	Was Mr. Tucker entitled to a hearing when he left the College.
Mr. Kula	Howard Tucker chose to resign rather than be fired. That was an option given to him. Theoretically, had the Board had leverage over President Kelleher, he could have resigned. Recall that there was documentation

	regarding Mr. Tucker's drinking in his office, and there were performance evaluations. He had been given a written warning.
Coroner	Hard to believe Dr. Pitman wasn't aware of the contract provision – did not know that there would have to be legitimate reasons for the Board to act.
Mr. Kula	I would agree. I expect he knew. I would be sure he knew.
Coroner	What do you know about Chairman Pitman having another attorney?
Mr. Kula	Well, Dr. Pitman did say that he had his own lawyer. According to the State Board Rules which govern community colleges, the Board must select a firm to handle legal matters. That company provides the legal advice to the Board and, upon request, to the President. If Dr. Pitman was getting other legal advice, as he says, there would be no standing for that attorney.
Coroner	Would another attorney from your firm represent the Board?
Mr. Kula	Mr. Clough, there's no way another attorney from our firm would ever handle the Board, under any circumstances, without clearing same with me. Furthermore, by the comments Pitman made, he's getting poor advice, whatever the source.
Coroner	Thank you. I guess we'll soon find out if the Board of Chosen Freeholders chooses to discipline the two of them.
Mr. Kula	Let me say something else. Had Mr. Kelleher gone before the Chosen Freeholders in a public session for a hearing on his termination or release of contract, I would have had to be the attorney representing the Board in *CJCC Board of Trustees vs. CJCC President J. Paul Kelleher*. Knowing what I know and embracing the integrity of Kelleher versus what Pitman and Harrison said under oath today, that would have made the hearing a circus. Pitman could have employed someone else, fired me, arguing I chose not to represent the Board. But he would have to

	have Board approval. If he gets that approval, and the Board goes to another law firm, be assured I would have chosen to represent President Kelleher.
Coroner	The College could have two legal firms?
Mr. Kula	That's right. It's possible. However, the College would pay both sets of attorney fees. I would think the other Board members would go nuts. Miss Rooney would have her pet story carried on the national wires and TV's 60 Minutes.

Martha Rooney was still making notes about Pitman's testimony. She perked up when she heard her name and 60 Minutes. Might be another story here, although she never watched the CBS show.

Mr. Smith	Mr. Coroner, may I comment here, sir?
Coroner	Of course, please do. Another sound legal opinion's a good thing.
Mr. Smith	Let me clarify what Mr. Kula has properly said. It would not be possible for the firm of Triano, Orr and Kula to represent both the College, meaning its Board of Trustees and the President. They would be on opposing sides of a legal issue.
Coroner	What would the Board have done?
Mr. Smith	In my opinion, Mr. Kula's firm would support him totally in whatever direction he would choose. That includes abandoning the Board and representing President Kelleher instead. That would have been the case, especially if Jack made his firm aware of the circumstances of the architect selection and other things. The Board would have to terminate Mr. Kula's firm as counsel and then approve a replacement law firm. Good luck with that one. The State Board might step in.
Coroner	Thank you. It appears the Chairman and the Vice Chairman drive the Board. Perhaps they all need a refresher orientation on Boardmanship and a presentation on presidential contracts in New Jersey.
Mr. Kula	Mr. Clough, every year at the reorganization meeting, President Kelleher would present me to the Board.

	This is the June meeting where they elect officers and approve the attorney contract for the next fiscal year. Mr. Kelleher always took time to introduce me. Dr. Greenleaf chose not to. J. Paul wanted the Board to know about this legal resource for him and them. Greenfield preferred to keep the resource silent.
Coroner	Not sure I understand. Why would the Board not want to know about this resource?
Mr. Kula	The Board Chairman and Vice Chairman knew. The others were told but relied on Dr. Pitman. President Kelleher proposed a professional development workshop on legal issues and accountability. I would have conducted it. Gladly. But each time he proposed it, Pitman said it wasn't necessary. The Chairman declared he wasn't about to spend public funds for such trivia. Nevertheless, the State Board recently mandated that Board members participate in a local legal training session every year. Better late than never, I suppose. Kelleher was ahead of his time on that one!
Coroner	Mr. Kula, for the record, could your firm have substituted another attorney for you if the Board requested that? Wouldn't the firm have to honor its contract to represent the College, even if you chose not to?
Mr. Kula	Mr. Coroner, my firm would have told the Board to shove it. No one would have taken the Board attorney role. Our agreement gives us an escape if we determine that representing the client is not in the firm's best interests.
Coroner	So, there's no provision to mandate that you represent the Board?
Mr. Kula	No, sir. We'd have a hell of a time in a court defending a client we can't support. The Partners would decide what to do, but I know these guys. There's no way they'd let me hang out to dry and take a sorry case like that one.
Coroner	Anything else, Mr. Kula?
Mr. Kula	Let me share something else that is pertinent to your questioning.

Coroner	Please do.
Mr. Kula	One of the first things Mr. Kelleher had the Board do when he became President was to establish a formal process for his annual evaluation. By law, Boards must complete a performance appraisal of their president each year in June, before the end of the fiscal year. Yet the State has no prescribed process or even requisite forms. They leave it up to local Boards. For all those years with Dr. Greenleaf, the Board just did a roll-call vote and called that an evaluation.
Coroner	They did not have a formal process?
Mr. Kula	Ironic, isn't it. Mr. Kelleher wanted to have a valid process based on objectives, ratings and written appraisals. He insisted. He had me show various models, and they agreed on the one currently in place.
Coroner	There would be a file in the Personnel office of those evaluations?
Mr. Kula	Of course. Mr. Kelleher's evaluations the past three years were excellent, including the one this June. I know. I facilitated the process. Even Dr. Pitman and Mr. Harrison praised his work. Their signatures are on the document.
Coroner	So, he had positive evaluations and they were documented?
Mr. Kula	Indeed. Know something else. In June, the Board agreed to petition to State Board to grant Mr. Kelleher a salary increase above what the other presidents were to receive.
Coroner	What happened?
Mr. Kula	Whether it was the architect selection, reassigning a local politician's cousin or other things, Pitman changed his tune five-six months ago. So, did Harrison. Nevertheless, Kelleher would have had those documents to support the case that the Board fired him without proper cause.
Coroner	Thank you very much, Mr. Kula. You can step away.

Arthur Clough shook Jack Kula's hand as he walked back to his seat. He opened his binder and withdrew a page with typed notes. Mr. Clough then spoke to the audience, "I now ask Dr. David Charles to re-take the witness stand."

Coroner	Dr. Charles, I have a few follow-up questions from your testimony earlier today. You are still under oath.
Dr. Charles	Certainly.
Coroner	You said the vials of Morphine contain 3 mg. Could Mr. Kelleher have taken the full amount if he desired, rather than a 2 mg. dosage?
Dr. Charles	Yes, he could. However, we have required counseling for patients taking this drug, including all cancer patients. No exceptions. In Mr. Kelleher's case, I felt, and still would argue, even today, that he was the best judge of his pain – when to self-administer and regarding the amount of relief to get from Morphine.
Coroner	Is that unusual? I mean, for the patient to control the meds?
Dr. Charles	That's not unusual for terminal patients before they end up in the hospital. We closely monitor the supply through the hospital's pharmacy. From what your officer gathered from that secret storage area in the bathroom, all the vials were accounted for. None was missing.
Coroner	Do you know if any of the returned vials were empty, suggesting that Mr. Kelleher took a greater dose?
Dr. Charles	The vial would be contaminated then, so probably not.
Coroner	Then please describe the process by which Dr. Kelleher would take his Morphine and how this would affect his body.
Dr. Charles	When Mr. Kelleher took the syringe and injected his arm, either arm, he would have had a few minutes before the medication would begin to dull his senses and diminish the pain. We advise our patients to take the medication before the pain becomes acute.
Coroner	Why is that?
Dr. Charles	Because there is a much greater likelihood that the patient will have a problem with the injection or will make a mistake.

Coroner	Thank you. Please proceed in describing the process.
Dr. Charles	As you know, there were needle marks in veins in his arms. Nowhere else. Because of the injection, it takes less time for the blood to reach the brain and initiate the effect. The blood enters the heart on the right side, which pumps it to the lungs, back to the heart on the left side and finally to the brain.
Coroner	Where would he complete the injections?
Dr. Charles	Could have been anywhere but from what you discovered, we know Mr. Kelleher kept the used syringes and empty medicine vials in the towel dispenser. Likely he chose to complete the Morphine injections there, in complete privacy. He would have placed the used meds inside the dispenser, closed the door and left the bathroom. I understand the door locked automatically if he pushed the thumb lock.

> May an Irish angel remove his hat and rest his weary feet beside your door.
> *Irish Leprechaun*

| Coroner | Let's talk about the alcohol consumption. We know he used old-fashioned glasses. That's what he kept in his office. Those glasses hold approximately 10 ounces. We were told he had at least three glasses of the 80-proof Irish Whiskey. With two fingers full, I'd estimate he ingested about 5 ounces per drink which would mean about 15 ounces of the whiskey. Perhaps more. Presumably, he did not ingest any food during this period. That's more alcohol than his body can successfully process in the time period. |
| Dr. Charles | The presence of the alcohol in his system sped-up the process, maybe caused him to black out. Plus, he would have experienced significant respiratory distress. The alcohol would have had a physical impact. The two are chemically reactive. Since, as you say, he could not process all of it in that time period, the excess would have flowed to the heart. That would lower his blood pressure. |

Coroner	Let's change the subject, Dr. Charles. From your studies, what's the presence of mind of those with terminal cancer regarding suicide?
Dr. Charles	Everyone's different. There's a definite escalation of guilt when the cancer goes from potentially or definitively curable, to that of eligible for surgery or chemotherapy and then to incurable. There's further acceleration of guilt when the diagnosis is death in a year or less, as in Mr. Kelleher's case.
Coroner	Why is that, Dr. Charles?
Dr. Charles	The patient feels burdened because he knows he can't fully take care of himself. Such reaction is only a matter of time. Strangely, they're not able to accept that their loved ones may welcome the neediness and embrace the opportunity to care for them. That's probably something we doctors should study more. Men are worse on this than women.
Coroner	Why the guilt?
Dr. Charles	Guilt is a feeling of blame. Could they have noticed the symptoms earlier? Now I'll be a burden to my family. Did my lifestyle choices contribute to the disease? Did I pass it on to my offspring? These are just some of the thoughts. Some terminal patients internalize the cancer's their fault. It's hard to let that go.
Coroner	Would you say that such was likely part of what was going on in President Kelleher's mind?
Dr. Charles	I expect so. Some cancer patients feel anger or resentment. They ask, why me? That was not J. Paul Kelleher. Let me also say, Mr. Clough, we don't know the health relationship between smoking and cancer, especially of the brain. Mr. Kelleher was a heavy smoker.
Coroner	Yes, he was. Mrs. Kelleher said he had cut back from three to two packs a day about the time he learned of his cancer. We can't be sure.
Dr. Charles	Smoking is certainly not a healthy habit, but we have no definitive studies that link smoking to heart or lung disease, let alone to cancer. The big tobacco

	companies argue there's no correlation. I thought it was a major event when the country adopted a ban on TV broadcast advertising about six years ago. I hear the Beverly Cinema no longer permits smoking during its movies, and I think that manufacturers now have to include a warning label on cigarette packs.
Coroner	Yes, it says *Smoking can damage your health*. But it's only a warning. Wouldn't scare people who smoke.
Dr. Charles	Ironically, his lungs were clear, but there was some damage to the throat. We cannot say that the smoking contributed to his death, if indeed there was no foul play.

The Coroner looked away for a moment. His thoughts remained on the suffering President Kelleher had to have experienced, being torn between his declining health, his job responsibilities and his family. The more Clough had investigated the case, and now the more he learned from testimony, the more he felt he could get into Kelleher's mind those last few weeks.

Coroner	Mr. Kelleher loathed the prospect of being a burden to his family and others. Would that be sufficient cause to take his own life, or speed along the dying process?
Dr. Charles	Who knows? At that extreme, one's guilt becomes pathological. I don't think Mr. Kelleher would allow himself to go to the extreme. He had things he wanted to address, to accomplish. He wanted to work until the end. Past the point when most patients would have abandoned their work due to the pain and side effects.
Coroner	We found a supply of the syringes and vials in just that one place – his office bathroom. Is it unusual for a patient to have one cache of the meds, especially when dealing with acute pain as Mr. Kelleher was?
Dr. Charles	Probably, but not in this case. Mr. Kelleher worked long hours. As much as he did not want his wife to know, he was likely more guarded with his sons. They are teen boys, with busy lives, so they probably didn't notice dad was ill and in pain. My observation is that

	he took the pain killer before he went home at night and then early in the AM at the office.
Coroner	What about the weekends?
Dr. Charles	If you ask Mrs. Kelleher, I imagine he told her he needed to go to the campus on Saturday and Sunday or run an errand. J. Paul told me that he and his wife had separate bedrooms those last months, giving him more privacy.
Coroner	Yes, that is what Mrs. Kelleher told me too. She thought it was because of the coughing and him not sleeping well.
Dr. Charles	I expect he asked her for it, not as spousal rejection.

The Coroner glanced over at Izzy Kelleher who had her eyes firmly closed. She knew that she had overplayed rejection as the reason for the separate bedrooms.

Coroner	What about when he wasn't on campus?
Dr. Charles	Mr. Kelleher may have hidden a couple of the vials in his briefcase for the weekend or an emergency. He may have disguised the vials and needles. All his vials were there, even the last two weeks with what we found in the towel dispenser. He looked to be very diligent in his dosages. If he did take vials home, he placed them back in that towel dispenser to return to us. All were accounted for.
Coroner	Thank you, Dr. Charles. You may step away.

Arthur Clough had completed questioning on the death of Mr. J. Paul Kelleher, President of Central Jersey Community College. Thirteen witnesses provided testimony during the Inquest. Several testified unwillingly. A few ignored the oath they had made and veered from the truth. Others offered crooked responses, setting in motion subsequent investigations of wrong doing outside the Courthouse and of perjury inside it. All that work would keep the Sheriff's Office busy for months, assuming the politicians did not decide he had uncovered too much of a good thing.

While wearing the Sheriff's hat, Clough had found the President's private notebook in a hidden desk drawer. He had found the President's Morphine vials and the hypodermic needles concealed on a make-shift shelf inside a paper towel dispenser. How would the Inquest have gone had he not made those discoveries? But he had.

He could thank Mr. Kelleher, posthumously – for his observations and disclosures. Few others would. More likely, the community, certainly Board members and politicians, would curse the dead President for the betrayals. That was a shame.

The Coroner was pleased he had tip-toed successfully through awkward question-and-answer moments where he had revealed suspicious relationships and phony alibis. He was equally delighted he had honored the private and irrelevant connections of others during the Inquest. There was no need to divulge that the County Commissioner and the President's Executive Assistant were having an affair or that Mrs. Wiegand had a lamentable one-nighter with the repulsive Fox.

Surely, he knew *Perry Mason* could not have done better.

Clough thought about how he had caused the professional statements of Clinical Pathologist David Charles, Chief of Campus Security Tyrone Jackson and College Attorney Jack Kula, to be incorporated into the official record. That was shrewd. He had nimbly brought to light Kelleher's efforts to juggle Morphine, whiskey and tobacco use and his efforts to struggle with the growing pain from the cancer.

The testimony had surfaced numerous issues for College governance and administration. He had exposed the need for policies on nepotism, multiple contracts, classroom exploitation, employee dating and the professional development of the Board. Without restrictive policy, abhorrent behaviors like that of Fox, with female students and unsuspecting women, might not be damning. Societal norms still favored the man in such cases and believed any classroom boorish behavior was a personal matter.

Maybe in his death, Mr. Kelleher had started a ground swell of changing campus norms. There would be no parade in his honor, or a building graced with his name. Not even a gold watch. No one would be singing *For He's a Jolly Good Fellow.* But just maybe there would be positive change, and lives would be better for it. Especially student lives.

Soon the Central Jersey Community College's Board of Trustees would initiate a search for a new President. If the Board retained its composition, especially with Pitman and Harrison as officers, the Board would likely hire a politician, someone who would yield on matters of personnel, finance and contracts. A Ph.D. and senior-level leadership experience would be irrelevant as credentials. Maybe integrity too.

If Pitman and Harrison got replaced, there was a good chance the College would conduct a truly bona fide national search. They might hire a consultant to guide the process or conduct candidate background checks. They might form a real Presidential Search Committee with representation from faculty, staff, community and even students. And all Committee members might actually get a vote.

Clough, nevertheless, was bothered there was no suicide note. It annoyed him too that Kelleher did not share his illness with his wife. Kelleher was peculiarly private, but how could he not include his wife and sons, especially toward the end?

Then there was Mrs. Kelleher. Why would his wife find solace with a scheming, self-centered basketball coach? Did her preoccupation with her own life blind her from seeing her husband's condition? Was the apparent indifference a product of their marital relationship at the time or something more sinister? Was Solomon sufficiently evil to cozy up to the wife in order to scorn and humiliate the husband? Evil enough to commit the murder of a dying man?

His mind reflected on his own marriage and what he had concluded after the divorce. It was not the passionate peaks or big sacrifices of intensity that made love endure. It was the small, day-by-day kindnesses, compromises and appreciations that kept the bond intact. He had forgotten to do that. His wife had too. Clough had lost that. He did not think J. Paul and Izzy Kelleher had.

Then there were the others. Was Pitman that mean and malicious to scheme around the President to force his resignation or something more wicked? What about those who had blatantly lied – Lieber, Hughes, Fishman, Winters. Candace Rodewald had lied too and committed a felony. She could pick a lock, but could she plan a murder by herself or with Wildwood? Bowens had skirted the truth more than once, but she refused to go down with Hughes. Why?

These were all questions spinning about in his head.

Clough reflected for that moment on how he might react if his doctor told him he was dying of cancer and had six months to live. His own financial affairs were far from organized, especially with the hurtful divorce that surfaced every nickel he was worth and penny he'd invested. The settlement had divvied up his pension. But he figured his finances were the least of his worries.

His eating habits were a real problem. He thought to himself: *Now would be a good time for me to give up the cigars and throw out most of the food in my pantry and refrigerator. Maybe I could start jogging or take the stairs at work rather than the elevator? I could reject the self-evident truth that a balanced diet is a donut in each hand or ice cream in the morning and again in the evening. Like the tree falling in the woods – if no one sees you eating it, are you really adding calories? You know, maybe it's time for me to look for a lady friend – to slap my hand when I grab unhealthy food.*

Now it was time to pull together the testimony and the results of his extensive investigations into his conclusions. Now it was time to provide the long-awaited conclusion – the Coroner's Summation.

THE INQUEST – THE CORONER'S SUMMATION

A man does not call a line crooked unless he has some idea of a straight line.
C. S. Lewis

As the Clinical Pathologist, Dr. David Charles, returned to his seat, Arthur Clough, the Monroe County Coroner, walked slowly back to the table where he kept his briefcase. Clough pulled out a document and studied it for a while after he rested it on the table.

He took only a couple of minutes, but to the people assembled in the Courtroom, it seemed like an hour. Then he broke the silence: "Ladies and gentlemen, I'd like to provide my conclusions for this Inquest and respecting the way Mr. Jacob Paul Kelleher died on the morning of Thursday, October 20, 1977."

Clough stood in front of the judge's bench, deliberately using the official locus of justice as a backdrop to his authority. He wanted no one to question what he was about to proclaim.

"From my investigation, we know Mr. Kelleher kept a doctor-prescribed supply of Morphine to ease the pain of the terminal cancer in his brain. He housed the drugs in his private bathroom, secretly preserving the meds, the used needles and vials in a paper towel dispenser. He kept the bathroom door locked and off-limits, even from custodians. No one else had access to the bathroom over this period. He used a penknife to open the towel dispenser when he needed relief from the pain. The bathroom door was closed and locked when they found his body."

The Coroner looked around the room and appreciated that he had the full attention of the audience – every single person focused their attention on every word he was saying. He felt like a medical doctor telling the tense family in the waiting room that the surgery was successful, or that the patient had died. Everyone listened intently, impatiently.

"It's significant that Mr. Kelleher's supply of the Morphine was consistent with the pharmacy records at St. Anthony Hospital," the Coroner added. "There's no reason to suspect he had any other supply of Morphine or other drugs. He had a high threshold of pain. He was managing the pain, and there was no evidence of a secondary supply of meds."

"In addition, we found no appreciable disturbance to the body, no trauma. There were no fingerprints inside the towel dispenser or in the bathroom other than Kelleher's. No incriminating finger prints in the office where the body was found. There would have been visuals on Kelleher's arms to show an intrusive syringe and evidential signs of a struggle, unless he had passed out."

The Coroner reflected momentarily on what he had just said, to be sure he had completed his thought process. Then he continued. "It is possible someone entered the bathroom, took the hypodermics and injected a lethal Morphine dosage. Miss Hart testified the bathroom door was open when she spoke with Mr. Kelleher after the Board Meeting. But it was closed when the body was found. Either he closed the door himself after taking his meds or his killer did."

"Someone with access to another supply of Morphine could have injected a fatal dose. That scenario is possible. Just not likely."

"Why would Mr. Kelleher have closed the bathroom door if he had injected himself with a potentially lethal amount of the drug? We know from testimony that the door was at least partially open. Why would he have bothered to shut the towel dispenser? Why turn off the lights in his office and the Board Room? Why not finish his glass of Irish Whiskey? And, why not leave a suicide note? These are still questions. We don't have all the answers."

The Coroner waited for a few moments before continuing. "Only Dr. Dandridge knew of Mr. Kelleher's terminal cancer. For many, hearing that today was the first time they knew. We can glean a great deal from their facial expressions to the news of the cancer."

"More likely, he was unwinding before heading home. He was considering all that had happened that evening, and all the visitors he had had. Imagine your Board Chairman comes to you in your office and says he has the votes to fire you. You know better, you understand your contract. But how horrible and, to top it off, you're dying of cancer. And no one knows it. You are alone. He was content being alone."

Clough took a big breath and swallowed hard. He knew he was about to offer a major pronouncement. "Therefore, I hereby provide the following conclusion:

> *From the completed physical examinations, as supported by my investigations and testimony here today, I am hereby dismissing the alternative that Mr. Jacob Paul Kelleher was murdered with intent and malice. There was no apparent homicide involved. While possible, the probability is most unlikely, and I choose to dismiss such as the explanation of how Mr. Kelleher died."*

The Coroner paused, as several people gasped. A few looked puzzled. Most everyone looked at another person to gauge reactions, as if they were unsure of the punchline of a joke or thought they might have misheard what he had said: *What did he say? Did I hear him correctly? Then how did he die?*

The Coroner waited for quiet before continuing his formal presentation.

"Ladies and gentlemen, let me now offer my rationale for rejecting the alternative that Mr. Kelleher's death was a homicide. Given the witness testimony today, we know there are people with motive. Some with opportunity. Let me speak to these persons and summarize my investigative conclusions."

"Let me first say that this investigation was odd. We have several duos or pairs of people with motive and opportunity, not just individuals. There were testimonies where one witness willingly created a false alibi for another. Thus, I considered murder for each individual, each person, as well as reflective of the pairings. There are some crazy collusions, contributing to the crooked behaviors."

"Let me offer the following remarks and conclusions on our suspect witnesses:

> **Mrs. Candace Rodewald** *admitted she broke into the President's Office to find his notebook. We found her fingerprints on the access door and the desk. But she did this after the President was dead. The fingerprints on the glass Shamrock were fresh and made after the office had been thoroughly cleaned. The woman's break-in leaves her vulnerable to criminal charges, and she was indeed guilty of poor judgment. But Mrs. Rodewald did not look to murder Mr. Kelleher, and she was not aware he was taking Morphine for the cancer. Had she realized his true impression of her, especially regarding the vacant*

Computer Center position, she would have lauded him, not given him an overdose. She would not have broken into his office.

Mr. Gene Wildwood admitted he was in the Board Room at the end of the October 19th meeting and that he sought the President's attention. He stated he intended to defend Mrs. Rodewald and lobby for her to get the Programmer position. He said he was aware Mrs. Rodewald had broken into the President's Office after Mr. Kelleher died. There is no identifiable motive for him to have murdered Mr. Kelleher, other than anger over Mr. Tucker's forced resignation. Indeed, he and Mrs. Rodewald were resentful that Howard Tucker had resigned. They blamed Mr. Kelleher even though it was Dr. Dandridge's recommendation. However, they blamed themselves even more for Mr. Tucker's drinking and his death. Mr. Wildwood did not lie in his testimony. Mr. Wildwood and Mrs. Rodewald will want to clarify their relationship. Both have some disclosing with their spouse relative to their infidelity. Such relationships happen. However, that is not, in this case, a transparent motive for murder.

Mr. Alan Fox, it would appear, has a clear motive. I chose not to call him to witness today even though he received a subpoena. There's an investigation already underway regarding his behaviors. I did not want to compromise his right to an unbiased trial should that be an outcome. Most likely Mr. Fox would have lost his job under Kelleher. The College may still fire the guy. Mr. Fox wanted to continue to hide his transgressions with students. Most importantly, Mr. Kelleher had already directed Mr. Winters to study Fox's grade reports and had told Personnel to seek advice from Mr. Kula and pursue disciplinary action. Killing Kelleher at that point would accomplish nothing. The horse was already out of the barn. There is no existing Board Policy or State Board Rule on student harassment, sexual or otherwise and in or out of the classroom. At the end of this Inquest, I will ask Mr. Kula to prepare a recommendation to the Board and determine the extent change is needed in each Collective Bargaining Contract to fully address this matter.

Mr. David Lieber is in serious trouble for taking payments and committing perjury today. His admission under oath that he under-represented Mrs. Wiegand in the contract with Media Visual Equipment is reprehensible but up to the College to review and discipline. His receipt of gifts or potential bribes is something that could place him in jeopardy, especially since this was with an out-of-state firm and involved federal dollars. But Mr. Lieber relied on President Kelleher for ego gratification and creative opportunities. He might not have liked some things Mr.

Kelleher did, but how could he be assured the new guy would pursue a similar parade of grant opportunities and keep Lieber in the spotlight? How could he know a new President would enable him to express his inventive mind and continue his problematic enterprises? Mr. Kelleher would not be surprised by the various charges Mr. Lieber will face.

Mr. Ralph Hughes and Miss Sally Bowens represent the Faculty Union and deserve special mention as a pair. The man of two names and two contracts – Mr. Ralph E. Hughes and Mr. R. Edward Hughes – will be unemployed and face charges from the authorities serving Columbia Community College. He may face the same from CCJC and perhaps from Trenton too. Ralph Hughes misrepresented his contract status and credentials. He lied under oath, as did his colleague, Miss Bowens. The man will face perjury and perhaps contempt charges. Mr. Hughes didn't need to manufacture an alibi for his whereabouts after the Board Meeting, but he felt he needed to hide his covert teaching. He chose to do so and lied. Mr. Kelleher said in his notebook that he knew who got up on the roof of the Administration Building to fly the helium rat. He used the contentious issue as reverse leverage in the negotiations. Miss Bowens and Mr. Hughes considered Mr. Kelleher a very worthy adversary who had the College's best interests in mind – not someone to kill. They would do well to remember that fact during subsequent negotiations, assuming they continue as faculty and represent the Faculty Union.

Vice President William Fishman and Mr. Richard Spurling are a twosome, a tag team, to use a wrestling term. These two gentlemen will be hearing from me in my role as Monroe County Sheriff. They have had lucrative, if nefarious behaviors underway that netted extra cash for themselves and severely disadvantaged students. Somehow, they survived past financial audits. They will not pass a subsequent one. An investigation will commence of the College's books by an outside audit firm that we will oversee. Given that the potential discrepancies involve federal monies, namely student scholarships, the investigation will probably take on a federal presence. Mr. Fishman lied under oath as to his whereabouts after the Board Meeting. Nevertheless, taking the life of President Kelleher would not have removed or reduced the scrutiny they were under or would be. They likely will also be among the terminated employees, as I am confident our County Commissioner will pursue legal redress himself or through the Board of Chosen Freeholders. The Board may want to reconsider their decision to name Mr. Fishman as Interim President.

Mr. Nathan Solomon, or *Coach Solly* as he prefers, told us how angry he continued to be toward Mr. Kelleher, even in the man's death.

He blamed the President for interfering with his coaching opportunity with the New Mexico university. But we know that the coach he would have been working with was not honest with him. We know Mr. Kelleher wanted this man to find a university position, not because he wanted to get rid of the guy but because he thought the College needed to resolve the funding of Intercollegiate Athletics. Mr. Solomon remains focused on winning basketball games, running his summer basketball camp and getting a university coaching position, probably in that order. He intentionally manufactured or at least distorted, a connection with the President's wife. He called it a collaboration, an alliance. That may have been his intent, but not that of Mrs. Kelleher. I would call it counterfeit affinity. However, there would be no advantage for him to murder her husband. The death of Mr. Kelleher works against him in many ways. He wanted to demean and humiliate Mr. Kelleher, not see him die. Unfortunately, in my opinion, Mr. Solomon remains a bitter man. It's that attitude that keeps him from becoming a university coach, not a president or his team's wins and losses.

Vice President Donald L. Winters admitted under oath that he hated President Kelleher. Hate usually masks other motives such as property disputes, revenge or greed. Hatred is merely sustained anger. He blamed Mr. Kelleher for not getting the CJCC Presidency. But he was not aware that Dr. Greenleaf had deceived him. Mr. Winters is tired, soured and hurt. Mostly he's angry with himself, even if he has trouble admitting that. He lied about his whereabouts after the Board Meeting but corrected his testimony later. I don't think Mr. Winters likes to lie, except to himself. Bottom line: He's not a murderer. The College would be wise to offer Mr. Winters professional counseling and personal leave out of appreciation for his years of service. Mr. Winters would be wise to take some time to determine whether he wants to retire, continue in administration, return to teaching or remain angry.

As for **Dr. Gerald Pitman and Mr. Charles Harrison**, I choose to discuss these two persons as another intriguing tag team. Accomplices may be a better term. The Chairman of the Board of Trustees, Dr. Gerald Pitman, with or without the Board Vice Chairman, Mr. Chuck Harrison, may have the most obvious motive and the most pressing opportunity. Dr. Pitman was embarrassed at the exposure of his scheme to receive payment for getting a local firm included in the architect selection process. His dental practice was diminished largely because of controversial practices and a string of complaints. He wanted, perhaps he needed, the money. We know his objective was to challenge the President's contract and fire the guy, not murder him. He was not aware of the cancer taking Mr. Kelleher's life. Mr. Harrison is proficient in magic, in making things appear and disappear. But he's not so good at lying. He's shown a willingness to work with others, no matter how crooked. Perhaps with new Board leadership, the incoming CJCC President will be able to lead the College. Hopefully he can do that without interference, respecting the Board's role in governance, not administrative intrusiveness. It's discouraging to discover that the Board Chairman found it proper to identify a mole in Mr. Lieber to dig up dirt on the President. Such unscrupulous actions should not be ignored by the authorities or by the public. This was not about needing a whistleblower. It is telling too that the entire Board, knowing what Dr. Pitman tried to do, still did not choose to censure him or Mr. Harrison. I should also point out that Dr. Pitman and Mr. Harrison may be receiving questionable legal consultation regarding contracts and their authority. However, that advice is not coming from Triano, Orr and Kula. Poor legal guidance is also not a motive for murder. I sincerely doubt a licensed attorney provided the so-called legal advice to Dr. Pitman. More than likely the advice came from an unreliable associate in his professional or crony peer group, maybe another dentist or a drinking buddy. Mr. Kelleher knew his contract; Pitman and Harrison did not. More likely, they chose to bluff.

Finally, **Miss Roseanne Hart** has had a great deal on her plate these past few months and endured considerable stress. She exonerated herself from potential perjury charges by being honest about her whereabouts and those of Mr. Fishman. Miss Hart proudly shared that the President often pressed her but respected her contributions and defended her against bigotry. She has apparently done some soul-searching. Hopefully, this Inquest will demonstrate the need for the College to conduct a systematic review of personnel policies, including faculty-student intimate interactions and dual employment. Having four unions and four Collective Bargaining Agreements cannot be an excuse for not having comprehensive and sound rules applicable to all employees. The times change and so does our society. College rules and policies must too."

Arthur Clough sighed noticeably. He put his notes back on the table next to his binder. The time was 5:55 PM. "I could go through a couple others," he said. "However, I choose not to do that. The bottom line, I rule, is that Mr. Kelleher's death was not due to foul play. His death was not a homicide."

"We know that once everyone left the Board Room and his office that night, Mr. Kelleher would have had time to inject himself, return the empty vials and used needle and shut the towel dispenser. He could have closed the bathroom door, returned to his desk and sat in his chair. He could have removed his shoes and deliberately placed them aside the desk. Knowing Mr. Kelleher, he may have planned to shine them again. He may have already shined them. He may have imbibed in more alcohol. Then when he felt the attack, he could have fallen from his chair onto the rug. He could have collapsed in the position he was found later that morning. A person can land on the floor in that curious position. I know. I've tried."

Arthur Clough thought to himself about how he had sat in the President's oversized desk chair when he was in his office earlier in the week and found the hidden notebook. He had intentionally collapsed and fallen to the floor to see what positions he would take once he hit the carpet. On the third try his right arm fell in the same position as Kelleher's had fallen – or had been placed – minus the *Marlboro* cigarette torch. On the fourth fall, while holding a pencil, his arm landed differently, but the momentum caused the chair to push back the way it was found that morning. His legs were tilted in the same direction.

Each time Clough found his body falling, his arms landed in slightly different positions but mostly with the right arm above his shoulder. Given that self-induced experiment, he knew he could not discount that the unusual position in which Kelleher's body was found could have been accidental. He knew the position would not necessarily be forced by Kelleher himself or by an assailant.

Clough also knew he would be very sore in the morning. He wasn't used to falling or anything remotely likened to exercise.

If only Deputy Diaz had been there to witness his vaudeville pratfalls. But he did not think his obesity would have made him fall in any other way onto the rug. The chair probably would have gone flying regardless.

Clough surmised that the President did not intentionally fall to the floor with a cigarette in his hand, lit and smoked at the time of the collapse. He thought to himself: *Why would*

I was summoned here this morning to meet J. Paul. Claim his soul. He's been haunted by me for a few months. Maybe this guy will carry his head too and ride a black horse in the darkness.

The Irish Dullahan

someone as organized as President Kelleher not extinguish the smoking Marlboro before falling, unless he was unconscious when he fell. He brought that expensive rug to his office, and he was fastidious with his cigarette ashes. For God's sake, the man used a separate ashtray in his car.

Clough concluded Kelleher had the attack while seated and then fell to the floor. He had not deliberately sprawled out on the carpet, as he died. Rather, he was unconscious and slowly dying as he crashed.

Clough smiled and laughed heartily at himself. He was about the same height as Kelleher but over 100 pounds heavier. He thought to himself: *If Kelleher was the After Photo for a diet product, I must be the Way-Before Photo.* He also thought: *Next time I do this, I'll get Chief Jackson to pretend he's Kelleher, not me. Then Diaz can pick up the lug, and I can just watch.*

The Coroner regained his focus for the Courtroom Inquest and continued his explanations. "President Kelleher could have left his shoes on the carpet carefully positioned under the desk before he injected himself. However, it may also be that he placed the shoes haphazardly on the floor, and somehow they ended up in that strange perpendicular position when the chair slid. The outstretched arm could have been deliberate, too, but with the trauma his body experienced, that would be unsubstantiated."

"To be sure, someone could have entered his office later, even after everyone including Dr. Pitman, Mr. Harrison and Miss Hart had left. Someone could have been waiting outside on the balcony, even though it was very cold that night. Someone might have found the bathroom door open, as Miss Hart said it was earlier that night. That person could have seen where the vials were hidden and forcibly used the hypodermic to inject Mr. Kelleher. Yet, there's no evidence of that happening."

The Coroner looked again at his notes to be certain he was directing his thoughts as he had planned. "We know several things from our investigation and today's testimony. Mr. Kelleher started to show the effects of the cancer. He started to slur his language and was jittery and occasionally irritable. The President tried to mask those symptoms and confuse others by reducing his interactions at meetings and by smoking. He disguised his symptoms by feigning that he was drinking more and increasingly under the influence of alcohol. That was a sham. He knew it. We can't judge why, but we know he wanted to camouflage his illness. He did not ingest nearly as much alcohol as those around him thought. That might have been the case that night, or that may have been when he did overindulge. I think he disciplined his drinking because he never wanted to lose control, even as he faced death. The one was a foil for the other. It gave him an excuse for the coughing and other symptoms of the cancer."

Arthur Clough took in a large breath of air as he reflected on how much he was alike the now dead College President. Then he resumed his statement. "Ladies and gentlemen, being in control was consistent with Mr. Kelleher's very being. A man like Kelleher wants to be in control of himself always, including when he's drinking and when he's in pain. I think we'd be wrong to underestimate his amount of physical self-control and vigilant reasoning."

"We often think of self-control in the framework of avoidance. Resisting the temptation to eat more than one cookie. Avoiding a second helping of ice cream. But self-control also is in play with self-regulation of emotions, including pain."

Arthur Clough had studied human behavior sufficiently to be confident of his observations. "Let me go on. Several people testified that Mr. Kelleher was drinking after the Board Meeting. Dr. Pitman said he saw Kelleher down two glasses of the Irish Whiskey and pour a third, with each glass, as he said, two fingers high. My theory is that Kelleher nursed those glasses to mask his behavior, to enable people to think his behavior was due to the liquor. Likely, he wanted people to exaggerate how much he was drinking to mask the symptoms from the cancer."

"Mr. Kelleher probably poured one or more drinks down the sink and then refilled his glass in front of others. Again, Mr. Kelleher never wanted to lose control. That was not his personality. The drinking kept people from being suspicious of his true illness, the cancer eating away his body and, more importantly for him, devouring his mind. He fumbled with words and slurred his speech, not because of the drinking but due to the cancer. But his ruse gave him time."

"As we learned from his hidden blue notebook, he was sensitive to those who were alcohol dependent, and he did not judge them. He supported Dr. Dandridge's decision on Howard Tucker's termination not because of the drinking. He supported it because of the effect on his performance and that of others in the Computer Center."

"Some people drink alcohol to release their emotions, take away inhibitions, even escape," Clough said with confidence. "A person like Mr. Kelleher doesn't drink to lose control. He drinks because he likes the bold taste. After all, he was a proud Irishman, with sons named Connor and Ian."

The Corner glanced at the audience and waited for the subdued laughs to subside before he continued. "Well, there must be other good folks of Irish heritage among us."

Then Arthur Clough resumed his emotionless explanations. "Most importantly for our observations today, Mr. Kelleher drank publicly to hide his emotions and self-regulate his pain. He knew that if he drank too much, he'd lower his inhibitions and make it harder to mask his feelings and symptoms. Then people would be far more curious about his condition, including those who were around him the most, like Mrs. Reynolds and Miss Bartell and even his wife and sons. But the alcohol still interacted with the Morphine and sped up the process."

The Coroner went back to the table to retrieve the notebook President

Kelleher had kept in his office. He held it up to the audience not unlike a preacher holding up a Bible during a sermon.

"A key to our investigation has to be this notebook Mr. Kelleher left in his office," Clough said. "He did not want just anyone to find the notes. He kept it hidden in a secret compartment in his desk drawer. He may well have left his shoes in the telling position to direct an investigator to them. But there's no proof. For all we know, he might have left the polished shoes in that position every night in fear the cancer might not permit him to return to the office in the morning. My understanding is that he came to work and went home wearing his *Asics* running shoes. He kept the *Johnston & Murphy* shoes at the office."

"As for the notebook itself, most people looking for an object in the desk would overlook the false drawer bottom. That's simply because they are not looking for a false bottom or anything out of the ordinary. People driving along are looking to avoid other cars. They may not see the bicycle or scooter. My guess is that the President used the false bottom when he knew his weeks were numbered."

"Deputy Diaz checked with the manufacturer of that particular desk," Mr. Clough continued. "She found that having a false bottom for one of the drawers was an option at purchase. Mr. Kelleher may have learned of that feature or discovered it accidentally, but it served his purposes."

"President Kelleher was content that, eventually, someone would discover the notebook. Perhaps Miss Bartell or Mrs. Reynolds. Perhaps his successor. He chose to record and track his thoughts as he persisted in trying to address the astonishing elements at the College. He knew the cancer was taking his life, and he did not want his private observations to fall into crooked hands while he was alive. He kept it there in the event he died before he could get to the desk and give it to the right person."

The Coroner placed the notebook back on the table before he continued. His thoughts for the moment drifted to the day before when he had uncovered the secret bottom of the desk drawer and found the journal: *Would this Inquest have taken a different turn had he not found it? Would he be reaching the same conclusions without those notes? Would not finding the notebook have changed the Summation, even the Death Certificate itself?*

"Let me point out something else," the Coroner continued. "There were no notes in the journal regarding his illness or dealing with the cancer. The notebook was focused on the College. Solely. It was not a *Dear Diary* of his thoughts, a daily or weekly account of his emotions or a chronicle of his illness. This was not the log of a ship's captain. That's significant. His notes were about the College. There isn't one word about his wife or kids. Nothing about how he felt facing death or reminiscing about his life. That is not a judgment, but a fact. It matters greatly to this Inquest. It mattered a great deal to his life. A diary would reveal his emotions, feelings. That is not what Mr. Kelleher chose to do with this blue notebook."

The physical examination of the body, Dr. Charles' partial autopsy and the toxicology reports had enabled Arthur Clough to conclude how Kelleher died. Clough's scrutiny of the Crime Scene analysis and uncovering the Morphine cache had made him skeptical of a homicide. But he could be wrong. He had to accept that.

"President Kelleher's notes contributed immensely to this Inquest, as we all would attest," the Coroner said as his focus returned to the Summation. "Mr. Kelleher uncovered behaviors of staff and others that we heard about today. We will review and investigate. Fines, employee discipline, even prosecution may result. That may not have been the ending Kelleher wanted, but he did want those illegal, unethical or crooked behaviors exposed. I'm convinced. We may have done that justice."

"That does not by itself tell me his mindset that fateful night was suicide or somber resignation to his fate. It tells me he focused on his job, on serving as President of Central Jersey Community College. Perhaps he should have concentrated more on his wife and sons or placed himself into a care facility. Perhaps he should have grabbed his family and gone on an ocean cruise or bought a Ford Thunderbird. Who can say or judge."

"An analysis of the hidden notebook reveals that President Kelleher's handwriting was slowly deteriorating, as pressure on his brain increased, along with the pain. His writings in the notebook of a year or so ago are strong and clear. He used complete sentences. We know that words were very important to him. Then you can see the pattern slowly worsening. Also, there were no notes that week of the October Board Meeting, including that night. The sentences got weaker over time. Scribbles of phrases, not entire sentences. That tells us his health was fading."

"I cannot say with conviction that his death was self-inflicted and thus Death by Suicide. Some elements suggest he was knowingly destroying his health, including the alcohol and tobacco indulgence or potentially over-indulgence. Yet, Mr. Kelleher was in social situations where others were drinking in their campus offices. I've already stated that he chose to mask his condition with the alcohol. Most suicides occur with firearms, not drugs and certainly not from alcohol or tobacco."

"We know Mr. Kelleher was in severe pain, which was eased by the Morphine injections. And, if I may add some levity, he told us he got some relief from eating canned pineapple."

"He was fully aware he was in the final months of his life. His will to live may have deteriorated. I don't think so as long as he could work at his desk."

Clough paused long enough to frame his next comment. He knew it would be controversial. "About half of people who commit suicide are diagnosed with a mental disorder. Unless there's a suicide note, and even with a note, there can always be a question as to whether the death was indeed self-inflicted. True, not everyone leaves a note. Most do. We know too that for every suicide resulting in actual death, the clear majority of suicide attempts fail."

"We also know that suicide is higher with cancer patients who were in remission and now find the cancer has returned. That, of course, is not the case with Mr. Kelleher. There is also a correlation with depression but, again, Mr. Kelleher did not seem depressed by his condition. He was stoic, dispassionate. He was strong, even at that last, brutal Board Meeting."

"Another factor pointing away from suicide is that Mr. Kelleher was raised Roman Catholic. The taking of one's life is considered an unforgiveable sin in that religion. He was not an overly religious man, and he became Protestant only after he married. As a Catholic myself, I suspect those childhood teachings were embedded in his mind. Of course, I don't know that. But there is a difference in the correlation of religion and suicide among different denominations."

Clough could see the agony on the faces of several people, given the topic was suicide and religion. "Ladies and gentlemen, many people who survive attempted suicide confess it was not that they wanted to die, but that they wanted to stop living. That may have been the case with Mr. Kelleher, given his astute understanding of his debilitation and imminent death."

"Yet, I doubt he wanted to stop living. Mr. Kelleher's life had purpose. He was dedicated to that end. True, he may have wanted to control his destiny and die under his terms. But those factors are not sufficient to convince me, without reasonable doubt, that he took his life."

"Therefore, I will complete the Death Certificate to show the following two conclusions:

(1) *The immediate cause of the death of Mr. Jacob Paul Kelleher was cardiac arrest following severe respiratory failure.*
(2) *The underlying cause was the convergence of a high-potency Morphine injection or injections into a vein or veins, with an elevated amount of alcohol in the system and acute, debilitating and eventually terminal cancerous cells in the brain.*

With that official pronouncement, Arthur Clough replaced his notes on the table. He took a deep breath and again addressed the audience in the Courtroom.

"Ladies and gentlemen, I would like to share a more general observation and ask for your indulgence as I do so. The words crook and crooked are used in many ways in the English language. We have a shepherd's crook, crooked teeth, crooked mile, crooked line, crooked miles, stiles and smiles and crookneck squash. There are crooked paths and crooked paintings on the wall. But we also have crook as in a dishonest person, a liar, thief, cheat or rogue. And we apply the word as synonymous with the word unscrupulous and refer to crooked elections and crooked politicians. The latter being redundant in the minds of many people."

"We are all too familiar with President Nixon's public statement four years ago in connection with the Watergate break-in of Democratic headquarters: *I am not a crook.* But we forget the statement he made in a TV interview with David Frost. Mr. Nixon said something like: *When the President of the United States of America does it, that means that whatever it is, is not illegal.* Or, in our context, it's not crooked when otherwise good people get involved in crooked actions."

"Can one be only a little crooked? Does it make a difference in our interpretation of crooked, if the person is a college president, a vice president, dean or faculty member? Does a Board of Trustees have a different threshold of crookedness? Does a Freeholder? A Commissioner? Does the end justify the means?"

"Folks, I don't have the answers, but as Sheriff and Coroner it's my job to discern when crooked behaviors occur. That is what I have tried to do today."

Arthur Clough cleared his throat to make a pronouncement. "Ladies and gentlemen, this concludes this official Inquest. I thank you, sincerely, for your participation, your time and patience. If there are questions or concerns, please see me after we adjourn or contact me at the office."

Arthur Clough, the Monroe County Corner, raised his arms over his head with his hands facing the audience in a petition of humility. He elevated his voice in deep and full resonance and pronounced, "Ladies and gentlemen, we stand adjourned."

There was a smattering of applause, as much out of thankfulness that the ordeal was over, as for the conclusions reached. Most people got up and swiftly headed for the door, as if leaving a movie at the end with the credits still playing. Some exited slowly, pondering what they had seen, as if waiting to read the credits. And, some remained in their seats, as if waiting for a second feature. A few scattered whispers were the only sounds in the room.

Some persons felt shame. Others relief. A few were disappointed that *Perry Mason* did not unmask the killer or that Gunsmoke's *Matt Dillon* did not save the distressed damsel or catch the bank robbers.

Some folks chose to believe a killer was still roaming the halls of the

College or stalking the streets of Monroe County. A few grasped the underlying significance of the Coroner's statement and that the Inquest had surfaced so many lies and deceptions.

The Coroner looked pleased with himself. He wondered what *Dr. Quincy ME* would say in his final remarks at an Inquest or if he had been in the Courthouse. No doubt Clough had fascinated many that day with his perceptions. He had astounded Monroe County with his astute analysis. *Dr. Quincy* would have been enormously impressed. *Matt Dillon* too. Perhaps Angie Dickinson.

Clough turned and walked over to where Izzy Kelleher was sitting. He reached for her right hand and cradled it within both of his bulky hands. He noticed the tears beginning to topple from her eyes, like tumbleweeds flowing across the plains.

"Mrs. Kelleher, Izzy, I'll complete this document upon leaving the Courtroom and in the presence of Mr. Smith," the Coroner said. "Having done so, if you are ready, or when you are, you may proceed with funeral arrangements. I apologize we took these weeks to complete the initial post-mortem exam, partial autopsy and Dr. Charles' toxicological analyses. I'm sorry I found it necessary to conduct this official Inquest and place this number of people on the witness stand and to . . ."

"Arthur, sir, do not apologize for doing your job," Mrs. Kelleher abruptly interrupted as she stared into his eyes. "The circumstances under which my husband died are extraordinary, especially with his terminal cancer. I was able to process his death and now better understand his state of mind. The Inquest exposed me to statements from his colleagues and a far better understanding of what he was dealing with. I can appreciate what he was trying to do at the College and all that mischief and deceit. You accomplished some things that would make my husband smile, and you know what happens *When Irish Eyes are Smiling: Tis like the morning spring and you can hear the angles sing. The Irish hearts steal your heart away. So, there's never a teardrop to fall.*"

Izzy released her hand and placed it on the Coroner's shoulder before she continued her response. "Arthur, I can never thank you enough. Don't you ever apologize to me."

"Izzy, you are gracious in your comments," Clough said. "Thank you. Is there anything I can do for you in my capacity as Sheriff or Coroner?"

Izzy released her hand from Clough's shoulder to reach for a tissue. Edith had already retrieved a couple. She handed one to Izzy and kept the other for herself. The widow wiped her eyes, one and then the other, no longer worried about smearing her makeup.

"One day soon, my sons will ask about what happened today," she began. "They'll want an explanation as to how their dad died. Thanks to you, Dr. Charles and others, I'll be able to provide that with confidence and compassion."

The widow looked around the empty Courtroom, as if looking for more of J. Pauls' guardian Irish Ghosts to appear. "And most of all," she added, "I can now accept the reality that no one harmed Pauly. I can now appreciate that there was no note and that he died quietly."

EPILOGUE

The Days that Followed
the Official Inquest

Glance into the world just as though time were gone and everything crooked
will become straight to you!
Friedrich Nietzsche

THE HOME OF MRS. IZZY KELLEHER

Saturday, November 19, 1977

Izzy Kelleher, the widow of the deceased J. Paul Kelleher, former President of Central Jersey Community College, was home on Saturday morning. This was three days after the Inquest. She was enjoying her second cup of coffee and a buttered slice of raisin toast. Connor and Ian were away at a friend's house for a sleepover, in which they undoubtedly did not sleep.

A partially smoked *Virginia Slims* cigarette rested in the ashtray, ash building at the tip. She looked at it and remembered what the Sheriff had told her about the cigarette her husband had in his fingers when his body was found. The one with his extended arm that looked like the Statue of Liberty's torch.

This was the first morning since her husband died that she was alone in the house. The only exception was the presence of sentinel Cerberus patrolling the backyard. Her Cerberus was the German Shepherd version, not the three-headed Irish one.

The widow had now had a month to deal with the death and categorize her emotions. Now she had to process all of it again, given the Inquest testimony, the conclusions she had formed and the Coroner's remarkable Summation.

Mrs. Kelleher had only two more days until Monday's funeral. The final chapter of her husband's life would be over. She was apprehensive about that moment, saying her last goodbyes and shedding another supply of tears. She had no idea who would show for the ceremony at Ewing Presbyterian Church. Pastor Bender, who had officiated at the Memorial Service, would lead the formality. She wanted it over.

Izzy had agonized over the editorial in the *Jersey Star* on Thursday, one day after the Inquest had ended. Reporter Martha J. Rooney had features on the dual teaching jobs for Mr. Ralph Hughes – *CJCC Faculty Collects Two Salaries* – and on the whereabouts of David Lieber and Donald Winters after the Board Meeting – *VP Says He Went to Strip Show*. For whatever reasons, she had not included any comments on the relationship of Candace Rodewald and Gene Wildwood or even mentioned that Alan Fox might be prosecuted. Perhaps she was just saving the juicier stories for the *National Inquirer* feed.

Mrs. Kelleher looked at the paper again before saying aloud: "What Inquest did they attend? Guess Jersey politics lives on and on. Sorry, Pauly."

She had invited only four speakers for the church service – Jack Kula, Dominic Panichi, Edith Reynolds and Tom Dandridge. The crypt ceremony afterwards would include brief remarks by Connor and Pastor Bender. She would share thoughts at both. She did not plan to say much, but she knew the words would come to her. Tears would come too.

J. Paul had wanted to be cremated. She knew that. Izzy had made the same decision for herself years ago. But he had been silent on what to do with the ash remains. He did not want them tossed into the ocean or left on the slopes of a mountain. That she knew. The widow Kelleher decided her husband's ashes would be placed in an urn and laid to rest in a niche at Forest Lawn Cemetery.

She chose a two-person cubicle niche where her ashes would join his one day. It was Forest Lawn's sentimental version of a double-wide. There was peace in having resolved his destination – hers as well.

The doorbell rang. Izzy was startled from her concentration on her husband's funeral and cremation.

It was unusual that anyone would be at the front door, let alone early on a Saturday. Neighbors and friends knew to come to the side door near the kitchen, the preferred entry for her and the boys.

By the time Izzy registered the ringing sound as her doorbell, it had sounded a second time. She shuffled to the door in her slippers after tightening the belt on her blue terry cloth robe. Two men were standing at her doorstep. One intruder, whom she did not know, was a man wearing a dark suit and tie. It was cold outside, but he had no topcoat. Just the black suit.

She recognized the dark-suited man as an attorney from the same firm as Jack Kula, but she had never met the man. The other person standing there, whom she knew all too well, was Arthur Clough. She recognized him because of the floppy hat.

She thought to herself: *Here's the Monroe County Sheriff and a dark-suited attorney at my front door on a Saturday morning. That can't be good news.*

"Good morning," Izzy said, opening the heavy decorative, wooden front door but keeping her right arm on the doorknob in case she needed to slam it. The glass storm door remained closed for now. "Hello, Mr. Clough," as she looked him in the eyes through the glass.

Clough wore a pair of jeans and his vintage pea coat, rather than his normal, wrinkled investigation wardrobe or his official Coroner Inquest garb. She turned to the dark-suited lawyer-man, "Do I know you, sir?"

Daily Editorial

The **Jersey Star**

It's Time to Move On

November 17, 1977

The day-long Inquest into the death of Central Jersey Community College's President ended yesterday evening. Some 30 people were called to witness, along with the medical doctor, Dr. Charles David, who had examined J. Paul Kelleher.

Dr. David found that Kelleher had terminal cancer and was injecting himself with Morphine for the pain.

The President had kept vials hidden in his office and kept knowledge of his cancer hidden from his wife and colleagues. Dr. David had given Kelleher six months to live when the cancer was initially diagnosed in June.

Coroner Arthur Clough called the witnesses and asked the questions, serving as both prosecutor and judge. Those who testified were under oath, same as a normal court case. Much of the questioning related to a diary that Mr. Kelleher had been keeping for the past year with notes on crooked behaviors of faculty and staff. Someone had broken into the office to steal the diary. The Coroner was able to dig into the truth and expose several people for less than honest answers.

We think he was a bit too invasive.

The Coroner concluded that Mr. Kelleher had not died from the hands of others or of his own intention. Rather, the Morphine had mixed with the alcohol in his system and caused cardiac arrest and respiratory failure. There was no suicide note. He would have died anyway in a couple months. Clough did not close the door on the possibility of a homicide, especially since someone had broken into the President's office. We don't either.

Board Chairman Dr. Gerald Pitman and Vice Chairman Chuck Harrison, prominent dentist and business man respectively, attended the Inquest and were called to testify. Both public servants praised Mr. Kelleher in their comments to the Editorial Board and noted that the College will be hard-pressed to find as qualified and dedicated a successor. There had been a dispute between the Board and Kelleher over selection of the architect for the $5 million Library, as Mr. Kelleher did not want a local firm to get the contract.

The Editorial Board thinks that was a mistake. Every construction project for the College, school system and public building in Monroe County should include local firms.

County Commissioner, Dominic Panichi, also testified, as did Vice Presidents Donald Winters and Bill Fishman and Head Basketball Coach, Coach Solly. Some faculty did too. We recently learned that the coach is a finalist for head coach at a New Jersey NBA team being formed.

We express condolences to Mrs. Kelleher and the family for their loss. With this behind us, we hope the Board and the new President will continue to press the state so that CJCC can finally become a university.

It's time to move on.

"Mrs. Kelleher, I apologize for being at your front door on a Saturday morning," said the visitor. "I have instructions to be here, to call on you unannounced. My name is Bradley Girard with the firm of Triano, Orr and Kula. You know Jack Kula from our firm. May we come in please?"

Izzy didn't think she had much of a choice. She decided not to ask either visitor if she did. She smiled, opened the storm door and motioned for Girard and Clough to enter her foyer. "Nice to meet you, Mr. Girard," she said. "I assume you and the Sheriff have news for me, likely about my deceased husband. Are you here to arrest me? Did someone confess to the murder?"

Seeing the hint of a smile from Arthur Clough, Izzy added: "Did I leave my purse at the Courtroom? Did I double-park somewhere? You got me!"

Mrs. Kelleher's attempt at humor was not successful. These guys were here on a serious mission. Izzy changed her approach. "Please, come into the living room and have a seat there on the couch. Can I get either of you a cup of coffee? Trust you've been well, Arthur, if still running around after Wednesday's crucial Inquest."

"I would appreciate that Mrs. Kelleher, if it's not too much trouble," Girard responded to the invitation. He placed his leather briefcase on the floor and took a seat in the middle of the tufted cream-colored twill fabric couch. Clough had no option but to choose the nearby leather recliner chair that probably had been J. Paul's favorite space.

Clough was not hesitant to request coffee as well. "Please, Izzy, I would very much appreciate a cup. Black's fine. This has been an unusual Saturday for me, and it's only 8:15 in the morning."

Bradley Girard reached inside his briefcase. He pulled out a large, brown Kraft pocket envelope with a mysterious and suspenseful aura. He undid the metal fastener and placed the envelope before himself.

Izzy went to her kitchen and poured two mugs of coffee, haphazardly grabbing two of the ones her husband had kept in his office at the College. She left the one with *Greatest Boss* on the shelf. She had no idea who gave him that infamous one, let alone why he kept it. She told herself: *Maybe he just thought it was fun. Perhaps he gave it to himself as a prank. Don't think I'll save this one very long. Should have left it with the others at the office yesterday.*

Mrs. Kelleher also had no idea what was about to be revealed to her by the two uninvited guests sitting in the living room. She had only yesterday ventured onto campus and into her husband's office. She chose that day to rummage through and collect his personal items, with Edith Reynolds and Samantha Bartell to bless what she took and didn't take.

She had seized the photos, ashtray, Irish artifacts and, of course, the *Waterford* Crystal Shamrock paperweight. She had abandoned the tacky reprints on the wall and the Governor's stock photo, but not without mocking them for the benefit of the two ladies and to lighten the mood.

She took J. Paul's framed diplomas, malfunctioning antique wall clock and high school gavel. She included the assorted mugs, the non-chipped ones, and his signature coffee cup and saucer. She had asked Edith to donate his shoes and the clothes closeted in the bathroom to the Salvation Army and discard the toiletries. Whatever else remained was left on purpose. Someone later could decide on a destination as being in or out of the trash. She didn't care. She had a dresser and closet of Pauly's clothes and shoes back at the house.

Izzy abandoned the Persian rug that supported the President's desk and chair, like a magic carpet, and that held his body when he died. As with the legends, the rug was to portray the power of its master, but she decided it could transport someone else. "Edith, just keep it here, sell it or give it away, as you prefer."

The widow sensed the Irish Spirits lingering in the office, preparing to tell their stories to the next occupant. Given the past several months, the apparitions had some fresh fables and original tales of the afterlife. *Would they receive Pauly into that world? Would an Irish Leprechaun dressed in green share a toast of Irish Whiskey when he arrived? Would those Irish eyes really be smiling?*

The wind had been blowing outside yesterday, creating a clatter of the office windows. The trees vibrated like harp strings playing an Irish folk tune, but out-of-tune. Through the dwindling leaves, she could make out the apparition of a headless figure riding a horse. The words sounded clear. *Your husband will be transported to the darkness and light of the afterworld. We've determined he'll spend eternity roaming the streets with everlasting blessings. That is, if you ever get him buried.*

Izzy had heard the story about how Arthur Clough had found her husband's journal in a secret desk compartment. She was convinced the Irish Spirits were responsible for the clues. How else did Samantha and Candace Rodewald and countless others go through the desk drawers and not find anything? Had to be.

Back in her kitchen, Izzy studied the two mugs before she poured coffee into them. One she had given Pauly on their vacation two years ago to St. Thomas, arranged through Global Travel. The other one had the Irish flag painted on it. Both did their function – held hot, lukewarm or cold coffee.

She wondered to herself: *How many had used those stained porcelain diner mugs while sitting in those God-awful faded, orange chairs? Why in the world had her husband never replaced those armchairs? Why had he not told her about the cancer? Why had she been so cold and oblivious about his health? How did he manage to inject the Morphine and she did not know of it? Did she ever suspect he was really sick? Why did Pauly only use a cup and saucer and not a mug?*

Izzy Kelleher re-entered the living room and presented her two guests with the brewed coffee. Neither man looked like he planned to drink any of it. There were other things to address. The display of manners and politeness was over.

"Mrs. Kelleher, let me first say how sorry I am your husband died," Bradley Girard, the attorney, shared without more pomp or circumstance. "Cancer can be just awful. I cannot fathom the pain Mr. Kelleher endured and the sorrow you and your sons must feel."

After completing the obligatory expression of sorrow, Girard began to frame the real purpose for the weekend intrusion. "I spent time with Mr. Kula after the Inquest to be sure I understood all that went on there," he said. "Whatever I missed, Mr. Clough filled in. Our Coroner was amazing and had a fateful mission the day of the Inquest."

Izzy felt another bout of sadness and remorse coming on. After sitting down, she said, "Thank you. I'm still processing that my husband would suffer as he did and keep the secret of his cancer. Hard to accept he didn't leave a note, an explanation for our boys. Perhaps leave an apology to them, if not to me. But, Mr. Clough says that does not typically happen, especially when it's not suicide."

The attorney repositioned the large, brown envelope before him on the coffee table, as if it were a restaurant menu and he, as the waiter, was serving himself. "Mrs. Kelleher, that's precisely why I'm here. Your husband contracted with me in July to serve as a private attorney. Accordingly, I've kept that a secret until now. He told me in confidence he was dying of cancer and had only months to live."

Mr. Girard paused to straighten his tie and his posture, more for effect than need. "I would like to go over the materials he left with me to give to you," he began. "I want to present these to you with the foreknowledge they may help in your grief and your understanding of what was happening in your husband's mind. Mr. Kula was unaware your husband hired me. Nor did anyone else in the firm. That was a condition of the contract."

Izzy took a sip of her coffee. The brew had lost its early-morning flavor and now served less as a soothing respite and more as a prop for the encounter with this attorney guy. "I'm surprised you would be here," Izzy confided. "I am not surprised Pauly would have a private attorney. It fits with his personality and aloneness, as well as his attention to detail and order. I don't mean that negatively. If he first saw you in July, Mr. Girard, and from what we learned at the Inquest, he'd known about the cancer for only a month. Did you see him again?"

Girard looked somewhat annoyed because the dialog was coming more from Mrs. Kelleher than from him. But he responded. "Yes, I saw him again in mid-August, and then at our final meeting September 28th, a Wednesday. He looked to be in pain, but his mind was sharp. He was lucid in his last conversation and directions to me."

Attorney Girard focused his attention momentarily on Arthur Clough. Then he continued. "While your husband did not direct me to do this, I thought it would be advisable to have Mr. Clough here this morning, given the nature of the Inquest and his official findings. I contacted him yesterday and asked him to meet me here. He has no prior knowledge of what this meeting is about or the contents of this large envelope. No one has. That's the way your husband wanted – what I agreed to do before I officially signed on as his lawyer."

"I am comfortable with Arthur being here," Izzy offered. "If what you are about to present is from Pauly, Mr. Clough should be here."

"Yes, I understand, Mrs. Kelleher," Girard shared. He looked at his coffee mug and thought about taking a swig but decided to stay on topic. "Mr. Kelleher left me with this envelope, the contents of which I am to formally present to you. I was instructed to deliver this only after the Death Certificate was officially signed and processed. Does that make sense to you?"

Izzy nodded in agreement, although she wasn't sure she could make sense of anything, especially coming early on a Saturday morning from a lawyer in a dark suit with a large briefcase and a suspicious envelope.

Girard continued. "There are three pieces inside this envelope, Mrs. Kelleher. Let me present them one-by-one."

Before speaking, the attorney pulled out two legal-appearing, multi-page documents. "These are two life insurance policies your husband established and wanted me to share with you. One is a $20,000 policy payable upon death, with the College Foundation as sole beneficiary. The payoff on the policy was contingent on death being a result of natural or accidental causes or illness and not of, or related to, a homicide or self-inflicted death. He knew that of course."

"Your husband set-up this policy in January 1975, to coincide with his appointment as President of the College," Girard continued. "This would have been over two years before he found out about the cancer. Had the Coroner determined that someone murdered your husband, or that it was suicide or that he knew of the cancer in 1975, the company would have canceled the policy. They would only have given you a fraction of the residual payments."

Arthur Clough then spoke up. "That's why you needed to wait until after the Inquest before delivering the envelope."

Girard wanted that codicil to sink in before he expanded on the other. "Mrs. Kelleher, the Coroner ruled that your husband died due to natural causes, even with the Morphine injection and alcohol in his system and the debilitating cancer. The policy is fully payable."

"I had no knowledge he'd set up this policy, but that's what Pauly would do," Izzy said. "He committed his career to that College. Leaving a financial legacy was likely very important to him. When he got the appointment as President, he got on his knees in this same room and told God he would dedicate himself to bringing CJCC out of disorder and into prominence. Pauly doesn't usually pray, so this was an exceptional moment of dedication. It was genuine. Perhaps it was a pact to himself, more than to God."

"Mrs. Kelleher, the only rider is that the money goes into an endowment," Girard responded. "Only the accrued interest is to be spent by the Foundation."

The attorney looked intently at Mrs. Kelleher. He knew he was about to share another stipulation to the Foundation gift. "Mrs. Kelleher," he began, "I need to tell you that he's named this the *Isabella Brooke Rhodes Kelleher Student Scholarship Fund.*"

Attorney Girard looked at Clough who simultaneously smiled and shook his head in sympathetic disbelief. His mind digressed: *This man had left the perpendicular shoes and clues in a dictionary for a false-bottom desk drawer concealing a personal journal. He kept the Morphine vials hidden in a towel dispenser. Now he even gives to the College in his death and dedicates the thing to his wife.*

Arthur Clough thought to himself: *Well, what other surprises does this Kelleher have up his sleeve? What else is in this mysterious brown envelope? One down. Two to go. No one seems to know. Had I known of the insurance policies and the payoffs, it might have affected my determination on his death. Glad I didn't know then. Doesn't change anything now.*

Girard hesitated and continued with his explanations. "Mrs. Kelleher, your husband established another term life insurance policy. This one is for you and your sons. He's had this one for twenty years, through Northeastern Mutual. Its value at death is $150,000. You're likely aware of this, as he told me you knew about it when you got married. He changed the beneficiary directives about ten years ago, with $40,000 to be set aside for Connor and Ian for their college education. The balance is for you."

"Pauly told me he'd started a term policy before we got married," Izzy explained. "But I never pressed him on what it was, or the company, much less the amount. Frankly, I'd not thought much about it. Lost track of it until now. But then who knew he'd die so soon, so damn young."

Mrs. Kelleher paused as if waiting for an answer to her question about who knew he would die young. There was no response. She resumed her comments. "Mr. Girard, I have not gotten with Jack or our financial planning guy to go over my husband's bank accounts, investments and financial estate.

Frankly, I wanted to get past the funeral next week. Pauly's had all that well-planned, as he did everything else. The only thing he did not plan well was his death and sharing his guilt and pain."

Attorney Girard was pleased he had brought Mr. Clough, so he would hear the details of the insurance claims. "Mrs. Kelleher, the policy for you and the boys had no contingency. The one for the College had a thirty-day wait period after his death to allow for investigation into how he died. I was directed to present these two policies to you after the Death Certificate was signed and the thirty-day period was over."

Arthur Clough felt it was his time to speak. "Mr. Girard, I remain resolute that my Inquest findings, my Summation and what I put on the Death Certificate are valid and accurate. Mr. Kelleher took out the policies before he knew he had the cancer. Was there an element of resignation that he was dying, that death was inevitable? Perhaps there was. Did he accelerate his death with the liquor, smoking and pain meds? I don't know. If he did those things to bring about death, we can't know for sure. In my mind, it does not matter. And as we know, there was no suicide note. The horrid cancer took his life."

"Thank you, Arthur," Izzy said with some relief. "You had an impossible task. No one could have done it better than you."

"Mrs. Kelleher, let me then present to you this legal envelope with a letter addressed to you," Girard interjected as he grabbed the remaining document. "There's a wax seal which I affixed when Mr. Kelleher was in my office on the afternoon of September 28, after placing the letter inside. That's less than a month before the night he died and another month from today."

Girard paused in his statement to check the expressions of the Coroner and the widow. That told him that neither had a notion there was a letter. "Your husband was of sound mind when we met. He instructed me to include this letter he was writing with the two insurance policies. He was unimpaired when he advised me on when to deliver the items to you. He was, however, coughing, and he slurred some words. Even then I did not know how severe the cancer was or how long before he'd be hospitalized."

The attorney held the envelope in one hand and pointed to the lettering and wax seal with his other hand. "Please see that the envelope is clearly marked: *To Present to Mrs. Izzy Kelleher – Private and Confidential.* He had me write that on the envelope the last time we met. And those are my initials, BAG, next to his, signifying I'd done so."

Clough studied the sealed envelope from across the room and asked, "Bradley, did Mr. Kelleher tell you about the contents of the letter?"

"No, he did not," Girard responded. "He said he wrote and typed it himself. He'd spent several weeks thinking about what he wanted to say to his wife upon his death, given the cancer was fatal. He didn't know how long he had. That's all. And, he didn't discuss the contents. He did say he'd written eight times or once or twice a week, the last one that Wednesday he placed the letter in the envelope. That was three weeks before his death."

Girard, Kelleher and Clough continued to look at the white envelope as if it were the final piece of a lengthy, complicated puzzle. Girard and Clough wished they had *Superman's* superpower of x-ray vision. Izzy wished she was alone.

Girard interrupted the moment by a final pronouncement. "Mrs. Kelleher, I need you to sign this certificate as having properly received these three documents. Arthur can witness, and we can be on our way."

Izzy scribbled her autograph on the consent form with only a cursory reading. She was growing impatient to rid her house of the morning visitors. She longed to resume her solitude. To make a fresh pot of coffee and play with Cerberus in the backyard.

She missed her boys. She missed playing racquetball. She mostly missed being married. She missed seeing her husband drive into the garage after work and explode into the house, as Cerberus greeted him at the door. She missed giving him a back scratch in the evening that turned into a back rub. She missed coming downstairs in the morning on weekends and finding fresh coffee already brewed, a piece of raisin bread perched in the toaster and a cheddar cheese omelet waiting to happen.

The widow regained focus, her composure and her manners. "Gentlemen, thank you for coming. This is a great deal for me to digest. I want to be alone when I open the letter, and I may not be ready to open it today or until after the funeral. I'm not one for immediate gratification."

Girard placed the signed certificate inside his briefcase. He and Clough simultaneously rose, as if they had scripted and rehearsed their exit. They looked with empathy at the widow and walked toward the front door. Izzy followed them, leaving the sealed, suspect envelope on the coffee table, as she once again tightened the sash on her robe.

Their departure was a solemn, sober denouement in the life of Jacob Paul Kelleher. The two men had delivered financial provisions and a communication to his wife as if Kelleher was reaching from death to life for one more moment.

Mrs. Kelleher extended her right hand to Bradley Girard and then to Arthur Clough. She gave Clough a cursory hug, as Girard opened the two doors and stood on the front stoop. "Again, thank you," Girard said. His billing for the day was complete, although he wrestled in his mind whether he should send a statement to the estate for that morning's legal work. He would, of course.

The two men walked toward their respective cars, as Izzy Kelleher stepped out into the chilly morning. "Next time you need me, Mr. Girard, call ahead," she shouted sarcastically. "This is Saturday morning!"

Izzy watched as the two men waved in acknowledgement and got into their respective cars. Clough looked back and smiled at Izzy. Impulsively, she shouted to him, "Hey Arthur, thank you for not asking just one more question."

Izzy returned to the warmth and sanctity of her house. She recaptured the mysterious envelope from the coffee table and walked back toward the kitchen before tossing it to the center of the table. She was in no rush to open it. She wanted time to process what had happened in her living room that morning.

As a little girl, Izzy had been the lone sibling on Christmas morning who was in no hurry to open Santa's presents. She was in no hurry to open this package, this letter, today, either.

The widow started another pot of coffee. It was not so much that she longed for a fresh cup, as for something to momentarily distract her. She could relax now, and the coffee would help. Cerberus had done his job and the Irish Spirits had now left her alone.

Izzy poked her head into the pantry to grab another piece of raisin bread to toast. Her eyes fixated on three *Dole* Pineapple cans, haphazardly stacked and precariously perched on the shelf next to the wooden bread box.

She clasped the three cans and patiently aligned them, one on top of the other. She adjusted their *Dole* labels to face forward, as her husband would have wanted. She did it out of love and honor. She did it as an impassioned and impulsive tribute.

Isabella Brooke Rhodes Kelleher clutched the top can of pineapple slices, as a wide-eyed child might cautiously cradle a fragile baby bird orphaned from its nest. Izzy placed the can on the kitchen table next to the ominous, unopened letter. The two unrelated items rested side-by-side for a few minutes.

Then Izzy grabbed the can-opener and a fork from her kitchen drawers. She cranked the opener and watched as it encircled the pineapple can, slowly carving out the tin top. Izzy pried open the lid with the fork as she'd seen her husband do many times. Ceremoniously she poked the fork into the top pineapple slice.

Mrs. J. Paul Kelleher held the juicy slice up to the morning sun. She looked at it for a while, the sun absorbing it and creating a brief sparkle. Then she leaned forward, closed her eyes and took a generous bite.

The widow would read the letter later, perhaps after she got dressed for the day.

Maybe after the funeral. Maybe after she hugged her boys or played fetch with Cerberus.

Maybe after she exchanged the coffee for a glass or two of wine.

Cerberus – Guarding the Gates of Hell

THE LETTER

To Present to Mrs. Izzy Kelleher – Private and Confidential
BAG
JPK

Like a morning dream,
life becomes more and more bright the longer we live,
and the reason of everything appears more clear.
What has puzzled us before seems less mysterious,
and the crooked paths look straighter as we approach the end.
Jean Paul

Monday, August 22, 1977

Izzy, I apologize for keeping my cancer from you and the boys. I didn't want to tell you or others right away. As the pain increases and Morphine becomes a friend, I decided to go without telling you, as long as I can tolerate what's happening to my body. Shame on me.

I want to keep working, keep addressing the agenda at the College. How we spend our time may depend on how much we have left. How does one balance the character of prolonging one's suffering and the character of curtailing a valued life? Now it's been two months since the cancer diagnosis.

I had thought I might write this letter long-hand, with my fountainpen, so it would be personal. But then my handwriting started to fail and I type better anyway. Always have. You know the story about when I was a high school senior, my mother made me take a typing class. One of the most valuable I ever had.

Plan to write every week as long as mind's still there and fingers work. Not sure which will go first. You know I type well. Consider this typed version as hugely personal. I made beer money in college by typing term papers for guys in the dorm. Perhaps I should have ditched the college administration career and been an editor and typist.

My cancer is in the front of the brain. As it enlarges, I can expect confusion and changes in my personality.That could be a good thing, as I've never been known for having much personality. Dr. Charles joked it might make me more agreeable to others, more pleasant. Humor can be a good thing, especially when one faces dying, particularly his way.

Doc said cancer would take over my vision and hearing too. That will happen later. My ~~m~~mind will be incoherent as if I had severe Alzheimer's. You know me. I'd prefer to lose my sight or hearing or have my right arm amputated than be deprived of my ability to think and reason clear~~ly~~ly.

If I take more pain-killers, drink more, smoke more, does it matter that I'm dying for God's sake. I don't want to go out with a rubber tube in my arm, sucking on a breathing straw, a nurse wiping my butt while I'm attached to a mass of life-sustaining contraptions, eating overcooked eggs and Jell-O squares.

I don't want to exist in a hospital bed under Morphine timed to a buzzer, my consciousness reduced to awareness that these cells are dividing uncontrollably in my head. Dr. Charles told me that as cancer progresses I will go to sleep at the end. Supposedly it's a peaceful death. We'll see. How does he even know? He's not dying.

Tuesday, August 30

Izzy, this is the second time I write in what will eventually amount to my last letter. I will finish one of these days before my mind stops or my fingesrrs fail me. I expect my comments will appear to you as a Stream of Consciousness – apologies to William James, James Joyce andd Virginia Woolf. The only coherence is that the words come from me without conventional transitions. When one is dying, there are no conventional or unconventional transitions.

I know you'll remember the day we went to dinner for our first date. We went to that Chinese restaurant where they had the inverted coffee maker at the table. China Pavilion. I got confused. I was nervous anyhow. the waiter had to show me how to press the plunger. He was concerned the plunger would not be straight when I pushed it down. You thought I was heroic.

When we got married, we ended-up with our rehearsal dinner at the same place. We gave fortune Cookies to all the guests. We made each cookie have a truism saying from European writers, by taking them apart and adding the saying before gluing them back. Some folks ate the stale cookie anyway. gGlue and all.

Have no idea why this Chinese food thing comes to mind. Funny how the mind rambles and recollects when the brain is damaged.

When you get this, you may want to contact Dr. David Charles who did the exam and determined I had a brain tumor. I was diagnosed with cancer in mid-June. The pain is increasing now to where it's affecting my daily life.But still I choose to keep it to myself. It'searly in my remaining time to live, so maybe when you get this I will have told you and we discussed it.

When I know death cannot be deferred longer, I may feel differently. The tumor compresses my brain. That's a hard visual to accept. Forgive me, Izzy. Forgive me, God, if you need to. What is peaceful if you're dying and must take a drugs to tolerate the pain?

As for the insurance money, use whatever amounts you feel are best for the boys, their education. I know you will. They're both on track to go to college, maybe even English majors. Do talk them out of that! Use the rest of the money for yourself. Take a lonhocean cruise with Ella or another female friend. Or treat the boys. Live it up. Be grateful for the years we shared, the two marvelous sons we raised. Then move on too the rest of your life. Find another love. Just not Solly or Fox.

Friday, September 2

Izzy, I've kept a notebook in my office the past year of ym thoughts on what happening at the College. Done it for the past year. If Samantha doesn't find it, or whomever, it's underneath a false bottom of a desk drawer. Right side, where I keep my dictionary. If no one's discovered it, retrieve it and give it o Jack Kula. Some observations may need to be verified. let him figure that out. Ask to get it back when he's done, as I know you like to read non-fiction. You can retain the Broadway and movie rights. Don't let Lieber negotiate the contract!

You may find this amusing, or disgusting, but I confiscated the Darvocet from when you had menstrual cramps.Those pills helped increase my pain tolerance, so I can stockpile morphine and defer doses until the pain's more severe. Hopefully, I can avioid avoid the hospital. Guess when you get this, you'll know if I did. Wanted Dr. Charles to thinkn I have high pain threshold. Hell, it hurts. I have a low threshold of pain but I pretend

I'm sorry to say too, when Connor broke his leg two years ago, he was given OxyContin for the pain. Some pills were left over. I swallowed two of those a day, until the bottell bottle was empty.

I'm finding it harder to type, even today. The brain's slow to dictatee to the fingers which keys to punch. You'll just have to excuse the typos, syntax and alll. I don't like to use the whiteout gunk and I can't retype the thing each time. Hard to see errors. Glad I can use this dictating thing in my office. Don'rt think Edith knows.

I've always been comfortaleable in my aloneness. Remember when I turned 35 and took a two-week outing in Outdoor Wilderness in NC, including two nights utterly alone in the woods. Solo.Some of my fellow adventurers freaked out – being by selves in the woods. I wrote poems and enjoyed being by myself. Had a marvelous solitary time. That's me. You have to have people around you. That's good for you.

I have missed runnning, running although most people would not label my movements around campus as running. My mother used to say getting older was a series of give-ups. She did not have a saying for what one gives-up when you have the Cancer. Running, eating and sleeping are on the list. Making lover tooo. Eventually you give up breathing. Maybe I should give-up the typing too? Sorry.

More than anything I missed our talks. Sitting on the couch together, your head on my lap. Your legs spread on the couch. As the problems at work increased, I zonedout when we did talk. We've had our share of peaks. You need to shared with someone, and I know I was not always therefor you. I was not jealous of your friends, just that they were a substitute for me. I was there.

Friday, September 9

Izzy, when I was a Vcie President I followed Dr. Greenleaf's lead. But when I became President and looked at everything, I found it was a pretty crookeded place. I expected problems, ordinary one. I found extraordinary dealings. Amazing how the change of hats from VP to President reveals so much crap, But my crooked college. Rather it is A Crookedd College. Are ohters.

I didn't see the problems as horrifying but as adversities to tacklel. I enjoy dealing with shit every day. Most edvery day. My paradise is in solving problems, not avoiding them or wishing they'd go away. My gratification's a constant work-in-progress, every day.

I regret I spent more time chugging Bushmills Irish by myself than sharing Bollo red with you. Might have been good for my waistline. I should have thrown away the Marlboros and started smoking your Virginia Slims. I smoke all those years and then will die of god damn brain cancer. I should have quite the cursing and the vulgar attempts at humor. Even though as an Irish guy, that's sacrilegious. Guilt has been a quiet and steady companion in my journey to this point since June.

By when you receive this letter, let's hope Fox, Hughes and Lieberr have met with the authorities and the District Attorney is making their lives miserable. There are notes on them in myjournal. Hopefully, Solly got that new women's pro basketball league job in Newark. Perhaps Winters will retire soon or go back into teaching. May Donald find peace in my eventual death. I'm afraid, Fishman will be prosecuted one day. Maybe soon.

I hope my successor valuess Edith and Samantha. If he doesnt' the Board probably got the selection wrong. If you are up to it, consider serving as a mentor to Samantha.She needs a friend now, as Dominic works out divorce. Siad he would. They deserve their love. Tehere relationship hasn't hindered her work.

Ive tried to find and champion solutions, yet knowing today's fixxxes fixes may be someone else's problems years from now. Those crooked problems are what I enjoy or guess enjhoyed doing. That's why I wanted to stay at it, if I could function reasonably well. As long as i could.

I blame myself for the lifestyle choices that led to the Cancer. It may have been something in the environment or my Irish heritage or our Jerseyk air. Certainly not the Tomato Piwe. The belief that the Cancer happens for a rason reason can be an attractive line of thinking. A logical mind says there must be a cause. I don't think so, at least not now. Maybe I will when I get closer to meeting Mr. Death. Or maybe Death has a doctorate.

Monday, September 12

I'm ashamed of the waytt I'd sometimes tease women before I became Presidentt. It came to mind with Fox seducing students. I was not into seduction. Know that. but I did exploit fellow employees just because they were females and vulnerable to someone like me. that was years ago when the male peer group encouraged that sort of stuff and sexual overtures were ignored. Four shame.

I had a chance to make amends, somewhat, when I toldRoseanne to draft Policy on sexual classroom behaviors because of Fox. What a creep We may be the first jersey college to do. But the Board may throw a roadblock. That's guilt I don't have to bare bear any longer. Thankyou, Mr. Cancer?

Hopefully, Roseanne will be able to orfganize a community Alcoholics Anonymouschapter on campus. That will enable employees, students and others who know "Bill W" to meet and address their situation and pursue help. I checked out this Bill. The AMA has concluded escessicve drinking is a disease, the rest of the world is not catching up. Most prefer to see alcohol abuse as a sign of a weakened personality,. Not soo.

Need board Policy so employees, including president, cannot have alcohokl in offices. I Yet here I sit her typing on this portable while sipping my whiskey. If you want, mention it to Kulaa. I forget a lotnow.

Share some of the notges with Panichi. Perhaps he can address the Board members whoo need to re replaced. Dominick told me Sheriff was good guy. Not to underestimat him. But don't share this letter with him or anyone. Let it go up in flammmes when I do.

Izzy, I could hardly write this letter without remembering my English Lit. Recall Hamlet, contemplating his death, says in his famous solillloquy.

To be, or not to be.

That"'s the question.

Whether it's nobler in the mind to sufor sufferr

The slings and arrows of outrageous fortune,

Or take arms against a sea of troubles,

And by opposing them, end them.

How Shakespeare died remains a mystery. He was 53 and may have been a vurus that ravaged his body and mind. But life expectacy was less than 40. Some claim it was alcohol and drugs.

Thursdaday, September 15

Izzy, I've always enjoyed this line from Macbethh, not realizing how I would interpret it years later:

Out, out, brief candle!

Life's but a walking shadow, a poor playre

That struts and frets his hour upon the stagee

And then is heard noo more.

tale Told by an idiot, full of sound and fury,

Signifying Nothing.

And, I like this quote from Oscar Wilde, except rt I'm not sure howi it applies when one is cremated, as I will bee or have already been when you read this. He was imprisoned and exiled as playwright. I imprisoned by The Cancer and being exiled from my work.

Death must be so beautiful.

To lie in the soft brown earth, with the grasses waving above one's head. list

To listen to silence and have no yesterdey, and no to-morrow.

To forget time, to forget life, to be at ~~piece~~ peace.

My version of Death, with earnst apologies to my Mr. Widle:

Death could be beautiful.

Ddying Dying certainly is not.

To have my ashes blend with Dust,

Flowers and veggies ~~gfowing~~ growing alongside.

To have had many yestredays.

But no more todays.

To remember time together with Izzy.

To remember my Irish sons.

To forget what I might do.

And be at peace.

Irish Ghosts are calling me home. Still feignt though.

Not listening yet. Hopefully my soul will elued the evil spirits. Tehre are still some of them trapped in my office here at the Collleg. They will vbe fluttering over my body when I die. If so, that's good news.

Friday, Septemberr 16

Couldn't finish Thursday. Early morning here so have some strength. Need to take something for The pain. Not good day. Much better today.

Got through Board meeting on Wednesday. Kula was teriffic. Got Pitman and Harrison really flustered.

Getting competent on these injexctions. That's why I come to the office on weekends. Don't want boys to see me.

How I yearn for a painless sleep. A head without an ache. A day without feeling I will fall over. Nevertheless, if you believe in righteoussness, the public will find out about what Pitman wanted. Probably won't happen. Sorry about being negative. You tried to get me to be more positive,but I couldn't listen. The glass could be filled.lord knows I tried to fill it. I have seen it mostly as half or almost totaly empty.

Thanks for understanding on separate bedrooms.

Samantha has been a wonder. Incredibly bright and perceptive. Hope sshe stays with college but might go back to cunty government.

Am so proud of what you have accomplished in your career. What I would have given to have had a professor like you when I was in college.

Sure do want my glass to be empty when die.

Supposed to see Dr. Charles today.

Need to understand how alcohol relates to the Morphine Im taking. Irish Whiskey likely interacts in a ver special way. I plan on that.

540

Wednesday, September 21

Bribe for PPitman over architect never came up In the Board's public meetng last Wednesday Saved embarrassment and ethical rebuke from county.The tension between us is going to worsen.makes death more welcome, given The Cancer. The increased pain does too. I did what had to do.

I should have told you earlier. I know but then I had to concentrate on the pain. How to handle it.

It may have looked likeI was drinking more but not so. I wanted people to think I was so that if I fainted or slurred speeech they would think it was the whiskey. Can't blame the Irish on that one. Poured down drain. Hope that doesn''t keep me from IRish heavens. Booze and morphine do not mix well either. I am told.

Glad I know that now. Will help at the end when I mix the two.

Dsappointed in Fishman. I knowhe cooked the books some, at least in financial aid. Imagin doing that to students. If they do an independent auditt, the errors will show up. Found out that he had a buddy in County who did the audit. He was sloppg. Let next president figre it out.

Have some notes in the notebook. Hidden bottom drawer on right. False bottom. Did I tell you that earleir.

Feel badly for Donald. He gave so much to this place. How do you inspire a guy like him after all these years. I was going to take him to lunch and invitge him to take a sabbatical but probably won't get to that before The Cancer takes me.

Sorry this day is a bummer. I have good days when think clearly and pain is tolerable. Other days, mask stuff going on in my head and hde out here.

Wednesday, Septemmberr 2778 28

I couldn't finish the one las tweek. Knew wanted to make this end of Sep as last day I wwrite. Head and fingers not doing gooood. Sorry. Need to get to lawyer guy.

My health worsening. Itry to mask The Cancer's pain with illusion that I'm drinking more. Not really. The Morphine helps I hide itin the bathroom behind the towel thing. Saved enough for the end. I hate myself for doing what I need to do when the time is right. Soon. Hard too, given Tucker wrapped himself around a tree. There's better way.

Tell Reuben and Dr. Charles for me about the hiding place. Not that I hoarded some of it for later. They were respectful and trusted me. But I cheatted The meds and empties are there.

Making injections in my arms is nota challenge Tha t parts easy. Can be addictived. Don't wanyt that. Won't die in a hospital Won't die dependent.

I want to finnish this letter and get to attorney for yo.u He's to give after the death Certificate is official.I don't think I have too many more weeks to live especially with pain of The Cancer.

Forgive the metafore but I plan todie with my shined shoes off, unlike a cowboy with his boots on. I liked cowbosys as a kid. Hopalong Cassady, Roy Rogers. Those guys never died. I prefer to sit in my office looking at the beautiful campus, not on some stupid horse with sagebrushes and wind blowing. Or a hospital and blank walls or hopeless machines. And a smoke in my fingers, Irish whisky in my hand, sitting in my office. Bottle empty.The meds will handle the rest. Take me away.

No idea why, but I reminded of the line from Nicholson's movie, One Flew Over Cuckoo's Nest "You're no crazier than the average asshole out walkingg streets." Guess Im the crazy one here.

That's it, my lovve. Don't fret on what I to do. Live your life fully.Let our sons live their lifes as well. Sorry I will miss. Do what you need to. That's peace. Let me leave you with this: May you always walk in sunshine. Never want for moore. May Irish angels rest their wings right beside your door

AUTHOR PROFILE

E. Timothy Lightfield, Ph.D., enjoyed a thirty-year career in higher education in Florida, Georgia, Illinois, New Jersey, North Carolina, South Carolina and Virginia as professor, researcher, chief academic officer, campus provost and president. He has a baccalaureate from Eckerd College, master's degree from the University of North Carolina at Chapel Hill and doctorate from Florida State University.

Dr. Lightfield has been honored by Phi Theta Kappa National Honor Society (CEO Award of Distinction), Association of Community College Trustees (National Executive Officer of the Year) and Alpha Beta Gamma National Honor Society (President of the Year). He was recognized with the Resolution of Merit from the Illinois General Assembly.

Dr. Lightfield has authored scholarly and research publications in sociology and higher education including the *Community and Junior College Journal, Educational Record, American Sociologist, Social Forces, Community College Review and Journal of College Student Personnel.*

Dr. Lightfield lives in Ponte Vedra, Florida, with his wife, Deborah, an artist and retired teacher and their wire-haired dachshund, Ella. The author has continued to teach and provide leadership to non-profit organizations and churches in organizational and resource development.

Tim enjoys SCUBA and long-distance swimming, pickleball, golf and cooking, especially for a local shelter. The pride of his life is grandson Jack Timothy, a future MVP right fielder for the Washington Nationals.